PENGUIN BOOKS

CHARLIE CHAN IS DEAD 2
At Home in the World

Jessica Hagedorn is an acclaimed novelist and National Book Award nominee, as well as a poet, playwright, and screenwriter. She was born and raised in the Philippines, and moved to the United States in her teens. She is the author of three novels, *Dream Jungle*, *The Gangster of Love*, and *Dogeaters*, and of *Danger and Beauty*, a collection of selected poetry and short fiction. Hagedorn is also the editor of the first *Charlie Chan Is Dead: An Anthology of Contemporary Asian American Fiction*.

CHARLIE CHAN IS DEAD 2

At Home in the World

• • •

AN ANTHOLOGY OF CONTEMPORARY ASIAN AMERICAN FICTION

REVISED AND UPDATED

Edited and with an Introduction by
Jessica Hagedorn

Preface by
Elaine H. Kim

PENGUIN BOOKS

PENGUIN BOOKS

Published by the Penguin Group
Penguin Group (USA) Inc., 375 Hudson Street,
New York, New York 10014, U.S.A.
Penguin Books Ltd, 80 Strand,
London WC2R ORL, England
Penguin Books Australia Ltd, 250 Camberwell Road, Camberwell,
Victoria 3124, Australia
Penguin Books Canada Ltd, 10 Alcorn Avenue,
Toronto, Ontario, Canada M4V 3B2
Penguin Books India (P) Ltd, 11 Community Centre, Panchsheel Park,
New Delhi—110 017, India
Penguin Books (N.Z.) Ltd, Cnr Rosedale and Airborne Roads, Albany,
Auckland, New Zealand
Penguin Books (South Africa) (Pty) Ltd, 24 Sturdee Avenue,
Rosebank, Johannesburg 2196, South Africa

Penguin Books Ltd, Registered Offices:
80 Strand, London WC2R ORL, England

First published in the United States of America by Penguin Books 1993
This revised and updated edition published 2004

5 7 9 10 8 6 4

Publisher's Note
These selections are works of fiction. Names, characters, places, and incidents either are the
product of the authors' imagination or are used fictitiously, and any resemblance to actual
persons, living or dead, business establishments, events, or locales is entirely coincidental.

LIBRARY OF CONGRESS CATALOGING-IN-PUBLICATION DATA

Charlie Chan is dead 2 : at home in the world : a new anthology of contemporary Asian
  American fiction edited with an introduction by Jessica Hagedorn ; with a preface by
  Elaine Kim.
     p. cm.
  "New, revised edition of Charlie Chan is dead"—Introd.
  ISBN 0-14-200390-5
  1. American fiction—Asian American authors. 2. American fiction—20th century.
  3. American fiction—21st century. 4. Asian Americans—Fiction.
  I. Hagedorn, Jessica Tarahata, 1949– II. Charlie Chan is dead.
  PS647.A75C484 2004
  813'.54080895—dc22   2003058225

Printed in the United States of America
Set in Electra with DINEngschrift
Designed by Sabrina Bowers

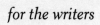

for the writers

PREFACE

When I was a kid back in the 1940s, I was always asked, "Are you Chinese or Japanese?" as if there could be no other options. There are over sixty different Asian groups in the United States today, from origins as diverse as Cambodia, China, India, Indonesia, Japan, Korea, Laos, Myanmar, Pakistan, the Philippines, Thailand, and Vietnam, as well as the islands of Polynesia—each with its own history, language, and culture. Some segments have been in the United States since the 1850s; others arrived only last week.

Asians are now the fastest-growing group in America, with a population projected to increase from eleven million last year to twenty million by 2020. But until quite recently, many Americans considered the United States either a white country or a black-and-white country.

ELAINE H. KIM is associate dean of the Graduate Division and professor of Asian American and comparative ethnic studies at the University of California at Berkeley. She has written, edited, and coedited such books as *Fresh Talk/Daring Gazes: Issues in Asian American Visual Art*, *Echoes Upon Echoes: New Korean American Writing*, *Dangerous Women: Gender and Korean Nationalism*, *Making More Waves: New Writing by Asian American Women*, *East to America: Korean American Life Stories*, *Writing Self, Writing Nation: A Collection of Essays on Dictee by Theresa Hak Kyung Cha*, *Making Waves: Writings by and About Asian American Women*, and *Asian American Literature: An Introduction to the Writings and Their Social Context*. She is a founder of Asian Women United of California, the Oakland Korean Community Center, and Asian Immigrant Women Advocates. She was born in New York City in 1942, but grew up in the Washington, D.C., area.

Since they really only recognized two possible races and were unaccustomed to thinking of Asians as part of the national human landscape, they could not imagine that an Asian could be American. They saw instead stereotypes and caricatures of sinister villains out to conquer the world, the brute hordes that blindly obey them, and exotic aliens of every description.

Asian Americans have a rich and sometimes troubled history in this country. In 1869, the transcontinental railroad was completed only with the blood and sweat of ten thousand Chinese immigrants. They also built roads, levees, irrigation systems, wine caverns—contributing to the phenomenal increase in the value of Pacific Coast land and, with the development of the railroad and refrigerator cars, American agriculture. By the early 1900s, Japanese Americans, who constituted a minuscule portion of the population, were crucial to the development of the nation's agriculture, producing up to 90 percent of truck crops on only 450,000 acres of land. The wealth of the country was also increased by Filipino migrant farmworkers, who moved with the crops from Alaska to Baja California. A segregated Japanese military unit that fought in Europe was the most highly decorated American unit during World War II, even though the young soldiers' families were being held in prison camps under suspicion of disloyalty to the United States. Individuals also made their mark: not many people know that a century ago, the nectarine was invented by a Korean American farmer or that the Bing cherry was invented by a Chinese American named Bing.

The nineteenth- and twentieth-century idea of America as a nation of immigrants did not include Asians or Latinos but had to do with Europe and the other side of the Atlantic. Historically, Asian immigrants were viewed as apart from white America. They were denied by law the right to become naturalized citizens, to own land, to intermarry; they were confined to segregated jobs and residential areas, and sometimes murdered, lynched, run out of town, or set adrift on the ocean.

Early Asian Americans worked together to challenge racism and social injustice. Chinese Americans fought every piece of racist legislation against them, sometimes all the way to the Supreme Court. And there were many: ordinances against laundries, laws against long hair, laws requiring a certain amount of cubic feet of air per Chinese person, a tax on being Chinese, laws against getting business licenses, laws against attending schools with whites or testifying against whites in court, laws against intermarriages, laws prohibiting Chinese from owning land, and, of course, laws against Chinese immigration or naturalization. Likewise, Japanese Americans participated in a long and ultimately successful legal battle for redress, reparations, and publicity about their unlawful internment during World War II. Filipino Americans built a spectacular labor movement that organized the poorest and most disenfranchised migrant agricultural workers in coalition with Mexican Americans from the 1930s through the 1960s. Among the many positive results of this is safer produce for everyone because of United Farm Workers' efforts to protect farmworkers from harmful pesticides.

Since the Immigration Act of 1965 eliminated national-origin quotas, there has been a new wave of Asian immigration that has increased the importance of learning about this diversity as a basic component of what it means to be American.

Unlike the earlier Asian immigrants, the newcomers are coming as families with the intention of settling down in America. About one-third are professionals, and the rest belong to the working class. Some have come looking for economic betterment. Others have fled unstable political and economic conditions in their homelands. Today, Asian workers continue to play a crucial and ever-increasing role in the food service industry as well as the garment industry. More than one-third of Silicon Valley's engineers are Asian American. Many small businesses across the country are operated by Asian immigrants, such as Korean dry cleaners, South Asian hotels and motels, Vietnamese nail salons, and Cambodian doughnut shops.

The enormous differences between Hmong refugees and fourth-generation Japanese Americans whose families have been in this country longer than many white Americans show us the diversity of Asian America. There is dramatic contrast between the more established Japanese and Chinese Americans and the Southeast Asian refugee communities. For every Asian American with an annual income of $75,000 or more, there is another making less than $10,000 a year. And while more than a third of all Asian Americans have at least a college degree, another 23 percent of those over twenty-five have less than a high school diploma. For every scientist or engineer, there is another making less than minimum wage.

In 2003, there were lots of activities going on to celebrate the Korean American centennial. I think it's fitting for us to settle on 1903, the year the first shipload of Korean immigrant sugar plantation workers landed in Hawaii, for several reasons. First, it places working class people at the center of the picture. Though the Korean immigrants to Hawaii were from a variety of backgrounds, almost all of them ended up in hard labor as sugar plantation workers. Because of racial barriers, many Korean Americans were unable to move into a wider range of work until the 1970s. Second, it reminds us of the importance of ethnic coalition. Koreans were deliberately recruited as strikebreakers by the planters, who wanted to halt Japanese plantation workers' demand for equal wages with whites. They kept workers in ethnically segregated work camps, but they could not prevent collaboration. The Japanese and Filipinos worked together to press for equal pay in spectacular strikes in 1909 and 1920, and by World War II the International Longshore and Warehouse Union (ILWU) in Hawaii was the model of multiracial labor organizing in the whole country. Finally, when we talk about assimilation, we usually think in terms of nonwhite people disappearing like raindrops into what we see as the ocean of mainstream white European American society. But this has not been the case in Hawaii. And, to my mind, Hawaii still remains a refreshingly working class kind of culture.

My grandmother somehow arrived in Hawaii around 1903 to work on the sugar plantations. She was apparently accompanied by my mother, who was an infant. My grandmother told my mother that she had left Korea because her husband, supposedly my grandfather, was a gambling man who had become angry at my mother's crying and had thrown a blanket over her. This, according to my grandmother's story, almost smothered her last living baby, since her supposed other children had all died already. In desperation, she told my mother, she grabbed her baby and stowed away on a ship bound for Hawaii.

I think that my mother believed this story all her life. But after I grew up and started reading about Korean history, I could see how impossible it was for an illiterate rural woman to leave Korea alone or with an infant in 1903 to travel thousands of miles across the Pacific Ocean to a place she knew nothing about and where she could not speak a word of the language.

After reading Korean history and studying gender relations in

Korea, I know that at least in the past most women couldn't leave husbands even if they were drunks, gamblers, and wife-beaters who brought home second wives and children from other women. And if wives ran away, they certainly didn't take their children with them. As for the story of the husband who threw a blanket on the last remaining baby—well, she probably said that so my mother would believe that she emigrated for her sake. That's a trick today's immigrant parents still use on their children to make us feel guilty and study harder: "I came here to suffer because of you."

What could the real story be? My mother looked like a mixed-race person, though she always thought of herself as Korean. I wondered: perhaps my grandmother was seduced or raped by a Russian soldier during the Russo-Japanese War. What would have happened to such a woman in Korea in 1903? If her situation were desperate enough, maybe she would take a chance when she heard about the ship bound for Hawaii. After all, aren't most immigrants to America unusual people, not just people with courage and a pioneering spirit but also people with a past from which they are escaping?

Unlike my mother, my father came from a landowning family. I have often marveled at how social classes that would never mix in the old country could mingle and marry in the New World. My father came to the United States as a foreign student in 1926, two years after complete exclusion of immigrants from Asia. He remained a student until World War II, when he was finally able to get a green card for working for the U.S. State Department against Japan. Not permitted to be naturalized for so many decades, he refused to become a U.S. citizen even after the law allowed it. When we traveled to Korea together, I would breeze through with my U.S. passport and then wait and wait for him to get through the line with his Korean passport. He lived sixty-three years in the United States and my mother lived here all her life, but they are buried in Korea because my father wanted to be there. After they died, I had the heartbreaking task of going through their belongings. Though their lives spanned continents and centuries, all that was left were some photographs of people I didn't know, some papers I couldn't read, and many harassing letters from the INS, which they kept for many years. That was almost the sum total, the proof of their American life.

Like some other Korean families of his time, my father's family is scattered across the globe. I have six cousins in South Korea, five cousins in North Korea, and five cousins in mainland China, most of whom have never met each other because the U.S. and the USSR had divided Korea in half and prevented movement between capitalist and Communist countries. My father went to Japan and on to the United States to study. His older brother went to China to fight in the resistance around the time of Japanese annexation. His younger sister became a Communist and went to North Korea to live in 1945. His younger brother was the only one who stayed in South Korea. This summer, I expect some cousins from Seoul, South Korea, and one cousin from Tientsin, China, to visit me in California. The cousins from Seoul speak only Korean. The cousin from China speaks only Mandarin. And I of course speak mostly English.

America is filled with people whose histories have deep and complicated roots. Their stories give us alternative views to the grand narrative of Western European progress, modernization, and enlightenment. Often, they directly contradict the fictions the United States tells about itself as a nation as benevolent abroad and inclusive at home. Especially for the racialized immigrant, moving to America brings opportunity for material comfort and liberating anonymity. But it also involves great pain and loss that must be recognized and acknowledged. Asian immigrant subjects are formed through racialization in the United States and colonialism, neocolonial capitalism, and imperialist wars in Asia. Their memories, histories, and experiences tell us a story quite different from the Hollywood versions of U.S. heroism that saved their homelands and adopted their orphans.

How many people in the United States are aware that one-sixth of the population of Luzon, the Philippines, was exterminated in the American attempt to put down the popular resistance during the Spanish-American War? How many people know that during the Korean War, U.S. bombs killed two to four million Korean people and burned to the ground every city, every village, every hut in northern and central Korea in an aerial war that presaged this year's attack on Iraq? Or that General Douglas MacArthur wanted to drop thirty to fifty atomic bombs from the Sea of Japan to the Yellow Sea, creating a "belt of radioactive cobalt" across the Korean Peninsula that would destroy anything that crossed it for ten generations? How many people have been told that the United States dumped two million tons of bombs on Laos—more than got dropped on Japan and Germany combined during all of World War II, making Laos the most bombed country per capita in the history of warfare? Or that twelve thousand villagers in Laos have been killed since 1973 because the estimated "dud rate" of 30 percent has left ten million unexploded bombs in Laotian soil?

The U.S. national narrative disavows that fact of American military, economic, and cultural colonization in Asia, from which Asian immigration directly emerges as the displaced and dislocated migrate to the very imperial center that disrupted their lives. The immigrant who wishes to close the chasm between herself and U.S. culture is obliged to leave by the door memories that contradict the story that America tells about itself. Finding a place in mainstream American life can mean denying her own history, for she must not recall what the United States as a nation seeks to forget, including the very existence of a U.S. imperialist project in her homeland as well as her own lived experiences of abjection and discrimination in the United States.

A history like the history of my family had no relevance at all when I was growing up in the United States. It was as if I had been dropped here from another planet. Schoolchildren in the United States still learn world history, as I did, with everything beginning in Greece and Rome. Sometimes, when thinking about today's Korean American communities, I also feel like an outsider. I have no extended family here and I don't go to church. My parents were unable to ever find work commensurate or even related to their education. Even I, who finished my Ivy League education one year before the passage of the Civil Rights Act of 1964, could only find work as a waitress in a Japanese restaurant, though I graduated with straight A's and was president of my class.

What ties Asian Americans of today to those of my day? Is it really true that race discrimination is a thing of the past, that now everyone can make it to the American dream, if they just agree to be good and work hard enough? I think that two threads connect us. One is exploitation of immigrant labor for maximization of profit for the captains of U.S. industry. The other is racialization of Korean and other Asian immigrants as outsiders to U.S. culture.

Linguistically and racially at odds with the United States' image of itself, Asians in the United States have traditionally been seen as eternal aliens. Today, Asians continue to be the object of law; there is an obsession to identify us by classification along a continuum from alien to citizen: as legal or illegal, U.S.-born or permanent resident, to manage the corrupting "foreignness" in the middle of America. In my grandmother's day, the labor was on sugar plantations and in fruit orchards. The racialization as outsiders meant being barred by law from immigration, citizenship, and intermarriage as well as from owning land or living in most neighborhoods or frequenting most restaurants, hotels, movie theaters, and barbershops. Now, it's highly trained professionals and technicians underemployed in service sector, small business, and technology industry work. And being thought of as an eternal foreigner today means being told you can't use your native language, being rendered invisible or represented as the evil enemy in the mass media, being suspected of spying, or being killed for the way you look. Really, Asians in the United States are distanced from U.S. culture either as the "yellow peril" taking over everything or as "model minorities" whose "successes" assure us that racism has been replaced by meritocracy and only laziness and inability hold back the black and brown.

The "model minority" stereotype conveniently ignores the fact that Asians usually have to have much more education and work much longer and harder than white Americans for the same outcomes. Or that Asian Americans pay a heavy price in terms of what they are obliged to give up or trade in for a place in U.S. society. Or that out of plain view is a multitude of immigrants from all over Asia in low-wage, low-mobility jobs in cleaning and food service; part-time and split-shift factory work in sewing, meatpacking, and electronics assembly; and prostitution.

How much have things changed since the old days? The students in my literature class this semester were born in the early 1980s. Still, I am amazed at how familiar their stories are. Min Chu, nineteen, who grew up in San Francisco, wrote:

> Third grade traumatized me. My white teacher was a racist. She never called on me and always put me in groups with people who couldn't speak English, though I spoke as well as anyone in the class. She treated my Mom like she was an alien from Mars. I would never go back to the third grade.

Another student, Susan K. Lee, nineteen, remembered excelling in English in Asia and then entering sixth grade in New Jersey:

As one of a handful of Asian girls in the school, I was tortured. I was called names like "chink" and "smarty-pants." Classmates asked "why do your eyes look like that?" and "how come your face is shaped that way?"

Daniel Hur, twenty-one, a student from Southern California, wondered if signs of Asian immigrant "success" might obscure something ominous beneath:

It's hard for me to believe that my dad . . . used to ride his bike randomly up and down Jefferson Boulevard in search of work. I cannot really picture my mother working in a huge sewing factory either. I was seven when we moved to a nicer neighborhood, and I figured that my family and most of my relatives were doing quite well. But when my uncle was 60 [and] was shot to death in the east L.A. deli where he worked, I realized that our being here in America is still highly problematic and that the struggle never really ends.

My students have dreams for the future that are not all about money and nice neighborhoods. As Julie Carl, nineteen, put it:

I live in a country that never considers me American, even though I was born here. My identity is being able to play a role in creating a safe, multi-racial, multi-cultural America. Not in that phony-politicians-looking-for-minority-votes way, but so that the concerns of every minority (racialized, gendered, poor, or of a different sexual orientation than most) get a legitimate forum. After all, my parents taught me that making waves is a good thing.

These students want to see themselves and other "minorities" in history and in literature.

As a rule, I think that when we read literature, we can enjoy and appreciate it all the more by learning as much as possible about social and historical context, without charging the cultural with the burden of representing, reflecting, or expressing the social and historical, which after all include aesthetic practices. Of course, we would be making a mistake to focus on *what* is being said so much that we neglect *how* it is being said, since in the best work the *what* and the *how* are entwined.

Indeed, looking at formal issues in Asian American literature and art very often reveals an aesthetic of disidentification that critiques representational modes like realism and naturalism as well as the concept of autonomous art separated from material conditions.

In my view, it is important to remember that Asian American artists write into a politics of representation that includes a long history of Orientalism in Western high and popular cultures. Assumptions about immigrant subjectivities and experiences are often rooted in notions of Western superiority. The underlying "truth" in Asian immigrant narratives in American literature has been the teleology of "progress" from Asia to America. Amy Tan's immigrant Chinese women escape the hell of Chinese misogyny into the paradise of American gender equality. Whether or not Maxine Hong Kingston meant *The Woman Warrior* to be the story of the coming of age of a Chinese American who emerges from the superstition-ridden ghost world of Chinese immigrants into the American world where floodlights are shone into dark corners, readers are conditioned to see "progress" from savagery to civilization. This helps explain the eagerness with which American publishers welcome novels about women escaping the horrors of the Chinese Cultural Revolution, the Cambodian "killing fields," the war-torn and chaotic Philippines or Vietnam, where women are supposedly killed for bearing mixed-race children or children out of wedlock, into the freedom and happiness of American life.

Asian American writers from the 1920s to the present have been encouraged by mainstream publishers and readers to function as a "cultural bridge" or a "bridge between two worlds," between "here" and "there," between the United States and Asia, between the West and the East, between American child and immigrant parent. This expectation presupposes a duality between two poles, eliding the inequality between them—for the fundamental and self-congratulatory supposition is that the "here" is always far better than the "there." No matter that the Asian American struggles not between two worlds but among at least three: mainstream America, imagined/remembered/revisited Asia, and the Asian American community that the other two sides do not acknowledge. No one expects Italian Americans, Greek Americans, or even Mexican Americans to serve as "bridges" or "cultural go-betweens," because Italian, Greek, and Mexican Americans are not viewed as eternally alien.

The work in this volume refuses the go-between, interpreter, bridge role. Instead, it mounts a critique of the kinds of totalizing representations that ultimately only describe the dominant. The writers here unearth buried stories that upend common assumptions about color, culture, and sexuality with unexpected voicings from unexpected locations. Together they show how very diverse Asian Americans are, in terms of ethnic and social class backgrounds and perspectives.

For many Americans, the most visible symbol of today's "new (and newly successful) Asian American" is the deracinated female news anchor. In general female news anchors are a homogeneous-looking-and -sounding lot, and Asian American female television news reporters are actively encouraged to look as much like the ever-familiar Connie Chung as possible. According to her interview in the documentary *Slaying the Dragon: Asian Women in U.S. Television and Film,* San Francisco news anchor Emerald Yeh's station fiddled with her hair and makeup until satisfied that she better approximated Chung, with what my students call "the plastic Asian Barbie doll look."

Even if an occasional character in *At Home in the World* bears some superficial resemblance to the Asian news anchor, concert pianist/violinist, or figure skater in the American popular imagination, readers might be surprised by what goes on inside that Barbie doll–like head. There are no "model minorities" here, but rather people of all kinds whose idiosyncratically raced and gendered views of the world are not often found in the American cultural arena. These are people with a past, people from both here and now and there and then who remember and dream about other worlds that have been subject to national forgetting. Their version of history requires them to be disobedient, rebellious, and unfaithful to the national narrative of American identity and viewpoint.

In these stories, we visit other terrains and other times: Sabina Murray's Indonesia, Ginu Kamani's India, and Linh Dinh's Vietnam. In Monique Truong's 1930s French village, everyone gapes at Binh, the *"asiatique"* live-in cook who accompanies Gertrude Stein and Alice B. Toklas on their sojourns in the Rhône Valley, where he knows he is regarded as "the sideshow freak." In "Mango," Christian Langworthy shows us American soldiers through the eyes of a prostitute's children during the Vietnam War.

We consider news headlines from new vantage points. In Bharati

Mukherjee's "The Management of Grief," we see the well-meaning but culturally ignorant *angrezi* social worker through the eyes of an Indian Canadian woman widowed when an Air India flight is bombed. In "Cunanan's Wake," Gina Apostol imagines a close relative of Andrew Cunanan's in the Philippines who wants to arrange a memorial service for him.

In "Red Wall," Sara Chin's Chinese American sound technician realizes that Jill, the British-born filmmaker she has accompanied to China, has already determined what the "story" will be. Jill is unable to see or hear the life all around her, and we are tantalized by what might have been revealed had the narrator been allowed to "open up [the] film."

> Jill . . . wanted a face that told it all. I thought she had it, many faces. Big, fat, thin, and small . . . But what she wanted was something we couldn't give her. The way she saw it, the face that told it all had to be a particular face . . . All I had to do was hold out my microphone and listen. Listen for the past to percolate up out of people . . . I used a . . . microphone that easily picked up half-digested meals, ill-cooked thoughts. Can you say that again? I would have to interrupt to get it right, a clean recording. It was my job to stand watch over memory, roll my tape out before it like a red carpet. I didn't have to worry about facts or truth. I could ponder other things. Things closer to my heart . . . Jill had to get the big picture, but I could indulge in the small moments . . . Jill needed to march straight through to her conclusion. . . . I loved the low ground, the things that people pushed offstage, the gossip, the dirt. I was looking for the heart, the trashy heart of history. After all, wasn't that where the unknown leaped out at you?

The artists in this collection give us another way of looking, a different take, as they remember and create history from occluded viewpoints that challenge both the textbook and the Hollywood versions. In Han Ong's "Fiesta of the Damned," a middle-aged Filipino American "failure" named Roger Caracera is on his way back to the Philippines to bury his father. On the same flight are American actors on their way to make a war film. Caracera knows that for them, Third World locales are conflated as jungle backdrops for the enactment of American manhood. Ultimately, we realize that Caracera's "failure" is actually his success in becoming a " 'No, boss' contrarian . . . unobliging, unrepentant."

These writers are "at home in the world" in the sense that they are not involved in an "identity" movement in search of cultural roots. At the same time, they are never quite "at home in the world"—thus their artistic attempts to disobediently claim and articulate the "trashy heart of history."

Elaine H. Kim
Oakland, California
March 2003

ACKNOWLEDGMENTS

I wish to thank Christine Bacareza Balancé for her excellent editorial assistance and critical insights. A big thanks, once again, to Elaine H. Kim for another kick-ass essay. My gratitude also extends to Quang Bao of the Asian American Writers' Workshop in New York City, Cynthia Gehrig of the Jerome Foundation, R.Z. Linmark, and Jan Schaefer for turning me on to several exciting new writers and stories I might have overlooked. Thanks of course to my editor, Jane Von Mehren, to Brett Kelly, Barbara Campo, and the team at Penguin Books. Last but not least, maraming salamat to my agent, Harold Schmidt.

CONTENTS

INTRODUCTION

TEN YEARS AFTER:
LOOKING BACK, LOOKING FORWARD

The original title for this anthology was inspired by the yellow-face movie detective Charlie Chan, a character created in 1925 by a white man named Earl Derr Biggers. In those creaky black-and-white film series of the thirties and forties, Charlie Chan was always played by white actors made up to look "chinky"—hair slicked back, taped eyelids, long, wispy, sinister mustaches. For some weird reason, the secondary character of Charlie's "Number One Son" was always cast with an actual Asian American actor. Nowadays, while Asians may be cast as Asians on the big screen, the only characters they are relegated to portraying are of the kung-fu fighting, tiger-crouching, hip-hop variety.

Ingrained in American popular culture, Charlie Chan is as much a part of the legacy of cultural stereotypes that continues to haunt, frustrate, and—dare I say it?—sometimes inspire us. Fu Manchu. The bucktoothed, apelike Jap wielding his bayonet. The cunning Dragon Lady. Tokyo Rose. The Placid Geisha. The indolent Filipino Houseboy. The Model Minority. Miss Saigon, tragic victim/whore of wartorn Vietnam. Weeping. Giggling, bowing, and scraping. Sexually available, eager to deceive or to please. As of 2003, you can add these stereotypes to the list: the belligerent Korean Grocer, the goofy Japanime Geek, and the campy, innocuous "Charlie's Angel." I must confess to a soft spot for kick-ass, kung-fu fightin' mamas, no matter how preposterous and absurd. Is Charlie Chan really dead? Probably not. According to the critic and scholar David Eng, Charlie's merely in a coma.

The 1993 *Charlie Chan Is Dead* anthology was created out of a need. As I said in my introduction to that first edition, "This is an anthology I created for selfish reasons; a book I wanted to read that had never been available to me." In the postwar Philippines of my childhood, I was educated in the literature and the ways of the Western world. Though we were also taught a few classics of Tagalog literature, the colonization of our imagination was, as I wrote in 1993, relentless and hard to shake off. I arrived in the United States in 1963—a displaced teenager, largely ignorant of the turbulent history and contributions of Asian Americans and other people of color in this country. I was Filipino American, yes. But what did that mean? I had no idea that Filipinos were exploited as cheap farm labor in places like Watsonville, Salinas, and Stockton; that they were firebombed and run out of town throughout the Western states by angry mobs that were threatened by loss of jobs; that Filipinos were once forbidden to marry white women, harassed openly, and even lynched for being involved with them. I was unaware of the signs that were prominently hung in California public establishments as recently as the 1930s: NO FILIPINOS AND NO DOGS ALLOWED. Unfortunately, these painful but illuminating bits of history were not part of either my early Philippine or later U.S. schooling.

There was one thing I always knew: I wanted to be a writer. I came from a family of voracious readers, art lovers, and storytellers. My dream of one day becoming a writer was encouraged. But what kind of stories and whose would I end up telling? How would I find my voice? In his eloquent and insightful *Letters to a Young Novelist*, the Latin American writer Mario Vargas Llosa asks, "What is the origin of this early inclination, the source of the literary vocation, for inventing beings and stories? The answer, I think, is rebellion. I'm convinced that those who immerse themselves in the lucubration of lives different from their own demonstrate indirectly their rejection and criticism of life as it is, of the real world, and manifest their desire to substitute for it the creations of their imaginations and their dreams."

Published in hardback in 1974 and in paperback in 1975, the first *Aiiieeeee!* anthology, edited by Jeffery Paul Chan, Frank Chin, Lawson Inada, and Shawn Wong, introduced the concept of Asian American writers to the world. There were only fourteen writers included in the anthology, but the energy and debate sparked by the editors' introductory essay, plus the provocative sampling of poems, plays, and stories by Carlos Bulosan, Louis Chu, John Okada, Oscar Peñaranda, Momoko Iko, and others was an absolute breakthrough as far as American writing was concerned. Much of my education as a writer, as I acknowledged in my original introduction, owes a big debt to this first *Aiiieeeee!*

In 1993, the timing seemed right for an Asian American fiction anthology of as hefty size and ambition as *Charlie Chan Is Dead*. There were forty-eight writers in that initial collection. An amazing range of age, literary styles, and backgrounds was represented in the stories and novel excerpts of such diverse authors as Meena Alexander, Peter Bacho, Jeffery Paul Chan, Fiona Cheong, Marilyn Chin, Kiana Davenport, Gish Jen, Cynthia Kadohata, Maxine Hong Kingston, Joy Kogawa, Alex Kuo, Russell Leong, Walter Lew, David Wong Louie, Darrell Lum, Laureen Mar, Ruthanne Lum McCunn, Bharati Mukherjee, David Mura, Fae Myenne Ng, Sigrid Nuñez, Amy Tan, Sylvia Watanabe, Shawn Wong, Yoji Yamaguchi, and John Yau.

Another strong reason to do the original anthology was the opportunity to feature work by young, wildly gifted, and daring writers who were largely unknown to a mass market readership. Lawrence Chua, the late Theresa Hak Kyung Cha, Kimiko Hahn, Cherylene Lee, Walter Lew, Jocelyn Lieu, R. Zamora Linmark, Ruxana Meer, Han Ong, John Song, Kerri Sakamoto, and Lois-Ann Yamanaka were being published in a major collection for the first time. The first edition of *Charlie Chan Is Dead* also celebrated many of the pioneer writers who had paved the way for my generation: Diana Chang, Carlos Bulosan, N.V.M. Gonzalez, Wakako Yamauchi, Hisaye Yamamoto, Bienvenido Santos, José Garcia Villa, and Toshio Mori.

Has anything changed or developed since the publication of the first edition? One thing is for sure—there are many more Asian American writers than ever before. It is exciting to look over the revised "Personal Bibliography" that I have assembled for this edition and note how many fine novels and collections of stories have been published since 1993. Some writers, like me, are first-generation Asian Americans, emigrating from places like China, Korea, Australia, Laos, Cambodia, India, or Pakistan, for example. Others were born on American soil, or are third-, fourth-, and fifth-generation Asian Americans. Obviously, the notion of "What is/What makes Asian American literature?" keeps expanding and evolving. South Asian, Korean, Filipino, and Vietnamese American writers have come into bloom in 2003 and are some of the strongest voices writing in the English language. As I write this, *Bamboo Among the Oaks*, an anthology of contemporary Hmong writing in English, edited by Mai Neng Moua, has just been published by the Minnesota Historical Society Press. It is, however, important to remember that the making of books isn't only about spotting trends or discovering the "next big ethnic thing," but also about digging deep into our past, unearthing long-forgotten treasures, recontextualizing and recognizing those who came before us and broke new ground. *The Anchored Angel*, a collection of the late José Garcia Villa's selected writings (including essays on his work by other writers and critics), happily falls into this category. Thanks to the efforts of editor Eileen Tabios and the ever-innovative Kaya Press, Villa's poems and stories have found a new audience since the inclusion of his minimalist fiction in the original *Charlie Chan Is Dead*.

Subtitled *At Home in the World, Charlie Chan Is Dead 2* once again brings together an array of fresh, vibrant, dissonant voices, alongside several writers from the first edition. Some—like Carlos Bulosan, Hisaye Yamamoto, Han Ong, Bharati Mukherjee, David Wong Louie, and Lois-Ann Yamanaka—are represented by different stories. Bold, confident, imaginative, and courageous, the forty-two writers in this anthology take us on a wild and unpredictable journey—from a humble village in the Philippine countryside to a discreet boutique in Hong Kong specializing in sinister sexual toys; from a posh celebrity estate in the Hollywood Hills to a cozy love nest in Boston; from a fashionable home in the Left Bank of Paris to a hovel in Saigon. We meet characters who are flawed, compelling, haunting, and unforgettable. They run the gamut—from the scrappy poor who live by their wits to the privileged, melancholy exiles who wander from city to city, consumed by loss and longing.

In Meera Nair's "Video," we encounter a feisty Muslim wife who decides she's had enough of her husband's shenanigans and stages an unorthodox rebellion. In Don Lee's "Voir Dire," we meet an ambivalent Korean American lawyer who's been assigned to defend a young, vicious, remorseless killer. In Eric Gamalinda's "Formerly Known as Bionic Boy," we meet an extraordinary exile from the Marcos-era Philippines, who is both blessed and cursed by his psychic powers. In Ka Vang's "Ms. Pac-Man Ruined My Gang Life," a tough Hmong teenager in Saint Paul, Minnesota, attempts to flee the dead-end violence of her troubled life. In Christian Langworthy's "Mango," we meet the sweet, mixed-race children of a prostitute in war-torn Vietnam, who have learned to take nothing for granted. In Monique Truong's "Live-in Cook," we meet Binh, a reserved young Vietnamese man, who is hired to cook for Gertrude Stein and Alice B. Toklas. In "Separation Anxiety," the gritty excerpt from Brian Ascalon Roley's novel *American Son*, we encounter two conflicted half-white, half-Filipino brothers. Tomas, the older brother, breeds attacks dogs and pretends to be a Mexican gangster. Gabe, the narrator and younger brother, is a gentle dreamer, yet also despises his Filipino half.

In "Mister Porma," R. Zamora Linmark has come up with another sly, witty story set in Hawaii—this time about a male beauty contest. Darrell Lum's hilarious "Fourscore and Seven Years Ago," written in pidgin English, is back. So is Bienvenido Santos's classic "Immigration Blues," which moves us with its unsparing yet tender characterizations of old-time Filipino bachelors seeking love in America. So is Shawn Wong's "Eye Contact," with its pair of sexy, knowing, almost-too-hip-for-their-own-good lovers, and Peter Bacho's revised version of "Rico." Marilyn Chin's angry, defiant voice in "Moon" is now paired with her new, just-as-sassy and ironic "Parable of the Cake." "The Brown House," by Hisaye Yamamoto, gives us a wry look at marriage, and what it means to be black and Asian in America. Bharati Mukherjee's "The Management of Grief" is an eerily prescient classic about the tragic aftermath of a terrorist bombing. Race and sex are examined in profound and unexpected ways as well, in Jhumpa Lahiri's "Sexy," Christina Chiu's "Doctor," and Peter Ho Davies's unsettling "The Hull Case." Karl Taro Greenfeld's "Submission" is an unflinching portrait of an ambitious, cunning young dominatrix in contemporary Hong Kong.

Despite, or because of, these fearful, post–9/11 days of economic uncertainty and political turmoil, the making of art and literature seems more precious and urgent than ever. Arts organizations, alternative presses, and literary collectives, such as Bamboo Ridge in Hawaii, Kaya Press and the Asian American Writers' Workshop in New York City, the Asian American Renaissance in Minneapolis, the Asian American Studies Center at UCLA, and the Keamy Street Workshop in San Francisco, are more vital than ever. Young Asian American writers flourish and grow in such supportive settings, and I have found that the impressive publications that come out of many of these cultural centers—collections of poetry, fiction, plays, oral history, and cultural studies—are great resources for anyone who cares about the past, present, and future of American literature.

As I write this introduction, suicide bombings have taken their grim and grisly toll in Bali, Baghdad, Jerusalem, Jakarta, Cotabato, and Bombay. Acts of terrorism and unspeakable violence have become routine. We're in a global, blood-drenched funk, cynical and despairing of the future. The sense of anxiety and blah in the air is almost palpable. Many of us go about our day-to-day tasks with a nagging, low-grade fever aching in our bones. We ask ourselves the usual obvious, unanswerable questions. What does all this frenzied carnage and destruction mean for our children and our children's children? But we go on. There are some things I cling to, some things I still believe. We write out of personal and often terrifying truths. For many of us, what is personal is also political, and vice versa. We continue to assert and explore who we are as Asians, Asian Americans, and citizens of the world. Yes, we read and we write as acts of resistance and rebellion, as Vargas Llosa says. But we also read and write to remember and to dream. We read and we write to arouse the senses. To lose ourselves, to escape. To walk in someone else's shoes. To empathize and understand. We write to reflect the beauty, cruelty, harmony, and chaos of the universe; we write to inflict the pain and shock and delight of recognition. We write to elicit sympathy, fear, or maybe both.

There are those of us who write simply because we must. All those voices singing, all those lovely ghosts dancing in our heads. The urge to create is essential, the same as the urge to live. Here, then, are the stories.

Jessica Hagedorn
August 27, 2003
New York City

CUNANAN'S WAKE

■ ■ ■

Gina Apostol

If it weren't for Budoy's wife Swanie, our *kapitana*, we would never have reached our pinnacle of achievement (as they say in the high school autograph books). We elected Swanie mayor because she made the best *lechon* in the village. She had perfected the art of basting a pig and transformed her talent into a cottage industry through government prizes and loans from the Women's Small Business Cooperative. She had a thief's cunning and a grandmother's tenacity—no one could outwit, outprofit, or outcook Kapitana Swanie. Her house soon became a meat packaging and distribution plant; her self-rotating Swanie Roaster™, patent number 87609-A, was exported to American cities, places like San Diego or Daly City.

In personal matters, however, Kapitana Swanie was not so lucky. For starters, she was married to Budoy. No offense, but though he was the strongest man in town, he wasn't the sharpest. He was a dreamer. The only profit he had to show for himself was the rise of his belly, a predictable account. He had given her one child and that was it: Joey.

Everyone knew about Joey but nobody talked about him. Once in a while, somebody would return from the city with some new snatch of

GINA APOSTOL was born in Manila, Philippines, in 1963. Her first novel, *Bibliolepsy*, won the Philippine National Book Award for Fiction in 1998. She has just completed her second novel, *The Gun Dealer's Daughter*. Her stories have appeared in various anthologies and journals, including *Flippin': Filipino Writing on America*; *Babaylan: An Anthology of Filipina and Filipina-American Writing*; and *Bold Words: A Century of Asian American Writing*. She lives in Dobbs Ferry, New York, with her daughter, Nastasia.

gossip, and small talk would follow. But we pitied Kapitana Swanie—and, to be honest, we feared Budoy, who used to be a bodyguard for Chinese gamblers. Nobody talked about Joey.

■ ■ ■

Benedicto Amolar, the college boy, came up from the city and accosted us with the news. He slapped Budoy's drinking arm with a newspaper, spilling his *basi*. "Hey—isn't this guy your cousin?"

"Careful, boy," Budoy warned. He whistled for Taranta and she emerged from behind the *puka*-shell curtain that separated her world from ours, dirt kitchen from dirt restaurant. Taranta was heavy with her fourth child, and her husband, the doctor, was fooling around with his fourth nurse-intern. Every time he had an affair, Taranta got pregnant, which made it easier for us to keep track of his indiscretions.

Benedicto jabbed at the headline: VERSACE MURDERED! "Look, it says the killer's from our province. Cunanan. Isn't your mother a Cunanan?"

"Maybe I didn't go off to some fancy school in Manila, but I can still read," Budoy grumbled. "And yeah, I read that. So what, Pig? Why don't you shut up and have a Coca? It's on me."

Benedicto was a skeletal yet handsome lad, with a haunted, tuberculous look. We called him Pig, for short.

Pig eased himself onto the bench.

Taranta came with a new pitcher of *basi* and a glass of Coke. She waddled over, oily as an emperor penguin. I watched the way her blouse stuck to her, a sheet of cellophane kissing the moon. I love every woman I see, even the ugly ones. I'm a connoisseur of humanity, its lumps and marks and tics. A woman bearing the burden of the world always has that potent look of sex and tragedy, desire and trauma, dread in love. Taranta's figure inspired my adolescent empathy, which began in the loins but flowered in the heart, or the liver—whichever was the seat of this greasy compassion. Her breasts jiggled as she sighed. And then she cleaned up the mess and clattered away, reeking of sizzling *pusit* and charcoal.

It was 7:30 in the evening, and we, too, had begun to stink, our moist flab giving off a humid excretion, a dipsomaniac spume. We were Taranta's favorite customers, early to drink and late to surrender, indulgence trapped in our flesh like banked smoke. We looked like drunks, we smelled like drunks, and we knew that one day we would die like drunks: soggy-headed, fetid, and unmourned. But none of that concerned us, at least not right then. Our wives and girlfriends were in their places, playing mayor or mayordoma, building up their self-esteem at our expense. But like I said, I love women, especially for their contribution to our longevity. How could the human race survive without their long-suffering, almost miraculous ability to revive and spawn, fuck and fornicate with, let's face it, beasts like us?

"So what?" Budoy said, examining Benedicto's newspaper. "Who cares? Everyone is crazy in America. All the killers who come from there—remember that one who made pickles out of fingers?"

"Yeah," I said. "Dahmer. Preserved their heads, too."

"And they killed John Lennon," Dadong added, bitterly. "Americans killed John Lennon."

I nodded. "In New York, they have a big park for him with strawberries."

Budoy spat out his betel nut and poured himself more *basi*.

"But this one's a Cunanan," Pig said. "He's your cousin. My aunt Toria said so."

"She does know your family," I said. "Ever since your uncle turned her down in '52, she's been taking notes."

Pig snatched the paper back from Budoy. "There's a bounty on his head."

We huddled around him. "You're right: FBI's Most Wanted. Ha! Takes a Filipino to escape the FBI—that's a Pinoy for you!"

Dadong lifted his glass. "*Yan ang* Pinoy!"

We shouted, clinked glasses. "*Mabuhay*! Long live Cunanan!"

"Even if he is a queer," Pig noted.

Budoy didn't share in our revelry. "So what?" he said. "So what if my mother's uncle's son lived in San Diego, America, and had a homosexual son who broke his heart? It must have broken his heart—sending that kid to an expensive Catholic school just so he could turn out *bakla*."

We talked it over, and in the end, we decided Budoy was right. Cunanan was the champion of TNT, *tago ng tago*, hiding for your life— the Filipino way of life in America—and for that, he deserved our respect. But beyond that, he was an American killer, and an American problem. America had brought him up.

Still, we sought him out in the papers again the next day. No one knew if he had ever even been to the Philippines, but the dailies liked the story. The fashion killer. They put his charming, fat-cheeked face on the cover every day, if only to announce that he was still on the lam—disappeared, somewhere, in the wilds of Florida or Illinois.

"Ha!" said Dadong. "They'll never get him."

We raised our glasses again. "*Mabuhay*! Long live Cunanan!"

The longer Cunanan remained free, the more sympathy I felt for him. Not for his Filipino name or troubled looks or his connection to our brooding friend Budoy or even the common cause we made with him in drink. It was the story of a hunted man, alone with himself. A man in the dark. It doesn't take much to move me, a lapsed Catholic, after all. I've kept the tenderness and lost the moral steel. My heart is a sissy. I didn't care about the killings or anything else that had come before his long, sunswept flight through Miami's summer. I rooted for him, I suppose, the way we all did, all of us drunks who knew too much about our own stupid lives.

Junior, the *barangay* captain, disagreed. "No tolerance, no pity. If I were in the FBI, I would just gun him down dead. That's what I'd do if I saw him."

Dadong shook his head. "Just gun him down dead? Your own countryman—your own cousin?"

"All the more reason. Disgrace to the Philippines. Shame on his country."

"Yeah, you'd shoot him with your cheap, second-hand Tokarev. Thing takes five rounds just to kill a rat," said Dadong. He was a reckless kid, just out of school, and he already had a belly.

Junior took out his precious gun, the gift his father had given him when he won the *barangay* elections despite not having finished elementary school. He pointed the barrel at Dadong, who froze. You could see that young Dadong's mind had partially scampered away—what was left of it, anyway, after all the booze.

Everyone got quiet. I imagined the headline. "Two Killed over Cunanan. Dateline: San D___." That was how our little town would have gone down in history. Then Budoy said, "Come on now, put it down, Junior," and Junior did.

■ ■ ■

CHARLIE CHAN IS DEAD 2

A few days later, Kapitana came to see us in the middle of the afternoon, agitated, as we sat sweating through our undershirts. We tried to be polite.

"He's dead!" she shrieked. "It's all over the papers!"

"It's on the radio," said Taranta from behind the *puka*-shell curtains.

The FBI had surrounded his hideaway boat with SWAT tacticians, but they were wasting their time. Cunanan didn't even put up a fight. He killed himself. "He buckled," Pig said.

We nodded.

"So what?" said Budoy. "Better to take your own life than be shot down like a wild boar."

"Too bad," said Dadong. "I thought he was going to get away."

Junior spat at him. "*Loko-loko*, all of you. He deserved to die. They should cook him on one of Budoy's spits, on a Swanie Roaster™. He's just a criminal."

"*Putang ina!*" said Budoy.

Junior reached for his Tokarev. "You want to stand up for your cousin?"

"He's not my cousin."

"He's your cousin, all right," said Junior. "Just like Joey is your son."

"*Putang ina!*" said Budoy, and he lunged for him.

If not for Swanie, who knows what could have happened? She smacked Budoy with a copy of *People's Tonight* and stared down Junior. No fury like a woman, especially one with the arms of a hog wrangler and the legal authority of a *kapitana*. That afternoon she had a mad look in her eyes, like a chicken that knows a rainstorm is coming. I had a *gallina* who looked just like her once—red-eyed, stiff-winged, stock still on a sunny afternoon.

Junior took a sip of his *basi*, and Budoy sat down.

"Now look here, Budoy, you're coming home with me. Family council." Kapitana Swanie was livid. "Taranta, can I see you tonight? I want to ask you a favor."

Aye-aye, Kapitana. All hail, Mayor Swanie Roaster™!

We took another swig in her honor.

■ ■ ■

I must admit I was disappointed by the headlines. He had his chance on the international stage, and he let us down. Dying like a coward in a ship's hold. If he'd brandished a bolo, at least he'd have shown defiance, a Filipino middle finger at the FBI. What kind of a macho killer was this? *Bakla*. A homosexual death. But I felt the injustice of my judgment. Here was the story of a man, after all, in the throes of terror, flinching like Dadong before a gun, wracked by despair and inner torment I could not fathom. Who knows what lurks? Who was I to judge? What is a man?

I don't think Kapitana Swanie had the temperament—or, perhaps, the ability—to contemplate these questions. She was a woman of action and accomplishment. And for her it was simple: he was family. She had to show her solidarity with cousin Pidok in San Diego, America. He had sent out a plea in the *Philippine Inquirer*. Then she could wash her hands of the whole business and get back to her life. *Basta*.

No one could ever quite figure out the chain of events, how our small town got dragged into a national story. Sure, if you think about it, all towns in the Philippines have their distinctions in the local heraldry. We all know about the red-shit residents of B___, producers of the best *basi*, and about the bolo-wielding wild men of C___, feared for their hotheadedness. They're famed in their vicinity, within the radius of jeepney and bus routes that carried pigs and pesticides from town to town, but unknown along Patranco North, which cuts a swath across provinces too remote for our prejudice. Even San D___, our fair village, has acquired its own reputation: we're known for our stupidity, for the morons and idiots in our midst. Maybe it's because we have no public school, though Kapitana has threatened to build one. Still, we hear about it every day at the bus stop, when the porters leap up to snatch a bundle of chickens from the roof, or help widows off the middle bench of the jeep. The minute the jeep is ready for the next passenger, the yelling and posturing begin—all in good fun, of course. "*Pula-pulang tae!*" we shout. Red shit, red shit! "*Mga bobo ng bayan!*" the passengers reply. No-read, no-write! They put fingers to their temples to denote the source of our fame, and we stone them until they disappear, rattling and laughing like diesel hyenas.

■ ■ ■

It was just after siesta, and we were gossiping about cockfights, Radyo Bombo, police calls, the election, and so on, when Budoy arrived with an announcement. He looked like shit, all stubbly face, bleary eyes, and dog breath, though he was dressed in a pressed polo shirt, cuffed pants, and church shoes, a black band wrapped around his sleeve.

"Boys, you are invited to a wake for my cousin," he said.

"Oh!" Dadong said. "Sorry to hear. Who is it, *bay*?"

"For cousin Pidok's nephew. The guy who died in Florida."

"For Cunanan?" I asked.

Junior made a loud grunt, as if to laugh.

"Yeah," Budoy said, looking down. "The Kapitana asked me to tell you."

"A wake for *loko-loko*—that killer?" Junior muttered, so only I could hear.

"Ssh," I said.

Pig couldn't stop smiling. This would score him big points with his friends in Manila. You want local color? Beat that! *Mga bobo ng bayan!*

"But you don't know him," said Dadong earnestly. "You never met him. It's like having a party for Madonna."

"If Madonna was a serial killer," Junior added under his breath.

Budoy grimaced. "It's the Kapitana, *bay*. You know Swanie: when she has an idea . . . I didn't want to do it. But he is my cousin, after all. And we're roasting two pigs."

Not one pig—two. That was like begging for attention, flattering our dignity. We went.

■ ■ ■

Cunanan's wake wasn't anything like the city papers reported: a huge fiesta, the whole town in attendance, fireworks. It was a sparse, lackluster affair, improvised at the last minute. Taranta was there, working in the kitchen as all three of her children ran around. (Her husband, the louse, was nowhere to be found.) The regular squad of professional mourners was there, looking just about ready to die themselves. There was the usual bunch of moochers, people who never missed a birth or a death or a saint's holiday. And then there was us: the drunks and louts, the great men of San D___.

The professional mourners had voices like pumice stones, gravelly and grating; I would carry them to purgatory just to shut them up. Flesh shriveled like coconut meat in the sun, they wailed lost names to a forgetful God. They were ordinary ladies, transformed by death into supplicants, holy though decaying. I took off my slippers and hat and ignored them. Like everyone else, I headed straight for the *basi* and the beer.

Budoy lumbered about for a while, one hand offering sweetcakes as the other brandished the spit—a menacing steel skewer. Then he went off to assemble the Swanie Roaster™.

When the first pig came through the door, stitched and stiff with the fruit in its mouth, lashed and wounded at the chest like a nude and tortured Saint Sebastian, the party perked up. Pig, the scholar, started strumming some Beatles song. Dadong stood and stretched his puny body, as if he were getting ready to sing. Junior fiddled with the karaoke machine. We reached the high point of the party, the pig in heat and karaoke in play. Junior and Dadong began their first duet. And in the middle of it all was Kapitana, in a black dress, black veil, and black shoes, as if she were going to light candles on All Souls' Day. She wore a black band around her sleeve, and her face looked as if she hadn't slept for weeks. I had already begun the first beer of the fifth round—or was it the fifth beer of the first round?—and I tried to remember what was going on.

Had the Kapitana gone mad? She was wearing Ray-Bans, just like Donatella Versace, the sister. Except that Donatella probably didn't have a porkbelly ridge swelling the georgette fabric of her clothes, or those stout arms—not unless she, too, trussed hogs for a living.

In Milan, the Versace family had held a funeral filled with dark Italian veils, a high mass with Elton John. The society pages of Manila's newspapers ran the photos as if it were the death of one of their own, Milan merely the capital's anagram, and Italy a province along Pantranco South. The expanded territory claimed by the papers had grown as Filipino immigration became bolder and more versatile: fishermen in Penang, cabin crews in the Caribbean, nurses in Denmark, translators in China, busboys in Brussels, telemarketers in Texas, housekeepers in Hollywood, phone technicians in Indonesia, basketball players in Dhahran. Even Italy was full of Filipinos dusting the Murano treasures of the rich. No wonder we felt the world was our home and Versace's abattoir our boudoir. Filipinos were everywhere: in the bedrooms, the privies, the boiler rooms, the cocktail parties, the kitchens, the bowers, the staterooms, and the sewers of the idle rich. We could swallow the world.

Thus, the newsmen in Manila should have scorned the festivities in Milan, to reflect the jaundiced eye, for instance, of an expatriate cook in a Roman home who can concoct all kinds of ravioli in her sleep but who dreams of adobo, who picks up Italian slang without a sweat but longs only for her humid home. Instead, there were articles about the funeral songs, the celebrities, and their exotic fashions. And then, later on, when they heard about the village of San D___—six ramps and a dust road off of the Southern Luzon Expressway—all they could muster was ridicule and cartoons. A wake for Versace's killer? The Township of Stupid: that was us.

■ ■ ■

"Boy," Junior turned to me, munching on a rib. "I always knew it. This family is mad. How she won the last election, I don't know, with that scandal over her *bakla* son, that girlie-boy Joey. They say he's wearing women's clothes on Roxas Boulevard, doing a show for the Japanese. Fake tits and sequins—*bakla*! Swanie screamed like a pig when she found out he had gone. She'll be voted out in the next election, mark my words."

A globule of fat dribbled from between his teeth and he poured himself another drink.

"And who are we going to vote for?" Dadong asked. "You?"

Junior just laughed.

"Ssh!" said one of the mourners, praying in another room. "Show some respect for the dead!"

Kapitana kept coming and going, from the yard to the house and back again. Minding the spit, bringing more drinks. Behind the Ray-Bans, her face was puffy, and I imagined her eyes were red. Taranta kept returning to replenish dishes, looking around all the time for her husband, and I kept my eyes on her, feeling a dull *basi* desire. The professional mourners were eating now, chewing loudly, claiming earthly dues for their heavenly services. Budoy sat patiently outside, keeping watch over the second pig. He looked gray from all the heat.

The Manila papers and Radyo Bombo and the pundits—they could laugh all they wanted, heap ridicule upon the backward people of San D___. But we knew we were separate from the rest of the world, separate from the Vatican's mumbo jumbo about burying the dead, separate from the lives of the fashion models in Milan; separate, even, from the rustle of newspapers in Manila's coffee houses, the rumble of trucks down Southern Luzon Expressway, the network of names along the tourist's chain of tannery-towns and dreamlace-weavers. We were separate, obscure, worthless—everyone knew that, even Joey, the prodigal son. But we lived for adventure. *Tago ng tago*, life to the lees!

As the wake wore on, and the ashen clouds of the roast yielded to the faint, sweetish smell of scorched vinegar and burnt fat, we moved outside, and even the professional mourners squatted with us, mixing Coca with their *basi*, chewing cigars, swatting flies. Songs regressed to a fevered languor, and Junior stood up to sing.

"*Cuando, cuando? Cuando, cuando?*"

Dadong banged on the guitar, trying to keep up with the karaoke.

"If you see him tell me when—*Cuando, cuando, cuando*—Jooooeey! Every moment's a daaay! Every day lasts a liiifetime! Oh my Joey tell me *when!*"

Junior strutted around like Harry Belafonte, holding the microphone like a torch. We clapped.

Then we saw, and we stopped clapping.

Kapitana stood behind Junior. She'd come up from the house to check our food, our drinks. It wasn't so much her sorrow that stopped us. There was something about seeing this fat, strong woman in Donatella's lace veil, shaking with anger, behind Junior, red-faced from all the *basi*. When we saw Kapitana, we saw the wild, keening face of a blind prophet in Ray-Bans. And then we heard the shout.

"*Putang ina!*"

Junior stopped, and we ducked.

We felt the shot more than we heard it—a whipcrack that split the afternoon in two. We scampered for safety, moochers and mourners alike, and we heard the reverberation like a blunt thud against a mattress spring. Chickens squawked in the bushes. In the distance, I thought I heard a bus groan. And when I looked up from my perch against a coconut tree, I saw benches overturned, the karaoke still spinning, sotto voce, and the splayed, shattered carcass of the denuded pig on its throne of banana leaves. Its gnawed ribcage was pierced through the center, where the absent heart would have been, but the head remained intact, the apple undisturbed.

Junior had escaped unscathed, still holding the microphone.

Budoy rushed in with ashes on his red face.

Kapitana threw the Tokarev at Junior and wailed, "One more word about Joey and you die."

The karaoke cranked: *"Cuando, cuando, cuando, cuando?"*

And I saw the headlines again: "Pig Shot at Killer's Wake. Dateline: San D___."

■ ■ ■

Temporary insanity, we say now. Kapitana Swanie got carried away that day, spending all that money on a wake for nobody—a boy who was no man. Later we applauded when the second *lechon* arrived. A specter of grief in a roast pig, mouth open to grip eternity. We crunched into its flesh with praise, goodwill, and greed, and washed it down with *basi*.

FASCINATION, GRAVITY, AND DEEPLY DONE KISS

■ ■ ■

Lisa Asagi

There was nothing at all significant that caused me to tell of this except for a sudden lapse in perception. How steam holds long enough to play against any conjured change in temperature, how a reaction can be so visibly shaken out of something as mundane as a shower in the middle of an ordinary evening.

■ ■ ■

Perhaps it was an inadequate amount of ventilation. Whatever the case, I had never found myself before in a room so vividly filled with vagueness, instilling an inertia normally reserved for a slipping off a very steep cliff. It had nothing to do with contemplation. I simply turned off the water, parted the curtains, and found myself not being able to find my towel. So unlike me. No not nude. Naked. In a fog. It could have been a smoke-filled room and my last moment. I could have died. But instead I am alone and worried about it.

■ ■ ■

There is a painting that hangs in a museum two miles from my apartment. It is a watercolor by Paul Klee. Smaller than what you'd expect from any book. Notepaper-sized. It's strange how wood frames pro-

LISA ASAGI is a writer and media artist. She is the author of two chapbooks — *Physics* and *Twelve Scenes at 12 a.m.* Although based in San Francisco, she is often found in Las Vegas, Los Angeles, London, and driving at odd hours around Honolulu, where she was born in 1966 and raised. At this writing, she is working on a book called *Isola*.

nounce the empty space that emerges from thin lines and segments of color. When you see them all lined up on the wall there is a strange sadness in the insect lines, deserts, and he wasn't even trying to be abstract. Some of them involve an image of a musical note called a fermata, which instructs a sustained pause, the prolongation of a tone, chord, or rest beyond its nominal value. He drew it on its side so it looked like a crescent moon. To musicians it is known as a bird's eye because of this elliptical shape.

■ ■ ■

Once, once I fell in love with a married woman. Once, I thought that this body she left me with was able to have her live within, absorbed like an ink bird on my thigh or some secret bullet. But this is not possible anymore because I cannot stop thinking about her. Cannot stop interfering with the nature of motion, have it grow out of me, let it envelop, encircle, then gradually expand until I am freed to be nothing but an atom already accustomed to the gravity in the next phase of its world. I stutter. I don't stare long enough. I eat too much, then I don't eat at all. I buy books and don't read them. I borrow books and read them. I walk around the block and can't decide the best time to cross the street. I practice falling in love with strangers. I practice falling in love with my friends. I practice falling in love because I know that this is the only way out. That perhaps one day, I will find myself hopefully lost with the gravity of a situation like her again. And then I will know why this feeling is brick red. That it is not my imagination. Because I have been practicing. Because maybe soon I will be able to say why there is a difference between secretly falling within a building of thought and actually free-falling quickly, a bright glance, the figure of a hand stretching outwards, the length of a deeply done kiss.

■ ■ ■

What's important. What's relevant. It always seems to depend on the minute of day or nonfiction to the point of some kind of rage. A storm in the eye.

■ ■ ■

"She was talking about her soul. She was talking about the angle of her soul. The one behind hindsight, the dashboard. That walking sleepless giant chasing shadows across tables of universes, knocking over chairs, twisting forks, teetering glasses. An animate angle that sweeps islands and airplanes into lips at the speed of sound, and swiftly closes as if an eyelid. The speed of light. You smiled. She was talking about fascination. She was thinking about desire, how it can only grow vivid once it is left long enough to feel itself as one thing. Original."

■ ■ ■

The storm in the eye of my life.

■ ■ ■

I know. It's odd. But I should say that it never felt anything close to abrupt at the time. Maybe I had been in love with her for three years. And maybe those years threw themselves into a wall and broke for two weeks, the strongest and loudest that ever happened to me. It scattered molecules, feathers in an atomic living room of a slowly disintegrating, slowly regenerating physically political world.

■ ■ ■

Strange but it happens.

■ ■ ■

Maybe if I start from the very beginning nothing will be lost and it would be okay. I think that if my body were a boat, to describe the ocean around me will mean that nothing will ever sink. Don't you agree?

■ ■ ■

Once there was an island that felt so alone it stopped. Got too involved with folding waves and how nothing happened to end this. It grew deaf and then violent. Then it could not tell the difference between land, flesh, blood and water. Coldness of a flame so far below the peacefulness of the Arctic Circle, it burned itself down to the wick just to spite the watchful eyes of time.

■ ■ ■

Wait a minute. That was drama. But this wants to be a story about semblance and difference between the object and subject of desire, the difference between a statue and a play, text and skin, music and motion, or an incredibly long sentence that says nothing about how one brief moment can go on to mean the world for a very long time.

■ ■ ■

So.

■ ■ ■

Soon the millennium will turn itself over and until then, anything can happen. The placement of the story, in the geometry of inclining angles, becomes strangely fixated into acute and recurrent sections. Where once was science, you distill chance. Whatever the call, you leave messages and send letters from the storm. Hope that if anything, they will find a course of reference beneath the cooling images, between the colorfully televised warnings of hurricanes and psychology. Maps were never useful in defending against tempests.

■ ■ ■

So you write if you can, you say:

■ ■ ■

wait.

■ ■ ■

or

■ ■ ■

Dear Miranda,

■ ■ ■

nobody told me this world
would be nothing but islands.
that you lived on an island around me.
that you would leave.
Sign it.

■ ■ ■

FASCINATION, GRAVITY, AND DEEPLY DONE KISS

Once I was walking down Sixteenth Street, heard a nocturne being played from a car at a stoplight and actually looked to see if it was her. It was the same nocturne that I asked her to teach me. Her father was a pianist, grew her around the mathematics of music and so notes would nestle into the corners of her ears. Like painters' eyes could absorb degrees of paint. She had this ebony baby grand piano and would play it at night after she thought I had gone to sleep. Three thousand miles and still I see her face in the sheets of glass, ceiling, walls of wood and plaster, cups of water, curved up like a glance. I don't want to think it, but sometimes I feel there is no such thing as land anymore. That maybe there are just boats who believe they are on rivers. Drifting on the same ocean all of the time.

■ ■ ■

It's so late. To some people it is just early enough. The sun is going to reappear within a matter of minutes. It has to. Motion as the habit that surrounds things that happen.

■ ■ ■

When I brush my teeth I realize that I am thirty-three years old. It is a very human feeling.

■ ■ ■

Run the faucet, then you don't. In an adult body, walk through the short hallway and into the angles assembled for an immediate future. Turn out the light and lie down.

■ ■ ■

It is a long fall into the fact that it is so late and uncomfortable, but you are accustomed to levels of tepidness. When it was too warm you grew fascinations. In these deepening days all you have are those feathers again. And you wander in them, months of curved knives.

■ ■ ■

I can't go to sleep. I don't have to. So then I will have to watch. You know, the earth is nothing but fire contained within itself by tons of ocean and degrees of cooled thickness, acres of rock. Every plot of land, horizontal then vertical, began as an island. They say that biology began on this planet as reaction to the accident. Survival. A self-taught, half-expected emotion whose logic was not understood until millions of afternoon proved enough to hold into evening.

■ ■ ■

I called her three days ago. Saw her a month ago in the post office. Then I saw her at a bus stop. She was standing in a Chinese take-out shop. Then sitting on the dryer in a laundromat. Then I remembered. It was so strange, but after I turned off the shower, parted the curtains and reached for my towel, I thought I saw her walk out of the bathroom. She left the door open.

RICO

■ ■ ■

Peter Bacho

When I was growing up in Seattle, Rico Divina was the baddest Filipino I ever knew, and I knew them all. Vietnam killed him. Not there, but it killed him nevertheless.

The last time I really saw him was August 1967, just before the start of my senior year in high school. I never thought those days would seem as distant and foreign as Burma, or Myanmar as some now call it, or even Vietnam. I was almost seventeen then, and Rico was a little more than a year older. We were both just starting to peer beyond the boundaries of the poor neighborhood that tied us down but also protected us and made us strong. It was home to Rico and me, and in my view, he ruled it.

Like many Filipinos, Rico was short and wiry, but he made up for it by being strong, fast, and clever—traits that earned respect even from the bloods, and they were always the hardest to impress.

White girls were a lot easier. He made them his specialty, particularly the long-legged blondes with ratted hair and heavy makeup. There were always a few at the weekly dances at the community center on Empire Way, hiding in the shadows of the dimly lit halls, their pale skin and high bouffants shining like beacons in the dark.

PETER BACHO was born in Seattle in 1950. He is the author of *Cebu*, *Dark Blue Suit*, and *Nelson's Run*, and one nonfiction work, *Boxing in Black and White*. Awards include an American Book Award, a Washington Governor's Writers Award, and the Murray Morgan Prize. Bacho is currently completing his third novel, *Entrys*.

Rico would always show up at dances alone, resplendent in his tight black slacks, matching black jacket, and felt hat with a narrow—the bloods called it "stingy"—brim. He also wore pointed Italian boots and a pink shirt with a high collar pressed to a sharp, thin edge. All that was missing was the Cadillac, which he wanted but couldn't come close to affording. So he arrived by bus, riding it like the prince of public transportation. I knew he didn't have a car, but it made no difference to the girls he left with, even if they had to pay their own fare.

According to Rico he was bestowing a favor. They were in it for the danger, he explained.

Filipinos always hired black bands; they carried a horn section in addition to two guitarists and a drummer. The extra section shrank each musician's share of the profit. But no matter; this was black music, not white, and the horns made it raw and powerful, something white bands could never do.

Rico loved the horns and the sweating black angels who played them. They were his rhythm-and-blues heralds, and once they kicked in on a tune, he'd scan the room and choose his partner. He never said anything, just looked at his girl for the night and nodded in the general direction of the dance floor. Invariably she would follow, because she knew who Rico was and she understood the rules. Out on the floor she could move and match the rhythm, and maybe even do it really well, as some white girls who were trying to pass for something else were able to do. But it was Rico's show, and he was its dark star.

If the music was slow, he'd hold the girl tight and softly sing the lyrics of lost or impossible love. With the horns setting the mournful mood, he'd roll her rhythmically with his right thigh between her legs, using it like a rudder to guide her, inches off the floor, as he leaned back. I told him once that I could always tell his dance partners; they walked funny, like they'd spent the day on horseback.

Rico changed with the song. To an upbeat tempo he'd skate halfway across the hall on one leg like James Brown, never a single pomaded hair ever out of place. He'd stop suddenly and do the splits, from which he'd just as suddenly rise to continue his journey to the other side. He defied gravity, just like James.

And just like James, his most obvious talents weren't suited for college. He had other skills, other potentials, but by the time public school was through ignoring him, I'm sure he wasn't sure what they were or even that they were.

Rico could dance and he could woo white girls. And there was one other thing: the boy could box. He was still an amateur, but the old guys like Tommy said he had "pro" written on the knuckles of both hands. Tommy, a part-time manager, also ran the Masonic Gym in downtown Seattle where Rico worked out. He'd once been a decent pro fighter, but, as Rico had put it to me, that must have been years ago, before electricity and pan-fried pork chops had turned his belly into mush. Fighting was something well-adjusted white folks didn't understand, but it was what the kids in my neighborhood did. Or even if they didn't, they thought about it all the time. I was more the thinking type, unlike Rico. As far back as I could remember, my mom had said: Think of your future, get an education, go to college. The future, from the day I began to read, was my own map. For Rico, Tommy was the first one to point him to a future, but the map, it turned out, was Tommy's.

■ ■ ■

The last time I saw Rico, he was honing his skills on a scared-looking Mexican kid in the small ring at the Masonic. I went down there that day because I'd heard a rumor that Rico had enlisted. He'd never said anything to me about it, and I wanted to find out.

I walked in at the split second Rico threw a perfectly timed right-hand counter at his opponent's head that, even with headgear and fat sparring gloves, managed to knock the kid hard against the ropes. It was the kind of punch that loosens your eyeballs and rolls them back under your brain. It was even more devastating because Rico threw it just as the Mexican was leaning into his own jab, the effect being doubled because he came onto the punch.

Rico, the old-timers said, was a natural counterpuncher. It's a rare gift that the boxing gods give to a few which allows them to attack when they sense an opening created by an opponent's offensive move. Rico had again displayed his gift; the sound of the punch, his perfect form, the sharp backward snap of the Mexican's head followed by his body's collapse into the straining ring ropes, all testified to it. The blurred sequence of events, witnessed by myself and the small circle of Masonic regulars, drew our collective "ooh."

We all knew an assassin was at work and, like any good assassin, Rico knew his work wasn't done. Seeing the Mexican draped helplessly against the ropes with his hands down was too good an invitation. He almost skipped like a schoolgirl to close the distance between himself and his prey, and he held his right hand back a bit more than usual. He had enough torque in that right to launch his victim on a straight trajectory, like one of Henry Aaron's line drives, to some southern point where Spanish was spoken. I knew it, and evidently Tommy did, too. Quickly, and despite his girth, Tommy scrambled into the ring and slid like a fat snake in what he had to know was a vain attempt to beat Rico to his launching spot. "Stop!" he screamed from his prone position as the right-hand rocket took off.

"Goddammit!" Tommy muttered a second later, still on the canvas. The Mexican's torso sagged deep into the taut ropes that strained and flung him face forward onto the canvas. The kid was out even before he landed on his nose and lips, not his landing gear of choice, around which a pool of blood quickly started to form. At the side of his face lay his mouthpiece, knocked loose by the impact.

Tommy was livid. He just lay there for a second, stunned and furious, looking at the prostrate body; his assistants, armed with smelling salts and towels, were already entering the ring. The old man rose, positioning himself close to Rico and in front of him. "Get outta' here!" he screamed, flapping his stubby arms for emphasis, slapping them repeatedly against his sides. With each smack, his heavy tits shook more than a stripper's. I started to giggle; he looked like he was trying to fly.

"You got it," Rico said calmly as he turned to go.

"And don't come back," Tommy added.

"Got that too," Rico said as he climbed between the ring ropes. He paused, one leg in the ring, the other out, and turned toward Tommy. "Too much garlic in that last batch of chops," Rico said in the same flat tone. "Smell like a gypsy queen."

"You're outta' here!" Tommy screamed, stung by the truth.

Rico started to walk toward the dressing room. "Startin' to look like one too, fatso," he said without looking back, but loud enough to be heard.

It wasn't the first time Tommy had yelled at Rico for losing control, for fighting instead of sparring. But I thought this really might be it— not because Tommy wouldn't take him back, a fight manager almost never turns away a potential moneymaker, and Tommy loved my friend's talent more than he loved pork chops—but because Rico himself had decided it was over. He wanted to leave with a bang. That was his way.

I wondered what he'd have to say as I followed him back to the dressing room. I opened the door slowly and saw him in the dim light, sitting on a stool, slumped in front of his locker. The cool of the room collided with the heat from his body, creating steam that covered him like morning fog. It was a little eerie. I stood by the door, waiting for him to turn and speak or do something to bring us back to more familiar terrain.

Finally, he looked over his shoulder and nodded at me. It wasn't much of a sign, but it was enough for the moment. "Goin' up in smoke, buddy," I said, trying to sound steady.

Rico paused and looked at himself. He chuckled. "Sure am," he said.

"What happened?"

"Fucker uppercut me," he said, "but Tommy didn't do shit. He knows the rules for sparring. Break clean. No cheap shots. Goddam Tommy. Can't count on him for nothin'." Rico pointed to a discolored spot on his neck. "That fucker nailed me," he said angrily. "He wanted to fight, so I fought. Nailed him back, too. Stapled his face to the floor."

I nodded. Rico laughed at the thought. The laugh almost put me at ease. I raised the question that had brought me to the gym in the first place. "I heard, man," I said quietly. "True story?"

There was no answer.

"Your mom called my mom and she don't want you to . . ."

Rico interrupted me, staring at the floor as he spoke. "Can't help it," he said. "Got nothin' goin' here."

It was the answer I didn't want to hear. I glanced around the room looking for someplace to sit. I felt heavy, like a bunch of men each the size of Buddha had jumped on my back and stayed there. I spotted a bench across the room and walked toward it.

"Damn," I said to myself as I sat down and buried my face in my hands. I'd known a lot of Filipinos from the neighborhood. Most were drafted; some enlisted. Most went to Vietnam. Some returned; others didn't. I knew our time was coming. That's just the way it was, and I accepted it. We all did. In that sense, we were like our fathers and uncles who had fought in Europe or in the Pacific—and if they were lifers, in

Korea, too. Like them, we asked no questions; couldn't even think of one to ask, much less expect an answer. For us, Vietnam had no moral ambiguities; the government called, and we went. Simple as that.

We vaguely hated communism, although we didn't know why. Fats Domino/the domino theory; knew one/heard about the other. Maybe related, but we weren't sure how. I didn't learn until much later that boys from poor neighborhoods like ours carried the flag into dangerous places for powerful, arrogant, and profoundly foolish old white men. But that was later. At sixteen I thought I'd go, too. I just wanted Rico to wait for us to do it together.

"Had to, Buddy," he said, using my nickname and interrupting my morose reverie. "Got no school. Got no job. Ain't colored, so I ain't got no black power let-your-hair-grow-out-don't-conk-it shit." I looked at him blankly. "What we got?" Rico asked angrily, referring to Filipinos in general and himself in particular. He got that way sometimes when he talked about his future, the one he was sure he didn't have. Rico stared at me straight and hard.

I scratched my head and scrambled; I wanted to throw a curve and back him off. "White girls," I finally said. " 'Specially blondes, tall long-legged ones."

Rico's laugh broke the momentum I'd thought was building to an uncomfortable point. "Yeah," he said, grinning. "Devil bitches, but I love 'em. Most bloods don't mess with 'em now, 'ceptin Sammy Davis." He smirked, then shrugged. "Leaves more for me," he said finally.

I felt confident enough to try to turn it serious again.

"Rico," I said quietly. "Don't go, at least not yet. There's ways . . . you know, deferments. White guys do it all the time. Like marriage . . ."

He shook his head no and looked at me like I'd lost it.

"Like college . . ." I said, trying again. I knew I was grasping, and I knew he knew.

He rolled his eyes. "Yeah, like I'm a perfect candidate, a goddam summa, whatever."

I was making no points and was getting a little desperate. "Your mom," I blurted.

That hit home. He gave me no quick answer. "I love her," he said finally. "But I'm eighteen, I'm signed, and I'm gone. The Marines own my butt now, not Mama."

So it was over. I knew then he'd closed the matter before I'd even had the chance to open it. I felt the Buddhas get heavier, and I sagged just a bit more.

Rico sensed this and tried his best to cheer me up. He smiled. "Hey, man, every Flip wants a gunfight," he said with bravado. "You know, our heroic dick-expandin' tradition, more shit to impress the ladies with and tell our kids and grandkids." His effort to cheer me didn't work. Undeterred, he tried another route. "I thought about leavin' and what I'd leave you," he said solemnly as he reached into his training bag. He found what he was looking for and handed it to me; it was a small black book. I looked at the book and reached to take it.

"Man, what's this?"

Rico feigned surprise. "Yo' mama raise you in a cave or somethin'? That book there's my address book—full of white girls, 'specially blondes. Ain't gonna be needin' it where I'm goin'. Gettin' me a new one anyway, full of Vietnamese writin' and female Vietnamese names." He mimed a drum roll with his hands. "I'm changin' my taste," he said. "Expandin' my horizons to find new pussy, goin' like Columbus where no Flip's ever been . . ."

"Damn, man, all right, okay," I said sharply, interrupting him. Rico was starting to talk trash I didn't want to hear.

He seemed to notice, or at least that's what I thought. "I've had this book a long, long time," Rico then said, sounding dead serious. It was hard to tell with him, but going to war wasn't a trifling thing, so I gave him the benefit of the doubt. Wrong move. I was tricked like a trout rising to a fisherman's fly.

"I got it years ago," he went on, fixing me with a sharp look. My intense focus told him I was hooked; it was all he needed to know. He paused dramatically before reeling me in. "Before my first shorthair," he said in a near whisper. His deadpan continued. "What the shit," he said as he shrugged his shoulders. "A boy's gotta' dream."

I couldn't help smiling, despite my sudden irritation and sense of impending loss. Rico didn't miss a step.

"That book there," he said, and he repeated himself for emphasis, "that book there even got a name."

It was too late. Like always, it was his dialogue, just like it was always his dance. I was his straight man and had to play along. I sighed. "What is it, man?"

CHARLIE CHAN IS DEAD 2

"Ho's I Know," he said, with a master's timing. Rico studied me, looking at my face for a sign of reaction. I didn't give him any. To my mind, this was too serious a moment.

"Oh," I said flatly. I held back and gathered my thoughts before speaking again. "So this is it?" I asked. I listened to myself uttering the words, creating the accusatory question. I'd miss him, which was all the more reason to keep the tone even. In our neighborhood, emotion was for sissies and not to be shown, even to friends. I thought I'd succeeded. I guess I hadn't.

"Hey," Rico said. "It ain't forever." His voice was softer. I looked at him closely and knew this time he wasn't setting me up.

"Man, come on by tonight," I said hopefully. "My folks, dinner . . . you know, a righteous goodbye."

"Can't."

For Rico, "can't" never meant "maybe." I pressed him, though, because I figured I had nothing to lose. I unloaded both barrels, or tried to.

"The folks, man," I started, "they . . ."

"Can't," he said again, with a firmness that ended any further appeal to my parents' affection. He looked at me and didn't speak until he was convinced I got the message. "Look," he said finally. "Got some time before I report and I'm gettin' outta' town, maybe to Frisco. Ain't never been there and I'd kinda' like to go, you know, like Cookie tried to."

Cookie was our friend, a young black kid we'd grown up with. All he talked about, once he figured out his dick wasn't just for pissing, was getting laid. He didn't care whether the girls were black, white, yellow, whatever—a fact attested to by his multicolored progeny and their angry grandparents who universally threatened to harm him. All he cared about was a girl's attitude, which he hoped was enthusiastic, and finding more eligibles and more places to hide.

Cookie knew Seattle was too small; he kept bumping into relatives of his lovers who wanted to kill him. The last, the brother of a Chinese girl, shot at him but missed. His frustrated assailant shouted at the fleeing Cookie that sooner or later he'd turn him into a barbecue slab and hang him from a hook. The image of his glazed flank hanging in the front window of a Chinatown restaurant frightened Cookie, and he decided it was time to go. He had to figure out where, and thought he'd discovered Heaven when he read about San Francisco and its sexual revolution.

When I last saw him he was growing his hair out, and I listened while he recited a litany of black-power phrases. He explained he was going to San Francisco to poke a commune full of white middle-class hippie girls who, by doing his black butt, would think they were promoting social justice. He'd figured it out. But just as he was about to leave, his draft notice came. Cookie died in Vietnam and never made it to Freakin' Frisco.

Rico didn't want to make the same mistake; I knew he had a good reason to leave, so I backed off and let the matter drop. He must have known I'd surrendered, and that giving up wasn't easy.

"Look," he said kindly, "it's hard, 'specially 'cause you and me are like this." He clenched his fist to illustrate. "You know, tight like brothers."

I looked at him and nodded agreement, feeling too sad to reply. "Guess this is it," I said, as I extended my hand. "Better get goin'."

He took my hand, pulled me toward him, and hugged me awkwardly. "Look," he said as he released me a moment later. "You're smart and you're goin' to Catholic school . . . college prep and takin' trig, Buddy. Me, I took shop, and it's the shop guys that's goin'. If the shit's still on in a year from now, get your butt in college. At least you can cut a deal, and if you go you'll be an officer with a safe job and a desk. Don't do like I'm about to do and go put yourself in a box."

He was silent for a minute, maybe more, but I knew it would end. I waited. He stared at the floor and breathed heavily. When he broke the silence, the tone of his voice was like a sudden hard jab, and so was his choice of words.

"Damn," he muttered without looking up. "Damn," he said again, louder this time, looking at me. "We're like brothers, you know, but we're different. 'Cause I'm the one that's gotta go." He paused again before speaking. "Buddy, you got hope. You got hope without ever havin' to leave town."

I was stunned and even unnerved. I wasn't sure if the anger in his voice was aimed at me or his situation. "Rico," I said, without really knowing what to say next. "I . . ."

"Better leave, man," he said, cutting me off. "We're cool, but I need to be alone. Gotta sort it out."

I just stared at him, blanked out by this new face on my old friend. I froze and stayed seated because I couldn't accept what I was hearing.

He returned my stare. "Man, you understand English?"

I did, and this time his tone—curt, cold, full of menace—made me rise and begin to take the first steps of my backward shuffle toward the door. I knew that tone well. I'd heard it directed at scores of childhood enemies, but I'd never thought I'd be the target.

He was no longer looking at me, but as I retreated I never took my eyes off him. To this day I'm not sure if it was for fear of what he might do, or for love of a friend I might never see again. I backed through the doorway, and as I did so, Rico became a picture in a frame, a sepia photo, an image in a seam of memory. Through the dim light, I saw him motionless, leaning forward, head bowed, this man with the moves. A seam of memory. Without a word to anyone, I walked out of the gym.

HOMECOMING

■ ■ ■

Carlos Bulosan

Already, through the coming darkness, he could see landmarks of familiar places. He stirred as he looked out of the window, remembering scenes of childhood. Houses flew by him; the sudden hum of human activity reached his ears. He was nearing home.

He kept his eyes upon the narrowing landscape. When the bus drove into town and stopped under the big arbor tree that was the station, he rushed from his seat and jumped onto the ground, filled with joy and wonder and mystery.

The station was deserted. He found the old road that ran toward his father's house. He walked in the darkness, between two long rows of houses. A little dog shot out from a house and barked at him. He looked at it with a friendly smile. He wanted to stop and pick up a handful of the earth of home, but thoughts of his people loomed large in his mind. Every step brought vivid recollections of his family. He was bursting with excitement, not knowing what to say. He walked on in the thickening darkness.

He had gone to America twelve years before, when he was fifteen.

CARLOS BULOSAN, self-taught Filipino writer and union activist, was born in Pangasinan, the Philippines, in 1911 and became the foremost chronicler of the Filipino/Filipino American struggle. Bulosan arrived in Seattle in 1930 and, until his death in 1956, he wrote in many literary genres. His best-known work is his autobiographical novel, *America Is in the Heart*, and *The Laughter of My Father*. Much of his fiction was published in the 1940s in *The New Yorker*, as well as *Harper's Bazaar* and *Arizona Quarterly*, and in an issue of *Amerasia Journal* devoted to his life and writings.

And now that he was back, walking on the dirt road that he had known so well, he felt like a boy of fifteen again. Yes, he was barely fifteen when he left home. He began to remember how one evening he ran like mad on this road with some roots that the herbalist needed for his mother, who was sick in bed with a mysterious disease. He had cried then, hugging the roots close to him. He knew that the fate of his mother was in his hands; he knew that they were waiting for him. . . . A mist came to his eyes. Reliving this tragic moment of childhood, he began to weaken with sudden tenderness for his mother. He walked faster, remembering . . .

Then he came to the gate of his father's house. For some moments he stood before the house, his heart pounding painfully. And now he knew. This was what he had come for—a little grass house near the mountains, away from the riot and madness of cities. He had left the civilization of America for this tiny house, and now that he was here, alone, he felt weak inside. He was uncertain.

For a moment he was afraid of what the house would say; he was afraid of what the house would ask him. The journey homeward had been more than eight thousand miles of land and water, but now that he was actually standing before the house, it seemed as if he had come from a place only a few miles away.

He surveyed the house in the dark, lost in his memories. Then he stepped forward, his feet whispering in the sand that filled the path to the house.

A faint gleam of light from the kitchen struck his face. He recalled at once that when he was young, the family always came home late in the evening; and his mother, who did all the domestic chores, served dinner around midnight. He paused a while, feeling a deep love for his mother. Then he crawled under the window, where the light shot across his face. He stood there and waited, breathless, for a moment.

But they were very quiet in the house. He could hear somebody moving toward the stove and stopping there to pour water into a jar. He found a hard object which he knew to be an empty box, and he hoisted himself on it, looking into the kitchen whence the lamp threw a beam of soft light.

Now he could see a large portion of the kitchen. He raised his heels, his eyes roving over the kitchen. Then he caught a quick glimpse of his mother, the old oil lamp in her hand. He was petrified with fear, not knowing what to do. One foot slipped from the side of the box and he hung in mid-air. He wanted to shout to her all the sorrows of his life, but a choking lump came to his throat. He looked, poised, undecided; then his mother disappeared behind a yellow curtain. His mind was a riot of conflict; he shifted from foot to foot. But action came to him at last. He jumped onto the ground and ran to the house.

He climbed up the ladder and stood by the door. His younger sister was setting the table, and his older sister, who was called Francisca, was helping his mother with the boiling pot on the stove. He watched the three women moving mechanically in the kitchen. Then he stepped forward, his leather shoes slapping against the floor. Francisca turned toward him and screamed.

"Mother!"

The mother looked swiftly from the burning stove and found the bewildered face of her son.

"It's me—Mariano—" he moved toward them, pausing at the table. "Mother!"

They rushed to him, all of them; the moment was eternity. Marcela, the younger sister, knelt before him; she was crying wordlessly. The mother was in his arms; her white hair fell upon his shoulder. Unable to say anything sensible, he reached for Francisca and said: "You've grown . . ."

Francisca could not say a word; she turned away and wept. The tension of this sudden meeting was unbearable to him. And now he was sorry he had come home. He felt that he could never make them happy again; a long period of deterioration would follow this sudden first meeting. He knew it, and he revolted against it. But he also knew that he could never tell them why he had come home.

They prepared a plate for him. He was hungry and he tried to eat everything they put on his plate. They had stopped eating. They were waiting for him to say something; they were watching his every movement. There were many things to talk about, but he did not know where to begin. He was confused. The silence was so deep he could hear the wind among the trees outside. Pausing a while, a thought came to his mind. *Father*: Where was father?

He looked at Francisca. "Where is father?" he asked.

Francisca turned to her mother for guidance, then to Mariano's lifted face.

Finally Francisca said: "Father died a year after you left."

"Father was a very old man," Marcela added. "He died in his sleep."

Mariano wanted to believe them, but he felt that they were only trying to make it easy for him. Then he looked at his mother. For the first time he seemed to realize that she had aged enormously. Then he turned to his sisters, who had become full-grown women in his absence. A long time passed before he could say anything.

"I didn't know that," he said, looking down at his food.

"We didn't want you to know," his mother said.

"I didn't know that father died," he repeated.

"Now you know," Marcela said.

Mariano tried to swallow the hot rice in his mouth, but a big lump of pain came to his throat. He could not eat anymore. He washed his hands and reached for the cloth on the wall above the table.

"I've had enough," he said.

Marcela and Francisca washed the dishes in a tall wooden tub. The mother went to the living room and spread the thin mat on the floor. Mariano sat on the long bench, near the stove. He was waiting for them to ask questions. His eyes roved around the house, becoming intimate with the furniture. When the mother came to the kitchen, Marcela took the lamp from the wall and placed it on one end of the bench. The light rose directly toward Mariano's face.

The mother paused. "Why didn't you let us know you were coming?" she asked.

"I wanted to surprise you," he lied.

"I'm glad you are with us again."

"We're very glad," Francisca said.

"Yes," Marcela said.

Then the mother closed the window. Mariano looked at Marcela, but the light dazzled him. Now he felt angry with himself. He wanted to tell the truth, but could not. How could he make them understand that he had failed in America? How could he let them realize that he had come home because there was no other place for him in the world? At twenty-seven, he felt through with life; he knew that he had come home to die. America had crushed his spirit.

He wanted to say something, but did not know where to begin. He was confused, now that he was home. All he could say was: "I came home . . ."

A strong wind blew into the house, extinguishing the lamp. The house was thrown into complete darkness. He could hear Marcela moving around, fumbling for matches under the stove. In the brief instant of darkness that wrapped the house he remembered his years in the hospital. He recalled the day of his operation, when the doctor had worked on his right lung. It all came back to him. Strange: unconsciously, he placed a hand on his chest. When the match spurted in Marcela's cupped palms, Mariano drew back his hand. He watched the lamp grow brighter until the house was all lighted again.

Then he said: "I wanted to write, but there was nothing I could say."

"We knew that," the mother said.

They were silent. Mariano looked at their faces. He knew now that he could never tell them what the doctor had told him before he sailed for home. Two years perhaps, the doctor had said. Yes, he had only two years left to live in the world. Two years: How much could he do in so brief a time? He began to feel weak. He looked at their faces.

Now it was his turn. Touching Marcela by the hand, he asked: "Are you all right? I mean . . . since father died . . ."

"I take laundry from students," Marcela said. "But it's barely enough. And sister here—"

Francisca rose suddenly and ran to the living room. The mother looked at Marcela. The house was electrified with fear and sadness.

"When students go back to their home towns, we have nothing."

"Is Francisca working?"

"She takes care of the Judge's children. Sister doesn't like to work in that house, but it's the only available work in town."

His heart was dying slowly.

"Mother can't go around anymore. Sister and I work to the bones. We've never known peace."

Mariano closed his eyes for a brief moment and pushed the existence of his sister out of his consciousness. The mother got up from the floor and joined Francisca in the living room. Now Mariano could hear Francisca weeping. Marcela was tougher; she looked toward the living room with hard, unsentimental eyes. Mariano was frightened, knowing what Marcela could do in a harsh world.

"Sister isn't pretty anymore," Marcela said.

Mariano was paralyzed with the sudden fear. He looked at Marcela. *Yes, she too was not pretty anymore.* But she did not care about herself;

she was concerned over her sister. He looked at her cotton dress, torn at the bottom. Then he felt like smashing the whole world; he was burning with anger. He was angry against all the forces that had made his sisters ugly.

Suddenly, he knelt before Marcela. He took her hands, comprehending. Marcela's palms were rough. Her fingernails were torn like matchsticks. Mariano bit his lower lip until it bled. He knew he would say something horrible if he opened his mouth. Instead he got up and took the lamp and went to the living room.

Francisca was weeping in her mother's arms. Mariano held the lamp above them, watching Francisca's face. She turned her face away, ashamed. But Mariano saw, and now he knew. *Francisca was not pretty anymore.* He wanted to cry.

"We were hungry," Marcela said. She had followed him.

Mariano turned around suddenly and felt cold inside when he saw Marcela's cold stare in the semi-darkness. What did he not know about hunger? *Goddamn!*

"I wish I . . ." he stopped. Fear and anger welled up in him. Now he could understand the brevity of their answers to his questions; their swift glances that meant more than their tongues could utter. Now he could understand his mother's deadening solemnity. And Marcela's bitterness. Now it dawned on him that his mother and sisters had suffered the same terrors of poverty, the same humiliations of defeat, that he had suffered in America. He was like a man who had emerged from night into day, and found the light as blinding as the darkness.

The mother knelt on the floor, reaching for the lamp. Mariano walked back to the kitchen. He knew he could not do anything for them. He knew he could not do anything for himself. He knew he could not do anything at all. This was the life he had found in America; it was so everywhere in the world. He was confirmed now. He thought when he was in America that it could not be thus in his father's house. But it was there when he returned to find his sisters wrecked by deprivation . . .

Mariano stood by the window long after they had gone to bed. He stood in the darkness, waiting. The houses were silent. The entire district was quiet as a tomb. His mother was sleeping peacefully. He turned to look at his sisters in the dark. They were sleeping soundly. Then noiselessly, he walked to the bed.

Mariano leaned against the wall, thinking. After a while a child began to cry somewhere in the neighborhood. Two dogs ran across the road, chasing each other. Then a rooster began to crow, and others followed. It was almost dawn.

Now Mariano sat still in the darkness, listening. When he was sure they were deep in sleep, he got up slowly and reached for his hat on the table. He stopped at the door and looked back. He found a match in his pocket and scratched it on the panel of the door. Then he tiptoed to his mother and watched her face with tenderness. As he walked over to his sisters, the match burned out. He stood between them, trembling with indecision. Suddenly, he walked to the door and descended the ladder in a hurry.

There were a few stars in the sky. The night wind was soft. There was a touch of summer in the air. When he had passed the gate, Mariano stopped and looked back at the house. The vision of his father rose in the night. Then it seemed to him that the house of his childhood was more vivid than at any other time in that last look. He knew he would never see it again.

MELPOMENE TRAGEDY

■ ■ ■

Theresa Hak Kyung Cha

S he could be seen sitting in the first few rows. She would be sitting in the first few rows. Closer the better. The more. Better to eliminate presences of others surrounding better view away from that which is left behind far away back behind more for closer view more and more face to face until nothing else sees only this view singular. All dim, gently, slowly until in the dark, the absolute darkness the shadows fade.

■ ■ ■

She is stretched out as far as the seat allows until her neck rests on the back of the seat. She pulls her coat just below her chin enveloped in one mass before the moving shades, flickering light through the empty window, length of the gardens the trees in perfect a symmetry.

■ ■ ■

The correct time beyond the windows the correct season the correct forecast. Beyond the empty the correct setting, immobile. Placid. Extreme stillness. Misplaces nothing. Nothing equivalent. Irreplaceable. Not before. Not after.

THERESA HAK KYUNG CHA, multimedia artist and author of *Dictee*, was born in Pusan, Korea, in 1951. At the time of her tragic death in 1982, Cha had been working on several projects, including a film and a book. In 1992–93, a retrospective of her video, film, and textual work was exhibited at the Whitney Museum in New York. *Dictee* has deeply influenced the works of many Korean and other Asian American women writers and visual artists.

■ ■ ■

The submission is complete. Relinquishes even the vision to immobility. Abandons all protests to that which will appear to the sight. About to appear. Forecast. Break. Break, by all means. The illusion that the act of viewing is to make alteration of the visible. The expulsion is immediate. Not one second is lost to the replication of the totality. Total severance of the seen. Incision.

April 19
Seoul, Korea

Dear Mother,

4. 19. Four Nineteen, April 19th, eighteen years later. Nothing has changed, we are at a standstill. I speak in another tongue now, a second tongue a foreign tongue. All this time we have been away. But nothing has changed. A stand still.

It is not 6. 25. Six Twenty-five. June 25th, 1950. Not today. Not this day. There are no bombs as you had described them. They do not fall, their shiny brown metallic backs like insects one by one after another.

The population standing before North standing before South for every bird that migrates North for Spring and South for Winter becomes a metaphor for the longing of return. Destination. Homeland.

■ ■ ■

No woman with child lifting sand bags barriers, all during the night for the battles to come.

■ ■ ■

There is no destination other than towards yet another refuge from yet another war. Many generations pass and many deceptions in the sequence in the chronology towards the destination.

■ ■ ■

You knew it would not be in vain. The thirty-six years of exile. Thirty six years multiplied by three hundred and sixty-five days. That one day your country would be your own. This day did finally come. The Japa-

nese were defeated in the world war and were making their descent
back to their country. As soon as you heard, you followed South. You
carried not a single piece, not a photograph, nothing to evoke your
memory, abandoned all to see your nation freed.

■ ■ ■

From another epic another history. From the missing narrative. From the
multitude of narratives. Missing. From the chronicles. For another
telling for other recitations.

■ ■ ■

Our destination is fixed on the perpetual motion of search. Fixed in its
perpetual exile. Here at my return in eighteen years, the war is not
ended. We fight the same war. We are inside the same struggle seeking
the same destination. We are severed in Two by an abstract enemy an
invisible enemy under the title of liberators who have conveniently
named the severance, Civil War. Cold War. Stalemate.

I am in the same crowd, the same coup, the same revolt, nothing
has changed. I am inside the demonstration I am locked inside the
crowd and carried in its movement. The voices ring shout one voice
then many voices they are waves they echo I am moving in the direction the only one direction with the voices the only direction. The
other movement towards us it increases steadily their direction their
only direction our mutual destination towards the other against the
other. Move.

■ ■ ■

I feel the tightening of the crowd body to body now the voices rising
thicker I hear the break the single motion tearing the break left of me
right of me the silence of the other direction advance before . . . They
are breaking now, their sounds, not new, you have heard them, so familiar to you now could you ever forget them not in your dreams, the
consequences of the sound the breaking. The air is made visible with
smoke it grows spreads without control we are hidden inside the white-
ness the greyness reduced to parts, reduced to separation. Inside an
arm lifts above the head in deliberate gesture and disappears into the
thick white from which slowly the legs of another bent at the knee hit
the ground the entire body on its left side. The stinging, it slices the air

it enters thus I lose direction the sky is a haze running the streets emptied I fell no one saw me I walk. Anywhere. In tears the air stagnant continues to sting I am crying the sky remnant the gas smoke absorbed the sky I am crying. The streets covered with chipped bricks and debris. Because. I see the frequent pairs of shoes thrown sometimes a single pair among the rocks they had carried. Because. I cry wail torn shirt lying I step among them. No trace of them. Except for the blood. Because. Step among them the blood that will not erase with the rain on the pavement that was walked upon like the stones where they fell had fallen. Because. Remain dark the stains not wash away. Because. I follow the crying crowd their voices among them their singing their voices unceasing the empty street.

■ ■ ■

There is no surrendering you are chosen to fail to be martyred to shed blood to be set an example one who has defied one who has chosen to defy and was to be set an example to be martyred an animal useless betrayer to the cause to the welfare to peace to harmony to progress.

■ ■ ■

It is 1962 eighteen years ago same month same day all over again. I am eleven years old. Running to the front door, Mother, you are holding my older brother pleading with him not to go out to the demonstration. You are threatening him, you are begging to him. He has on his school uniform, as all the other students representing their schools in the demonstration. You are pulling at him you stand before the door. He argues with you he pushes you away. You use all your force, all that you have. He is prepared to join the student demonstration outside. You can hear the gun shots. They are directed at anyone.

Coming home from school there are cries in all the streets. The mounting of shouts from every direction from the crowds arm in arm. The students. I saw them, older than us, men and women held to each other. They walk into the *others* who wait in *their* uniforms. Their shouts reach a crescendo as they approach nearer to the *other side*. Cries resisting cries to move forward. Orders, permission to use force against the students, have been dispatched. To be caught and beaten with sticks, and for others, shot, remassed, and carted off. They fall they bleed they die. They are thrown into gas into the crowd to be squelched. The police the soldiers anonymous they duplicate themselves, multiply in number invincible they execute their role. Further than their home further than their mother father their brother sister further than their children is the execution of their role their given identity further than their own line of blood.

You do not want to lose him, my brother, to be killed as the many others by now, already, you say you understand, you plead all the same they are killing any every one. You withstand his strength you call me to run to Uncle's house and call the tutor. Run. Run hard. Out the gate. Turn the corner. All down hill to reach Uncle's house. I know the two German shepherd dogs would be guarding one at each side, chained to their house they drag behind them barking. I must brave them, close my eyes and run between them. I call the tutor from the yard, above the sounds of the dogs barking. Several students look out of the windows. They are in hiding from the street, from their homes where they are being searched for. We run back to the house the tutor is ahead of me, when I enter the house the tutor is standing in front of him. You cannot go out he says you cannot join the D-e-m-o. *De. Mo.* A word, two sounds. Are you insane the tutor tells him they are killing any student in uniform. Anybody. What will you defend yourself with he asks. You, my brother, you protest your cause, you say you are willing to die. Dying is part of it. If it must be. He hits you. The tutor slaps you and your face turns red you stand silently against the door your head falls. My brother. You are all the rest all the others are you. You fell you died you gave your life. That day. It rained. It rained for several days. It rained more and more times. After it was all over. You were heard. Your victory mixed with rain falling from the sky for many days afterwards. I heard that the rain does not erase the blood fallen on the ground. I heard from the adults, the blood stains still. Year after year it rained. The stone pavement stained where you fell still remains dark.

Eighteen years pass. I am here for the first time in eighteen years, Mother. We left here in this memory still fresh, still new. I speak another tongue, a second tongue. This is how distant I am. From then. From that time. They take me back they have taken me back so precisely now exact to the hour to the day to the season in the smoke mist in the drizzle I turn the corner and there is no one. No one facing me. The street is rubble. I put my palm on my eyes to rub them, then I let them cry freely. Two school children with their book bags appear from nowhere with their arms around each other. Their white kerchief, their white shirt uniform, into a white residue of gas, crying.

I pass a second curve on the road. You soldiers appear in green. Always the green uniforms the patches of camouflage. Trees camouflage your green trucks you blend with nature the trees hide you you cannot be seen behind the guns no one sees you they have hidden you. You sit you recline on the earth next to the buses you wait hours days making visible your presence. Waiting for the false move that will conduct you to mobility to action. There is but one move, the only one and it will be false. It will be absolute. Their mistake. Your boredom waiting would not have been in vain. They will move they will have to move and you will move on them. Among them. You stand on your tanks your legs spread apart how many degrees exactly your hand on your rifle. Rifle to ground the same angle as your right leg. You wear a beret in the 90 degree sun there is no shade at the main gate you are fixed you cannot move you dare not move. You are your post you are your vow in nomine patris you work your post you are your nation defending your country from subversive infiltration from your own countrymen. Your skin scorched as dark as your uniform as you stand you don't hear. You hear nothing. You hear no one. You are hidden you see only the prey they do not see you they cannot. You who are hidden you who move in the crowds as you would in the trees you who move inside them you close your eyes to the piercing the breaking the flooding pools bathe their shadow memory as they fade from you your own blood your own flesh as tides ebb, through you through and through.

> You are this
> close to this much
> close to it.
> Extend arms apart just so, that much. Open
> the thumb and the index finger just so.
> the thumb and the index finger just so.
> That much
> you want to kill the time that is oppression itself.
> Time that delivers not. Not you, not from its
> expanse, without dimension, defined not by its
> limits. Airless, thin, not a thought rising even
> that there are things to be forgotten. Effortless. It

should be effortless. Effort less ly
the closer it is the closer to it. Away and against
time ing. A step forward from back. Backing
out. Backing off. Off periphery extended. From
imaginary to bordering on division. At least
somewhere in numerals in relation to the
equator, at least all the maps have them at least
walls are built between them at least the militia
uniforms and guns are in abeyance of them.
Imaginary borders. Un imaginable boundaries.

Suffice more than that. SHE opposes Her.
SHE against her.
More than that. Refuses to become discard
decomposed oblivion.
From its memory dust escapes the particles still
material still respiration move. Dead air stagnant
water still exhales mist. Pure hazard igniting flaming
itself with the slightest of friction like firefly. The loss
that should burn. Not burn, illuminate. Illuminate by
losing. Lighten by loss.
Yet it loses not.

Her name. First the whole name. Then syllable by syllable counting each inside the mouth. Make them rise they rise repeatedly without
ever making visible lips never open to utter them.

Mere names only names without the image not *hers*
hers alone not the whole of *her* and even the image
would not be the entire
her fraction *her* invalid that inhabits that rise
voluntarily like flint
pure hazard dead substance to fire.

Others anonymous *her* detachments take her place. Anonymous
against *her*. Suffice that should be nation against nation suffice that
should have been divided into two which once was whole. Suffice that
should diminish human breaths only too quickly. Suffice Melpomene.

Nation against nation multiplied nations against nations against themselves. Own. Repels her rejects her expels her from *her* own. Her own is, in, of, through, all others, *hers*. Her own who is offspring and mother, Demeter and Sibyl.

Violation of *her* by giving name to the betrayal, all possible names, interchangeable names, to remedy, to justify the violation. Of *her*. Own. Unbegotten. Name. Name only. Name without substance. The everlasting, Forever. Without end.

Deceptions all the while. No devils here. Nor gods. Labyrinth of deceptions. No enduring time. Self-devouring. Devouring itself. Perishing all the while. Insect that eats its own mate.

Suffice Melpomene, arrest the screen en-trance flickering hue from behind cast shadow silhouette from back not visible. Like ice. Metal. Glass. Mirror. Receives none admits none.

Arrest the machine that purports to employ democracy but rather causes the successive refraction of *her* none other than her own. Suffice Melpomene, to exorcise from this mouth the name the words the memory of severance through this act by this very act to utter one, *Her* once, Her to utter at once, *She* without the separate act of uttering.

TWO PARABLES:

PARABLE OF THE CAKE

■ ■ ■

Marilyn Chin

The Neighborwoman said to us, "I'll give you a big cake, little Chinese girls, if you come to the Christmas service with me and accept Jesus Christ, our lord, into your heart." We said, "Okay," and drove with her to the other side of the city and sat through a boring sermon when we should have taken the bus to Chinatown for our Cantonese lessons. Afterwards, she gave us a big cake that said "Happy Birthday, Buny" on it. She must have got it for half price because of the misspelling. My sister and I were really hungry after the long sermon, so we gulped down the whole cake as soon as we got home. I got sick and threw up all over the bathroom and my sister had to clean it up before Granny got home. Then, my face swelled up for two days on account of my being allergic to the peanut butter in the frosting. My sister was so afraid that I would croak that she confessed everything to Granny. First, Granny gave me some putrid herbal medicine, then she whipped us with her bamboo duster. She whipped us so hard that we both had red marks all over our legs. Then, she made us kneel before the Great Buddha for two hours balancing teapots on our heads.

MARILYN CHIN'S books of poems include *Rhapsody in Plain Yellow*; *The Phoenix Gone, the Terrace Empty*; and *Dwarf Bamboo*. She is completing a book of tales, in which "Moon" will be featured. Her work is anthologized widely, most recently in the *Norton Introduction to Literature*, and she was featured in Bill Moyers's PBS series *The Language of Life*. The recipient of a Fulbright fellowship, a Stegner fellowship, and a Lannan award, she currently codirects the M.F.A. program at San Diego State University. She was born in Hong Kong in 1955.

■ ■ ■

On Christmas Eve, Granny went to Safeway and bought a big white cake with Santa's face on it and made us go with her to the Neighborwoman's house. She placed the cake into the Neighborwoman's hands and said, "Peapod, translate this: Malignant Nun, we do not beg for your God." I didn't know how to translate "Malignant." And said politely, "Dear Missus, No beg, No God."

■ ■ ■

My sister and I both wept silently, embarrassed that my grandmother made us into a spectacle and ashamed that we had to lie to get out of it. Meanwhile, Granny was satisfied that we learned our lesson and decided to take her two favorite peapods to Chinatown for sweet bean dessert. We were the only riders on the bus that night; everybody else was probably home with their families preparing for a big meal. "Merry Christmas, ho ho ho, I am Santa's helper!" said the Bus Driver. He was wearing a green elf's hat, but we knew that he was really Mr. Riggers, the black bus driver. He gave us each two little candy canes. Granny scowled, "Tsk, tsk, ancient warrior in a fool's cap!" Then, we sat way in the back of the bus and Granny began singing our favorite song: "We will go home and eat cakies, little lotus-filled cakies," Granny sang. "We will eat sweet buns, sweet custard sweet buns!" she sang. "We will eat turnip squares, salty white turnip squares," she sang. "We will eat grass jelly, tangy green grass jelly. We will eat dumplings, soft, steamy dumplings." She was so jolly that we forgot our embarrassing episode and we sang with her, clapping hands. We sang and sang.

■ ■ ■

Granny would die a few years later, leaving us $3,000 under her mattress and a brand-new cleaver, still wrapped in Chinese newspaper from Hong Kong. We grew up into beautiful, clear-skinned young women. We worked hard in our studies, became successful and drove little white Mercedes. We learned nothing from our poverty, but to avoid poverty at all cost.

■ ■ ■

We had three failed marriages between us. Four nice children, whom we proudly raised with upper-middle-class values. We spent days and days at the mall buying shoes. We became born-again Christians. We feared love and loved no one, not even ourselves. We ended up with two dull but very kind husbands. We spoke of our grandmother with reverence but understood nothing, nothing, nada, nothing that she taught us.

■ ■ ■

Fa la la la la, little cakies, little cakies, little cakies . . . we drive around in our little white Mercedes all over southern California eating little cakies. Yes, let's put on the Ritz, sisters: little petits fours in pastels and rainbows . . . booze-soaked baba rhums, oooh yes, nuttynutty Florentines on little white doilies. . . . Oh sisters! Let's ghetto it! Ho Hos, Ding Dongs, pink and white Snowballs; let's suck the creamy hearts out of the Twinkies. Come hither, come yon, young Chinese girls. Come, let's drive around in our little white Mercedes eating cakies, little cakies. Come, let the crumbs fall down our chins and dance on our laps. Come, light light airy madeleines, come, creamy creamy trifles. Come, little cakies, little cakies. Come, the sweet, sweet hereafter.

TWO PARABLES:

MOON

■ ■ ■

Marilyn Chin

Moon was a little fat Chinese girl. She had a big, yellow face befitting her name. She was sad and lonely as were all little fat Chinese girls in 1991, and she had a strange, insatiable desire for a pair of trashy blond twins named Smith (no accounting for taste, of course). Every night she would wander on the beach in search of them, hoping to espy them taking a joyride around Pacific Beach in their rebuilt sky-blue convertible Impala: their long blond hair swept backward like horses' manes, their faces obscenely sunburnt, resembling ripe halves of peaches.

One chilly September evening the boys stopped to make a campfire on the beach; and Moon, feeling quite full and confident that day, descended upon them, waddling so fat, so round and shiny with seaspray. She offered them chocolate Macadamia nut clusters and began to sing, strumming a tiny lute-like instrument her grandmother sent her from China. She began singing in an ancient falsetto a baleful song about exiled geese winging across the horizon, about the waxing and waning of stormy seas, about children lost into the unknown depths of the new kingdom.

The boys were born and raised in "the valley" and were very unsophisticated. They were also functional illiterates and were held back twice in the fifth grade—and there was no way that they could have understood the complexities of her song. They huddled in that sporting male way and whispered surreptitiously, speaking in very short sentences between grunts or long, run-on sentences with ambiguous antecedents, so that Moon was not quite sure whether she was the subject of their discussion. Finally, the boys offered to give fat Moon a ride in their stainless steel canoe they got for Christmas (we know, of course, that they were up to trouble; you don't think that their hospitality was sincere, do you?).

Moon graciously accepted their invitation. Actually, she was elated given the bad state of her social life; she hadn't had a date for centuries. So the two boys paddled, one fore, one aft, with fat Moon in the middle. Moon was so happy that she started strumming her lute and singing the song of Hiawatha (don't ask me why, this was what she felt like singing). Suddenly, the boys started rocking the boat forcefully—forward and backward making wild horsey sounds until the boat flipped over, fat Moon, lute and all.

The boys laughed and taunted Moon to reappear from the rough water. When she didn't surface after a few minutes, it suddenly occurred to them that she was drowning; they watched in bemusement while the last of her yellow forehead bled into the waves. Finally, they dove in and dragged her heavy body back into the boat, which was quite a feat for she was twice as heavy wet than dry—and she was now tangled in sea flora.

When they finally docked, Moon discovered that the boys saved her only to humiliate her. It appeared that they wanted a reward for saving her life . . . a blood-debt, if you will. In this material world—goods are bartered for goods—and actions however heroic or well-intentioned in appearance are never clearly separated from services rendered. And in the American ledger, all services must be paid for in the end; and all contracts must be signed at closing bearing each participant's legal signature. Thus, the boys ripped off Moon's dress and took turns pissing all over her round face and belly saying, "So, it's true, it's true that your cunts are really slanted. Slant-eyed cunt! Did you really think that we had any interest in you?"

After the boys finished their vile act, they left Moon on the wharf without a stitch on, glowing with yellow piss. And she cried, wailed all the way home on her bicycle. Imagine a little fat Chinese girl, naked, pedaling, wailing.

When Moon got home her mother called her a slut. Her father went on and on about the Sino-Japanese war and about the starving girl-children in Kuangtung—and look, what are you doing with your youth and new prosperity, wailing, carrying on, just because some trashy white boys rejected you. Have you no shame? Your cousin the sun matriculated Harvard, your brothers the stars all became engineers. . . . Where are the I. M. Peis and Yo Yo Mas of your generation?—They sent her to bed without supper that night as a reminder that self-sacrifice is the most profound virtue of the Chinese people.

Up in her room Moon brooded and swore on a stack of Bibles that she would seek revenge for this terrible incident—and that if she were to die today she would come back to earth as an angry ghost to haunt those motherfuckers. With this in mind, Moon swallowed a whole bottle of sleeping pills only to cough them back up ten minutes later. Obviously, they didn't kill her. However, those ten minutes of retching must have prevented oxygen from entering her brain and left her deranged for at least a month after this episode (hey, I'm no doctor, just a story-teller, take my diagnosis with caution, please). Overnight, she became a homicidal maniac. A foul plague would shroud all of southern California, which, curiously, infected only blond men (both natural and peroxided types, those slightly hennaed would be spared).

For thirty days and thirty nights Moon scoured the seaside, howling, windswept—in search of blond victims. They would drown on their surfboards, or collapse while polishing their cars. . . . They would suffocate in their sleep next to their wives and lovers. Some died leaving a long trail of excrement, because whatever pursued them was so terrible that it literally scared the shit out of them. And not since Herod had we seen such a devastating assault on male children.

On the thirty-first night, the horror subsided. Moon finally found the Smith boys cruising in their sky-blue convertible Impala. They were driving south on the scenic coast route between San Clemente and Del Mar when she plunged down on them, her light was so powerful and bright that the boys were momentarily blinded and swerved into a canyon. Their car turned over twelve times. They were decapitated— the coroner said, so cleanly as if a surgeon had done the job with a laser.

Moon grew up, lost weight and became a famous singer, which proves that there is no justice in the universe, or that indeed, there is justice. Your interpretation of this denouement mostly depends on your race, creed, hair color, social and economic class and political proclivities—and whether or not you are a feminist revisionist and have a habit of cheering for the underdog. What is the moral of the story? Well, it's a tale of revenge, obviously, written from a Chinese American girl's perspective. My intentions are to veer you away from teasing and humiliating little chubby Chinese girls like myself. And that one wanton act of humiliation you perpetuated on the fore or aft of that boat of my arrival—may be one humiliating act too many. For although we are friendly neighbors, you don't really know me. You don't know the depth of my humiliation. And you don't know what I can do. You don't know what is beneath my doing.

RED WALL

...

Sara Chin

In Beijing, people are getting rich and riding around in chauffeured air-conditioning. Not so long ago, things appeared to be otherwise. I set down what I saw then. But was my experience an encounter with history, or with nostalgia? Is this just the sort of thing an American would mix up?

The long wall never quits. It goes on, one street to the next, Zhong-nanhai to Tiananmen. Lovers come, sit in its shade and, like the wall, they too go on and on, rapt in themselves, bicycles left by a tree, the traffic beyond flaring white.

Through the afternoon, people gather to buy an ice, cross the street. Buses come, veer away, yet nothing disturbs the long wall and its red shade. A march of leafy trees shelters it from the street.

I sit and watch a young soldier feed a popsicle to his girl. It's a treat to hide in the shade and eat an ice. The girl and her popsicle melt. The day's heat can only make them expire faster. The ice drips, the girl giggles over the smear on her lip. Her soldier takes out his handkerchief and applies it to her giggle.

Soon, an elderly couple approaches, two old Beijing men walking arm in arm. One swings a bag, the other leads with his belly. They pass the young lovers and come at me, hefty old men with shorts hauled up to their armpits, hair buzzed to their skulls. They cross in front of where

SARA CHIN was born in 1949 in Kiangsi, China, and raised in the United States. She lives in San Francisco, where she works on TV documentaries. She has written a book of short stories, *Below the Line*, and is now working on a novel.

I sit, big busy voices bowling along. They don't see they're going to trip over me until I pull back my feet. Even then they go on without a glance until a bump in the sidewalk, a crack in a thought, stops them suddenly. They turn to stare.

The lovers separate then. The girl, so flirty a moment ago, turns into a pudding face, the boy shrinks to a mere noodle. His uniform rumples, his handkerchief goes back to its pocket.

Boy and girl think the old men are looking at them, but I know they're not. The old men are staring at me. In the days before the city is entirely given over to the new, they have this look for the stranger in their midst. It's a stare that commits the whole body to its task, head up, chin out. The eyes do the calculating. They can tell whether the person stared at—like the donkey one might buy—has a set of teeth on her and enough meat to last a winter or two. This stare I recognize. I've prepared for it by wearing sunglasses. Large, expensive globes tinted to shield out UV and other rays. I've been to Beijing before. I know what to do: I smile. The old men stare. I smile again. Show a bit of teeth. They'll go now, I think, they've seen enough. But no. The old men suddenly rush me. Run me down like a barnyard chicken.

"Xiao Hung, Xiao Hung!" they shout, "What are *you* doing here!"

I jump. And behind me someone cries. Only then do I understand: it's the girl with the young soldier. The old men really have been staring at her, not me. She runs now, Xiao Hung, her flimsy dress streaking along the red wall, her soldier following. So much has changed since I was here before.

■ ■ ■

Before, I came to work. Before, I came to meet history, to shake its hand, look it in the eye. Hang a microphone over it, record it. Before, I didn't have time to come to the red wall and rest in its shade, stare at people as much as they stared at me.

A lifetime ago it seems, Jill called one day and startled me. She said, "Would you like to do something different?"

I didn't know what she meant, but soon enough she was talking me into my first trip to China. I wanted to go, there was no doubt about that. I had relatives everywhere and I wanted to see the great sights, but even so, Jill had to convince me; she wasn't offering an easy trip. She said, "The money's not quite in place yet, all of it, but it will be, you know. This is just too fantastic to pass up. They're all dying off! We've got to interview them now or we won't get them at all, at their age. Can you do it?"

She wanted me to work six weeks for nothing, filming on a bare-bones budget, pay deferred. The days would be long, with no overtime, but naps were guaranteed.

"Absolutely. They're all incapacitated after lunch, I don't know whether it's the lunch or the heat, though having eaten some of the lunches—"

Jill planned to travel all over: Shanghai, Beijing, a village here and there. "You'll get to see a lot, though it might be awful, too, some of it." She took pains to warn me as well as win me over. Jill was an old friend. She had given me my start, hiring me for a documentary series she had produced several years earlier.

"What do you mean?" I said. I had grown up in New Jersey, Jill in London; Jill had a different idea of awful than I did. Among other things, she liked marmite and fish and chips.

"You'll see," she said.

Before I left, Jill briefed me on what she wanted from China, "A simple story."

"Good," I was relieved. "It's not going to be another thriller then."

I remembered an exposé Jill had done on British intelligence. Something about fair trade, or was it "the" fair trade? Sex for secrets, where the sex had become worth a lot more than the secrets. Jill had left London for New York after the fallout from that show. That was also when she changed her name from Gillian to Jill. "More to the point, don't you think," she said.

"No, no," she assured me now, "I'm not going to go to China and make people drop their drawers—if that's what you're asking."

"You promise."

"Please. This one's not about smutty people. This one's history."

"From those who lived it."

"Exactly. That's the point. We're going to be educational."

Jill said this last without embarrassment. She was the only person I knew who could, and did, go on TV to say, "The purpose of film is to raise the general level." She said this on public TV, but even so . . .

Jill was tall, close to six feet, and liked to cultivate the attention she always got for her height and her looks. When she talked, people had a way of stepping back, inadvertently, to get a good view of her.

She sent me her script: "China Reborn." She was going to cover forty years of revolution up to the moment of what the communists called liberation, but what Jill decided to call birth. The birth, in 1949, of the new China, long and fraught, but made momentous the instant Chairman Mao stood atop the red wall and waved those famous hands.

"I've got loads of footage already," Jill said. "Newsreels, Shanghai melodramas—you name it, it's incredible."

Along with her script, Jill included a list of things she wanted me to know about China. Her list went like this:

General Li: Can we drug him? Antihistamine, of course. Otherwise, he'll come across as a crybaby. Age: 78.

Liu Bai and Liu Bing: Brothers. Fought the Japanese. Bai is a good talker, Bing is not. But Bai can't walk (knees shot to hell). Bing can. So—who to interview? I need a tour of their village. Someone who can walk and talk at the same time. Is this too much to ask? Age: Pickled.

Chen Xiao Lan: "Little Songbird of the Party." Will she sing for us? Age: Not apropos.

I packed for my trip: sound recorder, tape, batteries, microphones, cables, headphones. I took five cases. Then my mother called and I took six. The sixth was filled with clothes and gifts for relatives in China.

Before I left, my mother also sent me a briefing paper. Hers went like this:

Jiou-jiou, your uncle. My first brother. Don't be like his wife. Don't talk so loud.

Jiou-gunggung, your great-uncle. My mother's brother. Very old. Yell at him. His ears are no good, but he can eat. Everything.

Jiou po-po, your great-uncle's wife. She eats everything, too.

Gugu, your auntie. Your father's sister. If you are so short of time like you say, don't bother with her. If she sees you, you will not get away. Believe me.

San Jiou-jiou, your third uncle. Also my brother. But this one is younger than the other. This one is number three out of four. Like I am number one out of three. For girls. All my family, not your father's.

(Your father's side, you call him Shu-shu, okay?) This one, San Jiou-jiou, I have something special for.

I put these notes away in my bag and went off to China. Thoughts of the film, can Jill make it work; of my family, who should I see; and of the revolution, what will it tell me, going round in my head.

The first leg of my trip took me to Hong Kong. I slept most of the way, but woke as the plane dropped out of the clouds and the harbor appeared below, an expanse of global shipping, a skyline of dominant buildings. I thought of the memorable words from an otherwise un-memorable movie: "Thank you," the beautiful Chinese mistress said, "Thank you, Taipan. Thank you."

The plane whined. Skimmed rooftops, laundry, then—whump—it set me down.

Jill was already there. She'd gone on ahead to consult with Peter, our cameraman. Peter was a big guy, Cantonese, who said whatever he liked. His favorite game was insulting Jill. He called Jill "Missy." She called him "Boy." They knew each other from their early days in London, when both had been scrounging for film jobs. While Jill went on to become an inappropriate person at the BBC, alienating one executive after another, Peter found his niche shooting documentaries in London. He was able to do this for a number of years until his mother finally faked a heart attack and forced him home to Hong Kong to run the family business.

"Shirts," he said when I met him.

"Really?" I felt a bit confused, jet-lagged, probably. Jill had told me Peter owned a factory, but I couldn't recall how she had said making shirts and making films went together. Peter, on first meeting, didn't offer me a clue. He wasn't your stereotypical Hong Kong businessman. He didn't dress his hair, he didn't wear nice clothes, he wasn't pale, or neat. He was a slob. Big olive face set off by a frizz of hair, brown, kind of kinky. Maybe he had some Portuguese blood; he said his family came from Macao. When he walked, his pants slid off his hips. He had no waist.

I asked him, "You still making shirts? Is that what you do, mostly?"

"She didn't tell you?" Peter jerked a thumb at Jill. "I make my wife do it."

"Oh, it's not like that," Jill said. "She loves it. Making money."

"Of course. That's why she's my wife," Peter laughed a high-pitched laugh.

Later, Jill said, "That's Peter. When he came home, he kept shooting film, but his family said, is that all you learned in London? Coolie work? They told him, you run the factory. But he said, no, you find me a wife. Isn't that brilliant?"

Jill had us doing our first interview in Hong Kong. It was with an ancient couple who had worked for the YMCA, running leadership programs for Chinese youth. The Chinese half of the couple was a man from San Francisco Chinatown, and his companion—I calculated they'd been together since the 1960s—was from southern California, from pioneer stock he described as strict and Presbyterian.

They were Johnny and Earl. They looked like owls, short and round. Both stood on the backs of their heels and tilted their heads up to greet us when we arrived. At first, we couldn't tell them apart, not in the dim confines of their hall, but when they led us to the front of their apartment, where the light diffused from the harbor and sky outside gave everything within a pearly luminance, we could see Earl had the speckled head and Johnny the tufts of white. Though Peter said later, and he had the benefit of seeing them close-up through his camera, they really looked the same, their eyes were indistinguishably old and baggy.

"My father had the ranch and his the grocery," Earl pointed to Johnny.

"Bank," Johnny said. "The bank was the real business."

"Can you look here?" Peter held up a fist next to his camera. He was setting up for Earl's interview. Earl and Johnny had both gone to China when they were in their twenties. This would have been soon after the First War.

I hung a microphone over Earl. If he was any good, he was going to belong to the part of the film that dealt with Western influence in China. I put on my headphones.

"He's not sitting too low, is he?" Jill stuck a cushion behind Earl. We started filming. Earl talked about going to college and finding his calling there with the YMCA.

"Why the Y?" he said. He had a big voice and used it with vigor, as if to prove to us what he had been in his youth, a man who never saw a mountain he didn't want to climb. One wall of the apartment was covered with pictures demonstrating this: there was Earl in the Sierras, Earl in the Alps, Earl in Tibet. Earl with a leg up on every mountain he ever trod. "He got around, didn't he," Johnny said.

I turned Earl down on my tape recorder.

"Why the Y?" he said in more moderate tones, "Well, it was the greatest thing. In those days, it was like the Peace Corps. We got the best men, the best ideas and we put them together."

Earl slapped his hands into a sandwich. He spiked my recording.

"They were so hungry," he spoke of his Chinese students, "Anything we could get from home. Science books, magazines, why, they just snapped them up."

He grabbed a chunk of air. Jill, who sat facing him nodded, then smiled. She did this for every word Earl said, her smile the equivalent of a pat on the head, had Earl been a dog.

He lowered his head now and looked her in the eye, "They wanted change, those students, you bet. Change, which is progress, you know, no progress without change. You want something, you go get it. That's change. That's what I taught my students. And it's still the same today—some things don't change."

He sat up. Was this a digression coming on? I looked to Jill. She held up her hand. I looked to Peter, he stayed bent over his camera, but his leg moved to where Jill could poke him if she had to.

"Young people," Earl sounded a new and belligerent note, "young people—for them, change just comes natural. They don't want to sit still. And why should they?"

Jill dropped her hand. Peter stopped. I turned off. And Earl? He jabbed a finger in our collective eye. "Look," he said, "look at the students. The kids. That's who you should be filming today. Not us."

Earl was far more interested in the present than the past. "I hate old people who talk about the past," he told us at the end of his interview, "But—sometimes you have to. You're young, you people, and what you don't know, you need someone to tell you. I'm glad to do it." He went around and shook our hands.

When it was Johnny's turn, he talked about how his father and other Chinatown leaders, Chinese patriots, he called them, conspired to overthrow the foreign Manchu dynasty.

"People forget, but we really played a part. A big part. My father sang hymns. Went to a lot of meetings. And between the church, the

Six Companies, which ran all the businesses in Chinatown, and the family associations, my father raised more money than anybody else for the revolutionaries. He was very big on making China strong.

"Also, he started something, and this was very popular in Chinatown, if he knew you were a supporter of Dr. Sun Yat-sen and the Chinese republic—and he would know, because he was the one collected the money—well, he gave you a discount at his store. Then later at the bank, too, you got loans easier."

As Johnny talked, it became apparent that his father's investments to make China strong—a printing business, a cascade of banks—had done very well, even if China itself had not, and we were now enjoying one of the fruits thereof: Johnny's living room. A room that drew light from all of Victoria Harbor below, a room so big and comfortable Peter said he'd just as soon move in and shoot the rest of our interviews there, if only Jill would let him.

Johnny sat with his room stretching out behind him, a tapestry on the wall, a lamp farther back. He looked solid, seated in a deep armchair, but when he spoke, his voice came out frail and whispery. I had to turn the microphone up as far as I could for him.

"My father was someone you didn't say no to. He asked you to go to a meeting, you went to a meeting. He asked you to give a banquet, you gave a banquet. He asked you to give money, you gave money. He was tough, my father. Had to be. In his day, in the old country, you got your head chopped off, just for looking around. Or, if you went to the States, you could get run out of town, maybe killed, just for showing up there. Plenty of people were."

"Now. What else," Johnny rolled his eyes for a moment. "Oh. Ham-yu. Yes, how about ham-yu? You want to hear about the ham-yu?"

" 'Ham you?' " Jill asked.

I heard Peter click his camera off.

"You never heard of it?" Johnny smiled, "It's what every Cantonese mother cooks and what all the children love—"

Cut, cut, Jill flashed her hands. I kept rolling. Jill signaled again, but I looked away. Where was Johnny going with his ham-yu? I wanted to know. Tape was cheap. Tape was infinitely accommodating.

"It stinks," Johnny said. "Ground pork with salty fish, ham-yu. And that's what my mother fed Dr. Sun Yat-sen. Can you imagine? It was like giving George Washington stinky meat loaf.

"It was Father's fault. He didn't warn Mother, he just brought the Doctor home one day and that's all Mother had for supper. Ham-yu. Hahaha," Johnny started laughing, "Mother felt so cheap."

"I see," Jill said.

"No you don't," Johnny hiccuped. "Excuse me. You ask me about how we got rid of the emperor and all I can think of is this, ham-yu. Hahaha."

"Well, then, I guess we've got it," Jill stood up. "Thank you."

"No, listen, listen." Johnny held up a hand. "I think it's like this—you still on?"

He looked at Peter, me.

"It was like this: my father didn't like how in San Francisco they put you down if you were Chinese. At that time, it didn't help any to hear how bad China was doing over there. The famines, the country falling apart. People killing each other. Foreigners, too. My father said, 'Makes it worse for us here.'

"That's why he decided it was time for a change. That's why he started supporting Dr. Sun. Because he was fed up. Not on ham-yu, hahaha. But because, you know, it stinks—yes, that's it—everything stinks, and that's when you get it. Your revolution. When people are fed up. With the stink. Now, does that help?"

"Yes, yes. Thank you. So much."

This time Jill jumped at Johnny and hauled him to his feet before he could say more.

"Bull's-eye." Peter winked at me and started gathering up his camera gear.

Johnny and Earl first met through the YMCA in Shanghai in the 1920s. Their paths crossed and diverged several times thereafter. But with the communist victory in 1949, they both retreated to Hong Kong and there they eventually met again. "On the ferry," Earl said, "what a hoot." They'd been together ever since, served these many years by a skinny old amah who came out now and gave us tea when we were done.

"I was there, too," she yelled. "I was there."

The amah wanted to talk about how she had tricked the Japanese during the war, but Jill and Peter were too distracted to listen. They went off to film several boxes of old photos Johnny and Earl had collected during their years in China. This was a rare find, really, a cache of urban images from Shanghai, Chungking and Canton. I realized then that that was what Jill was after, the old photos. The interviews had been merely a chance to squeeze out more. Jill was always after more, a story here, a story there. But with Johnny going off the deep end about his ham-yu, Jill had only Earl's interview she could use now, what there was of it.

"About a roll and a half," Peter said.

As often happened, another story was left behind. If it were me—and I have to admit I love the tangential, the ephemeral, the gossip column as much as the main story, maybe more—if it were me, I would have asked Johnny and Earl about love and longevity. Their apartment was filled with mementos of their religious faith and their devotion to each other—photos, poems, hands clasped in worship and love.

Before we left, Peter took a still photo of Johnny and Earl sitting on their sofa. "Closer," Peter motioned them together.

"Like this?" Earl put an arm around Johnny and bared his teeth. We all laughed, though Johnny, who was proper, raised an eyebrow and shook off Earl's hand. If it were me, I would have asked them, how did you keep faith and friskiness alive?

After we interviewed Johnny and Earl, we flew to Canton, where we met Alice, our Chinese guide. There, Jill discovered Alice had booked us into the White Swan, the best hotel in Canton at the time.

"Whatever for?" Jill said, when she saw the gleaming white lobby and, below it, a little stream flowing under a bridge, past a tea shop. "I told you we didn't need a place like this."

Jill had made two earlier trips to reconnoiter locations and subjects for her film. She had worked with Alice on those, and afterwards returned home to report, "We have the perfect little translator." Now, however, she felt she had to eat her words. She said slowly and distinctly, "Alice, you understand, we are not Hollywood."

"Oh, yes," Alice replied. She was new to the business of guiding film groups around China, but she had worked on a big foreign picture before. "I understand," she widened her eyes, "but they have no room. At the other place."

"The other place—didn't we book them? Months ago?"

"Yes," Alice nodded.

"Well?"

"Maybe."

"Maybe what?"

"Maybe they think we're coming last month. Not this." Alice turned her palms up.

Jill stared at Alice's palms. They were pale and soft. "Oh," she said. Alice probably had done all she could. It was Jill who had negated her efforts, Jill who had decided at the last minute to delay filming by a month, and now with Peter, me, and two bellboys waiting on twenty cases of luggage, she, Jill, was hardly in a position to argue about what might have fallen through the cracks.

"Give me your passports," she said and held out her hand.

The next day, Jill sent Alice to deliver a packet of Sudafed to General Li, the weeping general. The rest of us took the morning off. Swam in a warm pool. Napped. Mid-afternoon, we set out for our interview with an intelligence officer Peter nicknamed "The Assassin."

Whenever possible, Jill interviewed in English, though sometimes the English got in the way, as it did on this occasion:

ASSASSIN: I did not kill myself.
JILL: You didn't commit suicide?
ASSASSIN: No. I did not.
JILL: What?
ASSASSIN: I did not kill. Myself.
JILL: No.
ASSASSIN: No.
JILL: I see. (pause) What *did* you do?
ASSASSIN: I was in charge. *I* did not kill.
JILL: But your unit, it was responsible for many deaths. You say so yourself. In your own book. See, "Confessions—"
ASSASSIN: No, no. That is revolutionary situation. Many people die in the revolution. I, I cannot save them.
JILL: But you were in charge.
ASSASSIN: Of course. I am intelligence officer.
JILL: So, if you were in charge, you could have stopped it. The deaths. You did not *have* to execute people.
ASSASSIN: That's what I tell you I never did!

Mr. Wu, our intelligence officer, had been the scourge of students during the 1930s and '40s, prisoner of the State after liberation, then a volunteer to settle a frontier region, then a sanatorium patient, then a forgotten man, then, finally and most recently, author of a Hong Kong bestseller, translated into English as *White Terror: Spymaster in Shanghai*. Mr. Wu, now shriveled as a mummy, but still sucking hard on a cigarette held at attention upright between thumb and forefinger. Mr. Wu sat under Peter's lights and tried to tell Jill that there was a genuine distinction between a man in charge and a man who killed. It was a distinction that mattered, for Mr. Wu was saying, hey, I'm not a thug. And he wasn't. As Alice told me later, though she didn't use these words, Mr. Wu didn't get to the top by killing people. He was already there. Where he came from, his family had called the shots, run the show. It had been that way for generations. What did he need to kill for? With his own hands? Mr. Wu was insulted by Jill's questions.

"How can he say what he said?" I asked Alice, "Isn't he afraid of—"

"What? At his age? Nobody listens to him," Alice wrinkled her nose.

She was disappointed, not with Mr. Wu, but with us. Disappointed that Peter was fat. And married. That Jill and I were women. Alice wasn't interested in what Mr. Wu or any of the old people we interviewed had to say, though she did become quite attentive, later on, when we filmed old generals in Beijing who arrived in their shiny Mercedes sedans.

Alice was twenty-six. She wanted to meet someone attractive. She had studied English with great discipline. Learned to speak it with hardly an accent. And not unreasonably, she expected her beautiful English to deliver more to her than it did when she got us, Jill, Peter, and me. Three not-so-up-to-date people in crumpled cottons.

At the airport while we were waiting for our luggage to come through, I caught Alice biting her lip and staring at our shoes. Peter's dirty tennies. My black Nikes and Jill's high-tops. Green, a Robin Hood green. These shoes dashed about and jiggled before the customs officials. I had never thought before what they said about us. How klunky they made us look. How low-powered. Our shoes squished and bulged where our feet bulged. Alice, however, wore neat patent-leather flats with pointy toes. They squeaked when she walked. They also squeaked when she wasn't walking. A mere shift in weight seemed to be enough to set them off. I had to tell Alice later not to wear these shoes while we were filming. They added an unwelcome commentary to my recordings.

■ ■ ■

General Li, the weeping general, was not insulted by the gift of Sudafed, as I had thought he would be. He was pleased, in fact. He told Jill he'd had his condition for years, and nothing had helped it. He was glad now to try something new. He'd already taken the Sudafed as Alice had instructed, translating from the directions on the packet when she delivered it. Could Jill see a difference?

"Yes," Jill lied, "I think so."

Peter whistled through his teeth. He set his camera up and took a long, hard look at the general.

The old man did have large, bulging eyes, as if he had been startled at some point and had never recovered. Jill asked him about the most wrenching moment of his life, when he had surrendered his nationalist troops to the communists during the civil war. She said, "Can you tell us about that, the surrender?"

She had newsreel footage of the general himself, younger by almost forty years, walking across a black and white field, wind rippling his shirt and his hair, leaving his brow exposed. His eyes are black in the white of his face. Is he squinting or tearing up? It's hard to tell. The picture jumps up and down. Crackles with white specks. I wish I could hear the general crossing the field, the two armies coming face to face, both dressed in drooping gray, a gathering of dark forms against a white sky, men falling into line, coming to rest. The general steps up, yields his gun.

"What did you say then?" Jill leaned into her question. I saw Peter zoom in for a close-up. I moved my microphone closer, too. Then we waited. The three of us. We waited because whatever the general would say, we had to be poised, camera rolling, sound rolling, to splice this moment to history. This was what we had come for, not the remaking of a great revolution—who would attempt that except as a major motion picture?—but this, this stalking of fugitive memory. We were here to stir up that beast, capture it on film as it streaked through the brush.

"What did you say?" Jill prodded.

"Nothing," the old man looked puzzled. "Nothing. We are like—" he held his arms far apart.

Was he talking about the two armies or about himself, the distance between the old man and the young, the one with eyes gone wet under our lights, or the other, forever reenacting his own demise?

Above the old general's desk there was a picture of the young man taken many years before fate claimed him. In the picture, the young man had the eyes of a matinee idol, dark and dreamy. He would sit for almost thirty years in prison.

■ ■ ■

We did three solid interviews after General Li. A political officer, a peasant, a soldier. Then a day off to wash clothes, do some shopping. Nothing more for three days except five reels of platitudes, which got us to Shanghai. Then a string of remarkable interviews with people who represented the cavalcade of idealists and opportunists, gangsters and workers, rich and destitute, those who had made Shanghai the great sinkhole of capitalism that it was in the old days.

One woman, a starlet of the 1930s, and later the dubbed voice for many Soviet films, said her specialty, before she joined the communists, was love and squalor. "They like me to cry." She bent her shoulders and heaved heartfelt sobs.

Jill was ecstatic. "Did you get that, did you?" she said later. She planned to use this shot with footage she had from a 1930s melodrama, showing the same actress sobbing in front of a young, handsome, and keenly distressed worker. He has just brought her the news her father has been killed. "By the soldiers!" the young man says, "They're coming—quick, quick." He pulls the beautifully weeping girl through a door.

Another woman spoke of a bleak childhood spent in a textile mill. Then there was the grizzled old man who talked of the day his comrades were mowed down. "We were just walking," he said, "dongdong-dongdong, then, wah," he brought his hand up suddenly and shot us all, Alice first—she was interpreting—then Jill, Peter, and, swinging his arm, me.

"Nineteen twenty-seven," he said, "and I was twenty-two." He chomped his teeth and glared at us.

When we finished with the proletariat in Shanghai we went on to the peasants in the south, to Jiangxi. Here the communists had had a base in the 1930s before they were forced out on their Long March to the Northwest. Jiangxi was poor and mountainous. But in the spring, when we got there, it was beautiful, the high fields yellow with flowering rapeseed, the paddy land rich as chocolate.

Peter wanted to stop and shoot along the way, at a market town, a ferry crossing, a mountain pass with a valley laid out in green and brown below. We were driving up to a village to interview some peasants there. Jill said there was no time to film GVs—general views—however spectacular they were.

Peter said, "Didn't you tell me you needed to show where all this was happening?"

Jill said, "No, I think I have it. On the old newsreels."

"What about transitions? Exteriors?"

"It's not that kind of film."

"You're not going to shoot anything else?" Peter's voice cracked. "Just talking heads? Talking Chinese?"

"Well, what else do I need? We *are* getting voice-overs. In English, my dear."

"Ooh luvly," Peter pitched his voice higher than usual. "That'll really make your film, Missy. Talking heads that aren't doing the talking."

At this point, I joined in. I was disturbed that most of my own efforts would end up in some netherland where original soundtracks go when they get mixed out of a show and replaced with voice-overs and uninspired music. I told Peter to quit harping about his shots. At least most of what he did would stay in the film. In fact, he was the film in a way that I couldn't be the sound.

"Tell her to use subtitles then." Peter got mad at me.

"Look, look," Jill intervened, "Didn't I tell you both? This is it. This is all I can give you: interviews, interviews, interviews. I don't have the bloody money for reconstructions. I can't give you the Long March, Peter."

"Who wants the Long March? All I'm saying is, open up your film. Get a shot of a village. Show the river they drowned in. The mountain that killed them. You know. It's what you're always talking about." Peter turned to me, "Isn't she?"

"Sure," I cribbed one of Jill's favorite lines, "Film is drama."

After this, Jill wouldn't speak to me for several days. She felt I'd betrayed her by siding with Peter. I felt I was merely asserting my rights democratically. Alice was fascinated by all this, by the way we tossed our opinions around. She would only smile when we asked her what she thought, really. We told her, if you're going to work on a film like this, where you don't make any money, at least you can have a good time and speak your mind.

Given the green light, Alice did start opening up little by little. Soon, with Peter's help—"Alice, Alice, you have a big rich boyfriend, hah-hhh?"—she had even produced a picture of an L.A. camera assistant she had met on her last job, a curly headed guy she was writing to now.

"Where is West Side?" she asked. "Near Disneyland?"

"Let me see," Peter took the picture Alice had pulled out for us. He made a face, "Aiya, don't waste your stamps on him."

We were like this at the beginning of our shoot, fooling around every day, with even our driver joining in. He had many questions for Jill, passed along through Peter or Alice, who translated. Questions about Jill's height. Her age. Her eligibility. And her hair. Is it really red?

"My god," Jill said, "Can't you see?"

"Hung Xiao-jie," the driver got quite chummy, "Miss Red." He was our movie star, cigarette plugged into his mouth, big smile sliding off the side of his face. "You don't like marry?" he turned to look at Jill as he drove straight for whatever was in front of us, a tractor, a truck. He had quickly realized this was the best way to get Jill's attention.

By our third week, however, the spark of being on the road, the seduction of it, the feeling of walking into high adventure akin to walking into a new relationship, had worn off and a certain dull inevitability set in. Jill didn't have the money to put us up in clean hotels, so we stayed in third-rate places. In the cities this hadn't been too bad. We often went to the good hotels to use a bathroom, drink coffee. But once we ventured into the countryside, it seemed we got up in the mornings, ate bread, bread so white it didn't even look like bread, then boarded our van, only to drive madly, horn blaring, to the next moldy bed, the next dripping toilet.

I remember a hotel in the south. One of those Soviet-style buildings that looked like it had been designed by somebody who built dams. It had a big dirty façade. Corridors wide enough to drive a pickup truck through, walls varnished a mucky brown, carpets well-greased. And rats gnawing in my room.

The first day there, I went out to pace the corridor and consider my options. That's when Peter appeared. He was carrying his camera, on his way back to his room.

"Did we shoot today?" I was alarmed that I might have missed something.

"Relax. I just liberated a roll of film, that's all. They back yet?" Peter inquired about Jill and Alice. They had gone off early in the morning to negotiate filming fees with local officials.

"No. You get any good shots?"

He made a face, "Looks like shit out there. The lake," he started down the corridor to his room.

I followed him, "You were going for exteriors?"

"What else? Missy's going to be happy she's got them later. But I wouldn't mention it now."

Peter went into his room and put his camera away. I watched. There must have been something about the way I was watching, an edginess, a certain tension that got to him, for when he finished what he was doing, he said, "Okay, okay. Come on."

He led me to the back of the hotel, to a big empty balcony. There I saw he had already set up a little survival unit for himself: a charcoal burner complete with palm-leaf fan, battered pot, and chopsticks lifted from the hotel dining room.

"Hungry?" he set me to work with the fan. While I tended the fire, he disappeared for a few minutes, then returned with a couple of packages of instant noodles, scallions, two eggs, and two bowls.

I leaned on the balcony wall and ate the noodles that Peter cooked for me. The city was a brown soup below. Blocks of red brick buildings. Dusty trees. I glared at all this, the ugliness down there and its unchecked sprawl into the distance, where, smack on the horizon, there rose a smokestack that failed to belch.

"You just can't see the smoke for all the smog," I said. "I bet you it's there, though."

"Probably," Peter shrugged.

"Did you see the dining room downstairs? The tablecloths?"

"Grease on grease."

"Yeah. But why?" I must have said this with some vehemence, more than I intended, for Peter stopped what he was doing then, drinking a bottle of pop, and squinted at me. "They're all standing around," I said.

"What's wrong, you want to make them work?" Peter smiled. "What do you care?"

I had become so intent on recording all the history I could on this trip, hooking straight into other lives with my microphones, and these lives coming back to me through my headphones; I'd listened so closely to the spit and gurgle of history that I had started to take everything personally. There were the good guys and the bad, the worker, the spy. There were the good deeds and the ignoble. The workers at the government guest house who wouldn't clean their tables had failed me in some way. They made me angry. Standing about picking their faces. What did I think the revolution was about? I don't know. But one thing for sure, I didn't want to touch its dirty linen.

Peter didn't like the dirt any more than I did, but he didn't care if things weren't living up to expectations. "They're going to do whatever they're going to do," he stuck his chin at the brown ether beyond our balcony. He wasn't worried about any day of reckoning, the communists could have Hong Kong. He had his own life.

"I got a house in Sydney," he said. "You come visit me, you'll feel better. We'll make a nice movie there, huh? Lots of beautiful scenery, Academy Award shots. And when we're done, I'll take you to Bondi Beach. You want to go to Bondi Beach?"

We left the city to go deep into the mountains. There, we interviewed peasants about their struggles with landlords and the armies that had swept through. Our best footage came from an old lady with the voice of a duck. We filmed her sitting on the threshing floor in front of her house, wet fields behind her and a boy on a water buffalo taking forever to cross through our shot.

"Xiao Hung, Xiao Hung," the old lady yelled at her grandson to get out of the way.

He whipped his buffalo up to where we were, got off and stood, gape-mouthed, listening to what the old lady had to say.

"They sold me," she described being handed over to right-wing troops. "Not even to a poor officer, but to a nobody. And me, I was pretty, too. Everybody said." The old lady wiped her face with the side of her hand. She was not crying; she was angry. "Sold to the cheapest fool around. Ai, he looked just like this one," she suddenly pointed an accusing finger at her grandson. The boy backed off, frightened.

"All right, all right," the old lady shouted at him. "You're a good boy." She was quite deaf.

When we returned to Shanghai, Jill heard she had received only part of the money she had counted on to complete her film. After her China shoot, she had originally planned to go on directly to Taiwan to interview the die-hard anti-communists there. Now she wasn't sure she could.

She cursed Johnny. Johnny, of Earl and Johnny in Hong Kong, had apparently promised the money she needed, some his own, some from his father's old connections, but none of it had showed up yet at Jill's bank in New York.

This news, coming after our argument about opening up the film, put Jill in a tough spot. She dropped a village she had planned to include. She pored over her schedule with Alice, trying to cut it down. And she spent an evening in my hotel room, talking compulsively about how she could make the film work. This was the film that was going to put her back on her feet, restore her reputation as the terrific filmmaker she knew she was.

"I'm not going to babysit any more people," she said. "Let them bollix up their own films. They're getting the credit for it anyway."

"What do you think? Can we make a film about China for the average Joe? Who is the average Joe?"

"I dunno." I was washing my socks at the time she insisted on bringing this up.

"Come on, you're American."

"He likes people?"

"Okay."

"And he identifies," I unplugged my wash basin, "with them."

"Christ," Jill flopped on my bed. She stared at the ceiling while the wash basin sucked the water down.

"Maybe," she said. "Maybe what I need is a face." She sat up.

"Isn't that what we've been getting all along? Mrs. Lu, Mr. Yang, Mr. Wu," I listed the people we had filmed.

"No, not them. A face that tells it all. About the revolution."

"All right, all right." I thought a minute, recalled the smile and the famous mole. I squeezed out my socks. "What about Mao?"

"Jesus," Jill almost came over and hit me. "Don't you think I have any original ideas?"

I had only meant to point out that she did have some powerful images, like the footage of the celebration at the founding of the People's Republic. All the big faces of the revolution are there, standing on that famous wall overlooking Tiananmen. And Mao, the biggest face of all, waves his hand and says in that funny voice of his, "Todaay . . . the Chinese People . . . have stood up."

I thought that told it all, but Jill said it wasn't enough.

■ ■ ■

"Wonderful, wonderful, wonderful."

Two days later, I had taken temporary leave of Jill and the tensions of her film. I was in Beijing by then, sitting in my uncle's apartment. This was my third uncle, San Jiou-jiou, my mother's favorite brother, the one she had said I must see. My uncle lived alone, his wife had died and his daughter worked in an industrial city to the north, yet he had a surprisingly large place to himself. He didn't have to share with another family, as far as I could tell. My uncle's apartment was plain, but adequately furnished with a big glass-covered desk in the main room and an arrangement of stiff chairs that looked out over a dusty courtyard.

I was sitting in one of the stiff chairs, showing my uncle the books I had brought for him: *The Lady of the Lake, The Big Sleep,* a Ross Macdonald, an Elmore Leonard, a Tony Hillerman. All Americans. And then, yes, the latest Le Carré, too.

"Wonderful, wonderful," my uncle stacked the books on his desk as if he were stacking coins. Next to the books was a bottle of cognac. I had brought this, too. "Very good. Together." My uncle pointed to the cognac and the books.

He had a paunch, but his hands were slim and fine as a woman's. "For diagnosis," my mother had told me. "Doctors there, they don't depend on tests, they use their hands. Like your uncle—he's the best."

My mother was not modest when she told me about her family and what I should be living up to. She had not added, though, that this uncle also had his vices and enjoyed them thoroughly. He lit up a cigarette now and took a long drag. I'd brought him Dunhills.

"Los Angeles," he smiled at me.

"Yes," I said.

"You went to school there."

"Uh huh."

"UCLA."

"Film school, yeah. Documentaries."

"It's good?"

"Mmm, I guess so—"

"Your mother says it's the best."

"Oh. Then it must be," I smiled.

My uncle laughed. He knew my mother's ways as well as I did. I'm sure he'd been receiving letters over the years recounting in detail this or that milestone passed. My mother, the only one in her family to go to the States, felt driven to make the most of her opportunities. This had made her high-strung and nervous, while my uncle, though he had suffered through the Cultural Revolution like so many others, had fared better in a way, that's what I thought. He had an assurance that my mother lacked. He knew Beijing was his world in a way that my mother could never feel New Jersey was hers. And he demonstrated this to me that very day, when he took me to his friend's house. The friend was an old and favorite patient of his.

"You went *there?*" Jill was astounded when I told her later.

"Yeah. It surprised me, too, but going there, it was like, nothing different, you know? We drove over and they waved us through a gate and inside, I lost track, but way in, we came to this place, kind of hidden, and we stopped, and this kid came out and he said, 'Uncle Liang, Uncle Liang.'

"He was just calling my uncle that, my uncle's not his real uncle. Anyway, he ran up and my uncle said, 'This is Mee-kee—as in Mickey Mouse.'

" 'Go get your cars,' my uncle tells Mickey and they went off, the two of them. They disappeared all of a sudden and left me standing in the driveway, with the guards looking at me. They didn't say anything, so I didn't say anything. I just stood there. Lucky thing the kid came back. He had two cars now and he wanted us to race them. Remote control. He wasn't real coordinated. I got bored. I was thinking about crashing my car into one of the guards just to see what would happen, you know? But that's when my uncle showed up. And that's when I met him."

"You're kidding."

"No, it was him. I swear, the guy who took over from Mao. What do they call him, the paramount leader? He's old, right? And short, real short." I drew my neck into my shoulders. "Like his pictures, exactly. You remember how he looked visiting Jimmy Carter in the White House. Anyway, I said, 'Sir,' I didn't know what else to call him. And he says, 'Thank you, thank you.' "

"To you?" Jill was incredulous, "What for?"

"I'm telling you—because I brought him what he needed. Knee braces."

"Knee braces?"

"Yeah. Made out of spongy cloth. You know, you wrap it round your knees and the velcro keeps it in place? It's what you get from your chiropractor."

"All right, all right—so then what?"

"Then he was happy. Because I brought him the braces. His knees have been giving out on him since the Long March."

"Terrific. He was so grateful to you he patted you on the back and he said, 'Good work, old girl.' Was that it?"

"No, come on. He wanted to talk."

"With you? About what?"

"Hollywood."

"Hollywood?" Jill's voice shifted a register.

"I'm not kidding. Really. He wanted to know how far it was from UCLA to—let's see—Disney, MGM, and Steven Spielberg. Major studios. That's what he had on this piece of paper. He just went down his list: how far to here, and here, and here. By car."

"Bullshit," Jill turned away.

"No, wait, wait. You're missing the good part. The old man's got a granddaughter, Mickey's older sister. Well, this granddaughter is going to UCLA, see? That's why the old man wanted to talk to me. Because his granddaughter is putting the squeeze on him. She wants to get rid of her bodyguard and get her own car. To make movies, she says. But the old man won't give her a car. He says she'll kill herself in it. Or use it to get drugs. Isn't that something?"

I thought I had delivered a great story to Jill, but once she believed me, she got upset that I hadn't talked to the old man about our film.

"You didn't ask him for an interview?" she was appalled.

"Well, it's not like I could," I said.

"You were there."

"Yes, but he set the agenda. He wanted to know about Hollywood. 'Why do you need a Porsche to make a movie? What's wrong with a Benz?' That's what he wanted to know. Not this," I waved my hand at the pile of luggage we had waiting on the curb. We were loading our van for another day's work. "He won't give us an interview just like that," I tried to reason with Jill. "Even if he is my uncle's patient. He's getting too old. He's got other things on his mind. You have to be like a major network before—"

Jill walked off and boarded our van.

She wanted a face that told it all. I thought she had it, many faces. Big, fat, thin, and small. Over the weeks, Peter had given her a gallery of film portraits. He was truly a master of his medium. He didn't light a subject so much as he found the perfect light to bring forth his subject, putting a peasant woman by her window, bright quilts behind her; sitting a famous general in a big chair, half his face falling into shadow, the other half swimming with his thoughts, in and out of watery sunlight.

Jill had all of this already in the can. But what she wanted was something we couldn't give her. The way she saw it, the face that told it all had to be a particular face: the face of a very high Party official. It wasn't enough that we had filmed bureau chiefs and the directors of cultural institutes. Old generals who had big houses in nice compounds with guards and drivers. These were not people to be sniffed at, but in Jill's view, if they were retired or only figureheads now, they were not quite first-rank. What she wanted was someone right from the inner circle, someone who could get her through that red gate into the heart of things, into Zhongnanhai, where only the select lived.

"What about Chou En-lai's wife?" I heard her say to Alice.

Jill spent the remaining days of our shoot huddled with Alice, usually in the front of our van. If she spoke to me, it was only to give instructions. Otherwise, she didn't want to be reminded that I had met the biggest fish of all and let him go.

I spread my gear and myself across the back seat of our van. We drove through the alleys of Beijing. Gray walls. Curved roofs. I was coming face to face with my own history for the first time.

I thought: Jill had to stick to facts. That was the problem. She had to make this history credible. But not me. All I had to do was hold out my microphone and listen. Listen for the past to percolate up out of people. And it would come up, sometimes with more gas than I could accept; I used a beautifully pristine German microphone that easily picked up half-digested meals, ill-cooked thoughts. Can you say that again? I would have to interrupt to get it right, a clean recording. It was my job to stand watch over memory, roll my tape out before it like a red carpet. I didn't have to worry about facts or truth. I could ponder other things. Things closer to my heart.

Like when we went to the village north of Beijing and interviewed the Liu brothers, the one who could walk but not talk, and the other who could talk but not walk. Two old guys we put in a cart and filmed as they took us around their village. From tunnel to trench to wall, Jill had to cover the sure ground, going from fighting the Japanese to shooting the local landlord. But me, I could step away for a moment. Catch the young man riding by on his bicycle, girlfriend on the back. She turns, her face ghost-white with astonishment, she is wearing the local make-up, garish, she turns too quick to look at me and throws her young man off balance.

"Xiao Hung, Xiao Hung," he cries as their bicycle weaves crazily down a rutted lane. White-washed walls on either side.

Jill had to get the big picture, but I could indulge in the small moments. Another day, our last day of shooting, we filmed the Songbird of the Party. She sang revolutionary songs for us. We filmed her in a hard, bright room, the glass doors to her bookcase jittering as a truck went by outside. I recorded her pure soprano; she was still quite youthful — black hair, lush lips — she had been only a young girl when she married a famous Party leader. He had passed on in the prime of his life. Of illness, Alice told me, not political intrigue.

I asked to use Madame's facilities after we were through, and her guard, a raw country boy from the look of him, led me down a hall to a door where he stopped and averted his face. I opened the door and walked through. Inside, there was a realm of private indulgence I hadn't seen in a long time: flush toilet — dressed the American way in something pink and fluffy — white bath, shiny faucets. There was a vase of flowers, plastic, by the curtained window. And a bar of soap, pink Dove, in a green soap dish. The towels were fresh.

Jill had to ask the Songbird about Yenan, the famous communist base in the Northwest, the one where many romances started and the one from which an ardent generation launched their final drive to power. Jill had to ask the Songbird about this, and then about her propaganda work. How she had spread the revolutionary message and advanced with the army as the communists swept to victory. We had come now, in the film's journey, to the end of the civil war, and Jill needed to march straight through to her conclusion. But I, I would have said, after I saw the oasis of the Songbird's bath, I would have said, "Tell me, madame, about your husband. I heard he was handsome, and apart from being a very reliable administrator, he was also a great ham and loved to write skits."

If I dared, I would have said this, for where Jill had to be high-minded,

I loved the low ground, the things that people pushed offstage, the gossip, the dirt. I was looking for the heart, the trashy heart of my history. After all, wasn't that where the unknown leaped out at you?

■ ■ ■

When I returned to Beijing some years later, I went back to the red wall and sat, waiting for something, I couldn't say what. I saw a girl and a soldier flirt over a popsicle. When they ran off, I waited through the afternoon and watched the light turn rosy, then gold. Soon it dropped to an afterthought and the old men went away, the checker players, too, the clerks in their white shirts, the visitors from out of town. When all had left and the city went dark, with only the dimmest street lights remaining, I walked around the wall.

Jill had finished her film and seen it broadcast to good reviews. Then Tiananmen came. And it seemed no longer possible to remember the past, except for the blood it left behind.

The revolution we had filmed, the old people we had talked to, they seemed as remote now as if we, the filmmakers—foreigners, no less— had made them up, their stories and their faces. As if we had written the script, cast the characters ourselves: "Landlords, anybody want to be a landlord?" And then directed the whole thing, badly at that.

"Mr. Mao, Mr. Mao, can we have you say it again?"

"The same?"

"Sure, don't change a thing."

(All rise) "Today, the Chinese People Have Stood Up."

I walked through Tiananmen and around the Forbidden City. The night had drained all color away, the red of the imperial wall, the green of the trees. I moved through a grayscape. A small bridge opened to the left. I crossed a pungent moat below. The great wall in front. I turned at its base and walked down a narrow path, squeezed between the wall, which rose thick and black to my left, and a row of squatter tenements tottering at the edge of the moat.

Perhaps it was the night and the calm it induced, the feeling of people retreating into themselves, so many mashed into a tiny space along that strip of wall, every inch animated with people washing, gargling, eating a late bowl of noodles, pissing, yet all of this done as if under some kind of blackout, no one talking above a murmur, only a bicycle whirring past.

Perhaps it was this, the grayscape without hard edges, the calm before sleep, that made it possible to reclaim illicit thoughts, retrograde emotions. I walked along that wall, everything dark but for the man who came out in pale pajamas and read under a dim street light, but for the chess players in their white undershirts, everything dark but for the green smell of the squash plants, the beans, the flowers planted so densely along the base of the wall. I walked by and a nostalgia took over.

It had no meaning, really, except that for me, stranger to the motherland, walking along the edge of that ancient wall, along the memory of a great past, I wanted to be able to claim it as my own, not only to claim it, but to believe it was indeed a splendid story, a story of more than blood and avarice, a story worth passing on.

I remember I waxed as nostalgic as the moon that night. I came to one end of the wall, crossed the moat, turned, and continued down another side. There were no tenements now, but bushes and trees planted along the moat.

I walked on imagining my history until I noticed the bushes I passed seemed to be taking on a life of their own. They shook, more than necessary—there was no wind. Then I noticed bicycles parked by the bushes, and here and there, I saw a bush that had acquired a limb, usually shod, and trembling. Soon I noticed the biggest bushes had motorcycles, not bicycles, as if some Darwinian law had decreed the biggest and best bushes got the biggest and best wheels. In this case, Suzukis.

What I saw walking along the wall was nothing grand and enduring. Just couples making out. Some law of perverse logic must have said that bushes grown luxuriant with leaves by day had to give shelter by night to couples with no other place to go, couples desperate to develop a people's history and pass it on to new generations. It was weird. A just exchange. The night's maneuverings stripped away my illusions, and in their place, what did I have? A little hot romance?

Was this why I went to the red wall each time I returned to Beijing? Like a camel to its oasis, a horse to its watering hole, maybe I first sought out that wall, drank in its splendor, rested in its shade, just so I could wait for a moment like this, suddenly, to claim me.

I came to the end of the wall. A tower hung over the water, a moon over the moat. Far away, there were firecrackers. It was the seventieth year of the Communist Party. It was a night made to hunt for love and history.

DOCTOR

. . .

Christina Chiu

M y first year out of med school, I started working at an eating disor-
ders clinic on the Upper East Side. I was twenty-six, a recovered
bulimic, understood the nature of the disorder, and felt that I could
make a difference. One of my patients, Laurel, came to us weighing
eighty-two pounds. She was five feet, five inches tall, and her sixteenth
birthday was in a month. Despite twelve days of treatment, she'd lost
another two pounds. Her pulse was down to forty-two beats per minute:
her blood pressure 80/50. She had an arrhythmia, which put her at risk
for heart failure.

Laurel was my last patient before the weekend. She had come to
me through Ma's friend Mary, who was the girl's aunt. I knocked at
Laurel's door. "It's Dr. Wong."

"One sec," she called. There was a rustling sound and the sharp
squeak of bedsprings. "Okay!"

I opened the door. Laurel's cheeks dipped inward, the bones pro-
truding against her taut skin. Her face was flushed. Droplets of perspi-
ration showed over her lip and throughout her thinning hair. Her
nostrils flared.

CHRISTINA CHIU is the author of *Troublemaker and Other Saints*. She is
the recipient of the Asian American Literary Award, the Robert Simpson Fellowship, the Claire Woolrich Scholarship, and the Van Lier Fellowship. Her
work has appeared in numerous magazines and anthologies, including *Tin
House*, *The MacGuffin*, and the *Asian Pacific American Journal*. She received
her M.F.A. from Columbia University and her B.A. from Bates College. She
was born in New York City in 1969.

Sit-ups again, I thought.

I noticed the fishbowl on the table beside the bed. The bowl contained a lone orange-and-black fish and a miniature white castle. The goldfish circled, searching the glass for a way out.

"Cute fish," I said. "Your mom bring it?"

Laurel shrugged. She was propped against a bunched-up comforter, her legs crossed and a foot bobbing in the air. She was reading *Romeo and Juliet*. The cover of the book was torn, the pages stained and crumpled.

Laurel whispered the sentences quickly, prayerlike, but with a passion that reeked of compulsion. The room's thermostat was set at seventy-eight degrees, and condensation fogged the windows. She wore a red woolly cardigan, a T-shirt, jeans, and thick athletic socks. The sweater hung from her gaunt shoulders.

"Does it have a name?" I asked, looking at the fish.

She gave me an eternally bored expression. "Yu."

I laughed—in Chinese, *yu* means "fish"—and Laurel's eyes darted up at me. There was a moment of recognition: Oh yeah, she's Chinese, too. She smirked; I was on the in. Finally, I thought, a connection.

"So how was the visit with your mom?" I asked, taking her pulse.

She shrugged again, shook her leg. "Same. Worried sick, blah, blah."

"Did you ask for something for your birthday?"

Laurel squinted at the fish. "She'd just say no."

"There's no harm in asking, is there?"

"You don't know Mom."

My nostrils tickled. My attention was suddenly drawn toward a corner of the room. One whiff, another. It was rancid food. Laurel's eyes darted from me to the bureau, then back to me. Her foot went still. "A dog," she stammered. "That's what I want."

I acknowledged her with a nod.

"A German shepherd," she said, clenching my hand. For someone so frail, she caught me off guard with the force of her grip. "But Mom's all like, 'Gain a few pounds first, and then we'll see.'"

I freed myself from her grasp and moved toward the bureau.

"Don't go in there," she said. "It's private." The panic in her voice made me want to take her in my arms, cradle her thinning bones to my body. You have your whole life ahead of you, I wanted to say. A lifetime of experiences to live for. But I could remember the terror. The chaos. Every moment painful and all-consuming.

"I'm sorry, Laurel. You know the rules." I opened the drawer. She quieted as I unraveled a towel filled with carrot bits, biscuit, browning lettuce, and rancid chicken.

"I didn't do it," she said, bolting out of bed. She knocked the table. Water splashed from the fishbowl. Yu banged into the castle and, stunned, drifted in place.

"How many days has this been going on?" I asked.

"I'm being framed. It's Katy. She hates me, the fat cow."

"Hey—come on." I rubbed Laurel's shoulder. She winced and shriveled from my touch. She sat back on the bed.

"Laurel, Dr. Brady's explained what's going on, right?"

She rolled her eyes.

"So you know your body's on the verge of—"

"Yeah, yeah—breaking down my muscles. Blah, blah."

"Internal organs like your heart."

"Blah, blah."

"And liver."

"Blah, blah."

"And brain," I said.

Her body grew stiff, and I knew she must be exerting every ounce of energy not to cry.

"You look scared," I said. "Are you scared?"

She nodded and turned away, and gripped the paperback with both hands. Veins puffed at her knuckles. "Everyone wants to make me fat," she said.

"I don't want that. Neither I nor Dr. Brady is going to let that happen to you."

Her brows creased with suspicion. She shrugged and took up her book. I touched her arm before she could go back to reading. "I'm not going to let your condition get worse without doing something about it, okay?"

She fidgeted, leafing through the book's pages, her foot shaking violently.

"We'll talk more about this on Monday," I said, rolling the towel into a ball. But I knew how it went. As soon as I walked out the door, she'd be counting sit-ups; by the time I got on the Bronx River Parkway, she'd be counting down from one hundred.

■ ■ ■

I exited the highway into town. The defroster cleared the cloudy wind-shield. My feet felt clammy. They were sweaty yet cold. At the super-market, I parked the car and headed inside. Wind sneaked down the back of my coat, making me shiver.

The store was brightly lit, and bustling with the after-work com-muter crowd. Cashier lines extended all the way into the dairy depart-ment. Half-filled metal carts cluttered the aisles, their loose wheels jangling like rusty tambourines. I resisted the urge to leave. Mark has had a long week, I told myself. The least I can do is have dinner ready when he gets home. I hurried up and down the aisles, filling a basket. I felt so hungry that I bit into an apple. Who knows what kinds of pesti-cides and germs were on it?

I was waiting at the checkout line when my cellular went off. "Hello?" I answered.

"Georgie?" Ma said.

I remembered I was supposed to deliver Uncle's allowance. The en-velope of cash was in the zippered pocket of my purse. "Oh, shoot."

"Ah-yah—you forgot?"

"I'm sorry. Things have been crazy lately."

"How could you forget? Uncle has nothing to eat."

I unloaded my groceries onto the belt. "I'll drop off some food. Mark can fix dinner while I'm out."

She quieted the way she always did at the mention of Mark. Neither Dad nor she was all that happy that I'd married a hei ren, but with time, I knew she'd get over it. Taking off for Hong Kong had been Dad's idea. "Mei mien zi," he'd said. "How are we to show our faces?"

This summed up what he'd told my sister, Amy, a born trouble-maker who, after a steady string of F's on her report cards, was caught shoplifting. He'd had her banished to a boarding school in New Hamp-shire. I felt bad, of course, since some of her problems must have stemmed from me—Ma and Dad constantly compared the two of us. "Georgie made straight A's when she was your age," they'd tell her. "Georgie got a perfect math score on the SAT."

Now, it was me, Georgianna, the one with the grades and scholar-ships and med school. *I* was the troublemaker.

"Make sure to go up with Carlos," Ma said. Carlos was the super at the St. Martin's. It had been a decent residential hotel when Uncle moved in years before, but now, as one of the few remaining welfare hotels, it had a reputation for crack deals and urine-stained hallways. Ma had tried to move Uncle elsewhere, but he wouldn't have it.

The clerk tallied the groceries. Prewashed salad, a baked chicken, French bread, and a large bag of apples. "When are you coming home?" I asked Ma.

"Ah-yah, I didn't tell you? Your father's buying an apartment."

My stomach bottomed out. They're gone for good, I thought. For good. Most people were leaving Hong Kong in droves, what with all the doubts about the Handover, but not my parents. They couldn't get there fast enough. I finished the last bite of apple, and felt hungrier than ever.

"In Wan Chai," Ma said. "Very nice."

Next to the cashier stood racks with magazines, candy, and every kind of baked treat you could imagine. Just looking at the Hostess cupcakes—chocolate with the promise of cream in the center—made my stomach growl.

No, I reminded myself. You're not hungry. You're upset.

I handed two packs of sugar-free gum to the cashier and then, after she had rung them up, ripped one open. I stuffed a piece into my mouth. Peppermint soothed my gums.

"There's everything," Ma said. "Any kind of food you like—zong tse or xi tse—just go outside and it's there."

I handed the cashier my credit card.

I heard Dad calling for Ma in the background. "Have to go, now," she whispered. I glanced at the cupcakes and casually tossed a two-pack onto the belt.

Dessert. Everyone needs dessert.

■ ■ ■

Mark was there when I got home. It was six o'clock and already dark out; I was acutely aware that my patients were sitting down to dinner. From outside our ranch house, I saw the changing light of the television. I entered through the kitchen, and put my purse and keys and the groceries on the counter. Mark had set the dining table with items from our registry: fine china, crystal glasses, silverware, cloth napkins. The lit candles were half melted. On each plate sat a tuna-fish sandwich and a large pickle. He had prepared mine the way I liked: quartered into triangles and with the crusts cut off.

Mark was asleep on the sofa. He'd changed into a T-shirt and sweat-pants. Back in school, he'd been so thin—"skinny," he called it—that he used to layer his clothes for bulk. Tonight, however, I noticed his Buddha belly peeking out from under the T-shirt.

I tiptoed to the couch, took a deep breath, and blew on his stom-ach. It made a loud, farting sound. "Hey," he said, awake now, his eyes pinkish and heavy with sleep. He sat up and yawned. I thought about Laurel, wondered how she was doing with dinner.

"Hey there—you all right?" he asked.

I sat facing him at the edge of the coffee table. "One of my pa-tients . . ."

"Up, up—get your head out of there. We worked last weekend. This one's for us, remember?" He sneaked a finger under his glasses and rubbed his eye. We'd planned to shop for the house (we still needed a television stand and a desk for the study), maybe see a show, possibly dine one night at his favorite French restaurant.

"Agreed," I said. "But—"

"But?" His glasses settled crookedly on his nose.

I leaned my head against his shoulder. "I forgot about Uncle."

He sniffed my hair, which, like my hands, must have smelled of hospital. "Can't it wait? The man's not going to starve, is he?" he asked.

"Hope not."

A vein at his temple pulsed. Even halfway around the globe, Ma and Dad were still plaguing our relationship. He yawned to cover his irritation and pushed himself up from the couch, his knees crunching loudly. He drew me to my feet. "Well, let's do it."

"Honey, thanks, but . . ."

"But?"

"Strangers frighten him."

"Never mind a black man like me, right?" He looked up to the ceiling, sighed, and I could tell he'd spoken before he could stop himself. "Forget I ever said that," he said. "Just go—get this over with already, all right?"

■ ■ ■

At the St. Martin's I double-parked in front of the building, my hazards flashing. I polished off a cupcake. My teeth sank through layers of soft chocolate cake into the cream core. Sweetness filled me up.

I stepped out of the car and wind sucked the crumbs from my coat. The St. Martin's as I'd remembered it was gone. The lobby window was cracked, and boarded on the inside with duct tape. The doorway smelled of urine. In the lobby, chipping paint revealed a layer of bluish wallpaper. The furniture consisted of a black imitation-leather ottoman, a desk chair, and a plastic lawn table. The elevator had an "Out of Order" sign. Carlos sat behind the front desk, feet propped on the counter and hands locked behind his head. His hair had grayed and thinned. He looked me over and nodded. "Your ma said you'd be comin'."

He labored to get up from the chair, and the springs squeaked under his weight. "Your face just like your ma's," he said. He searched through keys on a ring. When he found the one he was looking for, he locked his TV into a cabinet. We went upstairs. The red carpet stretched to the end of the hall. It was as spotted and matted as a sick tongue. The place reeked of body odor. "I'll wait here," Carlos said, at the stairwell.

"Thanks for waiting with me." I felt for the envelope of fresh bills.

Carlos noticed someone loitering on the landing above. "Eh—you wanna drink, do it in your own room," he said. He didn't take his eye off the guy until the door shut. "I wouldn't have it any other way. Now get going. I gotta get back to the desk soon, eh?"

I stepped to the end of the hall. Today's Chinese newspaper sat outside the door. A dark stain seeped out from beneath. I knocked lightly. "Uncle?"

"Harder," Carlos whispered.

I rapped again, the sound of my knuckles against steel echoing down the hall. "Hello? It's Georgianna."

I waited a moment. "Is he in?" I asked Carlos.

He shrugged and nodded at the foot of the door. "Should be. Paper's still there."

I tried again and again. My knuckles ached. I checked that the hallway was clear, then tried to shove the envelope through the crack under the door, but it snagged and ripped. Air streamed out warm and humid over my hands. It stunk of sour sheets.

"Shoot," I cursed, removing the torn envelope. I returned to the stairwell. "Would you mind?" I attempted a handoff.

Carlos shook his head. "Sorry. Too many kooks in here to be gettin' involved."

Right. I stuffed the envelope into the zippered pocket of my purse. Mark's going to flip, I thought. As if it weren't bad enough, what with the way Ma and Dad had treated him. Now this. I decided I wouldn't tell him. What could I possibly say, anyway? I went to give Uncle money but he refused to open the door? Tonight, when Mark asked, I'd say everything was taken care of.

Carlos cleared his throat. "You called?"

Called?

"Oh, you gotta call," he said. "Your ma always called."

■ ■ ■

Much too early on a Saturday morning, the phone rang and rang, drawing me out of a convoluted dream. It was about Uncle. He was ringing our doorbell. There were vague bits about sit-ups and cupcakes, sheets of newspaper blowing over the lawn. I remembered opening the door, to have his head roll off into my arms. Mark nudged me awake. He handed me the phone and dropped facedown into the pillow.

It took a moment for me to get my head straight. "Hello?" I said.

It was Nurse Anderson. Laurel had lost another half-pound. "Put her on watch," I said. "Dr. Brady in today?"

"Yes, Doctor."

"Have her meet with Laurel, before you assign staff," I said. "Notify me of any changes."

"Yes, Doctor."

When I hung up, I realized Mark was sprawled over three-quarters of the bed.

"You hog," I said, slapping his rear.

He looked up from the pillow, bleary-eyed: What was that you said?

"I'm sorry about last night." I rubbed his arm. "Strangers really do frighten him."

"Let's drop it." He shifted onto his side. "You're okay, I'm okay, we're okay." He drew me close and tried to wrestle and pin me to the mattress. I went for his underarms and tickled him until he flipped onto his back. "Stop, stop, I give up," he finally said. He was laughing so hard he could barely breathe.

The phone rang again. This time, I was short of breath when I answered.

"I'm so sorry, Doctor." It was Nurse Anderson, stammering with embarrassment. I could picture her going red in the face.

"What's the problem?" I asked.

"Laurel's mother is here. Dr. Brady tried to explain the possibilities of hyperalimentation. Mrs. Tung is adamant that we not perform the procedure. She wants to withdraw Laurel from the clinic."

"I'll be there in half an hour," I said. "Just keep her occupied until I get there."

Mark buried himself under the comforter. I kissed him through the duvet. "We'll do French tonight, okay?" I promised to make it up to him.

■ ■ ■

At the clinic, I found Mrs. Tung at Laurel's bedside. She was calm, smiling even, and feeding her daughter a spoonful of applesauce. "Choo-choo, choo-choo," she cooed. "Chew-chew for Mommy." Nurse Anderson flashed me this look—Guess who's getting taken for a ride?—then excused herself from the room. Laurel opened her parched lips, her egglike eyes focused on her mother's face. Between bites, she went back to reading out loud, her voice raspy and quick.

Today Mrs. Tung had on a purplish-black top and matching skirt. There was a crease of shriveled skin at the back of her neck. She reminded me of an overripe Chinese eggplant: slender and without sharp features. She heard me enter and turned. We greeted each other politely. Static danced in her hair, and her skin sagged around the eyes and mouth. She had the look of someone who had, as the Chinese say, tasted a bitter life.

"May I speak with you in my office?" I asked her.

"Yes, yes," she said, ready to feed her daughter another spoon of applesauce.

"Don't go, Mommy," Laurel pleaded. The goldfish swam up for air.

"I'll be right back," she said. Laurel started crying. Mrs. Tung glanced at me for reassurance. Should I? Panic showed in her eyes.

"It's just ten minutes," I said.

Mrs. Tung nodded and followed me out the door. "Ten minutes. Ten minutes and I'll be right back."

Laurel cried harder. She threw her book and screamed, "Grandma would never have dumped me in this place! She never would have left me!"

Mrs. Tung froze in the hallway. She shut her eyes, and before Laurel could witness more, I swung the door closed.

"You all right?" I asked, taking Mrs. Tung's arm.

She pulled away. "No tubes or pumps, hear me? Not for my daughter."

"It's a very minor procedure." I tried to keep my voice down. "We don't plan to implement it unless her condition gets worse."

Mrs. Tung shook her head. "My husband says no."

Your husband has yet to show his face, I thought.

I lowered my voice and explained. "Your daughter's very sick."

"She eats every bite," Mrs. Tung said. "Every bite I feed her."

I felt like shaking her. Can't you see? Your daughter's dying.

A gasping sound from Laurel's room caught our attention. Mrs. Tung looked at me. I nodded—Go ahead, open it. She stared at the door, took a breath, turned the knob. Laurel was on the floor, struggling with a sit-up, forcing elbows to knees. She shook from the strain. The grimace on her face—lined and weathered like that of a seventy-year-old—made me feel utterly helpless. Laurel's determined to die, I thought, and ultimately there's nothing I can do to stop her.

■ ■ ■

I found myself at the corner deli two blocks from the St. Martin's. It was close to five p.m. I'd missed breakfast and lunch, and my body was trembling. The store smelled of newspaper and fresh-brewed coffee. The aisles were stocked with colorfully wrapped candies, boxes of assorted baked goods, and bags of snack foods. From the freezer at the back of the store, I grabbed a bottle of diet Coke. I considered an apple for a snack, but then noticed a box of éclairs. In med school, I couldn't stay away from these. Six soft pastries, covered with chocolate and stuffed with creamy vanilla pudding.

One wouldn't hurt.

My cellular sounded, and I nearly jumped into a shelf of Tastykakes. I wondered what I would say if it was Mark. I'd told him I had more to finish up at the clinic, and so we'd meet at the restaurant at seven.

After the third ring, I lost my nerve and answered. There was a staticky, long-distance pause. "Ma?" I said. "Is that you?"

"Georgie?" she whispered. In the background, I could hear Dad's loud, guttural snore.

"What are you doing up?" I asked. "It's six in the morning over there."

"Getting old." I could picture her in her terry-cloth robe, pacing in the dark with a cigarette. "I worry," she said.

"Don't."

She exhaled. I thought of Laurel struggling with her sit-ups—up, down; up, down—and a longing ache stuck at the back of my throat.

"Oh, Ma. Everything's fine. I'm fine."

She sighed. "Uncle all alone in that place. So dangerous. If only we could find him some place in Chinatown."

Who's "we"? I wanted to say.

"He's fine," I told her.

She quieted. "Maybe you should take him out for food sometimes?"

"Never mind dinner," I said. "I can't get him to open the damn door."

"You didn't give him the money?"

"It's not my fault. This is my second time already."

"Ah-yah. You have to call first."

"I know that *now*." I told her I was, even as we spoke, on my way to the St. Martin's.

"Take good care of Uncle, uh?" she said softly, and from the tone, I knew they weren't coming back.

■ ■ ■

I called Uncle from the car. After an infinite number of rings, he finally answered the phone. I had just taken a bite of éclair. When I looked up from the wheel, there was a woman in the middle of the road. I braked. The woman dragged her treasures across the street. She turned to me and continued to talk to herself. Circles of rouge dotted her cheeks.

"Hello, hello?" I shouted into the phone.

"Ah?" Uncle stammered.

I swallowed the mouthful of éclair, and it went down like cardboard. "Uncle, it's me. Georgianna."

"Oh my God. Wong Lung Fang-ah?"

"Yes. It's Wong Lung Fang."

"Oh my God."

"I came by yesterday. Didn't you hear me knocking?"

"I was, oh, yes, taking a bath."

"Well, I'm on my way over. In fact, I'm just about there now."

Though it was already growing dark out, you could tell the St. Martin's must have been quite grand in its day. Its façade was covered with soot and streaked with stains, and sections of molding had chipped and cracked, yet the building's French Renaissance–style architecture gave it a certain historic presence. Several floors had wrought-iron balconies, which extended around the building. The windows were framed like doorways.

"Uncle? Hello?"

"Oh my God," he stammered. "Oh my God."

"Open the door, okay?" I said. I double-parked and entered the lobby.

"Ah?" he said. "Sleeping."

Open the door or I'll break it down with my bare hands, I thought, stumbling over an abandoned plastic doll and nearly twisting an ankle. The doll had long hair and open-and-close eyes.

"Uncle?" I repeated into the phone.

There was a click and the line went dead.

■ ■ ■

I was banging at the door when my phone rang. I kicked Uncle's newspaper aside and answered, "God damn it—hello!"

"Doctor?" Nurse Anderson peeped. "Doctor Wong?"

"Oh, hi," I said. My knuckles burned. "Sorry. I didn't mean to yell at you like that. What's up?"

"It's Laurel—"

I've lost her. Jesus, I've lost her.

"Cardiac arrest, but we were able to resuscitate," she said.

"What are her vitals? No, never mind, I'll be there in a few minutes." I hung up and headed for the stairwell.

"He comes out at night," Carlos told me, as I passed him on the landing.

"Excuse me?"

"Seven. Sometimes eight or nine."

I nodded and raced downstairs. Don't do this to me, Laurel, I prayed. You've got to fight this. In the car, my sugar-coated fingers stuck to the wheel. I raced uptown. Stores and fast-food restaurants blurred past.

■ ■ ■

At the clinic, I found Laurel in critical but stable condition. Dr. Brady and I discussed the possibility of surgery and the immediate changes in her treatment plan. She was now being fed intravenously at a rate of forty cubic centimeters an hour, which was to be increased gradually within the next two weeks to one hundred sixty cubic centimeters. This would be the equivalent of two thousand calories per day. From X rays, I could tell there was damage to the heart; the right ventricle had thinned to the point of possible hemorrhage. I was keeping Laurel in intensive care, but I knew that if she had another attack, there'd be little we could do to save her.

After meeting with Dr. Brady, I spoke with the cardiologist and then sent X rays to his department. Later I went to look in on Laurel in IC. The curtain was drawn partway around her bed. The cardiomonitor beeped: up, down; up, down. The infusion pump gurgled. IV dripped. An oxygen mask covered Laurel's nose and mouth. The Tungs were already there. Laurel seemed to be asleep, yet her mother was at her side reading out loud from *Romeo and Juliet*. Mrs. Tung held her daughter's hand. Mr. Tung was positioned at the foot of the bed. His briefcase was in one hand, his wife's purse and coat in the other. He looked from his daughter to the IV.

It had taken this to get him here.

Mr. Tung loosened his tie. The knot tipped off center. His eyes were glassy and dazed. It was a look I'd seen before: What did I do so wrong? How has it come to this?

Before I could stop myself, I ducked away, quickly gathered my things from the office, and hurried out of the clinic.

■ ■ ■

It was a miracle. Uncle was standing outside the St. Martin's when I arrived. The poor guy was staring at a piece of litter skipping over the sidewalk. His back was bent; his hands were tucked deep into his coat pockets. He was smaller than I remembered, overexposed to the elements. I tossed the pastry box into a garbage can. There was only one éclair left. My pants dug into the skin at my waist.

"Uncle?"

He remained still, frozen in his thoughts. I touched his shoulder and he flinched. He looked at me as if I were a ghost. "Si-mong, ah?"

"It's Georgianna, Uncle."

He blinked. "Wong Lung Fang-ah?"

"Yes. Wong Lung Fang. What are you doing out here?"

He scanned the ground at his feet. He seemed to be checking that he hadn't dropped anything.

"Have you eaten?" I asked. "Would you like to get dinner?"

His head rocked forward and back.

"Okay, how about that diner on the corner? I can smell burgers from here." My stomach throbbed painfully. It felt too full, like it might explode.

Uncle's head bobbed from right to left. "Ah," he muttered. His eyes shifted from the space in front of him to the diner. His hands came out of his pockets. He wrung them again and again. They were bloated and leathery, the nails thick and cracked, layered at the tips like eroded sandstone. I wondered if I could get him to a psychiatrist.

"You don't have to get a burger," I said, moving toward the diner. "You could get soup and a sandwich if you like. Or maybe a salad. You like chef salad?" I stepped inside and Uncle followed, pausing in the doorway, checking right and left, right and left.

The diner smelled of grease and burnt coffee.

"Sit and I'll be right back," I said, racing for the bathroom at the rear of the restaurant. There was barely enough time to get the toilet seat up. A mess of chocolatey cream forced its way up my gullet and exploded into the bowl. I hugged my arms around my stomach. Weakness drew me to my knees. When the retching stopped, I stared at the brown mixture swirling around and around, small particles clinging at the water's edge, and thought, It's back.

I flushed the toilet and wiped the tears from around my swollen, red eyes. I rinsed my mouth and spit. A brown spot stained the front of my shirt. I wiped it clean, only to create a large damp circle over my left breast. My knees ached. I glanced in the mirror, fixed a loose strand of hair, and told myself, Under no circumstances may that ever recur.

When I returned to the dining area, I heard the owner yelling out the front door. "What did I say about coming in here, huh?" Through the grease-streaked glass, I could see the curve of Uncle's back outside. His thin frame wavering in the wind.

I rushed to the front of the diner. "Excuse me," I said, tapping the owner on the back. "That man you are yelling at happens to be my uncle."

He looked me up and down. "So?"

"We were planning on dining here this evening."

"We close in fifteen minutes," he said, and slammed the door in my face.

Uncle stared at the spot in front of him on the sidewalk. His hands were low in his pockets.

"I'm so sorry," I told him. "Is there another place you'd like to go?"

We walked a block in silence and entered a Latino restaurant with glittery Formica tables and haggard polyester booths. The radio played a Spanish rendition of "Like a Virgin." At one table, a Latino family of three had started dinner. The woman was heavily made up with foundation and thick black eyeliner; her hair was pulled back into a long braid. Her daughter wore a ruffled pink party dress and had a pink ribbon in her hair.

Uncle and I took the booth closest to the bathroom.

"Chicken and rice? Chocolate milk?" the waitress asked from behind the counter. She had a chipped front tooth.

Uncle nodded. I said, "Just a diet Coke for me."

The waitress stuck her head through the sliding door that led to the kitchen. "Chicken rice, chocolate milk, diet Coke!" she shouted.

I laughed. "I like this place."

"There's music," Uncle said.

On the radio the singer switched into English: "Like a virgin, woh-oh-oh, like a virgin."

"Nice touch." I glanced at my watch. It was six-forty, and I knew I should call Mark.

Uncle's hands slid out of his pockets. He wrung them over the table. "Ah? Where's your ma?"

"Hong Kong," I answered. "I think they want to move back."

"Move? Oh my God." His hands circled around and around.

"It's okay. I'll bring anything you need." I slid the envelope across the table and placed my hand over his. Uncle leaped out of his seat. "Oh my God. Oh my God."

"Jesus," I said.

He glanced helplessly at his hands, wringing them faster.

Somehow I understood. "Here," I said, slipping the envelope into place. He nodded and disappeared into the bathroom. The waitress leaned back into the kitchen. "Keep warm," she yelled. She checked her nails, and reached into her apron pocket for a file.

From the bathroom, I could hear the faucets gushing, water splashing. I pictured Uncle compulsively washing his hands, and wondered whether medication might improve his condition. Would he agree to see a psychiatrist? Likely not.

Minutes passed. Finally I got up and knocked at the door. The waitress looked at me. When Uncle failed to answer, she went back to shaping her nails. I couldn't get Laurel out of my head. Those sit-ups and the expression on her face. Up, down; up, down. A bad feeling came over me.

My phone rang. I pulled the cellular from my purse and watched until it went silent. My hands trembled. I noticed chocolate cake on the counter.

"Do you have any fresh fruit—apples, maybe?" I asked the waitress.

"Fruit?" she said.

"Never mind." I placed the phone on the table. I could hear water splashing onto the floor in the bathroom. I ordered a piece of chocolate cake. Just one bite, I told myself.

After I'd devoured the cake, I knocked again. "Uncle? I have to go soon, okay?" By now the family of three had eaten, paid, and left.

Ten minutes later, Uncle used his feet to kick open the bathroom door. He had the timing down so that he didn't have to touch the door with his hands. The waitress mumbled something in Spanish and shook her head.

Uncle continued to wring his hands. His knuckles were red, almost steaming.

The food arrived. The waitress set Uncle's plate in front of him. She placed the glasses, pinched between her fingers, at the center of the table. Her thumb was in my drink. She dropped a clump of napkins near Uncle's plate.

"Excuse me," I said. "Do you have any utensils?"

"Utensils?"

The wringing stopped. From his pocket, Uncle withdrew a set of wood chopsticks. He fished them through the rice and hovered protectively over his plate.

"Oh," I said.

The woman shot me a look: You're the stranger here.

I excused myself to the bathroom. Everything was wet—toilet seat, walls, and ceiling. The mirror dripped. Streaks distorted my reflection. "Don't do this," I said. But carefully, so as not to touch anything, I leaned over the toilet and cried.

■ ■ ■

"You're not hungry?" Uncle asked, glancing up from his dish.

I felt weak all over. "My husband and I are going out for dinner tonight."

"Oh my God."

"It's okay. He'll wait."

"Ni?" You? he said. "Married?"

Great—Ma hadn't even told him. "Yeah. His name is Mark." I dug out a wedding photo.

"Oh my God."

"Yes, he's black."

He stared at the photo the way he had stared at the spot in front of him. "Si-mong," he whispered.

"Excuse me?"

"Ah," Uncle whispered thoughtfully. Suddenly everything seemed to make sense to him. He picked up the last grain of rice with his chopsticks, inserted it into his mouth, chewed patiently. He placed the tips of his chopsticks against the edge of the plate and with one hand pushed one chopstick over the other, over the other.

"Spanish?" he asked.

"Excuse me? Oh, you mean tonight? With Mark?"

"Mm."

"Probably French."

"Oh my God."

"You don't like French food?"

"Expensive," he said. "You should come here—cheap."

Uncle's chopsticks moved one over the other, the wood clicking softly, and I found the motion, the sound, strangely comforting.

THE HULL CASE

■ ■ ■

Peter Ho Davies

> Of modern North American cases, one of the earliest and
> most widely reported abductions occurred in the early
> sixties to a mixed-race couple in New Hampshire.
> —*Taken: Twelve Contemporary UFO Abduction*
> *Narratives*, K. Clifford Stanton

Helen is telling the colonel about the ship now, and Henry, sitting stiffly on the sectional sofa beside his wife, can't look up. He stares at the colonel's cap, the gold braid on the rim, where it rests on the coffee table next to the latest *Saturday Evening Post* and the plate of tunafish sandwiches Helen has laid out.

"What color were the lights, Mrs. Hull?" the colonel wants to know, and Helen says, "Blue."

The colonel makes a check mark.

"Baby blue," Helen adds. She looks at Henry, and he nods quickly. He thought the lights were a cop at first.

"Baby blue," the colonel repeats slowly, his pen scratching along. He's resting his clipboard against his khaki knee. His pants leg is crisply ironed, and his shoes glint. Henry wishes he could see what the colonel is writing.

"Is that usual?" he asks. "Blue lights? In these cases, I mean."

"I'm afraid I couldn't say," the colonel says.

" 'Cept I believe aircraft lights are usually red and white."

"Yes, sir."

PETER HO DAVIES was born in England in 1966 to Welsh and Chinese parents. He is the author of the story collections *The Ugliest House in the World* and *Equal Love*. Davies currently directs the M.F.A. program at the University of Michigan.

"Then this wouldn't be an aircraft?"

"That's what we're aiming to determine," the colonel says. "Sir." His smile reminds Henry of Richard Widmark.

There's a pause, and then Helen asks, "Won't you have a sandwich, colonel?" and the colonel says, "Thank you, ma'am. Don't mind if I do." He takes one and lays it on his plate, but doesn't take a bite.

Henry thought the lights were a cop at first. They'd already been stopped once on the drive back from Niagara. He could have sworn he'd been doing less than sixty. The cop had shone his flashlight in Henry's face—black—and then Helen's—white.

"Any trouble here, ma'am?"

"Not at all, officer," she told him, while Henry gripped the wheel with both hands.

■ ■ ■

It was meant to be a second honeymoon. Not that they'd had a first, really. They'd been married for seven years. Henry had been serving in Korea, a corporal in the signals, when he'd been caught in the open by a grenade. Helen was his nurse in Tokyo. He'd heard that some of the white nurses refused to touch the black GIs, but she didn't mind. The first day she gave him a sponge bath, he tried to thank her—not sure if he was more embarrassed for her or himself (he felt an erection pushing at the slit of his pajama pants)—but she told him not to be silly. He always remembered that. "Don't be silly." Like it was nothing.

"I'm just saying I appreciate it," he said, a little stung. "The nature of the race matter and all."

"The race matter doesn't matter to me," she told him briskly. "And it shouldn't matter to you." Later she came back and he asked her to scratch his back, below the shoulder blade where it itched him fiercely, and she did.

Perhaps it was the thought of losing his arm. He was so relieved when she told him they'd saved it. She'd been changing the dressing on his hand, unwinding the bandages from each fat finger. He whooped with joy. He asked her to have a drink with him. She said she didn't think so and his face fell, but then she laughed, her teeth as bright as her uniform. "Oh," she said, turning his hand over to wash it. "You mean after your release? Why, of course. I'd like that. I thought you meant now. You shouldn't be drinking now, not with your medication." And then she wound his hand up again in fresh white bandages.

Her tour had finished three weeks later, but she'd stayed on in Tokyo, and by the time his discharge came through, they were lovers. They ate sushi together and she wore beautiful multicolored kimonos and it all seemed perfectly natural. He'd been in the army for nine years, so he hung on to her now as the next thing in his life, and one night after a fifth of whiskey—"Why, Henry Hull, you're stinko"—he asked her to marry him. "Of course," she said, and he laughed out loud. *"Of course!"* They'd gone back to New Hampshire, where she had a job in a hospital in Manchester. He'd found work at the local post office, and they'd been married within the month.

They'd made a good life together. Helen's parents had been kind to him, after some reservations. "They know better than to try and stop me when I want something," Helen told him. Her brother called Henry a hero and a credit to his race at the small reception after their wedding at the town hall. Henry appreciated it, but it only reminded him that he was the one black man in the room. His own parents were long since dead, and his sister, Bernice, back in Summer Hill, had refused to come when she heard Henry was marrying a white woman. "What for?" she wanted to know, and when Henry said, "For the same reasons anybody gets married," she told him no, she didn't believe it.

Henry didn't know what to say to that. He could hear her kids, his nephews and nieces, in the background, yelling, and then a baby's sharp, sudden sobs.

"I gotta go," Bernice said. They hadn't talked since.

His brother, Roy, had been more sympathetic. "You and me been dreaming about white girls since we were boys. Bernice thinks that's all wrong and maybe it is, but a man's got to follow his dream. 'S only natural to want what you can't have." But Roy hadn't come either.

Henry and Helen did have a good life, though. Decent friends. Enough money. Helen had even taught him to skate. He liked his job, was proud of the uniform, and Mr. Rhodes, the postmaster, treated him well. The first week, when there'd been a little trouble over Henry's eating at the local sandwich shop, Mr. Rhodes had stepped across the street and told the owner that none of the postmen would be eating there again if Henry didn't. And just like that the shop integrated, although Henry told Helen he wouldn't have made anything of it himself.

"Why not, for Pete's sake?" she'd asked him, and when he shrugged she'd exclaimed, "You're too darned dignified for your own good sometimes."

He was the only black man he knew in Manchester, but he followed the news of lunchroom sit-ins and the Freedom Riders and joined the NAACP, although he was a lifelong Republican, like his father and his grandfather before him. He met more Negroes, but they all seemed a little shy of each other, almost sheepish. "Far as civil rights goes," one of them pointed out to him, "New Hampshire ain't exactly where it's *at*."

What nagged Henry was that it was all too good, unreal somehow, more than he deserved. He thought of his brother and sister and all the kids he'd grown up with. Why had he been the one singled out, plucked up by life and set down here? It made him a little scared to have something. Helen said he was just being superstitious, but he couldn't shake the idea. He thought one day he'd wake up, or someone would come along and take it all away. When Helen had miscarried the first time, the spring before, along with the worry for her, he'd felt an awful relief that finally something terrible had happened. He'd been so ashamed he hadn't known how to comfort her, except to keep trying. But when she'd miscarried the second time, that summer, he'd decided they couldn't go through it again. They'd been distant these last few months, Helen insisting she still wanted a child, had always wanted one, Henry doubtful, thinking *She wants one more now she maybe can't have one*, wondering if this was how she had once wanted him, wondering if he was no longer enough for her, which was why the idea of a trip to Niagara felt like such an inspiration.

Helen had laughed and called him a romantic but taken his hand across the dinner table.

■ ■ ■

The colonel wants to go back over the details again, as if he's trying to trip them up. "I thought you said it was cigar-shaped, Mrs. Hull?"

"From a distance," Helen says impatiently. "Up close, you could see it was a disk." She looks at Henry for support.

"We had a pair of binoculars along for the trip," he says. "I thought it might be a star at first. But when I pulled over at a lookout and used the glasses, whatever it was was definitely moving." The colonel is silent, so Henry hurries on, a little breathless but feeling that more is required of him. "A little later it came to me that I'd left the car running the first time while I leaned on the roof with the binocs. I thought the vibrations from the engine might have been the problem, see, so I pulled over again, stepped away from the car before I put the glasses on it. And it was still moving."

Henry wants the colonel to write this down, but his pen doesn't move. The colonel doesn't even ask him about the binoculars—his service issue 10 × 42 Weavers.

"Spinning," Helen says. "Don't forget it was spinning. That's what gave it the twinkling effect."

"Right," Henry says. "The lights that looked like they were moving across it from a distance were actually fixed to the rim." He makes a circling motion in the air with his index finger while the colonel stares at him.

"Did you write that down?" Helen asks, and the colonel blinks and says, "Yes, ma'am. I got it. 'Twinkling was spinning.' "

They had agreed before the colonel arrived that Helen would do most of the talking. Henry hadn't wanted them to tell anyone about what they had seen right from the start, but Helen insisted on calling her sister, Marge. Hadn't Marge seen a UFO herself in '57? Henry shrugged. He'd never believed Marge's story, but he knew Helen needed to tell someone, and Marge at least wouldn't make fun of them. But it hadn't stopped there. Marge put Helen on to a high school science teacher she knew, and he told her they should really notify the air force. Now here was the colonel with his clipboard. Henry hadn't wanted to meet him, but Helen had had a conniption fit.

"Henry Hull! How's it going to look," she said, "if I'm telling this story and my own husband won't back me up?"

Henry told her it wouldn't make any difference, but what he really thought was that nothing he said would help her, might even make her less believable. "You're a white woman married to a colored," he wanted to tell her. He didn't think anyone would believe them, but Helen wasn't having any of that. "Of course they'll believe us," she said. "So long as we tell the truth. We have to try, at least. You've no gumption, Henry, that's your whole trouble." It seemed so easy to her, but Henry had had to work hard to be believed most of his life.

Now he can see that Helen is getting tired of going over the same story again and again.

"I'm not telling you what it means," she says. "I'm just telling you what I saw. We were hoping *you* could explain it to *us*."

But the colonel just spreads his hands and says, "Sorry, ma'am."

"You act like we're lying."

"No, ma'am," the colonel says quickly. "I assure you."

Henry knows what's coming next. Helen wants to get on to the part inside the ship, the stuff Henry doesn't remember. He asked her not to talk about it, but she told him she couldn't promise. "What if it's a matter of national security?" she said. "It's our duty, isn't it? Think what it could mean for the future of everyone." So now she explains to the colonel how she only remembered this part later, in her dreams. Henry feels himself shrink, but the colonel just makes another scratch with his pen, and Helen starts to tell him about the aliens—the short gray men—and their tests.

"Gray?" The colonel looks from Helen to Henry, Henry to Helen.

"Gray," she says, and he writes it down.

"And short," she adds. "But not like dwarfs, like children."

In her dream, Helen says, she remembers them scraping her skin with a strange metal instrument. "Like a dentist might use, only different. It tickled," she recalls, without a smile. Then she remembers them pushing a long thin needle into her navel. "That really hurt," she says, "but when I cried out they did something and the pain stopped at once. They seemed sorry. They told me it was a pregnancy test."

The colonel, who has been taking notes with his head down, not looking at them, glances up quickly.

"Oh, of course I'm not pregnant," Helen says brusquely, and Henry sits very still. This is what he feared all along—that they wouldn't be able to keep their private business out of this.

"Have you ever heard of anything like it?" Helen asks. The colonel tells her he hasn't.

"You have no memory of this?" he asks Henry, who shakes his head slowly. He's racked his brains, but there's nothing. Helen can't understand it. "How can you not remember?" she cried the first time she told him, as if he were the one being unreasonable.

"Helen tells me I was in another room on the ship, drugged or something, but I don't recall." He wishes he could support her now, but also, in the back of his mind, he resents her dream, his weakness in it.

Helen presses on. She says she knows how it sounds, but she has proof. "I'm just getting to the best part," she says. "The part about Henry's teeth."

"Teeth?" the colonel says, and this time Henry sees a twitch to his lips that makes him feel cold inside.

"That's right," Helen says, and Henry can tell she's seething now. The aliens, she explains slowly, as if to a child, were surprised that Henry's teeth came out and Helen's didn't. "They didn't understand about dentures," Helen says. Henry feels his mouth grow dry. They have argued about this part. He didn't want her to tell it, but Helen feels it's the clincher. "How could we make that up?" she asked him last night. "Plus there's the physical proof."

"This was after the other tests," Helen says. "They were as curious as kids. I'm jumping ahead a little, but don't mind me. Anyway, after we were done, the one I think of as the doctor, he left the room, and the *grayer* one, the leader, he told me they were still finishing up with Henry. Anyhow, a few seconds later the doctor runs back in. He seems very excited and he asks me to open my mouth. Well, I don't quite know why, but I wanted to get this over with, so I obliged, and before you know it he'd pushed his little fingers in my mouth and he was pulling on my teeth. Well! You can imagine my surprise. I slapped his hand away quick as I could. He was pulling quite hard too, making my head go up and down. 'What do you think you're doing?' I said, and then he held out his other hand, and can you guess what he had?"

The colonel shakes his head slowly.

"Why, Henry's dentures. There they were, sitting in his little gray hand. Well, I snatched them up at once. I don't know what I was thinking. It made me so worried about Henry, I guess. That and the fact that he's always losing them, or pretending to lose them, anyway."

She pauses, and Henry thinks he should say something.

"They pinch me," he mumbles. "And they click. I don't like them so good."

Helen laughs. "I tell him he looks like a fool without them, but he doesn't care. He has such a fine smile, too."

Henry looks past the colonel's shoulder and out the picture window.

He does not smile. It's October, and the first snow is beginning to fall in the White Mountains.

"Anyway, I snatched them up, and then the leader started in about why my teeth were different from Henry's, so I had to explain all about dentures, about how people lose their teeth as they get older or, like Henry here, in accidents. I thought it was funny they were so flummoxed by dentures, but you know, now that I come to think about it, I don't remember seeing their teeth. They had these thin little slits for mouths, like I said before, and when they talked it was as if they didn't move their lips."

"Did they speak English?" the colonel asks. "Or was it more like telepathy?"

"Maybe," Helen says. "Like voices in my head, you mean? That certainly could explain it."

"And their fingers?" the colonel asks seriously. "Would you say they had suckers on them? Small pads maybe?"

Helen pauses and looks at him hard. "No," she says very clearly. "I would have remembered something like that."

There is an awkward pause before she goes on more brightly.

"Anyway, to cut a long story short, I thought the whole thing about the dentures was funny and I remember laughing, but it must have been one of those nervous laughs, because afterward when I looked at my hand where I'd been gripping them, I'd been holding them so tight that the teeth had left bruises." And here Helen holds out her hand to the colonel. He leans forward and takes it and turns it to the light. Henry can just see the crescent of purpling spots in the flesh of her palm.

Helen nudges him. Henry doesn't move for a moment, but then he decides. She's his wife. He'll try to help. He holds a handkerchief over his mouth and slips his plate out. He passes it to her, and with her free hand she places it in her palm so that the false teeth lie over the bruises. The denture glistens wetly, and Henry looks away in embarrassment.

"See," Helen says triumphantly. "Now that's evidence, isn't it?"

"It's something, ma'am," the colonel says, peering at Henry's teeth. "It's really something."

■ ■ ■

Henry has tried his damnedest to remember what Helen's talking about. But he can't do it. It's the strangest thing, he thinks, because he recalls the rest of the trip—start to finish—vividly.

They'd gotten up at five A.M., packed the car, and been on the road to Niagara by six. Henry wanted to get a good start on the day. It was September, peak foliage. "What impossible colors," Helen breathed, sliding across the seat to lean against him. "Better than Cinerama," he told her. He'd sung a few bars of "Oh, What a Beautiful Morning" and made her laugh, and she'd done her best Dinah Shore: "Drive your Chev-ro-lay, through the U.S.A." She'd got impatient with him the evening before for simonizing the car, bringing out the gloss in the two-tone paint job. Now, he saw, she was proud.

But when they stopped for brunch at a diner in upstate New York, Henry felt uneasy. The din in the place died when they entered, and the waitress seemed short with them. He ordered coffee and a dough-nut, but Helen had the short stack and took her time over her coffee. When he called for the check, she looked up and asked what his hurry was, and he said they still had a ways to go. Didn't he know she had to let her coffee cool before she could drink it? "Have a refill or a ciga-rette," she said, pushing the pack of Chesterfields across the table, but he told her a little sharply he didn't want either. He felt people watch-ing him. Helen finished her coffee and went to the bathroom, leaving him alone for five long terrible minutes. He could hear a child crying somewhere behind him, but he didn't turn to look. When she came back he hurried her out before she could retie her scarf, leaving a big tip. He had to stop to urinate fifteen minutes later and she made fun of him for not going earlier. "You're like a little boy," she said, and so he told her how he had felt in the diner.

"Oh, Henry," she said. "You were imagining it."

It made him mad that she wouldn't believe him, wouldn't take his word for it, but he didn't want to spoil the trip with a fight and he let her half convince him, because he knew it would make her feel better. He played with the radio, pushing buttons until he found some Harry Bela-fonte. Helen just didn't notice things the way he did. He loved her for it, this innocence, cherished it, though he couldn't share it (found his own sensitivity sharper than ever, in fact). That night when he stopped at two motels and was told that they were full, he didn't make anything of it, and when she said as they left one parking lot, "You'd think they'd turn off their vacancy sign," he just let it ride.

"Must be a lot of lovers in town," she added, and squeezed his thigh.

When they finally found a room at a place called the Falls Inn, she pulled him to her and he started to respond, but when she told him she'd forgotten her diaphragm, he pulled away.

"It'll be okay," she told him. "Just this once." She clung to him for a moment, holding him against her, before he rolled off. They lay side by side staring at the ceiling as if it were the future. After the second miscarriage, Helen had been warned that she might not be able to carry a baby to term. "We can't take the risk," Henry told her softly, but she turned away. "You're afraid," she said, curled up with her face to the wall. The knobs of her spine reminded him of knuckles. "I'm afraid of losing you," he said at last.

He told her he'd go out and get prophylactics, but driving around in the car, he couldn't. He stopped outside one store and sat for fifteen minutes, waiting for the other cars in the lot to leave, listening to the engine tick as it cooled. He *was* afraid of losing her, he knew, though the admission, so abject and ineffectual, shamed him. But behind that fear was another—a dim, formless dread of his own children and what they might mean for the precarious balance of his marriage, which made him shudder. There was one more car in the lot, but before it left a police cruiser pulled in, and Henry backed out and drove slowly back to the motel.

When they were first married, Helen used to call him by a pet name, Big, burying the tight curls of her permanent against his chest. He would stroke her neck and answer in the same slightly plaintive baby talk, "Little" or "Little 'un." It was how they had comforted themselves when they felt small and puny beside their love for each other, but remembering it now only made him feel hopeless before the childlessness that loomed over them. Helen was asleep when he got in, or pretending, and he lay down beside her as gently as possible, not touching but aware of her familiar warmth under the covers.

The next day had started better. They'd gone to the falls and been overwhelmed by the thundering white wall of water. They bought tickets for the *Maid of the Mist*. Henry bounced on the springy gangway and made her scream. They laughed at themselves in the yellow sou'esters and rain hats the crew passed out and then joined the rest of the identically dressed crowd at the bow railings. "Oh look," Helen said, pointing out children, like miniature adults in their slickers and hats, but Henry couldn't hear her over the crash of the falls. "Incredible," he yelled, leaning forward, squinting in the spray as if in bright light. He could taste the mist in his mouth, feel the gusts of air displaced as the water fell. Suddenly he wanted to hold his wife, but when he turned to Helen, she was gone. He stumbled from the railing looking for her, but it was impossible to identify her in the crowd of yellow slickers. He felt a moment of panic, like when she'd left him in the restaurant. He bent down to see under the hats and hoods of those around him, conscious that he was startling them but not caring. In the end he found her in the cabin, her head in her hands. She told him she'd thrown up. She didn't like boats much in general, she reminded him, and looking at the falls had made her dizzy. "I didn't want you to miss them, though," she told him, and he could see she'd been crying. He put his arm around her, and they sat like that until the trip was over. The other passengers began to file into the cabin around them, taking off their hats and jackets and hanging them on pegs until only Henry and Helen were left in theirs.

They had planned to go on into Canada that afternoon, the first time they'd been out of the country since Korea, but instead they turned around, headed back the way they'd come. It was late afternoon, but Henry figured they could be home by midnight if he got a clear run and put his foot down.

■ ■ ■

The colonel has a few more questions, and he asks if they'd mind talking to him separately. Henry feels himself stiffen, but Helen says, "Of course." He can tell she wants to go first, so he gets up and says he'll take a walk. He'll be back in about fifteen minutes. He steps out into the hall and finds his topcoat and hat and calls for Denny, Helen's dog. He walks out back first, and from the yard he can see Helen inside with the colonel. He wonders what she's saying as the dog strains at the leash. Probably talking more about her dreams. She thinks maybe the little gray men took one of her eggs. She thinks she remembers being shown strange children. They had agreed that she wouldn't talk about this, but Henry realizes suddenly he doesn't trust her. It makes him shudder to think of her telling these things to a stranger.

When he takes Denny around the front of the house, he is startled to find a black man in his drive, smoking. The young man drops the cigarette quickly when Denny starts yapping. He is in an air force uniform, and Henry realizes that this must be the colonel's driver. He feels suddenly shy. He tells him, "You startled me," and the young airman says, "Sorry, sir." And after a moment, that seems all there is to say. That *sir*. Henry lets Denny pull him up the drive, whining. The poor dog hasn't been out for hours and as soon as they're at the end of the drive squats and poops in full view of the house. Henry holds the leash slack and looks the other way. When they walk back a few minutes later, the airman is in the colonel's car. The windows are fogged. Henry knocks on the driver's-side glass.

"Would you like a cup of coffee?"

The airman hesitates, but his breath, even in the car, is steaming.

"I could bring it out," Henry offers, and the young man says, "Thank you." And it's the lack of a *sir* that makes Henry happy. He takes Denny inside and comes back out in a few minutes with two cups of coffee and climbs into the car with the boy. He sets them on the dash, where they make twin crescents of condensation on the windshield. When Henry sips his coffee, he realizes he's left his teeth inside with Helen, and he's suddenly self-conscious. He thinks he must look like an old fool, and he wants to be silent, keep his mouth shut, but it's too late. The airman asks him how he lost them.

"A fight," Henry says. And he tells a story he's never told Helen, how he got waylaid by a couple of crackers when he was just a boy. They wanted to know his mama's name, but for some reason he refused to say. "I just call her Mama," he said. "Other folks call her Mrs. Hull." But the boys wanted to know her first name, "her Chrustian name." Henry just kept on saying he didn't know it and then he tried to push past them and leave, but they shoved him back and lit into him. "I don't know what I was thinking," he says now over his coffee, "but it was very important to me that those fellas not know my mama's name. Mrs. Hull's all I'd say. I knew it, of course, although I never called her by it or even rightly thought of her by it. But I'd be damned if I'd tell them, and they beat the tar out of me for keeping that secret."

"Yeah, but I bet those boys got their share," the airman says, and Henry smiles and nods. He can't be more than eighteen, this driver. They talk about the service. The boy is frustrated to be a driver in the air force. He wants to fly. Henry tells him how he was put in the signals corps: "They liked having me fetch and carry the messages." The boy, Henry thinks, is a good soldier, and he feels a surge of pride in him. But then the coffee is finished and Helen is at the front door.

"Henry!" She doesn't see him in the car. "Henry!" He's suddenly embarrassed and gets out of the car quickly. "There you are," she says. "It's your turn."

Henry ducks his head back into the car to take the empty mugs and sees the airman looking at him strangely. "Eunice," he offers awkwardly. The young man's face is blank. "My mother's name. Eunice Euphonia Hull. In case you was wondering." He closes the car door with his rear, moves toward the house. Inside, he hands Helen the two mugs, and she takes them to wash up.

Back on the sofa, Henry sees that his dentures are lying beside the plate of sandwiches, but he feels uncomfortable about putting them in now.

The colonel asks him to describe his experiences, and Henry repeats the whole story. They'd been making good time until the cop stopped them around ten-thirty, and even then Henry had still expected to make it home by one. He explains how they noticed the lights a little after that and about twenty minutes later how they began to sense that the object was following them, how he had sped up, how it had kept pace. Finally he describes it swooping low over the road in front of them and hovering a hundred yards to their right. He'd stopped, still thinking it could be a chopper, and got out with the binoculars, leaving Helen in the still running car. But after getting a closer look he'd become uneasy, run back, and they had left in a hurry. They couldn't have been stopped more than ten minutes, but when they got home it was almost dawn, hours later than they expected.

"Mrs. Hull," the colonel says, "claims you were screaming when you came back to the car. About being captured."

Henry feels a moment of irritation at Helen.

"I was yelling," he says. "I was frightened. I felt that we were in danger, although I couldn't tell you why. I just knew this wasn't anything I understood."

He pauses, but the colonel seems to be waiting for him to go on.

"I was in Korea. I mean, I've been under fire. I was never afraid like this."

"These dreams of your wife's," the colonel asks. "Can you explain them at all?"

"She believes them," Henry says quickly. "Says they're more vivid than any dreams she remembers."

"Can you think of anything else that might explain them?"

Henry pauses. He could end it all here, he thinks. He looks at his dentures on the coffee table, feels the flush of humiliation. He opens his mouth, closes it, slowly shakes his head.

The colonel waits a moment, as if for something more. Then: "Any dreams yourself?"

"No, sir," Henry says quickly. "I don't remember my dreams."

The colonel clicks his pen—closed, open, closed—calls Helen back in, thanks them both for their time. He declines another sandwich, puts his cap under his arm, says he must be going, and they follow him out to where his driver holds the door for him. The car backs out, and they watch its taillights follow the curve of the road for a minute. Henry wonders if the colonel and his driver will talk. If the colonel will make fun of their story. The thought of the young man laughing at him makes him tired. But then he thinks, no, the colonel and the airman won't share a word. The boy will just drive, and in the back seat the colonel will watch him. Henry feels like he let the boy down, and is suddenly ashamed.

They stand under the porch light until the car is out of sight. "Well," Helen says, and he sees she's glowing, almost incandescent with excitement. "I think we did the right thing, don't you?" He feels his own mood like a shadow of hers. Bugs ping against the bulb and he flicks the switch off. In the darkness, they're silent for a moment, and then he hears the squeal of the screen door as she goes inside.

It's not late, but Helen tells him she's about done in. The interview went on for almost four hours. She goes up to bed, and Henry picks up in the living room, carries the cups and plates through to the kitchen, fills the sink to soak them. The untouched sandwiches he covers in Saran Wrap and slides into the refrigerator. He drops his dentures in a glass of water, watches them sink. Then he goes up and changes into his pajamas, lays himself down beside his already sleeping wife, listens to her steady breathing, dreams about the future.

A few weeks later they'll receive an official letter thanking them for their cooperation but offering no explanation for what they've seen. Henry hopes Helen will let the matter drop there, but she won't. She wants answers, and she feels it's their duty to share these experiences. "What if other people have had them?" They'll meet with psychiatrists. They'll undergo therapy. Henry shows symptoms of nervous anxiety, the doctors will say, but they won't know why. Eventually, almost a year later, under hypnosis, Henry will recall being inside the ship. He and Helen will listen to a tape of his flat voice describing his experiences. Tears will form in Helen's eyes.

"It's as if I'm asleep," he'll say on the tape. "Or sleepwalking. Like I'm drugged or under some mind control."

Under hypnosis, Henry will remember pale figures stopping their car. He'll recall the ship—a blinding wall of light—and being led to it, as if on an invisible rope, dragged and stumbling, his hands somehow tied behind him. He'll remember being naked, surrounded, the aliens touching him, pinching his arms and legs, peeling his lips back to examine his gritted teeth, cupping and prodding his genitals. It'll all come back to him: running through the woods, the breeze creaking in the branches, tripping and staring up at the moonlit trees. "Like great white sails," he'll hear himself say thickly as the spool runs out.

Afterward, he'll tell Helen in a rage he's finished with shrinks, but in the months that follow she'll call more doctors and scientists. She'll say she wants to write a book. Something extraordinary has happened to them. They've been chosen for a purpose. She'll talk to journalists. Henry will refuse to discuss it further. They'll fight, go days without speaking.

Tonight, in his dream, Henry wakes with a violent shudder, listens to his heart slow. He's lying in bed with Helen, he tells himself. He can feel her warm breath on his back. She rolls over beside him, the familiar shifting and settling weight, but then he feels the strange sensation of the mattress stiffening, the springs releasing. He opens his eyes and sees his wife rising above the bed, inch by inexorable inch, in a thin blue light.

DEAD ON ARRIVAL

■ ■ ■

Linh Dinh

I cannot wait to tuck an M-16 under my arm and pump a clip into the bodies of my enemies. I can see them falling backward, in slow motion, leaping up a little, from the force of my bullets. Die, Commies, die! Each day I stare at them in the newspaper, lined up in neat rows, some with their clothes blown off, their arms and legs bent at odd angles. I look at their exposed crotches, at their bare feet. (I cannot help myself: If I see a picture of a near-naked person, I look at the crotch first, then the face, if I look at the face.) Their captured weapons are also lined up in neat rows. Our soldiers can be seen standing in the background, neatly dressed, with their boots on. I cannot wait to get me a pair of black boots. Our national anthem begins like this:

> Citizens, it's time to liberate the country!
> Let's go and sacrifice our lives, with no regrets . . .

I'm willing to sacrifice my life and limbs for freedom and democracy.

■ ■ ■

My father is a police colonel. He answers only to Mr. Thieu, our president, and Mr. Ky, our vice president, and Mr. Khiem, our prime minis-

LINH DINH was born in Saigon in 1963, came to the United States in 1975, and now lives in Certaldo, Italy. He is the author of a collection of stories, *Fake House*, and several collections of poems, including *All Around What Empties Out*. His work is included in several anthologies, including *Best American Poetry 2000*.

ter, and Mr. Loan, his boss. (Yes, that Mr. Loan, the general who shot a Vietcong on TV. The Vietcong was an assassin who had killed many people that day. He was wearing a plaid shirt, a "caro" shirt.) Mr. Loan is very famous, a celebrity in America and in Europe. It's something to be proud of, having a father with a famous boss.

■ ■ ■

The Vietcong killed two of my uncles: Uncle Bao and Uncle Hiep. They killed my grandfather. That's all they do. Kill! Kill! Kill! They're born to kill. Mr. Thieu said, "Do not listen to what they say, but look at what they do."

■ ■ ■

My father was born a peasant. He's used to rustic ways. Although we have modern plumbing in our house, he routinely forgets to close the door when he sits on the toilet. If you walk into our house unannounced, you may catch him, just like that!, sitting on the toilet taking a dump with the door open.

■ ■ ■

My father encourages me to draw. He said, "Draw, Son, you're good!" He gave me a big brown envelope and said, "Remember to save all your drawings."

I would draw certain things over and over. A few months ago I drew tigers. I would draw a tiger over and over. Then I drew cowboys, a gunslinger wearing a plaid shirt (a "caro" shirt) and leather vest. Then I drew tanks, one tank after another. Lately I've been drawing ships.

■ ■ ■

There is a huge stranded ship in Vung Tau, with its prow stuck in the sand and its tail sticking out into the ocean. Inside this ship there must be thousands of fish that have swum in through the rusty gashes but are now stuck inside this huge stranded ship and cannot get out again.

■ ■ ■

Whenever I looked into the ocean, I would think, *There, just beyond my sight, is America. If the earth wasn't so round, I would be able to see it.*

■ ■ ■

The earth is divided into twenty-four time zones.

If you go east, you lose time. If you go west, you gain time.

If you go far enough east, you lose a whole day. If you go far enough west, you gain a whole day.

If you go far enough west you will end up where you started and it will be yesterday.

■ ■ ■

We have several words for America. We call it "Flag with Flowers." We call it "Beautiful Country." We call it "Country with Many Races."

■ ■ ■

So-called white Americans are really red (they look red). Black Americans are blue. Red Americans are yellow.

■ ■ ■

On Nguyen Hue Street is the tallest building in Saigon. I've seen it many times. I'd count: one, two, three, four, five, six, seven, eight, nine, ten, eleven, twelve! That's it: twelve! The tallest building in Vietnam has twelve stories.

■ ■ ■

I speak five languages. Aside from Vietnamese, I also speak French:
   "Foo? Shoo tit shoo? Le! La! Le! La!" Chinese: "Xi xoong! Xoong xi!" and English: "Well well?"

■ ■ ■

The hardest word to pronounce in the English language is *the*.

■ ■ ■

When people say "I'm buying a house," what do they mean by that? I mean, what store is big enough to hold a bunch of houses? Or even just one house? And how are you going to take a house home with you after you've bought it?

■ ■ ■

Although a dragon only has four legs, sometimes, when I drew him, I'd give him two extra legs.

■ ■ ■

The three nos of Communism: No God! No Country! No Family!

■ ■ ■

As me and my father were entering a restaurant—a fancy Chinese place where we go to eat lacquered suckling pig and swallow's nest soup—we saw my mother leaving with her new husband. I mean, as my father opened the glass door, we saw her standing right there, with her new husband.

■ ■ ■

There is a middle-aged Englishman in our neighborhood. He's always walking around, stooping a little—when you are so tall, you should stoop a little—wearing a pale-blue cotton shirt (with four pockets) and a pair of gray slacks, and carrying an old leather briefcase. He has deep-set hazel eyes and a nose like a shark's fin. He's married to a Chinese woman and cannot speak Vietnamese. Every time I saw him, I'd say, "Well well?"

If it weren't for the Vietcong, we'd probably be shooting at the Chinese. There are many Chinese in my neighborhood. They have their own schools and like to play basketball. There is a song:

> A Chinese asshole, it's all one and the same.
> The one who doesn't clean his asshole,
> We'll kick back to China.

Chinese movies are the best. I like *The Blind Swordsman*. He's blind and fights with a sword that's more like a meat cleaver. It's only half a sword really. It doesn't matter: If you know what you're doing, you can kill many people with only half a sword, even if you're blind.

■ ■ ■

In one movie, Bruce Lee, "The Little Dragon," fought a huge black man named Cream Java. I thought, *This is not very realistic, is it? I mean, my man, Bruce Lee, can't even reach this guy's face to punch him in the face.*

■ ■ ■

When I draw, I usually aim for absolute realism.

■ ■ ■

My favorite American movie is *Planet of the Apes*.

■ ■ ■

The best American band is called the Bee Gees. The second best American band is called the Beatles.

■ ■ ■

The "Country Homies," the hicks, don't listen to American music. They're embarrassed by it. It frightens them. As soon as you push "play," they become disoriented. These hicks, these "Country Homies," only know how to listen to folk opera.

This is how you get a cricket to fight better. You pick him up by one of his whiskers, then you spin him around a bunch of times. This will make him "drunk." You can also hold him inside your palms and blow into his face.

■ ■ ■

Some trees are so old that their branches sag and sag and sag until they reach the ground and become new trees. These new trees, in turn, also become so old that their branches sag and sag and sag until they reach the ground and become new trees. What you have, then, is an entire forest connected at the top, an upside-down forest, with the first tree in the middle.

■ ■ ■

Catholics are the best. All the important people are Catholic. The pope is Catholic. The president is Catholic. My father is Catholic. All the saints are Catholic.

There are many Buddhist kids in my school, which is a Catholic school. If their schools were any good, why would they go to a Catholic school?

■ ■ ■

What's a buddha?

■ ■ ■

I go to Lasan Taberd, an all-boys school run by Jesuits near Notre Dame Cathedral and JFK Plaza. In the plaza there is a large plaster statue of the Virgin Mary holding a globe with a little cross sticking out of it.

■ ■ ■

Last week I accidentally dropped all my colored pencils on the floor and Frère Tuan, our teacher, whacked me on the head with a ruler.

I like Frère Tuan. He called me Dinh Bo Linh once in front of the whole class. (My name is Dinh Hoang Linh.)

■ ■ ■

Dinh Bo Linh ruled from A.D. 968 to 979. He was a village bully before he became a warlord, before he became the emperor. He was known as Dinh the Celestial King.

To the north was China—Sung Dynasty. To the south was Champas—savages.

In front of the palace was a vat of boiling oil. Criminals were thrown into this vat.

This is how he died: Do Thich, a mandarin, dreamed that a star fell into his mouth. He thought this meant that he would become the next emperor.

One night, as Dinh Bo Linh and his son, Dinh Lien, were passed out, drunk, in a courtyard, Do Thich slashed their throats.

As soldiers searched for him, Do Thich hid in the eaves of the house for three days until he became very thirsty and had to climb down for a drink of water.

A concubine saw him do this and went and told General Nguyen Bac, who had Do Thich executed. His corpse was then chopped into tiny pieces and fed to everyone in the capital.

The capital was Hoa Lu.

Everyone loved Dinh Bo Linh. There is a poem about Do Thich:

A frog at the edge of a pond,
Hankering for a star.

I told my best friend, Truong, this story, and he said, "Did they eat his hair too?"

"Probably not."

"How about his bones?"

"Just the smaller bones."

"How do you eat bones?"

"You chop them up real fine and cook them for twenty-four hours."

Truong giggled. "How about his little birdie?"

"That they certainly ate."

"You liar!"

■ ■ ■

Truong said, "A penis is so ugly to look at, so disgusting, so unnatural. Why do we have penises?"

I said, "They may be ugly, but women love to look at them."

"No, they don't!"

"They love to touch them too."

"Who told you?!"

"They like to put it in their mouth!"

"You're sick!"

"I know what I'm talking about."

"Women are disgusted by the penis."

"You're an idiot."

■ ■ ■

Truong sits behind me in class. One time he said, "You just farted, didn't you?!"

"No, I didn't."

"How come I smelled it?!"

"I don't care what you smelled. I didn't feel it."

■ ■ ■

One of the kids in my class has neither the middle nor ring finger on his left hand. No one really knows what happened. Someone said he picked up his father's hand grenade and it blew his fingers off. Someone else said he lost his fingers in a motorcycle accident. Maybe he was just born that way. When we see him from afar—say, from across the schoolyard—we raise our fist, with index finger and pinkie upturned, to salute him.

■ ■ ■

There is another weird kid in my class. The skin on his face has the texture of bark and he cannot close his mouth properly. We call this kid "Planet of the Apes."

■ ■ ■

The Americans have made a special bomb called "Palm." It's like a big vat of boiling oil that they pour from the sky.

■ ■ ■

At school, during recess, we divide ourselves into gangs and try to kill each other. I have perfected a move: I feign a right jab, spin 360 degrees, and hit my opponent's face—surprise!—with the back of my left fist as it swings around—whack! So far I've connected with three of my enemies. I hit this one kid, Hung, so hard he fell backward and bounced his head on the ground—booink! Ha, ha! Blood was squirting out of his nose. He was taken by cyclo to the hospital, where he was pronounced Dead On Arrival.

Soon people will catch on to this move, which means that I will have to come up with another move.

■ ■ ■

It's important to overcome one's ignorance: Our cook, who's illiterate, once told me that a person gains exactly one drop of blood per day from eating. "Otherwise," she said, "where would all that blood go?"

She's very stupid, this woman, although an excellent cook. She knows how to make an excellent omelet with ground pork, bean threads, and scallions. She smells like coconut milk. Every now and then I stand near her as she squats on the kitchen floor snapping watercress and peer into her blouse.

■ ■ ■

I walked into the dining room and saw Sister Lan—that's the cook's name—sitting by herself. She wiped her face with a hand towel and smiled at me. Her eyes were all red. I said, "You're crying!"

"No! No! I'm not crying."

"Your eyes are all red!"

"I was chopping onions!"

I ran out of the dining room, screaming, "Sister Lan is crying! Sister Lan is crying!"

I told my grandmother about it and she said, "She's thinking about her boyfriend."

■ ■ ■

Once the foreskin of my penis got caught in the zipper of my pants as I was dressing to go to church. I screamed, "Grandmother! Grandmother!" and my grandmother ran over and pulled the zipper down. That was twice as painful as having my dick caught in the first place.

■ ■ ■

My grandmother is a good Catholic. She paces back and forth in the living room, fingering her rosary while mumbling her prayer—hundreds of Our Fathers and thousands of Ave Marias—as fast as she can.

I only pray when I've lost something. Once I lost a comic book—my Tintin comic book—and God helped me to find it. I mean: He didn't say, "There, there's your comic book," but as soon as I finished praying, I knew that my comic book was under a pile of newspapers in the living room.

My grandmother goes to church twice a day, once at five in the morning and once at three in the afternoon. Sometimes she makes me come along with her.

■ ■ ■

The worst part about going to church is having to hear the priest talk. You cannot follow him for more than a few seconds. It's very hot in there. You look around and all the people are fanning themselves, some with their eyes closed.

Father Duong can go on and on and on: "Charity is the key, a camel cannot walk through it. . . . Thirty milch camels with their colts, forty kine and ten bulls, forty she-asses and ten foals. . . . The Lord will give thee a trembling heart, the sole of your foot will not know rest. . . . And so many cows besides?"

■ ■ ■

A whale spat Jonah out into the desert. It was noon. The sun was blazing.

Jesus felt sorry for Jonah and gave him a gourd for shade.

Jonah slept under this shade.

When Jonah woke up, he was no longer in the shade because the sun had moved.

When Jonah became angry, Jesus said, "And so many cows besides?"

■ ■ ■

At the end of each sermon, Father Duong always says, "O Merciful Father, please bring peace to this wretched land." That's when you know it's almost time to go home.

■ ■ ■

As Father Duong walks toward the door, he shakes a metal canister at everyone. That's "holy water."

My patron saint, Saint Martin de Porres, was a black man.

■ ■ ■

Many beggars stand by the door outside the church. Once I saw my grandmother put a 200-dong bill into a blind man's upturned fedora, then fumble inside it for change totaling 150 dong.

■ ■ ■

I often think about getting married when I'm in church. About how I'll have to walk down the aisle in front of everyone. I'm not sure I'll be able to do that. I mean, what if you trip and fall as you're walking down the aisle?

■ ■ ■

To kiss a girl would be like eating ice cream. Her lips will be cold. Her teeth will be cold.

■ ■ ■

To kiss a girl would be like eating ice cream with strawberries, with the pips from the strawberries getting stuck between your teeth.

■ ■ ■

My father said, "Women are like monkeys. If you're nice to them, they'll climb all over you."

■ ■ ■

There's a saying: A French house, an American car, a Japanese wife, Chinese food.

■ ■ ■

My grandmother has told me this one story over and over (usually when we're having fish for dinner): During the famine of 1940, when the Japanese invaded, the villagers in Bui Chu, her home village, would place a carved wooden fish on the dinner table at mealtime "so they could just stare at it."

■ ■ ■

My grandmother is deaf in one ear because, as a little girl, she punctured an eardrum with a twig when an ant crawled inside her ear canal.

■ ■ ■

My grandmother said to me, "Are you going to be a priest when you grow up?"

■ ■ ■

My grandmother was trying to teach me how to tie my shoes. It's the hardest thing in the world, tying your shoes. I could never figure it out. My father screamed, his face red, "You're an idiot! An idiot!"

■ ■ ■

I would think about shooting my father, only to have to force myself to think, *I do not want to shoot my father*. Then I would think, once more, about shooting my father, only to have to force myself to think, again, *I do not want to shoot my father*.

FORMERLY KNOWN AS BIONIC BOY

■ ■ ■

Eric Gamalinda

He came out of nowhere, and vanished just as quickly. It was the time of comets, prophets, and paranoia. His timing couldn't have been better. Uri Geller was bending spoons in Russia, NASA was sending Beethoven symphonies to outer space. In Manila, where everything was bad news — the GNP plummeting like the wrecks of a space station, people letting hunger into their households like an unavoidable guest — he burst into the scene like a twist in a story. FEATS OF TELEKINESIS STUN CITY, the tabloids crammed on page one. In one of many TV interviews that followed, he dismissed all the hoopla and remarked: "Bending spoons is for kids." He was only thirteen years old. Bucktoothed, chubby (wearing a size-XL shirt), hair cropped close to the scalp ("I don't have the patience to deal with grooming"), his brown eyes a blur under the glaucomatous lens of Clark Kent spectacles, he was indifferent to attention, bored with journalists, and impatient with social pretensions: he walked out of an intimate dinner once, because he felt the conversation made the service too slow. They called him Bionic Boy, a term that amused him, because it made him sound extra-human, electronic, unreal. Wives of generals and mistresses of this coconut czar or that banana baron hosted brunches for him in palatial mansions in Forbes Park. He entertained them with what he considered parlor games — typing messages long distance on a sheet of paper locked in a file cabinet. Whenever he did that, they heard metallic sounds clicking out of his cranium. He couldn't tell them what did it.

ERIC GAMALINDA was born in Manila, the Philippines, on October 14, 1956. His recent publications include a novel, *My Sad Republic*, and *Zero Gravity*, a collection of poems.

One inquisitive matron suggested that they do a brain scan. He replied, "I suggest you invite a lab monkey to your next brunch." He wasn't as indelicate with the rest. He interpreted their dreams, and told them some of his own. Not grand, apocalyptic visions in Cinemascope, but simple things with profound settings: a bush whose bone-white blossoms all faced downward, a bright red room. They even asked him to perform some faith healing, but on this matter he was adamant: he thought faith healers were carnival performers, and that disease and its remedy should be left to science. He was, in other words, no threat to the hundreds of psychics who proliferated around the archipelago. Inevitably his talent reached the Palace, which was always on the lookout for divine affirmation. Imelda Marcos invited him for an audience, and he performed the usual parlor tricks. But he gave her one special performance: he made her see the extent of his powers. The palace collection of Douglas MacArthur's books flew from their shelves, their pages fluttering open in midair. Teacups rattled and teaspoons tinkled in perfect harmony. The shutters of the Malacañang Guest House whipped open, and *capiz* chandeliers swayed like galleons in an open sea. Imelda was so dazzled that she arranged for him to meet the president. But he knew the president would not be impressed with pyrotechnics. He offered instead to interpret Marcos's dreams. His interpretations were accurate and pertinent. He told the president where to keep his money, the condition of his bladder for the following week, the precise number of military casualties in the next Communist ambush. He predicted the aphelion of the regime within the next three years, marked by lavish parties, state visitors (including the pope), and foreign aid. And when Marcos told him he had dreamt of a young eagle diving into the South China Sea, he advised the president to yank the president's son off a plane that was flying in two hours. That plane, sans the presidential son, crashed soon after takeoff. No one survived. Immediately after that, Marcos gave him something even he had completely unexpected: the documents for his adoption into the presidential family. From then on he would have a room next to the palace gardens and would go by the name of Marcos. He accepted his fate gratefully, and also sadly, because he knew all this was temporary. Not just his life, but the life of the Marcoses as well. The sooner he told them, the better. He was convinced that they could all prepare for the end as one family. And so, one evening, when he thought the time was right, he told the family that, incredible as it may seem, the House of Marcos would fall one day. The family would not hear of it. They closed his room down and sent him away, and Imelda gave him money to keep quiet and to travel as far away as he could. She also gave him a threat: speak, and you die. Nothing was heard of him since then. Upon orders from the Palace, the press stopped mentioning his name. His presence vanished like the ancient layers of a palimpsest. Some say too much luxury killed his powers, and he became a sad, faceless citizen. Others say he found a job in Houston, where he helped NASA coordinate the trajectories of rockets in space. Still others insist there were several Bionic Boys, all claiming to be the authentic one. But the most plausible rumor of all was this: that he never existed at all, that the Palace invented him just as it had invented a lot of stories during its unhappy reign.

■ ■ ■

Look at one another short of breath, walking proudly in our winter coats.

Efren X looks out the window and remembers the song, but he can't recall how the next lines go. Things like this drive him crazy. Two stories below, people are braving the cold, rushing from nowhere to nowhere. Lispenard is one long muddy puddle under their boots. Trucks rumble on Canal Street, and his apartment shudders like a barrio in the rim of fire. Marjetica, the super of the building, is paddling about the room and saying, "Is too cold here. I send someone to check the heat." She is a stooped gray apparition, moving slowly, as though she has a hard time maneuvering her way in the physical world.

"It has to be cold, Marjetica," Efren says. "The goddamn computers need the cold. Like mayonnaise. Like ice cream."

"Computer will live, but you will die," Marjetica says. "One day I come here and find you frozen like ice cream, how you like that."

"Be sure to save before turning the computers off."

"You go out sometimes. Is spring."

"Still feels like winter to me. Never can tell when one season ends and another begins. Never learned to."

"Go meet people. Eat something. You never eat. Just cookies. Look at you, skin and skeleton. You talk to machine all the time."

"You know me inside out, Marjetica."

"Go out and meet people."

"It's too cold and the cold makes me socially inept."

"Don't understand your English."

"It's freezing out there."

"Not different here."

"Besides, I can't go anywhere. My doctor said so."

"Said what?"

"This new strain. This disease. It's some kind of pulmonary thing. My lungs, Marjetica. There's no fucking cure for it."

"Oh my," Marjetica says, edging towards the door.

"It gets worse and worse, but my doctor says most people actually do survive, but they need to stay indoors. It's very contagious."

"You see what I mean. I call my sister in Slovenia. She know all about lung sickness."

"No, Marjetica. Not even Slovenia . . ." He coughs into his fist for effect, the cough misting the bottom half of the lens of his glasses, like two gibbous moons. As soon as she leaves he picks up a microcassette recorder and presses the record button. "Brief but welcome intrusion from the lady who looks after this dump. I don't recall if I've talked about her before. Lives with a hundred cats, all strays. Claims they bring her good luck. Certainly brings to this building an overwhelming odor of urine. No one else in her life. Arthritic, simpleminded, believes anything I tell her."

The phone rings. It's Christina again. He listens as she speaks to the machine, her voice a hundred light-years away. "Wednesday morning at nine. They're taking her to court. Turn the goddamn TV on. It's gonna be televised. Pick up the phone, goddamit. Hello hello hello. Call you again soon."

"Well," he says aloud. "The problem is I don't have a TV anymore. I blew the thing up. Would darling Christina ever believe how I did it, I wonder." The recorder clicks off. "Shit." He pulls the cassette out and slips it in its case and tapes a label on it—#742—and places it on a shelf with several other tapes lining a wall of the apartment. "Acoustic padding," he says to himself. "Wall of sound." He slips in a new cassette and records: "Experiment number seven hundred forty-three. Will need to look passably presentable for this one. Shit."

■ ■ ■

At exactly half past nine that evening, after a hot bath and a shave, he puts on a fresh shirt and clean jeans, makes his bed, dims the lights and puts on some music—early Frank Sinatra. At five past ten, Poison rings his apartment, and he lets her in. She has hair the color of Mercurochrome and a freckled face that belies her twenty-eight years, a slight discrepancy with the nineteen years she claims in her ad in the *Village Voice*.

Efren shows her a clip of the ad as soon as she steps in. "You look exactly like your photograph," he says. She doesn't smile, but heads straight to the sofa, where, slumping, she suddenly seems smaller than she is. "I can't offer you a drink," Efren says. "Too cold to go out and get anything. Do you like the cold?"

"Two words," Poison says. "Take-out."

"No, I don't think so. I mean, it'd be such an imposition to ask people to deliver anything in this weather. I never really understood people who did that, order take-out in foul weather, that is. It just seems so inconsiderate."

"Yeah, but it's their job. Plus they get tips."

"Anyway, what I meant to say was, I apologize for not having anything to drink."

"I don't drink," Poison says. She has a voice that sounds like a whine, as though she never learned to speak properly until, say, age six. It's jarring and artificial. He likes that.

"Is Poison your real name?"

Poison laughs. "Of course it is."

"Who'd name their kid Poison?"

"It's my name, okay? I chose it myself. 'Cause that's what I am." When she talks she has a way of jerking her upper body forward, as though the slightest intake of air made her ample bosom too heavy to bear.

"Are those real?"

"What?"

"Those breasts. Are they real?"

"Of course they're real. What the fuck do you think they are, plastic?"

"Oh, I didn't mean anything like that. I mean they're just so lovely, that's all. Under the light of that lamp."

"Yeah, right. I need a drink."

"You said you don't drink."

"Gotta start sometime."

"You want some chocolate milk?"

"Jesus."

The doorbell rings again. Efren presses the buzzer and says, "Come on up."

"You expecting company?" Poison asks.

"Yes."

"You never said you were expecting company."

"I am."

Efren opens the door for Taylor. Taylor is a big black guy with a pretty face and close-shaved head.

"I was hoping you'd like Taylor," Efren tells Poison. "Just you and him."

"You pay extra," Poison says. "If you watch."

"It's a blind date," Efren says. "I wanted you to meet someone nice."

"The fuck you did," Poison says. "You gonna pay double."

Taylor sits across from her and throws a small plastic packet on the table. "What's the matter," he says. "You got a problem with black guys or something?"

"Yeah, I got a problem when it's not in the fucking agreement."

"Taylor never asks me to pay double. Taylor never asks me to pay anything."

"Well, tough. I'm not here to meet people, you know? What the fuck you trying to do?"

"Hey," Taylor says, spreading his arms out and hanging them on the back of the seat. "It's your business. I'm just a guest here."

"Well, why don't you two have a go at it," Poison says. "Maybe you'll like it."

"You shouldn't be so inflexible," Efren says. "You never answered my question."

"What?"

"Whether you liked the cold."

"I hate it, okay? Wish I were in fucking Bahamas. Or Israel. Anywhere but here. That good enough for you?"

"Do you like what you do?" Efren asks her.

"I dreamt about it since I was a kid, okay?" Her fingers have wandered towards the packet on the table, and now they are tracing the edges of it shakily.

"Go ahead," Efren says. "Taylor brought it for all of us."

She scoops the packet and tears it open viciously, like a bird of prey tearing a mouse. She dips a forefinger in and sticks it up her nose, inhaling deeply, closing her eyes.

"Good girl," Efren says.

"Price has gone down a bit this week," Taylor says. "I can get you more, if you like."

"It's a good time to have a habit," Efren says.

Suddenly Poison is choking. She wheezes and sneezes and spits out a glob of milky white spit. "Stupid fuck! It's fucking baby powder, you stupid fuck!"

"What?" Taylor picks up the packet, feels the powder with his finger, and says, "Fuck. Well, I'll be fucked."

"Yeah, you'll be fucked, you fuck, making me snort baby powder. Think I'm stupid, you fuck? Think you can get any fuck with this shit? I ain't fucking you, or you, or any fuck. You're not getting anything with this fuck."

Efren hands her a tissue. "Go home, Poison. You're no fun." He pulls out some bills and gives them to her.

"Well, yeah, fuck that. Blind date, my ass." She stuffs the bills in her jeans pocket. "You think you can get ass with baby powder, shove it up your ass, fucking faggots." She's still spurting a string of invectives as he shows her out, and when he shuts the door her voice, a sputtering of *fucks*, echoes through the hall. When he turns around Taylor is grinning under the lamp, his arms stretched out.

"Blind date, my ass," he says. "I told you she ain't gonna buy it."

"It was a surprise. People get interesting when they get surprised."

"Well, she didn't find it interesting, you know what I'm saying?"

"She seemed like a nice girl. Don't you think she was a nice girl?" Efren picks up the packet and smells the powder. "It does smell like baby powder, you know."

"Well, you told me to fill it with baby powder, that's what I did."

"Funny. Anyone could have told it from the smell."

"She seemed like she wasn't used to it."

"She's only nineteen."

"My ass."

He gives Taylor money and Taylor gets up to go. "You have a good life," Efren tells him.

"You're a fucking nut job, man," Taylor says. "But as long as you rich, you can be as fucked up as you want."

"Oh, I get it now," Efren says.

"What?"

" 'Wearing smells from laboratories. Facing a dying nation.' "

"Yeah, right. Well, you just have—"

"It's the lyrics of a song. From *Hair*. You remember *Hair*?"

"No."

"It's been running in my mind all day. It was driving me crazy. Does that ever happen to you, Taylor? Like you want to remember something, and it's just there, but it won't come out?"

"Happens all the time."

"And now I can't remember the lines after that. Of moving paper fantasies. That doesn't make much sense, does it? Then again the sixties never did. Or was it the seventies?"

"Yeah, man, whatever."

"Well, too bad we couldn't do anything tonight."

"You got my number, man."

■ ■ ■

The next morning, like a wake-up call, Christina is on the phone again. "Call her up, at least. You know where she is."

He buries his head under a pillow and groans. "Sweet Christina, how can I even think of calling up when I just blew two hundred bucks on an experiment that went nowhere?"

"Or if you can't, come to court tomorrow. She needs all of us. She cared about you, dammit."

"She still sends me money, like a good mom. You know that, Christina?"

"That's tomorrow at nine."

"And I want to make that money work, you know?"

"Be there."

"Do something useful, for a change. You think that'll help, my liposuctioned one?"

Two hours later he is heading for the subway station at Church. The wind is cold, the sky bright but full of tattered rags of clouds, and all along Canal muddy puddles gleam like costume jewelry. He takes the A train to Seventy-second, reading the paper all the while and looking up only when his stop is next. Since he moved to New York, he's always had this uncanny ability to know when his stop is next. It's an acquired instinct. You could blindfold him and shut his ears and he'd still know. He walks east to Central Park, and keeps on walking around and around the Great Lawn for a couple of hours until the wind gets colder and the sun hides behind ash-gray clouds and becomes a smear of light. He comes to a hot dog stand off the Delacorte Theater and asks for a hot dog with everything on it and a Classic Coke. A young Hispanic boy approaches him and asks for change. He picks out three dimes and hands them to the boy. The hot dog vendor, an Albanian immigrant with a scraggly mustache, says to the boy, "Go away now, get the fuck out of here." Efren tells him to make that two hot dogs and two Cokes. Then he catches up with the boy and gives him the extra order. The boy is taken aback. He extends his hands to accept the offer and then pulls his hands back, looking quizzically at Efren.

"It's a hot dog," Efren says. "You eat it. That nice man wanted to give it to you."

The boy takes the hot dog and the Coke with a smile that looks like a grimace.

"Come on," Efren says. "Let's eat by the lake. A picnic."

The boy doesn't seem inclined to do so, but he steps behind Efren, as though the meal put him in his debt.

"You got a name?" Efren asks him.

"Raul Echeverria," the boy says.

"A fine name. A gentleman's name. An honorable name. How old are you?"

The boys thinks for a while. "Twelve." And then, "Eleven."

"A fine age. A wonderful age. When I was eleven I tried to learn how to roller-skate. Do you roller-skate, Raul Echeverria?"

"No."

"Neither do I. Pulled my fucking arm out. A bad fall. Poor motor coordination or something. You got a family?"

"My father, my brother, and my uncle."

"Where do they live?"

The boy pointed north, vacillated, then pointed south.

"That narrows it down," Efren says. "Let's eat."

They sit on a bench by the lake. Ducks paddle towards the bank. Efren tears a piece of bread and throws it at them. They fight over the piece, creating ripples in the green water.

"Thank you for coming on such short notice," Efren addresses the ducks.

The boy chuckles.

"You have a nice smile, Raul Echeverria," Efren says. "You should do that more often. The world's not that bad."

"My father say New York is full of bad people."

"And he's probably right. But New York doesn't speak for the world. You tell him that. Tell him I said so."

"My father say don't come home."

"Why not?"

"Because I see him and Maria."

"Oh. I'm sure whatever it may have been, he and Maria wouldn't want you to stay out all night."

"He said he kill me. He hit me here." He rubs a hand against his belly.

"Does it still hurt?"

"No."

"Then you're okay. I think."

"You are doctor?"

"Jesus, no. What the hell am I? I guess I'm a scientist. A man of science. I conduct experiments. I set up situations, and I try to predict the outcome. To see what people do under certain situations. Do you know what I mean?"

"No."

"It's like this. I experiment with people. I don't stick pins into them or give them stuff or whatever. I just watch them. Well, I don't do just that. I sort of manipulate situations. You know what I mean?"

"No."

"Well, for instance, I walk down Broadway, and I see an old lady, and, out of the blue, I offer to help her cross the street. You know what happens when I do that? They get terrified. They look around for the police."

"That is science?"

"Oh, bright boy. I knew there was something in you. I could tell. How about this. I take the subway to Brooklyn. Past midnight. There's a drunk drooling on the train. There's no one else. He smells of piss. I walk to him and shake him awake and give him ten dollars. I go back to my seat. He staggers up, walks to me, sticks a knife to my ribs, and tells me to hand him all my money."

"To give ten dollars is stupid."

"Incredible. Raul Echeverria, you are wunderbar. You want a job? Analyze all my experiments or something. Wish I could pay you though. Hot dogs are probably all you'll ever get."

"Why you do it?"

"Good question. I don't know. I have a whole library of them, but I don't know what to make of it. An entire catalog of human responses. How about that? The only conclusion I've ever arrived at is that people can no longer respond to kindness. But that's pretty obvious. Did you know that humans are the only creatures capable of conceiving evil? Animals don't do that. Animals just want to survive. But that's pretty obvious too. So why do I do it? Don't know. I'm in a rut, Raul Echeverria. I'm a terrible failure."

By this time it's getting dark. The fading light turns everything blue and faintly luminous. Efren buttons his coat all the way up to his neck. "I'm going now. You go on home, too."

The boy doesn't move from his seat.

"You can't stay here all night," Efren says. "Come along."

They take the train back to Lispenard, sitting side by side and staring blankly at the ads on the train. They seem like a father and son whose constant companionship has absolved them of any further need for conversation.

On their way up to the apartment Marjetica pokes her head out and sees them.

"Marjetica, meet my little cousin, Raul Echeverria."

Marjetica's powder-pale face beams a radiant smile, which instantly fades to a look of concern. "But your lung sickness?"

"Gone. It's a miracle."

"Your cousin is from Philippines?"

"No, sweetheart. Dominican Republic. Or Puerto Rico. Extended family. It's a very long story. Good night."

In the apartment the boy looks at the wall of tapes and the disheveled mess of soiled clothes, towels, a blinking monitor, Coke liter bottles, and all the trappings of Efren's solitary life. He tries to turn the TV on.

"It doesn't work," Efren says. "I blew it up."

"What that mean, blew it up?"

"I don't know. I was just staring at it. There was this stupid game show or something, and I was too lazy to pick up the remote. So I was just staring at it and thinking I wish the thing would blow up, and it did. Zap. The screen went dead. It was so odd."

He pours some milk and opens a box of ginger snaps and a can of instant chocolate. "Suppertime," he says. He scoops the chocolate and drops little islands of it in two glasses and gives the boy a teaspoon to stir his milk. The chocolate clings to the spoon like mud. The boy licks the spoon clean and then drinks the milk.

After that Efren gives the boy an old sweater and says, "Here. Wear this. It's yours. You can keep it. What do you want to do now?"

"I want to sleep."

Efren clears the sofa of debris. The boy lies down and falls asleep immediately. It's as if a light just blinks out as soon as he lies down. He looks younger when he's asleep. Maybe he was lying about his age. Efren spreads a quilt over the boy. Then he spreads out a few things strategically in the room: his microcassette recorder, a Cross pen, his watch, his wallet. Then he goes to his bedroom and sleeps soundly, perhaps more soundly than he has in days. He sleeps late the next morning. It's cold and gray, the sun itself has a hard time getting up. Then he realizes what day it is. "Shit." He gets dressed, grabs his coat and ski cap, and walks to the other room. The boy is still sleeping, curled on the sofa. Efren picks up his watch and wallet. Then he decides to leave the watch. He closes the door gently behind him.

■ ■ ■

When he reaches City Hall there's a group of people, mostly Filipinos, already gathered at the steps. Several of them are carrying placards. One of the placards says: MAGNANAKAW! THIEF! Someone is dressed in a skeleton costume left over from Halloween. She is doing a kind of wriggling dance, waving her arms like a hula dancer. On her costume she has pinned a sign saying INANG BAYAN. MOTHERLAND. Police are trying to rein everyone in. Efren stands across from the demonstrators, behind the police line. A limousine pulls up. Flashbulbs spark like a short circuit. The crowd presses against the police ranks. From out of the limousine Imelda Marcos steps out. She is a tall, pale, imposing figure. "Putang ina mo, Imelda!" the woman in the Halloween costume yells. There's applause and then the heckler's booed down by another faction of the crowd. Efren edges his way closer to the police line. Imelda Marcos walks up the steps. She is wearing a low-cut gown, as though she's going to a ball. A décolleté, for Christ's sake, Efren says to himself. Her wrists are cuffed. She teeters upwards, assisted by her lawyer and bodyguards. As she passes the crowd she acknowledges with an almost imperceptible smile both curses and applause. Efren jostles for space. And then he is face to face with her. She looks straight at him. Straight in his eyes, her expression unchanging. Then she is swept up by journalists and guards and disappears into the federal courthouse. Efren catches a glimpse of the hem of her absurd gown; it has gathered some of the spring mud. The crowd soon rushes after them. Efren finds himself alone on the steps. Litter flies about him in small, tattered cyclones.

"Efren! Come inside, or you'll freeze to death!" It's Christina, bolting down the steps. "Where have you been? I've been going nuts calling you. I'm so glad you came. You look terrible. Jesus, you lost a lot of weight."

"You don't look so bad yourself."

"She wants to talk to you."

"What for?"

"She wants to confirm all those predictions. You know, about the outcome of the trial."

"Well, I'm sure she's getting good advice. Tell her lawyer to lose the hat."

"Be serious, Efren. She wants you."

"Why?"

"Because she trusts your opinion."

"I like the way you put it."

"I've never seen her so . . . *human*. It makes me so sad."

Efren laughs. "Sorry," he says.

"You've never forgiven her, have you?"

"Forgiven her for what, Christina?"

"For being you."

"She never made me what I am. I made me what I am."

"Come to her apartment, Efren. This afternoon. After the hearing. You know where it is. Fifth Avenue."

"Busy."

"Busy with what?"

"My science. My experiments."

"What can be more important right now—"

"See, Christina, there you go again. My experiments are important. They're the fucking most important thing I've ever done in my life. And nobody fucking gives a damn."

"Taping interviews? Talking to God knows what—Efren, this is the real world. You're in the real world now."

"All my life I wanted to know. You know that?"

"Know what?"

"What it is that goes on in that little thing inside people. The heart, for Christ's sake. The aorta. I want to know what goes on in that little machine. I want to do something useful. You know what that means, Christina?"

"My heart bleeds. Can you see that?"

"Jesus. You're beginning to sound just like her."

"What else do you want to know? It fucking bleeds. Just like she's bleeding now. We're all being tried here. Not just her. All of us. Do you understand?" She edges closer to him and looks in his eye. "Do you really think you're different from us all?"

"I can't do anything anymore. I just can't."

Christina holds his hands and then lets go. "I have to go in now. She needs all of us. Will you please please please be there?" She runs up the stairs, her heels clicking like ice.

He turns around and walks to the subway. Then, on second thought, he decides to walk home. He walks up Broadway, the bleak monotony of it, the hobos and the suits, the serpentine visa lines along the Federal Office Building, past the fortress of the police barracks on Lafayette, then turns left on Canal past the disheveled stacks of vegetables, the Vietnamese noodle houses, the Chinese bonsai shops, the unbearably human need to eat and fuck and defecate and prettify.

Finally, with some relief, he reaches the lesser frenzy of Lispenard. Back in his apartment he discovers that the boy has gone. He walks about, inspecting the objects he left behind. They're all there. The only thing missing is the sweater he gave the boy. He can't, for the life of him, remember what the boy looks like. Some day he'll pass him on the street and he won't recognize him. He picks up his recorder and switches it on, and sits thinking for a long time before switching it off. Then he slumps on the sofa. The remnants of last night's meal—the glass lined with a thin film of milk, the half-torn packet of biscuits—lie on the table. He stares at the spoon that's lying there. It's smeared with muddy chocolate that has dried and caked into streaks. He picks it up with the intention of dumping it in the kitchen sink. Then he changes his mind and puts it back on the table. He stares at it for a long time. It's beautiful, in a strange sort of way. Just the way it is.

SUBMISSION

■ ■ ■

Karl Taro Greenfeld

The boys on the wall catcalled as she passed. Tanned faces with flecks of peeling skin, crooked teeth, hooked noses, blood-rimmed eyes like old fish in a monger's stall, these were the features of horny, stoned, bored teenaged boys. And they stank, these boys did, of the ocean and brine and seaweed and their own sweat. They reminded Sandi of what was repellent about sex. The fluids. The smells. The saltiness. No wonder women demanded to be paid.

She didn't glance at them. Two years their senior, she had never really known the boys on the wall. Her own little brother, Mickey, was a good student, a potential engineer, consistently scoring in the high 90s at Chai Wan Secondary School #2. He never hung around with the surfers on the wall. They smoked cigarettes and hashish from crushed soda cans and executed little flip tricks on skateboards, the clicking sound of the urethane rolling over cracks in the pavement audible all

KARL TARO GREENFELD was born in Kobe, Japan, in 1964 of a Japanese mother and American Jewish father. Currently the editor of *Time* magazine's Asian edition, he is the author of two books of creative nonfiction, *Speed Tribes: Days and Nights with Japan's Next Generation* (1995) and *Standard Deviations: Growing Up and Coming Down in the New Asia* (2002). A former staff writer for *Time* and correspondent for the *Nation*, Greenfeld has spent much of his career reporting and writing about the Far East for *GQ*, *Outside*, *Men's Journal*, *Condé Nast Traveler*, *Vogue*, the *New York Times Magazine*, and other magazines. His nonfiction has been widely anthologized, most recently in *The Best American Non-Required Reading, 2002*. This is his first published work of fiction.

the way up the hill, even in the tiny dining room of her family's housing estate flat.

They ogled Sandi. With her feline eyes and condescending smirk, she frustrated and angered and aroused them. She had grown up in the same housing estate, swung and jungle-gymed in the same crummy rubber-matted play area and spent her springs and summers on the same dirty Shek-O beaches. They'd stood atop a Dumpster to spy on her peeing in the public bathrooms, seen her bush almost as soon as she had one. And now, suddenly, it's as if she didn't know them. For the boys, pulling their baggy Billabong T-shirts tight over bony chests and crouching with knees bent in the coiled human spring that is a skater about to ollie, she was the local bitch. So whenever she strolled by, her black Prada shaped like a doctor's bag but the size of a small suitcase under her arm, they reminded her that she was one of them.

"You slut."

No, she wasn't a slut. Because sluts gave it away. What the boys could never imagine was what was in the bag. The skin-tight vinyl cat suit, the crotchless panties, the dildos, the vibrators, the whip, the cat-o'-nine-tails, the plugs she would stick up a British investment banker's ass. All washed, cleaned, ready for lubrication and insertion. Could the boys on the wall handle that?

She boarded a mini-bus that wound up through the headlands and then down into Chai-wan, passed Northpoint, Quarry Bay and then along the harbor and into Central. As the driver, a middle-aged man with a face that seemed frozen in hang-jawed astonishment at how badly his life had turned out, swerved between taxis and trucks hauling bamboo pipes, Sandi ran through her calculations again. She had the same head for figures as her brother, only Sandi had never been able to stay interested in the abstractions of numbers without dollar signs attached to them. Now that the money was accumulating quickly, she was fascinated by the easy arithmetic of adding each day's take to the stash in her Standard and Chartered account. She'd quickly figured out she could charge more than the other girls: attractive Chinese dominatrixes were rare. They were actually more in demand than the wrinkled gweilos who hung around the shop. It was a matter of learning the technique, the knots and buckles and pulleys and straps. At first it was like taking a course in rock climbing. Master the equipment. Safety was paramount. You had to strap him in, make sure the customer was secure, test the straps and buckles before you winched him up. But she was learning. Steadily, slowly, from watching videos, reading magazines, visiting Web sites, doing doubles with some of the older girls. And her customers, they told her what worked and what didn't. This was a business, like any other, and she had to expect a certain amount of R&D, of sunk costs, there was that vinyl bodysuit, the dildos, it wasn't like you could go to a bank and take out a loan. But from here on it was all profit. And somewhere, at the end of all this, was Australia, Sydney, a paradise of S&M and dom-sub role-play. Where she could fist fifteen customers a day, pretty Aussie boys charged up on poppers with muscular chests and long, bulbous cocks and neatly trimmed pubes. She'd rent her own little flat in Paddington and finally get out of stinky, humid Hong Kong and away from her parents' tiny apartment, and frustrated, desperate Mickey hunched over his graph paper and tapping away on his Casio calculator and finally, once and for all, say good riddance to that bad rubbish who sat along the wall.

She worked in an office, she had lied to her parents, for an old gweilo woman who was often out of town and worked unconventional hours. Late evenings, Saturday afternoons, her mobile would buzz when Sandi was sitting down to dinner with her mother and father, chopsticks hunched over bowls of rice and steamed garupa and *dau-mieu*. A customer, one of her Pommie bankers, American computer geeks, French restaurateurs. They needed spanking, violation, discipline. They wanted to be strapped in, winched up, harnessed, saddled, ridden. Sandi would explain to her parents that her boss needed her and she would grab her Prada bag and head down the hill, past the beach and the boys on the wall, to the mini-bus stop or taxi stand and into town.

She stepped off the mini-bus near the Central Market, walking up the block to Lane Crawford and then the escalator up to Cavanaugh Street. The businessmen in their shirtsleeves, carrying their leather briefcases, the old ladies wheeling their collections of scavenged aluminum or cardboard, the teenage girls talking on mobiles, the shirtless construction workers taking a break from laying fiber-optic cable; the vista was numbingly familiar. Sandi felt she could slip into her fellow Hong Konger's minds at will, read their thoughts as easily as a Chiron scrolling news: the businessmen were scheming about money, the old ladies counting up their take in redeemables, the girls steadily compromising their standards so that in a year or two the prospect of marrying one of those businessmen wouldn't seem as depressing as it really was and the construction workers, well, they were thinking of fucking Sandi.

That's what bored her, actually, the same-sameness of it all. In Sydney, she had found, she really didn't know what those hook-nosed gweilos were thinking; oh, about sex, surely, because Sandi had concluded that was really all anyone thought about. You could throw in money, but wasn't that just sex in a different form, a fungible that was valued because of its ready convertibility to sex? But Down Under, who knew? Every withered, freckled, craggy, pallorous face was empty as a new bank account. That's what she fancied, after the stifling closeness of Hong Kong housing estate living. Her family's apartment was three bedrooms in name only, the rooms seemed small as airline seats, the smells and sounds of each family member permeated the whole place, so that Father's belches and Mother's sighing and Mickey's clicking away on his keyboard and scratching at his columns and rows of figures became the soundtrack of her life. They didn't need to speak anymore. It was as if they heard enough of each other when they were separated that when they came together, there was nothing to say. She always paid Mother the four thousand Hong Kong dollars they had agreed as her share of the communal housing and board bills before Mother even had a chance to ask for it.

As she walked into the shop, two of the old gweilo dominatrixes—they must have been in their mid-thirties—were sitting on the carpeted bench under the edible underwear and a selection of billy clubs. They were little better than prostitutes, Sandi reckoned, reduced to trolling the shop for middle-aged Chinese men who longed to revisit their colonial servitude. At first, when she got into the business, Sandi had listened to the old doms, eager to siphon their wisdom and advice, and intimidated by their ease and comfort with the vast array of equipment the shop provided in the dungeons let by the hour. She said hello in English and told the shop boy in Cantonese she'd like her usual chamber and to send in the sub when he checked in, an anxious, medium-height American with hair the color of sesame seeds. He'd be wearing an inexpensive-looking blazer and trousers. And he'd pay for the room.

At first, she'd made the mistake of having sex with the subs. They would beg her for it. Their reward, they would call it. And they would demand it petulantly. After being on the rack or in a pulley or strapped to a chair or suspended from a winch or locked in a cage for an hour or two, they would insist that they had been good boys and they should get their reward. As if Sandi was a doggy biscuit. They'd pout and sulk and say that for three thousand Hong Kong dollars they deserved it. And she'd relent, unzipping the crotch of her cat suit and squatting over them where they were tied down, or strapped up, and letting them lap at her hairy bush while she jerked them off. The old gweilo ladies smiled at each other when she asked about the rewards, and shrugged, telling her it was a matter of preference, clients, business. When she worked in tandem, she was surprised when the old dom, Madame Xonia, slid a condom over the balding Chinaman's cock and lowered herself onto him, riding him until he came and simpered, yes mistress, yes mistress. So she resigned herself to having to proffer her little biscuit to the subs.

Still it wasn't sex. This was masquerade, a kind of theater, or at least a spectacle. She was paid as much for her expertise as for her body. Those whores out in Mongkok, they were paid for allowing trespass, violation of their reproductive facilities, nothing more. There was a dignity in this, Sandi would insist, in knowing how to fasten the straps and tie the knots, to lay a fine silk rope between the subs' testicles and fasten it with a slip knot over the cock. That was a skill. One that paid well. And the more she learned, the more tribute she could demand. With her looks—whenever the new sub called, having been referred by the shop, they'd ask if she was pretty, "Very," she would say, her voice assured and confident, "very"—she had raised her rates: four thousand Hong Kong for the hour. And there was no longer any reward. At least not on the first few visits.

With this sub—the quiet American with dirty blond hair who insisted that his cock be tied up—she was settling into the routine. She let him in, led him through the dungeon and into the rest room. While he was showering, she checked herself in the mirror. She'd already changed, fastening the collar around her neck, slipping on the cat suit over the crotchless panties, pulling on the black stiletto boots. She removed a dildo, a small vibrator shaped like a giant diet pill and several Durexes from her bag, setting the sex toys and contraceptives atop the black, upholstered rack.

The sub would tell her about his sexual conquests—all lies, Sandi assumed, although she didn't care. He worked at a magazine, as a writer, he said, covering business, politics, Southeast Asia—again, not that she cared. He asked her if she read any magazines. *The Nutcracker*, she answered, *Leatherworks*, *BDSM Monthly*. Newspapers? he'd asked. *Mingpao*, *Apple Daily*. She gave a few names, but she really never read newspapers. They bored her. And they made her hands dirty with ink. He was frequently out of town. He once called her from Bangkok, as if they were friends, and told her he had to see her. She told him to call back when he was in Hong Kong. What did he think? That she would talk dirty to him while she was riding a mini-bus?

She told him his safe word: yellow. She would tie up his penis so that it was strapped to his stomach, pointing up at his navel. And she would whip it lightly with a riding crop. He moaned. He begged her not to stop. He told her he'd been a bad, bad boy, that while he was working at the magazine he would think of her and masturbate behind his desk, sometimes with the door open. Who knew who saw him? Sandi agreed that yes, that was bad and—thwack!—he had better not even think of stopping it.

"Because this is my cock, right?" Sandi said, poking at the fleshy little member with the riding crop—his penis reminded her of an elongated tube of pig's colon that you might find in an assorted noodle soup, mixed in with the pig's blood and rhubarb. "I own this cock. And if I tell you to touch yourself, you touch yourself."

"Yes mistress," he moaned. "Oh yes mistress."

■ ■ ■

Later, while she was browsing a rack of codpieces and chastity belts, she chatted with Xonia. Xonia was a part owner of the shop, though she would still frequently take a session or two or partner with another of the girls if the client wanted a threesome. Slightly built with medium-sized breasts and wavy, shoulder-length dyed-blond hair, Xonia was trying on a see-through camisole and turning before the mirror, commenting that she had to start working out again.

"I'm going all wobbly," she said as she bobbed up and down on the balls of her feet.

She'd been in Hong Kong more than a decade. Had seen advocates and chief secretaries and managing directors and magistrates pass through her dungeons. "Oh, you'd be surprised, you'd be surprised."

While Sandi fiddled with the lock on a male chastity belt, she listened as Xonia told her about her life in England, before she came to Hong Kong, about working for a pop star who was famous in the eighties, a now-forgotten, dreadlocked pretty boy with a few videos on heavy rotation on MTV—but this was before your time, Sandi, before Honkers even had MTV or Channel V. And how he was much smaller than he looked in the videos and how they would have these wild parties. He used to rent a villa in Ibiza or Mykonos, and they'd take drugs. Xonia never took drugs herself. They used to tease her for it. She'd drink tea and eat her chocolates while the rest of them were taking Es. This was before it became a big club drug, when you took it and stayed home and, well, just partied. By partying she meant having sex with multiple partners. One of the band or the pop star himself would come up to her and just tap her shoulder and off they'd go into one of the bedrooms and they'd screw, or they'd just cuddle. They didn't call them orgies then, nobody ever used those words. They were just parties.

"But I wasn't so wobbly then," Xonia said, examining her bum in the mirror.

Sandi tried to imagine Xonia as a younger woman, a Xonia in her prime. She may have been pretty once, in that fleeting gweilo way where a woman can be pretty for like fifteen minutes when she's nineteen and never catch a second glance again. How lucky she was to be Chinese, Sandi assured herself, her looks would last. And anyway, she had another thirteen years at least before she would be Xonia's age. But now Xonia was like an old scholar, someone to be venerated for her age and wisdom, but the lessons to be taken away were not necessarily those that came from Xonia's words, instead it was her life that Sandi took to be a cautionary tale. Stay in this business for too long, and you become an old whore, smelling of powder, stuffed into lingerie, hoping for customers.

Sandi looked at the price tag on the male chastity belt. A thousand Hong Kong dollars. "Do the subs like this?" She asked.

Xonia shrugged. "Some do, some do."

"And they can all fit?"

Xonia shook her head. "That's the point. The restriction. The imprisonment."

She would save the money, plunk it into her account, advance a thousand dollars closer to Sydney.

■ ■ ■

Her parents did wonder about her. Mickey had found her bankbook, had reported the vast amount that Sandi was socking away. What was she doing with the money? She didn't have friends. Appeared to have no interest in men. Came and went at strange hours and never told her parents where she worked. Was she seeing some gweilo? Was she taking drugs? There was no way to know what she was doing. Mickey, always eager to curry favor with his parents, offered to follow her into town. Mother deemed this too risky. What if Mickey got lost, became confused, was momentarily stupefied and turned into one of those boys who are deposited across the border in Shenzhen by anxious Hong Kong immigration authorities and go missing, becoming the subjects of TV Pearl documentaries. No, Mickey should stay close to home, working at his books and figures and earning his good grades so that maybe he could go to college in Canada. Mickey, the oldest son, was where his mother and father deposited their hopes. Sandi would end up married somehow, they told themselves, and why did a housewife need a secondary school degree? She was pretty, she would find some businessman or realtor or, at least, a lorry driver and they'd put their names down on a waiting list for a government flat, just as her mother and father had done, and when their names came up, they'd move in, beginning their lives, having kids, maybe get lucky and birth all boys. That's the way it worked. No reason why Sandi wouldn't eventually understand her place in the order of things.

What mattered was keeping Mickey out of trouble, away from those boys with hennaed hair and tattoos by the wall. He might win a scholarship, with a little bit of luck, some supplement for the family's meager savings to ease his passage to a good school in Vancouver. He'd marry some smart overseas Chinese woman, and . . . who knows? Maybe the whole family could move to Canada, get away from this housing estate, live in the cool air and fresh woodlands of Canada. Not that Sandi's mother had ever been to Canada, but she had watched the TV specials, seen the travel brochures. It was just so clean. Sandi had been to Australia. She paid for her own three-week vacation. But she never once told the family what it had been like. So Mother's dreams remained fixated on Canada, on Mickey going to school, on some giant crane built out of Mickey's skill with numbers and equations reaching across the

Pacific and plucking them up and out of Shek-O Housing Estates. Nothing should jeopardize that, especially with Mickey's exams pending, a procession of A-levels and SATs and ACTs for which he had been diligently preparing. He would score well on the maths, science, and history. His English scores, of course, might be lower. But surely the colleges would make an exception for a future engineer, for a precocious computer programmer. And he was such a hardworking boy, shut away in his room, scratching away with number two pencils on practice exams. The schools would see that and realize that not only was this a bright boy, but that he came from a good family that cared and would do everything necessary to ensure his future, *their* future.

When Sandi thought about Mickey, it was with a mixture of distaste and boredom. She accepted that he was the son, and therefore the vessel of so much parental aspiration, yet he was such a little dick, the kind of boy she had known by the dozen when she had still gone to school. Bright little mathematical machines, these boys became in her mind compendiums of statistics rather than human beings. Their scores, achievements, grades and results represented the reduction of character and desire to numbers on a page. Mickey stacked up well, Sandi knew, but there were so many like him, and what kind of life was that? Test well, and maybe you could go to college, test brilliantly and perhaps there was a spot for you overseas. She would get overseas on her own terms, by her own efforts, without having to sit for any stuffy exams.

That night, as she walked up from the mini-bus stop to her family's flat, she recalled the boy Mickey had been instead of what he had become. They'd spent every spring on the beach, before the summers and the crowds of tourists who would overrun their sand and waves, carving the whole cove into tiny fiefs of towel and beach chair. Mickey had been a bony kid, before the years of studying indoors had added layers of adolescent blubber, before his eyesight deteriorated and he needed glasses and he became pale as an Englishman's ass. She'd taught him how to bodysurf, how to catch the little waves and ride all the way to the shore. When typhoons were expected, the swells would be overhead and the local kids would ignore the high-numbered storm warnings and splash in the breakwater, catching lifts on the choppy waves. Even from here, as she walked up the hill, she could hear the surf, reminding her of the reckless freedom, of unheeded parental warnings and taking ownership of the nearly empty beach. The older kids would all be off surfing at Big Wave or Cap D' Aguilar and the beach would belong then to their crowd. You truly felt like a little emperor. The waves raising you up like you were in a palanquin, the weightlessness being for a moment terrifying and then, as you surrendered to it and lifted your head out of the foam, it was an intoxication, the rush of liberation. Mickey had loved the ocean, the beach, but he would only go in the water if Sandi was there, watching over him. What is it about the beach that can make a day seem as long as a season? You rode the water, lay on the sand, begged change for ice cream, built a castle, scavenged in the rocks, ignoring used rubbers and digging up broken glass polished by the waves, trashed compact discs turned pink by the saltwater, little black crabs with orange pincers. The spring wasn't as hot as the summer, so you could stay on the sand all day, heading into the water a dozen times, and each time that weightlessness as the waves picked you up.

But how many days like that had there really been? She now wondered as she rooted around in her bag for her keys. They had been in school during the spring, of course, and there were the rains that came, changing the color of the water to a murky brown and making the waves all chop and foam and too weak to carry them. There could only have been a few springs before the other boys began smoking cigarettes and sniffing glue. The older boys would already have been surfing. It now seemed that almost as soon as she was aware of gender, the tough boys began hanging around on the wall and taunting Mickey for being in his sister's charge. When they went to the beach then, Mickey would become tentative, not wanting to be seen with his sister but still too frightened to bodysurf without her. She would ride the waves and check on Mickey once in a while as he sat on the sand, picking up cigarette butts and bottle caps from around him but unwilling to even venture to the rocks, for fear the boys on the wall would make fun of him.

As she set down her bag in her room and could feel Mickey next door, could detect his heat and eagerness as he studied for his tests, which, she knew, were coming up next week, she now estimated there had been only four or five such good days, or perhaps even that was an exaggeration. Maybe there had only been one of those days on the beach, one afternoon, a few hours where they had been big sister and little brother and where they had felt free, before Mickey became this weird little droid who sat in his room all day working on figures and

Sandi became acutely aware of her body and gender and the universe of difference that implied between her and her brother. A whole life, an entire relationship, how could it rest on just those few hours?

■ ■ ■

One afternoon, after Mickey logged on and retrieved his SAT and ACT scores, the family indulged in a celebratory banquet. They had lunch at the Excelsior, the four of them. Father had even ordered shark's fin. And Mickey had been so smug, that little prick, sipping his soup and nodding as his mother went on about how proud she was and patted his little bowl-cut head. Sandi had swallowed her soup and felt practically invisible as the family wallowed in their good fortune at having such a son. His math scores had been the second best at Chai Wan #2, his science and history ACTs had also been impressive, in the top 2 percentile. It was as if the family's suffering and frugality had somehow been rewarded. Mother and Father seemed almost relieved at having been right. Unspoken during the previous months had been the question: What if Mickey didn't do well? What if his test scores were merely average?

But they weren't. He truly was a bright boy. And now the family's time was spent filling out financial aid forms and scholarship applications, for which Sandi, because of her better English, was always enlisted to help divine the meanings of the questionnaires, to ascertain which answers would magically open the purse strings of these universities. This was another exam, the family assumed, another shoal of trick questions which must be carefully negotiated in order to secure the right result. Nationality. Race. Religion. Family income. Family assets. Extracurriculars. An essay. The truth was irrelevant, everybody knew that. What did these colleges want? Sandi was entrusted to translate and extrapolate, and to alchemize the right responses. At one point she grew exasperated with the family's hand-wringing about the issue as they sat around the rickety wooden dining table beneath the Park 'n' Shop calendar, sipping tea and flipping through Cantonese primers on the subject of cajoling money from foreign universities. Why not just write the truth, she asked at one point. No one responded because that, of course, was out of the question.

The work took hours. Mickey would be, they decided, a minority among minorities. He wasn't a Chinese or a Hong Konger, but a Haka, a member of a minority that had fled China centuries ago and whose culture was in danger of vanishing. There was Haka blood in their family tree, as there was in so many Cantonese, so this was exaggeration rather than prevarication. But chinky is chinky, Sandi thought as she translated their lies. What Western institution would care if you were Haka or Cantonese or Fukkienese? They would only see chink, Sandi knew from her extensive dealings with gweilos. She kept this to herself as she dutifully wrote down the responses they dictated, while Mickey played Grand Theft Auto on his computer. The little punk was such a hero the family didn't even expect him to fill in his own applications. He was like a prizefighter resting up between bouts; becoming even chubbier as he dined on roast pork and duck prepared by his mother. He was dismissive when Sandi asked him what he thought they should write on the forms. It was suddenly beneath him now, a matter of clerical work fit for Sandi. The adulation of the clan had clearly gone to his head and made the little punk insufferable. His mother had boasted so vociferously to the other mothers in the housing estate that everyone now knew of the prodigy in their midst. A great student becomes a kind of celebrity in Hong Kong, Sandi knew, and now Mickey had achieved the kind of status accorded to local heroes. Even the boys on the wall ignored him now rather than make fun of him as he went by. In some way that they recognized, Mickey had become cool, his achievement in a distant field and venue according him their grudging respect.

The answers were contrived. Sandi wrote a dutiful essay dictated in Chinese by the family committee, a turgid piece of prose about duty and diligence and the virtues of hard work. It was a virtual repeat of the essays she had done for Mickey's original applications. Her suggestion that they write something about what it had been like growing up on the beach, with the waves and sand and the scavenging in the rocks, the feeling of weightlessness, of days that seemed to go on forever, was ignored in such a way that Sandi was made to feel stupid. The forms were filled out, photocopied, slid into their pristine envelopes, and sent via courier services to the various schools—the family's aspirations traveling in the bellies of cargo jets for eventual perusal and judgment by gweilos in far-away ivory towers.

■ ■ ■

Could Sandi come to a party? Xonia wondered. Five or six girls. A rich English banker in a house on the Peak. He liked subs, Xonia explained.

It would be very good money. He always paid well. Ten thousand an hour, probably four hours. Plus, if she was a good girl, a gratuity.

Sandi held her phone to her ear and weighed the proposition. She didn't like being a submissive, being bound and tied up and fondled and spanked. The loss of control unnerved her. Still, she quickly ran through the numbers, and forty thousand plus gratuity would push her bank account up even higher into the six figures. One job like this could save her weeks of sessions at the shop. And, lately, work had been slow. In the summer, so many of her regulars were out of town. She'd had to make do with responses to a classified ad she'd placed in a local giveaway magazine. It had killed her, using Mickey's computer to authorize the transfer from her account to the magazine's. There was, of course, a surcharge for these kinds of ads, the woman had explained to Sandi when she had booked. That had set her back a few thousand, and had made Sydney seem that much father away. And now, with Mickey's departure as imminent as the arrival of a propitious envelope bearing the news of acceptances, scholarships, financial aid grants, Sandi was more determined than ever to get out of Hong Kong. It had become, in her mind, a race to see who could leave first. She had to beat that little prick, to show her family that she too had plans, a vision, was good at something, even if she could never tell anyone what that something was. Her departure would be a resounding reminder that she too had aspirations and dreams and that Mickey wasn't the family's only success. Xonia gave her an address on Plantation Road and Sandi said she would be there.

It irked her that the boys on the wall still taunted her and now left Mickey alone. "Whore," they shouted. It was some small satisfaction that they too would hear of Sandi's emigration after the fact. Her absence would be a monument to their own inability to get themselves anywhere other than to the beach for the morning swell and then to the wall in the afternoon. Their collective subconscious could inscribe on the base of that blank monument their own failures—at schools, careers, love and sex—these losers had struck out in so many arenas they would need a pedestal as big as a school bus.

The modern white house was built onto the side of a hill so that the entrance hall was actually on the top flight and she had to descend to find her way to a living room with floor-to-ceiling plate glass windows looking out over Central, Victoria Harbor and, beyond that, Kowloon.

The house was the size of two dozen housing estate flats. Entire blocks of lower-middle-class Hong Kongers could have lived here, Sandi thought, whole families subdividing this living room into numerous flats. Yet only one man lived here, a banker, annoyingly tall yet slightly built, with sandy hair graying at the temples, a similarly grayish complexion, a shaved chest and legs and a semiflaccid penis poking out from a leather, crotchless G-string. A woman whose wrists were bound to a black nylon strap laced around a pulley screwed into the ceiling was panting and leaning so that the pulley took all of her weight. The Englishman held a wooden paddle in his hand and was spanking the girl. In between thwacks he was spitting on the red marks the paddle left on her buttocks.

There were five gweilo girls sitting at a sectional leather sofa around an intricately carved, dark wood coffee table. Each of them wore a chastity belt like Sandi had seen in the shop. They were younger and prettier than the doms who hung around the shop and she didn't recognize any of them. The girls were taking turns sniffing up a white powder sifted out on the glossy jacket of a heavy book about Chinese ceramics, before lying back, sipping from champagne flutes and then almost shouting at each other in Russian. Taking the scene in—the spanking, the drugs, the Russians—Sandi thought about turning around and leaving. This didn't seem safe. What she liked about her work was the control, the fact that she was in charge. This appeared reckless, like the beginning of a long and difficult evening, the whole goal of which was to reach uncharted sexual and psychological realms. This was the opposite of what attracted her to BDSM in the first place. And those Russians with their teased blond and brown hair, silicon tits and tireless appetite for drugs, there was about them an air of violent, mercenary willingness to do whatever it took for a big score. She turned to walk out and saw Xonia coming from the kitchen, wearing a black leather bustier, black panties and thigh-high patent leather boots. She was in full dom gear tonight.

"Sandi!" Xonia said, taking her by the arm, "How wonderful! Have you met the girls?"

And instead of leaving, Sandi thought about the money, about how many dull sessions with the American magazine writer it would take to equal just one night up here on the Peak. Just this one night and she could book her ticket, board that plane and get out of here forever, sky to sunnier climes where she could ply her trade among the better-equipped, more professional dungeons of Sydney and make a new life away from the housing estates, the boys on the rock, the same-sameness of it all. She let Xonia guide her back into the room.

The Englishman looked up. "Oh, wicked, wicked, that's what we've needed: a Chinese girl."

Xonia took her down another staircase to a bedroom where Sandi could change, handing her a chastity belt. Sandi slipped out of her black skirt, white blouse and cotton panties, stashing them in her Prada bag, which she zipped up and took the precaution of hiding in a closet behind a dehumidifier. Who knew what these people were capable of? She stepped into the chastity belt, the shiny aluminum feeling like she had a saucepan strapped to her thighs. Pushing the nylon belt with its steel clasp into a slot on the side of the crotch plate, she heard a metallic click and then realized Xonia hadn't given her the keys. Checking herself in the mirror, her small breasts bobbing as she tied her hair back in a tight bun, she didn't like the faint look of fear she saw in her own eyes, an unfamiliar diffidence that she hadn't seen in herself since her own adolescence. She wanted to get this over with as soon as possible.

Back in the living room, Xonia gave a roll call of Russian names. Jenyas and Natashas and Annas. Sandi listened politely, taking a seat on one of the sofas, sipping from a champagne flute she was offered. The Russians nodded at her, appraising her with quick up and down looks as if calculating what portion of tonight's proceeds this newcomer might be entitled to. There was murmuring of "Chinoise," and then the girls went back to their banter in Russian, pointedly ignoring Sandi.

"He's a gentleman," Xonia said from behind her, placing a hand on her shoulder. "Nothing to fear, darling, nothing to fear."

Sitting naked in the house's frigid air gave her goose bumps. The banker went on with his spanking and spitting, pausing occasionally to check his own erection and stroke himself. He seemed to not even notice the rest of the girls waiting on the sofa; in his single-mindedness he reminded Sandi, somehow, of Mickey and his relentless studying toward a goal. A rack was rolled in. Then a black table like a pommel horse on which the sub lay face down with a padded mask over her eyes and her arms and legs strapped and spread. One by one the Russians took their turns, standing for a moment while the Englishman would dig a key ring from his pocket and motion for Xonia to unlock the chastity belt. Their pubes were always darker than the dyed top hair, Sandi noticed, and depilated to thin little strips like follicled racing stripes. Xonia would apply a pair of nipple clamps and a dog collar. Sandi could tell the clamps weren't that tight by the girls' indifferent reactions to their placement. Breathing heavily from his exertions, the Englishman would do a quick once-over of the girl in question, asking her name and then order her into the black pommel horse where Xonia would strap her down, making sure the restraints were tight.

There was a production line aspect to the whole affair, an industrialization of sadomasochism that left Sandi feeling uneasy. The Englishman, his wispy, dirty-blond hair now bobbing with each thwack, was the foreman of this assembly line of abuse. The decibel level of the women's gasps was his quality control. The red welts on their bottoms his finished products. When each girl was let out of the restraints, gingerly rubbing her bottom as she walked back to the sofas, he would pause to admire his handiwork. "Thank you, master," each girl would sigh in accented English. And they would quickly wet a finger in their mouths, dip it into the cokey on the table and then apply some of the powder to their stinging posteriors to numb the pain. When they sat back down, it was on their knees rather than backsides.

It soon became apparent that Sandi was to be the last. Each of the Russians was being called up in succession. There was still time to withdraw, Sandi figured. She could pull Xonia aside and demand the key to her belt. By now, however, she began to feel competitive with these dismissive Russians. She hated the idea that she would seem weak compared to them, that by taking her leave she would confirm to them her inferiority. She'd never encountered this before, this sort of overt racism in the BDSM world. If anything, because Chinese doms were so rare, she had always been treated exceptionally well, and because of her looks been able to charge even more than her gweilo counterparts. In Sydney, of course, she'd been an exotic, and accorded the appropriate amount of respect. She had relished that feeling of being different but superior, so unlike the sensation she had in Hong Kong of being yet another statistic in the great masses of Cantonese. And again, she thought about the money that would ease her ultimate flight. If that meant a few minutes of discomfort at the hands of this obsessive Englishman, then she figured she could stand a little pain.

The fear she felt, that she had detected earlier in herself, was the cold fear of the inevitable, that this machine of abuse was relentlessly working its way toward her, that she would be taken in and fed down the conveyer belts toward the paddle and spit out, damaged but much, much richer. Perhaps this would be the end of her career. She could take her money, move to Sydney and start anew, away from the BDSM scene, get a normal job, do something in the straight world, become a bartender or waitress, commence a regular life. There would be a certain logic to that as well. And it would be fresh and adventurous and even that life's banalities would seem exciting and challenging to her, occurring in that far-away, dry climate among a taller, more expansive race of men and women. She could marry one of those gweilos with their tooty voices and huge feet. She'd never thought about that before: raising a family Down Under. Kids who would grow up and know wide streets and spacious rooms and fine weather and clean beaches. She imagined it as being a way to make everything right with her life, to erase the unfairness of being born a girl instead of a boy, to free the next generations from the tyranny of her own. That possibility, of changing not just the locale but the content of her life, now added to the trepidation inspired by this den of clinical punishment. This house, with its whores and john and violence all in the name of commerce, its hierarchy of gweilos and Chinese, its presumption that pain could be bought and sold like a commodity, it represented everything that was wrong about Hong Kong. The city demanded this pain from its inhabitants in the form of tiny apartments and dead-end lives, and in return you received a wage, some small salary for your hurt and suffering. Wasn't that why her parents were so eager to have Mickey go overseas? They too understood this but had never actually put words to those thoughts. As she watched the spanking, she came to see that this was Hong Kong in microcosm, everything about the place reduced to one night of suffering. The girls kept on plowing through the cokey and drinking. Sandi, despite Xonia's imploring, turned down the drugs. She guessed that would only draw her in deeper, make her even more complicit in this whole affair.

A crescendo of sorts had been reached. The last of the Russians had been duly thwacked. The Englishman had worked up a tremendous sweat so that his sallow skin now glistened. His penis now stood at a jaunty sixty-degree angle as he turned around, breaking open a pack of pills and swallowing one with some water. "I'm ready now," he said with his back to the sofa.

Xonia crooked her index finger back and forth toward Sandi, and Sandi took her place in front of the Englishman. Just as Xonia undid the chastity belt, the Englishman turned around and exhaled. Sandi caught his rank, sour-dairy breath full on her face as she saw his reddened, fatigued, stoned eyes. They didn't even seem like eyes, but rather like two clumps of eye-shaped wax stuck into his sockets. The pupils were dilated yet dull. The jaundiced, yellowy whites marbled with veins. She'd seen these sorts of eyes before, on the boys who stood by the wall. When they were stoned, after they'd been in the water all day, their eyes had a similar pointless cruelty. Then he said exactly what the boys would always say, "You whore."

He looked her up and down, his bitter breath coming faster. "You hairy little Chinese whore."

Sandi didn't wax herself to the extreme degree of the Russian women, and so by contrast her mons seemed positively hirsute compared to her predecessors. "Clamp her. Strap her in." And Sandi's breasts were clamped, pinching her nipples so that they stung a little bit. If this was as bad as it got, she could take it. Think of the money. Think of her future. She was splayed on the pommel horse, a mask placed over her face, arms and legs strapped down by the heavy buckles. The world was black now. She could still smell the Englishman's breath, could hear his exhalations accelerate as he arranged himself behind her. She had the sensation of falling, sliding down and into some sort of machine of terror. This was real fear, not the playacting kind she drew out of her customers at the shop. This was out of control.

As the spanking began, at first a vibrating stinging that emanated from her buttocks and up her sides, and then an emanating round, burning sensation that seemed to jump from her rear to her head, making her skull ache each time the paddle connected, she tried to hold firm to the positive images in her mind. Sydney. Her future. A beach somewhere. A long, sandy cove where it was always sunny, bright, breezy. A day that went on forever. But the pain soon pushed everything else out. She would never do this again. Never. This was it.

Then, miraculously, the Englishman paused in his paddling.

"Strap one on, mistress," Sandi heard him say.

And then lips on her ears. "I'll pick a small one," Xonia whispered. "It'll be lubed. Just relax."

"No," Sandi said. No one had given her a safe word and she had forgotten to ask for one. She listened as buckles were unclasped. The Englishman was breathing heavily.

"Fuck that little Chinese ass."

"What's the safe word?" Sandi asked.

There wasn't one. She lay there, exposed, strapped down, as vulnerable as an abandoned sand castle on a beach full of malicious boys. There is a realm of panic and fear that goes beyond reason and emotion. She cried and pleaded. Stop this, please, Xonia, stop this. She would have licked boots to escape from this. She knew what was coming, she'd seen the movies. She had never let anyone do that to her. And as much as she'd ever thought about it, it was to decide she would never, ever do that.

There was some shuffling about behind her, and the prodding head of something at her rectum, and then a painful sliding sensation, a sharp stabbing that felt neither pleasurable nor painful but simply violating, something going in where stuff should only go out.

"Just keep breathing, darling," Xonia whispered from behind. "If you relax it's easier. Think of the money."

She detected the rest of the girls going quiet and watching. Sandi tried to keep perfectly still as Xonia worked the dildo in and out. Xonia, despite being complicit in Sandi's betrayal, was trying to be gentle, choosing a slim phallus, lubing it, easing it in. She had herself, at different times, been the receiving end.

Hold on, Sandi told herself. It will finish. Someday, at some point, this feeling will stop and I'll be out of here, away from these people, gone from this city, free.

"Pull out, mistress," the Englishman said. "She needs to know her master."

The sounds of a condom package being peeled open. She felt his damp legs on the inside of her thighs as he took up position behind her. He would be much bigger than the dildo Xonia had used. She heard the Russian girls laughing now. This, apparently, was turning out to be a good joke.

Sandi screamed and began fighting against the restraints, panicking, bucking against the leather. A plug like a belted squash ball was stuck in her mouth and buckled behind her neck. She couldn't scream. She concentrated on breathing through her nose. She tried to think about the money.

■ ■ ■

Now she hung around with the boys on the wall. She wore baggy T-shirts and long Bermuda shorts and whenever the crushed-up grapefruit soda can with the smoldering chunk of hash was passed around she took greedy hits from it, bogarting the pipe so long that one of the boys would eventually grab it from her. She had become the beach wench. The "Shek O" grinder, one of the boys called her.

Mickey had left for college in Vancouver. Now it was only her. When her parents passed by the wall, her mother on her way to do the shopping and her father on his way back from work, they'd avert their eyes rather than look at Sandi. Not because she was an embarrassment, but because she was always so angry with them. But was it really their fault? If Mickey had won a scholarship, generous financial aid, this would have been different. But there were so many bright students in Hong Kong, in China, in all of Asia, that the universities told them they would welcome Mickey, but he would have to pay his own way. Did they really have a choice? Where else could they find the money but in Sandi's account? And rather than ask her, they'd simply told Mickey to transfer the money from Sandi's account to her parents', and from theirs to the university's.

One morning, Sandi had logged on to check her balance. Nothing.

She pulled on a pair of jeans and walked to the beach and waited by the wall. It was spring. The boys were just getting back from the morning swell.

BABY

■ ■ ■

Philip Huang

S uch a warm night, not a wisp of fog. This is not now, this is 1972. All over the city, windows are being opened or left open and sounds drift out: music, water running, the tiny clinking of dishes you might mistake for the twinkling of stars overhead. In San Francisco's Mission District, above a bookstore, a little apartment begins its vigil over Valencia Street. Now a bit of breeze gets caught in its curtains, hiding and fussing, hiding and fussing like a toddler in its mother's skirt, so that from the street it looks like a bashful sort of flirtation and, alternately, the fluttering gaze of someone falling toward sleep, a little nap you didn't plan for but don't object to either.

On this pleasant night, in this little apartment on Valencia Street, the shower is running and the story has already begun.

■ ■ ■

When he opened the bathroom door, steam rushed all around him and Baby felt like he was stepping off a spaceship into a dreamy, alien atmosphere: a cloud of moist, feeble thoughts through which the dark voice of a candle throbbed and retreated, throbbed and retreated.

He lay down on the bed and closed his eyes.

"Happy birthday," a voice says.

PHILIP HUANG's work has appeared in *Queer PAPI Porn* and *Take Out*, and he was the winner of the 2000 Poz/Artery Poetry Contest. He gives countless thanks to the writers in his life—Tim Arevalo, Tyne Balance, Joel Tan, Napoleon Lustre—and dedicates this story to all those who write because they have to, even if they don't want to. He was born in Taipei, Taiwan, in 1975.

"I'm twenty," Baby says. "God. Twenty. Twenty, I'm twenty," he practiced saying.

Above him, Baby heard a match being lit, then the sucking in of breath.

A hand offered him a joint and Baby toked deeply.

"I got a problem," he said. "I've fallen in love."

"Uh-oh," said the voice wearily. "What's the name of this man? Geronimo? Egg Foo-Young?"

Baby giggled and smoke burst from his nostrils. "Look what you made me do. Stop talking about him," he said, and yawned and stretched. "You don't know nothing about love."

"I don't?"

"Do you?"

"I do. I do. And you do?"

"Oh yes. Ooh, yes, yes, yes."

"What's he do to you that's so special?" A palm ran down Baby's chest. "Bet I could make you forget him altogether." A mouth closed over Baby's mouth and Baby felt the bed sink away beneath him.

When he opened his eyes, he looked at Samuel for a long minute, suddenly stoned.

"This is the decade it's all going to happen," he told Samuel.

"What's going to happen?" Samuel asked, earnestly. "Tell me."

Baby thought about it. "Oh. Just everything."

"*Everything*," Samuel repeated, and the two of them stared up at the ceiling happily.

■ ■ ■

His mind a train, and in that moment of smoke and tonnage and screaming iron, no matter how brief, he might believe he might be lifted up and away, up and away—

Baby fell on top of Samuel, whose back felt hot and cooked.

Still here. Train come and gone.

He traded stares with the pimple at the base of Samuel's neck.

"I'm going in the kitchen," Baby declared absently.

Samuel nodded into the pillow.

What a comforting word. Yes, of course, I'm going in the kitchen. A kitchen, a hearth. A *home*. The rest could be imagined so long as you had a kitchen.

But there really wasn't a kitchen, as in a separate room. There was a living room, a square of wood floor the size of two parking spaces, two tall, narrow windows, an old brown sofa, and, in one corner, a fridge and a squat stove, like two giant sucked caramels. Baby padded quickly across the wood floor and pulled a bottle of rum from the freezer.

Back at the home, they had a *mess hall*. All stainless steel, like those tables where you cut dead people up. Everybody called it "the home," but that was wishful thinking if he'd ever heard one. He saw what happened to those boys who got picked up by foster families, heard the stories when they ended up back in the home meaner than ever.

He was sixteen when they turned him out. He had packed up some of his clothes and navigated through the crowd of boys smoking on the steps ("Good-bye, good-bye!" they had called, slapping hands) and then walked to a diner a little ways into town and sat down at the counter next to a trucker who was wiping a plate with a piece of toast. "You must've been hungry," Baby had said. (Was this how men talked to each other?) "Still am," the man had replied.

And just like that, a ride out of town.

And just like that, a ride out of any town.

And invariably, when the day's driving had been done and the truck pulled into some desolate eave, a hand would clap behind Baby's neck.

"Now. How's about some company for the night?" they'd ask, not really asking.

Well, blow jobs could mean company, too, Baby supposed. A company that hired anyone who applied. Anyone at all.

One town, then another, some no more than a gas station and few stands of pies or produce. Some no more than a sign on the side of the road: Rushfield, Golden Rod, Bear Creek, Fairfield. After Fairfield, Modesto.

Modesto, the name of a humble magician.

They (Baby and a trucker nicknamed, improbably, Isotope) had arrived in Modesto near midnight, and Baby hopped off and walked across a gravel lot toward the john while the truck was filled up for the last leg of the run toward the Bay. The john was a little concrete deal set before a huge expanse of darkness, and for the single yellow bug light dangling from its eave, Baby couldn't see where he was headed. He didn't have to piss that badly, but he was aching for a little of the snort the last trucker had given him. As he walked closer to the john, he began to make out the lean knife of a figure spliced into the cone of light, so thin it might be a girl, propped against one wall of the john, smoking a cigarette with a careful indifference that Baby immediately recognized. He walked slower, trying to see if the figure would look up. It didn't. There was a danger, Baby fingered the blade in his pocket, but he knew it wasn't that sort of danger. He passed the figure, and still it didn't look up. Baby rounded the corner and went into the john. It was surprisingly clean inside, and smelt of bleach and lime. A bright white place, humming with light. He thought of the figure outside. The dark slit of it.

When he stepped out, he fished a cigarette from his pocket.

"You got a light?" he asked the figure.

It looked up.

Baby took a breath. He took it right out of his own lung.

It was a boy, all right.

Instead of pulling out a match or a lighter, instead of even pulling the cigarette from his mouth and offering it to Baby, the boy leaned forward and brought his face close to Baby's, slowly, until the tips of their cigarettes, extending from their lips, touched.

That was it. They were lit. Every dream, all their years ahead: lit.

A shepherd to follow.

Samuel.

Oh Samuel.

Baby wiped his mouth now and felt his way back to the bed and slipped under the covers. Samuel turned toward him and grunted deeply, a happy sound. Baby's own skin felt clean, but Samuel's was still cooked. Outside, on the street below, he heard the heavy doors of a truck unsticking, boots landing on the sidewalk, then the door shutting. Through the window, he could see the panes of the glass on the building across the alley, the drowsy eyelets of their curtains backlit by lamps.

It struck Baby that this was a moment not quite happening, a dream that would haze into white at any moment. This whole life of theirs so far, this sweet night, just a glimmer, without substance, and when he came to he would have to say, "Yeah, man, thanks for the light," and walk off again into the night, across the gravel, back onto Isotope's blue metal truck, and never look back from whatever point he might be now, instead. (And not what they had done either, back in the john, on top of the sink, pulling and pulling at each other slowly, the gorged skin of the moment popping faintly around them. No. Not that either.)

The thought fascinated him, and he blinked to see if it were really true. Then Samuel coughed, a sound so real and ordinary that Baby smiled and cupped Samuel's cock until it nodded off and coiled lazily into his hand, and then he felt himself fall asleep with his nose along the lip of Samuel's right ear.

■ ■ ■

Baby was ten again. His mama was yellow and Sheriff was white.

Black women, some hoisting infants on their hips, floated looks above Baby's head and tisked-tisked.

Look at her, their eyes said to each other. *Who she think she is now? Woman like that, who never needed nothing, this yellow whore who never left her plot of land by the railroad where she raised that mongrel of a child ("Look at this child. Damn near a negro. Damn near."), this woman nobody can remember being acknowledged by so much as a nod, who was rumored to have a slanted twat so maybe that's why a nigger would want to touch her ('cause an unschooled nigger was nothing if not curious)—who she think she is now? A nobody. Nobody.*

Still, nobody deserved what she got.

This slip of a body that Sheriff's men had dragged out from beneath her own house and covered with a sheet when they didn't know what else to do with it, that someone (*a man, you can bet, yes'm, a man, a jealous man*) had hog-tied and slit open and stuffed in the crawl space of her own house, so cut up you couldn't tell that the sheet over it was white originally till someone told you, so cut up even Sheriff held a handkerchief over his nose—

Covered up, but not before the women could get a good long look at what they had compared themselves to, standing nude before their long mirrors, and what their men would've crawled over broken glass to get a sniff of.

■ ■ ■

They slept a little while, then Baby woke Samuel and got dressed and went to the bar on the corner.

Not much to look at. Just a little bitty place with a wood dance floor and lightbulbs the owners smoked out over a candle. A place so half-minded but stubborn, so airy but insistent, it felt like hot shallow breaths on the back of your neck all the time. That's what you walked into, a room poised on the edge of sex, electrified with the possibility of what could happen between men, those deep silent fucks for which time stopped and plunged, and stopped again.

The white boys, all fucked up on something scary, propped against the walls with their johns, would look up once in a while to watch the colored boys make like they were dry-fucking on the dance floor. And, Baby, if he felt like, would throw them a look like a hock of spit—like Yeah? So what?—without losing the roll of Samuel's pelvis against his own.

Samuel had grown tall and wide, shoulders like volleyballs wrapped in cotton: a flagship, a mast cutting high and steady through eddies of men on the dance floor. Half the eyes in the room were on him. The other half were on Baby.

For Baby, though short, possessed a density, a thickness, that spoke of power, like the arc of a bow just drawn back. Half-cocked. Ready to spring. Above all that, Baby had the indifference of a man who was used to being looked at. Men looked at him and their mouths went sour from sucking on their own tongues, their noses ached with sniffing.

If anyone knew the choreography of Baby's body, it was Samuel.

For it was Samuel's body that traced out the complex logarithms for Baby to follow.

For when they danced, they talked with their hipbones in a language only people born with the dance could understand.

Hold still. Now grind.

I'm slowing down, where are you?

Give me more.

Careful what you wish for.

Give it. Give it.

You sure you want it?

I do. I do.

People in the room still?

For when Baby danced with Samuel, the walls of the room, the floor beneath, all fell away, ribbons from a box that held only him and his.

■ ■ ■

Sheriff bent down and looked Baby in the eye.

"You know what this is?" Sheriff touched the metal star on his chest. "You know what this means, boy? Means I got a right to ask questions and people got an obligation to answer me. Baby, look at your mama there. Look at her and think real hard about what I'm going to ask you because I'm only going to ask once. Baby: Where's your daddy at?"

Baby didn't answer. He wasn't ever supposed to talk to a white man, even when asked a question he knew the answer to.

His daddy was a soldier. His daddy had said to his mama, "Soon-hee, this is a table. This is a kettle. And that there's a baby." His mama had said, "Table. Kettle. Baby." All his life, Baby never knew another name. His daddy had said that morning, "Baby, you go outside and play. Look what a fine day it is. It's a fine day, ain't it? Go outside and play. I need to have a word with your mother." Then he had winked and patted Baby's tummy and guided him out the door.

So what does a white man, a sheriff at that, know about what a black man is capable of? Baby looked at the railroad tracks running all the way down to the sky until something on the edge of his vision rustled.

The mass under the sheet had managed to sit up, bolt-straight, and lift an arm. She was pointing at the railroad. Her jaws moved up and down. She looked at her son and pointed at the railroad more intently.

Baby tried to help. *Yes, Mama. That's right. The train. That's where he went. The train.*

Her eyes darted between Baby and the horizon. Still she pointed, like a young child trying to show a parent where the monster was hiding. The air was hazy with flies, the trees clogged with anything else born out of the Mississippi mud that's small enough to fly. Baby tried to please his mother by looking where she pointed, to show he understood. After a while, he realized it wasn't the railroad at all he was looking at, but the long ragged range of Samuel's spine.

■ ■ ■

For it was Samuel who knew of the tea saucer on Baby's back that was filled with cream. That was soft, runny cream left out in sunlight, the one sure mark that he was something other than black.

No one knew where to place a man like Baby, with his dusty high yellow skin and his hair real straight in some parts and real kinky in others, with his one eye hooded and the other a clean blade of almond.

It wrapped him, the passing glances of folks on the street hardening into approximating stares, the nebulous and impenetrable skin of an atom.

Samuel was a quarter Indian himself, but you couldn't tell by looking. Bones cut so sharp and skin so dark, his head seemed in silhouette even in full light, all apples and angles. Kissing the skin of a boy like Samuel, that's the glimpse of evil. Skin so oiled and dark you run the danger of seeing your own face in it, seeing your ugly please me please me face that no one ought to see lest you turn to salt.

Samuel said his mother's people a few generations back hunted buffalo, though Baby knew that buffalo haven't been free on the continent to hunt for well over a century. They made stuff up as they went along if someone wanted a story. If Samuel's people hunted buffalo, then Baby's people built the Great Wall of China. ("Maybe that's how they built that damned wall, with buffaloes.")

Samuel always laughed that if they had a kid together, they'd end up with one hell of a wrong-looking child.

Well, children weren't something too much on Baby's mind. What's he want with a child anyway? But you talk long enough about something that you don't have, never going to have, and it starts to mesh right into the grain of your life so that you forget what fiction is. If Baby drank a beer at breakfast, Samuel would frown and say, "Aw, now, Papa, what kind of example is that for our girl?" If Samuel left some toenails on the pillow, Baby would chide, "I can't be cleaning after you once that child comes!"

Sometimes when he was alone, Baby would sense something vague just to the left and back of him, some sense of a round-headed child, a little girl maybe, sitting there waiting to get her hair braided. And he'd touch his throat and laugh at himself for thinking such a ridiculous thing and then feel a little ache after.

■ ■ ■

Baby said: *I'm sorry. I didn't know what he was doing to you in there. I thought he was making love to you in there.*

His mama was standing now, on the steps of the porch. She was barely grown, Baby thought, barely a woman. She dipped her head and fanned the back of her neck with her hand. Open gashes draped her torso. Bones gleamed from beneath the wounds like the eyes of animals hiding in her body. Her breasts peeled to either side of the longest gash and the thick hairs of her genitals were clotted with blood.

Baby fetched a glass from the house and filled it with water from the pump, but she didn't want any. She seemed preoccupied. Again and again, she rubbed at her wrist, her palm. Killing time. Waiting.

And he might have mistaken it for a twitch, but there was no mistaking. She winked.

■ ■ ■

Samuel whined at breakfast about the milk being too cold.

"Too cold? You getting fussy on me, or you just getting fussy on me?"

"I ain't kidding, Baby. Something about my head, I don't know what, but that cold is hurting my head, like right here, right at the back of my neck." He rolled his head to demonstrate.

"Oh," Baby said dismissively. "I get that, too, when I eat ice cream too fast. Just take small sips then. Be a good boy."

Samuel didn't argue but sat holding the back of his neck. With his other hand, he raised the glass to his lips and took small sips like Baby said. A good boy.

Samuel had to be down on the corner by quarter to eight each morning to catch the Muni to BART, an easier schedule than when he was just a packer and had to be there at six. Now he took care of orders and worked a clean nine to six shift. Baby himself flitted through jobs, gas stations and restaurants, mostly in the gray cold months of the year, but when the weather brightened, as much as it does in the city, he said his farewells to employment. It wasn't that they had money, had the luxury of unemployment. They were making it month to month as it was, but it was certainly more than they were used to: Samuel was union now, and making good-enough wages to keep them both afloat for the moment.

Mornings Baby woke with Samuel's skin hot against his own, sometimes opening his eyes to find them blinking against Samuel's cheek. Usually he woke first, and he might watch there a moment and not touch his lover's face nor soothe his lover's low murmurings against whatever dream (the final hour of dreaming being the most vivid and breathless). And if Baby could not resist touching, either the hair or the face, he might have a little more time before Samuel's body began to wake, the tiny trembling moving up and up him until his eyes burst open and his torso heaved with breath and a yawn unclotted from his throat, all parts of one grand, luxurious, agonizing motion, as though he were pierced through and through and they were looking eye to eye, if not in love then in recognition.

Waiting on a couple of eggs on the stove and some toast in the oven while Samuel showered and shaved, the coffee poured and in hand, Baby settled into the first pose of being separated for the day. His legs crossed at the thighs for the cold, the coffee mug halfway to his lips, his mind trying to work out the knot of some dream he might've had the night before.

After Samuel left for work, Baby liked to sit in the window, one leg up, the ashtray beneath the raised thigh, and watch the street beginning to wake: cars with music drifting out as they passed, children traveling in bubbling clusters, the grocer across the street setting out displays of oranges on the sidewalk. And if it was summer, Baby liked to place his chin on his knee and wait for a nap to take him closer to noon.

Then maybe to the park, but maybe just see what the old bookstores and record shops might have that he hadn't seen before. He'd set out of the house with a sense of adventure, though his adventures, usually, never extended past the ten-block area of his neighborhood: the Mission. What mattered was the sense of mischief, a sense of freedom to invent his daily persona: he could be the bemused stroller, taking delight at every window front, sitting anonymously good-natured in a Mexican diner; or he could be something darker, at the station, posing the practiced casual pose from his old loitering days, cataloging the real hustlers who worked the station's men's room, washing their hands for long minutes, checking the shine of their hair in the mirror along with prospective johns. Occasionally one of them would try to catch Baby's eye, but immediately they'd know him for what he was, and there's nothing worse, nothing, than one whore propositioning another.

Oh, the lores he invented for himself, the selves he imagined.

The persistent drowsiness like a hand about his waist.

Every day like this, the hours laid out before him, a large ballroom scattered with old furniture, all worn uniquely to his form, and he could sit here and there, here and there, by the window, against a building, on a bus. When asked how his day was, Baby did not recall much of anything except these kinds of poses.

This undocking, this drifting through the day: it was a present he gave himself. A person could let himself wander anywhere he pleased, so long as he had a harbor to return to each night.

■ ■ ■

That evening Baby met Samuel at the Sixteenth Street Station like he always did Fridays, but Samuel wasn't there. After half an hour, Baby walked home alone, muttering to himself. *Ever heard of a phone? Ever heard of calling someone to say you going to be late?*

"Brother!"

Baby hadn't seen the man or the commotion behind him. Two blocks up a crowd had taken over the street, dancing in the dimming light. Too festive to be another war protest.

The man who called out to him looked overjoyed. His blond hair was wrapped to approximate a head of dreadlocks. The man threw up his hands to imitate a goalpost, so excitedly that he nearly fell over. "It's over, bro. It's over!" he cried.

That was the thing. No men left in this town except fags, college students, and hippies.

Baby tried to walk past but the man kept at his side.

"I mean, shit! Haven't you heard yet? Saigon?"

Baby stopped. "What about Saigon?"

"Saigon fell! It's over! The war, man. You know, the war's over!"

When Baby didn't react, the man paused and took a good look. Sometimes the angle of lighting brought out the narrowness and up-wardness of Baby's eyes, accentuated the wide cheeks that sloped into the corners of his mouth. And a yellow streetlight could bring out certain tinctures of his skin—

"Hey," the man said. "You guys won. Congratulations." He joined his fists together at his chest and made a little bow at Baby and then skipped off toward the crowd.

Crazy-ass cracker.

What the hell was there to celebrate? He didn't follow the war too closely but Baby knew it was lots of black boys out there in the jungle, and black boys who got their legs blown off, and boys kids who just plain died, in the mud, in the jungle, pieces of them left to be found and cataloged and a letter sent. And on the flip side, Vietnam. He'd seen enough villages on fire, seen enough dirty crying children to last him another lifetime. The whole thing was a mess. So, again, what the hell was there to celebrate?

And this was a thought that came uniquely to Baby: how you gonna talk about who won and who lost to a man that came from two peoples who, in another generation, in another war, had been bent on putting bullets through each other's heads?

He turned the corner and took the long route home to avoid the crowd, shaking his head. The wind was lifting leaves off the ground. He wanted Samuel.

■ ■ ■

"Finally." Samuel had shrugged the night they had arrived in San Francisco. Samuel was fifteen, a year younger than Baby, but he'd crisscrossed the country three times over already and decided they should spend some time in Frisco, while the weather was nice.

They were standing in the lobby of an old hotel like those you see in old movies with comic, fumbling bellhops. Curls of wood climbed the tall, domed ceiling, dull brass panels gazed serenely from the elevators, and the parched paper on the walls swirled with so many flowers that Baby's nose twitched with the acrid scent of open roses. Just beyond, there might be a grand ballroom. Thin pale women in beaded dresses might spill laughing from the elevators at any moment. But everything looked heavy, as if logged with water.

Baby whispered, "Where are we?" He didn't want to disturb the old men asleep on velvet armchairs by the mute TV.

"The Tenderloin," Samuel explained simply.

Baby smoothed the legs of his jeans and patted down his hair as they approached the counter.

"We need a room," Samuel told the clerk, a fat, redheaded boy reading something on his lap.

"We charge by the hour, not the quarter or the half hour. One minute into the hour and we charge you full," the clerk recited to the women in his magazine.

"We need two weeks."

"First and last day deposit now. Room open on the sixth floor. Shower and toilet located at the end of the hall. Cash only and don't leave nothing on the sheets," the clerk told them.

The elevator gave a sigh when they told it to move. Samuel asked, "Those truckers, they ever give you money? D'you ever ask?"

"Sure. Sometimes."

"Good enough," Samuel said.

Nights were for work, but days were for themselves. Sometimes they'd have enough money for a stretch of three or four days for themselves. For bare-chested naps in Dolores Park, chess games at the wharf, scenes from a movie, a montage of summer days. It wasn't the sort of heat Baby was used to in Mississippi, nothing that bred flies and baked trees and blurred your sightline. It was a heat that lulled you, sang to you in deep clear chords with its palm on your belly. They didn't have to work every night. If they worked, they worked simultaneously, sometimes as a team. That way, neither of them would ever have to sleep alone.

One week passed. Then another. Pretty soon, a whole month. The weather started turning chilly earlier and earlier in the day, Baby remembered. Then one morning, when he staggered home from a john, placing one foot in front of another up all those steps that seemed both shallow and deep, down the dark hall whose doors oozed at him like the bellies of large animals, when he finally steadied the nauseating swilling of time long enough to work the complex machinery of the doorknob, Samuel was not there. Baby stood in the little room for a long, long time and then the floor rose and rose until it pressed against his face and the last thing he remembered thinking, so lucidly and calmly he could hear it even now:

Well, that's the trouble with being sheep.

He had known it all along. He had known how it would turn out. And now here it was.

But he had been wrong, wrong. For a hand had reached into his deep white sleep and pulled him up by the collar.

And then that hand slapping his cheeks.

And then Baby's own voice screaming, accusing.

And then Samuel's voice: "No, no. I didn't. I'm right here."

And Baby bobbed to the surface.

Samuel had turned out Baby's elbow and found the tiny clot nestled inside there like a beetle. But there had been no questions, no more words. There would be time for all of that later.

Time for all of that later.

Were they ever that young? That memory wavered uncertainly in his account of their life so far, tied off from the years that followed, like a knot in a clown's balloon. For the Samuel who had strode confidently to the hotel counter, who slipped like a bug through a hungry city and its lymph nodes of truck stops and men's rooms, the Samuel who could be drenched with the breaths of breathless men, that Samuel seemed to Baby now too youthful and confident to have ever been real. But more than that, and this saddened him: also irretrievable, like a toy lost in the water, like, yes, a childhood game that they've had to give up for this life without magic.

Baby sighed now as he climbed the last flight of stairs.

That was why he clung to Samuel so. They were utterly alone in the world, in the sense that no one else knew the grimy, exciting fairy tale, the furious youth that they had stepped out of once, once upon a time.

■ ■ ■

When Samuel walked in through the door, he looked so limp and chewed up that Baby couldn't find the heart to be angry.

"I'm sorry," Samuel said, sagging against the door. His voice wobbled. "I just plain fell asleep. Can't explain it. Rode all the way out across the Bay before I woke up." He sniffled and rubbed his nose. "You mad?"

Baby looked him up and down.

Samuel asked for a kiss.

"Hells no," Baby said. "And don't you look to get me sick too."

But he lighted a kiss on Samuel's forehead and put him to bed.

In the kitchen, Baby hummed along with the rice as he chopped up a leek to go in with the mushrooms. *Sure is a nice feeling to have your man in bed. Sure is peaceful to have your man be asleep and not be fussing over how much butter you cook your own damn mushrooms in.*

Another voice said, Amen, and Baby nodded.

When he tried to wake Samuel for dinner, he got waved away. "Let me get some sleep," Samuel said heavily. "I'll be fine by tomorrow, I promise."

Baby felt Samuel's forehead. Hot. Definitely hot.

"Sure," he said. "Sick gets what sick wants."

It was early enough to be restless, and Baby had counted on going to the bar with Samuel, but now it looks like he's staying home. It's different when a sick man's in your bed. Can't be hopping all over town when a sick man's in your bed.

Summer nights meant music and long shiny trucks and tough young men in tight jeans, the most beautiful boys he's ever seen, under the window. This time of year, the night air was cool and pleasant, like the cool of a chilled beer can just under your nose. Young men called to each other, to passing cars. Young men who escaped the draft for lack of papers or eyebrows, the same young men who looked tough and available on the benches of Dolores Park. Baby tipped the bottle to his mouth and listened to their friendly greetings.

Hey. Where you been, where you going?

No place, man, no place.

After the dishes, Baby went through the pantry: beer nuts, canned olives, bean spread, bags of salty stuff. That Samuel, he'd eat frosting from a can all three meals if you let him. Behind a gallon jug of salsa, Baby found a tiny box wrapped in red. Sneaky, Baby thought. He had half a mind to open it, but his birthday wasn't more than a week away. If he can wait twenty-four years for this birthday, he can wait a few more days. He put the box back and tried to watch TV, but it was all the same, on every channel: news of Saigon, women running, dragging babies, running toward the embassy, mashed against an iron gate like pressed flowers. Baby yawned and finished his beer and turned off all the lights, washed up, and slid into bed naked.

Samuel felt like a loaf of dough left to rise under a heavy towel. Instinctively, his head turned away and revealed his neck. Baby placed his face into the crook made there, but he couldn't sleep.

■ ■ ■

Distinctly he recalled the cushion of his mother's body underneath him, her tiny steps blurring after a while into flight, that teenage body blowing down the streets, the world blowing by, the two of them born along the ground

What's that word? Buoyant. Buoyancy.

Did she run like that, with a baby strapped to her back like a bundle of kindling, a baby that she could hold up to the powers-that-be at the embassy and push on a plane to anywhere, anywhere at all, because, after all, that baby was one of their own, even if she weren't—

No. She didn't have to. Because his daddy married her. He married her when he didn't have to, when he could've left her to rot and starve in the fields his men had left smoking with bodies.

It had been a clean, safe passage.

"This is a table. This is a chair. And that there's a baby."

"This is a railroad, Baby. You know what a railroad really is?" his daddy would ask, then laugh his deep laugh. They would squat at the edge of the tracks, Baby between his daddy's knees, their fingers on the steel rails, waiting. Then the tremor, a tiny bird heart beating, and Baby would look into his daddy's face. "Now? Is that it? Now?" But his daddy's face would be calm, his eyes closed. The tremor grew more and more, a bird heart, then the heart of some larger animal, a dog's, then a horse's, the feather and fur and hide growing thin until it seemed the heart was beating bare in their palms, until their fingers, still on the rail, began to shake, the dense wall of sound washing closer and closer. "Now?" Baby would ask, getting scared, his legs growing soft. A boy had been killed on the tracks the summer before, his shoe caught between the wood ties. "Now?" The conductor started to blow his horn, once, then twice, then just let it wail, but his daddy would only shush him and press his fingers to the steel.

"Trust me, child. Not yet, not yet—"

Then at the last possible minute, Baby felt his body lifted upwards and backwards, into the air, as if blown by the wind from the passing train, blood rushing through the cords of his little neck, his heart lurching and pumping clots of thoughts and his daddy screaming "Hallelujah!" but then, just then, his feet would land on the coarse gravel again and his daddy's arms would unwind from his torso, and it would grow peaceful and still and green again.

"Wasn't that something?" his daddy would say, his voice near tears. "Something, wasn't that? Remember that feeling, Baby. Remember it. Anytime you think you know what fear is, anytime you forget what the joy of living is, remember that feeling. And you remember that I pulled you back. Me, your daddy. Never trust anyone else to do the same for you."

Eventually the silence took over Baby's mind. Such quiet and darkness, he couldn't tell how much time had passed since he first lay down. He imagined the ceiling was the surface of a sea and they were deep below, where all there is to do is concentrate on the act of breathing. Gently he slipped off Samuel's underwear and tucked his hand where the thighs branched.

■ ■ ■

But Samuel wasn't better by morning, nor the day after that. The whole weekend he stayed in bed and let Baby play mother. Baby cooked up some tea he bought at the herbal pharmacy down the street. He helped Samuel into the bathtub and sponged him. *Who's my baby? Who's Baby's baby?* On Thursday evening, Samuel felt good enough to get up and move around. Just as well, cause it was Baby's birthday and he was going to cook up a heap of a meal.

Samuel leaned against the side of the fridge with a glass of wine— no, with his third glass of wine—and watched while Baby chopped and boiled and washed. A small ham was sitting royally in the oven, a pot of rice simmering with its clean easy smell.

Baby put down his knife and wiped his hands on his apron. "Twenty-four," he said. "Lord."

"Did I ever tell you," Samuel began. "Did I ever tell you how beautiful you are?"

A radio was playing the next floor down, sad and far away. Why was it that far-away music always sounded so sad? The lightbulb, yellow and failing, flickered absently.

Baby picked up his knife. "You drunk, that's what you are."

"Beautiful ain't even the word for it. God damn."

"Leave me alone if you don't want to help me cook."

Samuel circled Baby's waist and kissed his ears. "You want to do something crazy?"

He started grinding his crotch against the cheeks of Baby's ass. He reached around and pressed lightly on each of Baby's nipples.

"You want to?"

Baby's dick stiffened against the sink. His mouth turned up with thoughts of something illegal and wet. He turned around in Samuel's arms and pressed himself into Samuel's crotch.

"Well, do you?" Samuel asked.

Baby could feel Samuel begin to rise under his pajamas. "Maybe. Maybe not."

Samuel moved down onto one knee.

Baby let out a peal of laughter. "Shit," he said. "You just want to give some head." He began to unzip his unfurling crotch, but Samuel's face, just below, was full of piety instead of flirtation, earnestness instead of foreplay.

"Baby, quit. I'm being serious here," Samuel said, but didn't continue. He stole a look at the ceiling, which, Baby supposed, was the closest Samuel ever came to being religious.

"Let me tell you a story," Samuel said.

"A story," Baby repeated. "You're serious."

"Yes, I'm serious here. Okay, a story. There was this man once," Samuel said. "This boy, actually, this kid who thought—

"Wait, that's dumb. Okay, wait. Geese. No, wait," he said, and then stopped. "Wait."

Baby waited. Samuel got this way sometimes when he drank.

"Okay," Samuel continued. "Remember when we just arrived here, living in that hotel? You remember?"

Baby nodded suspiciously.

"There was one night when I'd headed out the door thinking I was just going to find a john, make some quick cash, whatever. But then a bus came, and I thought, sure! And then another bus came and I thought, why not! I don't know. I just kept going and going, one transfer after another, not really sure what I was doing, but all the time doing it just the same. I thought, Baby don't need me. He'll be fine. And what I need *him* for?

"Baby, you know how geese, when they're born, their minds get stuck on the first thing they see, be it their mother or an alarm clock, and they follow it forever? Baby, I saw that was starting to happen with you, you were starting to get stuck on me, and Lord knows if you follow me I'll lead you someplace awful. That's what I was thinking."

Baby's vision milked over. "Why are you telling me this?"

"I'm telling you this because I came back. Because I knew I had to. And wasn't I right? Wasn't I? When I opened the door, I thought you were dead, Baby, dead! But then you started screaming, you remember? Screaming, You fucker! You fucking left me! Didn't you! Didn't you!" Samuel tried to laugh at this, but he only managed to clear his throat. "And I thought, Yes, yes I did. And then, No, no. I couldn't have, could I? Could I have?"

Baby leaned back, hoping the counter was still there. His knees were turning to dough and liquid pushed up his throat, but Samuel caught him square in the eye and held him.

"Listen, Baby. I been thinking. I been thinking a lot, 'specially these few days when you been taking care of me. Listen to me, Baby. I'm telling you this. I'm telling you this is how it is." He looked down a second and when he looked back up, he was sober. "This is it right here. You and me. Two people get so used to making a life together they don't want nothing else. Maybe there ain't nothing else out there. Maybe all there is is in this room, right here, right now."

Baby could have said lots of things. He could have argued or said something smart. But he just stood there like someone dumb, holding out his hand like a begging cup as Samuel slid the ring onto his finger.

You follow me. You follow me forever.
Baby said yes, yes.
Won't be no place awful, I can promise you that.
Baby thought, yes, good, promise.
You a married lady now.
Amen.

Tell me, Baby. Tell me why. Why's a man got to kill a woman like that?
Sheriff's voice trailed off. He looked sadly down at his palms, and Baby knew suddenly what he hadn't wanted to know, what he had known all along, about that white man and his white heart beating beneath his metal star.

Then Baby was off.

Not so much running but slipping along the smooth rails. He could hear the train though it was miles off now, the shudder of the wood ties beneath like the timbre of a low growl that tired more and more. When the house, too, disappeared, he stopped and untied the bundle from his back, and carefully, carefully he peeled back the first layer of pale cotton. But there was only another layer, and another, and then only a tangle of cloth in his hands. Where were the bright eyes, the tiny fists? Where was Samuel?

A dream. Samuel was next to him, a thick lump under the sheet. Baby placed a palm on the sheet to calm himself but there it was, there it bloomed, under his hand, spreading in a circle, spreading wider and wider. His palm came away wet and red.

No no no no no—

Another dream.

■ ■ ■

New Year's Eve.

The air outside was wet and cold and thin, almost not enough air to breathe. Baby sat in the window watching Widow Matthews caning down the street with her eyes set dead ahead of her, determined to fight the wind and gravity itself. If the weather was warmer, Baby would've dangled out the window and called out to her, but now she seemed just another old woman trying to get herself home before dark. Her steps were labored, just left of sync.

Heavy.

Yes ma'am. That's the feeling.

A whole new decade was coming tonight but Baby felt just tired. More like something was ending.

Samuel settled between Baby's legs with a blanket around himself, his face turning orange with the sunset. Baby fed him a bit of wine from his own glass. After a while, they fell asleep. After a little while longer, they were on the bed making love.

Samuel felt a little skinnier, it was true.

Maybe a lot skinnier. Flesh ain't what it used to be. Samuel's skin, that fearful oiled skin, now took on a dullness and a thinness, like cigarette paper near the cherry, like Widow Matthews's cloudy eye. Holding Samuel sometimes felt like holding his own bouquet of knees, and Baby imagined they were two elderly folks resting up for the remainder of their days. Then he thought, Why, we ain't even thirty yet!

Baby tried to remember what they used to feel like to each other naked, but he couldn't. Body grows with you. It was gradual, like an iceberg. You keep your eye on it and it don't seem to move at all, but if you look away and look back—

Baby entered Samuel gently, gently.

Who's moving? Who's still? That's sugar rising through cake, gin sinking through water. Can't tell what's one and what's the other.

They fell asleep again and again, weaved under and over white dreams. In the distance, firework and guns popped faintly.

"Happy New Year's," one of them whispered.

"The eighties," Samuel practiced saying. He said it again, and this time it was as though he were looking at something he'd always heard about and liked to see.

They kissed and folded again into sleep.

Baby was dreaming of Samuel's face seen that first time outside the truck stop john, bathed in yellow like a wash of sepia tone, the sad and sweet quality of a time and place you could ache for but never see again. Another lifetime. That was what struck him. What had struck him, what he had already felt, all those years ago, on the edge of Modesto, a sense of nostalgia so sudden and fleeting that he had no choice but to chase it.

And the man next to him now was surely not the same boy. Not quite.

Baby heard himself sighing in the dream.

"Bad dream?" Samuel asked.

"Yes. A bad dream."

"Do they find him this time? Whoever killed your mama?"

"No. They never do."

"Oh," Samuel said. "Poor Baby," he cooed. And then, "Tell me again. What's it look like?"

"Oh, real cute."

"He?"

"She."

"Is she smart?"

"Oh, real smart. Reads anything you give her."

"That's good. That's beautiful."

They laced hands over Samuel's heart.

In this way, a third person entered their lives.

In this way, Baby and Samuel became parents.

■ ■ ■

When Samuel died, tall blond grass grew up around the bed.

Baby's mother came and stroked his hand.

Poor Baby—

Is a train coming, Mama?

Poor little Baby.

She took out a bit of rope and made a loop around his wrists. He put his chest to the ground and she made a loop around his ankles.

He's gone, Mama. So you were wrong. He didn't kill me. Maybe I killed him.

After a few minutes, when he didn't hear anything else, Baby knew his mama had left him for good.

People in the room still?

It's over, bro. It's over.

What's over?

You know. The story. This is how it ends.

Slivers of sunlight, like knives seen edge on, cut through the slats of wood above, crawling closer as the sun wound across what had to have been a spectacular sky.

Beneath him, the softest earth, though nothing grew.

See? Didn't I promise you? That if you followed me, it won't be no place awful, Baby.

That's the price, ain't it? You love someone and it don't ever end. Not even when he does.

Baby knew, too, what he should have said to Sheriff.

You ask me where my daddy went? You'll never know where. No one will. He jumped on a train that come passing by after he killed Mama and he somewhere far. He was scared. He seen his own face in Mama's skin, seen such evil, the only thing he could do was cut it up.

But who killed who, I ask you.

I begged my daddy to take me with him but he wouldn't. He said the strangest thing. I still remember it. He said, There's a story here you don't want to know and I don't want to tell. He said, You know what a railroad is? A railroad is a piece of the ladder God climbed to heaven after Creation and then kicked to the ground after. Touching the tracks is like touching a piece of sacrament, a piece of His hem. And being on a train is just man's way of trying to get to heaven without really earning it. That train's going to run and run, but it won't never pull in anyplace.

Now what kind of life is that?

What kind of life you suppose that is for my Baby? For my sweet, sweet Baby—

■ ■ ■

Such a warm night, not a wisp of fog.

A sleight of hand, a magic trick. If you blink, if you cough, you've missed it.

In their little apartment on Valencia Street, Baby and Samuel are lying on the bed, talking softly.

"This is the decade it's all going to happen," Baby says. What does he mean? He doesn't know what he means.

"What's going to happen?" Samuel asks. "Tell me."

"Oh," Baby says, after a moment. "Just everything."

"*Everything*," Samuel repeats.

And the two of them look up happily at the ceiling where they don't see what's already beginning to happen, to unfurl, a thought like a sheet of scrim, how it waves and opens and opens and opens. A banner. A painting. They can't see it.

In the painting he will go to the bed. He will kneel there and not move, an entire day, an entire night, whispering into the cooling clay of Samuel's cheek.

Can you hear me? If you can hear me, Samuel, I love you—

But Samuel can't hear. He is far away. When one is so close to the end, what he hears is the darker song.

It doesn't matter. Baby goes on whispering.

I love you, he tells Samuel, *I love you, I—*

Do.

WHO'S IRISH?

■ ■ ■

Gish Jen

In China, people say mixed children are supposed to be smart, and definitely my granddaughter Sophie is smart. But Sophie is wild, Sophie is not like my daughter Natalie, or like me. I am work hard my whole life, and fierce besides. My husband always used to say he is afraid of me, and in our restaurant, busboys and cooks all afraid of me too. Even the gang members come for protection money, they try to talk to my husband. When I am there, they stay away. If they come by mistake, they pretend they are come to eat. They hide behind the menu, they order a lot of food. They talk about their mothers. Oh, my mother have some arthritis, need to take herbal medicine, they say. Oh, my mother getting old, her hair all white now.

I say, Your mother's hair used to be white, but since she dye it, it become black again. Why don't you go home once in a while and take a look? I tell them, Confucius say a filial son knows what color his mother's hair is.

My daughter is fierce too, she is vice president in the bank now. Her

GISH JEN is the author of two novels, *Typical American* and *Mona in the Promised Land*, as well as a collection of stories, *Who's Irish?* Her work has appeared in *The New Yorker*, the *Atlantic Monthly*, and other magazines, and in numerous anthologies, including *The Best American Short Stories of the Century*. She has received grant support from the National Endowment for the Arts, the Guggenheim Foundation, the Radcliffe Institute for Advanced Study, the Lannan Foundation, and the Fulbright Program. She currently holds a Strauss Living from the American Academy of Arts and Letters. She was born in New York City in 1955.

new house is big enough for everybody to have their own room, including me. But Sophie take after Natalie's husband's family, their name is Shea. Irish. I always thought Irish people are like Chinese people, work so hard on the railroad, but now I know why the Chinese beat the Irish. Of course, not all Irish are like the Shea family, of course not. My daughter tell me I should not say Irish this, Irish that.

How do you like it when people say the Chinese this, the Chinese that, she say.

You know, the British call the Irish heathen, just like they call the Chinese, she say.

You think the Opium War was bad, how would you like to live right next door to the British, she say.

And that is that. My daughter have a funny habit when she win an argument, she take a sip of something and look away, so the other person is not embarrassed. So I am not embarrassed. I do not call anybody anything either. I just happen to mention about the Shea family, an interesting fact: four brothers in the family, and not one of them work. The mother, Bess, have a job before she got sick, she was executive secretary in a big company. She is handle everything for a big shot, you would be surprised how complicated her job is, not just type this, type that. Now she is a nice woman with a clean house. But her boys, every one of them is on welfare, or so-called severance pay, or so-called disability pay. Something. They say they cannot find work, this is not the economy of the fifties, but I say, Even the black people doing better these days, some of them live so fancy, you'd be surprised. Why the Shea family have so much trouble? They are white people, they speak English. When I come to this country, I have no money and do not speak English. But my husband and I own our restaurant before he die. Free and clear, no mortgage. Of course, I understand I am just lucky, come from a country where the food is popular all over the world. I understand it is not the Shea family's fault they come from a country where everything is boiled. Still, I say.

She's right, we should broaden our horizons, say one brother, Jim, at Thanksgiving. Forget about the car business. Think about egg rolls.

Pad thai, say another brother, Mike. I'm going to make my fortune in pad thai. It's going to be the new pizza.

I say, You people too picky about what you sell. Selling egg rolls not good enough for you, but at least my husband and I can say, We made it. What can you say? Tell me. What can you say?

Everybody chew their tough turkey.

I especially cannot understand my daughter's husband John, who has no job but cannot take care of Sophie either. Because he is a man, he say, and that's the end of the sentence.

Plain boiled food, plain boiled thinking. Even his name is plain boiled: John. Maybe because I grew up with black bean sauce and hoisin sauce and garlic sauce, I always feel something is missing when my son-in-law talk.

But, okay: so my son-in-law can be man, I am baby-sitter. Six hours a day, same as the old sitter, crazy Amy, who quit. This is not so easy, now that I am sixty-eight, Chinese age almost seventy. Still, I try. In China, daughter take care of mother. Here it is the other way around. Mother help daughter, mother ask, Anything else I can do? Otherwise daughter complain mother is not supportive. I tell daughter, We do not have this word in Chinese, *supportive*. But my daughter too busy to listen, she has to go to meeting, she has to write memo while her husband go to the gym to be a man. My daughter say otherwise he will be depressed. Seems like all his life he has this trouble, depression.

No one wants to hire someone who is depressed, she say. It is important for him to keep his spirits up.

Beautiful wife, beautiful daughter, beautiful house, oven can clean itself automatically. No money left over, because only one income, but lucky enough, got the baby-sitter for free. If John lived in China, he would be very happy. But he is not happy. Even at the gym things go wrong. One day, he pull a muscle. Another day, weight room too crowded. Always something.

Until finally, hooray, he has a job. Then he feel pressure.

I need to concentrate, he say. I need to focus.

He is going to work for insurance company. Salesman job. A paycheck, he say, and at least he will wear clothes instead of gym shorts. My daughter buy him some special candy bars from the health-food store. They say THINK! on them, and are supposed to help John think.

John is a good-looking boy, you have to say that, especially now that he shave so you can see his face.

I am an old man in a young man's game, say John.

I will need a new suit, say John.

This time I am not going to shoot myself in the foot, say John.

Good, I say.

She means to be supportive, my daughter say. Don't start the send her back to China thing, because we can't.

■ ■ ■

Sophie is three years old American age, but already I see her nice Chinese side swallowed up by her wild Shea side. She looks like mostly Chinese. Beautiful black hair, beautiful black eyes. Nose perfect size, not so flat looks like something fell down, not so large looks like some big deal got stuck in wrong face. Everything just right, only her skin is a brown surprise to John's family. So brown, they say. Even John say it. She never goes in the sun, still she is that color, he say. Brown. They say, Nothing the matter with brown. They are just surprised. So brown. Nattie is not that brown, they say. They say, It seems like Sophie should be a color in between Nattie and John. Seems funny, a girl named Sophie Shea be brown. But she is brown, maybe her name should be Sophie Brown. She never go in the sun, still she is that color, they say. Nothing the matter with brown. They are just surprised.

The Shea family talk is like this sometimes, going around and around like a Christmas-tree train.

Maybe John is not her father, I say one day, to stop the train. And sure enough, train wreck. None of the brothers ever say the word *brown* to me again.

Instead, John's mother, Bess, say, I hope you are not offended.

She say, I did my best on those boys. But raising four boys with no father is no picnic.

You have a beautiful family, I say.

I'm getting old, she say.

You deserve a rest, I say. Too many boys make you old.

I never had a daughter, she say. You have a daughter.

I have a daughter, I say. Chinese people don't think a daughter is so great, but you're right. I have a daughter.

I was never against the marriage, you know, she say. I never thought John was marrying down. I always thought Nattie was just as good as white.

I was never against the marriage either, I say. I just wonder if they look at the whole problem.

Of course you pointed out the problem, you are a mother, she say.

And now we both have a granddaughter. A little brown granddaughter, she is so precious to me.

I laugh. A little brown granddaughter, I say. To tell you the truth, I don't know how she came out so brown.

We laugh some more. These days Bess need a walker to walk. She take so many pills, she need two glasses of water to get them all down. Her favorite TV show is about bloopers, and she love her bird feeder. All day long, she can watch that bird feeder, like a cat.

I can't wait for her to grow up, Bess say. I could use some female company.

Too many boys, I say.

Boys are fine, she say. But they do surround you after a while.

You should take a break, come live with us, I say. Lots of girls at our house.

Be careful what you offer, say Bess with a wink. Where I come from, people mean for you to move in when they say a thing like that.

■ ■ ■

Nothing the matter with Sophie's outside, that's the truth. It is inside that she is like not any Chinese girl I ever see. We go to the park, and this is what she does. She stand up in the stroller. She take off her all her clothes and throw them in the fountain.

Sophie! I say. Stop!

But she just laugh like a crazy person. Before I take over as baby-sitter, Sophie has that crazy-person sitter, Amy the guitar player. My daughter thought this Amy very creative—another word we do not talk about in China. In China, we talk about whether we have difficulty or no difficulty. We talk about whether life is bitter or not bitter. In America, all day long, people talk about creative. Never mind that I cannot even look at this Amy, with her shirt so short that her belly button showing. This Amy think Sophie should love her body. So when Sophie take off her diaper, Amy laugh. When Sophie run around naked, Amy say she wouldn't want to wear a diaper either. When Sophie go *shu-shu* in her lap, Amy laugh and say there are no germs in pee. When Sophie take off her shoes, Amy say bare feet is best, even the pediatrician say so. That is why Sophie now walk around with no shoes like a beggar child. Also why Sophie love to take off her clothes.

Turn around! say the boys in the park. Let's see that ass!

Of course, Sophie does not understand. Sophie clap her hands, I am the only one to say, No! This is not a game.

It has nothing to do with John's family, my daughter say. Amy was too permissive, that's all.

But I think if Sophie was not wild inside, she would not take off her shoes and clothes to begin with.

You never take off your clothes when you were little, I say. All my Chinese friends had babies, I never saw one of them act wild like that.

Look, my daughter say. I have a big presentation tomorrow.

John and my daughter agree Sophie is a problem, but they don't know what to do.

You spank her, she'll stop, I say another day.

But they say, Oh no.

In America, parents not supposed to spank the child.

It gives them low self-esteem, my daughter say. And that leads to problems later, as I happen to know.

My daughter never have big presentation the next day when the subject of spanking come up.

I don't want you to touch Sophie, she say. No spanking, period.

Don't tell me what to do, I say.

I'm not telling you what to do, say my daughter. I'm telling you how I feel.

I am not your servant, I say. Don't you dare talk to me like that.

My daughter have another funny habit when she lose an argument. She spread out all her fingers and look at them, as if she like to make sure they are still there.

My daughter is fierce like me, but she and John think it is better to explain to Sophie that clothes are a good idea. This is not so hard in the cold weather. In the warm weather, it is very hard.

Use your words, my daughter say. That's what we tell Sophie. How about if you set a good example.

As if good example mean anything to Sophie. I am so fierce, the gang members who used to come to the restaurant all afraid of me, but Sophie is not afraid.

I say, Sophie, if you take off your clothes, no snack.

I say, Sophie, if you take off your clothes, no lunch.

I say, Sophie, if you take off your clothes, no park.

Pretty soon we are stay home all day, and by the end of six hours she still did not have one thing to eat. You never saw a child stubborn like that.

I'm hungry! she cry when my daughter come home.

What's the matter, doesn't your grandmother feed you? My daughter laugh.

No! Sophie say. She doesn't feed me anything!

My daughter laugh again. Here you go, she say.

She say to John, Sophie must be growing.

Growing like a weed, I say.

Still Sophie take off her clothes, until one day I spank her. Not too hard, but she cry and cry, and when I tell her if she doesn't put her clothes back on I'll spank her again, she put her clothes back on. Then I tell her she is good girl, and give her some food to eat. The next day we go to the park and, like a nice Chinese girl, she does not take off her clothes.

She stop taking off her clothes, I report. Finally!

How did you do it? my daughter ask.

After twenty-eight years experience with you, I guess I learn something, I say.

It must have been a phase, John say, and his voice is suddenly like an expert.

His voice is like an expert about everything these days, now that he carry a leather briefcase, and wear shiny shoes, and can go shopping for a new car. On the company, he say. The company will pay for it, but he will be able to drive it whenever he want.

A free car, he say. How do you like that.

It's good to see you in the saddle again, my daughter say. Some of your family patterns are scary.

At least I don't drink, he say. He say, And I'm not the only one with scary family patterns.

That's for sure, say my daughter.

■　■　■

Everyone is happy. Even I am happy, because there is more trouble with Sophie, but now I think I can help her Chinese side fight against her wild side. I teach her to eat food with fork or spoon or chopsticks, she cannot just grab into the middle of a bowl of noodles. I teach her not to play with garbage cans. Sometimes I spank her, but not too often, and not too hard.

Still, there are problems. Sophie like to climb everything. If there is a railing, she is never next to it. Always she is on top of it. Also, Sophie like to hit the mommies of her friends. She learn this from her playground best friend, Sinbad, who is four. Sinbad wear army clothes every day and like to ambush his mommy. He is the one who dug a big hole under the play structure, a foxhole he call it, all by himself. Very hardworking. Now he wait in the foxhole with a shovel full of wet sand. When his mommy come, he throw it right at her.

Oh, it's all right, his mommy say. You can't get rid of war games, it's part of their imaginative play. All the boys go through it.

Also, he like to kick his mommy, and one day he tell Sophie to kick his mommy too.

I wish this story is not true.

Kick her, kick her! Sinbad say.

Sophie kick her. A little kick, as if she just so happened was swinging her little leg and didn't realize that big mommy leg was in the way. Still I spank Sophie and make Sophie say sorry, and what does the mommy say?

Really, it's all right, she say. It didn't hurt.

After that, Sophie learn she can attack mommies in the playground, and some will say, Stop, but others will say, Oh, she didn't mean it, especially if they realize Sophie will be punished.

■ ■ ■

This is how, one day, bigger trouble come. The bigger trouble start when Sophie hide in the foxhole with that shovel full of sand. She wait, and when I come look for her, she throw it at me. All over my nice clean clothes.

Did you ever see a Chinese girl act this way?

Sophie! I say. Come out of there, say you're sorry.

But she does not come out. Instead, she laugh. Naaah, naah-na, naaa-naaa, she say.

I am not exaggerate: millions of children in China, not one act like this.

Sophie! I say. Now! Come out now!

But she know she is in big trouble. She know if she come out, what will happen next. So she does not come out. I am sixty-eight, Chinese age almost seventy, how can I crawl under there to catch her? Impossible. So I yell, yell, yell, and what happen? Nothing. A Chinese mother would help, but American mothers, they look at you, they shake their head, they go home. And, of course, a Chinese child would give up, but not Sophie.

I hate you! she yell. I hate you, Meanie!

Meanie is my new name these days.

Long time this goes on, long long time. The foxhole is deep, you cannot see too much, you don't know where is the bottom. You cannot hear too much either. If she does not yell, you cannot even know she is still there or not. After a while, getting cold out, getting dark out. No one left in the playground, only us.

Sophie, I say. How did you become stubborn like this? I am go home without you now.

I try to use a stick, chase her out of there, and once or twice I hit her, but still she does not come out. So finally I leave. I go outside the gate.

Bye-bye! I say. I'm go home now.

But still she does not come out and does not come out. Now it is dinnertime, the sky is black. I think I should maybe go get help, but how can I leave a little girl by herself in the playground? A bad man could come. A rat could come. I go back in to see what is happen to Sophie. What if she have a shovel and is making a tunnel to escape?

Sophie! I say.

No answer.

Sophie!

I don't know if she is alive. I don't know if she is fall asleep down there. If she is crying, I cannot hear her.

So I take the stick and poke.

Sophie! I say. I promise I no hit you. If you come out, I give you a lollipop.

No answer. By now I worried. What to do, what to do, what to do? I poke some more, even harder, so that I am poking and poking when my daughter and John suddenly appear.

What are you doing? What is going on? say my daughter.

Put down that stick! say my daughter.

You are crazy! say my daughter.

John wiggle under the structure, into the foxhole, to rescue Sophie.

She fell asleep, say John the expert. She's okay. That is one big hole.

Now Sophie is crying and crying.

Sophia, my daughter say, hugging her. Are you okay, peanut? Are you okay?

She's just scared, say John.

Are you okay? I say too. I don't know what happen, I say.

She's okay, say John. He is not like my daughter, full of questions. He is full of answers until we get home and can see by the lamplight.

Will you look at her? he yell then. What the hell happened?

Bruises all over her brown skin, and a swollen-up eye.

You are crazy! say my daughter. Look at what you did! You are crazy!

I try very hard, I say.

How could you use a stick? I told you to use your words!

She is hard to handle, I say.

She's three years old! You cannot use a stick! say my daughter.

She is not like any Chinese girl I ever saw, I say.

I brush some sand off my clothes. Sophie's clothes are dirty too, but at least she has her clothes on.

Has she done this before? ask my daughter. Has she hit you before?

She hits me all the time, Sophie say, eating ice cream.

Your family, say John.

Believe me, say my daughter.

■ ■ ■

A daughter I have, a beautiful daughter. I took care of her when she could not hold her head up. I took care of her before she could argue with me, when she was a little girl with two pigtails, one of them always crooked. I took care of her when we have to escape from China, I took care of her when suddenly we live in a country with cars everywhere, if you are not careful your little girl get run over. When my husband die, I promise him I will keep the family together, even though it was just two of us, hardly a family at all.

But now my daughter take me around to look at apartments. After all, I can cook, I can clean, there's no reason I cannot live by myself, all I need is a telephone. Of course, she is sorry. Sometimes she cry, I am the one to say everything will be okay. She say she have no choice, she doesn't want to end up divorced. I say divorce is terrible, I don't know who invented this terrible idea. Instead of live with a telephone, though, surprise, I come to live with Bess. Imagine that. Bess make an offer and, sure enough, where she come from, people mean for you to move in when they say things like that. A crazy idea, go to live with someone else's family, but she like to have some female company, not like my daughter, who does not believe in company. These days when my daughter visit, she does not bring Sophie. Bess say we should give Nattie time, we will see Sophie again soon. But seems like my daughter have more presentation than ever before, every time she come she have to leave.

I have a family to support, she say, and her voice is heavy, as if soaking wet. I have a young daughter and a depressed husband and no one to turn to.

When she say no one to turn to, she mean me.

These days my beautiful daughter is so tired she can just sit there in a chair and fall asleep. John lost his job again, already, but still they rather hire a baby-sitter than ask me to help, even they can't afford it. Of course, the new baby-sitter is much younger, can run around. I don't know if Sophie these days is wild or not wild. She call me Meanie, but she like to kiss me too, sometimes. I remember that every time I see a child on TV. Sophie like to grab my hair, a fistful in each hand, and then kiss me smack on the nose. I never see any other child kiss that way.

The satellite TV has so many channels, more channels than I can count, including a Chinese channel from the Mainland and a Chinese channel from Taiwan, but most of the time I watch bloopers with Bess. Also, I watch the bird feeder—so many, many kinds of birds come. The Shea sons hang around all the time, asking when will I go home, but Bess tell them, Get lost.

She's a permanent resident, say Bess. She isn't going anywhere.

Then she wink at me, and switch the channel with the remote control.

Of course, I shouldn't say Irish this, Irish that, especially now I am become honorary Irish myself, according to Bess. Me! Who's Irish? I say, and she laugh. All the same, if I could mention one thing about some of the Irish, not all of them of course, I like to mention this: Their talk just stick. I don't know how Bess Shea learn to use her words, but sometimes I hear what she say a long time later. *Permanent resident. Not going anywhere.* Over and over I hear it, the voice of Bess.

WAXING THE THING

■ ■ ■

Ginu Kamani

When I first came to Bombay to work in a beauty salon, I didn't understand anything. They told me to wax, so I waxed: legs, arms, underarms, stomachs, foreheads, fingers, toes. It's like a game for me. I cover the skin of the ladies with hot wax, then quickly-quickly take it all off with a cloth, almost before they notice that it's there. It reminds me of my village school, where I used to draw on the wall with chalk, then quickly wipe it off before the teacher found out. For me it's all very strange, what goes on with these rich-rich city ladies, but I mind my own business. I'm just a simple village girl. Everything about the city is strange to me, so what's one thing more?

There I was, minding my own business, when one day this Mrs. Yusuf, whose legs I was waxing in the private room, asked me if I would come to her house to wax her *thing*. I was so stupid, I asked her to her face, "What is this *thing*?"

Born in Bombay, India, in 1962, GINU KAMANI moved with her family to the United States in 1976. She is the author of *Junglee Girl*, a collection of short stories, and coauthor of the play *The Cure* along with Joel B. Tan. A writing fellow with the Sundance Institute, and an instructor of creative writing in the Mills College M.F.A. program, she is currently working on a series of novellas, as well as a book of essays on taboo-breaking filmmakers. Her interests in mentoring new writers include work in the high school classroom through a California Arts Council grant, and a sexual storytelling workshop with members of HIV/AIDS care groups in India. Also a filmmaker, she currently has two video documentaries in postproduction.

Now she was already lying there with her sari pulled up to her stomach, and her legs bent at the knees, and I was trying not to look at her big white panties that she was shamelessly showing me through her wide-open legs, when suddenly she stuck one finger inside of her panties and pulled the material down and showed me all her hair *there*. I felt so ashamed! All this time, I didn't know that the ladies wax down there.

This Mrs. Yusuf said, very sweetly, that only young girls like me are pure enough in the heart to wax it down there. Naturally she wanted me to go to her house to do this delicate job. In a salon, anyone can walk into the private room, even when the curtain is pulled. Some of the other waxing girls told me that they don't do such type of work. Why shouldn't I? If they want to pay me better than at the salon, and on top of that, pay for my taxi here and there, then what do I care?

So I did the work for Mrs. Yusuf, and she told her friends, and before I knew it I had more work waxing things than arms and legs and all. All the ladies like me better because I'm not married. They tell me that marriage will make me rough, like a man, and then I won't be able to do the delicate job.

All our Indians, you know, are so rough and hairy. The shameless Indian men are always scratching themselves between the legs because of the Bombay heat, but the ladies don't have to, because their skin down there is cool and clean. And definitely the smell is also a little less.

I never knew how many kinds of smells could come out of these city ladies' things! Even though they wash night and day and remove every single hair from their bodies, I tell you, some of them smell down there like an armpit. I tell them to put a little baby powder, or maybe even some eau de cologne on the day that I'm coming, otherwise I have to breathe through my mouth so the smell won't drive me crazy. I never used to notice such smells before, but day in and day out putting wax between their legs, I can't help it, my nose has become very nosey.

I'm not so nosey that I ask them questions or anything, but these ladies tell me anyway about why they like to be waxed down there. These thin-thin ladies like Mrs. Nariman and Mrs. Dastur say that it makes them feel clean, because there's no hair for anything to get stuck to down there. Then the gray-hair ladies like Mrs. Patel and Mrs. Loelka say it makes them feel like innocent little girls again, and they even talk with giggly high voices. But worst of all are the lazy fat ones like Mrs. Singh and Mrs. Vaswani, who tell me it's so much better than getting a massage, giving so much more energy to the body, keeping the blood going all day and all night.

Mostly I don't listen to what they say, but one lady, Mrs. D'Souza, told me a very sad story. She said that she was married so many years and her husband never liked to do the man's work in her and so they had no children. Finally she got angry and asked him what was wrong with him and he said that it was all her fault, that the hair on her thing was so rough that it poked like pins right into his skin so he couldn't come near her. Poor man! Since then this lady makes me wax her thing every week, even when I can't find one single hair. The whole time, she lies there saying prayers to Mother Mary. At least these days someone like Mrs. D'Souza can wax. In olden days what must have happened to these poor ladies?

My mother in the village still lives like in olden times. I tried to explain to her that I do waxing to make money, but she just can't understand. She stays in the house all day, covered from head to toe in her cotton sari, so how will she understand? These city ladies are not like that. They understand everything, or how else would they all get rich-rich husbands?

My poor mother—it's so shameful—doesn't even wear panties. And she sits with her legs wide open. All the old women are like that. They're so shameless, they don't even *want* to wear anything down there. Without panties, how can a modern girl control her monthly mess? When my mother was young and she got her monthly bleeding, she just sat in one corner and spread this mud between her legs until it mixed with the blood and became hard, a lid made of clay to close her upside-down, bleeding "pot." When she stood up, the hard clay cut into her skin like a knife. For five days she was like that, sitting in one corner with a pile of mud, playing with herself like a mad girl. After the five days, when she tried to break the mud, the hair from down there would be stuck in it and she would pull the hair right off. How she would scream! My god, you would think it was the end of the world. Why such a big fuss over a few hairs? That's the difference, I tell my mother, between her and the big ladies. If she knew what was good for her, she would have pulled *all* the hair out.

The ladies definitely want all their hair out. They make me check again and again for even one single hair that I missed. It's not so easy, you know, unless I shine a torch on it, and anyway, who says I want to look down there? In the beauty salon they told us, if you're plucking a lady's eyebrows, don't look into her eyes; if you're threading her upper lip, don't look into her mouth; so if I'm waxing the thing I don't look inside there!

Of course it's my job to get all the hair out, but I can't help it, sometimes the hair just won't come out. I try once or twice, but these fussy ladies are never satisfied. For half an hour I have to feel around bit by bit for any leftover hair, and then even if I find it, how can I wax just one hair? So I have to try to pull it out with my fingers, but even that is impossible because by then the skin has become all sensitive and slippery and sliding.

That Mrs. Yusuf, my god, the way she shouts! "I can feel it, I can feel one hair, not there, other side, in the front, no, no, feel properly, grab the skin with one hand and pull with the other, try again, just wipe your fingers if they're sliding, don't think you can rush away without finishing your job," and on and on. What to do? I don't like digging around in there because I know it's where babies and all come from. But I don't grumble because the fussy ladies always give a good tip. Thank god they are not all like that or I would have to spend the whole day waxing and cleaning the thing of just one of them!

Not that they are in any hurry. They can just lie there all day, I tell you. At least I don't have to work at night, because the ladies only like me to wax during the day. I have to finish before the husband comes home, because the man doesn't like his wife to be locked in a room with some outsider.

Sometimes when there is a new lady who wants me to go over to do her waxing, she will ask, "How do I know that you will do a good job? It requires such talent and if you do anything wrong, I'll have to go straight to hospital." So first I give the new lady the names of some other ladies that I work for, so she can call and find out. And then I tell her that I wax my own thing, not just others', so there's no need to worry. All of them, when they hear this, are so shocked! I'm just a poor village girl, so what do I need to wax for? As though you have to be rich to do it! Am I not a woman like them? Can't I be beautiful like them? If my own sister's husband likes it, then won't mine also want it?

I went back to my village for my oldest sister's marriage, and just to teach her how ignorant she is, I took some wax and clean cloths, and I waxed her. What a fuss that stupid girl made! I had to sit on top of her so she wouldn't run away. But then after the wedding, her husband wrote to me that I should come back to the village and wax his wife again, because everyone in the village tells him he's lucky to have such a clean high-class woman. Until I return, my sister is pulling the hair out from down there one by one with her fingers.

Everyone has something that they can wax, so why not me? I only wax myself once in a while. It's not so easy for me. To wax down there, since I can't bend down to see properly, I have to sit on a mirror. Who would think I would ever look at my own thing? Even all those big-big ladies never look at their thing . . . and me, I've seen so many dozens by now.

"Don't wax it yet, you're not married!" the ladies keep saying. "You're still thin and pure and innocent, and you're not *prepared* like a married woman for what happens down there. You'll start feeling wrong feelings between your legs and then no man will take a chance with you. That's why we don't let our unmarried daughters wax down there." I tell you these ladies think they know everything. I am going to have a love marriage, and have enough money saved so that I can give a good dowry. What husband will say no to that?

The real reason these ladies don't allow their young daughters to wax down there is because then the daughters will want to have love marriages! And then all the life's work for these rich-rich ladies will go to waste, because if Indian girls are allowed to marry whichever man they want, then who will marry the ladies' good-for-nothing sons? They're very clever, these rich ladies. But very stupid also. They force their daughters to be beautiful so they can arrange a match with a rich boy, but in the end they are marrying off their girls to boys who are exactly the same as their fathers, who make this and that excuse and don't touch one finger to their wives who are waxed clean and ready from head to toe.

So every day, there is plenty of business for the beauty salon, giving these ladies manicure, pedicure, facial, waxing, haircut, massage . . . And then some simple village girl like me will come along who doesn't know anything and they will cunningly find some way to get her to wax their thing. And when they feel something down there which makes them feel like human beings, then they're happy.

But who wants to listen to what I have to say? So I keep my mouth shut and do my work. When the time comes to get married, I will have saved enough money so my husband can treat me well. Until then, I am living without worries, so what do I care?

BECCAH

from *COMFORT WOMAN*

■ ■ ■

Nora Okja Keller

On the fifth anniversary of my father's death, my mother confessed to his murder. We had been peeling the shrimp for his *chesa*, slicing through the crackling skins, popping the gray and slippery meat, ripe as fruit, into the kitchen sink. My mother, who was allergic to my father's favorite food, held her red and puffy hands under cold running water and scratched at her fingers. "Beccah-chan," she told me without looking up, "I killed your father."

My mother picked at her hands, rubbing at the blisters bubbling between her fingers. I turned the water off and wrapped her hands in a dish towel. "Shh, Mommy," I said. "Don't start."

"Never happen like this," she said, trying to snap her fingers under the cloth. "I had to work at it."

I led her to the kitchen table, clearing a place for her by pushing the stacks of offerings we planned to burn after I ate the remembrance feast my mother made to appease my father's spirit. My father died when I was five, and this yearly meal, with its persistent smell of the ocean, and the smoke and the ash that would penetrate our apartment for days after we burned the Monopoly money and paper-doll clothes, supplanted my dim memories of an actual man. Even when I unearthed the picture I had of him from my underwear drawer, stealing a look, I

NORA OKJA KELLER is the author of *Comfort Woman* and *Fox Girl*. Born in Seoul, Korea, in 1965, She lives in Hawaii with her husband and two daughters. She received the Pushcart Prize in 1995 and the American Book Award in 1998, and is currently at work on her next novel.

saw him less and less clearly, the image fading in almost imperceptible gradations each time I exposed it to light and scrutiny.

What stays with me, though, is the color of his eyes. While his face, his body, sit in shadows behind the black of the Bible he always carried with him, the blue of his eyes sharpen on me. At night before I fell asleep, I would try to imagine my father as an angel coming to comfort me. I gave him the face and voice of Mister Rogers and waited for him to wrap me in that cardigan sweater, which would smell of mothballs and mint and Daddy. He would spirit me away, to a home on the Mainland complete with plush carpet and a cocker spaniel pup. My daddy, I knew, would save my mother and me, burning with his blue eyes the Korean ghosts and demons that fed off our lives.

But when he rolled me into the sweater, binding my arms behind me, my father opened his eyes not on the demons but on me. And the blue light from his eyes grew so bright it burned me, each night, into nothingness.

■ ■ ■

I don't remember what I felt the day my mother told me she had killed my father. Maybe anger, or fear. Not because I believed she had killed him, but because I thought she was slipping into one of her trances. I remember telling her, "Okay," in a loud, slow voice, while I listed in my head the things that I needed to do: call Auntie Reno, buy enough oranges and incense sticks to last two weeks, secure the double locks on the doors when I left for school so my mother couldn't get out of the house.

Most of the time my mother seemed normal. Not normal like the moms on TV—the kind that baked cookies, joined the PTA, or came to weekly soccer games—but normal in that she seemed to know where she was and who I was. During those times, my mother would get up when she heard my alarm clock go off in the morning, and before I pressed the second snooze alarm, she'd have folded the blankets on her side of the bed, poured hot water for the tea, and made breakfast: fresh rice mixed with raw egg, shoyu, and Tabasco. After eating, we'd dress and then walk down the water-rotted hallway of our building, past the "three o'clock" drunk asleep on the bottom stairs, to the bus stop. Instead of continuing straight to school, I'd wait with her until the number 8 came to take her to Reno's Waikiki Bar-B-Q Hut, where she worked as fry cook and clean-up girl.

The days my mother was well enough to catch the bus, I would eat all of my school lunch at one time instead of wrapping half of it to eat before bed. Working at Auntie Reno's, my mother was able to bring home leftovers from the daily special; Auntie Reno, who isn't a blood relative, was good to us in that way: she always made sure we had enough to eat.

I have a habit I picked up from those small-kid days, one that I can't seem to shake even now. Before eating my meals, I set aside a small mound of rice—or whatever I'm eating—as a sacrifice for the spirits or for God, in case either exists. Even eating out with friends, I push the food around on my plate, severing a small portion, and think the prayer I have prayed ever since I can remember: "Please, God—please, spirits and Induk—please, Daddy and whoever is listening: Leave my mother alone."

■ ■ ■

I loved my mother during the normal times. She laughed and sang songs she made up. Instead of telling me to clear my papers and books off the table for dinner, she'd sing it to me. We'd play *hatto*, and while she dealt the cards, she'd sometimes tell me stories about my father or Korea—stories that began "Once on a time" but occasionally hinted at possible truths. And she'd sit and watch me do my homework, as if I were the TV, and mumble about how smart I was, so smart that could I really be her daughter? Though I used to grumble at her—"What? What you staring at? I got two heads or something?"—inside I was really loving it, seeing how she smiled, how she looked at me.

But always, no matter how many piles of rice I left for the gods, no matter how many times I prayed, there came the times when—as Auntie Reno used to say—the spirits claimed my mother.

When the spirits called to her, my mother would leave me and slip inside herself, to somewhere I could not and did not want to follow. It was as if the mother I knew turned off, checked out, and someone else came to rent the space. During these times, the body of my mother would float through our one-bedroom apartment, slamming into walls and bookshelves and bumping into the corners of the coffee table and the television. If I could catch her, I would try to clean her cuts with

Cambison ointment, dab the bruises with vinegar to stop the swelling. But most times I just left her food and water and hid in the bedroom, where I listened to long stretches of thumping accentuated by occasional shouts to a spirit named Induk.

■ ■ ■

It was worse when I was younger. When my father died, leaving us as guests of his most recent employers, at the Miami Mission House for Boys, my mother cashed what was left of his estate—several pieces of family jewelry, pearls mostly, and shares in a retirement village—paid off his hospital bills, and tried to return to Korea. She got as far as Hawai'i when—not knowing anyone, broke, and with a young child to care for—my mother had to put me in school and find work. I remember my mother drifting in and out of under-the-table jobs—washing dishes in Vietnamese restaurants, slinging drinks in Korean bars on Ke'eaumoku—stringing together enough change to pay the weekly rent on a dirty second-floor apartment off Kapi'olani Boulevard. I remember the darkness of that apartment: the brown imitation-wood wall paneling blackened from exhaust from the street, the boarded-up windows, the nights without electricity when we could not pay the bill. And I remember nights that seemed to last for days, when my mother dropped into a darkness of her own, so deep that I did not think she would ever come back to me.

At Ala Wai Elementary, where I was enrolled, I was taught that if I was ever in trouble I should tell my teachers or the police; I learned about 911. But in real life, I knew none of these people would understand, that they might even hurt my mother. I was on my own. At least until Auntie Reno discovered my mother's potential.

■ ■ ■

The way Auntie Reno tells it, she was the only person who would hire my mother. Though my mother could speak English, Korean, and Japanese—which was a big plus in Waikiki—she had no real job skills or experience. "Out of dah goodness of my heart, I wen take your maddah as one cook," Auntie Reno told me. "Even though she nevah even know how for fry hamburgah steak."

The first few months on the job, my mother did well, despite the oil burns on her arms and face. Then the spirits—Saja the Death

Messenger and Induk the Birth Grandmother—descended upon her, fighting over her loyalty and consciousness. During these times in which she shouted and punched at the air above her head, dancing as if to duck return jabs, I was afraid to let her out of the house, both because she might never come back and because—like a wandering *yongson* ghost finding its way back to its birthplace—she might. After roaming the streets, she could have led everyone back to me, the one who would have to explain my mother's insanity. Each morning during her spell, I locked the door on her rantings and ravings, and each afternoon I raced home, fearful of what I'd find when I slipped back into our apartment.

The day Reno found out about my mother, I had just come home from school to find her dancing. At first I thought that she was back to normal, having fun listening to the radio or trying out a new American dance step, the bump-and-grind the teenagers were doing on *Bandstand* every week. But then I noticed the silence. Arms flailing, knees pumping into her chest, my mother danced without music. She must have been dancing a long time in that hot, airless apartment, because she was drenched in sweat: her hair slapped against, then stuck to her blotchy face, and water seeped from her pores, soaking the chest and underarms of her tunic blouse.

"Mom," I yelled at her. When she didn't look at me, I tried to grab one of her arms. She wrenched herself away and kept dancing.

"I got something for you to eat." I held up the part of my school lunch that I had wrapped in a napkin and brought home: half of my pig-in-the-blanket and a peanut butter cookie. I could not remember the last time she ate. I remember hoping that she had eaten while I was at school, but when I checked the refrigerator and the cabinets, whatever food we had seemed untouched.

She danced away from me, hearing music I could not hear, dancing and dancing until her rasping gasps for breath filled the air and permeated each bite of pig-in-the-blanket I took. The food tasted like sweat and hot air, but I ate because I was hungry and because I could not let it go to waste. I ate everything, not even saving any of the cookie to place on the shrine on top of our bookshelf, because I was mad at the spirits and at God for taking my mother away from me.

While I tried to do my homework and my mother continued to dance, Auntie Reno came pounding at our door. "Let me in," she bellowed. "I know you in dere, Akiko! You slackah! You lazy bum! You owe me for leaving me short so many days!"

I ran to the door and yelled through the crack: "Mrs. DeSilva-Chung, my mom is sick."

"Lie!" she yelled back. "How come when I wen call, I heard her laugh and laugh and den hang up?"

"Uh," I answered, trying to remember if I had forgotten to unplug the phone before I left for school.

Sweet Mary, the woman who lived next door, kicked the common wall between us so hard that the dishes in our sink rattled. "Shaddup!" she screeched through the walls. "I goin' call dah police! Whatchu think this is, Grand Central Station?"

Mrs. DeSilva-Chung, my Auntie Reno, yelled back, "Eh, *you* shaddup!" but she stopped banging the door and made her voice real sweet: "If you don't let me in, Rebeccah honey, I dah one goin' call dah police."

I unsnapped the locks and pulled the door open. "Won't you please come in?" I told her. Behind me, I could hear my mother panting and wheezing.

"Ho," Auntie Reno said as she pushed her way past me. The blue-and-silver scarf she had wrapped around her poodle-permed head snagged on the doorframe. "Goffunnit," she grumbled, yanking the scarf away from the frame. She folded the scarf over her hair, tucking the tight curls under the cloth. "Where's your maddah?" she growled, and when she looked up and saw my mother twirling in her see-through clothes, Auntie Reno breathed, "Ho-oly shit," and let the scarf float to the floor.

I closed the door and watched Auntie Reno watch my mother. A spider's line of spittle swung from my mother's gasping mouth as she swayed from the top of the coffee table. When she finally dropped to the ground, her chest heaving as she gulped air, Auntie Reno said, "Wow. I never seen that before."

"Shut up!" I marched over to where my mother lay and folded my arms across my chest. "She's not crazy!"

Auntie Reno looked at me, then blinked her eyes slowly, so that I could see the wings of her sparkly-blue eye shadow. "Honey girl, no one evah told you nevah jump to conclusions?" She walked forward. Stopping in front of me, she bent down and touched my mother's face.

My mother's eyes opened. "Why have you come here? Dirty person from a house full of mourning, tend to your own mother: Teeth are biting at her head, and rats are nesting at her feet."

Auntie Reno gasped. "What dah hell dat crazy woman saying?"

"Bad girl, bad daughter!" Rolling into a crouch, my mother yelled at Reno. "You pretended to take care of her, wiping her drool and her *gundinghi*, but you only wished for her to die! You only wish to save money for yourself. You wouldn't buy your mother a decent bed in life, and look, now, you won't buy her one in death—"

"No!" I rushed forward to put a hand over my mom's mouth. "She doesn't know what—"

Auntie Reno waddled quickly to the door. "I jus' go now. Uh, I call her wen she feeling better." She bent to pick up her scarf.

Before I could stop her, my mother rushed toward Reno and grabbed the scarf. She twined it around her own neck, closed her eyes, and started to rock back and forth on the cushions of her feet. "You, Baby Reno, you always wanted dis scarf. So did your sister, but I nevah wanted for you two for fight over um. 'Bury it wit me,' I told you. You made me one promise, you good-for-nuttin', and still you wen tell yoah sister I gave um to you."

Reno dropped to her knees. "Oh my God," she groaned. "Eh, Mama, wasn't li' dat, I swear on your memory."

"Mommy, stop," I said, jumping up to untangle the scarf from her neck. I pulled it from her, felt the sweat that had soaked into the material, and offered it to Reno. "I'm sorry," I said. "My mother is sick, and sometimes she just starts talking about nothing, rambling on about anykine stuff."

"Try wait, Mama—please no leave me again." Auntie Reno crawled to my mother's feet. "Mama? Akiko-san? Please," she whispered, "you can tell me anyting else?"

My mother hummed, then went to lie down on the couch.

Reno wiped at her eyes, smudging her makeup, and listened for a while to my mother's monotonous buzzing. "Your maddah might be one crazy lady," she said, holding up her hand when she thought I would protest, "but she got dah gift. She was right, you know." She glared at me, knotting the scarf in her fist and quickly adding, "Not about everyting: my maddah did say I could have dis as one—whatchu-call—keepsake; my sistah only tink I was suppose to bury em wit dah body. But—and I stay shame for dis—I nevah put my maddah's remains where she asked, and now the city moving all dah graves where my maddah stay. Tractahs digging em up now."

When I frowned, inching away from her, Reno scowled back. "You dense or what? Don't you get it—dat's dah teet' stay biting at her head." She crossed her legs, leaned forward to prop her chin in the cup of her hands, and studied my mother. When my mother's eyes drifted shut and her breathing settled into a rumbling rhythm, Auntie Reno spoke: "All my life, I heard about people like dis. You know, my maddah said dis kinda thing supposed to run in our family, but I nevah seen anyone wit dah gift dis strong." She touched the tip of her finger to my mother's forehead. "Some people—not many, but some—get dah gift of talking to the dead, of walking true worlds and seeing things one regulah person like you or me don't even know about. Dah spirits love these people, tellin' em for 'do this, do that.' But they hate em, too, jealous of dah living."

■ ■ ■

Auntie Reno likes to say she saved my mother and me from life in the streets, and I suppose she did. "Out of dah goodness of my heart, I'm telling you," the story goes, "I became your maddah's manager. I saw how she could help those in need, and I saw how those in need could help your maddah and you." Which is true, I guess, but Auntie Reno also saw a way that she could help herself.

Whenever the spirits called my mother to them, Auntie Reno insisted I dial her beeper, punching in 911 to let her know my mother had entered a trance. After the lunch crowd and before the dinner rush, Auntie Reno would phone the people who waited sometimes for months for my mother to deliver messages to and from the city of the dead. Then Reno closed the store and rushed over to our place.

While my mother wandered through the rooms talking to ghosts, Auntie Reno would place the large ceramic Wishing Bowl and a stack of red money envelopes on the coffee table, and I would stack oranges and light incense sticks in the corners of the apartment. Auntie Reno, who asserted that atmosphere was just as important as ability, hung bells and chimes and long banners of *kanji* on our walls. When I asked her what the characters meant, she shrugged. "Good luck, double happiness, someting like that."

Then we'd catch my mother, dress her in a long white or blue or yellow robe—whichever one we could throw over her body without protest from the spirits—and turn on the music that would start my mother dancing. She liked heavy drumbeats, and once she got going, my mother could tell all about a person and the wishes of the dead that circled around her.

It got to be that whenever my mother slipped into her spells, we'd have people camping in our kitchen and living room and out in the apartment hallway, all waiting for my mother to tell them about the death and unfulfilled desire in their lives. "Your father's mother's sister died in childbirth, crying out the name of the baby who died inside her," she'd tell one elderly customer with a growth in her uterus, "and she hangs around you, causing sickness and trouble, because she is jealous of all your children and grandchildren." Or she'd tell someone else that her husband was cheating on her because of her bad breath, caused by the vindictive first-wife ghost who died craving a final bite of *mu kimchee.*

For each of the seekers, my mother would pray and advise. And before they left, she would fold purified rock salt, ashes from the shrine, and the whispers of their deepest wish into a square of silk as a talisman against the evil or mischievous or unhappy spirits inhabiting their homes. In return, to ensure the fulfillment of their wishes, they folded money into a red envelope and dropped it into the Wishing Bowl.

And milling through all the mourners-in-waiting—the old ladies with their aching joints and deviant children, the fresh-off-the-boat immigrants with cheating husbands and tax problems, and, later on, the rich middle-aged haoles looking for a new direction in life—was Reno, who served tea or soda and collected the fee between her shifts at the restaurant.

Everyone seemed so respectful of my mother, so in awe of her, and Auntie Reno played it up, telling people my mother was a renowned fortune-teller and spirit medium in Japan and Korea. "Akiko Sonsaeng-nim," she'd say, attaching the Korean honorific to my mother's name—something she would never do when my mother was conscious—"stay famous in dah old country."

Auntie Reno's words impressed so many people that customers would wait for hours in the dank hallways and decrepit stairwells. Finally the apartment manager, fearful of the potential liabilities and lawsuits related to substandard housing and building codes, evicted us. And Auntie Reno saved us from the streets once again, informing us that my mother's share of the money enabled us to put a down payment on a small house in Waipahu, Kaimuki, Nu'uanu, or—if we weren't too choosy—Manoa Valley.

As long as my mother's trance lasted, Auntie Reno would show up at our door every morning before I went to school, leading a new gathering of people. After she organized the customers, packing them tight against the railing and down the stairs so that the line coiled from our second-story apartment into the alley below, she'd pull me aside and hand me a pastry and a small bag of money collected from the Wishing Bowl.

Always, when I went to hide the money in my room, I'd slip out a dollar bill, roll it tight as an incense stick, and lay it in an ashtray on the dresser. Careful to hide from Reno's eyes, I'd strike a match and burn the money for the spirits. Then, pulling out my father's picture, I would begin to pray to my only connection in the spirit world. "Please please please, Daddy. I'll give you everything if you give my mother back." I begged, reasoning that as a dead preacher, my father would be able to get God to intercede on my mother's behalf, or—as a spirit himself and in collusion with the other vengeful ghosts holding my mother captive—he might be persuaded by my own burnt offerings and bribes to free her.

■ ■ ■

When my mother began talking about how she killed my father, I thought that the spirits were coming to claim her again. "Stop, Mommy," I said, rubbing the shrimp juice from her fingers. "You don't know what you're saying." At ten, despite all the people coming to hear her talk this way, I was still afraid that someone would hear my mother's craziness and lock her up. It wasn't until I reached high school that I actually started hoping that that would happen. "You're not yourself," I said loudly.

"Quiet!" My mother smacked my hand, just as she did when I couldn't memorize the times table. "Who else would I be? Pay attention!" She took the dishcloth, folded it into a rectangle, then a square, smoothing the wrinkles. "I wished him to death," she said. "Every day I think, every day I pray, 'Die, die,' sending him death-wish arrows, until one day my prayers were answered."

"Oh God," I groaned, my eyes rolling toward the back of my head. "So you didn't actually, physically kill him. Like with a knife or something."

She whacked my hand again. "I'm teaching you something very important about life. Listen: Sickness, bad luck, death, these things are not accidents. This kind stuff, people wish on you. Believe me, I know! And if you cannot block these wishes, all the death thoughts people send you collect, become arrows in your back. This is what causes wrinkles and make your shoulders fold inward."

She looked at me slouching into my chair, shoulders hunched into my body. I straightened up.

"Death thoughts turn your hair white, make you weak and break you, sucking out your life. I tell you these things," she said, touching my hair with her blistering hands, "to protect you."

She leaned toward me, and as she bent forward to kiss or hug me, I could see veins of white hair running through her black braid. Before she could touch me, I pushed away from the table, turning toward the sink to prepare the shrimp for the annual meal that made my mother's hands crack open and bleed.

■ ■ ■

I look at myself in the mirror now and see the same strands of white streaking across my dark head. I squint, and the lines in the corners of my eyes deepen, etching my face in the pattern that was my mother's. And I think: It has taken me nearly thirty years, almost all of my life, but finally the wishes I flung out in childhood have come true.

My mother is dead.

SEXY

■ ■ ■

Jhumpa Lahiri

It was a wife's worst nightmare. After nine years of marriage, Laxmi
told Miranda, her cousin's husband had fallen in love with another
woman. He sat next to her on a plane, on a flight from Delhi to Montreal, and instead of flying home to his wife and son, he got off with the
woman at Heathrow. He called his wife, and told her he'd had a conversation that had changed his life, and that he needed time to figure
things out. Laxmi's cousin had taken to her bed.

"Not that I blame her," Laxmi said. She reached for the Hot Mix she
munched throughout the day, which looked to Miranda like dusty orange cereal. "Imagine. An English girl, half his age." Laxmi was only a
few years older than Miranda, but she was already married, and kept a
photo of herself and her husband, seated on a white stone bench in
front of the Taj Mahal, tacked to the inside of her cubicle, which was
next to Miranda's. Laxmi had been on the phone for at least an hour,
trying to calm her cousin down. No one noticed; they worked for a
public radio station, in the fund-raising department, and were surrounded by people who spent all day on the phone, soliciting pledges.

"I feel worst for the boy," Laxmi added. "He's been at home for days.
My cousin said she can't even take him to school."

JHUMPA LAHIRI was born in 1967 in London, England, raised in Rhode Island, and currently lives in Brooklyn. She has published fiction in *The New
Yorker*, *Agni*, *Story Quarterly*, and elsewhere. In 2000, she received the Pulitzer
Prize for fiction for her collection of short stories, *Interpreter of Maladies*, in
which this story appears. Her acclaimed first novel, *The Namesake*, was published in 2003.

"It sounds awful," Miranda said. Normally Laxmi's phone conversations—mainly to her husband, about what to cook for dinner—distracted Miranda as she typed letters, asking members of the radio station to increase their annual pledge in exchange for a tote bag or an umbrella. She could hear Laxmi clearly, her sentences peppered every now and then with an Indian word, through the laminated wall between their desks. But that afternoon Miranda hadn't been listening. She'd been on the phone herself, with Dev, deciding where to meet later that evening.

"Then again, a few days at home won't hurt him." Laxmi ate some more Hot Mix, then put it away in a drawer. "He's something of a genius. He has a Punjabi mother and a Bengali father, and because he learns French and English at school he already speaks four languages. I think he skipped two grades."

Dev was Bengali, too. At first Miranda thought it was a religion. But then he pointed it out to her, a place in India called Bengal, in a map printed in an issue of *The Economist*. He had brought the magazine specially to her apartment, for she did not own an atlas, or any other books with maps in them. He'd pointed to the city where he'd been born, and another city where his father had been born. One of the cities had a box around it, intended to attract the reader's eye. When Miranda asked what the box indicated, Dev rolled up the magazine, and said, "Nothing you'll ever need to worry about," and he tapped her playfully on the head.

Before leaving her apartment he'd tossed the magazine in the garbage, along with the ends of the three cigarettes he always smoked in the course of his visits. But after she watched his car disappear down Commonwealth Avenue, back to his house in the suburbs, where he lived with his wife, Miranda retrieved it, and brushed the ashes off the cover, and rolled it in the opposite direction to get it to lie flat. She got into bed, still rumpled from their lovemaking, and studied the borders of Bengal. There was a bay below and mountains above. The map was connected to an article about something called the Gramin Bank. She turned the page, hoping for a photograph of the city where Dev was born, but all she found were graphs and grids. Still, she stared at them, thinking the whole while about Dev, about how only fifteen minutes ago he'd propped her feet on top of his shoulders, and pressed her knees to her chest, and told her that he couldn't get enough of her.

She'd met him a week ago, at Filene's. She was there on her lunch break, buying discounted pantyhose in the Basement. Afterward she took the escalator to the main part of the store, to the cosmetics department, where soaps and creams were displayed like jewels, and eye shadows and powders shimmered like butterflies pinned behind protective glass. Though Miranda had never bought anything other than a lipstick, she liked walking through the cramped, confined maze, which was familiar to her in a way the rest of Boston still was not. She liked negotiating her way past the women planted at every turn, who sprayed cards with perfume and waved them in the air; sometimes she would find a card days afterward, folded in her coat pocket, and the rich aroma, still faintly preserved, would warm her as she waited on cold mornings for the T.

That day, stopping to smell one of the more pleasing cards, Miranda noticed a man standing at one of the counters. He held a slip of paper covered in a precise, feminine hand. A saleswoman took one look at the paper and began to open drawers. She produced an oblong cake of soap in a black case, a hydrating mask, a vial of cell renewal drops, and two tubes of face cream. The man was tanned, with black hair that was visible on his knuckles. He wore a flamingo pink shirt, a navy blue suit, a camel overcoat with gleaming leather buttons. In order to pay he had taken off pigskin gloves. Crisp bills emerged from a burgundy wallet. He didn't wear a wedding ring.

"What can I get you, honey?" the saleswoman asked Miranda. She looked over the tops of her tortoiseshell glasses, assessing Miranda's complexion.

Miranda didn't know what she wanted. All she knew was that she didn't want the man to walk away. He seemed to be lingering, waiting, along with the saleswoman, for her to say something. She stared at some bottles, some short, others tall, arranged on an oval tray, like a family posing for a photograph.

"A cream," Miranda said eventually.

"How old are you?"

"Twenty-two."

The saleswoman nodded, opening a frosted bottle. "This may seem a bit heavier than what you're used to, but I'd start now. All your wrinkles are going to form by twenty-five. After that they just start showing."

While the saleswoman dabbed the cream on Miranda's face, the man stood and watched. While Miranda was told the proper way to apply it, in swift upward strokes beginning at the base of her throat, he spun the lipstick carousel. He pressed a pump that dispensed cellulite gel and massaged it into the back of his ungloved hand. He opened a jar, leaned over, and drew so close that a drop of cream flecked his nose.

Miranda smiled, but her mouth was obscured by a large brush that the saleswoman was sweeping over her face. "This is blusher Number Two," the woman said. "Gives you some color."

Miranda nodded, glancing at her reflection in one of the angled mirrors that lined the counter. She had silver eyes and skin as pale as paper, and the contrast with her hair, as dark and glossy as an espresso bean, caused people to describe her as striking, if not pretty. She had a narrow, egg-shaped head that rose to a prominent point. Her features, too, were narrow, with nostrils so slim that they appeared to have been pinched with a clothespin. Now her face glowed, rosy at the cheeks, smoky below the brow bone. Her lips glistened.

The man was glancing in a mirror, too, quickly wiping the cream from his nose. Miranda wondered where he was from. She thought he might be Spanish, or Lebanese. When he opened another jar, and said, to no one in particular, "This one smells like pineapple," she detected only the hint of an accent.

"Anything else for you today?" the saleswoman asked, accepting Miranda's credit card.

"No thanks."

The woman wrapped the cream in several layers of red tissue. "You'll be very happy with this product." Miranda's hand was unsteady as she signed the receipt. The man hadn't budged.

"I threw in a sample of our new eye gel," the saleswoman added, handing Miranda a small shopping bag. She looked at Miranda's credit card before sliding it across the counter. "Bye-bye, Miranda."

Miranda began walking. At first she sped up. Then, noticing the doors that led to Downtown Crossing, she slowed down.

"Part of your name is Indian," the man said, pacing his steps with hers.

She stopped, as did he, at a circular table piled with sweaters, flanked with pinecones and velvet bows. "Miranda?"

"Mira. I have an aunt named Mira."

His name was Dev. He worked in an investment bank back that way, he said, tilting his head in the direction of South Station. He was the first man with a mustache, Miranda decided, she found handsome.

They walked together toward Park Street station, past the kiosks that sold cheap belts and handbags. A fierce January wind spoiled the part in her hair. As she fished for a token in her coat pocket, her eyes fell to his shopping bag. "And those are for her?"

"Who?"

"Your Aunt Mira."

"They're for my wife." He uttered the words slowly, holding Miranda's gaze. "She's going to India for a few weeks." He rolled his eyes. "She's addicted to this stuff."

■ ■ ■

Somehow, without the wife there, it didn't seem so wrong. At first Miranda and Dev spent every night together, almost. He explained that he couldn't spend the whole night at her place, because his wife called every day at six in the morning, from India, where it was four in the afternoon. And so he left her apartment at two, three, often as late as four in the morning, driving back to his house in the suburbs. During the day he called her every hour, it seemed, from work, or from his cell phone. Once he learned Miranda's schedule he left her a message each evening at five-thirty, when she was on the T coming back to her apartment, just so, he said, she could hear his voice as soon as she walked through the door. "I'm thinking about you," he'd say on the tape. "I can't wait to see you." He told her he liked spending time in her apartment, with its kitchen counter no wider than a breadbox, and scratchy floors that sloped, and a buzzer in the lobby that always made a slightly embarrassing sound when he pressed it. He said he admired her for moving to Boston, where she knew no one, instead of remaining in Michigan, where she'd grown up and gone to college. When Miranda told him it was nothing to admire, that she'd moved to Boston precisely for that reason, he shook his head. "I know what it's like to be lonely," he said, suddenly serious, and at that moment Miranda felt that he understood her—understood how she felt some nights on the T, after seeing a movie on her own, or going to a bookstore to read magazines, or having drinks with Laxmi, who always had to meet her husband at Alewife station in an hour or two. In less serious moments Dev said he liked that her legs were longer than her torso, something he'd observed the first time she walked across a room naked. "You're the first," he told her, admiring her from the bed. "The first woman I've known with legs this long."

Dev was the first to tell her that. Unlike the boys she dated in college, who were simply taller, heavier versions of the ones she dated in high school, Dev was the first always to pay for things, and hold doors open, and reach across a table in a restaurant to kiss her hand. He was the first to bring her a bouquet of flowers so immense she'd had to split it up into all six of her drinking glasses, and the first to whisper her name again and again when they made love. Within days of meeting him, when she was at work, Miranda began to wish that there were a picture of her and Dev tacked to the inside of her cubicle, like the one of Laxmi and her husband in front of the Taj Mahal. She didn't tell Laxmi about Dev. She didn't tell anyone. Part of her wanted to tell Laxmi, if only because Laxmi was Indian, too. But Laxmi was always on the phone with her cousin these days, who was still in bed, whose husband was still in London, and whose son still wasn't going to school. "You must eat something," Laxmi would urge. "You mustn't lose your health." When she wasn't speaking to her cousin, she spoke to her husband, shorter conversations, in which she ended up arguing about whether to have chicken or lamb for dinner. "I'm sorry," Miranda heard her apologize at one point. "This whole thing just makes me a little paranoid."

Miranda and Dev didn't argue. They went to movies at the Nickelodeon and kissed the whole time. They ate pulled pork and cornbread in Davis Square, a paper napkin tucked like a cravat into the collar of Dev's shirt. They sipped sangria at the bar of a Spanish restaurant, a grinning pig's head presiding over their conversation. They went to the MFA and picked out a poster of water lilies for her bedroom. One Saturday, following an afternoon concert at Symphony Hall, he showed her his favorite place in the city, the Mapparium at the Christian Science center, where they stood inside a room made of glowing stained-glass panels, which was shaped like the inside of a globe, but looked like the outside of one. In the middle of the room was a transparent bridge, so that they felt as if they were standing in the center of the world. Dev pointed to India, which was red, and far more detailed than the map in *The Economist*. He explained that many of the countries, like Siam and Italian Somaliland, no longer existed in the same way; the names had changed by now. The ocean, as blue as a peacock's breast, appeared in two shades, depending on the depth of the water. He showed her the deepest spot on earth, seven miles deep, above the Mariana Islands. They peered over the bridge and saw the Antarctic archipelago at their feet, craned their necks and saw a giant metal star overhead. As Dev spoke, his voice bounced wildly off the glass, sometimes loud, sometimes soft, sometimes seeming to land in Miranda's chest, sometimes eluding her ear altogether. When a group of tourists walked onto the bridge, she could hear them clearing their throats, as if through microphones. Dev explained that it was because of the acoustics.

Miranda found London, where Laxmi's cousin's husband was, with the woman he'd met on the plane. She wondered which of the cities in India Dev's wife was in. The farthest Miranda had ever been was to the Bahamas once when she was a child. She searched but couldn't find it on the glass panels. When the tourists left and she and Dev were alone again, he told her to stand at one end of the bridge. Even though they were thirty feet apart, Dev said, they'd be able to hear each other whisper.

"I don't believe you," Miranda said. It was the first time she'd spoken since they'd entered. She felt as if speakers were embedded in her ears.

"Go ahead," he urged, walking backward to his end of the bridge. His voice dropped to a whisper. "Say something." She watched his lips forming the words; at the same time she heard them so clearly that she felt them under her skin, under her winter coat, so near and full of warmth that she felt herself go hot.

"Hi," she whispered, unsure of what else to say.

"You're sexy," he whispered back.

■ ■ ■

At work the following week, Laxmi told Miranda that it wasn't the first time her cousin's husband had had an affair. "She's decided to let him come to his senses," Laxmi said one evening as they were getting ready to leave the office. "She says it's for the boy. She's willing to forgive him for the boy." Miranda waited as Laxmi shut off her computer. "He'll come crawling back, and she'll let him," Laxmi said, shaking her head. "Not me. If my husband so much as looked at another woman I'd change the locks." She studied the picture tacked to her cubicle. Laxmi's husband had his arm draped over her shoulder, his knees leaning in toward her on the bench. She turned to Miranda. "Wouldn't you?"

She nodded. Dev's wife was coming back from India the next day. That afternoon he'd called Miranda at work, to say he had to go to the airport to pick her up. He promised he'd call as soon as he could.

"What's the Taj Mahal like?" she asked Laxmi.

"The most romantic spot on earth." Laxmi's face brightened at the memory. "An everlasting monument to love."

■ ■ ■

While Dev was at the airport, Miranda went to Filene's Basement to buy herself things she thought a mistress should have. She found a pair of black high heels with buckles smaller than a baby's teeth. She found a satin slip with scalloped edges and a knee-length silk robe. Instead of the pantyhose she normally wore to work, she found sheer stockings with a seam. She searched through piles and wandered through racks, pressing back hanger after hanger, until she found a cocktail dress made of a slinky silvery material that matched her eyes, with little chains for straps. As she shopped she thought about Dev, and about what he'd told her in the Mapparium. It was the first time a man had called her sexy, and when she closed her eyes she could still feel his whisper drifting through her body, under her skin. In the fitting room, which was just one big room with mirrors on the walls, she found a spot next to an older woman with a shiny face and coarse frosted hair. The woman stood barefoot in her underwear, pulling the black net of a body stocking taut between her fingers.

"Always check for snags," the woman advised.

Miranda pulled out the satin slip with scalloped edges. She held it to her chest.

The woman nodded with approval. "Oh yes."

"And this?" She held up the silver cocktail dress.

"Absolutely," the woman said. "He'll want to rip it right off you."

Miranda pictured the two of them at a restaurant in the South End they'd been to, where Dev had ordered foie gras and a soup made with champagne and raspberries. She pictured herself in the cocktail dress, and Dev in one of his suits, kissing her hand across the table. Only the next time Dev came to visit her, on a Sunday afternoon several days since the last time they'd seen each other, he was in gym clothes. After his wife came back, that was his excuse: on Sundays he drove into Boston and went running along the Charles. The first Sunday she opened the door in the knee-length robe, but Dev didn't even notice it; he carried her over to the bed, wearing sweatpants and sneakers, and entered her without a word. Later, she slipped on the robe when she walked across the room to get him a saucer for his cigarette ashes, but he complained that she was depriving him of the sight of her long legs, and demanded that she remove it. So the next Sunday she didn't bother. She wore jeans. She kept the lingerie at the back of a drawer, behind her socks and everyday underwear. The silver cocktail dress hung in her closet, the tag dangling from the seam. Often, in the morning, the dress would be in a heap on the floor; the chain straps always slipped off the metal hanger.

Still, Miranda looked forward to Sundays. In the mornings she went to a deli and bought a baguette and little containers of things Dev liked to eat, like pickled herring, and potato salad, and tortes of pesto and mascarpone cheese. They ate in bed, picking up the herring with their fingers and ripping the baguette with their hands. Dev told her stories about his childhood, when he would come home from school and drink mango juice served to him on a tray, and then play cricket by a lake, dressed all in white. He told her about how, at eighteen, he'd been sent to a college in upstate New York during something called the Emergency, and about how it took him years to be able to follow American accents in movies, in spite of the fact that he'd had an English-medium education. As he talked he smoked three cigarettes, crushing them in a saucer by the side of her bed. Sometimes he asked her questions, like how many lovers she'd had (three) and how old she'd been the first time (nineteen). After lunch they made love, on sheets covered with crumbs, and then Dev took a nap for twelve minutes. Miranda had never known an adult who took naps, but Dev said it was something he'd grown up doing in India, where it was so hot that people didn't leave their homes until the sun went down. "Plus it allows us to sleep together," he murmured mischievously, curving his arm like a big bracelet around her body.

Only Miranda never slept. She watched the clock on her bedside table, or pressed her face against Dev's fingers, intertwined with hers, each with its half-dozen hairs at the knuckle. After six minutes she turned to face him, sighing and stretching, to test if he was really sleeping. He always was. His ribs were visible through his skin as he breathed, and yet he was beginning to develop a paunch. He complained about the hair on his shoulders, but Miranda thought him perfect, and refused to imagine him any other way.

At the end of twelve minutes Dev would open his eyes as if he'd been awake all along, smiling at her, full of a contentment she wished she felt herself. "The best twelve minutes of the week." He'd sigh, running a hand along the backs of her calves. Then he'd spring out of bed, pulling on his sweatpants and lacing up his sneakers. He would go to the bathroom and brush his teeth with his index finger, something he told her all Indians knew how to do, to get rid of the smoke in his mouth. When she kissed him good-bye she smelled herself sometimes in his hair. But she knew that his excuse, that he'd spent the afternoon jogging, allowed him to take a shower when he got home, first thing.

■ ■ ■

Apart from Laxmi and Dev, the only Indians whom Miranda had known were a family in the neighborhood where she'd grown up, named the Dixits. Much to the amusement of the neighborhood children, including Miranda, but not including the Dixit children, Mr. Dixit would jog each evening along the flat winding streets of their development in his everyday shirt and trousers, his only concession to athletic apparel a pair of cheap Keds. Every weekend, the family—mother, father, two boys, and a girl—piled into their car and went away, to where nobody knew. The fathers complained that Mr. Dixit did not fertilize his lawn properly, did not rake his leaves on time, and agreed that the Dixits' house, the only one with vinyl siding, detracted from the neighborhood's charm. The mothers never invited Mrs. Dixit to join them around the Armstrongs' swimming pool. Waiting for the school bus with the Dixit children standing to one side, the other children would say "The Dixits dig shit," under their breath, and then burst into laughter.

One year, all the neighborhood children were invited to the birthday party of the Dixit girl. Miranda remembered a heavy aroma of incense and onions in the house, and a pile of shoes heaped by the front door. But most of all she remembered a piece of fabric, about the size of a pillowcase, which hung from a wooden dowel at the bottom of the stairs. It was a painting of a naked woman with a red face shaped like a knight's shield. She had enormous white eyes that tilted toward her temples, and mere dots for pupils. Two circles, with the same dots at their centers, indicated her breasts. In one hand she brandished a dagger. With one foot she crushed a struggling man on the ground. Around her body was a necklace composed of bleeding heads, strung together like a popcorn chain. She stuck her tongue out at Miranda.

"It is the goddess Kali," Mrs. Dixit explained brightly, shifting the dowel slightly in order to straighten the image. Mrs. Dixit's hands were painted with henna, an intricate pattern of zigzags and stars. "Come please, time for cake."

Miranda, then nine years old, had been too frightened to eat the cake. For months afterward she'd been too frightened even to walk on the same side of the street as the Dixits' house, which she had to pass twice daily, once to get to the bus stop, and once again to come home. For a while she even held her breath until she reached the next lawn, just as she did when the school bus passed a cemetery.

It shamed her now. Now, when she and Dev made love, Miranda closed her eyes and saw deserts and elephants, and marble pavilions floating on lakes beneath a full moon. One Saturday, having nothing else to do, she walked all the way to Central Square, to an Indian restaurant, and ordered a plate of tandoori chicken. As she ate she tried to memorize phrases printed at the bottom of the menu, for things like "delicious" and "water" and "check, please." The phrases didn't stick in her mind, and so she began to stop from time to time in the foreign-language section of a bookstore in Kenmore Square, where she studied the Bengali alphabet in the Teach Yourself series. Once she went so far as to try to transcribe the Indian part of her name, "Mira," into her Filofax, her hand moving in unfamiliar directions, stopping and turning and picking up her pen when she least expected to. Following the arrows in the book, she drew a bar from left to right from which the letters hung; one looked more like a number than a letter, another looked like a triangle on its side. It had taken her several tries to get the letters of her name to resemble the sample letters in the book, and even then she wasn't sure if she'd written Mira or Mara. It was a scribble to her, but somewhere in the world, she realized with a shock, it meant something.

■ ■ ■

During the week it wasn't so bad. Work kept her busy, and she and Laxmi had begun having lunch together at a new Indian restaurant around the corner, during which Laxmi reported the latest status of her cousin's marriage. Sometimes Miranda tried to change the topic; it made her feel the way she once felt in college, when she and her boyfriend at the time had walked away from a crowded house of pancakes without paying for their food, just to see if they could get away with it. But Laxmi spoke of nothing else. "If I were her I'd fly straight to London and shoot them both," she announced one day. She snapped a papadum in half and dipped it into chutney. "I don't know how she can just wait this way."

Miranda knew how to wait. In the evenings she sat at her dining table and coated her nails with clear nail polish, and ate salad straight from the salad bowl, and watched television, and waited for Sunday. Saturdays were the worst because by Saturday it seemed that Sunday would never come. One Saturday when Dev called, late at night, she heard people laughing and talking in the background, so many that she asked him if he was at a concert hall. But he was only calling from his house in the suburbs. "I can't hear you that well," he said. "We have guests. Miss me?" She looked at the television screen, a sitcom that she'd muted with the remote control when the phone rang. She pictured him whispering into his cell phone, in a room upstairs, a hand on the doorknob, the hallway filled with guests. "Miranda, do you miss me?" he asked again. She told him that she did.

The next day, when Dev came to visit, Miranda asked him what his wife looked like. She was nervous to ask, waiting until he'd smoked the last of his cigarettes, crushing it with a firm twist into the saucer. She wondered if they'd quarrel. But Dev wasn't surprised by the question. He told her, spreading some smoked whitefish on a cracker, that his wife resembled an actress in Bombay named Madhuri Dixit.

For an instant Miranda's heart stopped. But no, the Dixit girl had been named something else, something that began with P. Still, she wondered if the actress and the Dixit girl were related. She'd been plain, wearing her hair in two braids all through high school.

A few days later Miranda went to an Indian grocery in Central Square which also rented videos. The door opened to a complicated tinkling of bells. It was dinnertime, and she was the only customer. A video was playing on a television hooked up in a corner of the store: a row of young women in harem pants were thrusting their hips in synchrony on a beach.

"Can I help you?" the man standing at the cash register asked. He was eating a samosa, dipping it into some dark brown sauce on a paper plate. Below the glass counter at his waist were trays of more plump samosas, and what looked like pale, diamond-shaped pieces of fudge covered with foil, and some bright orange pastries floating in syrup. "You like some video?"

Miranda opened up her Filofax, where she had written "Mottery Dixit." She looked up at the videos on the shelves behind the counter. She saw women wearing skirts that sat low on the hips and tops that tied like bandannas between their breasts. Some leaned back against a stone wall, or a tree. They were beautiful, the way the women dancing on the beach were beautiful, with kohl-rimmed eyes and long black hair. She knew then that Madhuri Dixit was beautiful, too.

"We have subtitled versions, miss," the man continued. He wiped his fingertips quickly on his shirt and pulled out three titles.

"No," Miranda said. "Thank you, no." She wandered through the store, studying shelves lined with unlabeled packets and tins. The freezer case was stuffed with bags of pita bread and vegetables she didn't recognize. The only thing she recognized was a rack lined with bags and bags of the Hot Mix that Laxmi was always eating. She thought about buying some for Laxmi, then hesitated, wondering how to explain what she'd been doing in an Indian grocery.

"Very spicy," the man said, shaking his head, his eyes traveling across Miranda's body. "Too spicy for you."

■ ■ ■

By February, Laxmi's cousin's husband still hadn't come to his senses. He had returned to Montreal, argued bitterly with his wife for two weeks, packed two suitcases, and flown back to London. He wanted a divorce.

Miranda sat in her cubicle and listened as Laxmi kept telling her cousin that there were better men in the world, just waiting to come out of the woodwork. The next day the cousin said she and her son were going to her parents' house in California, to try to recuperate.

Laxmi convinced her to arrange a weekend layover in Boston. "A quick change of place will do you good," Laxmi insisted gently, "besides which, I haven't seen you in years."

Miranda stared at her own phone, wishing Dev would call. It had been four days since their last conversation. She heard Laxmi dialing directory assistance, asking for the number of a beauty salon. "Something soothing," Laxmi requested. She scheduled massages, facials, manicures, and pedicures. Then she reserved a table for lunch at the Four Seasons. In her determination to cheer up her cousin, Laxmi had forgotten about the boy. She rapped her knuckles on the laminated wall.

"Are you busy Saturday?"

■ ■ ■

The boy was thin. He wore a yellow knapsack strapped across his back, gray herringbone trousers, a red V-necked sweater, and black leather shoes. His hair was cut in a thick fringe over his eyes, which had dark circles under them. They were the first thing Miranda noticed. They made him look haggard, as if he smoked a great deal and slept very little, in spite of the fact that he was only seven years old. He clasped a large sketch pad with a spiral binding. His name was Rohin.

"Ask me a capital," he said, staring up at Miranda.

She stared back at him. It was eight-thirty on a Saturday morning. She took a sip of coffee. "A what?"

"It's a game he's been playing," Laxmi's cousin explained. She was thin like her son, with a long face and the same dark circles under her eyes. A rust-colored coat hung heavy on her shoulders. Her black hair, with a few strands of gray at the temples, was pulled back like a ballerina's. "You ask him a country and he tells you the capital."

"You should have heard him in the car," Laxmi said. "He's already memorized all of Europe."

"It's not a game," Rohin said. "I'm having a competition with a boy at school. We're competing to memorize all the capitals. I'm going to beat him."

Miranda nodded. "Okay. What's the capital of India?"

"That's no good." He marched away, his arms swinging like a toy soldier. Then he marched back to Laxmi's cousin and tugged at a pocket of her overcoat. "Ask me a hard one."

"Senegal," she said.

"Dakar!" Rohin exclaimed triumphantly, and began running in larger and larger circles. Eventually he ran into the kitchen. Miranda could hear him opening and closing the fridge.

"Rohin, don't touch without asking," Laxmi's cousin called out wearily. She managed a smile for Miranda. "Don't worry, he'll fall asleep in a few hours. And thanks for watching him."

"Back at three," Laxmi said, disappearing with her cousin down the hallway. "We're double-parked."

Miranda fastened the chain on the door. She went to the kitchen to find Rohin, but he was now in the living room, at the dining table, kneeling on one of the director's chairs. He unzipped his knapsack, pushed Miranda's basket of manicure supplies to one side of the table, and spread his crayons over the surface. Miranda stood over his shoulder. She watched as he gripped a blue crayon and drew the outline of an airplane.

"It's lovely," she said. When he didn't reply, she went to the kitchen to pour herself more coffee.

"Some for me, please," Rohin called out.

She returned to the living room. "Some what?"

"Some coffee. There's enough in the pot. I saw."

She walked over to the table and sat opposite him. At times he nearly stood up to reach for a new crayon. He barely made a dent in the director's chair.

"You're too young for coffee."

Rohin leaned over the sketch pad, so that his tiny chest and shoulders almost touched it, his head tilted to one side. "The stewardess let me have coffee," he said. "She made it with milk and lots of sugar." He straightened, revealing a woman's face beside the plane, with long wavy hair and eyes like asterisks. "Her hair was more shiny," he decided, adding, "My father met a pretty woman on a plane, too." He looked at Miranda. His face darkened as he watched her sip. "Can't I have just a little coffee? Please?"

She wondered, in spite of his composed, brooding expression, if he were the type to throw a tantrum. She imagined his kicking her with his leather shoes, screaming for coffee, screaming and crying until his mother and Laxmi came back to fetch him. She went to the kitchen and prepared a cup for him as he'd requested. She selected a mug she didn't care for, in case he dropped it.

"Thank you," he said when she put it on the table. He took short sips, holding the mug securely with both hands.

Miranda sat with him while he drew, but when she attempted to put a coat of clear polish on her nails he protested. Instead he pulled out a paperback world almanac from his knapsack and asked her to quiz him. The countries were arranged by continent, six to a page, with the capitals in boldface, followed by a short entry on the population, government, and other statistics. Miranda turned to a page in the Africa section and went down the list.

"Mali," she asked him.

"Bamako," he replied instantly.

"Malawi."

"Lilongwe."

She remembered looking at Africa in the Mapparium. She remembered the fat part of it was green.

"Go on," Rohin said.

"Mauritania."

"Nouakchott."

"Mauritius."

He paused, squeezed his eyes shut, then opened them, defeated. "I can't remember."

"Port Louis," she told him.

"Port Louis." He began to say it again and again, like a chant under his breath.

When they reached the last of the countries in Africa, Rohin said he wanted to watch cartoons, telling Miranda to watch them with him. When the cartoons ended, he followed her to the kitchen, and stood by her side as she made more coffee. He didn't follow her when she went to the bathroom a few minutes later, but when she opened the door she was startled to find him standing outside.

"Do you need to go?"

He shook his head but walked into the bathroom anyway. He put the cover of the toilet down, climbed on top of it, and surveyed the narrow glass shelf over the sink which held Miranda's toothbrush and makeup.

"What's this for?" he asked, picking up the sample of eye gel she'd gotten the day she met Dev.

"Puffiness."

"What's puffiness?"

"Here," she explained, pointing.

"After you've been crying?"

"I guess so."

Rohin opened the tube and smelled it. He squeezed a drop of it onto a finger, then rubbed it on his hand. "It stings." He inspected the back of his hand closely, as if expecting it to change color. "My mother has puffiness. She says it's a cold, but really she cries, sometimes for hours. Sometimes straight through dinner. Sometimes she cries so hard her eyes puff up like bullfrogs."

Miranda wondered if she ought to feed him. In the kitchen she discovered a bag of rice cakes and some lettuce. She offered to go out, to buy something from the deli, but Rohin said he wasn't very hungry, and accepted one of the rice cakes. "You eat one too," he said. They sat at the table, the rice cakes between them. He turned to a fresh page in his sketch pad. "You draw."

She selected a blue crayon. "What should I draw?"

He thought for a moment. "I know," he said. He asked her to draw things in the living room: the sofa, the director's chairs, the television, the telephone. "This way I can memorize it."

"Memorize what?"

"Our day together." He reached for another rice cake.

"Why do you want to memorize it?"

"Because we're never going to see each other, ever again."

The precision of the phrase startled her. She looked at him, feeling slightly depressed. Rohin didn't look depressed. He tapped the page. "Go on."

And so she drew the items as best as she could—the sofa, the director's chairs, the television, the telephone. He sidled up to her, so close that it was sometimes difficult to see what she was doing. He put his small brown hand over hers. "Now me."

She handed him the crayon.

He shook his head. "No, now draw me."

"I can't," she said. "It won't look like you."

The brooding look began to spread across Rohin's face again, just as it had when she'd refused him coffee. "Please?"

She drew his face, outlining his head and the thick fringe of hair. He sat perfectly still, with a formal, melancholy expression, his gaze fixed to one side. Miranda wished she could draw a good likeness. Her hand moved in conjunction with her eyes, in unknown ways, just as it had that day in the bookstore when she'd transcribed her name in Bengali letters. It looked nothing like him. She was in the middle of drawing his nose when he wriggled away from the table.

"I'm bored," he announced, heading toward her bedroom. She heard him opening the door, opening the drawers of her bureau and closing them.

When she joined him he was inside the closet. After a moment he emerged, his hair disheveled, holding the silver cocktail dress. "This was on the floor."

"It falls off the hanger."

Rohin looked at the dress and then at Miranda's body. "Put it on."

"Excuse me?"

"Put it on."

There was no reason to put it on. Apart from in the fitting room at Filene's she had never worn it, and as long as she was with Dev she knew she never would. She knew they would never go to restaurants, where he would reach across a table and kiss her hand. They would meet in her apartment, on Sundays, he in his sweatpants, she in her jeans. She took the dress from Rohin and shook it out, even though the slinky fabric never wrinkled. She reached into the closet for a free hanger.

"Please put it on," Rohin asked, suddenly standing behind her. He pressed his face against her, clasping her waist with both his thin arms. "Please?"

"All right," she said, surprised by the strength of his grip.

He smiled, satisfied, and sat on the edge of her bed.

"You have to wait out there," she said, pointing to the door. "I'll come out when I'm ready."

"But my mother always takes her clothes off in front of me."

"She does?"

Rohin nodded. "She doesn't even pick them up afterward. She leaves them all on the floor by the bed, all tangled.

"One day she slept in my room," he continued. "She said it felt better than her bed, now that my father's gone."

"I'm not your mother," Miranda said, lifting him by the armpits off her bed. When he refused to stand, she picked him up. He was heavier than she expected, and he clung to her, his legs wrapped firmly around her hips, his head resting against her chest. She set him down in the hallway and shut the door. As an extra precaution she fastened the latch. She changed into the dress, glancing into the full-length mirror nailed to the back of the door. Her ankle socks looked silly, and so she opened a drawer and found the stockings. She searched through the back of the closet and slipped on the high heels with the tiny buckles. The chain straps of the dress were as light as paper clips against her collarbone. It was a bit loose on her. She could not zip it herself.

Rohin began knocking. "May I come in now?"

She opened the door. Rohin was holding his almanac in his hands, muttering something under his breath. His eyes opened wide at the sight of her. "I need help with the zipper," she said. She sat on the edge of the bed.

Rohin fastened the zipper to the top, and then Miranda stood up and twirled. Rohin put down the almanac. "You're sexy," he declared.

"What did you say?"

"You're sexy."

Miranda sat down again. Though she knew it meant nothing, her heart skipped a beat. Rohin probably referred to all women as sexy. He'd probably heard the word on television, or seen it on the cover of a magazine. She remembered the day in the Mapparium, standing across the bridge from Dev. At the time she thought she knew what his words meant. At the time they'd made sense.

Miranda folded her arms across her chest and looked Rohin in the eyes. "Tell me something."

He was silent.

"What does it mean?"

"What?"

"That word. 'Sexy.' What does it mean?"

He looked down, suddenly shy. "I can't tell you."

"Why not?"

"It's a secret." He pressed his lips together, so hard that a bit of them went white.

"Tell me the secret. I want to know."

Rohin sat on the bed beside Miranda and began to kick the edge of the mattress with the backs of his shoes. He giggled nervously, his thin body flinching as if it were being tickled.

"Tell me," Miranda demanded. She leaned over and gripped his ankles, holding his feet still.

Rohin looked at her, his eyes like slits. He struggled to kick the mattress again, but Miranda pressed against him. He fell back on the bed, his back straight as a board. He cupped his hands around his mouth, and then he whispered, "It means loving someone you don't know."

Miranda felt Rohin's words under her skin, the same way she'd felt Dev's. But instead of going hot she felt numb. It reminded her of the way she'd felt at the Indian grocery, the moment she knew, without even looking at a picture, that Madhuri Dixit, whom Dev's wife resembled, was beautiful.

"That's what my father did," Rohin continued. "He sat next to someone he didn't know, someone sexy, and now he loves her instead of my mother."

He took off his shoes and placed them side by side on the floor. Then he peeled back the comforter and crawled into Miranda's bed with the almanac. A minute later the book dropped from his hands, and he closed his eyes. Miranda watched him sleep, the comforter rising and falling as he breathed. He didn't wake up after twelve minutes like Dev, or even twenty. He didn't open his eyes as she stepped out of the silver cocktail dress and back into her jeans, and put the high-heeled shoes in the back of the closet, and rolled up the stockings and put them back in her drawer.

When she had put everything away she sat on the bed. She leaned toward him, close enough to see some white powder from the rice cakes stuck to the corners of his mouth, and picked up the almanac. As she turned the pages she imagined the quarrels Rohin had overheard in his house in Montreal. "Is she pretty?" his mother would have asked his father, wearing the same bathrobe she'd worn for weeks, her own pretty face turning spiteful. "Is she sexy?" His father would deny it at first, try to change the subject. "Tell me," Rohin's mother would shriek, "tell me if she's sexy." In the end his father would admit that she was, and his mother would cry and cry, in a bed surrounded by a tangle of clothes, her eyes puffing up like bullfrogs. "How could you," she'd ask, sobbing, "how could you love a woman you don't even know?"

As Miranda imagined the scene she began to cry a little herself. In the Mapparium that day, all the countries had seemed close enough to touch, and Dev's voice had bounced wildly off the glass. From across the bridge, thirty feet away, his words had reached her ears, so near and full of warmth that they'd drifted for days under her skin. Miranda cried harder, unable to stop. But Rohin still slept. She guessed that he was used to it now, to the sound of a woman crying.

■ ■ ■

On Sunday, Dev called to tell Miranda he was on his way. "I'm almost ready. I'll be there at two."

She was watching a cooking show on television. A woman pointed to a row of apples, explaining which were best for baking. "You shouldn't come today."

"Why not?"

"I have a cold," she lied. It wasn't far from the truth; crying had left her congested. "I've been in bed all morning."

"You do sound stuffed up." There was a pause. "Do you need anything?"

"I'm all set."

"Drink lots of fluids."

"Dev?"

"Yes, Miranda?"

"Do you remember that day we went to the Mapparium?"

"Of course."

"Do you remember how we whispered to each other?"

"I remember," Dev whispered playfully.

"Do you remember what you said?"

There was a pause. " 'Let's go back to your place.' " He laughed quietly. "Next Sunday, then?"

The day before, as she'd cried, Miranda had believed she would never forget anything—not even the way her name looked written in Bengali. She'd fallen asleep beside Rohin and when she woke up he was drawing an airplane on the copy of *The Economist* she'd saved, hidden under the bed. "Who's Devajit Mitra?" he had asked, looking at the address label.

Miranda pictured Dev, in his sweatpants and sneakers, laughing into the phone. In a moment he'd join his wife downstairs, and tell her he wasn't going jogging. He'd pulled a muscle while stretching, he'd say, settling down to read the paper. In spite of herself, she longed for him. She would see him one more Sunday, she decided, perhaps two.

Then she would tell him the things she had known all along: that it wasn't fair to her, or to his wife, that they both deserved better, that there was no point in it dragging on.

But the next Sunday it snowed, so much so that Dev couldn't tell his wife he was going running along the Charles. The Sunday after that, the snow had melted, but Miranda made plans to go to the movies with Laxmi, and when she told Dev this over the phone, he didn't ask her to cancel them. The third Sunday she got up early and went out for a walk. It was cold but sunny, and so she walked all the way down Commonwealth Avenue, past the restaurants where Dev had kissed her, and then she walked all the way to the Christian Science center. The Mapparium was closed, but she bought a cup of coffee nearby and sat on one of the benches in the plaza outside the church, gazing at its giant pillars and its massive dome, and at the clear-blue sky spread over the city.

MANGO

■ ■ ■

Christian Langworthy

1

My brother and I were the sons of my mother's clients. We never knew
their names. Whenever we asked our mother about them, she wouldn't
say much. She just said they were both killed in the war between the
North and the South. She said one father died in a helicopter accident;
the other was ambushed while crossing a bridge. Mother told the same
story to all of our neighbors, and often smiled as she recounted the details. She never cried when she told these stories. Mother even laughed
once, when she admitted to a woman how she loved my brother's father
more than she loved mine.

Mother's clients were all around us, on the street corners and in
the pool halls. They were prison guards, truck drivers, mechanics,
and pilots. They were sergeants and majors, captains and corporals.
They lived on the military bases, in their Quonset huts and in clusters
of green tents. I watched them as they performed their duties in the
prisons, on the streets, or on the landing zones. I watched them pilot
their Huey and Chinook helicopters. My brother and I caught the
bubble gum they threw from the back of deuce-and-a-half trucks as

Born in Danang, Vietnam, in 1967, CHRISTIAN LANGWORTHY is the author of a chapbook of poems entitled *The Geography of War*. His fiction and
poetry have been selected for anthologies such as *Bold Words, Both Sides Now,
Watermark, Premonitions, Poetry Nation, Tilting the Continent, Vietnam
Forum,* and *Asian American Poetry*. He is currently writing a novel, from
which this story is excerpted.

their convoys rumbled by. I was fascinated with the soldiers and their weapons of war. They were my heroes.

Sometimes I took my brother out to the streets to imitate the way the soldiers walked and carried their rifles. We played war games on the streets with the neighborhood boys. Every military piece of trash that we found became a prized possession: belt buckles, brass shells, helmet liners, or canteens. But the most prized items were live rounds. We would try to fire the rounds, striking the priming caps with nails or dropping them off rooftops onto cement. Sometimes we unscrewed the bullets from their brass casings and used the black powder to make firecrackers that we lobbed like grenades over the neighbors' walls.

We pretended to be soldiers. We marched on the streets with the men in the green uniforms. In the afternoons, we staged gunfights and skirmishes in deserted alleys. Sometimes we marched down to the canal or to the harbor and pretended that we were being shipped off to war and, like soldiers, we waved good-bye to our loved ones.

My mother's clients talked to us in a language we didn't understand. They patted our shoulders and handed us candy. The men who stayed for more than a day bought us toys like boxing gloves and battery-powered jets. My mother would leave during the day and come back late at night. If she returned with a client we would hear whispers and hushed voices.

One afternoon, in the height of the rainy season, my brother and I slept in the back room of the bungalow behind a makeshift bamboo partition. It was dark in the bungalow when we were awakened, suddenly disturbed. Through the pattering of the raindrops, we heard voices groaning. Being curious, we both crept out to the front room, which was lit by a hurricane lamp. On a table in the center of the room, a soldier was bending over Mother. My brother and I approached the table and walked around it. Mother told us to go back to sleep, but we ignored her and watched. She was wearing a blouse, but was naked from the waist down. The soldier's green trousers hung around his ankles. His hips moved up and down like he was trying to climb on top of her. We circled the table several times. We giggled. We hoped to catch them kissing. The soldier said something, and Mother yelled at us, "Dung! Sa! You're not done napping!"

We ran to the back room, where we pretended to be asleep. Lying on our mats on the floor, we heard the man yell at Mother and then we heard the door slam shut.

Sa and I waited for Mother in the back room. We heard her as she put on her pants. It was so quiet that I could hear water from the rain gutters dripping into the cistern behind the bungalow. I tried to count each drop as it plunked into the cistern. After a while, we peeked around the bamboo partition. Mother sat at the table. She was counting stacks of bills by the light of the hurricane lamp. She looked at us and, without a word, went back to her counting. We moved around her with tentative steps. A cold draft slid through the open doorway into the room, and it seemed Mother's anger would never end. Geckos darted through the doorway. The rain fell harder, drumming on the tin roofs of the shantytown. The alley was flooded. The water came right up to our door. I heard a bread boy clapping teak sticks as he slogged his way through the rain.

"Baguettes!" he yelled, followed by the clap, clap of his sticks. Mother went to the bungalow door to answer his call. She bought two loaves of bread and paid him with a fresh, stiff bill. She pulled the loaves out of a damp paper bag and the room filled with the smell of yeast. Mother always did nice things for us after spending time with her clients. We broke the loaves in half and crumbs of crust fell to the floor. The baguettes were still warm and a happy feeling rose inside me. I felt it coming up as I ate the bread. I looked at Sa. He was happy too. Mother's anger was gone, and she let us sit next to her at the table as we ate.

Monsoon season passed. The men in the green uniforms entered and left our lives. They parked their Jeeps on the street, dusted themselves off with their field caps and trampled down our alley. They stepped out of rickshaws and looked toward our bungalow with their hands hidden in their pants pockets or tucked behind the buckles of pistol belts.

Mother usually went to her clients and left us to ourselves, but increasingly, they were sleeping in our bungalow. Sometimes from behind the bamboo partition, I heard their movements throughout the night. My ears strained to catch every little sound as they shifted the weight of their bodies—every rasp of an elbow as they brushed against each other on the sleeping mats. Sometimes my ears caught each moan or grunt, and each word they whispered. But occasionally, the roar of the jet bombers and the blades of the helicopters somewhere in the sky masked the sounds that they made.

Eventually, Sa and I associated the sounds of the helicopters with the presence of the soldiers, her clients. Sometimes the helicopters flew so low over the treetops we could see the faces of the pilots. On some days, we saw the soldiers who sat inside the helicopters with rucksacks on their laps and rifles between their knees. Whenever I heard the helicopters, I ran out from the bungalow to see if a soldier was nearby.

Sometimes in the evenings when Sa and I came home from the streets, we found Mother entertaining her clients. One man wrestled with us after he had wrestled with Mother. Another man was taken away by MPs who knocked on our door in the middle of the night. Whenever we could we slept with Mother, but the soldiers took most of her nights. It was only during the afternoons when temperatures were too hot to do anything that Mother napped with us in the cool air of the bungalow and held us in her arms.

One day, Sa and I came home to escape from the midday heat. A soldier was with Mother. She told us that he was staying for a little while. There was something about the way he looked at Mother that I did not like—the way his teeth showed, or how he rested the knuckles of his fists on his hips. My stomach felt sick. Sa went into the bungalow and lay down, but I ran out down the long alley and back into the street.

I searched for a stick, a long piece of metal, anything, but all that I could find was an ice cream stick broken lengthwise down the middle. Wielding the ice cream stick like a knife, I headed back to the bungalow. I stomped past a small garden plot and local water well with its iron pump handle down. Mother and her client had come out to look for me. I confronted them near a neighbor's clothesline, where some white bedsheets hung.

"I'll kill you," I shouted at the soldier and waved the ice cream stick threateningly. "Go away."

The soldier didn't understand what I had said, but he understood my body language. He laughed and nervously slapped a field cap against his thigh. Mother was furious. She was about to hit me, but the soldier stopped her. He pulled money from his pockets and extended his hand. He said something in his foreign language. I saw the colorful bills he waved in front of my eyes. I looked at the soldier and then at Mother. The white bedsheets billowed behind her. "Take it," she said.

I grabbed the money. I ran to the nearest street vendor, where I bought a pop pistol and a packet of red strip-paper ammo. Tearing open the plastic packet, I loaded the pistol with a strip of ammo. All afternoon, I ran up and down the streets, past the comic book stands, past the shoeshine boys and girls, and I shot at people. Then I ran to the temple grounds and shot the monks sitting on moss-covered steps guarded on both sides by stone dragons. I scampered across the railroad tracks into the local market and shot the merchants squatting over baskets of squid and shrimp. I shot the cloth vendors unrolling bolts of silk and linen. Then the lanes between the vending stalls became too crowded, so I left the market to roam the streets again and kept shooting until it was safe to go home.

2

Days passed. I wondered if the soldier who gave me money would ever come back. I wondered about the war. I didn't know what it was about, but I was told that the Communists were bad. Sometimes Sa and I talked about the war and what kind of heroes our fathers might have been.

We didn't see much of the war, though it was never far away. It was on the other side of the canal, over the hills in the mountains and jungle. We never saw the battles or the skirmishes in the swamps and paddies. To us the war was the distant thunder of howitzers, the shudder of our bungalow door, the helicopter blades whipping the air. It was green and yellow star clusters flaring across the moonless skies, the prison searchlights and the air raid sirens. It was the sand-filled burlap bags of the bomb shelter and the faces of strangers springing from the dark under the lantern light. The war was the muffled reports of assault rifles somewhere in the jungle, the cadences of soldiers marching through the streets of Da Nang. It was orange-robed monks leading funeral processions through streets littered with the fresh dung of oxen.

Sometimes the war was sticks of incense burned for prayer, sometimes olive-green tin cans of C rations labeled with black stars. Sometimes it was canisters of spilled chemicals and sun-blistered barrels of tar in the slums and shantytowns where we lived. But the war was mostly news over the radio and stories overheard from our neighbors. Stories of the death of a son, father, or distant cousin. Stories like the one Mother told of how our fathers died. I imagined what must have happened to my father as Mother told neighbors her version of the story. While my mother and her friends drank tea in the afternoons and read the veins of tea leaves held over candles to tell their fortunes, I saw my father crossing a bridge over a narrow river. I saw the hump of the rucksack on his back, his ammo clips, and his rifle. I imagined the pineapple grenade arcing in the sky and bouncing on the wooden planks of the bridge. Then Mother would tell the story of how Sa's father died: how he had run from an exploding helicopter on a landing zone and how a rotor blade had cut off his head.

We never knew for sure if the stories were true, but we assumed our fathers died the deaths of heroes. Sometimes we thought our fathers were still alive, that they walked the streets of Da Nang. We thought that they would pull up in a Jeep or jump out of a helicopter that landed nearby. We wanted to find our fathers. We often searched the faces of the soldiers patrolling the streets and sometimes we mistook a client for a father. Whenever Sa and I were alone with Mother, we asked her about our fathers. We asked her about them during the typhoons that trapped us in our bungalow.

Once during a typhoon, as Mother lit sticks of incense to pray to the Buddha in our bungalow, Sa asked her if she had a picture of his father. She shook her head, knelt down, and prayed for our safety. Though she said no, we always wondered if she had the photographs. We wondered if she hid the photographs in a footlocker given to her by one of her clients. She kept it locked up in a far corner of the bungalow and was always careful to guard its contents from our eyes. The footlocker was a box full of secrets. As the typhoon winds ripped up the corrugated tin roofs of the shantytown and flung the roofs like paper into the air and whipped the rain against our door, we begged Mother to let us see what was in the footlocker. Then we asked her questions about our fathers and questions about America.

"What did he look like?" we each asked her, as the typhoon winds howled and water seeped underneath the door.

"You'll see one day," she said.

Over the course of the typhoon, we haggled her with more questions, but her answers were always brief and vague while she pretended to be busy counting her bills and coins and stuffing them in empty tea boxes stacked up against the bungalow wall that faced the Buddha.

The typhoon ended. The floodwaters receded from the alley, and we could walk out to the streets again. The men in the green uniforms returned to the doorsteps of our bungalow. They strolled down our alley dressed in fatigues, wearing web belts and shoulder harnesses and holstered pistols. They jumped off the backs of deuce-and-a-halves in the various greens of their camouflage, in drab olive-green fatigues with deep pockets and worn-out mechanic's greens mired with oil and dirt from repairing the engines of tanks or working under the bellies of Hueys and Chinooks. They knocked on our door in the amber green of shirts and trousers burned by the hot steam of the ironing press. They stepped out of Jeeps in the emerald green of dress uniforms worn for traveling or staying in the garrison. Sometimes they approached our bungalow with smiles, but most often with stern looks and tired eyes.

They were the men in the green uniforms, the men who threw us gum, patted our shoulders, and brought us toys. But when they came to see our mother, they slipped off their black boots and their pressed uniforms. When they left, their uniforms were creased and crumpled. Sometimes Sa and I spied on Mother and her clients through the cracks of the bamboo partition. As the clients undressed, we saw them change from green to the color of the chameleons that we caught on rocks as they changed from emerald to stone.

Mother ventured out and left us to ourselves. Sa and I emerged from the bungalow excited about the flooding and the wreckage. We played in the retreating waters of the flooded dumps. We surfed on broken doors floating in the knee-deep waters. We forgot about our fathers, forgot about America until we came back home and saw a client leaving our bungalow. I liked the typhoons because my mother stayed home with us and because the clients were absent. Without them, it was just the three of us waiting out the storms.

One day soon after the storms, when the cement blocks of our bungalow walls were still wet, Sa and I walked to the neighbor's rain gutters and showered under the run-off. With our clothes wet, our hair matted down, and our rubber sandals squeaking, we started down the alley towards home. The tomato vines had been stripped of their leaves, and all the fruit was crushed and scattered across the muddy ground. The bushes of chili peppers and grapefruit trees were usually shaded. Now, with the broad leaves of the banana trees ripped to shreds, they sat exposed to the hot sun.

As we approached the patio, we saw that a dark-haired soldier was stretched out in our hammock. His field cap covered his face. One arm rested on his stomach and the other hung off the side of the hammock. The fingers of his hand gripped the blue plastic straps of a pair of roller skates. The metal skates shone in the sun. I looked at Sa, and I knew that we wondered the same thing: maybe this soldier was one of our fathers. As we stepped closer, our sandals squeaked. We stood beside the hammock and looked down at the dark-haired soldier. He seemed to be asleep. The bungalow door was open. I knew Mother was inside and would come out at any moment. The soldier had a dark tan and curly black hair. Suddenly, he kicked up his feet, sat up, and grabbed Sa in one swift movement. He smiled and laughed—his laughter infectious. He picked up the roller skates and pointed toward Sa's bare feet. Smiling, Sa took off his sandals, and the soldier strapped the skates on for him. Then he gripped Sa's arms and pushed him backward on the patio cement. I laughed. The soldier let him go. Sa stood stiffly with his arms out and his knees locked straight, then kicked his legs and rolled until he tumbled onto the cement.

Mother came out of the bungalow and handed the soldier a glass of lemonade. With ice in it, the glass was sweating in the heat of the afternoon. Mother must have gotten the ice from the market. It was rare that she bought blocks of ice, which had been wrapped in burlap bags and stored in sawdust. But occasionally she bought it when she crushed green tea leaves and made iced tea, and among her utensils was an awl that she used for chipping it. I looked at the dark-haired soldier and at the chips floating in the glass. I thought he was one of our fathers because he was special enough to get ice in his glass.

"Can I have some ice?" I asked. I knew there was a whole block somewhere in the bungalow.

"Me too!" said Sa, who slipped on the roller skates and nearly fell face first on the cement patio.

Mother went into the bungalow. We heard her chipping the block, heard each strike of the awl. The dark-haired soldier pushed Sa around some more. He rolled back and forth on the patio and bounced from wall to wall.

When the chipping sound stopped, Mother appeared at the door with two chunks of ice and gave them to us. The chunk was so cold in my hand that I kept switching it from one hand to the other. I bit off a small piece, and the ice was so cold on my teeth that they hurt.

The dark-haired soldier drank from his glass of lemonade. Sa rolled around clumsily on the patio and fell again, bumping into the soldier's legs. As the soldier tried to haul Sa onto his feet, some of the lemonade spilled from his glass and left a wet spot on his trousers.

Mother put her hands on my shoulders. She patted me on the head and looked into my eyes.

"Take Sa down the street to the sidewalk," she said. "And practice riding the skates." She gave me some money. "You can buy a drink from the vendors when you're both thirsty."

Sa held onto my arm to keep himself steady as he stepped off the patio, and I pushed and pulled him up the alley and out into the street. I looked back down the tunnel of the alley, toward the patio and the hammock. Mother and the soldier had disappeared into the bungalow.

It didn't take us long to learn how to roll around on the skates without falling down. We took turns skating and chasing each other down the sidewalk and the hard-packed dirt of the street. It was so hot that we skated only in the shaded sections of the sidewalk. The streets were quiet while everyone took an afternoon nap, so we skated back and forth down the whole length of the sidewalk. We started out slowly and then we skated faster. The ball bearings in the wheels hissed. We kicked our feet behind us, pushed ourselves forward, and felt the wind of speed against our cheeks.

We skated until we were thirsty and then we went to the vendors. We stood by as the vendor crushed sugarcane for our drinks by drawing the stalks through two wooden rollers. While we waited, he cut off two small slices and gave them to us to chew on.

When we were tired from the sun and the skating, we headed back to the alley. The door to the bungalow was shut. I had on the roller skates, stepped onto the patio, and skated to the door. I tried to open it, pulling and yanking on the doorknob, but it was locked. I heard my mother's voice whispering inside. I pounded on the door with my fists.

"Let us in," I said. "We're home."

No one answered. No one came to the door. I pounded harder, and as I slammed my fist again, the skates kicked out from under me. I stuck my arm out straight to cushion my fall. When my hand hit the cement, a sharp pain shot up from my elbow. I screamed. Sa pounded on the door, shouting, "Come out! Dung broke his arm!"

The door opened, and Mother came out. She was pulling her shirt over her pants and she looked down at me while I cradled the injured elbow with my other arm.

"What did you do?" she said. Her client stood behind her. The pain in my elbow hurt so much that I could barely speak. I swallowed a big gulp of air. I tried not to cry in front of the soldier.

"He slipped and fell on his arm," Sa said. "I think he broke it."

Mother got down on her knees and squeezed my elbow. "Does that hurt?"

"It hurts," I said, almost in a whisper.

She tried to straighten my elbow. I screamed. The dark-haired soldier knelt beside me. He pressed his fingers into my tender elbow. I winced and screamed again. Then he probed my bony arm, touching gently. When he finished, he looked up at my mother and shook his head.

"Your arm isn't broken," she said. "You jammed it."

The soldier said something to my mother and then walked quickly out to the alley. When he came back, he held some blue cloth in his hands.

"He's going to put your elbow in a sling," my mother said. She saw the fear in my eyes.

The soldier lifted my injured arm, wrapped the blue cloth under my elbow, and tied the sling around my neck. He smiled, and his brown eyes were bright in the afternoon sun. He said a few things to Mother, disappeared into the bungalow, and came back out. I knew he was about to leave, but when he turned to say good-bye, he brought his arms from behind his back and gave me a tea box sealed with green tape.

"There's a gift for you inside," Mother said. "But you can't open the tea box until your elbow heals."

I waited for a week. My elbow still hurt a little, but my mother said I could open the box. I took a knife, cut the tape, and pulled out something with green bands and moving dials.

"A watch!" I said.

"Now you can tell time," my mother said as she stitched a patch over a hole on my brother's shorts.

"How can I do that?" I asked.

"I'll show you," she said. "See the little hands?"

"What hands?"

She pointed to the face of the watch. "These little things. They're called hands."

"They don't look like hands," I said. "They look like needles."

"Okay, then. The little needle shows the hours. The big needle shows the minutes."

"What are hours and minutes?" I asked.

"Ways to tell the time," she said. "Days are made of hours and hours are made of minutes."

"How many hours in a minute?" I asked.

"Minutes are smaller," she said, laughing. "Hours are made of minutes."

"Then why is the big needle the minutes? Shouldn't the big needle be the hours?"

"Because minutes happen faster," she said, exasperated, and continued her stitching.

I didn't understand the concept of time. I only knew the passing of days and nights between Mother's leaving and her eventual return. I knew the moments between the arrival and departure of my mother's clients, when they entered and left our alley.

We never knew where Mother's clients came from. Sa and I knew only that the land, the air, and the sea brought them. We watched them as they lumbered under the weight of their war gear and marched down the loading ramps of cargo planes and rode into town on trucks and Jeeps.

We cheered them as they disembarked from the decks of warships and landed on our coast with their rifles and steel pots and field caps shielding their eyes. We watched them as they jumped from the bellies of helicopters hovering over the landing zones and flattening the marsh grass into a carpet. We spied on them while crouched behind the grassy berms bordering the landing zones. We watched them loading crates of weapons and boxes of ammo and medical supplies into the backs of deuce-and-a-halves.

On many afternoons, we stood outside the gates of the prison or the army base on the other side of town and studied the soldiers, their uniforms and equipment. In a game that we played, we categorized them into the foot soldiers and the sailors, the men who drove tanks, the pilots who flew jets and helicopters. Then there were the soldiers our fathers must have known: the ones who patrolled the jungles and never came back. We spotted the soldiers who worked as cooks in the mess halls, and the soldiers who guarded the prisons, and the ones who worked in the Quonset huts and never were killed.

I knew time as the moments Sa and I roamed the streets and harbors and watched the men of war—the men who sometimes strolled down our alley. Time was when we peeked through the cracks in the bamboo partition at Mother and her clients. Time was the number of water drops plunking into the cistern. That was all I knew of seconds, minutes, and hours. Though I didn't know how to read the moving hands, I knew that it was a gift, that the watch was mine.

AHJUHMA

from NATIVE SPEAKER

■ ■ ■

Chang-rae Lee

I thought it would be the two of us, like that, forever.

But one day my father called from one of his vegetable stores in the Bronx and said he was going to JFK and would be late coming home. I didn't think much of it. He often went to the airport, to the international terminal, to pick up a friend or a parcel from Korea. After my mother's death he had a steady flow of old friends visiting us, hardly any relatives, and it was my responsibility to make up the bed in the guest room and prepare a tray of sliced fruit and corn tea or liquor for their arrival.

My mother had always done this for guests; although I was a boy, I was the only child and there was no one else to peel the oranges and apples and set out nuts and spicy crackers and glasses of beer or a bottle of Johnnie Walker for my father and his friends. They used to sit on the carpeted floor around the lacquered Korean table with their legs crossed and laugh deeply and utterly together as if they had been holding themselves in for a long time, and I'd greedily pick at the snacks from the perch of my father's sturdy lap, pinching my throat in just such a way that I might rumble and shake, too. My mother would smile and talk to them, but she sat on a chair just outside the circle of men and politely covered her mouth whenever one of them made her laugh or offered compliments on her still-fresh beauty and youth.

Born in Seoul, Korea, in 1965, CHANG-RAE LEE is the author of two novels, *A Gesture Life* and *Native Speaker*. He has won the Hemingway Foundation/PEN Award, among other honors, for *Native Speaker*, and was selected as one of the twenty best American writers under forty by *The New Yorker*. He lives in New Jersey with his family and teaches at Princeton University.

The night my father phoned I went to the cabinet where he kept the whiskey and nuts and took out a bottle for their arrival. An ashtray, of course, because the men always smoked. The men—it was always only men—were mostly friends of his from college now come to the States on matters of business. Import-export. They seemed exotic to me then. They wore shiny, textured gray-blue suits and wide ties and sported long sideburns and slightly too large brown-tinted polarizing glasses. It was 1971. They dragged into the house huge square plastic suitcases on wheels, stuffed full of samples of their wares, knock-off perfumes and colognes, gaudy women's handkerchiefs, plastic AM radios cast in the shapes of footballs and automobiles, leatherette handbags, purses, belts, tinny watches and cuff links, half-crushed boxes of Oriental rice crackers and leathery sheets of dried squid, and bags upon bags of sickly-sweet sucking candy whose transparent wrappers were edible and dissolved on the tongue.

In the foyer these men had to struggle to pull off the tight black shoes from their swollen feet, and the sour, ammoniac smell of sweat-sopped wool and cheap leather reached me where I stood overlooking them from the raised living room of our split-level house, that nose-stinging smell of sixteen hours of sleepless cramped flight from Seoul to Anchorage to New York shot so full of their ranks, hopeful of good commerce here in America.

My father opened the door at ten o'clock, hauling into the house two huge, battered suitcases. I had just set out a tray of fruits and rice cakes to go along with the liquor on the low table in the living room and went down to help him. He waved me off and nodded toward the driveway.

"Go help," he said, immediately bearing the suitcases upstairs.

I walked outside. A dim figure of a woman stood unmoving in the darkness next to my father's Chevrolet. It was late winter, still cold and miserable, and she was bundled up in a long woolen coat that nearly reached the ground. Beside her were two small bags and a cardboard box messily bound with twine. When I got closer to her she lifted both bags and so I picked up the box; it was very heavy, full of glass jars and tins of pickled vegetables and meats. I realized she had transported homemade food thousands of miles, all the way from Korea, and the stench of overripe kimchee shot up through the cardboard flaps and I nearly dropped the whole thing.

The woman mumbled something in an unusual accent about my not knowing what kimchee was, but I didn't answer. I thought she was a very distant relative. She didn't look at all like us, nothing like my mother, whose broad, serene face was the smoothest mask. This woman, I could see, had deep pockmarks stippling her high, fleshy cheeks, like the scarring from a mistreated bout of chickenpox or smallpox, and she stood much shorter than I first thought, barely five feet in her heeled shoes. Her ankles and wrists were as thick as posts. She waited for me to turn and start for the house before she followed several steps behind me. I was surprised that my father wasn't waiting in the doorway, to greet her or hold the door, and as I walked up the carpeted steps leading to the kitchen I saw that the food and drink I had prepared had been cleared away.

"Please come this way," he said to her stiffly in Korean, appearing from the hallway to the bedrooms. "Please come this way."

He ushered her into the guest room and shut the door behind them. After a few minutes he came back out and sat down in the kitchen with me. He hadn't changed out of his work clothes, and his shirt and the knees and cuffs of his pants were stained with the slick juice of spoiled vegetables. I was eating apple quarters off the tray. My father picked one, bit into it, and then put it back. This was a habit of his, perhaps because he worked with fruits and vegetables all day, randomly sampling them for freshness and flavor.

He started speaking, but in English. Sometimes, when he wanted to hide or not outright lie, he chose to speak in English. He used to break into it when he argued with my mother, and it drove her crazy when he did and she would just plead, "No, no!" as though he had suddenly introduced a switchblade into a clean fistfight. Once, when he was having some money problems with a store, he started berating her with some awful stream of nonsensical street talk, shouting "my hot mama shit ass tight cock sucka," and "slant-eye spic-and-span motha-fucka" (he had picked it up, no doubt, from his customers). I broke into their argument and started yelling at him, making sure I was speaking in complete sentences about his cowardice and unfairness, shooting back at him his own medicine, until he slammed both palms on the table and demanded, "You shut up! You shut up!"

I kept at him anyway, using the biggest words I knew, whether they made sense or not, school words like "socioeconomic" and "intangible," anything I could lift from my dizzy burning thoughts and hurl against him, until my mother, who'd been perfectly quiet the whole time, whacked me hard across the back of the head and shouted in Korean, *Who do you think you are?*

Fair fight or not, she wasn't going to let me dress down my father, not with language, not with anything.

"Hen-*ry*," he now said, accenting as always the second syllable, "you know, it's difficult now. Your mommy dead and nobody at home. You too young for that. This nice lady, she come for you. Take care home, food. Nice dinner. Clean house. Better that way."

I didn't answer him.

"I better tell you before, I know, but I know you don't like. So what I do? I go to store in morning and come home late, nine o'clock, ten. No good, no good. Nice lady, she fix that. And soon we move to nice neighborhood, over near Fern Pond, big house and yard. Very nice place."

"Fern Pond? I don't want to move! And I don't want to move there, all the rich kids live there."

"Ha!" he laughed. "You rich kid now, your daddy rich rich man. Big house, big tree, now even we got houselady. Nice big yard for you. I pay all cash."

"What? You bought a house already?"

"Price very low for big house. Fix-her-upper. You thank me some-day . . ."

"I won't. I won't move. No way."

Byong-ho, he said firmly. His voice was already changing. He was shifting into Korean, getting his throat ready. Then he spoke as he rose to leave. *Let's not hear one more thing about it. The woman will come with us to the new house and take care of you. This is what I have de-cided. Our talk is past usefulness. There will be no other way.*

In the new house, the woman lived in the two small rooms behind the kitchen pantry. I decided early on that I would never venture in there or try to befriend her. Her manner unnerved me. She never laughed. She spoke only when it mattered, when a thing needed to be done, or requested, or acknowledged. Otherwise the sole sounds I heard from her were the sucking noises she would make through the spaces between her teeth after meals and in the mornings. Once I heard her humming a pretty melody in her room, some Korean folk song, but as I walked toward her doorway to hear it better she stopped immediately, and I never heard it again.

She kept a clean and orderly house. Because she was the one who really moved us from the old house, she organized and ran the new one in a manner that suited her. In the old Korean tradition, my presence in the kitchen was unwelcome unless I was actually eating, or passing through the room. I understood that her two rooms, the tiny bathroom adjoining them, and the kitchen and pantry, constituted the sphere of her influence, and she was quick to deflect any interest on my part to look into the cabinets or closets. If she were present, I was to ask her for something I wanted, even if it was in the refrigerator, and then she would get it for me. She became annoyed if I lingered too long, and I quickly learned to remove myself immediately after any eating or drinking. Only when a friend of mine was over, after school or sports, would she mysteriously recede from the kitchen. My tall, talkative white friends made her nervous. Then she would wait noiselessly in her back room until we had gone.

She smelled strongly of fried fish and sesame oil and garlic. Though I didn't like it, my friends called her "Aunt Scallion," and made faces behind her back.

Sometimes I thought she was some kind of zombie. When she wasn't cleaning or cooking or folding clothes she was barely present; she never whistled or hummed or made any noise, and it seemed to me as if she only partly possessed her own body, and preferred it that way. When she sat in the living room or outside on the patio she never read or listened to music. She didn't have a hobby, as far as I could see. She never exercised. She sometimes watched the soap operas on television (I found this out when I stayed home sick from school), but she always turned them off after a few minutes.

She never called her family in Korea, and they never called her. I imagined that something deeply horrible had happened to her when she was young, some nameless pain, something brutal, that a malicious man had taught her fear and sadness and she had had to leave her life and family because of it.

■ ■ ■

Years later, when the three of us came on Memorial Day for the summer-long stay with my father, he had the houselady prepare the apartment above the garage for us. Whenever we first opened its door at the top of the creaky narrow stairs we smelled the fresh veneers of pine oil and bleach and lemon balm. The pine floors were shimmering and dangerously slick. Mitt would dash past us to the king-sized mattress in the center of the open space and tumble on the neatly sheeted bed. The bed was my parents' old one; my father bought himself a twin the first year we moved into the new house. The rest of the stuff in the apartment had come with the property: there was an old leather sofa; a chest of drawers; a metal office desk; my first stereo, the all-in-one kind, still working; and someone's nod to a kitchen, thrown together next to the bathroom in the far corner, featuring a dorm-style refrigerator, a half-sized two-burner stove, and the single cabinet above it.

Mitt and Lelia loved that place. Lelia especially liked the tiny secret room that was tucked behind a false panel in the closet. The room, barely six by eight, featured a single-paned window in the shape of a face that swung out to a discreet view of my father's exquisitely land-scaped garden of cut stones and flowers. She wrote back in that room during the summer, slipping in at sunrise before I left for Purchase, and was able to complete a handful of workable poems by the time we departed on Labor Day, when she had to go back to teaching.

Mitt liked the room, too, for its pitched ceiling that he could almost reach if he tippy-toed, and I could see he felt himself bigger in there as he stamped about in my father's musty cordovans like some thundering giant, sweeping at the air, though he only ventured in during the late afternoons when enough light could angle inside and warmly lamp every crag and corner nook. He got locked in once for a few hours, the panel becoming stuck somehow, and we heard his wails all the way from the kitchen in the big house.

"Spooky," Mitt pronounced that night, fearful and unashamed as he lay between us in our bed, clutching his mother's thigh.

Mitt slept with us those summers until my father bought him his own canvas army cot. That's what the boy wanted. He liked the camou-flaging pattern of the thick fabric and sometimes tipped the thing on its side and shot rubber-tipped arrows at me and Lelia from behind its cover. We had to shoot them back before he would agree to go to bed.

When he was an infant we waited until he was asleep and then deli-cately placed him atop our two pillows, which we arranged on the floor next to the bed. We lay still a few minutes until we could hear his breathing deepen and become rhythmic. That's when we made love. It was warm up there in the summer and we didn't have to strip or do anything sudden. We moved as mutely and as deftly as we could bear, muffling ourselves in one another's hair and neck so as not to wake him, but then, too, of course, so we could hear the sound of his sleeping, his breathing, ours, that strange conspiring. Afterward, we lay quiet again, to make certain of his slumber, and then lifted him back between our hips into the bed, so heavy and alive with our mixed scent.

"Hey," Lelia whispered to me one night that first summer, "the woman, in the house, what do you think she does at night?"

"I don't know," I said, stroking her arm, Mitt's.

"I mean, does she have any friends or relatives?"

I didn't know.

She then said, "There's no one else besides your father?"

"I don't think she has anyone here. They're all in Korea."

"Has she ever gone back to visit?"

"I don't think so," I said. "I think she sends them money instead."

"God," Lelia answered. "How awful." She brushed back the damp downy hair from Mitt's forehead. "She must be so lonely."

"Does she seem lonely?" I asked.

She thought about it for a moment. "I guess not. She doesn't seem like she's anything. I keep looking for something, but even when she's with your father there's nothing in her face. She's been here since you were young, right?"

I nodded.

"You think they're friends?" she asked.

"I doubt it."

"Lovers?"

I had to answer, "Maybe."

"So what's her name?" Lelia asked after a moment.

"I don't know."

"What?"

I told her that I didn't know. That I had never known.

"What's that you call her, then?" she said. "I thought that was her name. Your father calls her that, too."

"It's not her name," I told her. "It's not her name. It's just a form of address."

It was the truth. Lelia had great trouble accepting this stunning ignorance of mine. That summer, when it seemed she was thinking about it, she would stare in wonderment at me as if I had a gaping hole blown through my head. I couldn't blame her. Americans live on a first-name basis. She didn't understand that there weren't moments in our language—the rigorous, regimental one of family and servants—when the woman's name could have naturally come out. Or why it wasn't important. At breakfast and lunch and dinner my father and I called her "Ah-juh-ma," literally *aunt*, but more akin to "ma'am," the customary address to an unrelated Korean woman. But in our context the title bore much less deference. I never heard my father speak her name in all the years she was with us.

But then he never even called my mother by her name, nor did she ever in my presence speak his. She was always and only "spouse" or "wife" or "Mother"; he was "husband" or "Father" or "Henry's father." And to this day, when someone asks what my parents' names were, I have to pause for a moment, I have to rehear them not from the memory of my own voice, my own calling to them, but through the staticky voices of their old friends phoning from the other end of the world.

"I can't believe this," Lelia cried, her long Scottish face all screwed up in the moonlight. "You've known her since you were a kid! She practically raised you."

"I don't know who raised me," I said to her.

"Well, she must have had something to do with it!" She nearly woke up Mitt.

She whispered, "What do you think cooking and cleaning and ironing is? That's what she does all day, if you haven't noticed. Your father depends so much on her. I'm sure you did, too, when you were young."

"Of course I did," I answered. "But what do you want, what do you want me to say?"

"There's nothing you *have* to say. I just wonder, that's all. This woman has given twenty years of her life to you and your father and it still seems like she could be anyone to you. It doesn't seem to matter who she is. Right? If your father switched her now with someone else, probably nothing would be different."

She paused. She brought up her knees so they were even with her hips. She pulled Mitt to her chest.

"Careful," I said. "You'll wake him."

"It scares me," she said. "I just think about you and me. What I am . . ."

"Don't be crazy," I said.

"I am not being crazy," she replied carefully. Mitt started to whimper. I slung my arm over her belly. She didn't move. This was the way, the very slow way, that our conversations were spoiling.

"I'll ask my father tomorrow," I stupidly said.

Lelia didn't say anything to that. After a while she turned away, Mitt still tight against her belly.

"Sweetie . . ."

I whispered to her. I craned and licked the soft hair above her neck. She didn't budge. "Let's not make this something huge."

"My *God*," she whispered.

■ ■ ■

For the next few days, Lelia was edgy. She wouldn't say much to me. She wandered around the large wooded yard with Mitt strapped tightly in her chest sling. Close to her. She wasn't writing, as far as I could tell. And she generally stayed away from the house; she couldn't bear to watch the woman do anything. Finally, Lelia decided to talk to her; I would have to interpret. We walked over to the house and found her dusting in the living room. But when the woman saw us purposefully approaching her, she quickly crept away so that we had to follow her into the dining room and then to the kitchen until she finally disappeared into her back rooms. I stopped us at the threshold. I called in and said that my wife wanted to speak with her. No answer. "Ahjuhma," I then called to the silence, "Ahjuhma!"

Finally her voice shot back, *There's nothing for your American wife and me to talk about. Will you please leave the kitchen. It is very dirty and needs cleaning.*

Despite how Ahjuhma felt about the three of us, our unusual little family, Lelia made several more futile attempts before she gave up. The woman didn't seem to accept Mitt, she seemed to sour when she looked upon his round, only half-Korean eyes and the reddish highlights in his hair.

One afternoon Lelia cornered the woman in the laundry room and tried to communicate with her while helping her fold a pile of clothes fresh out of the dryer. But each time Lelia picked up a shirt or a pair of shorts the woman gently tugged it away and quickly folded it herself. I walked by then and saw them standing side by side in the narrow steamy room, Lelia guarding her heap and grittily working as fast as she could, the woman steadily keeping pace with her, not a word or a glance between them. Lelia told me later that the woman actually began nudging her in the side with the fleshy mound of her low-set shoulder, grunting and pushing her out of the room with short steps; Lelia began hockey-checking back with her elbows, trying to hold her position, when by accident she caught her hard on the ear and the woman let out a loud shrill whine that sent them both scampering from the room. Lelia ran out to where I was working inside the garage, tears streaming from her eyes; we hurried back to the house, only to find the woman back in the laundry room, carefully refolding the dry laundry. She backed away when she saw Lelia and cried madly in Korean, *You cat! You nasty American cat!*

I scolded her then, telling her she couldn't speak to my wife that way if she wanted to keep living in our house. The woman bit her lip; she bent her head and bowed severely before me in a way that perhaps no one could anymore and then trundled out of the room between us. I suddenly felt as if I'd committed a great wrong.

Lelia shouted, "What did she say? What did you say? What the hell just happened?"

But I didn't answer her immediately and she cursed "Goddamnit!" under her breath and ran out the back door toward the apartment. I went after her but she wouldn't slow down. When I reached the side stairs to the apartment I heard the door slam hard above. I climbed the stairs and opened the door and saw she wasn't there. Then I realized that she'd already slipped into the secret room behind the closet.

She was sitting at my old child's desk below the face-shaped window, her head down in her folded arms. When I touched her shoulder she began shuddering, sobbing deeply into the bend of her elbow, and when I tried to coax her out she shook me off and dug in deeper. So I embraced her huddled figure, and she let me do that, and after a while she turned out of herself and began crying into my belly, where I felt the wetness blotting the front of my shirt.

"Come on," I said softly, stroking her hair. "Try to take it easy. I'm sorry. I don't know what to say about her. She's always been a mystery to me."

She soon calmed down and stopped crying. Lelia cried easily, but back then in our early days I didn't know and each time she wept I feared the worst, that it meant something catastrophic was happening between us, an irreversible damage. What I should have feared was the damage unseen, what she wouldn't end up crying over or even speaking about in our last good year.

"She's not a mystery to me, Henry," she now answered, her whole face looking as though it had been stung. With her eyes swollen like that and her high cheekbones, she looked almost Asian, like a certain kind of Russian. She wiped her eyes with her sleeve. She looked out the little window.

"I know who she is."

"Who?" I said, wanting to know.

"She's an abandoned girl. But all grown up."

■ ■ ■

During high school I used to wander out to the garage from the house to read or just get away after one of the countless arguments I had with my father. Our talk back then was in fact one long and grave contention, an incessant quarrel, though to hear it now would be to recognize the usual forms of homely rancor and still homelier devotion, involving all the dire subjects of adolescence—my imperfect studies, my unworthy friends, the driving of his car, smoking and drinking, the whatever and whatever. One of our worst nights of talk was after he suggested that the girl I was taking to the eighth-grade Spring Dance didn't—or couldn't—find me attractive.

"What you think she like?" he asked, or more accurately said, shaking his head to tell me I was a fool. We had been watching the late news in his study.

"She likes *me*," I told him defiantly. "Why is that so hard for you to take?"

He laughed at me. "You think she like your funny face? Funny eyes? You think she dream you at night?"

"I really don't know, Dad," I answered. "She's not even my girlfriend or anything. I don't know why you bother so much."

"Bother?" he said. "*Bother?*"

"Nothing, Dad, nothing."

"Your mother say exact same," he decreed.

"Just forget it."

"No, no, *you* forget it," he shot back, his voice rising. "You don't know nothing! This American girl, she nobody for you. She don't know nothing about you. You Korean man. So so different. Also, she know we live in expensive area."

"So what!" I gasped.

"You real dummy, Henry. Don't you know? You just free dance ticket. She just using you." Just then the housekeeper shuffled by us into her rooms on the other side of the pantry.

"I guess that's right," I said. "I should have seen that. You know it all. I guess I still have much to learn from you about dealing with women."

"What you say!" he exploded. "What you say!" He slammed his palm on the side lamp table, almost breaking the plate of smoked glass. I started to leave but he grabbed me hard by the neck as if to shake me and I flung my arm back and knocked off his grip. We were turned on each other, suddenly ready to go, and I could tell he was as astonished as I to be glaring this way at his only blood. He took a step back, afraid of what might have happened. Then he threw up his hands and just muttered, "Stupid."

A few weeks later I stumbled home from the garage apartment late one night, drunk on some gin filched from a friend's parents' liquor cabinet. My father appeared downstairs at the door and I promptly vomited at his feet on the newly refinished floors. He didn't say anything and just helped me to my room. When I struggled down to the landing the next morning the mess was gone. I still felt nauseous. I went to the kitchen and he was sitting there with his tea, smoking and reading the Korean-language newspaper. I sat across from him.

"Did she clean it up?" I asked, looking about for the woman. He looked at me like I was crazy. He put down the paper and rose and disappeared into the pantry. He returned with a bottle of bourbon and glasses and he carefully poured two generous jiggers of it. It was nine o'clock on Sunday morning. He took one for himself and then slid the other under me.

"*Mah-shuh!*" he said firmly. *Drink!* I could see he was serious. "*Mah-shuh!*"

He sat there, waiting. I lifted the stinking glass to my lips and could only let a little of the alcohol seep onto my tongue before I leaped to the sink and dry-heaved uncontrollably. And as I turned with tears in my eyes and the spittle hanging from my mouth I saw my father grimace before he threw back his share all at once. He shuddered, and then recovered himself and brought the glasses to the sink. He was never much of a drinker. *Clean all this up well so she doesn't see it,* he said hoarsely in Korean. *Then help her with the windows.* He gently patted my back and then left the house and drove off to one of his stores in the city.

The woman, her head forward and bent, suddenly padded out from her back rooms in thickly socked feet and stood waiting for me, silent.

I knew the job, and I did it quickly for her. My father and I used to do a similar task together when I was very young. This before my mother died, in our first, modest house. Early in the morning on the first full warm day of the year he carried down from the attic the bug screens sandwiched in his brief, powerful arms and lined them up in a row against the side of the house. He had me stand back a few yards with the sprayer and wait for him to finish scrubbing the metal mesh with an old shoe brush and car soap. He squatted the way my grandmother did (she visited us once in America before she died), balancing on his flat feet with his armpits locked over his knees and his forearms working between them in front, the position so strangely apelike to me even then that I tried at night in my bedroom to mimic him, to see if the posture came naturally to us Parks, to us Koreans. It didn't.

When my father finished he rose and stretched his back in several directions and then moved to the side. He stood there straight as if at attention and then commanded me with a raised hand to fire away.

"In-jeh!" he yelled. *Now!*

I had to pull with both hands on the trigger, and I almost lost hold of the nozzle from the backforce of the water and sprayed wildly at whatever I could hit. He yelled at me to stop after a few seconds so he could inspect our work; he did this so that he could make a big deal of bending over in front of me, trying to coax his small boy to shoot his behind. When I finally figured it out I shot him; he wheeled about with his face all red storm and theater and shook his fists at me with comic menace. He skulked back to a safe position with his suspecting eyes fixed on me and commanded that I fire again. He shouted for me to stop and he went again and bent over the screens; again I shot him, this time hitting him square on the rump and back, and he yelled louder, his cheeks and jaw wrenched maudlin with rage. I threw down the hose and sprinted for the back door but he caught me from behind and swung me up in what seemed one motion and plunked me down hard on his soaked shoulders. My mother stuck her head out the second-floor kitchen window just then and said to him, *You be careful with that bad boy.*

My father grunted back in that low way of his, the vibrato from his neck tickling my thighs, his voice all raw meat and stones, and my mother just answered him, *Come up right now and eat some lunch.* He marched around the side of the house with me hanging from his back by my ankles and then bounded up the front stairs, inside, and up to the kitchen table, where she had set out bowls of noodles in broth with half-moon slices of pink and white fish cake and minced scallions. And as we sat down, my mother cracked two eggs into my father's bowl, one into mine, and then took her seat between us at the table before her spartan plate of last night's rice and kimchee and cold mackerel (she only ate leftovers at lunch), and then we shut our eyes and clasped our hands, my mother always holding mine extra tight, and I could taste on my face the rich steam of soup and the call of my hungry father offering up his most patient prayers to his God.

None of us even dreamed that she would be dead six years later from a cancer in her liver. She never even drank or smoked. I have trouble remembering the details of her illness because she and my father kept it from me until they couldn't hide it any longer. She was buried in a Korean ceremony two days afterward, and for me it was more a disappearance than a death. During her illness they said her regular outings on Saturday mornings were to go to "meetings" with her old school friends who were living down in the city. They said her constant weariness and tears were from her concern over my mediocre studies. They said, so calmly, that the rotten pumpkin color of her face and neck and the patchiness of her once rich hair were due to a skin condition that would get worse before it became better. They finally said, with hard pride, that she was afflicted with a "Korean fever" that no doctor in America was able to cure.

A few months after her death I would come home from school and smell the fishy salty broth of those same noodles. There was the woman, Ahjuhma, stirring a beaten egg into the pot with long chopsticks; she was wearing the yellow-piped white apron that my mother had once sewn and prettily embroidered with daisies. I ran straight up the stairs to my room on the second floor of the new house, and Ahjuhma called after me in her dialect, "Come, there is enough for you." I slammed the door as hard as I could. After a half hour there was a knock and I yelled back in English, "Leave me alone!" I opened the door hours later when I heard my father come in, and the bowl of soup was at my feet, sitting cold and misplaced.

After that we didn't bother much with each other.

I still remember certain things about the woman: she wore white rubber Korean slippers that were shaped exactly like miniature canoes. She had bad teeth that plagued her. My father sent her to the dentist, who fitted her with gold crowns. Afterward, she seemed to yawn for people, as if to show them off. She balled up her hair and held it with a wooden chopstick. She prepared fish and soup every night; meat or pork every other; at least four kinds of *namool*, prepared vegetables, and then always something fried.

She carefully dusted the photographs of my mother the first thing every morning, and then vacuumed the entire house.

For years I had no idea what she did on her day off; she'd go walking somewhere, maybe the two miles into town though I couldn't imagine what she did there because she never learned three words of English. Finally, one dull summer before I left for college, a friend and I secretly followed her. We trailed her on the road into the center of the town, into the village of Ardsley. She went into Rocky's Corner newsstand and bought a glossy teen magazine and a red Popsicle. She flipped through the pages, obviously looking only at the pictures. She ate the Popsicle like it was a hot dog, in three large bites.

"She's a total alien," my friend said. "She's completely bizarre."

She got up and peered into some store windows, talked to no one, and then she started on the long walk back to our house.

She didn't drive. I don't know if she didn't wish to or whether my father prohibited it. He would take her shopping once a week, first to the grocery and then maybe to the drugstore, if she needed something for herself. Once in a while he would take her to the mall and buy her some clothes or shoes. I think out of respect and ignorance she let him pick them out. Normally around the house she simply wore sweatpants and old blouses. I saw her dressed up only once, the day I graduated from high school. She put on an iridescent dress with nubbly flecks in the material, which somehow matched her silvery heels. She looked like a huge trout. My father had horrible taste.

Once, when I was back from college over spring break, I heard steps in the night on the back stairwell, up and then down. The next night I heard them coming up again and I stepped out into the hall. I caught the woman about to turn the knob of my father's door. She had a cup of tea in her hands. Her hair was down and she wore a white cotton shift and in the weak glow of the hallway night-light her skin looked almost smooth. I was surprised by the pretty shape of her face.

"Your papa is thirsty," she whispered in Korean, "go back to sleep."

The next day I went out to the garage, up to the nook behind the closet, to read some old novels. I had a bunch of them there from high school. I picked one to read over again and then crawled out through the closet to turn on the stereo; when I got back in I stood up for a moment and I saw them outside through the tiny oval window.

They were working together in the garden, loosening and turning over the packed soil of the beds. They must have thought I was off with friends, not because they did anything, or even spoke to one another, but because they were simply together and seemed to want it that way. In the house nothing between them had been any different. I watched them as they moved in tandem on their knees up and down the rows, passing a small hand shovel and a three-fingered claw between them. When they were finished my father stood up and stretched his back in his familiar way and then motioned to her to do the same.

She got up from her knees and turned her torso after him in slow circles, her hands on her hips. Like that, I thought she suddenly looked like someone else, like someone standing for real before her own life. They laughed lightly at something. For a few weeks I feared that my father might marry her, but nothing happened between them that way, then or ever.

The woman died sometime before my father did, of complications from pneumonia. It took all of us by surprise. He wasn't too well himself after his first mild stroke, and Lelia and I, despite our discord, were mutually grateful that the woman had been taking good care of him. At the time, this was something we could talk about without getting ourselves deeper into our troubles of what we were for one another, who we were, and we even took turns going up there on weekends to drive the woman to the grocery store and to the mall. We talked best when either she or I called from the big house, from the kitchen phone, my father and his housekeeper sitting quietly together somewhere in the house.

After his rehabilitation, my father didn't need us shuttling back and forth anymore. That's when she died. Apparently, she didn't bother telling him that she was feeling sick. One night she was carrying a tray of food to his bed when she collapsed on the back stairwell. Against her wishes my father took her to the hospital but somehow it was too late and she died four days later. When he called me up he sounded weary and spent. I told him I would go up there; he said no, no, everything was fine.

I drove up anyway and when I opened the door to the house he was sitting alone in the kitchen, the kettle on the stove madly whistling away. He was fast asleep; after the stroke he sometimes nodded off in the middle of things. I woke him, and when he saw me he patted my cheek.

"Good boy," he muttered.

I made him change his clothes and then fixed us a dinner of fried rice from some leftovers. Maybe the kind of food she would make. As I was cleaning up after we ate, I asked whether he had buried her, and if he did, where.

"No, no," he said, waving his hands. "Not that."

The woman had begged him not to. She didn't want to be buried here in America. Her last wish, he said, was to be burned. He did that for her. I imagined him there in the hospital room, leaning stiffly over her face, above her wracked lips, to listen to her speak. I wondered if she could ever say what he had meant to her. Or say his true name. Or request that he speak hers. Perhaps he did then, with sorrow and love.

I didn't ask him of these things. I knew already that he was there when she died. I knew he had suffered in his own unspeakable and shadowy way. I knew, by his custom, that he had her body moved to a local mortuary to be washed and then cremated, and that he had mailed the ashes back to Korea in a solid gold coffer finely etched with classical Chinese characters.

Our gift to her grieving blood.

VOIR DIRE

■ ■ ■

Don Lee

O n Sunday afternoon, when Hank Low Kwon returned to his house
in Rosarita Bay, he found a note tacked to his front door. "You don't
think I *read?*" it said. The note was unsigned, but he knew it was from
Molly Beddle. No doubt she had seen the newspaper article, small as it
was, summarizing the first day of the trial, and was miffed that he had
mentioned it only tangentially to her. It was clearly his biggest case in
four years as a public defender.

He had been working at his San Vicente office all day and didn't
know where Molly would be. He tried her at her loft, at the sports center and gym, and then, on a hunch, dialed the marine forecast—northwest at twenty-three knots, gusting to thirty—and was certain he would
find her at Rummy Creek, her favorite windsurfing spot.

From Highway 1, he turned onto a dirt fire road that cut through a
barbed-wire fence with no trespassing signs, bumped down half a mile
of scrub grass, wound past the Air Force radar station, and then arrived
at the headlands bordering the ocean. Molly's truck was there, parked

DON LEE, a third-generation Korean American, was born in Tokyo in 1959.
He is the author of the short-story collection *Yellow*, which won the Sue Kaufman Prize for First Fiction from the American Academy of Arts and Letters.
Winners of a Pushcart Prize and an O. Henry Award, his stories have been
published in *GQ, Manoa, Bamboo Ridge*, the *Gettysburg Review, Glimmer
Train, New England Review*, and elsewhere. He has been the recipient of fiction fellowships from the Massachusetts Cultural Council and the Saint
Botolph Club Foundation. Currently he lives in Cambridge, Massachusetts,
and is the editor of the literary journal *Ploughshares*.

among a handful of cars, and Hank stepped to the edge of the cliff to look for her.

It didn't take long. She was flying across the water, feet in the board's straps, hooked to the boom in her harness, raking the sail back so far, she was almost lying flat—a human catamaran. She carved the board into a sweeping turn, executing a smooth laydown jibe, and raced back to shore. She jibed again, accelerated toward a small wave, and launched off its lip, swooping fifteen feet into the air, and then touched down without missing a beat.

Hank sat on a tree stump and watched her. Molly had once described the feeling she got out there, sometimes flailing, struggling just to keep her balance and hang on to the boom, and then getting into a slot where everything fell into place, hydroplaning on the tail of the board, lightly skimming over the chop. At that moment, going as fast as she could, it was effortless. She could take one hand off the rig, let her fingers drag in the water. She could look around, catch a little scenery—the cypress and pine atop the bluffs, the kelp waving underneath the surface. It was glorious, she had said, and as Molly, finished for the day, waded to the sand, as Hank climbed down the cliff to meet her, he could see the quiet elation in her face, the contentment of a woman who knew what she loved in this world.

But then she spotted Hank. She dropped her board and sail and marched toward him, sleek and divine in her sleeveless wetsuit. Without a word, she punched her fist into his arm, stinging him so hard with surprise, he fell to the ground. He looked up at her, half laughing. "I can't believe you did that," he said.

"Did it hurt?"

"Yes, it hurt. Like a son of a bitch."

"Good. I feel better now," she said, and helped him to his feet.

■ ■ ■

The indictment was on two counts: Penal Code Section 187, second-degree murder, punishable by fifteen years to life, and Section 273a, Subdivision (1), felony child abuse, punishable by one to ten. The previous summer, Chee Seng Lam, a cocaine addict, had beaten his girlfriend's three-year-old son, Simon Liu, to death with an electrical cord, whipping the boy, according to the medical examiner, more than four hundred times.

On Friday at San Vicente Superior Court, before the weekend recess, Hank had given his opening statement. He had told the jury that Lam was not a child abuser; he had never intended to harm Simon Liu that night. Indeed, he hadn't even known it was Simon he was hitting. High on cocaine, hallucinating wildly, he had believed he was lashing at—trying to protect himself from—a nest of snakes, thousands of them.

Drugs alone could not eliminate culpability. To win an acquittal, Hank would have to prove that the coke had made Lam delusional and paranoid, even when he wasn't under the influence—in other words, that he had developed a latent mental defect—and because of it, he was incapable of knowing or understanding the nature and quality of his act, or of distinguishing right from wrong—the legal definition of insanity in California.

"You believe him?" Molly asked as she hosed the salt off her gear in his driveway.

"I don't know," Hank said. "I'm not sure he's smart enough to have made it up."

"Does he have a history of violence?"

"Not against the kid, but yeah, he was your basic piece of shit." Chee Seng Lam had twenty-two prior arrests, mostly as a juvenile, when he had been a member of the Flying Dragons gang: aggravated assault, extortion, burglary, receiving stolen property, gun and drug possession, a couple of other assorted goodies, none of which would ever be revealed in court, since Hank had gotten his record suppressed.

"I guess you won't have too many character witnesses," Molly said.

"His dealer liked him."

Molly restrapped her shortboards on the rack of her truck. She had been a ten-meter platform diver in college, but she was in better shape now, at thirty-five, than she had been at her competitive peak, although most people never suspected it. Largely, this had to do with how little she cared about her looks. She had a sweet, guileless face—eyes set wide apart, a plump mouth, long, wispy blond hair—yet she never wore makeup, and her skin was always sunburned in patches, bruised, scratched, her lips chapped. In the rumpled sweaters and khakis she preferred, she was deceptively ordinary. Solid and thick-boned, one would think; maybe even a little overweight.

But of course, underneath the baggy attire, it was all muscle and power. Besides windsurfing, Molly skied, kayaked, rock climbed, and occasionally entered a triathlon for fun. She had degrees in biomechanics and sports science, and she was now the head diving coach at San Vicente University, where she had put together a championship program.

Her energy and fitness both attracted and overwhelmed Hank, who'd become, in his late thirties, a bit paunchy and prone to bronchitis. Yet, for all their differences, they got on remarkably well. They had met at the grand opening of Banzai Pipeline, the Japanese restaurant on Main Street. Hank had grown up in Hawaii with the owner, Duncan Roh, a surfer Molly knew from Rummy Creek.

They had been seeing each other for a year and a half now, and recently they had agreed that they would move in together at the end of the summer, when their current leases expired. Both divorced, they were careful not to attach undue significance to the decision. They knew enough not to ask the other for compromise, not to be too preoccupied about defining a future, which had become difficult of late, since Molly was now ten weeks pregnant.

She adjusted the nozzle on the garden hose and took a sip of water. "Would you mind if I came to the trial?" she asked.

"Why would you want to?"

"I want to see you at work. I've never been to a trial."

"You might make me more nervous than I already am," he told her. This was partially true. Out of the two-hundred-fifty-some cases he had handled, only twenty had gone to a jury—a routine track record in the public defenders' office, where the motto was plead 'em and speed 'em.

"Your ex-wife never went to court?"

"Didn't care for the clientele."

Molly pulled her T-shirt over her head.

"What are you doing?" Hank said. He rented a mildewy two-bedroom cottage near Rummy Creek, and his neighbors were out and about.

Molly bent over and sprayed water on her hair, then squeezed it into a ponytail.

Hank noticed a cut on her bicep. "You're bleeding," he told her. He didn't think she should have been windsurfing at all, but pregnancy hadn't slowed her down a bit—no morning sickness, no fatigue.

Molly examined the gash on her arm, then licked the blood and kissed him. "Have you been smoking today?" she asked. "You taste like smoke."

"That's what I like about you. You don't nag. Why don't you put your shirt back on before someone gets a cheap thrill."

She looked down at her breasts. "Amazing. I actually have tits now," she said. "They're so swollen. Feel them."

"Are they tender?"

"A little. You don't want to feel them?"

He handed back her T-shirt. "You really want to come to the trial?"

"Would it disturb you that much?"

"I guess not," he told her. "But it'll be embarrassing to watch."

"Why? Is your case that weak?"

"No, you don't get it," he said. "I think I'm going to win."

■　■　■

Last summer, on June 23, Ruby Liu drove down from Oakland to San Vicente with her son. She had been looking forward to spending the weekend with Chee Seng Lam, but right away they argued. Lam was irritated she'd brought Simon. "He say Simon noisy," she testified. "He say Simon need discipline."

Later, she and Simon fell asleep in the bedroom while Lam stayed up in the living room, listening to music on his headphones. At approximately one A.M., Ruby awoke and saw that Simon was no longer at her side. She walked down the hall and discovered Lam whipping her son with the cord to his headphones. She pushed Lam away. Simon was moaning, his eyes fluttering, and then he stopped breathing. She called 911. By the time the E.M.T.s arrived, Simon was dead.

From the standpoint of the law, Ruby's testimony was devastating, but she wasn't entirely effective as a witness. She spoke in a rehearsed monotone, eyes down, body impassive and contained, and it was hard to fathom a mother not betraying a single hint of emotion as she related the death of her only child. She seemed to be hiding something. She seemed to be lying.

What everyone but the jury knew was that Ruby Liu was a prostitute and a junkie. She mainlined speedballs—a combination of heroin and cocaine—and she had gone to Lam's apartment that weekend to get high with him. She could have easily been indicted on a slew of negligence charges, so it was no surprise that she had agreed to testify for the prosecution.

"Did Mr. Lam ever hit Simon before?" Hank asked her.

Ruby glanced at the assistant district attorney, John Boudreau, then said no.

"Not once? Maybe an isolated spanking?"

"No."

"So he never hit Simon, or spanked him, or slapped him. Not once. He never even raised his voice to him, did he?"

"He say Simon noisy. He say he need discipline."

"You keep repeating that. Did he say this to you in English or Chinese?"

Ruby blinked several times, trying to choose. "English," she declared.

"How good would you say Mr. Lam's English is?"

"He speak English."

"Is he fluent, or is his English somewhat broken, like yours?"

"Same as me, maybe."

"Can he read and write?"

"Not good."

"Have you ever heard him use the word 'discipline' before?"

She squirmed. "No."

"Are you sure he said 'discipline,' or did someone suggest the word to you?"

"Objection," Boudreau said.

For the next two hours, Hank had Ruby describe Lam's escalating drug use over the five years she'd known him, how eventually he would freebase cocaine for up to twenty hours at a time, sometimes going six days without sleep, obsessed with getting and smoking the coke, ignoring all else.

Increasingly, his behavior became more erratic. He saw bugs, tadpoles. On his body, coming out of his skin, on other people. Without warning, he would slap and scratch himself, claw his fingernails into his arms until he bled. Then he began seeing snakes. Diamondbacks, corals, water moccasins, copperheads, black mambas, cobras, tree vipers—he identified fourteen varieties from library books Ruby stole for him. Lam weather-stripped his doors and sealed every window, covered the heating vents with screens. He would often drop to all fours with a flashlight and a propane torch, hunting for the snakes, burning the floor and furniture.

Once, he beat a sofa cushion with a stick, trying to kill the baby cottonmouths he said were slithering out of it, rending the cushion apart for an hour and a half without pause. He heard voices, he saw ghosts. He thought the government was dumping the snakes into his apartment to kill him, and he drilled peepholes in the walls, bolted a security camera above his front door, and installed listening devices in nearly every room. He would not leave his apartment. Repeatedly, Ruby tried to convince him that the cocaine was making him hallucinate, but he refused to believe her. She was crazy, he said.

"Was he freebasing cocaine the night Simon was killed?"

"Yes."

"When you discovered him standing over Simon in the living room, did you yell at him to stop?"

"Yes."

"And did he respond to you in any way?"

"No."

"So he appeared to be in a trance?" Hank asked.

Ruby frowned. "I don't know," she said. "No."

"Like the time with the sofa cushion?"

"Objection," Boudreau said. "Asked and answered."

Hank withdrew the question and said instead, "Where were the headphones?"

"What?"

"He was holding the cord to his headphones, but where were the headphones themselves?"

"I don't know. His neck, maybe."

"Mr. Lam often spent all night doing cocaine while he listened to music on the headphones?"

"Yes."

"Would you say, then, that when Simon walked in, Mr. Lam must have jumped up in a panic, thinking these snakes—"

Boudreau cut him off. "Calls for speculation, Your Honor," he complained, his face flushing. Boudreau had some form of psoriasis, and whenever he was nervous or rattled—which was all the time—his skin bloomed red. Boudreau asked only one question in his redirect: "Did you ever see Mr. Lam selling drugs?"

"Yeah, he sell drugs."

Hank stood up. "Did he sell drugs to make a profit," he asked, "or just to support his own habit?"

Ruby looked dumbly at Hank. She was exhausted. "Habit, okay?" she said.

After a lengthy sidebar at Hank's request, the judge, Eduardo Gutierrez, instructed the jury that the issue of selling drugs was pertinent only to the defendant's state of mind, not his character. "The fact that Mr. Lam might have sold drugs does not prove he has an inherent disposition to engage in criminal conduct," Gutierrez said, remarkably deadpan.

■ ■ ■

Lam wore a striped button-down shirt, which was one size too large for him, a tie, and pleated pants—nothing too fancy, but neat. His hair was cut above the ears, and he was clean-shaven. Since he was small and thin to begin with, he looked, by design, harmless—a far cry from the ponytailed, hollow-eyed menace to society Hank had met nine months earlier, when Lam had been released from Cabrillo State Hospital.

In a conference room next to the holding pen, Hank gave Lam a cigarette. Smoking wasn't permitted anymore, but everyone ignored the rule. "You do good," Lam said. "Better than I think."

"I covered all the necessary points."

"No, really. Before, I think you *stupid*."

Hank was used to this reaction. No one had any respect for public defenders—not judges, prosecutors, cops, not the public, least of all clients. "Don't get too smug," he said. "We've got a long way to go."

Lam blew on the tip of his cigarette, reddening the cherry. "Blondie your girlfriend?" Lam said. He'd seen Molly with Hank during a recess. "*Low faan* girlfriend, huh? No like Chinese girls?"

Hank flipped through the pages of his notepad. Like everyone, Lam assumed that Hank was Chinese. He had a Chinese-sounding name, but he was actually Korean, born and raised in Haleiwa, on the North Shore of Oahu, where his father was a Presbyterian minister.

Lam helped himself to another cigarette. As he was lighting it, Hank noticed his eyes—glazed and dilated. "You're stoned," he said.

"Naw."

"Bullshit."

"Just a little pot."

"You idiot. I told you to stay clean."

"You see Ruby? I betcha Valium," Lam said. "Good thing I never marry her. She lie first, you know. Say Simon my baby. But I know. I slap her. My baby? *My* baby? She cry. Boo hoo. Mistake. Big mistake. I'm not *stupid*. Right, Hankie?"

Hank looked at Lam, who was grinning, clowning. "When we get back in the courtroom," he told him, "you don't smile, you don't laugh. You don't act bored or slouch in your chair. Look serious and remorseful. Look like you feel bad about what you've done."

■ ■ ■

They were stuck in traffic on Highway 71, coming over the hill from San Vicente to Rosarita Bay. During rush hour, it sometimes took two hours to travel the fifteen miles home.

"I don't think I can make it to the rest of the trial," Molly said.

"No?" Hank asked. She had only attended two days.

"I've got too much work to do."

This was an equivocation, Hank knew, but he was relieved nonetheless.

"Do you think they assigned this case to you because you're Asian?" Molly asked.

"That's rhetorical, right?"

"Because they thought it'd help with the jury?"

"Partly them, mostly the client."

Molly tugged on her seat belt strap, pulling it away from her chest. "You ever wonder what makes people go in one direction and not another?"

"What do you mean?"

"All the little things that add up. I was thinking about Lam and his girlfriend, the model minorities they turned out to be. Aren't you curious about that?"

"I used to be. Not anymore."

"Why not?"

Hank shifted into neutral; they weren't going anywhere. "There's this strangely poetic phrase in the California Penal Code. Malice can be implied if circumstances show 'an abandoned and malignant heart.' Day in and day out, that's what I see. Some people are just evil."

"That's a charitable view of the world. I thought you were such a liberal."

"Given enough time, we all become Republicans."

Before moving to Rosarita Bay, Hank had spent ten years working for a small, progressive law firm in San Francisco, specializing in immigration cases and bias suits. He had always been a true believer—a "left-wing, bleeding-heart pagoda of virtue," his ex-wife, Allison Pak, used to say. He hadn't known what he was getting into four years ago, becoming a public defender. He had been fired up about the presumption of innocence and due process, about the racial inequities of the judicial system. Now he represented muggers, drug dealers, wife beaters, carjackers, arsonists, thieves, rapists, and child molesters. They were almost always guilty, they were all junkies, and if by some technicality Hank was able to get them off, they'd go right out and do the same thing, or worse.

He told Molly about one of his first cases in Juvenile Court, a ten-year-old San Vicente kid who, as he was riding down the street on his BMX bicycle, swung a pipe into a man's face. No reason. Didn't know him, didn't rob him. Just felt like it. Hank found out some things about the kid's background—broken home, physical abuse—and thought he deserved another chance. A month later, the kid participated in a home invasion. He raped and sodomized a six-year-old girl with a broomstick, a beer bottle, and a light bulb, which he busted inside her, and then, for good measure, hammered a few nails into her heels.

"You're having a crisis of faith," Molly said.

"Is it that obvious?"

"It's just this case. You'll get over it."

"You're horrified by it. How can you not be? I'm defending a baby-killer."

They finally crossed Skyview Ridge and headed downhill to Rosarita Bay. Hank rolled down the window and breathed in the chaparral and the ocean. Rosarita Bay was part of San Vicente County, but this side of the peninsula mountains, the Coastside, was a remote outpost in the tundra compared to the industrial Bayside city of San Vicente. To Hank, it was well worth the commute to be out of the fray.

They stopped by Hank's cottage to pick up one of his suits, then went to Molly's loft, which was in a converted cannery next to the harbor. Once inside, Molly said, "I have to pee. It's incredible how many times I have to pee these days."

There was a mini-trampoline on the floor, near the foot of her bed, and on the way to the bathroom, Molly nonchalantly hopped onto it and did a forward flip. She grinned back mischievously at Hank.

For a while, the trampoline had been an instrument of ritual. Whenever Molly wanted to make love, she would bounce off the tramp, tumble through the air, and flop onto the bed. "Time to make Molly jolly," she'd say. Sometimes, growling: "Tiger Lily want her Moo Shi Kwon."

At first, Molly's sexual assertion had unnerved him. When they began dating, she had been subdued and uncomfortable, and he had been certain, each time he called her, that she would not see him again. At the end of their fourth date—another disaster, he had thought—he drove her home and lightly kissed her cheek goodnight. She stayed in the car, cracking her knuckles. "That's it?" she suddenly blurted. "You mean you're *done* with me?" Then she had ravished him, taking him inside to the loft and stripping him of his clothes.

With Molly, all roads originated in the body. Her entire life, she had spoken through it—joy found in challenging limits and conquering the elements, being fearless, perfect, indomitable. There were no moral ambiguities in her life. What she did was pure.

When she came out of the bathroom, she joined Hank on the couch, and he massaged her feet, kneading his thumbs into her instep.

"Hank," she said, "why don't you want this baby?"

When she had first revealed she was pregnant, he had told her he would support her either way, but it was her decision to make. He wouldn't say it explicitly, but it was clear he favored an abortion. "I just wish it was something we'd planned," he said to her now.

"Is it because I'm not Korean?"

"God, no," Hank said. "Where'd that come from?"

She wiggled her toes, signaling for him to switch feet. "I think I saw your ex-wife today."

"What?"

"At the courthouse. One floor up. The bathroom across the hall was being cleaned, so I went upstairs."

"Are you sure it was her?" Hank asked. Molly had seen photographs of Allison, but had never met her.

Molly nodded. "She's very pretty."

■ ■ ■

The photographs hurt. There were five of them—all color eight-by-tens—and they sat on Boudreau's table for the next two days as he called up the firemen who were first on the scene, the E.M.T.s who tried to revive Simon, and the police officers who arrested Lam. With each witness, Boudreau brought out the photographs and asked, "Do they accurately and fairly depict the condition of the boy as you found him?" And each of these grown men, these veterans of daily, horrific violence, would wince looking at the pictures, then choke out yes.

Each of them confirmed that Lam had pointed to the headphone cord when questioned what he beat Simon with, that he had kept repeating he wasn't a child beater, and that though he seemed agitated, he was coherent, even asking to change his clothes and put on his shoes before being cuffed. He did not mention any hallucinations. Not a word about snakes.

The county medical examiner testified that he had counted 417 separate and distinct contusions and abrasions, and the cord was consistent with the injuries. At some point, he said, the cord must have been doubled up, which would explain some of the U-shaped marks. The official cause of death was swelling and bleeding of the brain caused by trauma, which forced the brain into its base and cut off breathing functions.

"You also found a large lump on the back of his head?" Hank asked.

"A blunt force injury on the occipital lobe."

"Was it caused by the cord?"

"No. Most likely he fell backwards to the floor and hit his head."

"He tripped and fell down."

"Or he was pushed."

"Could the fall have rendered Simon unconscious the whole time?"

"That's impossible to determine."

"Is it *possible*, however?"

"I suppose."

"Could the fall, bumping his head, have been the actual cause of death?"

The M.E., seeing where Hank was going, smirked and said, "Unlikely."

"But it's possible?"

Boudreau objected, and Gutierrez had them approach. "You know better than to challenge proximate cause," he told Hank. "Move it along."

Hank held up the plastic evidence bag containing the headphones. "It's been stipulated that this cord is ten feet long, but only one-sixteenth of an inch wide. *With* the headphones, it weighs less than three ounces. Wouldn't you say it's pretty ineffective as a weapon?"

"It seemed to do the trick."

"But considering how light it is, it's rather awkward to use as a whip, isn't it? Even doubled up?"

"I wouldn't know."

"Did the injuries indicate a repetitive motor motion?"

"Obviously."

"The same action, over and over, like a mindless robot?"

"I can't make that characterization."

"But you *are* an expert on injuries resulting from the application of specific weapons?"

"I am that."

Hank showed the M.E. two photographs of Lam's living room and passed copies to the jurors, which was decidedly risky, since they would spot the V.C.R.s stacked in Lam's apartment and might surmise, correctly, that he had been fencing them. "If Mr. Lam really wanted to inflict pain, 'discipline' someone, as it were, wouldn't the baseball bat—right here in the photograph, right next to where they found the deceased—wouldn't it have been more effective?"

"That depends," the M.E. said.

"What about this broomstick here? Or this belt?"

The M.E. sighed. "Mr. Kwon, a piece of dental floss, tightened around a tender part of the body, could be more excruciating than many more obvious methods of torture. Its general innocuousness as an implement of hygiene does not remove its lethal potential. What happened to this boy was brutal, and it caused him unimaginable pain, and it killed him."

■ ■ ■

"Maybe wrong before," Lam said in the conference room. "Maybe you really stupid."

Hank lit a cigarette. Lam, wanting one, motioned to Hank, who ignored him.

"Hey," Lam said. "C'mon."

Hank forcefully slid the pack across the table, bouncing it off Lam's chest.

Lam tsked. "Be nice."

"Tell me something," Hank said. "How do you know Simon wasn't your kid?"

"Huh?"

"What makes you so sure he wasn't your son?"

"You crazy? Ruby whore. She slam heroin with needle. Always use condom. No want AIDS, you know."

"You had no feelings for him?"

Lam shrugged. "Make noise. Run run. Break stereo. Always cry. No food. No toy. Little whore baby. Ruby no care. You think Simon become doctor? Maybe lawyer, like you? Better dead."

In the medical examiner's photographs, Simon's entire body—all two feet, thirty pounds of him—had been covered with welts and bruises and cuts, only the palms of his hands and the soles of his feet spared.

Hank watched Lam brush a stray cigarette ash from his shirtsleeve.

A few days ago, Hank had found a pregnancy book in Molly's loft, hidden in a cupboard. He had read a passage in the book that she had underlined. At twelve weeks, the fetus would be fully formed. It would have eyelids, thirty-two tooth buds, finger- and toenails. It would be able to swallow, press its lips together, frown, clench its fists. It would be, at that point, two and a half inches long.

"It sickens me to think I might let you walk," he told Lam.

"Too bad. You have job."

"I find myself asking what would happen if I slipped a little, made a mistake here and there."

"No choice. You have job. You do best."

"Maybe I already fucked up on purpose. You were right about the medical examiner. I'm usually smarter than that."

"No, you too much goodie-goodie. You never do that."

"No?"

"Naw."

"The funny thing is, you wouldn't be able to tell. No one would. If I'm not blatantly incompetent, no one would ever know."

Lam giggled, then slowly quieted down, growing uncertain. "Better not," he said. "Better not, you fuck."

"Who would it hurt?"

■ ■ ■

They got their drinks at the bar and snagged a table near the front window. The restaurant was crowded—a popular hangout for those who worked at the courthouse.

"This place is a pit," Allison said.

"There's not much else around here," Hank said.

"I hate San Vicente."

Hank had checked the dockets and had found his ex-wife upstairs, representing a consulting firm that was being sued for breach of contract.

"The details would put you to sleep," she told Hank. She was still hoping to settle.

They caught up a little. It had been about a year since they'd run into each other. Allison looked good, crisp in her starched white blouse and silk suit. Her hair was longer, chin-length now, parted in the middle and tucked behind her ears. She'd had a short blunt cut before, which had pronounced her sucked-in cheeks and skinny frame, making her seem even more acerbic and severe than she was.

They had been divorced for three years, almost as long as they had been married. They had been mismatched from the beginning, always getting into fights about politics and money ("kuppie," he would call her—Korean yuppie), trading indictments about his moronic crusades and her nauseating self-absorption, epitomized, he felt, by her refusal to have children. They had mistaken their hostility for passion and stayed together longer than they should have.

She was now living in San Francisco with a wealthy developer named Jason Chu, an A.B.C., American-born Chinese, who, coincidentally, had been trying for the last decade to build a $50 million monstrosity in Rosarita Bay: two hundred houses around a golf course, a shopping mall, a hotel and conference center, and a fake lighthouse.

"Is he still trying to get that passed?" Hank asked. "He'll never get it to fly. Not in Rosarita Bay."

"How can you live there?"

"It's nice."

"It's hicksville. You might as well be in the Farm Belt," Allison told him. "Jason says it's racism, the reason why he can't get zoning. In your former life, he might've been a client of yours. Get this. I read him the article about your trial, your lovely Mr. Lam, and Jason said, 'That can't be right. Chinese don't do drugs.'"

"Ha."

"How's your diver friend? Martha?"

"Molly. Don't try to be cute. You know her name."

"So, how are things going?"

"She's pregnant."

"*Well*," Allison said expansively. "Congratulations. You're finally going to be a pa*pa*."

"Maybe not," Hank said.

"What do you mean? You knocked her up by *accident*?"

"I don't know how it happened."

"I'm guessing it was a Freudian spurt. It's what you've always wanted, isn't it? Do you love her?"

Hank lit a cigarette.

"I thought you quit," Allison said.

"I did."

"Well, do you? Love her?"

Hank nodded.

"Enough to marry her one of these days?"

He nodded again.

"What gives, then?"

Hank tried to flag down the waitress for another drink, but she didn't notice him. He hesitated, then asked Allison, "Why didn't you want a child with me?"

"I thought it was because I'm a selfish bitch. Because I'm—"

"Don't start."

"I always hated that about you. Your moral superiority. What made you think you were so much better than everyone else? Now look at you, with this scumbag Lam. That'd be quite a precedent if you win. Negate culpability for anyone on drugs. Some way to save the world."

"Do we have to do this?"

"No, I suppose not," Allison said. "But you could've let me enjoy myself a bit longer." She reapplied lipstick to her mouth.

Hank fiddled with his empty drink glass. "Did you think I wouldn't be a good father?"

She turned to him. "No, I never thought that," she said, softening. "What's going on with you? What are you afraid of?"

"These days, everything."

"I don't like seeing you like this. It's fun beating you up once in a while, but only if you fight back."

"Ironic, isn't it?" Hank said. "I used to think not wanting a child was selfish. Now I think wanting one is."

■ ■ ■

His defense took four days. He had a narcotics detective testify that, contrary to Boudreau's suggestions, Lam was not a dealer of any consequence. The paraphernalia found in his apartment was used for freebasing, a somewhat antiquated method of smoking coke, reserved for connoisseurs and hard-core addicts. Instead of heating cocaine hydrochloride powder with baking soda, which would yield crack, Lam separated the base with ether and a propane torch. Freebase was purer than crack, but no dealer today went through the trouble of producing it. It took too long, and it was dangerous. And although crack houses had precision scales and surveillance equipment like Lam's, most dealers did not have any reason to monitor the *inside* of the house. There was also no currency found in the apartment, no vials or plastic pouches that were the usual receptacles for distribution.

Three of Lam's friends corroborated Ruby's testimony about Lam's bingeing habits, paranoia, and snake fixation, but all three, when cross-examined by Boudreau, were impeached rather comically. Each claimed he had never bought any drugs from Lam, never saw him sell drugs to anyone else, didn't know where he got them, didn't smoke with him, simply went to the apartment to watch TV.

A neighbor recalled seeing Lam scamper out to the street one evening in his underwear, bleeding profusely, screaming. She called the police, who took him to the hospital. Lam told the admitting nurse he'd run through a sliding glass door, trying to get away from the snakes. He was transferred to the county mental health clinic, where he'd been held five previous times for acute cocaine intoxication.

The Chinese officer who had booked Lam on June 23 recounted their conversation in the police station. Lam spoke to him in Cantonese and insisted he had not known it was Simon he was hitting, he'd seen snakes, that he would have never done anything to hurt the kid.

Finally, Hank brought Dr. Jeffrey Winnick to the stand. Winnick, a psychopharmacologist, studied the effects of cocaine on human behavior. He was a frequent consultant to the F.B.I. and the D.E.A., and he had testified in over five hundred trials, mostly—Hank emphasized—for the prosecution. By chance, Winnick had been doing research at Cabrillo State Hospital when Lam was taken there to test his competency. Over the course of four months, he interviewed Lam three times a week for a total of seventy hours.

"Did you arrive at an opinion about Mr. Lam?" Hank asked.

"In my opinion, Mr. Lam was psychotic on June twenty-third and could not appreciate the wrongfulness of his actions. In my opinion, he did not know it was Simon he was beating."

He explained to the jury the psychopathology of freebasing. Because the surface area of the lungs was equivalent to a tennis court, smoking cocaine allowed the drug to enter the bloodstream almost instantaneously, affecting the brain within eight to twelve seconds. The initial effect was as a stimulant, creating a feeling of confidence and euphoria. As one's tolerance increased, however, dysphoria occurred, prompting more frequent usage, which led to paranoia.

"People often begin to have hallucinations at this point," Winnick said, "the most common of which is cocaine bugs. Their brains are firing so fast, these bursts of light—snow lights, they're called—flash in the corners of their eyes, and they think they're seeing things that aren't there, that keep escaping when they turn to look. At the same time, their skin feels like it's prickling, because cocaine constricts the blood vessels, and the combination leads them to believe there are things crawling on them—bugs or worms, or, as in Mr. Lam's case, snakes—and they'll scrape their skin or try to catch them. Since they're wide awake, they'll be absolutely convinced these hallucinations are real, and they'll have delusions beyond the period of intoxication. This stage is referred to as cocaine paranoid psychosis, and it can be latent for months or even years after the last use of cocaine."

"Did Mr. Lam's cocaine habit progress to this stage?"

"Yes. His entire world revolved around trying to prove the existence of these snakes and trying to capture and kill them. He was terrified of them."

"Is cocaine paranoid psychosis caused by an organic disturbance to the brain?"

"Yes."

"So you would say that this is a mental defect?"

"Absolutely."

"Was Mr. Lam suffering from this mental defect on June twenty-third?"

"I am certain that he was."

■ ■ ■

The jury took two days to reach a verdict, and in the end, they did what was right. Legally, they felt obliged to acquit Lam of child abuse, but they could not absolve him completely of killing Simon. Nor could they find him insane and send him to the relative comfort of a state institution. They convicted him of voluntary manslaughter. Gutierrez sentenced Lam immediately to the maximum term—eleven years.

Hank went to Molly's loft and told her the news. "I should resign," he said.

"Why?"

"I did a great job. On the evidence alone, the jury should've found him not guilty. But they didn't, and I'm relieved. What does that say about me as a public defender?"

"It says you're human. It says Lam got a fair trial."

"With early release, he could be out in six years. He killed a three-year-old kid. Is that fair?"

They went to Banzai Pipeline for sushi, and then stopped by the Moonside Trading Post to rent a couple of videos before returning to the loft. Between movies—two mindless comedies Molly hoped would distract him—Hank popped in the videotape of Molly competing in the N.C.A.A. diving championships fifteen years ago.

"Why are you watching that again?" Molly asked, coming out of the bathroom.

The first time Hank had seen the tape, it had been a revelation, the image of her then. She had saved her best dive for last—a backward one and a half with three and a half twists, ripping the entry, barely bruising the surface. As the crowd erupted, Molly had pulled herself out of the pool. She had knocked the side of her head with the heel of her hand, trying to get the water out of her ear, allowing herself only a small, victorious smile.

"Can you believe I was ever that young?" Molly said. She moved over to the couch, straddled Hank's thighs, and sat on his lap. She locked her arms around his neck. "I have something to tell you," she said. "I decided this a while ago, but I wanted to wait until after the trial. I've decided to have this baby no matter what. With you, without you, regardless of how you feel."

"I suspected as much."

"But I'm hoping you'll be there with me. Do you think you will?"

Hank looked at Molly—her large blue eyes, the freckles across her cheeks, the blond down of eyebrows and lashes. "I don't know," he said. He thought of her standing on the ten-meter platform, not a single tremor or twitch, taut and immortal in her bathing suit. "Our worlds are so different," he said. "You deal with human beings at their highest potential. I see them at their worst."

"What does that mean?"

"How can I say I'll be able to protect this child, when I'm putting people like Lam back on the streets?"

"You can't. But that's the risk we'd have to take. Don't you think it'd be worth the risk?"

They watched the second movie, then fell asleep together. For how long, he did not know. A black, dreamless sleep. Then he awoke to the bed shaking. An earthquake, he thought, as he lay on his back, opening his eyes to the ceiling, scared.

But it was Molly, standing over him at the foot of the bed. "Don't move," she said. He saw her body toppling, breaking the plane of inertia, then falling toward him, gathering speed as she brought her hands together, arms rigid, palms flat. An inch before his face, she split her hands apart, and he felt a rush of air as they brushed past his ears. "You ever do this as a kid?" she asked, holding herself over him. "Admit it. You want this baby."

"What are you doing?"

She stood up and fell again. "Confess."

"I can't be coerced," he said.

"You sure?" She got off the bed. "Don't move."

She walked to the middle of the floor, then turned around. She took two steps, ran toward the trampoline, and bounded into the air. Her back was arched, arms swept out in a swan dive. She was coming right at him. He watched her, staying still. She was going to crush him, he knew. Eventually, she would crush him.

NO BRUCE LEE

■ ■ ■

Russell Charles Leong

In the heat of a Los Angeles afternoon a Latino with a torn satchel and a Filipino nurse in a rumpled white uniform wait for the bus. Empty-handed, I stand a few feet behind them. Sundays mean those hours I reserve on the Day of Rest for those spare, routine actions that serve to tide me through the coming week.

Number 376, the downtown bus, stops. I get on, picking a side seat in the rear. The brown plastic seat facing me is impervious to knives, most scratches, and even to the L.A. aerosol-paint graffiti. It's made to last. The bus speeds through Santa Monica and West Los Angeles, stopping occasionally for passengers, mostly Salvadoran or Mexican or Black. The same mix. I note my own strong round kneecaps, not thin and pointed like a white man's, but sturdy, attached to muscle, to the punch and gravity of the bus, the street, the earth. Another time I might have felt like kicking my feet out, or dancing with them, but not today.

I am sweating. The cool, camphor smell of the Tiger Balm salve that I had dabbed on a fleabite under my ear before leaving my room vibrates in my nostrils. The Chinese medicine was an orange paste, but for me its smell was green.

RUSSELL CHARLES LEONG is the editor of UCLA's *Amerasia Journal* and an adjunct professor of English at UCLA. *Phoenix Eyes and Other Stories* received the American Book Award, and *The Country of Dreams and Dust* received an Oakland PEN Josephine Miles Literature Award. Leong's stories and poems on Buddhism, sexualities, and migration have been translated in Nanjing, Taipei, and Shanghai. He was born in San Francisco in 1950.

I reflect on this anomaly. Color and smell can deceive me, can make my senses palpitate after things foreign and imaginary. Which is worse, I cannot decide, warm color or cool odor.

The bus, I know, will carry me past the rich greenbelt of Beverly Hills, then southward to the Jewish section with its seedy rest homes and bakeries. Eventually it will reach the flat expanse of Olympic Boulevard lined with Korean signs and shops. The Korean alphabet is not sinuous and cursive like Chinese or Japanese, but stolid, rather no-nonsense, like Korean food—meat, fish, and hot pickles. The bus will speed on. Korean signs will transform themselves into svelte Spanish syllables for burrito and taco stands replacing the Korean cafes and bars. The giant 76 gas station sign on Figueroa Street will loom in my face, an orange and blue eye surveying all traffic to the inner city. Thus, a Sunday afternoon will be a third spent by the time I reach downtown.

In the aisle, a man camouflaged in green army fatigues weaves in and out between the standing passengers. His hair is the color of rust and he holds a red transistor radio in his hand. Muttering "chrissakes" to no one in particular, his voice becomes louder at the lack of atten-tion. His eyes appear gray and as opaque as smoke. He sports a plastic hospital wristband, probably from the county hospital. He looks at each passenger intently but they look through him. The man snorts, turning to the Latina woman next to him, who presses her child closer to her body and uses her grocery bag as a shield. The man repeats him-self. "If you don't understand English—go back to where you came from. Christ. To where you belong. Chrissakes."

The bus driver turns his head once but does not say a word.

■ ■ ■

I am most honest with myself on Sundays, when I make the lone bus ride downtown, have a coffee and lemon creme pie at Lipton's, and then return on the same bus going the opposite direction. At one time, I could afford bar hopping, Sunday Chinese tea brunches, real woolen slacks, and two pairs of shoes per year. Under the dim lights of any bar, I would pass for an eternal thirty. But as the summers came and went, the sunlit days seemed longer. The happy hours that began at four or five o'clock in most places grew interminable. The brightness of L.A. summers began to hurt my eyes. I squinted more. Vanity did not permit me to wear either clear or tinted glasses. Finally, I had to curtail my bar hopping. I found myself bringing home bottles of gin purchased at the discount liquor store near my apartment. I began to get careless. Even the expensive cologne could not hide the liquor that slackened my skin and soured my breath. With each emptied bottle my countenance and authority had gone. The length of time I could hold on to any job became shorter and shorter.

■ ■ ■

The quake had been the last straw. I could not sleep, thinking of the brick apartment complexes on my block that had been condemned by the city building inspectors. Each day as I passed the red-tagged buildings I could see the bricks out of kilter and the drywall of the rooms inside exposed by gaping cracks. The domed roof of an Armenian bakery was fully exposed to the sky. I felt as naked and vulnerable as the warped structures around me.

■ ■ ■

One evening in June I had ended up at the downtown Greyhound terminal. I had two hundred dollars in cash in my wallet and a small duffel bag with shirts, underwear, and socks. I fumbled with a fifty-dollar bill, the price of a round-trip fare, then folded it neatly into my imitation alligator billfold and stuffed it into my back trouser pocket. It caught on a seam so I pushed it further down. I would walk a few blocks in the cool evening air before making the long bus ride home. It was really a dirty street, I decided, after side-stepping a mound of damp slop. A drink might lift my spirits. I harbored the hope that the right mix of alcohol would realign the complex code of my brain and heart and ease the burden of my uneventful life.

Catty-corner, I spied a neon bar sign with a flaming green palm tree suspended over a blinking red island. I started to walk toward it. The Oasis was one of the last businesses not yet boarded up on a block slated for demolition by the city redevelopment agency. At the swinging double doors I almost collided with the two cops coming out. Once inside, I took a moment to adjust my eyes to the murkiness. Jukebox rap raced with the familiar pulsing of my heart. On the torn red vinyl stools sat mostly Black males, of varying ages, and a few Spanish-speaking men. The black-and-white tile floor was heavily worn, revealing an older orange floor beneath, the color of Tiger Balm ointment. A hand-lettered sign above the jukebox stated:

> No men in costumes or cut-offs above the knees. No prostitution.
> No selling of drugs. We have the right to refuse service to anyone.
> Signed: The Management.

Before surveying the bar I laid down my duffel on the counter and ordered a brandy and water. The Christian Brothers tasted sour and watery at the same time. I gulped it down quickly. I was the only Asian. The Blacks seemed to be enjoying themselves, bantering and laughing. Despite the sign, I noticed two men of indeterminate ethnicity with white powder covering their beardless skin, dressed in unisex green polyester hot pants and blouses. Their narrow hips and muscular calves gave their sex away. There were no women.

A young Black man to my left started to speak to me. He insisted that I reminded him of Bruce Lee, the martial arts star.

"Yes, he died at thirty-three and so did I," I told the Black. He chuckled and slowly sipped his rum and Coke, watching me intently from beneath his short-cropped curls. Perhaps he had some Indian blood in him, I thought, glancing at the oblique angle of his eyes. I thought better than to ask and instead ordered another rum and Coke for him.

"Bruce man, thanks for the drink. You don't look Korean or Jap to me. Your eyes are bigger. You're a Chinaman I bet."

"Close. I am Chinese."

" 'Scuse me, my man. 'Chinaman' is like a honkie calling me a nigger, ain't it?"

"Depends. Forget it. Whatever name I am, I am for tonight."

"So watcha up to, Bruce?"

"I was planning to go to San Francisco to visit some relatives. But they can wait. The city will be there unless there's an earthquake tomorrow."

■ ■ ■

I had planned to go to San Francisco to visit my mother's sister, an aging spinster who lived in Chinatown. But I vacillated, better to save the money and buy a new pair of shoes. My aunt, whom I had not seen for ten years, had raised me while my parents worked. It was she who had fed me canned applesauce over hot rice, slapped me on the hands, forced my tiny fingers around the hard ceramic Chinese soup spoon. She turned angry if I spilled the contents of the spoon. At a later age, pressed into the Chinese Christian language school in Chinatown, I learned to handle a skinny bamboo brush quite decently. My aunt would lift the transparent writing paper and examine each character, stroke by stroke, and tell me what was right or wrong about it. Where she obtained the knowledge she never told me, but one time she read my palms and said that I was destined to become famous with my hands.

"A three-star chef or a major screenwriter?" I asked. She did not answer. That was the first and last time she had predicted the future for me. Wisely, she left the other lines on my hands unread.

I could imagine the chagrin on her face if I told her I could no longer hold down a job. I decided that she could wait.

■ ■ ■

Before I left my room this morning I had clipped down my fingernails with the nail clipper I had picked up at the drugstore. At a furious pace, I started on the pinky and worked my way to the thumb, left hand to right. My hands were small and pared down, almost to the bone. My rather flat and now fleshy face belied thin hands.

It had become a ritual, this paring of nails down to a point, so that the tender pink flesh was raw and flinched at handling salt or citrus fruit. Satisfied with the minute bleeding and inflammation that sometimes occurred when my fingernails were too short, I swathed them in imaginary bandages. In a sense, it was an effort to punish myself for the good life that my hands had failed to create in forty-four years. Paring down my nails made the tips of my fingers all the more sensitive to changes in heat, cold, acidity, salinity, and texture. Seawater almost devastated my freshly cut fingertips.

To curb my passions—that was the intent—but not to the point of numbness. On the contrary, to the point of realization and pain. My fine-boned hands, which had served thousands of restaurant customers, had not paid off as handsomely as I'd planned. Two years ago I was fired as the head maitre d' at Flamingo West, the Chinese supper club on Sunset Strip. I had worked there for almost ten years. It was an expensive, dreary tourist trap, with Sichuan shrimp and sweet and sour spareribs that glared purplish under the ornate Chinese lamps. In its favor, however, the place possessed a sweeping view of the Hollywood Hills. The tips were good. My old coterie of friends and acquaintances, who loved sipping the Flamingo West's giant margaritas and nibbling greasy shrimp, scattered, moved to Florida, had strokes, or just became more miserly with their affections and their cash.

During my hours off I had learned to cater even more closely with my hands. I even put an ad in the gay papers: "Experienced Asian American masseur with western hands and eastern touch. Total sensuous body massage, versatile. In and out calls." But my amateur massages weren't all that good. My clients preferred a younger man for the sexual services that were usually demanded with a rubdown. In recent years they were harder to please with their peculiar demands. Their tips grew meager. Some wanted their asses slapped before they could get excited; others wanted me to wear a jockstrap or a leather cock ring while giving them a massage on specific parts of the body—usually the feet, butt, or nipples. One client who tipped me well lived in a mansion in Hancock Park, an elegant enclave for "old-monied" WASPS. The neighborhood streets were lined with pepper and oak trees fronting brick and stucco buildings. I usually entered the house through the "merchants'" side entrance and pressed the door chime. The door opened electronically. I'd make my way to the small elegant study on the first floor that faced the garden. He would have already drawn the linen shades and dimmed the lights. Under bound gilt volumes of Pushkin, Tolstoi, London, and Mark Twain, he'd be in his pajamas drinking a vodka tonic.

"Take off your leather jacket, dear, it's hot today," he'd always say, whether it was summer or winter, handing me the white envelope. Without speaking, I'd pocket my fee and do what he wanted. In my white tanktop and tight Levi's, torn at the crotch, I would tease him until he grew excited. I would walk over to his chair, take the drink out of his hand and help him finish it, leaving his hands free to fondle my body. He'd lower his head. I'd stroke the strawberry blond toupee below my belly, as he began to methodically unbutton my Levi's with his teeth. Under my pants I wore a jock of black matte rubber with a chrome zipper that he'd bought me. With my free hand I would take the flat wooden paddle, almost like the one I used to scoop rice at home, and begin to slowly tap at his shoulders, until his pajama top fell to the carpet. Half-closing my eyes, I'd work my way down his body, until his skin was flushed and glistening with sweat. Another vodka would dull my senses, four was my limit. That's all I would do, standing over him, my legs straddling his shoulders and heavy pink flesh until, with a loud moan, he would come, using a black towel to wipe himself off. I had refused, however, to wear a silken kimono outfit and formal wig that he had supplied to celebrate his sixty-third birthday—along with a braided leather whip. "M. Butterfly" was not in my repertoire, though I did use the whip on him, gently, that night.

"Happy Birthday," I said, whacking him nicely on the back of his thighs and splashing the remains of my last drink over his body. Sometimes I wished that I was a blind masseur so that I could feel impartial toward all flesh.

■ ■ ■

"As I said, man, you sure do remind me of Bruce Lee. More and more. Let me get you a drink. Carlos, get this Chinese man another," he said, drawing out the last few words.

Carlos brought over another brandy and water.

"Thanks for the drink. My turn to ask your name."

"Brother Goode. Goode for tonight, and ba—ad tomorrow! And yours?" he asked, extending his hand.

"Hell, why not just call me Bruce. I'm beginning to like that name."

"Bruce, just look at yourself in that mirror over there."

I turned to the mirror and laughed. "My face is so red I probably look more like Mao. Goode, are you a native of L.A.?"

"Let's just say I've been here a long, long time. But my folks are originally from Louisiana. They call us Geechies down there."

"Geech . . . what?"

"In the ol' days, folks used to say that the Blacks and the Indians and the Whites got down together and what all turned out was Geechies. I got some Indian blood in me. So my color is red, 'specially when I can catch some rays. But not as red as you." He grinned. "As I was saying, I'm Brother Goode. Ask anyone around here." He poked the guy on the bar stool next to him. "Ed, what do you say now? Am I, or am I not, Brother Goode?"

Peering at the two of us from under his white baseball cap, Ed was noncommittal. "Good as you can be. Which ain't saying much."

I laughed, and studied Brother Goode under the red bar light. His face was smooth and delicate, with high cheekbones and hair that had been processed to give it a fine copper sheen. Late twenties, at most, I thought. After something, I suspected, but attracted, I continued to listen.

"You see, Bruce, I was in the Orient, in Okinawa. Naha. Stationed there in ninety. I dig Orientals. I myself had the craziest, the best Oriental chick in the whole world. Haru was her name."

"So, you have girlfriends?"

"Yeah. Back then. But you know how fast things can change for a man. Changing every day. Anyway, some chicks are fine. Some are real bitches. Some men are fine. Some of them are bitches too." He shrugged. "Now take yourself for instance, you're cool. Nice skin, I bet."

"Yeah? Not as smooth as yours, Brother."

"Skin against skin. One picture's worth a thousand words, that's what you Orientals say, don't you?" He smiled.

"It's getting late. I got to run. I enjoyed talking with you, Brother, but the last bus going back to Hollywood leaves at 1 A.M."

"Why leave now? It's only eleven o'clock. You scared of this joint? Of all of us niggers here? Of another earthquake and this damn building falling on you? Brother Goode will take care of you. Don't you worry yourself 'bout that now. You got any weed?"

"I don't smoke."

"Look, I got me a nice little room down the street. The Alonzo Hotel. Chinaman owns it, I think."

"I don't know it. As I said, I hardly ever come down here. First time in this bar. I'm going by bus to San Francisco."

"But now you're not. C'mon. What's a lone Chinaman gonna do this time of night anyway?"

"You win," I laughed. "Bartender, another one for this young man and one for me. Soda back. Goode, you make sense. But who's kidding who? I'm old enough to be your father. Bruce Lee's father for that matter. And I . . ."

"Every man for his self, Bruce."

"Let's just finish our drinks and call it a night."

We wound up having three more drinks for the road never taken. It was well past one o'clock. I rested my arm on Brother Goode's shoulder and let myself be dragged out of the bar before the cops kicked both of us out. Goode half-carried and half-pushed me down the street to the hotel, up the stairwell, and along the dingy hallway. We reached the room and stumbled in.

"Bruce, now watch yourself. Just take it easy here while I help you get those clothes off. Why are you looking at me so strange. You feelin' okay?"

"Very tired. But I'm not drunk. I'm very okay . . . No. I'm not okay. But I just ought to be getting home." I started to rise from the bed, then fell back.

"You're in no shape to do anything. Not even fuck, man. You just lay back while I run down the hall for a second." Yielding to common sense and weariness, I kicked off my shoes and closed my eyes. The door opened and shut again. I smelled the sweetish odor of marijuana. My eyes scanned the angles of his face and shoulders as he grinned and exhaled, blowing smoke at me. Inhaling, I felt my body relax. He began to stroke my chest and I stretched my fingers over the small of his back.

■ ■ ■

Morning light through the torn paper window shade turned the pinkish bedspread into flame. I stirred, turned to my side, and saw a triangular expanse of copper shoulder beside me, topped by disheveled reddish curls. Then I remembered that I was with Brother Goode. I saw that the man beside me was holding his dark flaccid cock in one hand. A small square of burnt tin foil and a match lay between us on the sheet. Maybe it wasn't what I remembered. Coke or Ecstasy or something else that I didn't know. I reached back toward my trouser pocket. Feeling nothing but my own flesh, I spied my pants folded neatly on the metal chair near the window.

I rose, tiptoed to the chair, and stuck my hands into the back pocket of the trousers. Anxious fingers yanked the wallet out. I quickly scanned the bills—two fifties, a couple of twenties and tens left after the drinks.

"You Koreans. All you think about is your money gettin' ripped off. I should have figured that out before I brought you . . .'"

I spun around and the wallet dropped to the floor. Brother Goode wore a contemptuous smile, hand propping up his head.

"Uh, no, I was checking to see whether I had enough change for bus fare. I'm on unemployment, ya know."

"Don't jive me, yellow mother fuck. . . . Here I half-dragged your flat ass home. Didn't even mess with it and you think I took your money."

"No, no. It's just that I'm not a rich man."

"Who said anything about being a rich man? You're simple. SIM-PLE."

"You got me wrong. I'm really thankful. Uh, how about going out to get some breakfast. On me. Really, I'm sorry. In this part of town you have to be a little careful."

"Who you sayin' sorry to? Not to me. But you should know one thing. You ain't no Bruce Lee. Not your face or your body."

"I never said I was, Brother. You said it."

"Brother? Bruce Lee? Shit, get outta here."

"Look—you want breakfast or not?"

Brother Goode turned his head, puffed up his pillow, and retorted. "I am stayin' right here. In my room. You get on home. But don't look too carefully in that mirror, Pops."

I threw on my shirt and pants, socks and shoes. I picked up my duffel and checked my wallet again, making sure it was lodged tightly in my back pocket. I made my way to the corridor. Downstairs, I nodded at the Asian manager, who threw me a look of disdain.

■ ■ ■

The bus swerves to avoid hitting a pickup truck loaded with plantains and oranges, jolting me out of an intense sweat-and-camphor somnolence. I wipe my forehead with my perspiring right hand and push the thinning black bangs to one side. The bus reels and groans along its predestined course.

The man with the transistor and hospital wristband and the Latina with the child get off at the same stop. The child is dressed for church in a white lace dress and matching bib, reminding me that today is the Day of Rest.

LATE BLOOMER

from **WAYLAID**

∎ ∎ ∎

Ed Lin

I was about twelve years old when I knew I had to get laid soon. No more of this jerking off. That was for fags.

The idea had been put into my head by Vincent, a Benny from Brooklyn. Bennys were young whites who came down to our hotel in the summers to pollute New Jersey's shores. They didn't go to college and worked in factories or as secretaries. All of them were from Bayonne, Elizabeth, Newark, or New York, hence the name.

Vincent and I were sitting on the office couch playing Warlords when he turned to me and said, "You gotten laid yet?"

"Nah. Not yet."

"Well, why not? You're like eleven, right?"

"I'm twelve," I said, straightening my back.

"Yeah, whatever, you should get laid. Girls were all over me when I was like eight. I was all over them, too." Vincent scratched his right side and his nipples visibly hardened. I never saw him with a shirt on, but he never shivered when he slipped into the frigid air of the office, wearing only a pair of tight black trunks and aquarium-blue flip-flops.

I had on a New Orleans Mardi Gras T-shirt that I found in one of the rooms and a pair of Yankees shorts. Imitation leather slippers

---

ED LIN, who is half Chinese and half Taiwanese, was born in New York City in 1969 and grew up in New Jersey and Pennsylvania. He has held a wide variety of jobs, including managing a financial-news Web site, moving boxes in a warehouse, and lifeguarding. He plays bass in the Asian American rock band Raven Steals the Light, which released its CD in early 2003. *Waylaid*, his first novel, was published by Kaya in 2001.

from Taiwan left treads on the top of my feet where the straps criss-crossed.

"What for, Vincent?"

" 'What for?' What the fuck kind of question is that?" He punched playfully at my arm. "What for! For getting your dick wet!" I hit the reset button on the Atari and starting pounding away at Vincent's war-lord.

"Hey hey hey!" he yelped as he fumbled to pull up the controller, which had slipped into his crotch.

■ ■ ■

This was Vincent's fourth straight weekend at our hotel. Vincent always wanted Room 59, because he was born that year and because it was close to the pool. It was also far from the office, which was important because he was sneaking in his two cousins with his girlfriend so he could pay the two-person rate instead of the four-person rate, which was ten bucks more. Vincent told me because we were friends and we had an understanding between us.

Vincent was in his early twenties, with a face that was long and nar-row like a skinny tree trunk. Thick black hair was cropped short and stood straight up, like magnified photos of stubble before the razor cuts the chin clean. He was "Vincent," never "Vinny," because "Vinny's" was the name of some pizza joint and it wasn't the real Italian pizza anyway. You needed a fork and a knife to eat real pizza. Real Italian pizza was thicker and had more stuff in it. Vincent had never had real Italian pizza, but that was the first thing he was going to eat when he got to Italy, where his grandfather was from. Vincent was working at some construction job his uncle got him, but at night he was studying to be a cop. He was going to take me to Coney Island in his squad car one day. We were going to ride the Cyclone and eat hot dogs.

■ ■ ■

I had moved the Atari and the television into the office because it got so busy during the summertime that it didn't make sense to stay inside the living quarters and walk into and out of the office every five minutes for every BING! BING! BING! of the desk bell. Nobody hit that bell just once. Besides, it was June, and the temperature was cranking up. The office was air-conditioned and our living quarters weren't. It had to be that way because my parents said it wasn't worth air-conditioning the living quarters. But if the office wasn't kept cold, customers would think the air conditioners in the rooms didn't work.

I spent a lot of time on the office couch. Vincent would drop in to hang out and play Atari with me when his girlfriend was pissed at him, which was usually a few hours on Saturday morning and a few more hours on Sunday morning.

I liked having someone to play games with. I was an only child and my parents could never tell if I was playing Atari or watching television, even if there were blocky tanks, planes or spaceships firing at each other on the screen. They wouldn't have had time to play games even if they knew how. Friends, forget about it. No one wanted to hang out at our hotel. And it was too busy for me to ever leave for long enough to have friends outside of school.

■ ■ ■

"I'm going to win again," I yelled.

I felt like such a loser when Vincent talked about girls. Vincent always talked about his fucking adventures—how he fucked his married neighbor who was forty but was as tight as a twenty-year-old, and how he fucked three sisters in three days and two of them were virgins. I preferred hearing his stories to having him ask me who I was fucking. I only had stories about me winning fights, which I did often enough because I was big for my age, but I knew I was letting him down.

"I know you kids are fucking in school. I know you are."

"I only heard about the two retarded kids, and I don't even think they meant it," I said.

Vincent laughed. "Retarded pussy! Shit, pussy's pussy, who cares. You gotta like someone in school. I know you do. Some girls already start developing, you know? Their asses kinda turn out like fenders and the headlights, you know they're going on high beam." His warlord flickered and died. Defeat was drawn out in crude, blinking video blocks. "Some little Oriental girl? You been keeping her a secret? You give her some bamboo? You slip it to her?"

"Naw, I'm the only one in my school. Anyway, Chinese girls are ugly. I like blondes. Or redheads if they don't have too many freckles." Vincent shook his head from side to side, keeping his pupils fixed on me.

"I fucked Chinese girls. Goddamned cute. I fucked one last week, that's why Patty's pissed at me. I just told her."

"Then why are you still with Patty? You can just go out with someone different every weekend. She just gives you too much shit." I was thinking that when I was old enough, I would be fucking left and right because there were so many women wanting cock in the world. Maybe I was old enough now, since I was getting hard-ons all the time. If I found a dynamite bombshell, I'd make her my girlfriend. But Patty was no bombshell. She had huge tits, but her nose drooped down like the mascot on the Moosehead Beer label. I never told Vincent that.

"Why am I still going out with Patty? Because I love her. You know, I really do. I'm gonna marry her. We're gonna have kids and everything." His mouth narrowed into a scythe. "But she don't have no chain on my dick. I don't gotta pull in the leash until the ring's on the finger. Then we'll see."

I knew all about the powerful drive of horniness from reading the letters in *Penthouse* and *Swank*, but never having had sex lent a certain mystique to it all, especially stuff like S&M or ass fucking. It was like reading about being weightless in space; this one astronaut woke up to find a hand wrapped around his neck and tightening. But it turned out to be his own hand.

"I know this girl here who will suck your dick for ten bucks. We used to take the same bus together. She don't fuck, but you can cum on her tits, she don't care. Her name's Chris or Karen and she's in Room 30," said Vincent. He threw his head back like a horse tossing its mane. "I know you've got at least ten bucks."

I saw the girl in Room 30. She couldn't ever get me hard.

He traced my look of skepticism with his eyes and drew the wrong conclusion.

"No, it's okay. She doesn't care about you Orientals." His hands on his thighs flipped to open palms.

I felt a pin slip into my stomach. Vincent's a friend, I told myself, he doesn't mean anything.

I hit reset on the Atari and the game began again. "Hey, c'mon now! That's not fair!" Vincent put up a fight for a few seconds, then tossed his controller onto the couch next to me.

"So, anyway, you have to get laid," he said, running a single finger through his hair. Vincent looked at the office clock, which was a large plastic-molded Marlboro sign with a dial in the middle of the second *o*. A cowboy in spurs leaned against the *M*. It was a quarter to eleven.

Vincent got up and stretched, cracking bones in his lower back. "Maybe Patty's cooled off by now. Remember what I tell you. I'll be disappointed if you don't get laid by the end of the summer. Real fucking disappointed." He wagged a finger at me and pulled at his waistband. "Or maybe you'll turn queer on me, or something. Maybe you're fag bait already!"

Right then, Peter Fiorello walked into the office with Mrs. Fiorello. The Fiorellos were the first regulars I'd met—they were both retired, and they'd been coming down to our place since we'd bought it. Each of them kissed Vincent on the cheek. They were old enough to be Vincent's parents, maybe even his grandparents. The three of them together in a semiembrace looked like a spaghetti sauce commercial. The only thing missing were the aprons and wooden spoons.

Peter Fiorello's shrunken patch of short white hair looked like a knit cap. Peter would walk around shirtless in the summer, exposing old tattoos on his chest and arms, blued and blurred beyond recognition. His tits were smeared with excess red and brown paint, hanging against his chest like dried mud. Peter wore a gold chain with a religious pendant on it and dark shades. I never saw him with his shades off or without a smelly, smoldering cigar in his hand. He smiled often, flashing two rows of rotten corn kernels.

Mrs. Fiorello was loud, large and annoying. She had big pouffy hair, with plump breasts and stomach to match. Her skin was covered with impossibly dense freckles. There must have been a thousand dark brown dots per square inch all over the massive surface area of her body. Seeing her in a one-piece bathing suit that didn't even show that much skin took away my faith in God.

The Fiorellos were the hotel's only steady customers through the four seasons. They lived somewhere in New York, but there were too many loud blacks and Puerto Ricans up there. They wanted to come to our hotel at the Jersey shore where they could relax and talk to us nice Chinese people.

"Watch this man. He's going places," Peter said, wrapping an arm around Vincent's waist and stroking Vincent's neck with his free hand. He liked Vincent and touched him so much it was worrisome.

"Peter, you tell the boy to listen to what I say, okay?" said Vincent, making a meaningless gesture at me with his right hand.

"You listen to Vincent, he's going to be on top. He's the man to look out for," Peter said.

"Vincent is a good boy. If you turn out like him, your mother will be really proud," said Mrs. Fiorello. Vincent winked, extracted himself, and walked around the Fiorellos. His slippers made sucking sounds as he walked back to Room 59.

"I used to look like that," said Peter, standing at the office window. He leaned back and rubbed the scraggly white fuzz on his chest.

"Now you're twice the man, Peter," said Mrs. Fiorello, patting at his stomach.

"You see this? You see this? Always a compliment with a nitpick. Always a slap with a kiss." He tapped his cigar, and his nose twitched as he winked from behind his impenetrable shades, which were as dark as a wet blackboard.

"Oh, stop, Peter!" said Mrs. Fiorello, taking a playful swat at his face.

Listening to the Fiorellos talk would run like an old stand-up routine, complete with elbowing and winks:

"These cigars really aren't bad for you," he might start.

"Peter never inhales. He only breathes out, so it's okay."

"You know, she'll be the death of me, not these things. Cigars are a habit you can break, but women always break you first."

"Peter doesn't need to be broken. All those years of being in the navy broke you. He cleans so much around the house, I feel like I'm the one making a mess. I just watch the television and put my feet up."

"She puts her feet up on my back when I'm scrubbing the floors. It's abuse, I tell ya. You people know how to treat your women. Put them in their place in China."

"Peter!"

"It's true, they can't even walk next to their husband, they have to walk behind them."

"They have such pretty dresses, the Chinese women. Doesn't your mother have any like that? She should wear them. Pretty and silk."

The Fiorellos would always have that angle, throw in something about China or Chinese food, as if I couldn't follow the conversation if they didn't. Mrs. Fiorello turned to the television screen. "This is a computer game, right? You shouldn't play this anymore, they rot your brain. I read it in *Newsweek*."

"They develop motor skills and improve hand-eye coordination," I said, using my prepared answer from the video-game magazines. "They also keep kids off the street and out of trouble. Video games don't require parental supervision, unlike many movies, and nobody gets hurt playing them. They're also good for children who don't have any playmates."

Mrs. Fiorello rolled her eyes and dropped to the couch next to me. I felt the creaky frame give a little and the seat cushion grow tight. "You think you're so smart. Just wait until it's too late," she said. After a heavy sigh, she added, "Is your mother in?"

"Hold on a sec," I said. I turned off the Atari and walked back into the living quarters. I went into my parents' bedroom and shook my mother awake. It was about time for her to get up, anyway. I could tell by the hotel's log that she'd been up until five renting rooms, but six hours of sleep was more than enough. Today was going to be another busy day for the hotel, and there were rooms we needed to clean. In a few minutes, she was fully dressed and in the office. I heard an exaggerated but brief greeting exchanged amongst the three of them.

I shut the door to the office, feeling the heat of the living quarters. I followed the worn path on the living room rug, between a lopsided couch and a bare TV stand, back to my room. Talking to Vincent had made me think about this girl from school I liked, Lee Anderson. She had blond hair and green eyes and was so cute, I couldn't help but look away when she caught me staring, which was about every two minutes. Even though she was just twelve like me, I could tell that Lee was going to be a perfect girl when she grew up. She was already past a B cup, and her long, soft blond hair curled at her shoulders. Her body was growing in all the right places, and she was looking pretty damn sexy.

When we were in second grade together, she'd drunk beer from her Thermos and couldn't wake up after naptime. Maybe things would go easier for me if I got her drunk again. Beer could make a lot of things possible.

But I got the feeling she liked me, too. Maybe she had a speck of dust in her eye the day I thought she winked at me. So what if it was. She was definitely going to be mine. I felt warm each time Lee smiled or said my name. She'd probably just let me get into her pants sober. Get my dick wet.

I pulled out my Monopoly set and took an issue of *Cheri* from under the game board. I reread the letters. Women driving, walking, or sitting alone were dying to get naked and suck and fuck.

Some mornings I woke up with my own hand wrapped around my cock.

■ ■ ■

The hotel was beautiful once, back in the 1950s.

I know because I'd found a box of old color pamphlets in the crawl space that ran under the complete length of the hotel. The pictures were in soft, faded colors—the blues were baby blues and the reds were pink. Flying wooden ramparts painted gleaming white connected the tips of the two parallel wings of the hotel like a big suspension bridge. Voluptuous cars iced with chrome looked like they could have driven out of Arnold's parking lot on *Happy Days*. Men wore suits and hats, and women had scarves and gloves.

Three decades went by. It was the 1980s.

The ramparts were now rotting in stacks in the thickly wooded area that pressed up against the outside of the even- and odd-numbered wings. The hotel was laid out like the letter U, with the office at the bottom. An asphalt driveway ran the entire inside length of the letter, from the four-lane interstate highway that led to the beaches, to the office, and then back.

The big cars had been replaced by beat-up Datsuns and Thunderbirds that crawled around the parking lot like insects with a leg or wing torn off.

Men had ditched their suits and hats, and women their scarves and gloves. Now they wore a unisex uniform of T-shirts and jeans, or bathing suits and cut-offs in the summer. Their faces were desperate for sex, for love, for another smoke; men with a few days of stubble, women with uneven layers of makeup. Their hard eyes and harder mouths would only loosen up with booze or some pot.

■ ■ ■

I don't remember much of life before the hotel. I was born in New York City, but we moved out to the Jersey shore and bought the place when

I was just a kid. The sellers were a white couple with a son about my age.

I remember racing slot cars with that other little boy while our parents hammered out the details of the sale. The handheld controllers smelled like blown-out birthday candles as they heated up. If you didn't let off on the trigger on the turn, the car would fishtail and flip off the track. Our parents were talking in the kitchen with the door closed. I couldn't hear what they were saying as the cars whined around and around, but I could see them through the plate glass window.

My father was standing at the dining table, sleeves rolled up. He was slightly shorter than my mother, with a ruddy complexion that made him look like he was drunk or really mad, but he was never in either of those states. He had curly black hair, which was a little unusual, but his eyes and wide cheeks tagged him as Chinese. He was poring over the blueprints of the hotel, examining the structure and soundness of the plan, and figuring out how salvageable the hotel was in its current state of disrepair. Was that when my parents hammered out the details of renting out rooms to hookers and johns?

The main reason why my father had wanted the hotel was because he wanted to have his own business. Like all his classmates from Taiwan who had come to the United States, he had been passed over for promotions at the civil-engineering company he'd been working at. His boss had told him his English wasn't good enough, but after a few months with some textbooks, he found out that none of the engineers, including his boss, really knew proper spelling or grammar. He ended up making a lot of corrections in the firm's reports. My mother told me they'd given him a bottle of champagne when he left, which he poured out in the street before throwing the bottle into the gutter.

After we moved into the hotel, he was always covered with rust or flakes of rotted wood. There were burn holes in his pants, holes that corresponded to scars on his skin. He'd slip into the crawl space because of a leaking pipe or a sinking bathroom floor and solder and nail away, surfacing only for food before heading back down. I would join him down there sometimes, but my main job was handling the front desk. My father never wanted to deal with customers. Unlike my mother, he was embarrassed about his English, though his was much better than hers.

When the hotel filled up in the summer, we could just lock the office door and put the closed sign in the window. When the fall arrived, we had to scrounge for business. We needed to keep the office open and unlocked to get all the business we could.

The bulk of the business during those times was the three-hour rental.

On the weekends, during the school year, my mother would lay down a folded comforter behind the counter for me and set an alarm clock by the bell. She would leave the office light on, telling me to turn my head and close my eyes, and it wouldn't keep me up. Late nights were prime john time, and if the light was out, they might think the place was closed and go to another hotel or use our parking lot. My mother was too tired from watching the office the whole week while I was in school and needed to catch up on sleep on the weekends. As a woman, I'm sure she also didn't relish the thought of being in the same room as the cock side of the money equation.

Some nights I just couldn't sleep, even if no one came all night. When that happened, I would read the letters sections of sex magazines, which I could easily hide in the folds of the comforter when I heard a customer coming in.

■ ■ ■

I first saw the letters in an issue of *Hustler* when I was about seven. When I was with my mom, she'd thrown out all the porn right off the bat, making sure to rip it up in front of me. But that time, I found it under the bed, and shoved it under my shirt before she saw.

That magazine had an article on how to find hotels that charged hourly rates. It recommended going to non-chain hotels close to train stations. Or you could pick up hookers by the train stations late at night and they would know which hotels to go to. A fuckhole wasn't only a cunt; it was also a place to hole up and fuck. Like our hotel. After reading the article, I wondered how much it would cost for me to get laid with a hooker, and how much money was in the cash drawer.

When I was ten, a john I was renting a room to told me he was picking up girls by the New Jersey Transit station in nearby Asbury Park. They wore short skirts and long coats, and carried open umbrellas.

After all my years at the hotel, I'd never seen any hookers—not their full bodies, anyway. They wouldn't prance around the parking lot afterwards, trying to pick up more tricks. The most I ever saw was a dim face between the dashboard and sun blind of a car pulled up outside the office. Sometimes they'd be smoking or fixing their makeup.

The john told me they were $20, $5 extra to fuck them up the ass and $5 more for swallowing. So a room and a no-frills prostitute were $40 in total.

"It's worth it to get laid, isn't it?" he asked, as he filled out a registration card, moving as fast as he could make up the information. He was wearing a dark brown corduroy jacket, a grimy button-down shirt, and dark slacks. Silvery hair cascaded into the gap between his lobster-red neck and his loosened collar. He looked like he was about fifty.

"Are they pretty?" I asked. He laughed.

"I'm not looking for Miss America, but they're pretty for black girls. The white ones are kind of ugly."

"But how good is it?"

"How good is it? It's great. It's like following through on a good clean punch."

"What does it feel like?"

"What does it feel like . . ." He was smiling. "Look, kid, just give me the goddamn key."

■ ■ ■

I fell asleep once with the fifth anniversary issue of *Celebrity Skin* over my face and I didn't hear the alarm go off. It was a lot softer than a BING! The clock alarm went on for so long, my mother got up and came into the office. I hadn't fully awoken until she swatted my face with the rolled-up magazine.

"You go to hell, you look at these pictures!" she screamed, now kicking at my shoulders as I scrambled to my feet.

"I was just reading the letters!"

"You go to hell! Where did you get this from!?!?"

"I got it from cleaning the hotel rooms!"

"You don't touch this anymore! You go to hell!" She never said anything more about porn mags and I continued to add to my collection. But from that day on, I would bring only my schoolbooks to read at night and left the magazines in my room. That way, she wouldn't have to see them.

I once asked my mother why anybody would want to rent one of our hotel rooms for just three hours.

"They tire from driving," she said. "They want lie down and take little nap." We were distant enough to let that howling wind of a lie exist between our worlds. And it let me know it was okay to lie to her, too.

■ ■ ■

Late Friday was big for hourly rentals. The husbands could always say they were trying to finish up some work at the office before the weekend.

At one in the morning, there were about a dozen rooms that had to be cleaned to be rented out again.

I yawned and rubbed my eyes before picking up a plastic bucket in each hand and followed my mother out the office door. She held a bundle of folded sheets, pillowcases and towels. My mother had a mop of straight black hair that dangled down to her shoulders. As we walked along the curved part of the U-shaped driveway, the light from the outdoor spotlights reflected in the smooth crescents in her hair.

When we got to 11A, my mother knocked on the door to make sure they had left.

Once upon a time, 11A had been 13, but then it had been changed so the rooms on the odd-numbered wing went from 11 to 11A and then to 15. Nobody wanted to rent a room 13. Like they wouldn't get lucky or something if they did.

My mother opened the lock with the master key and turned to look at me.

"You have everything, right?" she asked. I nodded and shook the buckets.

One of my buckets held a few spray bottles of bathroom cleaners, air fresheners, and rug cleaners. A worn toilet bowl brush dangled over the side of the bucket, the bristles pressed flat against the battered wire rim.

My other bucket was packed with soap, rolls of toilet paper, and sheaves of sanitary labels. The soap bars were slender white rectangles embossed with "THANK YOU" on one side, like we were thanking our customers for taking a shower and trying to be clean. The soap lathered up about as well as a Lego block and would break into pieces if you tried to use it more than once. Our toilet paper was so thin you'd feed fingers up your ass.

Each hotel room was basically the same except that some of the black-and-white televisions had rabbit-ear antennas and some had inverted wire coat hangers. The rooms all had a simple desk, a nightstand, and a chair made of pressed wood. Push on any of the furniture the wrong way and it would splinter apart. There were burn marks on the desks and nightstands, even though each room had chipped-glass ashtrays. The two windows had shades as heavy as burlap. When they were closed, they blocked out sound and light and also the view of the parking lot.

The bed consisted of flimsy metal frames and creaky box springs with broken slats of wood topped with a doughy mattress. Two limp pillows slouched against the pressed-wood headstand. Some of the headstands had stickers on them with instructions on how to operate the vibrating motor for a quarter, but the motion devices had been ripped out and thrown away long before we'd owned the place. The wall-to-wall carpeting looked like every marching band in the country had dragged flour sacks of grime across it. Every color in the carpet was corrupted into a different shade of dark green.

The bathroom tile wasn't much better, but at least we provided soap and clean towels. We weren't classy enough to have vials of shampoo because we ordered from the economy section of our supplier catalog. Only the standard and luxury sections had shampoo.

I sat on the edge of the bathtub and scrubbed at the gunk in the shower with the toilet brush, shaking a can of some no-name imitation of Ajax so that it snowed into the scummy tub. I scrubbed again.

I looked at myself in the bathroom mirror. My hair was straight like my mother's, but about twice as thick. It stuck out sideways at odd angles like clumps of crabgrass. My eyes were bloodshot and my face looked old and tired.

I finished with the toilet and slipped a paper label around the folded rim and seat cover. I shook the toilet brush into the sink, then scrubbed it against the edges of the sink and the faucet handles.

My mother had been stripping the sheets off the bed. When she stopped, I turned to see what was the matter. She was looking at a dark spot on the mattress and frowning.

"We have to flip this one," she said, nodding her head towards the stain in the other lower corner. I pulled at the seam of the fabric until I could get a good hold on the thick, mushy mattress, then helped her wrestle it off the crooked bed frame. Most of the mattresses and bed frames were from a demolition company that would strip everything out of a house before pulverizing it.

Soon the mattress was turned upside down and pushed back into place. There were dark brown stains—all near the same area as the wet one—on this side of the mattress, too. Some were oval-shaped, some looked like warped coffee-cup stains, and others looked like little amoebas with several pseudopodia. They were dry, though, and that was all that was important. My mother unfurled the new sheets and threw them on top.

The wet come stains were now on the underside of the mattress.

MISTER PORMA

■ ■ ■

R. Zamora Linmark

Definition of "Porma" from Bonifacio Dumpit's
Decolonization for Beginners: A Filipino Glossary

Porma, adj: 1. Formal attire. 2. Proper. 3. Well-bred.

DRUMROLL

Voice-over: Live from C'est Si Bon at the Pagoda Hotel, welcome to the Third Annual Mister Porma Pageant.

Spotlight sweeps across the grand ballroom, brushing the coifs of the boisterous crowd. The bubble of light halts center stage, where a man is flashing a wide grin, awaiting recognition and adulation.

Voice-over: Please welcome this evening's host: Dave Manchester.

A haole transplant from Los Angeles, Dave Manchester has graced fashion magazine covers and appeared in numerous TV and print ads in Hawaii, Japan, and the continental United States. He's featured in a forthcoming issue of *Gentleman's Quarterly.*

"Aloha and *magandang gabi po* to everyone. I am Dave Manchester, your host for this evening."

Decked in a see-through barong Tagalog shirt and black Armani trousers, the Irish-American model swaggers across a stage decorated with banana leaves.

The poet and novelist R. ZAMORA LINMARK is the author of *Rolling the R's*, which he's adapting for the stage, and *Leche.* Born in Manila in 1968, he grew up in Hawaii and now divides his time between the United States and the Philippines.

"*Mga kababayan.*" Dave pauses to translate what "countrymen" is to those who do not know Tagalog. "Without further ado, here are the five finalists of the Third Annual Mister Porma Pageant in the traditional opening parade."

Blackout.

Silence.

Bright lights. Music. The theme from *Hawaii Five-O* by the Exotic Orchestra of Arthur Lyman.

The Big Five make their dramatic entrance from behind the banana tree:

Honolulu-born Virgilio "Virgo" Salcedo is first; pure Ilocano; twenty-two years of age; attending Honolulu Community College, majoring in auto mechanics.

Next, Arturo "Art" Dwayne Pascual Johnson, twenty-four, born at Clark Air Force Base in Angeles City, Pampanga; half African-American, half Visayan; has lived all over the United States, Japan, Germany, and Korea; currently a pre-law student at the University of Hawaii, Manoa campus; resides in Schofield Army Barracks with his parents;

Then, Filipino-Hawaiian Shane Kawika Lacaran, twenty-two, freshman at Kapiolani Community College (Diamond Head campus), hopes of becoming a veterinarian or an orthopedic surgeon;

Then, Kenzo Kahoku'okalani Parubrub-Kajiwara, twenty-three, of Hawaiian-Okinawan-Filipino descent, presently in his last semester at Connecticut College in New London; majoring in modern dance;

And last but not least, Manila-born Vince Formoso De Los Reyes, who is twenty-three years of age and of Filipino-Spanish-American descent. Nervous, Vince pauses to wipe the sweat coursing down his face.

"Right on, Vince."

"Go, Vince."

"I love you, son."

Am I hallucinating? Vince wonders.

No, he isn't. Those four words that went in one ear but refused to go out the other belong to none other than his mother, Carmen Formoso.

Vince should've known better, should've braced himself for Carmen's last-minute appearance ("apparition" is more like it), should've obeyed his sixth sense, which went on red alert as soon as he entered the spotlight, when his nervousness was quickly replaced by an agitation caused by the strong force emanating from the third row to his right, a presence clamoring for his attention.

"Kick ass, son," cheers Carmen, who resembles a Mexican telenovela actress. All her three children—Vince, Jing, and Alvin—inherited her huge eyes that can speak about love and hurt in a hundred languages.

What the hell is she doing here? A stupid thought—considering the Mister Porma finalists were featured last night on Emme Tomimbang's TV show, *Island Moments*.

Vince scans the front rows for his father, doesn't see him; only his sister, Jing, his brother, Alvin, and Maggie, his mother's perky aerobics instructor, had all seen Emme's show.

Tune Mom out, Vince thinks. If I want to leave this rock, I must block her out of my mind, erase her from my memory. Erase her and Dad and Jing and Alvin and Dave and Maggie.

Focus.

"Come on, dude, hurry up."

Focus.

"Shut up and let the guy speak."

Go!

"Last December, I completed my B.A. studies in film and literature at the University of Hawaii in Manoa and graduated with highest honors."

The mention of "highest honors" elicits awe from the audience.

Charged with adrenaline and confidence, Vince leaves the spotlight, thinking: Hello, East Coast; good riddance, Honolulu.

But Virgo, Art, Shane, and Kenzo are just as determined to take home the title of Mister Porma. Who wouldn't be? They've come this far, having beat out one hundred forty-five other applicants (breaking last year's record by twelve, according to pageant coordinator Evangeline Encarnacion).

In order to qualify, the applicant had to be at least twenty years old, of Filipino descent (copy of birth certificate), a resident of Hawaii, and, as stated in Section 1G of the contract, "of good moral character, never engaged in any activity which could be characterized as dishonest, immoral, immodest, indecent, or in bad taste."

Virgo and Art return to the dim-lit stage and pose with their arms folded over their chests.

The audience goes wild.

A loud noise from the stereo speakers (a record needle screeching on vinyl?) cues Vince and Shane to walk downstage, holding bamboo sticks.

"Oh, man, not the tinikling again." The room breaks out in laughter.

Also known as the Philippine bamboo dance, the tinikling is the most overperformed opening number in Asian American pageant history. Every contestant must've danced in and out of those poles enough times to do it blindfolded. It was used in the first two Mister Porma pageants. Fortunately, this year, the pattern was broken. Thanks to Edgar Ramirez, this year's choreographer. As he told the Big Five in their first rehearsal, "No more bamboo dancing!"

Bright lights flood the stage as the music begins: an instrumental medley of Paula Abdul dance tunes from her *Shut Up & Dance* CD, with Edgar supplying appropriated lyrics at the last minute because he could not get permission from ASCAP.

Vince takes a deep breath, then rolls his eyes to Virgo making the sign of the cross.

Kenzo, the fifth finalist, will make his entrance later. What's more important is that the four finalists remember the mambo.

According to the five-dollar program, the opening dance number is a tribute to Leonard Bernstein's *West Side Story*. Instead of the Jets and Sharks, however, the friction is between Da Manong and United Stars gangs of Kalihi, Honolulu. Vince and Virgo represent Da Manong gang, immigrants seeking a better life in Hawaii. They are identified by the iron-on sticker of the Philippine flag on their shirts. The United Stars consists of Art and Shane, who, like the WASPy Jets, are locals protecting their territory from FOBs; they wear red-white-and-blue bandannas around their heads.

Vince and Shane begin swaggering sideways downstage while Art and Virgo taunt each other backstage.

The beat picks up. Shane swings his stick and nearly whacks Vince on the face.

Vince narrows his eyes. "Come on, man," he sings, "do you really wanna / fight me / forever?"

Shane nods, motions Vince to screw the sticks, brah, and fight him like a man. Vince accepts the challenge, tosses the stick to the floor, then spits at him.

Grinning, Shane wipes the thread of spit across his face with the back of his hand.

A push-and-shove match ensues. Biceps and triceps flex. Hands ball into fists.

Shane throws a right straight punch and misses. Vince smirks, does the mambo and then the cha-cha. Seeing an upper-cut opening, he seizes it.

Shane hunches over; the audience gasps with him.

Vince ambles over to Shane, who is trying to rise. "Hey, man, you okay?" he whispers, unsure if Shane is acting or not.

"You fuckin' fag." Shane's fist heads straight for Vince's crotch.

Vince grunts as Shane's knuckles land on his right hip.

"That blow is low / almost TKO," Art and Virgo chant. Now, it's their turn to rumble in the spotlight.

"You just like him," Virgo sings to Art. "Just by your eyes / can tell they fulla lies."

Track change.

Art punches Virgo in the face. Virgo tackles him. The two bear-wrestle downstage. Vince and Shane join them. The crowd rises, stands on their seats to watch the brawl.

"Vibe-o-lo-gy," Paula Abdul, the former LA Lakers cheerleader-turned-choreographer-turned-diva, sings in the background.

The stage transforms into a snake pit with bodies writhing, tossing, pinning and getting pinned.

Throughout the "Vibeology" number, Vince, Shane, Art, and Virgo get so wrapped up beating each other up that they forget who the enemy is. Pounce, grab, takedown. And the battle over who owns Kalihi is now buried in an avalanche of sweat.

The mood changes from funk to light rock. Spotlight on Kenzo, suspended in midair, hovering over the bodies. On his back, huge feathered wings he attempts to flap.

"Prometheus is coming / and he's calling your name," Kenzo sings as he descends onto the stage. "The world's collapsing / time to make your peace."

"Peace be with you / Also with you," Vince, Shane, Art, and Virgo chant to each other. They rise from the floor and sing about forgiveness.

The end unites them. Joining hands, they bow, then rush backstage to remove torn shirts, wipe off sweat, and apply Mercurochrome to cuts and scratches.

"And there you have it, ladies and gentlemen, the opening song and dance number as choreographed by last year's Mister Porma, Edgar Ramirez," Dave says. "While the Big Five get ready for the talent portion, let me take this opportunity to thank our cosponsors."

AND NOW A WORD FROM

JENNIFER'S KAMAYAN ("Over a hundred Philippine regional dishes. Ilokano way, Tagalog way, Visayan way, any way you want 'em. Just name 'em, we'll cook 'em, you'll dig 'em. Eighteen great locations to serve you"); PINOY SAVINGS & LOAN ("Avail of our 'Lolo and Lola' retirement plan for the elderlies. Member: FDIC"); "Make no mistake cuz all it takes is one take JUN'S TAKE-ONE, home of the one-hour passport and VISA photos," located on North King and Kalihi Street"; "Come visit us at RICHARDSON, SMITH & YAMASHITA and take advantage of our multilingual staff. No fee if no recovery. Call for free consultation."

SLAM

"Talent is a major trait of Filipinos," Dave says. "How many of you have heard the saying that a Filipino is not a Filipino if he cannot dance, act, and sing?"

Amens from the audience.

Arturo inaugurates the talent portion by rapping to Run-DMC's *Walk This Way*, followed by Virgo, who offers a five-minute demonstration on the Philippine national sport—the sipa. "It is our version of the hackey sack," Virgo explains. "Like tennis, sipa can be played in singles or doubles." Next is Shane, dragging a Soloflex Nautilus machine onstage. "For my talent portion, I going show you guys the proper body mechanics to do push-ups, pull-ups, and sit-ups so you guys no injure your backs, okay?" Kenzo takes the stage next to perform an avant-garde dance number that fuses hula and Butoh, a postwar Japanese dance that requires a lot of patience from the audience.

Draped in a bedsheet over a white-painted body, Kenzo spends an hour and forty-five minutes in catatonia while a silver-painted *kumu*, a Polynesian-looking man who resembles the Michelin Man, bangs his gourd and chants about haoles without souls, haoles who don't have any respect for the land.

Throughout Kenzo's postmodern/postmortem dance, most of the audience abscond to smoke cigarettes on the patio, replenish their system with caffeine, piss, move their bowels, retrieve messages from their GTE voice mail, run across the street to McDonald's for a quick value meal.

Then it's Vince's turn.

He enters the stage, clutching a book in his hand and humming a Frank Sinatra tune.

He sets the book on the podium and opens it to the dog-eared page. Kenzo's out of the race, for sure, he thinks. He went way over the fifteen-minute time limit. Art couldn't rap for shit to save his half-Filipino, half-black ass. As for Shane? Since when is back injury prevention considered a talent? And Virgo's hackey-sack exhibition?

Vince looks straight ahead and plants an imaginary dot.

"*Let America be America again,*" he begins, emphasis on "be."

"*Let it be the dream it used to be,*" he continues, emphasis on "dream."

"*America never was America to me.*" This time, the emphasis is a balled-up fist that unfolds as he pleads, "*Let America be the dream the dreamers dreamed.*"

Pause.

He then speaks of bearing slavery's scars and of being the poor white "*fooled and pushed apart,*" the red man driven from the land, and the immigrant clutching hopelessness in the land of the free.

By the time he tells them with trembling voice that "*he's the man who never got ahead, the poorest worker bartered through the years,*" the audience is in rapture.

"*Sure,*" he says, cockylike, "*call me any ugly name you choose; the steel of freedom does not stain*" (emphasis on "ugly," "choose," and "stain").

Despite its anger, the poem ends on a hopeful note: "We, the people, must redeem our land," he says, "the mines, the plants, the rivers, and make America again!"

In awe, the audience rewards him with a five-minute standing ovation, taking him by surprise. Sure, he's gotten everyone's undivided attention by the second stanza. Sure, his anger has provoked a chorus of Amens and Ain't that the truths, mostly from military personnel who are there to cheer for Art. And, sure, he's gotten that kind of reception before, having recited the Langston Hughes poem way back in high school at a speech tournament, where he placed second in the dramatic interpretation category and made the coach of the speech team, Mrs. Tanigawa, Farrington High School's "Teacher of the Year." But that was 1985, when he performed it in front of drama teachers and high school actors rather than active members of the Filipino community who were expecting him to dance the hula or the tinikling, sing a tune from *Miss Saigon* or a kundiman folk song, pull rabbits out of a hat, kick a sipa, kick anything, do anything ethnic. But to read a poem by Langston Hughes that talks shit about the land of the free, opportunities, Medicare, and food stamps?

Though seemingly confident, Vince feared they'd accuse him of being an ungrateful immigrant. Boo his ass off the stage. Tell him to get the hell outta America if he hates it that bad. Put him on the spot. Reprimand him for rocking the boat that once carried his ancestors out of the jungle.

Why, son, why make waves out of a pond?

But a five-minute standing ovation? Why? Vince wonders, then tells himself: Why not?

"Boy, what a performance!" Dave says. "And there you have it, ladies and gentlemen. The talent portion, which accounts for one-third of the overall score. Now, before we move on to the Q and A, I want to introduce our distinguished panel of judges."

THE BIG FISHES

Emme Tomimbang, entrepreneur and host of *Emme's Island Moments.* Manny de la Cruz, Manila's fashion czar and founder of Fashion for Life, an AIDS benefit. Merle Kim, lounge singer and winner of three Po'okela awards (Hawaii's version of the Tony minus the

"Trophy Donated by Beretania Florist" engraved on the plaque). Danilo Buenaventura, First-Runner-Up Mister Ambassador to the Philippine Islands 1990. And Dr. Bonifacio "Bonny" Dumpit, emeritus professor at the University of Hawaii of Manoa and author of a dozen books, including *Decolonization for Beginners: A Filipino Glossary* and *Mr. and Mrs. John and Marcia Law.*

RAMP

"We now come to my favorite part of the program: the runway modeling competition," Dave says. "Worth a third of the overall score, the judges are looking for the three-C factor: charm, confidence, composure."

The Big Five take turns strutting to Madonna's "Vogue." With their collars up, they do half-turns center stage and thumb-on-chin poses, then face the screen to admire their composites, courtesy of Jun's Take-One studio.

TRY REPEAT

Dave: We now come to the interview portion, worth a third of the overall score. Each candidate has fifteen seconds. *(Pause)* Let's start with Shane Kawika Lacaran. Shane, your question comes from Manny de la Cruz.

Manny: Shane, are you for or against same-sex marriage?

Shane (Speaks in pidgin English, a chop suey island vernacular peppered with Polynesian and East Asian words): Can repeat the question?

Manny: Are you for or against same-sex marriage?

Shane: I feel that marriage is a very serious thing and that gays shouldn't do it just for tax purposes or health insurance and stuff like that cuz marriage is real holy. I don't have anything against guys who like other guys but we gotta carry out God's order, which is for us guys to procreate. *Mahalo nui loa.* And *malamalama* the *aina.*

Dave: Yes, Shane, *malamalama* the *aina.* That means love for the land, ladies and gentlemen. Next, we call on Vince De Los Reyes, please step up to the mike. Your question comes from Danilo Buenaventura, who was last year's first-runner-up titleholder.

Danilo: Vince, if you had twenty-four hours left on earth, where would you go and why?

Vince: I'd want to spend it in the Philippines. (*Pause. Waits till the applause subsides*) I think that one should never forget his roots. To quote the immortal words of Dr. José Rizal, Philippine national hero, a Filipino who does not know where he came from will never know where he is going. Thank you.

Dave: Thank you, Mr. De Los Reyes. And now, Mr. Salcedo—

Virgilio: Call me Virgo.

Dave: Very well, Virgo. Your question is from Miss Emme Tomimbang.

Emme: Virgo, how does one go about breaking negative stereotypes?

Virgo: One way of breaking stereotypes is by simply ignoring them. Stereotypes, like labels, I think, are there to serve and perpetuate the white man's hierarchical structure, thank you.

Dave: Now let's ask Kenzo Kahoku'okalani Parubrub-Kajiwara to come on down and answer Professor Dumpit's question.

Kenzo: (*Mutters*): Shit.

Professor Dumpit: Kenzo, what is the difference between acculturation and assimilation?

Kenzo: Pardon me?

Professor Dumpit: What is the difference between acculturation and assimilation?

Kenzo: Assimilation is about . . . (*Stops to think*) adapting! Assimilation is about adapting to a new culture, a new place, whereas acculturation refers more to adopting another culture, to embracing another culture. (*Thunderous applause*)

Dave: Boy, that was a hard one. Thank you, Kenzo. I now call on Art Johnson. Miss Merle Kim, do you have your question ready?

Merle (Nods): The U.S. military leases on Subic Naval and Clark Air Force bases expire this coming September. Do you think the Philippines should allow the United States to renew their lease?

Art: That's an excellent question, Miss Kim. I think that, yes, the Philippines should allow the U.S. military to retain its bases in Subic and Clark. (*Pause. Waits till the applause subsides*) The bases play a significant role in the Philippine economy, which hasn't been doing well for the last twenty years. Should the Philippines decide to end its treaty with the United States, thousands and thousands of Filipinos who depend on the bases for their income will suffer. Thank you.

THE IMPORTANCE OF BEING FIRST RUNNER-UP

Volunteers from Farrington High School's Leo Club appear onstage with five towering trophies (courtesy of Jennifer's Kamayan Restaurant) beside the Big Five. Then, MISS PETITE SAMPAGUITA and MISS ASIA PACIFICA walk onstage carrying sashes. Dave comments on how resplendent the two ladies look in their Maria Clara gowns with stiff butterfly sleeves. Edgar makes his entrance next, pushing a cartload of koa bowls that serves no purpose other than storing coins, keys, bills, and condoms.

"And here he is, ladies and gentlemen," Dave announces, "our reigning Mister Porma 1990, Edgar Ramirez."

Edgar waves to the audience, then hands Dave an envelope.

"I have here, ladies and gentlemen, the names of the winners."

Virgo makes the sign of the cross, Kenzo closes his eyes, Vince crosses his fingers, Art tightens his lips, and Shane looks lemur-eyed at Dave.

Drumroll.

"Stand by, gentlemen." Dave tears open the envelope. "Let's start with the fourth and third runner-ups. Both will receive a weekend stay at the magnificent Turtle Bay Resort, a trophy, and a koa bowl." He pauses to look at the finalists, then, in one breath, says: "The fourth runner-up is Shane Kawika Lacaran and the third runner-up is Kenzo Kajiwara."

Applause.

"The second runner-up will receive a five-hundred-dollar savings bond plus four days and three nights in Kalaupapa, Molokai. And the winner is . . . Virgilio Salcedo."

Applause.

"And then there were two," Dave says. "Hmmm."

"Quit stalling, Haole."

Ignoring the racial slur, Dave turns to Vince and Art. "I am now going to read the name of the first runner-up, also known as Mister API, or Ambassador to the Philippine Islands. In addition to the trophy and koa bowl, Mister API will receive a cash prize of one thousand dollars plus an all-expense-paid trip for ten days to the Philippines. Mister Porma, as you already know, will receive a cash prize of three thousand dollars and live rent-free for a year in Woodside, Queens. Wow." Dave whistles. "Now, in the event that Mister Porma cannot fulfill his duties for whatever reason, Mister API automatically becomes Mister Porma."

Beat.

"The title of Mister API goes to—"

Drumroll.

"Vince De Los Reyes. This year's Mister Porma is Arturo "Art" Dwayne Pascual Johnson!"

In the audience, a factory of murmurs:

"What? The black guy won?"

"Pro-base, that's why."

"Are you sure he's Filipino?"

"Of course he is. Look how flat his nose is."

Dave motions Art to march downstage. "The stage is yours, Mister Porma 1991," Dave says. "So go and say hello to your new world."

POSTPAGEANT STRESS DISORDER

Vince likens the feeling of losing the Mister Porma title to the emotional plunge one gets while coming down from a cocaine high. As photographers aim their shots at the new reigning Mister Porma, Vince knows why he, and not Art, is going to Manila. Of the Big Five, Art sold the most tickets, which explains why almost one-third of the ballroom is occupied by Filipino and African-American soldiers and their dependents.

Sayang that he lost to Art; he's got his mind set on winding his alarm clock six hours ahead, Eastern Standard Time, instead of eighteen hours, Third World Time. As early as New Year's Eve, he's made a vow that before 1991 ends, he's wrapping up his thirteen-year relationship with Honolulu and moving to a place far, far away. Away from the land of Aloha spirit, extended families, Las Vegas air-and-room-with-meals specials, one-night stands, failed relationships that should've been one-night stands, and SPAM (only Guam consumes more cans of luncheon meat per annum than Hawaii). To a city whose politics are cut-and-dried, and not middle road like Hawaii. Beneath its veneer of pro-Democrat pro-Liberal stance, Hawaii is as middle road as middle road can get, falling somewhere between conservatism and political correctness.

So when Edgar invited himself over to Vince's condo two weeks ago to hand him the guidelines to the only pageant for Filipino men in America, Vince flat out told him: "You fuckin' kidding me, right?"

Edgar shook his head. "If you start now, you can mail your packet by the end of the week."

"Are you getting commission for torturing me?"

"I thought you wanted to get the fuck out of this rock, Vince."

"I do."

"Then join the freakin' pageant," Edgar snapped. "I cannot guarantee you the Statue of Liberty, braddah, but it's your ticket out of Gilligan's Island."

What better reasons could Edgar have given his best friend? How much more convincing did Vince need? Edgar was right: Mister Porma was Vince's way out of the Gathering Isle of Oahu. But more than that: it was free.

COLD-HEARTED

■ ■ ■

David Wong Louie

His father had disappeared. Opened the freezer, pulled out two steaks, and was gone. His mother had said so. A woman incapable of lies. Driving south across the Sound, Lawrence Lung remembered how Genius used to run his seashell-thick thumbnail along the plastic wrap that covered the supermarket steaks, tracing the T-shaped bones. "Best money can buy," he would say. This was nothing but a father imparting the facts of life to his son. So when his mother called him, the youngest of four, only boy, and closest to home, the fact of the steaks did not faze him. What did though was the suit. She said he was wearing his suit. And where could he be going in his suit, she wanted to know? It was the only one he owned, a decades-old, double-breasted number straight off the set of *The Untouchables*, with lapels as broad as shark fins, raspberry and navy pinstripes on dark gray wool cloth. There were the photos of Genius, taken in his early days in the U.S.: suit, white hat, cigarette, a mischievous light in his eyes. This was the man he sent across seas to the wife he left in Hong Kong. He wore it on special occasions, weddings, banquets, funerals, the day Lawrence was born. He seemed taller in the suit, more substantial, even though he had obviously bought it a size or two too big, expecting to grow into the wide shoulders and waist, the long sleeves and pant legs, and from an early age Lawrence knew it would one day be his by default, the three sisters

---

DAVID WONG LOUIE is the author of *Pangs of Love*, a collection of short stories, and *The Barbarians Are Coming*, a novel. He teaches in the Department of English and at the Asian American Studies Center at UCLA. He was born on Long Island, New York, in 1954.

posing no competition, his inheritance, and that was just fine, he thought, as long as it did not come with the man inside.

■ ■ ■

As soon as he got home Lawrence went straight for the refrigerators. It was his habit, how it was to be at home. One refrigerator, then the next, opening the doors and looking, but knowing there was nothing in there he'd want to eat. As his mother repeated the story of the vanishing husband, the very same one she had told him, almost to the word, over the phone, he moved busily back and forth between these obese twins, set side by side, one's motor whirring on, then the other's. On a good day, if he were lucky, he might find a bottle of Coke stuffed among the paper bags of oranges, greens, and roots; the bundles of medicinal herbs, twigs, bark, berries, and what looked like worms bound with pink cellophane ribbon; there were see-through packages of black mushrooms and funky salted fish; wrappers of duck sausage and waxy pork bellies; take-out boxes with scraps of roast pig, roast liver, roast ribs; jars of oysters, shrimp, wood ears, lily buds; and dishes and bowls, of metal and porcelain, stacked one on top of the other, holding left-overs that had been reheated and re-served so many times not a trace of nutrients or flavor lingered in their pale cells. It was barefoot food, food eaten with sticks, under harvest moons. Rinse off the maggots, slice, and steam. It was squatting in still water food, water snake around your ankle food. Pole across your shoulders, hooves in the house food.

It was among the embarrassments of his youth. Thanks to his oldest sister, Lucy, the family flirted from time to time with real food. What real people ate. With forks and knives, your own plate, your own por-tions, no more dipping into the communal soup bowl. Food from boxes and cans. The best were Swanson TV dinners. Meat loaf, Salisbury steak. He was convinced Salisbury steak was served in the White House every night. Meat in one compartment, vegetable medley in another, apple crisp next door. What a concept! Everything had its own house or its own room. That was how real people lived. By the time Lawrence was eleven, he had cooked his first meal: roast beef, Green Giant canned corn, Betty Crocker instant mashed potatoes, Pillsbury Pop 'n' Fresh rolls. Call it the march of generations.

They were not a family of big eaters. Lily and Patty pecked. Lucy consistently left half her rice. Lawrence and his parents were the family jaws, though since his operation his father had slacked off from his usual two-bowl pace. Consider this then: as the household was presently constituted there was a three-to-two diner-to-refrigerator ratio.

Lawrence was partly responsible for the excess. He had helped his father bring the second refrigerator home. It happened one New Year's Eve, Lawrence returning from school to find his sisters already pressed into service of the new year, scrubbing and dusting and vacuuming every inch of the store for that clean start, just as they would for the same reason wash their feet and hair later that night. In the kitchen his mother was frying the New Year's fish, a porgy for the ancestors, while his father sat like an ancestor himself, stolid, in a nimbus of smoke, his hand serving his Lucky Strikes up to his lips, the cigarette like a thick stick of incense, the action like a prayer to his own spirit.

"Where have you been?" his father asked, pouring a cup of hot water into a bowl of broken saltines and evaporated milk. He had been awaiting his return and motioned for Lawrence to eat.

When he finished they went out to the backyard, the parking lot, and Pop handed Lawrence the keys to the family car. Pop did not drive and Lawrence only had a learner's permit. Lawrence turned the ignition, the engine churned, started, and stalled. Ma stuck her head out the metal door; the expression on her face was a hybrid of hurt and confusion, and before she could utter a word the engine turned over and Lawrence gave her the gas and she roared at Ma, and Pop yanked down on the bill of his orange hunting cap and tapped the gearshift, signaling Lawrence to go.

Lawrence was a good driver even without a license. He liked the idea he and his father might get into trouble together. Bad boys. He didn't see how he could lose: "He made me do it, Officer," he would say, his finger like a gun at the earflap on Pop's cap. And now he got to drive without the encumbrance of his nervous driver's ed teacher or his bossy sisters. For the briefest instant Lawrence wondered why his father had not enlisted one of his sisters, and that way kept things legal, instead of waiting for him to come home from school. But hadn't Pop always waited for Lawrence? Waited for a son as his wife delivered girl after girl after girl; waited for the son to mature into a second pair of hands to help him with his chores; waited for him to turn into a set of wheels. He knew that was all there was to it. He knew that he wasn't singled out as someone special, someone necessary.

Lawrence played with the radio dial and he was pleased, impressed even, by how adept he was at the maneuver. He switched on the heater, the blower on *high* then *lo*, and tried the wipers and upped the volume on the radio. When somebody honked he honked back; long blasts, as if to say, "YOU'RE WELCOME. I LIKE THE WAY YOU DRIVE TOO!" After the rush of that first honk, he clutched the steering wheel at the ten o'clock and two o'clock positions and braced for his father's fierce bark or flying hand or both. But there was no reprimand, no thwack to the back of his head. For a split second he felt cheated. He glanced over at Pop. He was sitting on the edge of the vinyl seat, gripping the dash with both hands, his body so rigid one high-pitched screech and he'd shatter like glass. It was then Lawrence realized that in the car the rules that governed their life together had changed. Their common ground had shifted, a tremor enough to make you stop and reevaluate your days. As illegal as he was in the car it looked far worse for his father. Whatever advantage Pop might have claimed by virtue of his age he had forfeited when he slid in next to Lawrence and told him to go.

Then he told him to stop. They were in the middle of a tree-lined street of brick houses and, up ahead at the intersection, businesses, including a laundry run by a family friend. Lawrence eased off the brake, letting the car roll; it only stood to reason that "stop" meant at the corner. "Stop," Pop said. "We've arrived."

"What do you mean? Arrived where?"

Pop looked over his shoulder, out the rear window, and Lawrence put the car in reverse, driving to meet his father's gaze.

"We've arrived," Pop said excitedly, once, twice. He bounded from the car, circled past the front end, crossed the street. Lawrence had never seen him so frisky. There on the curb he grabbed the handle of a discarded refrigerator, as if he were shaking its hand.

It was colder outside than it could ever be inside a refrigerator.

"How do you like it?" his father asked.

Lawrence had never thought of a refrigerator as something you liked. It was just there, like your arms or your teeth. He shrugged.

"I won it," he said. "It's all mine."

Lawrence wasn't sure but he thought he heard bragging in Pop's voice. And why shouldn't he brag, he reasoned, a refrigerator is—if nothing else—impressive for its size. Then he quickly recognized that this particular refrigerator was no prize from *Let's Make a Deal*. It was nothing more than a big piece of junk. What had he won but hundreds of pounds of garbage? It was an old Frigidaire with rounded corners like a bar of soap and a dent where its heart would be if this were the body of a man.

His father removed a homemade dolly from the trunk of the car. Double-thick plywood and black supermarket carriage wheels. Then a length of coarse rope. "Two are always better than one," Pop said. "Has to be that way, except maybe in the case of children." He was pleased with himself, making a joke at others' expense, as the cigar-smoking men in tuxedos did on television. Then he said in English, "I have two kit, I feed two mouth. I have four kit, I feed four mouth. I have two refrigerator, we have more food to eat. Hey, *goong hee faht toy*." He chuckled. "This way New Year start off in very good style."

Snow started falling, large heavy flakes. Lawrence and his father inched the refrigerator off the curb and onto the dolly positioned in the gutter, the icy snow acting as a lubricant. "Does this thing work?" Lawrence asked.

"It has to work," he said. "It's all mine now! Good machine better than money. Money you spend; no more; all gone. Paper turn into air. But a machine like this refrigerator is different. If I keep it full up, it always give you plenty good food to eat."

Following his father's directions Lawrence backed the car inches shy of the Frigidaire. Pop lashed the refrigerator to the car's bumper, then twined a draped bedsheet over it. "Chinese people don't like to show off," his father said, addressing the look of disapprobation Lawrence wore. "We don't want to call attention to ourselves. I don't want people to say, Oh look at that big shot, he must have won that nice refrigerator."

Even from his sixteen-year-old's perspective Lawrence was dubious about his father's scheme. Such an opinion was fully consistent with others he held for whatever his father did or whatever he put his mind to doing. Pop's intentions and deeds arrived in Lawrence's brain like the sight of a man who tips his hat and reveals a head of blue hair: the man is a whole human being, bearing all the requisite parts, but at the same time everything about him feels wrong, patently untrustworthy.

Lawrence put the car in drive. The tug at his rear made him feel suddenly important, heroic. The enormous weight, the mystery beneath the white sheet, his father's winnings and how he would not brag on it to the world, the big snow and hard wind, the wipers barely keeping pace with the storm, the wheels' flimsy contact with the road.

His father was smoking, more relaxed now than he was before, and when his son reached for a cigarette fully expecting his hand would be slapped away Pop tilted the package to facilitate the maneuver.

"One time," his father said, flicking his steel lighter in his son's direction, as if it were a cigar in celebration of the birth of a son, the sheet-swathed baby riding in back.

When Lawrence turned his head to catch the light, when his eyes momentarily left the road, when he sucked in the first big smoke and coughed into his hand, the traffic light changed from yellow to red without his notice, and the snow-slick road itself seemed to move, as he honked his horn and slammed on the brakes in this winter world with its white cars and white roads and white headlight beams. All he could see in his panic was the black word "STOP!" like soot stamped on his mind's eye and all he could feel was shame building like a fire under his collar, a heat as mean as hardware on a burning door, and all around him he could smell it: the tobacco, the metal, the vinyl, the heater, the sudden aging of the man and the boy within the compartment.

Cars everywhere were honking. Theirs had skidded nearly perpendicular to the traffic flow. He could have killed them both, they came that close to crashing. And before his heart stopped racing and the pulse in his temples calmed, once that slow wave of relief and gratitude had passed, he saw how the worst could have just happened, and how he couldn't even blame Pop for it, and how Pop couldn't really pin this one on him.

When he started the car again he felt a lightness. A release, your opponent in a tug-of-war letting go. In the rearview the Frigidaire was free between lanes of traffic. A snowman adrift on wheels. A car swerved to avoid it. The car's driver sped up until their cars were rolling side by side and the driver honked his horn impatiently and Lawrence motioned for Pop to lower his window and he did and the driver and his buddy stared into their car, two men with blue eyes who seemed to own the road, and the driver sneered, "Oh, it's just some crazy chinks," and as they laughed at his father—they couldn't have been laughing at Lawrence—Lawrence came to the quick conclusion that these two thugs were right, there was something unerringly Chinese about hauling this useless machine, a won-at-cards slant-eyed prize, garbage-picker special, tethered to the car like Gregory Peck on the back of the Great White Whale; he could not imagine his friends and their dads doing likewise in their Electras or Continentals. Then as the other car peeled away in the slickness his father stuck his orange-hunting-capped head out the window, bracing himself with his Lucky Strike hand, and shouted, "Fuck you!" without a trace of accent, and flipped them off with his free hand, the right one, the one that lit the matches and in anger struck the blows. It was all too much for Lawrence. If Pop had a hold of that car he would have torn loose the hood, tossed the engine into their laps. Instead he had a hold of Lawrence, his hot words ripping a hole in his chest as fresh and smoky as the one those men just shot through his boy soul.

They parked and curbed the refrigerator. Pop told him to telephone one of his road-legal sisters. He brought out a palmful of change and let Lawrence pick his own coins for the call. This was unexpected, something new, dipping into his personal till, like drawing blood, and he didn't flinch. Lawrence could smell the metal warmed by the heat of his leg. Drawing twice, two nickels.

Through the storm Lawrence walked to a pay phone, called home, and when he returned to his father he was standing beside the Frigidaire, both covered with snow. He wondered why he had not taken shelter inside the car but decided not to ask. He wanted to remember his father's imitation of a real man, the man with the dangerous voice, the man with a palm of silver.

They sat in the car. Lawrence suggested they wait at Uncle Law's place, Pop's friend's laundry up the block. Warm and steamy, fragrant with pressed cotton. Maybe even score a cup of hot tea. But Pop wouldn't bite. He had lost face, his only son having failed him.

When Patty arrived, Pop stuffed a five-dollar bill in Lawrence's jacket and zipped the pocket. A surprise reward. Perhaps he wasn't so disappointed after all. Then his father and sister drove home. Lawrence was left guarding the refrigerator, and even as day darkened, and cold cut crosswise against his cheeks he did not stray from his post.

When Pop returned with the upholstery man neighbor and his truck he said Lawrence was *saw-saw* for waiting outside by the refrigerator rather than waiting in the car. "Did you think it was going to run away?" he asked. After a protracted struggle they loaded the refrigerator onto the truck. As he was about to climb into the cab, his father grabbed Lawrence by his jacket sleeve. Pop would give thanks now, Lawrence thought, for a job well done, mission accomplished. Pin a medal on his chest, plant a kiss on his cheek, shake his hand firmly, tousle his hair. Robert Young and Fred MacMurray, slippered and piped, their depthless compassion and broad streaks of sanity, as white as their starched shirts. Right then, in the exhilarating moment of antic- ipation, the upholstery truck's idling motor was music, its blue-burning oil perfume. But what Pop did was unzip Lawrence's pocket and filch the five-dollar bill—a tip for the upholstery man.

Later that night after the New Year's Eve feast and the chores and the homework, when everyone was washing their feet before sleeping into the next year and all the sinks and pails were occupied, Pop filled his refrigerator's vegetable drawers with hot soapy water and rolled up his pants and plunged his blue-white feet in and said, "Who said it's good for nothing?" He had cleaned his prize with Comet cleanser, scrubbing away dirt as well as paint, and defended it against the girls' wisecracks, and by now had shed whatever diffidence he felt when he first introduced this newest member of the clan. Then he plugged the Frigidaire in and sat there, with the door open, soaking his feet, wiping down its insides, using a rag and soapy water from the vegetable bin. No one could see his face but Lawrence was on to him. Cut off from the rest of the family, his father basked in the refrigerator's chilled air, in its silvery vapors, and the glow of its measly light. What Lawrence saw in his father's gentle cleaning of each egg holder's deep dimple was kindness, and the pang Lawrence felt, like fingers fanning in his throat, was envy, and the motor's hum were murmurings of love. And he wondered then, if he'd ever be so brave as to love like that. A ma- chine or the man.

FOURSCORE AND SEVEN YEARS AGO

■ ■ ■

Darrell Lum

Sixt grade, we had to give da news every morning aftah da pledge al-
legence and My Country Tis of Dee. "Current events time," Mrs.
Ching tell, and she only call on maybe five kids fo get extra points, so
first, you gotta raise your hand up and hope she call on you. You
should always try be ready wit someting fo say cause sometimes nobody
raise up their hands cause nobody went listen to da news on da radio or
read da newspaypah last night so if you raise your hand, guarantee she
call you. Bungy Lau was always waving his hand almost everyday fo
give news. And if only get one chance fo tell da news left, Bungy give
you da stink eye and raise his hand mo high and wave um and almost
stand up awready fo make Mrs. Ching see him. Us guys and most
times da girls too, dey jes put their hands down cause we no like Bungy
get mad at us. Mrs. Ching try look around da room for see if get anybody else she can call besides Bungy but by den we all stay looking
down at our desk so she gotta call Bungy cause he da only one left,
yeah? And Bungy he stand up, he big you know, and he stay cracking
his knuckles and he no mo one paper or anyting and we know dat he
going to give da wrestling results from da night before.

"Las night at da Civic Auditorium, fo da Nort American Heavy-
weight Belt, Nicky Bockwinkle pinned Curtis 'da Bull' Iaukea in two

---

Born in Honolulu, Hawaii, in 1950, DARRELL LUM is a fiction writer and
playwright whose work has been one of the pioneering voices of Hawaii literature. His stories celebrate the everyday lives of island people, growing up
"small kid times," and the use of pidgin. He and Eric Chock founded the literary journal *Bamboo Ridge* in 1978, which features the work of Hawaii writers.

outa tree falls and retained da Nort American Belt. In tag team ackshen 'Mister Fooge,' Fuji Fujiwara and da Masked Executionah was disqualified in a minute and thirty seconds of da first round fo using brass knuckles dat da Executionah went hide in his tights."

"Da cheatah!" Jon go tell and everybody went laugh at him. Mrs. Ching shush da class.

"Da duo of Giant Baba and da Southern Gennelman, Rippah Collins retained their tag team title."

Once I thot dat I would try dat too and I went listen to da radio, KGU Sports, da night before fo get da winners and I wrote um down because no fair if Bungy hog all da points just by giving the wrestling results. Dat wasn't news, was all fake. My fahdah said wrestling was like roller derby, all fake.

Anyway, da time I was going give da wrestling results, Bungy was looking at me cracking each knuckle in his fingers first one hand den da uddah and I went look down at my paypah wit da winnahs and da times and I thot maybe I better give da news about how da Russian Yuri Gagarin went around in space instead. After I was finished, Bungy raised his hand and said dat da Indian guy, Chief Billy White Wolf went fight Beauregarde, da guy dat always stay combing his hair and he took Beauregarde in two minutes of the third round with a half Nelson. Exact what I had on my paypah! I saw Mrs. Ching marking down our points in her book.

One time, Mrs. Ching went ask me if I like get extra points. She said she would gimme extra points if I get all dressed up like Abraham Lincoln and say da Gettysburg Address to da fift graders. I nevah like but she said I had to go cause I was da best at saying um las year. I still nevah like cause look stoopid when dey pin da black construction paper bow tie and make you wear da tall construction paper hat but she said it was one privilege fo say da speech and dat she would help me memarize um again. Ass cause when I was in da fift grade everybody had to learn da ting and had one contest in da whole fift grade and I went win cause everybody else did junk on purpose so dat dey nevah have to get up in front of da whole school, dressed up like Abe Lincoln. Shoot. I nevah know. I nevah know dat da winner had to go back da next year and say um again to da fift graders either.

■ ■ ■

Everyting was diffrent. In da sevent grade, you change classes l'dat and had all dese rules and j'like da bell stay ringing all da time. Had da warning bell before school start, had da real bell, and had da tardy bell. And da bells between classes and da tardy to class bell and da first lunch bell and da second lunch bell. And you had to tuck in your shirt-tails and wear shoes.

Bungy was Benjamen now. I knew cause his muddah and my mud-dah went make us go Chinese school summer time and we had to be in da first grade class wit all da small kids even if we was in da sixt grade going be sevent. Anyway, whenevah da teacha call Bung Mun, he tell, "My name Benjamen!" So da teacha try say "Benjamen" only ting come out "Bung-a-mun" and Bungy gotta tell again, "Benjamen!" Ass how I knew his name was Benjamen now. But most guys still yet called him "Bungy" even if he nevah answer.

And Charlene Chu had braces so she nevah smile anymore, not dat she used to smile at us anyways. Bungy, I mean Benjamen, would yell at her, "Hey, metal mout, you can staple my math papers wit your teet?" And all of a sudden, she had tits. Sixt grade nutting. Sevent grade, braces and bra.

Benjamen would always wear slippahs still yet even if he was sup-posed to wear shoes. He tell he get sore feet but his feet always stay bus up cause he like to go barefoot. His feet so ugly and dirty and stink, da nurse no like even look at dem, she jes give him da slippah pass. And if you had to go batroom during classtime you had to get one batroom pass. And had library pass and cafeteria pass and if you work cafeteria you had to wear da paper cap or if you get long hair da ladies make you wear da girls hairnet and you had to wear covered shoes. Even had dis yellow line painted on da stairs and down da middle of da hallway all ovah da school and you had to go up only on da right side and go down on da uddah side. Dey could nab you and make you stand hall for doing stuff like going down the up side of the stairs. Crazy yeah?

If you gotta stand hall you gotta go da vice-principal's office before school, recess, lunch time, and after school fo so many minutes and stand in da main hallway of the school facing the wall. Ass where every-body walk pass so dey can razz you anymuch dey like cause you no can talk when you standing hall. I tink Mr. Hansen went make up da rules. He was dis tall, skinny haole guy, mean-looking buggah. But he nevah do da dirty work. If you got reported to the office, you had to see da vice-principal, Mr. Higuchi. He was one short, fat guy you had to go see if you was tardy or went fight and somebody said he da one who paddle you. Bungy said watch out if you gotta go his office and he close da door. Anyway, when Higuchi tell you you gotta stand hall, he take you to your spot and he take his pencil and he make one dot on da wall and he tell, "Dis is your spot. Don't take your eyes off it." You no can talk or look around cause every now and den he come out of his office and walk up and down da hallway real soft fo check if you still dere and you not fooling around.

So in da sevent grade, I wised-up. Had me and Jon and Bungy left in da classroom spelling bee. Da winner had to represent da class in da school spelling bee and no ways we was going make "A" in front da whole school.

"Tenement," Miss Hashimoto said.

"T-E-N-A-M-E-N-T," I went spell um.

"T-E-N-T-E-M-E-N-T," Bungy went spell um.

"T-A-N-E-M-E-N-T," Jon said.

"This is easy, you guys," Hashimoto went tell.

"Nah, S-L-U-M!" Bungy went tell.

"Okay, nobody got um. Next word, syncopate."

"S-I-N-K-O-P-A-T-E," I went tell real fast. I was trying fo spell um as wrong as I could cause I nevah like spell um right by accident. Miss Hashimoto went sigh real loud.

"Definition please," Bungy went jump right in. He throw da ack him.

"To shorten or produce by syncope."

"S-Y-N-C-O-P-A-T-E . . ."

"Yes!" Miss Hashimoto said. She sounded relieved.

"E!" Bungy went yell. He knew he went spell um correct. He went spell um again, "S-Y-N-C-O-P-A-T-E-E."

Jon was laughing and I was telling, "No fair! He had two chances. Da first one was good! Was correct." Hashimoto looked pissed, she caught on. "If you boys don't shape up and start being serious I'm just going to dock your grade and send all three of you to the finals."

It ended up being me. I tink da uddah two guys was still yet missing on purpose but everytime came to me, Hashimoto went gimme me da eye and made her mout kinda mean and I could feel my heart loud in my throat and she everytime had to say, "Louder, please. Repeat the spelling." And I would spell um different jes in case I spelled um correct da first time and she would say, "Correct!" even when I tink I went spell um wrong. So I was da one.

When I was up on stage, da principal, Mr. Hansen, was pronouncing da words and he went gimme "forefathers" in da first round. I went spell um "F-O-R-F-A-T-H-E-R-S" and I knew I had um wrong by da way Miss Hashimoto went look at me when I went look out at the seats and saw my homeroom class. I knew she was tinking I did um on purpose but actually I was figuring on staying fo a coupla rounds fo make um look good before I went out. When I got back to my seat on stage I went look at her and I tink she was crying. She had one Kleenex in her hand and she was wiping her eyes. I felt *bad*, man. Wasn't my fault. I was really trying dat time. I went aftah school fo tell her sorry I went get out on da first round and she started crying again. I wanted to cry too cause I neyah mean to make da teacha cry. I hate Hashimoto fo making me go up dere in da first place. Bungy and Jon was smartah den me. My ears was hot, j'like dey was laughing at me.

Mostly da teachas was all dese old futs. But we heard dat had one cute new speech teacha, Mrs. Sherwin and dat she was one hot-cha-cha. Gordon Morikawa said da eight graders said she was good-looking. He said dat how many times Jimmy Uyehara went catch da bone while he was giving one speech cause when you give one speech you gotta go to da front and she go to da back and sometimes when she cross her legs can see her panties. "Naht," I couldn't believe dat. Besides I said, "She must be *old* if she married, she *Mrs.* Sherwin, yeah?"

Anyways we all wanted to see what she was going be like cause anyting was bettah den having chorus wit Miss Teruya who was one young old fut, and mean. She whack you wit her stick if she tink you not singing loud enough and if you no memarize da words, she make you stand next to da piano and sing solo. One time we went spend one whole class period practicing standing up and sitting down when she give da signal cause she no like when everybody stand up or go down crooked.

Da first day of da second semester we switched from chorus to speech and we went to her room and everybody was quiet cause was j'like da first day of school again. Bungy kept poking me in my back wit one book. "She cute," he whispered to me, "I heard she cute!" even though we nevah even see her yet. Some of da girls went turn around and give him stink eye and tell him, "Shhhh!" He jes went stretch out his legs and tell loud, "You tink Charlene Chu wear falsies?" I donno if he knew she was walking in da door but everybody went laugh when Charlene came through da door. Jon guys was trying fo be quiet but dey was all trying fo grab da small paperback dat Benjamen was reading behind his social studies book, *Lady Chatterley's Lover*. Jon said dat was one hot book and only da guys in their club could read um. Jon sat in front of me, and Benjamen sat behind me, so I had to pass da book back and fort between dose two guys. Nevah look like one hot book. I went look inside and nevah see no hot parts.

"Dat's because you donno which page fo read," Jon told me afterwards, "Benjamen get um all written down in his Pee Chee folder." Dey was passing da book back and fort reading da good parts all da way in social studies and now in speech. I wanted to read um too but if you stop and read um, Benjamen start kicking your chair until you pass um on. Dey was still yet passing um around when Mrs. Sherwin walked into da room and threw her cigarette case on the desk.

"Okay class, let's begin." She looked like one nint grader or little older maybe and she was wearing one short dress and everytime her bra strap was falling out and she tuck um in.

"Whoa, she smoke," Bungy was telling Jon, "She smoke!"

"See, I told you she cute," he said in my ear and put da hot book on my desk. I was supposed to pass um on to Jon but even though I was poking Jon wit da book, he nevah turn around and take um cause Sherwin went start class and he nevah like her see. I went put um undah my folder but I started fo get nervous about what if I get nabbed for having one hot book. Probably gotta stand hall for da rest of da year.

We went watch her reaching up to write her name high at da top of da board "Mrs. Sherry Sherwin—Beginning Speech" in one loose, half-printing, half-script style. She was skinny and we was watching her ass and her arm and she even write sexy and all da boys started to adjust their pants in their seats. Even her name was sexy . . . Sherry . . . Sherwin. She turned around and we watched her lick her lips with da tip of her tongue. Da girls was looking at her and den turning around and looking at da boys. Dey probably was jes jealous.

Da rest of da time was regular. Pass out books, write your name on da card and hand um in and she gave us work on da first day, man. Was boring da beginning part so I started to read da hot book. Dis time

Benjamen wasn't kicking my chair and Jon went forget about getting um, so I went read um. Mostly was about dis creepy gardener guy and he was trying fo get dis young girl. He was peeking in her window or something and was checking out her tits and he was reaching for his dick, da book call um his "member" and somebody went kick my chair real hard and I went drop da book and quick Benjamen went kick um undah my chair. "Stoopid!" he went hiss at me. Sherwin went look up at us.

■ ■ ■

Turn out, Sherwin was the sevent-grade adviser and when came time fo the first canteen, she told the boys that we had to learn the etiquette of asking a young lady to dance. She made us practice.

"Make sure all the girls get to dance," she said. "If any of my boys notice wallflowers, I expect you to say . . ." She looked around da room and went call on me, "Daniel?"

"May I have dis dance," I mumbled.

"And ladies, how should you reply? Charlene?" Sherwin said.

"Why I'd *love* to, Daniel," Charlene said, all sassy. All da guys laughed.

"Whoa, Dan-yo! Maybe she going make you dance wit Charlene!"

"Maybe Charlene going ask you fo dance!"

Charlene straightened up and tucked her blouse tightly into her skirt. She looked at me disgusted. I wonder if dey was falsies?

"Whas one wall-fla-wah?" Jon asked.

"Stoopid," Benjamen said, "da ugly ones!"

Jon raised his hand. "Geez," Benjamen said, "he going ask someting stoopid," and he put his head down.

"Yes, Jon."

"So what if we no like dance wit da wall-fla-wahs?"

"Then you have to dance with me," Mrs. Sherwin said. "Would you like to dance with me, Jon?"

"Oh, no! Ah, I mean yes. Ah, I mean it would be an honor m'am."

"Don't gimme that bull," Mrs. Sherwin said laughing. "I just want to see you out on the floor, dear. Kicking up those heels."

I wouldn't mind dancing wit her. I was looking at my shoes. If I had Beatle boots, maybe she would dance wit me. Evans said that if you had real shiny shoes you could look up the girls' dresses. No wondah he was always rubbing the top of his shoes on the back of his pants legs. He had Beatle boots with taps and stomped on anybody with new shoes. Scuffed um up and said, "Baptize!" Like how he baptized everybody after they came back to school with a fresh haircut. Everytime he sweep his hand around my ears and tell, "Ay, whitewalls!" Evans had sideburns and a sheik cut, a razor-trimmed cut around his ears that made his head look like a black helmet, hard and glistening with pomade, swept into a ducktail in the back.

"And boys," Mrs. Sherwin was saying, "if I catch you combing your hair in the dance, I'm going to confiscate your comb. Get a nice haircut before the dance and comb your hair in the bathroom." Once, I got nabbed with my comb, da long skinny kine, sticking out of my pocket and Sherwin took um cause she no even like *see* one comb. She told me I had to come back after school if I wanted um back. So I went after school fo get um back and when she went open her drawer, had ukubillion combs, all hairy and greasy and probably had real ukus on top.

"Which one is yours?" she told me.

"Uh, ass okay, I foget which one was mine," I said even though I could see mine, right dere, on top.

"You don't need to comb your hair anyway," and she went rough up my hair and I could feel her hand go down the bristly back of my neck, almost like how Benjamen baptize you.

"Eh, no make," I said. Felt good though. Could smell her perfume. Spicy. I felt hot. I wish I had one sheik cut. But I couldn't cause nutting was growing in front my ears. I no like when da barber jes buzz um off. I like get one sheik cut but I no mo nuff hair over dere to shave. Costs fifty cents more, too. Even my father no get one sheik cut. He get the 85 cent special at Roosevelt Barbershop, one time around da ears wit da machine and scissors cut on top. Pau fast.

Every time my fahdah go cut hair, I gotta go too. Even if I no like. Geez, I hope nobody see me cutting hair. Da barbah guy, Fortunato, still take out da booster seat, one old worn-out board dat he put across da arms of da chair and I gotta sit on um cause da stuff fo crank up da seat stay broken.

Da only good ting was da barbah shop was next to da theater dat showed hot movies. Hard fo look at da pictures when you stay wit your fahdah but you can look look side-eye at da Now Playing and Coming Attractions posters. "Alexandra the Great 48 in Buxom Babes!" and

"Physical Education!" Couple times I went put da *National Enquirer* inside one of the old magazines, *Soldier of Fortune* or *Guns and Ammo* or *Field & Stream*, and read the main story, "My Bosom Made Me a Nympho at Twelve." I read um so many times I almost memarized um. Had this picture of one kinda old lady bending over and could see down her dress but I knew that couldn't be one picture of da girl cause she nevah look like she was twelve and no ways you could have tits that big. Maybe trick photography. Sometimes when my fahdah stay in da chair and I stay waiting my turn, Fortunato stop cutting and quick I look up fo see if he nab me but he only stay listening to da D.J. on da radio talking Filipino. Fast, excited. He jes suck his teeth and make one "tssk" sound and cut again. And I would look at da picture again and try to imagine dat it was Mrs. Sherwin but I only could see Charlene's face in dat picture, bending ovah. Smiling at me, her braces shiny, glistening. Whoa, da spooky.

THE MANAGEMENT OF GRIEF

▪ ▪ ▪

Bharati Mukherjee

A woman I don't know is boiling tea the Indian way in my kitchen. There are a lot of women I don't know in my kitchen, whispering, and moving tactfully. They open doors, rummage through the pantry, and try not to ask me where things are kept. They remind me of when my sons were small, on Mother's Day or when Vikram and I were tired, and they would make big, sloppy omelets. I would lie in bed pretending I didn't hear them.

Dr. Sharma, the treasurer of the Indo-Canada Society, pulls me into the hallway. He wants to know if I am worried about money. His wife, who has just come up from the basement with a tray of empty cups and glasses, scolds him. "Don't bother Mrs. Bhave with mundane details." She looks so monstrously pregnant her baby must be days overdue. I tell her she shouldn't be carrying heavy things. "Shaila," she says, smiling, "this is the fifth." Then she grabs a teenager by his shirttails. He slips his Walkman off his head. He has to be one of her four children, they have the same domed and dented foreheads. "What's the official word now?" she demands. The boy slips the headphones back on. "They're acting evasive, Ma. They're saying it could be an accident or a terrorist bomb."

BHARATI MUKHERJEE was born in 1940 in Calcutta, India. Having lived in Toronto and Montreal, she came to the United States in 1961 to attend the University of Iowa, became a citizen in 1988, and now teaches at the University of California at Berkeley. She is the renowned author of numerous works of fiction, including the prizewinning *The Middleman and Other Stories*, from which this story is taken. Her most recent novel is *Desirable Daughters*.

All morning, the boys have been muttering, Sikh Bomb, Sikh Bomb. The men, not using the word, bow their heads in agreement. Mrs. Sharma touches her forehead at such a word. At least they've stopped talking about space debris and Russian lasers.

Two radios are going in the dining room. They are tuned to different stations. Someone must have brought the radios down from my boys' bedrooms. I haven't gone into their rooms since Kusum came running across the front lawn in her bathrobe. She looked so funny, I was laughing when I opened the door.

The big TV in the den is being whizzed through American networks and cable channels.

"Damn!" some man swears bitterly. "How can these preachers carry on like nothing's happened?" I want to tell him we're not that important. You look at the audience, and at the preacher in his blue robe with his beautiful white hair, the potted palm trees under a blue sky, and you know they care about nothing.

The phone rings and rings. Dr. Sharma's taken charge. "We're with her," he keeps saying. "Yes, yes, the doctor has given calming pills. Yes, yes, pills are having necessary effect." I wonder if pills alone explain this calm. Not peace, just a deadening quiet. I was always controlled, but never repressed. Sound can reach me, but my body is tensed, ready to scream. I hear their voices all around me. I hear my boys and Vikram cry, "Mommy, Shaila!" and their screams insulate me, like headphones.

The woman boiling water tells her story again and again. "I got the news first. My cousin called from Halifax before six A.M., can you imagine? He'd gotten up for prayers and his son was studying for medical exams and he heard on a rock channel that something had happened to a plane. They said first it had disappeared from the radar, like a giant eraser just reached out. His father called me, so I said to him, what do you mean, 'something bad'? You mean a hijacking? And he said, *behn*, there is no confirmation of anything yet, but check with your neighbors because a lot of them must be on that plane. So I called poor Kusum straightaway. I knew Kusum's husband and daughter were booked to go yesterday."

Kusum lives across the street from me. She and Satish had moved in less than a month ago. They said they needed a bigger place. All these people, the Sharmas and friends from the Indo-Canada Society, had been there for the housewarming. Satish and Kusum made homemade tandoori on their big gas grill and even the white neighbors piled their plates high with that luridly red, charred, juicy chicken. Their younger daughter had danced, and even our boys had broken away from the Stanley Cup telecast to put in a reluctant appearance. Everyone took pictures for their albums and for the community newspapers—another of our families had made it big in Toronto—and now I wonder how many of those happy faces are gone. "Why does God give us so much if all along He intends to take it away?" Kusum asks me.

I nod. We sit on carpeted stairs, holding hands like children. "I never once told him that I loved him," I say. I was too much the well brought up woman. I was so well brought up I never felt comfortable calling my husband by his first name.

"It's all right," Kusum says. "He knew. My husband knew. They felt it. Modern young girls have to say it because what they feel is fake."

Kusum's daughter, Pam, runs in with an overnight case. Pam's in her McDonald's uniform. "Mummy! You have to get dressed!" Panic makes her cranky. "A reporter's on his way here."

"Why?"

"You want to talk to him in your bathrobe?" She starts to brush her mother's long hair. She's the daughter who's always in trouble. She dates Canadian boys and hangs out in the mall, shopping for tight sweaters. The younger one, the goody-goody one according to Pam, the one with a voice so sweet that when she sang *bhajans* for Ethiopian relief even a frugal man like my husband wrote out a hundred dollar check, *she* was on that plane. *She* was going to spend July and August with grandparents because Pam wouldn't go. Pam said she'd rather waitress at McDonald's. "If it's a choice between Bombay and Wonderland, I'm picking Wonderland," she'd said.

"Leave me alone," Kusum yells. "You know what I want to do? If I didn't have to look after you now, I'd hang myself."

Pam's young face goes blotchy with pain. "Thanks," she says, "don't let me stop you."

"Hush," pregnant Mrs. Sharma scolds Pam. "Leave your mother alone. Mr. Sharma will tackle the reporters and fill out the forms. He'll say what has to be said."

Pam stands her ground. "You think I don't know what Mummy's

thinking? *Why her?* that's what. That's sick! Mummy wishes my little sister were alive and I were dead."

Kusum's hand in mine is trembly hot. We continue to sit on the stairs.

■ ■ ■

She calls before she arrives, wondering if there's anything I need. Her name is Judith Templeton and she's an appointee of the provincial government. "Multiculturalism?" I ask, and she says, "partially," but that her mandate is bigger. "I've been told you knew many of the people on the flight," she says. "Perhaps if you'd agree to help us reach the others . . . ?"

She gives me time at least to put on tea water and pick up the mess in the front room. I have a few *samosas* from Kusum's housewarming that I could fry up, but then I think, Why prolong this visit?

Judith Templeton is much younger than she sounded. She wears a blue suit with a white blouse and a polka dot tie. Her blond hair is cut short, her only jewelry is pearl drop earrings. Her briefcase is new and expensive looking, a gleaming cordovan leather. She sits with it across her lap. When she looks out the front windows onto the street, her contact lenses seem to float in front of her light blue eyes.

"What sort of help do you want from me?" I ask. She has refused the tea, out of politeness, but I insist, along with some slightly stale biscuits.

"I have no experience," she admits. "That is, I have an MSW and I've worked in liaison with accident victims, but I mean I have no experience with a tragedy of this scale—"

"Who could?" I ask.

"—and with the complications of culture, language, and customs. Someone mentioned that Mrs. Bhave is a pillar—because you've taken it more calmly."

At this, perhaps, I frown, for she reaches forward, almost to take my hand. "I hope you understand my meaning, Mrs. Bhave. There are hundreds of people in Metro directly affected, like you, and some of them speak no English. There are some widows who've never handled money or gone on a bus, and there are old parents who still haven't eaten or gone outside their bedrooms. Some houses and apartments have been looted. Some wives are still hysterical. Some husbands are in shock and profound depression. We want to help, but our hands are tied in so many ways. We have to distribute money to some people, and there are legal documents—these things can be done. We have interpreters, but we don't always have the human touch, or maybe the right human touch. We don't want to make mistakes, Mrs. Bhave, and that's why we'd like to ask you to help us."

"More mistakes, you mean," I say.

"Police matters are not in my hands," she answers.

"Nothing I can do will make any difference," I say. "We must all grieve in our own way."

"But you are coping very well. All the people said, Mrs. Bhave is the strongest person of all. Perhaps if the others could see you, talk with you, it would help them."

"By the standards of the people you call hysterical, I am behaving very oddly and very badly, Miss Templeton." I want to say to her, *I wish I could scream, starve, walk into Lake Ontario, jump from a bridge.* "They would not see me as a model. I do not see myself as a model."

I am a freak. No one who has ever known me would think of me reacting this way. This terrible calm will not go away.

She asks me if she may call again, after I get back from a long trip that we all must make. "Of course," I say. "Feel free to call, anytime."

■ ■ ■

Four days later, I find Kusum squatting on a rock overlooking a bay in Ireland. It isn't a big rock, but it juts sharply out over water. This is as close as we'll ever get to them. June breezes balloon out her sari and unpin her knee-length hair. She has the bewildered look of a sea creature whom the tides have stranded.

It's been one hundred hours since Kusum came stumbling and screaming across my lawn. Waiting around the hospital, we've heard many stories. The police, the diplomats, they tell us things thinking that we're strong, that knowledge is helpful to the grieving, and maybe it is. Some, I know, prefer ignorance, or their own versions. The plane broke into two, they say. Unconsciousness was instantaneous. No one suffered. My boys must have just finished their breakfasts. They loved eating on planes, they loved the smallness of plates, knives, and forks. Last year they saved the airline salt and pepper shakers. Half an hour more and they would have made it to Heathrow.

Kusum says that we can't escape our fate. She says that all those people—our husbands, my boys, her girl with the nightingale voice, all those Hindus, Christians, Sikhs, Muslims, Parsis, and atheists on that plane—were fated to die together off this beautiful bay. She learned this from a swami in Toronto.

I have my Valium.

Six of us "relatives"—two widows and four widowers—choose to spend the day today by the waters instead of sitting in a hospital room and scanning photographs of the dead. That's what they call us now: relatives. I've looked through twenty-seven photos in two days. They're very kind to us, the Irish are very understanding. Sometimes understanding means freeing a tourist bus for this trip to the bay, so we can pretend to spy our loved ones through the glassiness of waves or in sun-speckled cloud shapes.

I could die here, too, and be content.

"What is that, out there?" She's standing and flapping her hands and for a moment I see a head shape bobbing in the waves. She's standing in the water, I, on the boulder. The tide is low, and a round, black, head-sized rock has just risen from the waves. She returns, her sari end dripping and ruined and her face is a twisted remnant of hope, the way mine was a hundred hours ago, still laughing but inwardly knowing that nothing but the ultimate tragedy could bring two women together at six o'clock on a Sunday morning. I watch her face sag into blankness.

"That water felt warm, Shaila," she says at length.

"You can't," I say. "We have to wait for our turn to come."

I haven't eaten in four days, haven't brushed my teeth.

"I know," she says. "I tell myself I have no right to grieve. They are in a better place than we are. My swami says I should be thrilled for them. My swami says depression is a sign of our selfishness."

Maybe I'm selfish. Selfishly I break away from Kusum and run, sandals slapping against stones, to the water's edge. What if my boys aren't lying pinned under the debris? What if they aren't stuck a mile below that innocent blue chop? What if, given the strong currents. . . .

Now I've ruined my sari, one of my best. Kusum has joined me, knee-deep in water that feels to me like a swimming pool. I could settle in the water, and my husband would take my hand and the boys would slap water in my face just to see me scream.

"Do you remember what good swimmers my boys were, Kusum?"

"I saw the medals," she says.

One of the widowers, Dr. Ranganathan from Montreal, walks out to us, carrying his shoes in one hand. He's an electrical engineer. Someone at the hotel mentioned his work is famous around the world, something about the place where physics and electricity come together. He has lost a huge family, something indescribable. "With some luck," Dr. Ranganathan suggests to me, "a good swimmer could make it safely to some island. It is quite possible that there may be many, many microscopic islets scattered around."

"You're not just saying that?" I tell Dr. Ranganathan about Vinod, my elder son. Last year he took diving as well.

"It's a parent's duty to hope," he says. "It is foolish to rule out possibilities that have not been tested. I myself have not surrendered hope."

Kusum is sobbing once again. "Dear lady," he says, laying his free hand on her arm, and she calms down.

"Vinod is how old?" he asks me. He's very careful, as we all are. *Is*, not was.

"Fourteen. Yesterday he was fourteen. His father and uncle were going to take him down to the Taj and give him a big birthday party. I couldn't go with them because I couldn't get two weeks off from my stupid job in June." I process bills for a travel agent. June is a big travel month.

Dr. Ranganathan whips the pockets of his suit jacket inside out. Squashed roses, in darkening shades of pink, float on the water. He tore the roses off creepers in somebody's garden. He didn't ask anyone if he could pluck the roses, but now there's been an article about it in the local papers. When you see an Indian person, it says, please give him or her flowers.

"A strong youth of fourteen," he says, "can very likely pull to safety a younger one."

My sons, though four years apart, were very close. Vinod wouldn't let Mithun drown. *Electrical engineering*, I think, foolishly perhaps: this man knows important secrets of the universe, things closed to me. Relief spins me lightheaded. No wonder my boys' photographs haven't turned up in the gallery of photos of the recovered dead. "Such pretty roses," I say.

"My wife loved pink roses. Every Friday I had to bring a bunch home. I used to say, Why? After twenty odd years of marriage you're still needing proof positive of my love?" He has identified his wife and three of his children. Then others from Montreal, the lucky ones, intact families with no survivors. He chuckles as he wades back to shore. Then he swings around to ask me a question. "Mrs. Bhave, you are wanting to throw in some roses for your loved ones? I have two big ones left."

But I have other things to float: Vinod's pocket calculator; a half-painted model B-52 for my Mithun. They'd want them on their island. And for my husband? For him I let fall into the calm, glassy waters a poem I wrote in the hospital yesterday. Finally he'll know my feelings for him.

"Don't tumble, the rocks are slippery," Dr. Ranganathan cautions. He holds out a hand for me to grab.

Then it's time to get back on the bus, time to rush back to our waiting posts on hospital benches.

■ ■ ■

Kusum is one of the lucky ones. The lucky ones flew here, identified in multiplicate their loved ones, then will fly to India with the bodies for proper ceremonies. Satish is one of the few males who surfaced. The photos of faces we saw on the walls in an office at Heathrow and here in the hospital are mostly of women. Women have more body fat, a nun said to me matter-of-factly. They float better.

Today I was stopped by a young sailor on the street. He had loaded bodies, he'd gone into the water when—he checks my face for signs of strength—when the sharks were first spotted. I don't blush, and he breaks down. "It's all right," I say. "Thank you." I had heard about the sharks from Dr. Ranganathan. In his orderly mind, science brings understanding, it holds no terror. It is the shark's duty. For every deer there is a hunter, for every fish a fisherman.

The Irish are not shy; they rush to me and give me hugs and some are crying. I cannot imagine reactions like that on the streets of Toronto. Just strangers, and I am touched. Some carry flowers with them and give them to any Indian they see.

After lunch, a policeman I have gotten to know quite well catches hold of me. He says he thinks he has a match for Vinod. I explain what a good swimmer Vinod is.

"You want me with you when you look at photos?" Dr. Ranganathan walks ahead of me into the picture gallery. In these matters, he is a scientist, and I am grateful. It is a new perspective. "They have performed miracles," he says. "We are indebted to them."

The first day or two the policemen showed us relatives only one picture at a time; now they're in a hurry, they're eager to lay out the possibles, and even the probables.

The face on the photo is of a boy much like Vinod; the same intelligent eyes, the same thick brows dipping into a V. But this boy's features, even his cheeks, are puffier, wider, mushier.

"No." My gaze is pulled by other pictures. There are five other boys who look like Vinod.

The nun assigned to console me rubs the first picture with a fingertip. "When they've been in the water for a while, love, they look a little heavier." The bones under the skin are broken, they said on the first day—try to adjust your memories. It's important.

"It's not him. I'm his mother. I'd know."

"I know this one!" Dr. Ranganathan cries out suddenly from the back of the gallery. "And this one!" I think he senses that I don't want to find my boys. "They are the Kutty brothers. They were also from Montreal." I don't mean to be crying. On the contrary, I am ecstatic. My suitcase in the hotel is packed heavy with dry clothes for my boys.

The policeman starts to cry. "I am so sorry, I am so sorry, ma'am. I really thought we had a match."

With the nun ahead of us and the policeman behind, we, the unlucky ones without our children's bodies, file out of the makeshift gallery.

■ ■ ■

From Ireland most of us go on to India. Kusum and I take the same direct flight to Bombay, so I can help her clear customs quickly. But we have to argue with a man in uniform. He has large boils on his face. The boils swell and glow with sweat as we argue with him. He wants Kusum to wait in line and he refuses to take authority because his boss is on a tea break. But Kusum won't let her coffins out of sight, and I shan't desert her though I know that my parents, elderly and diabetic, must be waiting in a stuffy car in a scorching lot.

"You bastard!" I scream at the man with the popping boils. Other passengers press closer. "You think we're smuggling contraband in those coffins!"

Once upon a time we were well brought up women; we were dutiful wives who kept our heads veiled, our voices shy and sweet.

■ ■ ■

In India, I become, once again, an only child of rich, ailing parents. Old friends of the family come to pay their respects. Some are Sikh, and inwardly, involuntarily, I cringe. My parents are progressive people; they do not blame communities for a few individuals.

In Canada it is a different story now.

"Stay longer," my mother pleads. "Canada is a cold place. Why would you want to be all by yourself?" I stay.

Three months pass. Then another.

"Vikram wouldn't have wanted you to give up things!" they protest. They call my husband by the name he was born with. In Toronto he'd changed to Vik so the men he worked with at his office would find his name as easy as Rod or Chris. "You know, the dead aren't cut off from us!"

My grandmother, the spoiled daughter of a rich *zamindar*, shaved her head with rusty razor blades when she was widowed at sixteen. My grandfather died of childhood diabetes when he was nineteen, and she saw herself as the harbinger of bad luck. My mother grew up without parents, raised indifferently by an uncle, while her true mother slept in a hut behind the main estate house and took her food with the servants. She grew up a rationalist. My parents abhor mindless mortification.

The *zamindar*'s daughter kept stubborn faith in Vedic rituals; my parents rebelled. I am trapped between two modes of knowledge. At thirty-six, I am too old to start over and too young to give up. Like my husband's spirit, I flutter between worlds.

■ ■ ■

Courting aphasia, we travel. We travel with our phalanx of servants and poor relatives. To hill stations and to beach resorts. We play contract bridge in dusty gymkhana clubs. We ride stubby ponies up crumbly mountain trails. At tea dances, we let ourselves be twirled twice round the ballroom. We hit the holy spots we hadn't made time for before. In

Varanasi, Kalighat, Rishikesh, Hardwar, astrologers and palmists seek me out and for a fee offer me cosmic consolations.

Already the widowers among us are being shown new bride candidates. They cannot resist the call of custom, the authority of their parents and older brothers. They must marry; it is the duty of a man to look after a wife. The new wives will be young widows with children, destitute but of good family. They will make loving wives, but the men will shun them. I've had calls from the men over crackling Indian telephone lines. "Save me," they say, these substantial, educated, successful men of forty. "My parents are arranging a marriage for me." In a month they will have buried one family and returned to Canada with a new bride and partial family.

I am comparatively lucky. No one here thinks of arranging a husband for an unlucky widow.

Then, on the third day of the sixth month into this odyssey, in an abandoned temple in a tiny Himalayan village, as I make my offering of flowers and sweetmeats to the god of a tribe of animists, my husband descends to me. He is squatting next to a scrawny *sadhu* in moth-eaten robes. Vikram wears the vanilla suit he wore the last time I hugged him. The *sadhu* tosses petals on a butter-fed flame, reciting Sanskrit mantras, and sweeps his face of flies. My husband takes my hands in his.

You're beautiful, he starts. Then, *What are you doing here?*

Shall I stay? I ask. He only smiles, but already the image is fading. *You must finish alone what we started together.* No seaweed wreathes his mouth. He speaks too fast just as he used to when we were an envied family in our pink split-level. He is gone.

In the windowless altar room, smoky with joss sticks and clarified butter lamps, a sweaty hand gropes for my blouse. I do not shriek. The *sadhu* arranges his robe. The lamps hiss and sputter out.

When we come out of the temple, my mother says, "Did you feel something weird in there?"

My mother has no patience with ghosts, prophetic dreams, holy men, and cults.

"No," I lie. "Nothing."

But she knows that she's lost me. She knows that in days I shall be leaving.

Kusum's put her house up for sale. She wants to live in an ashram in Hardwar. Moving to Hardwar was her swami's idea. Her swami runs two ashrams, the one in Hardwar and another here in Toronto.

"Don't run away," I tell her.

"I'm not running away," she says. "I'm pursuing inner peace. You think you or that Ranganathan fellow are better off?"

Pam's left for California. She wants to do some modelling, she says. She says when she comes into her share of the insurance money she'll open a yoga-cum-aerobics studio in Hollywood. She sends me postcards so naughty I daren't leave them on the coffee table. Her mother has withdrawn from her and the world.

The rest of us don't lose touch, that's the point. Talk is all we have, says Dr. Ranganathan, who has also resisted his relatives and returned to Montreal and to his job, alone. He says, whom better to talk with than other relatives? We've been melted down and recast as a new tribe.

He calls me twice a week from Montreal. Every Wednesday night and every Saturday afternoon. He is changing jobs, going to Ottawa. But Ottawa is over a hundred miles away, and he is forced to drive two hundred and twenty miles a day. He can't bring himself to sell his house. The house is a temple, he says; the king-sized bed in the master bedroom is a shrine. He sleeps on a folding cot. A devotee.

■ ■ ■

There are still some hysterical relatives. Judith Templeton's list of those needing help and those who've "accepted" is in nearly perfect balance. Acceptance means you speak of your family in the past tense and you make active plans for moving ahead with your life. There are courses at Seneca and Ryerson we could be taking. Her gleaming leather briefcase is full of college catalogues and lists of cultural societies that need our help. She has done impressive work, I tell her.

"In the textbooks on grief management," she replies—I am her confidante, I realize, one of the few whose grief has not sprung bizarre obsessions—"there are stages to pass through: rejection, depression, acceptance, reconstruction." She has compiled a chart and finds that six months after the tragedy, none of us still reject reality, but only a handful are reconstructing. "Depressed Acceptance" is the plateau we've reached. Remarriage is a major step in reconstruction (though she's a little surprised, even shocked, over *how* quickly some of the men have taken on new families). Selling one's house and changing jobs and cities is healthy.

How do I tell Judith Templeton that my family surrounds me, and that like creatures in epics, they've changed shapes? She sees me as calm and accepting but worries that I have no job, no career. My closest friends are worse off than I. I cannot tell her my days, even my nights, are thrilling.

She asks me to help with families she can't reach at all. An elderly couple in Agincourt whose sons were killed just weeks after they had brought their parents over from a village in Punjab. From their names, I know they are Sikh. Judith Templeton and a translator have visited them twice with offers of money for airfare to Ireland, with bank forms, power-of-attorney forms, but they have refused to sign, or to leave their tiny apartment. Their sons' money is frozen in the bank. Their sons' investment apartments have been trashed by tenants, the furnishings sold off. The parents fear that anything they sign or any money they receive will end the company's or the country's obligations to them. They fear they are selling their sons for two airline tickets to a place they've never seen.

The high-rise apartment is a tower of Indians and West Indians, with a sprinkling of Orientals. The nearest bus stop kiosk is lined with women in saris. Boys practice cricket in the parking lot. Inside the building, even I wince a bit from the ferocity of onion fumes, the distinctive and immediate Indianness of frying *ghee*, but Judith Templeton maintains a steady flow of information. These poor old people are in imminent danger of losing their place and all their services.

I say to her, "They are Sikh. They will not open up to a Hindu woman." And what I want to add is, as much as I try not to, I stiffen now at the sight of beards and turbans. I remember a time when we all trusted each other in this new country, it was only the new country we worried about.

The two rooms are dark and stuffy. The lights are off, and an oil lamp sputters on the coffee table. The bent old lady has let us in, and her husband is wrapping a white turban over his oiled, hip-length hair.

She immediately goes to the kitchen, and I hear the most familiar sound of an Indian home, tap water hitting and filling a teapot.

They have not paid their utility bills, out of fear and the inability to write a check. The telephone is gone; electricity and gas and water are soon to follow. They have told Judith their sons will provide. They are good boys, and they have always earned and looked after their parents.

We converse a bit in Hindi. They do not ask about the crash and I wonder if I should bring it up. If they think I am here merely as a translator, then they may feel insulted. There are thousands of Punjabi-speakers, Sikhs, in Toronto to do a better job. And so I say to the old lady, "I too have lost my sons, and my husband, in the crash."

Her eyes immediately fill with tears. The man mutters a few words which sound like a blessing. "God provides and God takes away," he says.

I want to say, But only men destroy and give back nothing. "My boys and my husband are not coming back," I say. "We have to understand that."

Now the old woman responds. "But who is to say? Man alone does not decide these things." To this her husband adds his agreement.

Judith asks about the bank papers, the release forms. With a stroke of the pen, they will have a provincial trustee to pay their bills, invest their money, send them a monthly pension.

"Do you know this woman?" I ask them.

The man raises his hand from the table, turns it over, and seems to regard each finger separately before he answers. "This young lady is always coming here, we make tea for her and she leaves papers for us to sign." His eyes scan a pile of papers in the corner of the room. "Soon we will be out of tea, then will she go away?"

The old lady adds, "I have asked my neighbors and no one else gets *angrezi* visitors. What have we done?"

"It's her job," I try to explain. "The government is worried. Soon you will have no place to stay, no lights, no gas, no water."

"Government will get its money. Tell her not to worry, we are honorable people."

I try to explain the government wishes to give money, not take. He raises his hand. "Let them take," he says. "We are accustomed to that. That is no problem."

"We are strong people," says the wife. "Tell her that."

"Who needs all this machinery?" demands the husband. "It is unhealthy, the bright lights, the cold air on a hot day, the cold food, the four gas rings. God will provide, not government."

"When our boys return," the mother says. Her husband sucks his teeth. "Enough talk," he says.

Judith breaks in. "Have you convinced them?" The snaps on her cordovan briefcase go off like firecrackers in that quiet apartment. She lays the sheaf of legal papers on the coffee table. "If they can't write their names, an X will do—I've told them that."

Now the old lady has shuffled to the kitchen and soon emerges with a pot of tea and two cups. "I think my bladder will go first on a job like this," Judith says to me, smiling. "If only there was some way of reaching them. Please thank her for the tea. Tell her she's very kind."

I nod in Judith's direction and tell them in Hindi, "She thanks you for the tea. She thinks you are being very hospitable but she doesn't have the slightest idea what it means."

I want to say, Humor her. I want to say, My boys and my husband are with me too, more than ever. I look in the old man's eyes and I can read his stubborn, peasant's message: *I have protected this woman as best I can. She is the only person I have left. Give to me or take from me what you will, but I will not sign for it. I will not pretend that I accept.*

In the car, Judith says, "You see what I'm up against? I'm sure they're lovely people, but their stubbornness and ignorance are driving me crazy. They think signing a paper is signing their sons' death warrants, don't they?"

I am looking out the window. I want to say, *In our culture, it is a parent's duty to hope.*

"Now Shaila, this next woman is a real mess. She cries day and night, and she refuses all medical help. We may have to—"

"—Let me out at the subway," I say.

"I beg your pardon?" I can feel those blue eyes staring at me.

It would not be like her to disobey. She merely disapproves, and slows at a corner to let me out. Her voice is plaintive. "Is there anything I said? Anything I did?"

I could answer her suddenly in a dozen ways, but I choose not to. "Shaila? Let's talk about it," I hear, then slam the door.

■ ■ ■

A wife and mother begins her new life in a new country, and that life is cut short. Yet her husband tells her: Complete what we have started. We who stayed out of politics and came halfway around the world to avoid religious and political feuding have been the first in the New World to die from it. I no longer know what we started, nor how to complete it. I write letters to the editors of local papers and to members of Parliament. Now at least they admit it was a bomb. One MP answers back, with sympathy, but with a challenge. You want to make a difference? Work on a campaign. Work on mine. Politicize the Indian voter.

My husband's old lawyer helps me set up a trust. Vikram was a saver and a careful investor. He had saved the boys' boarding school and college fees. I sell the pink house at four times what we paid for it and take a small apartment downtown. I am looking for a charity to support.

We are deep in the Toronto winter, gray skies, icy pavements. I stay indoors, watching television. I have tried to assess my situation, how best to live my life, to complete what we began so many years ago. Kusum has written me from Hardwar that her life is now serene. She has seen Satish and has heard her daughter sing again. Kusum was on a pilgrimage, passing through a village, when she heard a young girl's voice, singing one of her daughter's favorite *bhajans*. She followed the music through the squalor of a Himalayan village, to a hut where a young girl, an exact replica of her daughter, was fanning coals under the kitchen fire. When she appeared, the girl cried out, "Ma!" and ran away. What did I think of that?

I think I can only envy her.

Pam didn't make it to California, but writes me from Vancouver. She works in a department store, giving make-up hints to Indian and Oriental girls. Dr. Ranganathan has given up his commute, given up his house and job, and accepted an academic position in Texas where no one knows his story and he has vowed not to tell it. He calls me now once a week.

I wait, I listen, and I pray, but Vikram has not returned to me. The voices and the shapes and the nights filled with visions ended abruptly several weeks ago.

I take it as a sign.

One rare, beautiful, sunny day last week, returning from a small errand on Yonge Street, I was walking through the park from the subway to my apartment. I live equidistant from the Ontario Houses of Parliament and the University of Toronto. The day was not cold, but something in the bare trees caught my attention. I looked up from the gravel, into the branches and the clear blue sky beyond. I thought I heard the rustling of larger forms, and I waited a moment for voices. Nothing.

"What?" I asked.

Then, as I stood in the path looking north to Queen's Park and west to the university, I heard the voices of my family one last time. *Your time has come*, they said. *Go, be brave.*

I do not know where this voyage I have begun will end. I do not know which direction I will take. I dropped the package on a park bench and started walking.

FOLLY

▪ ▪ ▪

Sabina Murray

Kees Bouman stood alone in the sala of his house. The breeze, which
had earlier bowed the tops of the palms, was suddenly quiet and the
only sound was the clock as it shuddered to each tick. Middle age was
making him contemplative, he thought, because with each forward
step of the clock, second by second into a modern future, Bouman felt
the jungle struggle forcefully against it. Here in the tropics there was
one endless season that cycled on and on, then circled back onto itself
like a serpent eating its tail. He felt like the first, or maybe the last, man
on earth. His evening tea was not waiting on the table and his daughter, Katrina, was not ready to serve it.

Bouman went to stand at the door. The orange sun was sinking fast
behind the topmost brushes of the palms. There was a soothing *hush
hush* of waves, out of sight from where he stood. A bird excited by the
final moments of the day let forth a rattling cackle, beat the warm air
with its wings, then followed the sinking sun into the jungle. If his wife
had still been alive, she would have stood on the doorstep and started

SABINA MURRAY was born in Manila in 1968 and grew up in Australia and
the Philippines. *The Caprices*, a collection of short stories based on the Pacific
campaign of World War II, was published in 2002 and awarded the
PEN/Faulkner Prize in 2003. The author of the novel *Slow Burn* and the
screenplay for *Beautiful Country*, her stories have appeared in *Ploughshares*,
Ontario Review, *New England Review*, and other magazines. She is a former
Bunting Fellow at Harvard University and a recipient of a major grant from the
Massachusetts Cultural Council. Murray is currently the writer in residence at
Phillips Academy, Andover.

yelling. One call from her and the entire household would have leaped to attention, come running across the swept dirt of the compound. The very chickens would have cackled to life. That gnarled pony tied to the post would have raised his head in respectful attention, but Bouman could only transfer his weight from one bare foot to the other, adjust the waist of his baggy pants, and hope that someone would notice him so forlorn and bereft of tea.

He smelled chicken curry. Bouman looked to the cooking shack and was surprised to see Katrina exit. She was wearing her new white kabeya, the one embroidered in a floral motif, which had been very costly; she was hurrying through the compound's center with such speed that she lost her slipper and had to go back for it.

"Katrina!" called Bouman.

She stopped, stunned and seemingly guilty. "Father?"

"Where is my tea?"

Katrina put her slipper on and turned back in the direction of the cooking shack.

"What is this nonsense?" he called again.

"Father, we have a visitor."

"A visitor?"

"He's on the veranda. I'll bring the tea there."

Bouman raised his eyebrows in resignation. He hadn't heard anyone on the veranda but now on reentering the living room he could hear the low voice of Aya, the housekeeper, chattering away. He peeked out the door and sure enough, seated at the table—on which someone had set a large stinking bunch of frangipani—was a young native in brilliantly pressed colonial whites. Bouman looked at his own bare feet and baggy batik pants with some amusement. His European shirt, made from coarse local cotton, was frayed at the collar. Bouman felt a certain pride in all of this, especially the way that it would annoy Katrina, the way her immaculate dress was annoying him. Aya was squatting on the floor next to the visitor's ankles. Her elbows rested on her knees and she absently swatted the air in front of her face for mosquitoes.

When Aya noticed Bouman she jumped up straight.

"Tea," she said, embarrassed.

"Oh, forget the tea," said Bouman. "Gin now and some limeade for our visitor."

"Mr. Bouman . . ." The visitor was now standing, his hands clasped behind his back, his head at a respectful incline.

"Yes, I am Bouman. And you?"

"I am Tan Lumbantobing. I deeply appreciate your hospitality."

"I can take no credit for that," said Bouman. "But I am not so rude as to deny that the hospitality of my daughter and my housekeeper is correct and admirable." Bouman smiled. He was actually relieved at his guest, better than a European planter, who would be eager for fresh sympathy over disease and sullen workers. "You will not mind if I call you Tan?"

The young man smiled.

"Are you a visitor or a customer?"

"That depends on what you're selling."

"You are looking for weapons and gunpowder." Bouman shook his head. "Excuse my frankness, but I am an old man and don't want to die not having spoken my mind." Bouman was just forty-five, but felt a great deal older. The sun had creased his skin and the army had calcified his joints, which made him seem old at first but, on closer look, permanent.

The drinks arrived and Bouman poured himself a glass of gin. Tan was smiling at his hands in subtle, respectful silence.

"I would offer you gin, but I suspect your religion forbids it. If you care to help yourself, go right ahead."

Tan took the glass of limeade. He sipped and nodded at Bouman. "This is very refreshing," he said.

"Yes," said Bouman, "refreshing. I prefer my beverages steeped and aged—pickled berries," he said, raising the gin, "or dead leaves soaked in hot water."

Katrina appeared at the door with the tea. She set it down on the table and wiped her hands on her skirt. She was flushed and distracted.

"Sit down, for heaven's sake. Have some tea. Have some gin, if you like." Katrina did not move. She looked from the guest, back over to her father, then at her hands. She was paralyzed with embarrassment.

"Where's the food?" said Bouman to his daughter.

"It will be ready soon," Katrina whispered.

Bouman took a mouthful of gin and closed his eyes. He smiled. "She is a quiet girl," he said to Tan, "but good. She is nothing like her mother, who was wild and, in my opinion, better. I find it hard to believe that there was something that could kill that woman, but there was. And now she is dead ten years."

"You are lucky to have a daughter to care for you," said Tan.

"Yes. Yes, I am." Bouman drank again. "And you, where is your family?"

"My father is in Aceh. My brother is also on a buying expedition. He has gone to the west."

"How are you traveling?"

"By prahu."

"I saw none."

"My brother has taken the boat with him. I do not mean to tax your hospitality, but your housekeeper told me that I could stay in a room in the manager's quarters. It is only for one week."

"You are welcome to stay as long as you like." Bouman did not care what Tan did with his time. "You are from Aceh?"

The young man nodded.

"A relative of the raja?"

"Yes."

"I trust he is alive and well?"

"Alive, but not well."

Even better, thought Bouman. "Did he speak of me?"

"Only to say that during the war, you had been on opposite sides, but if there was one Dutchman in Sumatra who could give me a straight answer, it was you."

"I was on the side of pepper. That's what we fought for in Aceh. Many lives were wasted, uselessly, on both sides. I will not have the stuff on my table."

"Pepper?"

"Pepper and war, so if we must talk of arms, we will do so after we eat." Bouman spun his glass on the table.

"You lost your fingers in Aceh?" asked Tan.

Bouman raised his right hand. The thumb was solid and his fore- and middle fingers had survived the war, but the other two were sheared right off. The shadow of Bouman's altered hand fell across Katrina's face. "During the war, but not because of it. A bull elephant frightened by the conflict entered camp. Some were trampled and in the effort to kill it, a stray bullet took off my fingers."

"I am sorry that you lost your fingers."

"Oh, I still have them, and later, if I've had enough of this stuff"—Bouman raised his glass—"I will show them to you."

Katrina looked shyly at her father. She had an overbite and when she was uncomfortable, struggled to get her mouth closed over her teeth. Despite this, she was pretty. Bouman thought she had taken the best physical traits of her mother, the gentle brow, the broad cheeks, the unblemished skin that glowed in the sun. From him, she had inherited horsy European teeth—at odds with her small jaws—and social awkwardness. At seventeen she looked more womanly than her full-blooded native peers. She also lacked their guile and awareness. Bouman noticed sadly that Tan had taken a few cautious glances in Katrina's direction and that her burning cheeks and anxiety had been noticed and seen as encouragement.

During dinner Katrina cowered behind the floral arrangement. When Tan thought Bouman so involved with his food that he was not being watched, he slid the flowers slightly to the left with the tip of his knife to take a better look at the girl. She was concentrating on her food, taking the tiniest bites. When she saw Tan watching her, she met his eyes frankly and nervously. It was not he who rattled her, it was her father. Bouman ate fast, without conversation, and loudly. To keep up Tan choked down the chicken and bitter squash, which was spicy and good, only clearing his throat with water. The entire meal took ten minutes. Katrina was not even halfway through her food when the men stood up together and went to stand by the railing to smoke, or in the case of Tan, to pinch a little betel nut, as was his custom after dinner.

"I sent her to Batavia for school," said Bouman, smoke pouring out the corners of his mouth. The two men stood now on the edge of the veranda and a bright moon hit the water and the trees, lighting everything with a pleasing, silver glow. "When she chooses to speak, she can speak in Dutch and French." He smiled at his daughter, who had overcome her shyness enough to smile back. "She came back with a taste for embroidered cloth and now wants me to buy her a piano. I can no longer eat with the simple smell of meat. Now I must be menaced at the table by bouquets of these tough, native flowers whose cheap perfume makes the food taste like shampoo."

"Women like pretty things," said Tan. Bouman took in Tan's soulful eyes and long-fingered, elegant hands. His hair had a sheen to it. Bouman laughed.

"And men," he said, "care only for drink, and barring that, war." Here Bouman gazed knowingly at his guest.

"I don't need to darken this evening with business," said Tan. "I am enjoying your hospitality and I can wait until tomorrow."

"Why," said Bouman suddenly, his face gripped in a smile, "why do you think that I have weapons?"

Tan nodded a few times and turned to his host, who was now only inches from his face. "I know that you have supplied hunters with weapons. They have come out of the jungle with elephant, rhinoceros, tiger, boar. They have taken their heads mounted back to Europe. And you have supplied the cartridges to this end."

"No more hunters for me," said Bouman.

Tan was poised to speak, but then changed his mind. He raised his limeade in a quick, silent toast.

"What were you going to say?"

"What do you mean?"

"Be frank with me. It is the only way to get what you want."

"I don't intend to be disrespectful."

"Of course not."

"You are the supervisor of the trading post."

"Ah. And you would like to speak to the owner?"

Both Tan and Bouman looked up the coast, where a mere two hundred feet away there was another house, much like Bouman's, only this one was still and dark. "Peter Versteegh is on a hunt," Bouman said.

"When did he leave?"

"Five years ago."

"When do you expect him back?"

"I don't," said Bouman. "He was foolishly hunting with a stout businessman from Marseille, someone he knew from the trade. They were hunting orangutan. I suspect the Batak got them, that Versteegh's bony head is gracing a chieftain's mantel as is that Frenchman's. He had a very plump head and impressive mustaches. Even I could see the value in collecting a head like that . . ."

"Father!"

"Ah. She speaks. I'm sorry to offend." Bouman laughed. "Go get some sweets for our guest. I'm sure we have something."

Bouman waved Katrina off. She reluctantly pushed away from the table and the chair legs ground loudly across the floor. Bouman saw her look at Tan with complete frustration and Tan smiled back.

"The Frenchman," whispered Bouman as Katrina left, "had little appreciation for life. He shot an ape and brought it in. It was a female, lactating. He'd lost the infant and didn't seem to care. I went out looking for the baby. I went out for hours, all night, with a lantern. Call me sentimental, but I know what it's like when a child loses the mother."

"Do you really think the Batak killed them?"

"You know better than I do their beliefs, that the ancestors come back as animals—elephant, tiger, and orangutan. Even death is not permanent. I saw little value to the lives of Versteegh and this Frenchman. His name, I remember, was Guillotte. Yes. And they are dead."

"But you say they are still hunting?"

"I wrote to Guillotte's family saying that I doubted he would return. And as for Versteegh, his native wife is still living in the house. Why would I write to his cousins in Holland? They would come and sell this and where would I go? And why should they have this place? You cannot put the value of our little house, our compound, and small business into guilders. Besides, is it not a romantic thought that the Dutchman and Frenchman are wandering through the heart of Sumatra chasing an elusive ape who stays always two steps ahead?"

"A pretty myth," said Tan. "You are romantic, from another time. You forget that it is 1922, that the ways of the ancestors, yours and mine, have long been buried with them. I don't mourn that. Change is good."

"Change?" said Bouman sadly. Katrina appeared in the doorway with a plate. She had picked more blossoms and arranged these in with the rice cakes and wafers. "If I could make this evening last indefinitely, I would do it."

The prahu returned six days later. Bouman had convinced Tan that he had no weapons for sale. Bouman had a half-dozen rifles and countless boxes of cartridges, but Tan was unwilling to name his enemy and rampaging bull elephants were no longer the problem they'd been twenty years earlier. Bouman decided to give the boy a good deal on some bolts of cotton. He'd thrown in a few pairs of embroidered slippers for the boy's relatives, offered gin and tobacco, which had not been of interest, and an immense cooking pot (for boiling missionaries, Bouman had joked), which Tan had thought would be useful. Bouman was just coming out of the warehouse when he saw Tan running down the steps of the house. A figure appeared in the doorway immediately afterward, wiping her eyes with the back of her hand. Tan stopped and turned, then he ran back up the stairs and embraced her. In his shock, Bouman wanted to believe that the woman was Aya, who, gnarled as she was, could offer occasional sexual gratification. But no. It was Katrina, and a cold chill slowly took over Bouman's heart.

When Tan entered the warehouse Bouman was sitting at his desk. There was a box of ammunition by his feet. A dozen rifles leaned against the wall. Bouman sat at his desk, his face covered by his hands. Tan could see the man trembling and at first thought that he had been moved to tears, but when Bouman lifted his head, his eyes were clearly fired with anger. Bouman stood up.

"You were a guest in my house and you have deceived me."

"My intentions are honorable."

"Who is the judge of that?"

Tan was silent. "You know my family . . ."

"That they are rich, powerful—yes, I know that. And I tell you that you will never have my daughter. Take the guns. Leave. Never come back."

"She wants to go with me."

"What does she know of what she wants? She is seventeen years old." Bouman picked up a rifle and swung it gracefully to point into Tan's face. "I am offering you the gun. You take the muzzle or the trigger."

Tan was silent.

"I will kill you. I have killed dozens of men in my time and not once has my sleep been disturbed."

■ ■ ■

Bouman watched the prahu round the promontory and thought with a cautious satisfaction that he would never see the boy again. No doubt, Katrina was in tears and would not speak to him for months. His household was in disorder. Aya would be glaring at him from behind the posts of the house, going about her daily tasks with more than the usual menace; she would be spitting in his food. Bouman shook his head. A stiff breeze stirred the water and the palms dipped and swayed. More than the usual monkey chatter was going on overhead. The birds dipped and swooped with unusual urgency. On the ground Bouman saw the ants coursing fervently in streams. There was the burn of electricity in the air. At the edge of the horizon a beam of lightning flared, leaving the margin a menacing dark purple. Bouman sighed deeply, baring his teeth at the world. He knew he was in for trouble.

■ ■ ■

About many things, Bouman had been wrong. He was wrong to think that his father-love could satisfy his daughter and wrong to think that he would never see Tan again. By the time the young man returned he was no longer a young man and Bouman had seen so many things—more than twenty years had passed—that he questioned every reality. The very nose in the center of his face was up for debate, as far as he was concerned. But as he squatted and smoked in the burned-out square of earth that had once been his house, he somehow knew that the prahu dipping over the edge of the water, rising up like the sun, bore his old acquaintance, Tan. And Bouman thought, in an uncharacteristically mystical way, that his new clairvoyance meant that his life was drawing to a close.

Tan had lost the colonial whites and was now wearing the baggy batik trousers of his people, those and a European shirt of coarse cotton, with a belt of ammunition slung from shoulder to hip. There was silver in with the black, but he looked much the same. Bouman got up and threw his cigarette. He cocked his head to one side. Tan hesitated, stopping twenty feet from where Bouman stood. To his surprise, Bouman laughed.

"I told you not to come back or I would kill you, but it is you who are armed and I have nothing but these two imperfect hands." Bouman splayed his eight fingers up for inspection.

"How can it be," said Tan, "that you have not changed?"

"A mystery," Bouman shrugged. "I am wiser now and so I will ask you to dinner, to have some tea with me, because I now know what an enemy looks like." Bouman laughed again.

"I thought you were dead," said Tan. "I myself looked in all the nine camps of Sumatra. I had my people check every Javanese camp, every Dutchman."

"Did you not think I might be lost under a different name? And the islands are full of Dutchmen."

"Eight-fingered Dutchmen?" said Tan.

"So thinking I was dead, you came back for my daughter, but it is she who is dead."

Tan was silent.

"That saddens you."

"The Japanese killed many."

"Many, but not her. I have you to blame for that."

"Me?"

"Katrina died in childbirth." Bouman closed his eyes. He heard again Katrina's frightened screams. He remembered Aya's desperate butchery. "Come. Have tea." The Dutchman gestured for Tan to follow. "You can send me back to Holland after dinner."

Bouman had moved into the manager's small house. He walked quickly and Tan followed, two steps behind, his hands resting nervously on his ammunition belt and gun. The sloping thatch roof was repaired with ragged sheets of tin, probably the work of Bouman. He no longer seemed to have anyone in his employ, not even Aya, who would have made her presence known had she been there. Leaning up against a tree to the right of the hut was an ornate carved door, blunted and polished by exposure. Tan recognized the door as belonging to the original house and wondered what had inspired Bouman to move it from the flames that had no doubt engulfed and destroyed all of his former dwelling. The hut backed onto a wall of vegetation—a development of the last twenty years—and was shadowed and dreary. A few tough vines had lassoed the roof and beams, and soon the hut would be dragged back into the jungle.

Bouman cooked now. He could offer Tan a weak chicken and vegetable broth. Tan set his gun down and took a stool at the table. The sun was low and forced its way inside in blades of harsh light. Soon they would need to light candles. Bouman lit a flame beneath the pot and stirred the chicken. He was whispering to himself, almost singing to the soup. Tan looked cautiously around. There was a hammock in the corner and a sleeping mat rolled up, leaning against the wall. A case of gin (or what had once been a case of gin) acted as a side table and set on that was a greasy candle and, of all things, a Bible. There was a large wooden box on the floor, blackened by the fire, and it took Tan some moments to realize that it had once been a clock.

"You see, I have survived the war," said Bouman, setting the soup before his guest, "but only in pieces."

"Where were you?" said Tan.

"Here."

"Here? The whole war here? Mr. Bouman, how can that be? All the Dutch were transported."

"But the French were not. Remember, Vichy is an ally of the Golden Prosperity Sphere." Bouman smiled slyly, then, reaching behind him to a splintered shelf, he found a passport. He handed it to Tan.

Tan opened the passport. There was Bouman's picture—an old picture, to be sure, where Bouman's fine blond hair actually reached his forehead in a bank rather than one sharp point in the center—the name *Jean Guillotte*, and the birthplace, *Marseille, République de France.*

"Very clever," said Tan. "And how did you survive the natives?"

"I hear a trader down the coast was buried alive," said Bouman with a smile. "But I am lucky. So much sadness puts people off," he said. "They say the ghost of Katrina wanders here, that she will steal your heart as her heart was stolen."

Just then a shadow passed by the window and Tan thought he'd seen her, Katrina, although thinner and darker. He turned quickly to Bouman.

"And you," said Bouman, "do you think Katrina still walks here?"

There was an awkward moment of silence, then a figure appeared in the door, a young woman carrying an infant strapped across her in a batik sling.

"This is Karen," said Bouman.

Tan stiffened. The young woman looked Tan up and down, then turned to Bouman, who gave an almost imperceptible nod. This woman was nothing like the shy Katrina. She was darker and Tan realized with a shock that this was his genetic donation. Her eyes met his boldly and it seemed that she recognized him for who he was. Her hair was not brushed but matted into one huge knot at the nape of her neck. Tan calculated that she must be twenty-three years old, but she looked a good deal older. This Karen squatted by the table. She did not seem to care that there was a visitor, but looked at her father with some slyness and satisfaction.

Tan had anticipated another situation altogether, where he was in charge, but now Bouman and the woman were grinning at each other across the table in an exclusive way that could easily be taken as clairvoyant. No, thought Tan, madness. He took a spoonful of soup and began planning his departure.

The soup was odd, slightly bitter, with a nutty aroma that he could not place. People ate many strange things during the war and in the deprivation following. Tan wondered if perhaps the soup had been flavored with wood. Just then the baby, which Tan had pushed to the back of his mind, stirred in the sling and began wailing. The woman shifted on her ankles, clucking anxiously, then produced one skinny breast that she popped into the baby's mouth. She moved the sling slightly to accommodate this action and Tan saw the baby's sharp eyes and square face, the thick shock of vertical hair that was not a family trait, the paler skin.

Tan looked to Bouman.

"Yes," said Bouman, "the father is Japanese, but she does not know who. She was not as lucky as me. She spent the war in Batavia as a comfort woman. She'd always wanted to go to Batavia, like her mother, for schooling."

"I am sorry," said Tan, stuttering over the phrase.

"Irony," said Bouman and smiled. "My greatest fear was that men would steal my girls, but look, ruined for anything, delivered permanently into my hands, given back to me, my lovely girls, by men."

Tan shook his head sympathetically. "She does not speak?"

"She," said Bouman, "has nothing to say."

The baby had fallen back asleep while nursing and Karen pulled up to the table, taking a seat and a bowl of soup close to Bouman's right elbow.

"Tell me," said Bouman, "what you plan to accomplish by this visit. I am no longer a trader, everything is gone, except for a small stash of gin and some rat poison."

"I will be honest with you," said Tan. "I thought you were dead. I was worried what would happen to Katrina, because of her Dutch blood. In Java, the Allies have herded all the Dutch into protection camps." Tan glanced sideways at Bouman, who, in the old tradition, was speedily slopping up his soup. "They have been forced to hire Japanese troops to protect them."

"Protect them?"

"From the Indonesians."

"Indonesians?" said Bouman, looking slyly up from the bowl. "And who are these Indonesians? Before we got here, there were no Indonesians. There were Dayak, Batak, Asmat—headhunters and cannibals selling their daughters for glass beads. And now, you are Indonesian? Can you tell me that you love the Balinese as brothers? That you find the negro of Irian Jaya anything but a terrifying barbarian?"

Tan felt a chill at the base of his spine. "What can I tell you that will satisfy you?" said Tan. "There is nothing just in this world, but some things are essential to improvement in the future and we must take the bitter to achieve the sweet."

"You speak like a politician."

"I am a politician," said Tan. "You would like something more direct? Your time has passed. You have profited in another's country, which is equivalent to theft, and I would rather see you leave, but could easily kill you and feel justified."

"You support the devil Sukarno."

"Sukarno," said Tan with a cryptic smile, "supports me."

There was silence after that, maybe a whole fifteen minutes without a word said. Karen stood up to spill more soup into everyone's bowl and Tan continued eating, despite the odd flavor, because he was tired of speaking to Bouman. Bouman was insane and this woman, Tan's daughter, and the little Japanese baby, Tan's grandson, were strangers and more than that, beyond the realm of his plan of noble return and rescue. What would he do with these people, inextricably bound to him by his own folly, by accidents of blood and union? Bouman was drinking a tall glass of gin. Tan saw that Karen too was drinking and thought of his other daughters, perfect ladies protected in yards of fabric, manners. They would never recognize her and they would despise their father's indiscretion. Tan closed his eyes, unwilling to imagine further the sequence of ideas.

"Do you remember," said Bouman, interrupting the moment of peace, "how I once told you that if I had enough of this"—Bouman raised his glass—"that I would show you my fingers?"

"Yes, yes I do. I remember that."

Bouman got up and went to the far corner of the room, where the hammock was slung from the beams. Bouman ducked under it and began to rifle through some belongings that cluttered the top of a crude set of shelves. He lit a candle and long shadows began to dance across the wall, animated by each breeze that shivered the flame. Tan could see from the man's clumsiness that he had had a lot to drink. Karen watched her grandfather for a moment, her face softening, but then growing blank. She stood up and took the baby from the sling. She rocked it softly, then offered the baby to Tan. Tan was chilled. He did not want to hold the child; he shuddered, then realized he had never been in a position to be so cruel.

"I can see you love your baby," said Tan, finally relenting, extending his arms, and taking the child who, from his estimate, was about four months old. Karen smiled slightly, but her eyes were filling with tears. She snatched the baby back and began desperately cooing at it, even though the baby seemed peaceful and content.

Tan stood up. He had had enough for one evening. His blood pressure, he thought, must be soaring, because he was dizzy and heavy pounding had begun in his ears. He was also a bit short of breath. He looked over at Karen. To his surprise, she too seemed to have difficulty breathing. Her lips were pulling at the corners and Tan saw that she had no teeth.

"Here they are," said Bouman with satisfaction. "Sit down, Tan. It will all be over soon."

Tan sat down. Bouman was holding a yellowed linen handkerchief. He unfolded this ceremoniously until the two shriveled, leathery fingers were revealed. The nails were brown with age and the fingers had curled, which made them look alive. Bouman set them down on the table.

"To what do I owe this honor?" asked Tan. He was feeling sweaty and weak. Something must have been off in the soup because his intestines were seizing up and he felt suddenly cold.

"This honor? I would like to be buried whole."

"Why?" asked Tan unsympathetically. "Are you dying?"

"We are all dying," answered Bouman. His voice sounded distant and muffled.

"Age," said Tan, "has made you philosophical."

Bouman laughed. "No, no. We are all dying. I have poisoned us by putting arsenic in the soup."

The next morning Aya crept into the compound. She had heard the Japanese were finally vanquished and was worried about the old Dutchman, who was an idiot and a drunk, but not evil. She also missed soap and cigarettes, which at this juncture she preferred to betel. Most compellingly, she wanted to know if Karen, who was a daughter to her, had survived the war. Many nights she had stayed awake with her heart pounding, vibrating down to her very wrists, remembering the soldiers dragging Karen by her hair as she struggled to get her feet beneath her. She remembered Bouman's strong arms holding her back, whispering, "Aya, they will kill her if we protest. Let them go. It will not be long before we are liberated."

Aya stood in the burnt square of what had been the house. Versteegh's dwelling was gone too. There was a cigarette half smoked, carelessly tossed into the ruins. She picked this up, smoothed it straight, then stuck it behind her ear for later. Bouman was still alive, still smoking, still wasting tobacco. There was a prahu anchored close by and on it she could just make out the outline of men moving about. Why would a boat be moored so close without Bouman in attention? Perhaps the Nationalists had taken over.

"Bouman!" she called. "Bouman, sir, where are you?"

In response, Aya heard the caterwauling of an infant. Aya's blood froze. The sound was coming from the manager's hut. She was not one to be overwhelmed by superstition, but her first thought was that a spirit was tricking her, using the most compelling sound known to woman to draw her into the hut. Who knows what evil awaited her there?

"Bouman, sir!" she called again. "Bouman!"

A canoe had set off from the prahu angling for shore. Aya watched the rise and dip of paddles, the sun glinting off black hair and sweating arms, the sun brightening the surface of the water in bladelike light and purple depressions. She felt the heat beginning slowly in the day, rising up through the earth. Aya found a match in her pocket that she had managed to secure before coming to the house. The baby was still crying. She lit the half cigarette. When it was burned clear to her fingers, she would make the short walk to the manager's hut. She would boldly greet whatever evil awaited her. She was an old woman and tough. Was there something stronger than she? What secrets and horrors were there that these old bones did not remember, recorded in the very stuff, ringed in the marrow and shell as years are told in the trunks of trees?

VIDEO

■ ■ ■

Meera Nair

Naseer lay beside his wife in the dark and wished he had never seen that video. He blamed it for all the trouble they had been having lately. He knew Rasheeda was angrier than she had ever been in all their years of marriage. Ever since he first asked her the question, she had flung her silence at him. But that was only during the day, in front of the rest of the family. At night, after the children were asleep, she hadn't been so quiet. Now, with his blood cooling, he thought of mollifying her as he had done for many nights lately, and making her understand with clear, logical, unemotional explanations why he needed her to do this for him. She was his wife, for God's sake. He had rights, didn't he?

"Rasheeda! Listen—" he began.

"Fifteen years we've been married and now you want me to do this—this thing!" His wife sat up abruptly, reached for her nightgown, and thrust her head into it.

Oh God, here she goes again.

"Allah, please put some sense into this man. Is this a good thing to ask your wife to do? I've had three of his children and now he asks me for this . . ." Her voice was muffled but the aggrieved tone came through loud and clear.

MEERA NAIR was born in Kerala, India, in 1963. She has an M.A. from Temple University, Philadelphia, and an M.F.A. from New York University, where she was a *New York Times* Fellow. Her debut collection, *Video*, was chosen by the *Washington Post* as one of the best books of 2002. She lives in Brooklyn, New York.

She acts as if she has a Star TV channel blasting directly into Allah's living room. As if He's just waiting there, eager to listen to Madam Rasheeda. Naseer knew the situation was serious, but he couldn't help smiling in the dark.

"Allah, he has gone mad. His body's noise is louder than any voice of reason," Rasheeda continued.

Why does she talk so loud? Naseer twisted his head around to make sure the door to the children's bedroom was closed. She will probably wake the children and his brothers and their wives and his mother the way she's carrying on. Surely his brothers didn't have troubles like his: a recalcitrant wife who sat up in bed at night and belligerently talked to her God.

He looked at her now as she sat marooned in the middle of the bed. The light from the streetlamp filtered through the cotton curtains, turning her broad back pale blue. It was hot and still and Naseer shivered involuntarily as the sweat on his legs dried.

A few nights ago, he had even cited the teachings of the mullahs exhorting Muslim wives to listen to their husbands in all things. But then she was hardly the sort to be frightened by the mullahs, not with her direct line to Allah.

"But Allah, I'll tell you one thing. Never shall I submit to this man's whims. I'll do my duty as a wife, but where is it written that I have to do such things?" Rasheeda's monologue showed no signs of flagging.

That last bit was for his benefit, not Allah's, thought Naseer as he reached for his pajamas at the foot of the bed. And what was this about doing her duty as a wife? When she was in bed with him, she didn't just lie there hating it like some other women he had heard about. He should know. She liked the stroking and rubbing all right. Not that there had been too much of that lately. Take tonight. He hadn't cared to slip his hand down her body and finish her off. He'd asked her right in the middle of it all, gasping the question at her, shameless in his need. But once again she said no, shaking her head from side to side, her eyes tightly closed. So he had ended it quickly and not bothered with her at all. But it wasn't right, and he didn't like it. Naseer shifted uncomfortably on the far side of the bed. He liked his fingers being swallowed up in her slopes and ridges and bumps, in that hidden, miniature landscape all her own. He liked having her face turned up at him, her eyes gone far away to the place where her feeling was building. He liked her giggling, embarrassed because she thrashed about so much. She'd always giggled, ever since the first time, a few months after their wedding when he had finally stumbled on how to pull her across the threshold of fear and nervousness to pleasure.

Her complaints to Allah done at last, Rasheeda lay down, taking care to not brush against him in the muggy dark. Everything had been fine right until the moment he sat down on the black rattan chair in Khaleel's shadowed living room and the video player was turned on.

■ ■ ■

Naseer had gone over to his cousin Khaleel's place to ask his opinion about a new van he wanted to buy. He'd use it to deliver hardware supplies from his store to customers who phoned in their orders. One had to move with the times. Khaleel had his own auto repair shop and could pick out a bad vehicle from a good one by merely listening to the sound of its engine, like a doctor to a patient's chest. Nusrat, his second brother's wife, had called loudly after him from the kitchen window as he opened the gate and stepped out into the street. "It's kababs tonight, so don't be late. You know how Rasheeda won't eat without you."

Adnan, thin and gangly, with Rasheeda's fine, flyaway hair, was playing cricket in the street in front of the house. After a quick sideways glance confirming that his father had stopped to watch him, he gazed seriously at the ball. Old Janaki Ram was sitting on his stoop in his striped undershorts, customary teacup in hand.

"Your boy is hitting four after four today," he said. Naseer smiled and rubbed at his beard to hide his pride.

A few minutes into Adnan's turn at the wicket, Naseer started down the street and Adnan lifted his hand off the bat for a second in farewell. Naseer fought an impulse to tell Adnan to go home before it got too dark. He was fourteen and Naseer didn't want to embarrass him in front of his friends.

The street barely managed to squeeze between the buildings that lined its length. The houses scrunched up against each other and in the shadows of the late evening they seemed to draw closer together, huddling over the street like gossipy old women. The houses around here had hardly changed from when his father's father had first moved in here. Naseer looked up affectionately at the lacy wooden balconies, their curlicued railings still overhung with the saris housewives had forgotten to take inside from the sun. As he walked he greeted the men resting from the heat on the porches, old men who, with the memories of his father still fresh in them, expected him to stop and inquire respectfully about the gout or kidney stones or unemployed son they suffered from.

Here and there transistor radios played softly, the tinny voice of Lata Mangeshkar singing a song about being stricken sleepless by love. One stanza flowed into another, accompanying him from porch to porch all the way down until he turned the corner onto Khaleel's street.

Here the houses around him were newer. Bright whitewashed walls shouldered up against worn stone flared and dimmed in the light of passing cars. A shiny black Fiat jutted out of a gate, taking up street space. Khaleel's place was the last one, just before the street curved away at an angle.

When Naseer got to the door the house was dark, yet he could see the TV's staccato flicker in the living room through the opaque windowpane. At his knock the TV was switched off. Khaleel took his time to answer the door.

"Oh! It's you. I thought it was Baba come back from Madras early," Khaleel said, wiping his palm down the front of his shirt.

Khaleel's father had a twenty-year-old property dispute that came up for a hearing every few years and took him away from home. The old man's tenacity had become a joke in the family.

"I rented a VCR for the day—thought I'd watch some films. You know how Baba is so strict and all, not allowing us to do anything." Khaleel moved aside to let Naseer in.

"All the women kissing men in broad daylight in front of the children, this TV sheevee will destroy the country yet . . ." Naseer mimicked his uncle's disgruntled old man's voice.

Khaleel didn't laugh as he usually did.

Looking at his cousin now, Naseer thought, as he had many times before, how strange it was that all the men in his family were short and wiry and bearded.

"So what're you watching? Anything with Amitabh in it?" Naseer loved the actor. When *Sholay* had been released, he had seen it five times.

"No," Khaleel said. "Come on in and see for yourself."

When Khaleel switched on the VCR, there were two foreigners on the screen—a woman and a man. The man lay on the bed and the woman knelt between his legs. White skin, golden hair, smooth nakedness. She bent down. Then she opened her mouth over him. After one frozen minute of incredulity, everything inside Naseer contracted. He put his hands over his stomach as if to contain the faint tremors he felt starting. He watched the woman, her movements sometimes languid, sometimes frenzied, her cheeks working. It was unbelievable that any woman would admit a man inside her face, to touch her tongue and her teeth and the inside of her cheeks. The two of them seemed bound together in some extreme ecstasy, the man watching the woman looking at him. They took a long time to finish. Watching the man as he arched on the bed, Naseer felt as if he was about to lose control and slide off the chair trembling and moaning—right there in Khaleel's mother's living room with its bright blue carpet and showcase filled with the ceramic dogs her daughter had sent from Dubai.

Naseer got up abruptly and mumbled something to Khaleel about coming back another time. Moving toward the door, Naseer saw himself reflected indistinctly on the TV screen, his shadowy form moving closer as he neared the set. Khaleel barely acknowledged his departure, and his eyes, glittering in the blue light, remained riveted on the screen.

Outside, Naseer leaned against the wall and breathed deeply. He could feel the rough stubble of its surface pressing against his shoulder blades and back through the thin muslin of his kurta. The wall was uncomfortably warm.

He couldn't bring himself to walk just yet, not with this hot weight in him, as if everything inside had descended to settle around his lower stomach and thighs. It was almost pain but not quite, he thought, shocked at the great scrabbling need that stretched down his middle. There had been a time when he was twenty-three and just married to Rasheeda when he could go four times a night. The greediness of a recent virgin—that's what it had been. The need had been a constant unfulfilled thrum in him. Now here it was again, as if someone had plucked hard at a taut string that ran from his head down to his toes.

When he finally pushed himself away from the wall and started walking home, he felt grateful that the old men on the stoops had gone inside to their dinners. He had heard the boys who hung around the college cafeteria snicker about things like this a long time ago, but it had always remained some mythic thing that occurred elsewhere, not in a home, not on an ordinary bed.

Back at home he found Rasheeda in the bedroom getting fresh nappies for the baby.

"Oof, oh! Husband! Stop it! Everybody's waiting for their dinner downstairs and you're doing nonsense things," she laughed, brushing him aside, a little surprised at his sudden ardor. Then she hurried away, the cloth triangles swinging from her hands.

He stood in the middle of the bedroom, reluctant to go down and face the clattering crockery and noisy children in the dining room. What if he rented a VCR and the film himself and got Rasheeda to watch it with him? No. It was impossible—the only TV they owned was in the living room and his mother watched *Understanding the Koran* on it in the afternoons, her silver head nodding sleepily, her fingers slipping now and then off her prayer beads.

At dinner Rasheeda caught him looking at her as she returned from the kitchen with a refill of the kababs and smiled absently in his direction. The oil from the biryani had left her lips slick and shiny. The older children, who had been fed earlier and sent into the living room, fought for control over the TV. Today was Wednesday and that meant *Baywatch*. Naseer knew his brothers would join the kids to watch the serial after dinner.

"Bhai-jaan must have snacked at Khaleel's—he's hardly eating anything at all," Nusrat announced archly. Everyone turned to look at Naseer and he had to nod yes and scramble to name a snack. He got up hurriedly from the table. Farhana stumbled up behind him and stood clutching desperately at his legs for an instant before plopping down onto her behind. She drew breath to wail. He picked her up and went into the living room to order his sons up to bed—he didn't want them watching half-naked women cavort on the beach.

The children bribed and nagged into going to bed and alone with his wife at last, Naseer could feel Rasheeda's pleased astonishment at his impatience.

"Wait, wait, let me turn off the light," she said, reaching for the lamp.

"No. Wait," he said. He put his hands on her hips and pulled her down with him on their bed. Then he pushed himself away from her and took a deep breath. "I saw this video at Khaleel's," he began and stopped. He wanted to say the words carefully, lucidly, even though whole sentences and phrases had jostled in his head all through dinner and the interminable conversation with his brothers afterward. "It was foreign and they were, you know, doing it." He felt embarrassed but determined. This had to be said.

"Allah! Cheee! Toba toba, so *this* is what you were doing," Rasheeda looked at him, her mouth contracting in disgust.

"Listen, I have never seen anything like this . . ." He pressed on. He told her about the video, about the woman and what she had done for the man. Just saying the words excited him. He felt relieved. Now she knew too. The knowledge of this disturbing, fascinating new thing was no longer in his head alone.

Rasheeda moved away and watched him gravely, warily, as he struggled on, trying to explain the moment, the things he'd felt.

In the end, his telling ragged at the edges, he blurted out what he wanted. He knew, even as he stumbled over the words "me" and "mouth," that they came out all wrong, as if they were not meant to be said aloud between them there in their bedroom of fifteen years.

Rasheeda's face contorted in shock and she jumped off the bed as if the sheets were on fire. After a first strangled sound of surprise she stood silent.

"No." She said it quietly. Just that one word, thrown down firmly in front of him without any explanation attached. "No," she said again as she lay down heavily and turned her back to him, her nightdress rustling in the dark. Then, after a long silence in which he willed himself to calmness and was about to fall asleep—"Never."

From then on it had been the same story—every night a repetition of tonight. Her "no" was all-encompassing, leaving him without space to maneuver or argue. All she gave him was that word, and it stood steadfast against all his attempts to wear it down, as unassailable as a mountain made of glass.

Yet every day in his head the blonde woman's mouth stretched itself wide and pink over him and would not let him rest.

■ ■ ■

Sitting behind his counter in the hardware store, Naseer looked at the men who came in asking for hinges and light fixtures and wondered if he was the only man in the world who had spent all these years so pathetically ignorant of this pleasure. Surely all sophisticated men enjoyed it. It was his father's fault for forcing him to marry at twenty-three.

Naseer had wanted other things. Nodding over his college books through the long, humid nights, he had imagined himself, standing bareheaded under a pitiless blue sky, building the dam that would put sweet water in the earthen pots of the villagers and green their fields. Just like Dílíp Kumar in the movie *Naya Daur*. But he was the eldest son, ordained to carry on the family business, and Naseer couldn't bring himself to break his father's heart. So, instead of Naseer, his brothers had become engineers. They were the ones who sat in high-ceilinged government offices, dusty with stacks of forgotten files, and approved plans to build other buildings exactly like the ones they worked in. Now, with his father gone, they accorded him the respect they would have given his father. It made him more distant than ever from them.

Naseer told himself he was deeply unhappy. The craving wouldn't let him be and he felt betrayed by this discontent. He had struggled to be pleased with his lot over the years. Even when he was forced to take on the business, he had taught himself to find satisfaction in the idea of some unknown house, somewhere in the city, growing older, held together by his hinges and latches and nails, the doorknobs pushed open day after day by children and the children's children, the curtains pulled back on his curtain rings. There was a kind of immortality in it. Now Rasheeda had spoiled it all. Why couldn't she behave as wives should?

■ ■ ■

Rasheeda started sending his breakfast out of the kitchen with Aliyeh, the youngest sister-in-law, who kept her sari-covered head bowed respectfully as she quickly set his omelet down on the table, poured his tea, and scuttled back into the kitchen. As if he was a guest who had overstayed his welcome, thought Naseer.

Ever since his mother had ceremoniously handed over the keys to her after Siddiq was born, Rasheeda had run the household. She had slid expertly into the role of matriarch, although she'd been barely thirty-one, as if she had practiced running a household of seven adults, five children, and three maids secretly over the years.

Nowadays, as she walked past him pretending to be busy with the children, he resented that she could always find things to do in the confused bustle of communal living. With his brothers, their wives, or the children always around, he could never get her alone. At night, he was usually asleep by the time she finished ironing school uniforms or discussing tomorrow's menu or whatever it was she did down there to delay coming upstairs.

Some nights he stayed awake, fighting sleep. But the more he tried to persuade her, the more adamantly she condemned this ungodly practice, vociferously calling upon Allah to intervene. Naseer couldn't stop asking either, couldn't just let it be. It's like an unending game, he thought. Only whatever move he made Rasheeda was already there, anticipating him, ready with her defense.

At mealtimes, Naseer imagined he could feel the eyes of the other women on him. Could Rasheeda have dared tell them about what was going on between them? She wouldn't, would she? Violate the quiet yellow warmth of their bed, throw it open for all to peer and comment? His thoughts brought on a great, bursting pressure in his chest.

Yet in the evenings he couldn't wait to get back home. It was a relief just to have Rasheeda somewhere nearby where he could at least watch her face. And her mouth.

When his parents had found him Rasheeda, he had said yes without a demur. It was his mother who had asked the marriage broker, "Do we really want such a highly educated daughter-in-law?" She had been uneasy with the fact that Rasheeda had passed high school. But his father had surprised him by insisting on the match.

Naseer saw Rasheeda on the evening of their wedding only after the Kazi, his interminable mumbling incantations finally done, decreed he could see the bride.

He had gone into the zenana, the women's hall, where she sat surrounded by her relatives and friends, the women whispering and shimmering around him in their yellow and green silks. One of Rasheeda's oldest aunts held a long-handled mirror under her bowed head, carefully angling it inside her dupatta so that he would see only her face and nothing else. He never forgot that first glimpse of her face framed by the veil, the mirror filled suddenly with large sloping eyes and pale pink mouth. Clumsy as he bent over to peer at the mirror, he had stepped on her skirt, and she had put her hand out quickly to tug the material away. Her hand had lain there for an instant, white and forlorn, before it retreated under her heavy, embroidered shawl. A faint, damp mark was left behind on the rose silk where she had touched it, and he was overwhelmed by a sudden compassion. He had wanted to tell her then not to worry—everything would be all right.

Sometime during the all-important first night, Naseer asked her to stand next to him and was surprised to discover that he was only half an inch taller than she was. In spite of her nervousness, she had laughed. The rest had come slowly, in awkward fits and starts. He was gentle with her and she patient with him. Just as he mapped her body, he cataloged her peculiarities—the faint, fair down on her legs, the way her arm pressed the pillow to her face in the morning, shutting out the day for a few minutes more.

Then the children arrived. First Adnan, then Siddiq, and the last one, Farhana, a wriggling, big-bottomed baby girl. Over the years they fit into each other. Now when he reached for her at night it was like driving down the road to the store. He knew when to take the curve, which pothole to avoid, and where to stop. He hadn't wanted much more. Until the woman in the video opened her glistening mouth.

■ ■ ■

It was the twelfth of June and Rasheeda's birthday. It was time they solved this impasse, he decided. He called in the afternoon and told her he had tickets to the latest Aamir Khan movie.

"How many?" she asked, her voice unsmiling on the telephone.

"Just you and me," he said firmly. On the rare occasions they went out to the movies or a restaurant, all the brothers and their wives would go together, piling into the old green van, everyone teasing Aliyeh, the youngest sister-in-law, forcing her onto her husband's lap.

When he went home to pick Rasheeda up, there were giggles from the kitchen. She sat quietly by him until he finished his tea and samosas. A woman's love can be measured by how many samosas she urges you to eat, he thought. She did not force any upon him this time.

"Good samosas. Okay. Let's go, the movie begins at six thirty," he said, all bluff and hearty, hoping she would play along, at least in front of the sisters-in-law, who looked over at them from time to time.

"Why this sudden good mood? This movie and everything?" Rasheeda didn't smile back.

She must know that he was trying to get back to where they were, before she'd stopped talking to him, he thought.

"Well, it is your birthday, isn't it?" he said. He had bought her a present but didn't want to give it to her in front of the other women. Nusrat would have had something catty to say for sure.

Rasheeda didn't answer, but she didn't argue either, just got dressed quickly and walked out with him, flinging a stream of instructions over her shoulder on what to give each of the children for dinner. On her silk sari, flowers spread over her breasts like purple hands.

The entire family came out, crowding around the gate to see them off. Farhana began to cry.

"Enjoy yourselves," Nusrat smirked. Aliyeh bent down and smoothed Rasheeda's sari over her calves one final time.

"It's not as if we're going away for three years, is it?" Naseer grumbled.

"Shh, it's okay. We don't go out alone together every night," Rasheeda said.

■ ■ ■

Back from the movie, Naseer stood in front of the mirror in their bedroom and drew Rasheeda to him.

"We still look nice, don't we?" he said. In her high heels, she was slightly taller than he was.

"I like your shorter beard," she said, so he rubbed it against her cheek. His hands stroked her wide hips and pulled her against him.

"I must do something about my weight," Rasheeda said, but he shook his head.

"Imagine if you were thin and bony like that heroine in the movie. I like large portions." He slipped his hands under her breasts and hefted them in the mirror. Rasheeda's hands came up to pull his away, but she was laughing, her face soft and forgiving.

Later, Naseer did all the things she liked: rubbing her back in widening circles, dragging his thumb slowly across her armpit. He took his time, teasing her, starting her up and slowing her down and starting her up again, until she was desperate and insistent against his palm.

Naseer lay awake for two hours after Rasheeda fell asleep. He felt hollow and dissatisfied. The lovemaking between them had been decent. But he couldn't help wondering how much better it might have been if she had lowered her mouth to him, taken him slowly into her mouth. He hadn't brought it up this time because he was afraid she'd stop talking to him again.

Next to him Rasheeda shifted onto her back. A few minutes later she started snoring softly. Naseer smiled. She was always indignant when he told her she snored, as if it were somehow his fault for even bringing it up. He put his hand on her shoulder. A push onto her side always made her stop. Not that she'd know or wake up. His mother liked to say that Rasheeda could sleep through an earthquake. Yet when Farhana was younger, she'd scramble up even when the baby just burped in her sleep. It was amazing how women could switch themselves off and on like that.

Rasheeda smacked loudly in her sleep and her mouth fell open. Watching her, Naseer felt himself become hard even before the thought was fully formed in his head.

He slid off the bed, his heart pounding. He walked around to Rasheeda's side, fumbling with the string of his pyjamas. Her mouth was slack and agape and she did not wake up even when he knelt awkwardly with his knees next to her face. He leaned far over her head and tried to direct his cock safely inside her mouth. His knees were trembling so hard that he had to grip the headboard with his other hand—even then he slid off the edge of the bed a few times. Then he was in. Was he touching the roof of her mouth?

Just then Rasheeda woke up and stared at him looming over her, his crotch in her face. In her shock Rasheeda's lips closed automatically over him. She made a strangled sound. He thought confusedly of pulling out, but he could not. Not then. Afterward, he couldn't remember when he thought she wouldn't mind or how he held her sleep-dazed head still and ignored her struggling. It was all over in seconds anyway. She got up, ran into the bathroom, and didn't come out for a long time.

I could have touched her brain if I'd wanted to, he thought, feeling excited and mellow at the same time. I was so close to where she lives, not somewhere down there far away; I was more inside her than I've ever been. Then he fell asleep even as he was thinking that he would never be able to sleep.

Rasheeda was still in the bathroom when he woke up in the morning. She hadn't come out even when he left for the store, three hours later. When he came back in the evening, Nusrat, who over the years had developed a certain degree of familiarity with him, took it upon herself to have a word with him. Rasheeda had stayed in the bathroom the whole day.

"She refuses to go to a doctor, says there's nothing wrong with her," she said, looking genuinely worried.

Rasheeda went to the bathroom twelve times the next day. Ten times the third. She did not stop frequenting the bathroom even after a week, yet she refused to see a doctor. Naseer, frightened for her life, even brought one to the house. The doctor, a small, skinny man who looked as if he'd received his degree only months ago, stood nervously in their bedroom, clutching his brown leather medicine bag to his crotch.

"I am fine, Doctor-saab, please go away," Rasheeda yelled from the bathroom.

"Get a *peer*. They know about these strange afflictions, this nonstop diarrhea and suchlike things," the doctor stuttered and fled.

Naseer couldn't bring himself to summon any sorcerers with their magic cures into the house. Maybe she would get better on her own, he thought.

But Rasheeda wouldn't stop. She claimed the outside bathroom for herself. It stood next to the small vegetable garden in the backyard and had been abandoned after the new bathrooms with concealed plumbing were built. She gave herself up to its white-tiled interior at regular intervals. Every hour on the hour, like the BBC. Right in the middle of tying bows in Farhana's hair, she would set her comb down and hurry to the bathroom. Halfway to the greengrocer's down the road, she would stop and head back to the house, overcome by her colon.

Yet nothing else seemed to be the matter with her.

Naseer could hear the sisters-in-law talking and laughing in the kitchen as he ate his breakfast alone. "The whole day she's in the bathroom, but she doesn't look sick or lose weight," they would say. "It is sort of unnatural, don't you think?"

He had to admit it was true. Rasheeda's plump white arms and open luminous face still looked as desirable as ever as she pushed past him, hurrying toward the bathroom.

Since Rasheeda didn't get any sicker, the household adapted quickly, resilient as always. This peculiar new bump was absorbed quickly and ironed flat into its texture. Rasheeda's vigils in the bathroom soon ceased to be an event and became part of her Rasheedaness, protected from comment by their very familiarity and repetitiveness. Even the children tired of shouting "She went ten times today" at him the minute he returned from work. His brothers didn't offer their irritating commiseration anymore.

The children came home from school and went straight to the outdoor bathroom, confident of finding Rasheeda there. They stood outside the door to talk to her.

"Gunjan stole my orange. I hate him," Siddiq would say. He hoarded complaints like sweets.

"The math teacher is horrible. You come and tell the principal that he shouldn't give us so much homework." Farida, Nusrat's little princess, could appeal only to Rasheeda, since her mother didn't believe in coddling children.

"I need ten rupees to pay the PT fees tomorrow." Even Adnan, his initial embarrassment forgotten, leaned against the outer wall of the bathroom and held shouted conversations with her.

"Never mind, I'll give you another orange tomorrow . . . Don't talk about your teacher like that. Have you no respect? . . . Adi, ask your father for the money." She'd answer each of them, serene and inviolate, firmly embedded in their world.

Gradually, as the days became weeks, even the vegetable sellers and fishmongers pushed their handcarts to the back gate near the bathroom and Rasheeda. They would lean over the gate and make their appeals.

"Fresh tomatoes, four rupees, Bibiji. Ekdum fresh!" the vegetable wallah would shout.

"Three is quite enough," Rasheeda would bargain with zest, and they'd give in easily, bemused by this new method of commerce.

"Only for you, Bibiji, don't tell anyone else, only for you three rupees." The transaction concluded, the vegetable wallah or fish wallah would go up to the kitchen and get the payment from Aliyeh or Nusrat.

For a time there was the problem of the keys. As the eldest daughter-in-law, only Rasheeda had the honor of carrying the keys to the pantry and the cupboards. Since the doors were kept carefully locked against the pilfering servants, Aliyeh and Nusrat had to trek down to the bathroom and Rasheeda every time they needed supplies.

One day Naseer saw Nusrat standing outside the bathroom door, tapping her foot impatiently. When she saw him, she muttered under her breath. The next morning Naseer sent a carpenter he knew to cut a small door in the center of the larger one. Rasheeda, temporarily out of the bathroom, said nothing, but she came out from the kitchen to watch him as he planed the sides of the small square of wood and attached hinges and a latch. She offered him tea when he was done, the carpenter reported when Naseer asked him, his voice as studiously casual as Naseer's. Naseer almost started to say that now all Rasheeda had to do was pass the key through the hinged door to whoever came knocking, but he caught himself in time. No need to add to the gossip that was surely circulating already. That evening Rasheeda brought Naseer his tea and set it on the table before him silently. He raised his head eagerly but she walked away before he could say a word.

One Sunday afternoon, when Rasheeda was taking her siesta, Naseer walked around the vegetable garden and, after making sure no one was watching, peered into the bathroom. It was hot inside the dingy room, with a thick, spongy heat that reflected down from the tin roof. On the ledge beside the commode were seashells, a bottle of glue and some pasteboard, someone's half-finished math homework, a recipe in Urdu, and the small transistor radio he had given her. She's destroying our marriage because she wants to listen to Hindi songs in the toilet, he thought. She had metamorphosed even as he watched, like the women in the fairy tales of his childhood, who turned into houris or winged ponies if a man dared to spy on them. Only he was dislodged. Everything else went on as normal. The TV was loud in the living room—the entire family was watching *Star Trek*. He couldn't understand the fascination with weird-looking space travelers. His life was in shambles; there were objects collapsing inside him, shivering apart like a dilapidated house struck by a cannonball, and they were watching TV.

Rasheeda had left his bed the second day after her visits to the bathroom began and now slept with the children, who were delighted; within minutes she had turned it all into an exciting game. Some nights he would hear them giggling behind the door in the other room.

Lying awake at night, he stared at the faintly luminescent square of the window and struggled to form the sentences he wanted to say to her in the morning. He would wake up and she would be gone, sucked into the everyday chaos of the household. He imagined himself marching into the kitchen to drag her out and confront her with the state of their marriage. But the thought of his sisters-in-law looking up aghast at him—the omnipotent, respected elder—made him cringe at the potential embarrassment of it all. In the meantime, Rasheeda continued to orbit around the toilet like a penitent devotee seeking absolution.

As the days passed, even the ladies of the neighborhood resumed their customary afternoon visits. They sat with their teacups in the shade of the tamarind tree in front of the bathroom and talked about other housewives who weren't there. Rasheeda would go in and out of the toilet, and the conversations would continue uninterrupted. Naseer had had the roof of the outhouse tarred so now it was a lot cooler inside.

Miriam, one of the young women down the road, had started dropping in more frequently than the other housewives. Her brand-new husband listened more to his parents than to her, she pouted, the color rising in her cheeks.

"It's as if I am nobody, just someone he can . . . you know . . . and then ignore." She caught the end of her blue dupatta between her teeth and stopped. The listening women sighed sympathetically. They knew.

One afternoon, Rasheeda called Miriam close to the door of the bathroom. Miriam smoothed a few strands of hair away and pressed her ear to the door. All the straining women could hear was a low mutter from inside. Miriam had a secret smile when she left. A few days later Miriam was back—all glow and giggles. Whatever Rasheeda had advised had worked like a charm. He's my little puppy dog now, Miriam crowed.

That was the beginning of it. Later, when there were lines of young women waiting to talk to Rasheeda in the bathroom, the original story was repeated proudly by Miriam. I was the first, she'd say, walking importantly through the small knots of women waiting to recount their troubles to Rasheeda. They told her things they wouldn't tell their best friends. Most of the talk was about husbands and in-laws, the trials and tribulations of living in joint families. Sometimes all some embattled girl wanted to hear was her own voice. They called Rasheeda *Sandaz Begum*—Madam Bathroom—affectionately. All she did was dispense commonsense advice. But the women kept coming back.

To Naseer this meant that he saw Rasheeda even less than before. She spent even more time in the bathroom. There were even more people who demanded her attention now. His mother, disgusted by the goings-on in the backyard, called him into her room and said some sharp words to him.

"Who does your wife think she is? Some kind of guru or what? What is all this khoos-poos whispering with women in the backyard? Would your father have tolerated all this nonsense?" She spat a thick brown stream of tobacco into the silver spittoon beside her bed.

One Saturday, after he had spent an hour watching the women murmur in front of the bathroom from behind the curtains of his bedroom window, Naseer realized that each of these women had probably spoken longer with Rasheeda than he, her husband in the eyes of Allah, had in the past few weeks.

Rasheeda banned consultations on Sunday so she could do whatever she did in the bathroom in peace. When she came out to prepare the evening meal, he cut a four-inch-square out of one of the bathroom's wooden walls and covered the opening with steel mesh.

■ ■ ■

"It will make it easier for you to hear the women's complaints," he told Rasheeda the next day, putting his mouth close to the mesh. He had stood in line behind the women for twenty minutes. When they saw him, they hurriedly veiled their heads and shifted in embarrassment at having this man in their midst, not knowing whether to stay or leave. But he didn't move, not even when his brothers and their wives peeked out at him from the windows of the house. Now the children took their places, some standing on tiptoe to look over the balcony wall. Except Adnan. He had left the house the moment Naseer stepped into the back garden. As he got closer to the mesh, Naseer imagined Rasheeda looking at his face framed in the square, open and naked to her gaze in the sunlight. When he finally peered in, blinking from the sun, he could see only her dim form and little else in the gloom. She turned toward him abruptly, startled by his voice.

"Just wanted to make it easy for you to hear the women's complaints," Naseer repeated. She looked at him and said nothing. He thought he saw her nod. After a few moments Naseer left his place in the line and walked back to the house.

At dinner that night, Rasheeda reached across the table and heaped a ladleful of rice onto his plate. When Naseer looked up at her, she was looking back at him. Before she turned her face away to answer one of the children, he was quite sure he saw her mouth twitch gently at the corners.

FIESTA OF THE DAMNED

■ ■ ■

Han Ong

Forty-four, Filipino, a failure, the American returner Roger Caracera was ferrying his father's body back to Manila. He would deliver it to the festive grief of the Caracera clan, who would make sure, before interring it into an awaiting hole at Quezon City's Kalayaan Cemetery, to provide services that would give the man one last taste of the family's money.

It was on the plane, his father's coffin in the cargo hold (to the back? at the side? below them?) that Roger Caracera'd first heard of it.

■ ■ ■

Harvey Keitel on the very flight they were on, himself en route to the Philippines.

He was about to shoot a movie financed by Twentieth Century-Fox called *Fiesta of the Damned*, based on the very successful book of the same name which recounted the final heroic hours preceding the rescue of American survivors of the Death March to Bataan. His costars, variously on their way or awaiting Mr. Keitel's appearance in Manila, were John Travolta, Robert De Niro, Samuel L. Jackson, James Caan, and Bert Convy. This was the fifth production in as many months to be

HAN ONG is the author of a first novel, *Fixer Chao*, as well as a playwright. His plays include *Watcher*, *Middle Finger*, *The Chang Fragments*, *The L.A. Plays*, and *Swoony Planet*. He was born and educated in the Philippines, and came to the United States as a teenager. He has been awarded a MacArthur Fellowship. "Fiesta of the Damned" is excerpted from a forthcoming novel entitled *Beneficiary* (working title).

shot in the Philippines; the others also based on best-selling accounts and regurgitating, as *Fiesta of the Damned* hoped to, one more episode of World War II by which could be memorialized a peak period of American manhood, filled with decisive action unencumbered by feminine ambiguity; and whose tagline was therefore, as Roger Caracera knew, having had more than a passing acquaintance with the same sentiment voiced by bar geezers he'd sat next to over the course of a drinking lifetime: Ahhh, Those Were the Days . . .

Direction would be courtesy of a twenty-three-year-old kid genius best known as an acolyte, and archival overseer of the films, of the late Stanley Kubrick. He was also a quarter-Filipino and had cast the aging Filipino superstar Nora Aunor and the newcomer matinee idol Arsenio "Paduy" Macapagal in sizable supporting roles in the interests of flushing the Philippines out of the narrative and historical background into, well, if not exactly the foreground, then, the *"ummm, sea-level and not sunken like buried treasure."* Miss Aunor and Mr. Macapagal would be playing a mother and son caught in the maws of the Japanese-American conflict, the former an unwilling whore to the Japs and the latter a messenger between the insurgent anti-Jap native forces and the American army who, through the course of the story, is caught and forces his beloved mother to trade her freedom for his life. Until they are rescued near the end by men led by Harvey Keitel playing General Douglas MacArthur.

Any of the information not available through the gossip that passed down from first class and which was further augmented by the thrilled stewardesses could be found in the in-flight magazine in an article bearing the title "Philippines: Hot Hot Hot!," which, besides its comprehensive coverage of the recent popularity of the Philippines as a Hollywood outpost, was pocked again and again by the mystery-giving phrase *"jungles of the Philippines."* Repeatedly, even when he was forced by a sudden seething that was a compound of bitter humor and voluptuous horror to read no further and only skim the article, the phrase kept snagging his eyes. Its reference point, the center from which it radiated, turned out to be the rerelease in the upcoming year of the "cinematic masterpiece" *Apocalypse Now*, this time with half an hour of extra footage and newly retitled *Apocalypse Now Redux.*

The film had been shot "in the jungles of the Philippines." During production there had been "delays exacerbated by storms in the jungles of the Philippines." Martin Sheen, one of the principals, suffered a "heart attack in the middle of the jungles." Budget overruns costing "enough to transform the jungles into whole cities." Cast and crew "stranded in the jungles of . . ." "Beautiful and treacherous Philippine jungles." "Napalm dropped on the jungles of . . ." Marlon Brando finding a "counterpart to his beloved Polynesia in the jungles of . . ." "Conradian habitats of the provinces of the Philippines": reading which, Roger Caracera imagined whole acreages of trees like an endless expanse of paper towels having to sop up and sop up a steady stream from the cut veins of American guilt. Had he seen the movie?

Yes. He remembered now. He'd been on coke and speed at the time. And the movie had kept fucking with his high. That was all he'd remembered of it. He'd gone having heard it was a great movie to trip on, much like *2001: A Space Odyssey* and that Disney movie with Mickey Mouse as Merlin the Magician had been for previous generations. And instead he'd been rewarded with the debut of the gremlin that had, from that moment on, taken up residence directly over his lungs, sitting on his chest with the sole intention of crushing the breath out of him.

Looking up from the magazine, he saw the man seated next to him flashing a smile. It turned out that the man was among the crew headed for the *Fiesta of the Damned* set in Manila.

■ ■ ■

Forty-four, Filipino, a failure, the American returner was restored to his childhood home in Makati, where he slept in his long-ago bedroom. Outside the windows of the room, which was on the second floor, was a calamansi tree. The leaves and branches had begun to scrape at the windows with regularity, vanes announcing the arrival of the monsoons. At night they made a sound that brought him all the way back to childhood. Their insistent *krrk-krrk* against the steel guards added to the shadows the lights on the property caused them to cast on the walls of his room gave them the same power they had had when he was a boy: giant skeleton fingers endeavoring to claim him for the devil.

His father, wanting to pacify him, had once ordered the tree to be pruned. About the boy it was known that he had an imaginative and artistic nature, perhaps overly so.

It was a rude shock to be recalled to the tenderness of his enemy. Across the tunnel of years his father's act was revealed to be a grand gesture, something which he couldn't have realized then, and which, knowing it now, was weighted with an extra pain: he hadn't deserved it; and his father had been fully justified, in later years, in his rancor against Caracera, forever having to tabulate the costs of such largesse against the meager shows of sentient gratefulness from a boy locked inside the room of his private resentments.

■ ■ ■

Three klieg lights were stood up along the periphery of a vacated shot, shining the diffuse light of an overcast, rainy day with the help of paper filters—exactly the kind of day outside the Manila Hotel. The day's shoot was to have involved General MacArthur's dalliance with a local beauty at the hotel. Now, it seemed, Keitel had gone AWOL.

At the center of the lit area was the door to a room and surrounding it a little patch of wall and corridor. But whatever human scene was supposed to be enacted there had been temporarily postponed while various technicians—untrustworthy-looking men wearing the Hawaiian shirts and cargo shorts of a perpetual lunch break/vacation—futzed and fumbled with the various metal boxes and wires and bulbs and hinged pieces of equipment that were omnipresent and imposing, as at a scene of a scientific experiment, so that Roger Caracera came to understand, implicitly, that the entire moviemaking process was about the mastery of gadgetry and that art, if it happened, would at best be on the sly. The equipment predominated and the actors were to be rushed in, milked of their functions, and then rushed out. In fact, the actors, once commandeered to the set, would be expected to behave like machines: replicating their performances take after take; breakdowns were allowed for the machines but not for them (it was expected that this rule would not apply to Keitel and the other big "names" and that they could, just like the technicians, take their time to finish up their endeavors). The schedule, though tight, allowed for both the malfeasances of these lead actors (whose erraticness was an extension of their gifts) and of the technicians (who were protected by all-powerful unions). The latter moved their pieces of equipment noisily, in a way that made clear their control of the set. Among them was the guy who'd invited Caracera to watch the day's shooting, but who had not taken notice of his guest sitting in a corner on a canvas chair with a backrest that read CRAFT SERVICES.

Taking advantage of the break, the young director, who looked like an angleworm, twerpy and overcaffeinated, was busying himself with the press. HBO had a camera crew waiting. So did PBS. Meanwhile, Twentieth Century-Fox had also sent their own camera team and they were now being treated to some serious disquisition by the young man who, to his credit, looked unoverwhelmed. He answered questions with sweeping hand gestures like a majordomo indicating all that he sat on and smoothly controlled. It occurred to Caracera that the boy must know that the interview footage—along with the dailies—would be screened for his bosses and so had to act up to his role as, in effect, overseer of a budget in the tens of millions. Surely they were looking for some reason to fire him and he would not let them have the satisfaction? Surely his age and relative lack of experience had been a source of worry to them from the very beginning? Perhaps he'd gotten on the helm through the backing of one of the stars—who'd hoped that the young man's relationship with Kubrick would roughly be tantamount to the passing of the torch of genius to this generation; and who, furthermore, never having had the chance to work with the master, would get the chance now, at least by association?

Art was one thing, however; economics and accounting, another. The boy was trying to overcome the undeniable physical fact of his boyishness with a lowered voice and an assurance to his bosses that they were all on the same track and that the movie he would deliver would be one long action sequence; however, this message was couched in counterproductive vocabulary that would be sure to send the executives back on the lot after their eject buttons. The young man talked of things being "perspectival" and "unmediated by the tangle of cerebration and sophistry," and of the episode being depicted in the movie as an "opportunity for the reinstatement of a kind of headlong and heedless trajectory that had its apotheosis in the fifties, say, with the movies of men like Ford and Fuller."

Clearly, thought Caracera, restraining himself from going over to advise the man, the young director should save his choicest bullshit for the PBS crew. While for his bosses, his language should match up with his stated intention: straightforward and unencumbered.

Seated on both sides of Caracera were people with tape recorders and steno pads in their laps, awaiting their turn. In the meantime they were brushing up on questions they intended to ask and on background notes for the production, which they'd been provided by a female assistant. Caracera had one too. He'd been mistaken for one of them and had been handed a sheaf of these notes, which he now went over lazily.

He expected, for some reason, to find the phrase "jungles of the Philippines" in these notes and was surprised to be told instead of how the production had had to choose between Vietnam and the Philippines for its location. The Vietnamese, Caracera figured, were returning the favor for *Apocalypse Now* when the Philippines had been chosen to stand in for their country.

So the Vietnamese government had offered free accommodations and other incentives to woo the production. The burgeoning Vietnamese tourist trade desired the further boost of a Hollywood connection. But in the end, the Philippines had been where four of the last five Asian-themed U.S. movies were shot, and, on the strength of that recommendation, had won out over Vietnam.

This seemed the only thing of interest to be gleaned from the notes, which were otherwise filled with biographies of the personnel involved, a plot synopsis, and a brief historical sketch of U.S. intervention in the Philippines—culminating in a jingoistic defense of American foreign policy, which seemed to Caracera more wishful and nostalgic than anything.

Suddenly, the journalists who had been busy scribbling into their pads looked up.

Activity was starting up again. This was indicated by the sudden hush that was heard to descend, as if a machine whose job it was to create an enveloping blanket of noise had broken down. It was the same kind of silence, awed and a little fearful, that ought to be followed by the entrance of a dignitary. Keitel, perhaps, or his cohorts. But the white actors dressed in military garb were not known to any of the people Caracera was grouped with. With them, walking several steps behind and apart, were Filipinos. Only after they too stepped into the hot ring of the lights, which were being turned up, was it understood that they were actors, needed for the postponed shot. At everyone's tails, managing their movements, was a Filipino production assistant wearing an overlarge T-shirt that read, comically, UNICEF, above low-slung, wide-hemmed black jeans. He gave the impression of having not much to do and was trying to do it as visibly as he could.

Names were being called out. A bunch of phrases, including "Quiet on the set." Here came the young ringleader, conferring with his director of photography in a loud technicalese, which he gave the impression of enjoying, knowing perhaps that it shut out everyone else.

The actors were being arranged by the production assistant to flank the doorway where the camera was pointed. Military men and some Filipino insurgents, it looked like, waiting for the general to finish up with his Filipina beauty—who, if his history lessons sufficed, Caracera remembered to have been the gift from a grateful nation to the victorious liberator.

Not once did the director check up on his actors. Instead, his style was to have another assistant yell "Action" for him, and then look not at the live scene but rather at its magnetized ghost in a monitor that flickered in front of where he sat and which was attached to the camera through a series of wires snaking on the floor.

Before Caracera, the scene being played was at once ordinary, the dialogue businesslike, and yet, because of the knowledge of its double being preserved for posterity, highly compelling.

Not once were the Filipino actors heard to utter anything until near the end, and only one of them seen to open his mouth: "Yes, boss."

The scene was ordered "Cut!" by the same assistant. Once more, the director and DP were seen to consult. Once more, "Action!"

Turning to the screen this second time, where the image literally flickered and pulsed, and the actors were rendered bluish, Caracera noticed an X mark at the very center, and to demarcate the edges of the film frame, a square drawn in a thin line that reminded Caracera of a spiderweb. Again and again, the scene was ordered reperformed. Not once was the camera moved for another angle. What was so special about the scene—which involved the military men conferring with each other, waiting for the general to finish with his native paramour? Unable to wait any longer, they finally entrust the sentinel's duty to one of three Filipino men, leaving to attend to other matters. The curious sameness of scene after scene, during which breaks the director did not offer a single adjustment, owed to an obsessiveness Caracera found hard to account for. Perfectionism, to be traced back to the young director's apprenticeship with the notoriously exact Kubrick?

Two of the three Filipinos—the ones with no lines—were positioned to the rightmost side, so that their bodies jutted outside the excluding web.

"Yes, boss." Yet again. "Yes, boss."

The modifying word before the word "story," in this instance, being "historical." And so Filipinos instructed to perform as "history" has shown them to. Acquiescent, subjugable. Could this be what the overflow of pride in the Filipino press regarding a new, strengthened amity between this country and the United States, exemplified by this fifth in what was hoped would be an ongoing series of movies, was about? "Yes, boss."

Roger Caracera himself had no talent for acquiescence and at its sight received the prickled flesh of fear, repugnance. The man he had come back to help bury had been a bully, with whom he had had no word for eighteen years. In one moment, picking up the phone, eighteen years had gone up in smoke.

There had been thick curtains pulled over the windows of one of the bedrooms in his sister's San Francisco house, mansion, really, where the man lay dying. Only a thin wand of light was being let in, and this light had seemed to Roger Caracera, the prodigal son, the black star of his father's disappointed life, to have been like a surgical finger of blame that the man, by choosing to be sequestered in that room, had been hoping to escape entirely. He felt just like this light, an intruder from the outside world disturbing the quiet scene of not-yet-death. With him in the room, looking on with tentativeness, was his older brother and older sister, the two successful children of the union of Jesus and Teresa Caracera. They were their father's children—go-getters, moving with American upward thrust while retaining their Filipino obedience, their filial seriousness. The brother a banker, the sister a pediatrician. In them, the wealth of their Philippine adolescence was carried over, perpetuated, even bettered.

Roger Caracera was more his mother's son. And the woman, from whom the father had wrested his children to move abroad, was now left rotting in some mental institution somewhere in Manila. The son shared in his mother's erraticness, her lack of ambition. Next to his siblings, this lack, this juniorness, was a refutation.

There was the dead man in his bed. It was one of those hospital beds that you could adjust to make the patient sit up. There was the dead man sitting, looking at him as he slowly, fearfully made his way to the dead man's bedside.

He didn't know what to think. His mind was blank. He was conscious only of the room being no place and any place at the same time, aware that this dreaded reunion was taking place exactly as he'd imagined it once, long ago: inside the abstract realm of imagination, with the antagonist of his life helpless, deprived of the strongest weaponry of words, so that he, Caracera, was free to decide the outcome of the encounter to his satisfaction, to triumph, in other words. And yet, Caracera had felt untriumphant, reduced to mere tears. The same tears that were on his brother's and sister's faces. The three of them knew the general meaning of the scene—a conciliation, a tying up—but he felt that there were deeper secrets that eluded them. They knew that the man was dying and that, by living, by not following him to the grave, they had finally become, too late in their lives, their own selves. They were crying for the tardy knowledge as much as for the man's suffering.

The man had thin greenish tubing up both nostrils. This tubing was connected to an oxygen tank that had a circular meter with a needle inside it that went up and down with each tiny breath. As Caracera approached he noticed that the needle went up and down with alarming speed, as if the man was afraid Caracera meant to harm him. Caracera's sister Socorro had rushed to the dead man's side, coddling him. But he had hit—more like patted, actually—her hands away.

Caracera noticed too the man's arm, which had been stabbed into to connect him to two IV drips: one to kill pain, the other to deliver food. There were a few other bruises in the vicinity of where the IVs joined his arm and Caracera surmised that perhaps the man had tried to disentangle himself previously. This had made him break into more tears. He didn't know why it should be this and not anything else.

Made weak by pain and further slackened by medication, his father's mouth could not move enough to form coherent words, only sounds—communicating the cumulative weariness of waiting for death. So all the talking had been on Caracera's end.

What did he have to say?

Lies, mostly. Compelled by the occasion to embellish on his threadbare accomplishments. He taught writing at Columbia University—having failed as a writer, he had had no choice but to lower himself to instructorhood; and, adjudging from that sequence of compromise, had been compelled to stay unhappy for the rest of his life. And though he had the courage to confess what he did for a living, he tried to improve upon the paltry reality by inventing successes for his students—youngsters beginning to be published in famous magazines and acquiring book contracts—which by implication traced back to him.

His father was unable to reply to any of his assertions, but the man seemed to be grateful and maybe even a little proud.

During his time away from the family, Caracera had become a true adult, that was to say, cynical, unremorseful, self-propping, oblivious to the past, and perhaps a little destructive in the present; nourished by the distance, he had become the perfect nobody—not father, not brother, not husband, and certainly not son—but in the end, it was in his father's power to give to Caracera's "accomplishments" a sudden reverse image, a revelatory, shaming flip side: so that he was not, in fact, nobody, but rather conventionally, comfortingly (to the dead man) and sadly (to himself), "somebody": a success by his attachment to, not his separation from, people, because look, wasn't he, by his own admission, connected to his students, the effector, fatherlike, of their success in the world?

Twenty minutes into their first meeting in nearly two decades, the man had expired, dropping his head away from the side where his children had gathered, and towards the curtained window, as if finally able to face the evaluation he had been so afraid of all his life.

"Yes, boss."

Yet again the scene was replayed. The white soldiers conferring and while they did, the Filipinos—were they actually native insurgents? could they be hotel staff?—waited. Waited for the one line.

It was not only because of his father's death that he had dreaded his return to this country. Now, in front of him a veritable demented show created by a rewind-happy zombie, he knew another, more compelling reason.

"Yes, boss." "Jungles of the Philippines."

It had only taken him two short days to reacquaint himself with the overwhelming humility, the subjugability of the countrymen around him—on the streets, as he passed them by in the family car; and today. They evinced a palpable quality of Catholic prostration too that he had long since surpassed. That had been why reading "Philippines: Hot Hot Hot!" had been so mortifying. He had felt sure that, after having been spoiled by the States, he too would succumb to using the same imagery that he had regarded with such suspicion in that article, was sure, knowing well his lack of fortitude, that he would, made aghast by reacquaintance with this country, turn into the newest shiny exemplar off the assembly line of the Ugly American.

Sooner or later he would have to face his relatives and he would have to say to them, as Harvey Keitel would in a penultimate scene in *Fiesta of the Damned*: *I have returned*. Would it be understood that he was speaking only for his father?

"Yes, boss."

"Cut!"

Already he was practicing the answer he would be required to provide the family, to what was sure to be their ceaseless questioning. His favorite word, which his family, especially his father, had given him many occasions to use.

Are you back for good?

No.

But you'll be able to stay a while?

No.

Don't you miss life here?

No.

How soon are you going?

As soon as he's buried.

But aren't you curious to find out what your father has left you in his will?

No.

SHIPS IN THE NIGHT

▪ ▪ ▪

Ruth Ozeki

Baby slept in the eaves, under the rafters. Her room was shaped like a wedge of cake on its side, so that when she lay in bed and looked up at the steeply pitched ceiling, she felt as though a lid were being slowly lowered on top of her. She had grown so tall in the months since they moved to Vancouver that now, if she pointed her toes, the tops of her toenails scraped against the angle. When she brought this up at breakfast, Guy's answer to the problem was,

"*C'est facile, Bébé*. We will chop off ze legs."

Cayenne frowned. "Don't tease her," she said. "He's just kidding, Baby."

Guy whinnied though his nose. He was smoking a joint, which was all he ever had for breakfast. Baby ate dry Froot Loops from a bowl because Cayenne had forgotten the milk.

"Oh, lady! *Comme tu est bête*," Guy said, taking a toke so that the words came out strangled. "Not ze legs of *Bébé*. Ze legs of ze bed."

But Cayenne didn't get it. Guy rolled his eyes and exhaled. "I will cut a few inches from ze legs of ze bed," he explained through the smoke. "So we will gain in length what we lose in height."

Born in New Haven, Connecticut, in 1956, RUTH OZEKI began her career in the arts as a set designer for low-budget horror films, and later swapped severed limbs and exploding heads for the more subtle horrors of Japanese television production. She has made several award-winning independent films, including *Halving the Bones* and *Body of Correspondence*. Her first novel, *My Year of Meats*, evokes the darkly comic chaos of commercial meat and media production. Her second novel, *All Over Creation*, is about potatoes.

Guy had been in engineering school until he did too many psyche-delics and dropped out, sometime back in the sixties. He was older than Cayenne. He was not Baby's father, but she liked him. She liked the way he pronounced her name. *Bébé*. His name was pronounced *Gee* because he was <u>Q</u>uebecois.

Baby's bed was just a mattress on a sheet of plywood, supported with two-by-fours that Guy had nailed together after she'd seen the rat on the floor. He had drilled holes into the plywood, "So it can *breeze*," he said. They were living off his unemployment checks while Cayenne worked on her romance novel. It was going to make them a lot of money, Cayenne said, and Baby believed her. Cayenne didn't know about engineering, but she knew about romance. She'd named herself for a pepper, after all. It would look good on the jacket of her book—no last name, just *Cayenne*, in big, raised gold letters. They'd been living with a guitar player in El Paso, and every-thing was very romantic—*muy caliente*—until it wasn't anymore, so they moved on.

■ ■ ■

"You don't have to take that shit," Cayenne said, gripping Baby's wrist. "Remember, you don't have to take it lying down." She pushed Baby into the front of the Chevette and slammed the door, then she went back for their stuff. Baby watched through the car window as Cayenne humped the broken suitcase across the yard. Her long India-print skirt dragged in the dust and tangled around her ankles. One of the suitcase latches came undone, spilling some of the contents—a torn shawl, a platform sandal. For a moment Cayenne looked like she was going to cry, but she picked up the sandal and threw it at the car, instead.

The skin on Baby's arm hurt. There were red marks like a rope burn and a smear of blood from the cut on Cayenne's knuckle. Baby licked her thumb and rubbed away the blood, then she spread the road atlas across her bare knees. The cover was sticky from spilled Coca-Cola. She fingered the tattered pages.

The car slumped as Cayenne got in. Baby opened to the map of the whole United States and waited, but Cayenne just sat there, frozen, clutching the steering wheel and staring straight ahead. Her hand was still bleeding. There was a bruise below her eye.

Baby traced the nation's veins, its blue and red arteries, with a dirty finger. "Where are we going, anyway?" she asked, finally.

Cayenne sighed, let her forehead drop to the wheel. "I'm sick of the whole damn country," she muttered. They sat there for a while longer. Suddenly she sat up. "Hey!" she said. "Canada! What do you think?" She turned the key in the ignition and gunned the engine. "Buckle up, Baby. We're going straight to the top!"

■ ■ ■

When they first moved in with Guy, into the little wooden house, it was exceedingly romantic. "Oh, Baby," Cayenne whispered. "What do you think? Fuck America, right? Canada is *awesome!*"

She gripped Baby's hand and pulled her up the narrow stairs, opening every door. The floor creaked and the lintels were crooked. It used to be the carriage house, built behind the main house where the Chinese landlord lived. Baby's window looked out the back, down into the wide alley that the carriages once used. Now it was mostly delivery trucks and garbage trucks and Dumpsters.

Cayenne gazed out past the dirty rooftops, splattered with seagull shit, to the ragged, snowcapped ridge just visible beyond. "The vast north!" She sighed. "Can't you just feel it? Look at those mountains! We got room to *breathe* here, Baby."

Her eyes were like hot stars on Baby's horizon.

■ ■ ■

Baby remembered the stars.

"It's all about experience," Cayenne said, as she drove the battered Chevette through the star-filled desert night. "Real life experience. A writer needs that, don't you think?"

Baby nodded.

"I've got it figured out, see? The heroine is from Texas. From El Paso. Maybe she's the daughter of a rich oilman, who falls in love with a musician . . . What do you think?"

Baby turned to face her mother, scrunching down in the seat and stretching out her legs so that her feet were in Cayenne's lap. The window knob dug into her backbone. "Is she beautiful?"

"Of course," Cayenne said. "Is your door locked?"

Baby twisted and punched down the button. "How beautiful?"

"Extremely beautiful. The most beautiful girl in all of Texas. She's got flaming red curls and a temper to match. Like you, Baby. She gets her looks from her mother."

Cayenne's profile was the only thing that stayed the same—her face, encircled by the moon and the stars, framed against a landscape and blurred by speed.

"The musician guy . . . is he a guitar player?"

"Hmm," Cayenne said, tilting her head. "That's a good idea. Do you think he should be?"

"Yeah," Baby said. "A guitar player creep."

Cayenne glanced over at Baby. "You glad we left El Paso, hon?"

Baby nodded.

"Well, I think you're right," Cayenne said. "We needed some distance. You can't write about a place until you leave it behind."

■ ■ ■

The old glass pane in Baby's window looked like it was melting. When she knelt on her mattress and stared down into the alley below, everything seemed molten, a wavering underwater world with big steel Dumpsters like rusting shipwrecks, and girls like gaudy fishes flitting up and down.

It was called the Stroll, Guy told her. At one end was Hung Lung Enterprises, a chicken-processing plant that filled the alley with the sweet stink of death when the wind came warmly off the Burrard Inlet. The seagulls rode the pockets of air, perching on splintery wooden poles that rose and tilted like a forest of crosses. Dotted with ceramic insulators, their trussed limbs supported the great looping strands of high-voltage wire, heavy and rubber-coated, that attached the house to the grid, just below Baby's window. The wood on the sash had swollen, leaving the window stuck slightly ajar, so that when the wind blew off the alley, Baby could lie on her back in bed and watch the curtain lift and settle above her.

Cayenne had made the curtain out of a worn housedress that she'd found at the Union Gospel Mission Thrift Store.

"Look, Baby!" she said. "It's antique! Can't buy fabric like this anymore." She held the dress up to herself. "I don't know. Do you think it's too domestic?"

The thin yellowed fabric was decorated with blue cornflowers and smelled like the thrift store, of vinegar and mold. When puffs of wind billowed the curtain above Baby's face, it was like looking up a mother's dress, except that mothers didn't wear housedresses anymore. They wore sweatpants in pastel colors and plus sizes. Cayenne had pointed out the moms, crossing America. They had names like Madge and Dot and Gert, Cayenne whispered. Terrible names. Not romantic.

■ ■ ■

Standing in line at a convenience store late one night, waiting to pay for gas, Baby found a little booklet called, What to Name Your Baby.

"What's the Texas girl's name?" she asked.

Cayenne was looking at a People *magazine, but now she put it down. "Let me see that." She flipped through the booklet, then pretended to return it to the rack. Instead, she slipped it into Baby's pocket and gave her a quick hard smack on the head.*

"I thought I told you to stop touching everything," she said loudly, so the cashier would hear. "Get out to the car and wait for me."

As she pulled out from the parking lot, Cayenne reached over and rumpled Baby's hair. "What a team!" she said.

"That hurt," Baby said, sulking, but Cayenne just laughed and flicked on the dome light. "Go on," she said. "Start with the L's."

Baby flipped through the booklet. "Liz?"

"Boring."

"Laverne?"

"Cheap." Cayenne frowned. "L's should be sensual. Like love." She curled up her tongue, touched the tip to her teeth, and Baby could hear it vibrate. "Can't you hear the difference, Baby?"

■ ■ ■

In the alley, Baby watched the girls as they scratched through the gravel. "Like chickens," Guy said. "Looking for stash." Couch grass cracked the asphalt in patches, grew up and then went to seed. The girls came in from the prairie provinces, Guy told her. They were not much older than Baby, from places like Moose Jaw or Cut Knife or Qu'Appelle.

"C'est la ville terminale," Guy croaked through the smoke he held in his lungs. "It iz Terminal City, Bébé! End of ze line."

Across the alley, rickety wooden steps led up to the Golden Happiness Printing Company, and underneath, to the clatter of the presses, the girls did things with men. Rhythmic. Fast. Sometimes they did it behind the Union Gospel Mission, on broken sofas that leaked stuffing in tufts.

When a storm came in from the Pacific and rattled the glass, Baby lay in bed and listened to the electrical poles creak. The wires swung like heavy rigging on a pitching ship. Now and then, she would hear the rat in the wall, and when it rained, the girls in the alley would start to swear, their high heels clicking faster as they ran to the eaves for shelter. The summer Baby turned fourteen, she felt the restless breath of the alley play across her face as she watched the curtain swell.

Sometimes when Guy was doing a deal downstairs, Cayenne would come and lie on her bed, and they would gaze out the window together. "It's like we're princesses," Cayenne whispered. "Imprisoned in a tower while the whole world passes us by."

Down below, homeless men pushed shopping carts across the gravel. They crawled over the Dumpster's tall steel walls and dropped down inside. When too many went in at once, a fight would break out. Like a tangle of rats, they rose to the surface, wrestling for a prize—a torn sweater, a broken toaster.

"Look at that," Cayenne said, leaning into Baby. She cupped her chin in her hands. "What do you suppose he wants with that toaster?"

Under the streetlight, a hooker in a Spandex tube dress was doing jumping jacks in stiletto-heeled shoes. Her ankles wobbled and she toppled off the edges.

"She's doing aerobics," Baby said. "She's got a needle in her mouth."

"That's enough," Cayenne said, trying to close the curtain, but Baby opened it again. The girl hiked her dress up to her waist and folded over like she was hinged.

"No," Cayenne said, pulling Baby back from the window. "Don't look."

But Baby shook her off. The girl was bending over, doing something down below, then her knees buckled and she plopped down, bareassed, in the gravel. Her legs were splayed, and the hypodermic needle stuck out from her groin beside the patch of pubic hair, but she had already forgotten.

Cayenne sat at the edge of the bed. Her shoulders were slumped, and she rubbed her temples. "I'm going back to work," she muttered.

"What about your novel?" Baby asked.

Cayenne looked up quickly. "That's what I meant. What did you think I meant?"

"Nothing," Baby said. "You said work. I—"

Cayenne held up her hand. "I don't want to know." She got to her feet and stood in the doorway. They listened to the whore moaning, *Come on! Come to Mama* . . .

Cayenne's voice was low and charged. "I would *never* do that," she said. She crossed the hallway to the bedroom that she shared with Guy. After a while, Baby heard the clack of the typewriter keys. Slow, one letter after another. Then a pause. Barely a word even. Certainly not a long word. One worth any money at all.

■ ■ ■

A narrow patch of kitchen garden, which had once been a backyard lawn, separated the carriage house from the landlord's house in front. On one side lived the Wongs, and on the other side lived the Fongs, and the landlord was a lady named Lily. They were always screaming at each other in Cantonese across the chain link that separated their gardens. Lily lived with her mother and a man who, Guy insisted, was a former Politburo cadre from the Guang Dong Province and had once shared a bottle of *mi jiu* with Li Ping.

"He's Triad now," Guy said. "A real gangster."

"*Ce n'est pas vrai,*" Cayenne said. She was trying to learn a little French from Guy so she could use it in her novel. She had typed out the first chapter, and now she was reading it at the kitchen table. Next to her was an advertisement she had torn from a magazine for a company that published novels. Cayenne was going to send them her chapter.

"It iz the truth," Guy protested. "Mrs. Wong told me so."

"She doesn't speak English," Cayenne said. "And you don't speak Cantonese."

"*Kam tin tin hei hou . . .*" Guy sang.

"What's that?" asked Baby, giggling.

"*It iz a fine day today.* What do you say, Bébé? *Hoi sam ma?*"

"I don't understand."

"*Are you happy?*" Guy said. "Say it. *Hoi sam ma?* It means, *Do you open your heart?*"

Cayenne rustled her pages and rolled her eyes. "I'm trying to concentrate," she said.

■ ■ ■

Lily worked at Hung Lung Enterprises, boning chickens. Mrs. Wong got up early and cut the guts out of fishes. Her garden was overgrown with vegetables—*bok choy, yu choy*, snap peas and chards. She dug her kitchen scraps right into the earth. Whenever Baby left the little house, she had to pass Mrs. Wong, squatting outside with her sleeves rolled up, doing something wet and violent to food. She scrubbed black earth off white radishes as fat as legs, cracked ribs of pork, scaled red snappers for luck, decapitated turtles for longevity. Sometimes when Baby went out to buy cigarettes for Cayenne, Mrs. Wong would wipe her forehead with a bloodstained knuckle and call out to her—*You! You!*—hoisting herself to her feet and parting the tendrils of the pea vines that climbed up the chain link. She had a gap-toothed smile that squeezed her eyes into crescents as she thrust things into Baby's hands—a dusty bunch of mustard greens, the head of a cabbage. Guy told Baby she must always accept the gift and always say thank you. She could say, "*Tao-che,*" which meant, "I appreciate you many times."

One day, Mrs. Wong hauled a garbage bag from the house. The bag smelled raw and leaked blood, and Baby recoiled into the hydrangeas.

"*You! You!*"

Baby took the bag, holding it away from her. "*Tao-che,*" she remembered to whisper, and Mrs. Wong smiled and nodded.

"What the fuck—?" Cayenne said, as blood dripped on to the linoleum.

"Fish heads!" Guy cried. He pushed back his chair. "It's Chinatown, Bébé!" He and Cayenne had been weighing marijuana, but now he cleared the table, flung open the cabinets and started pulling out spices—star anise, dried dates, bone-white shark cartilage. The fish heads slithered from the garbage bag, sticky and wet. An hour later Guy lifted the thick lid from a steaming clay pot, ladled out large bowls and set them on the table. Baby stared at her fish head, resting on a nest of noodles. It stared balefully back.

"Eat!" Guy cried, poking his chopsticks into the fish's cheek.

Steam rose off the bowl, into her face. Baby pushed it away. "It's gross!" she said.

Guy reached over and skewered the large milky eyeball. He waved it in front of Baby.

"Stop it," Cayenne said. "Stop tormenting her."

Guy shrugged and popped the eyeball into his mouth. He closed his eyes, grunting with pleasure. His lips moved as he sucked, and his forehead was greasy with sweat and steam. He opened his eyes and spit out a hard white kernel the size of a small pearl.

Baby pushed back her chair and ran upstairs to her room. From her bed, she heard Cayenne complaining, and then Guy declared, "*Bien*. If she must eat hamburgers, then take her back to America."

Their voices dropped, and after a while it was quiet, and all Baby could hear was the wind in the alley and the dry sporadic cough of an asthmatic hooker. The sound made her feel lonely, like she wanted to cry. The coughing continued. Baby lifted the curtain and looked out into the dusk. A girl was standing alone in a cone of light cast by the streetlamp. She was weaving and dancing—two steps to the left—cough—two steps to the right. Her head looked like a balloon on a string, bobbing and partly deflated.

Baby heard the stairs creak, then footsteps. Guy's voice was low. Cayenne giggled. "Shhh!" she said. The door to their bedroom clicked shut behind them.

Outside, the girl had started to wheeze and gasp for air. She dropped to her knees and spat. Baby wanted to call Cayenne to come and see, but she didn't. The girl clutched her stomach and looked toward the moon. She caught sight of Baby instead.

"Hey!" she called.

It was the hooker from before, the one with the needle. Now Baby could see she was just a kid, Native, maybe fourteen or fifteen years old. She was wearing bike shorts that hugged her rear end in a way Baby admired. Her black hair was razored into a bad shag. It may have been a trick of the streetlight or the watery flux of the windowpane, but as the girl stared upward, it looked like her eyes were crossing and uncrossing as she swayed from side to side.

"Hey you!" the girl called. "Up there. Yo, Princess!"

In a tower, Baby thought. Like Cayenne said. Sounds were coming from the bedroom. The house seemed to tremble when Cayenne and

Guy made love. Baby could hear her mother moaning, *"Oh, Guy, je t'aime . . ."* but she was faking. Baby could tell. Guy was no longer romantic. Baby wondered where they'd wind up next.

The street was silent, so she pulled back the curtain. The girl was still there, and now she moved her arm in a big, inviting arc.

"Come down here!" Her voice was thin behind the warped glass.

Baby shook her head.

"What's your name?"

Baby didn't answer.

"I'm Lulu," the girl said. "You got any money?" She started to wheeze again. "I gotta get to the hospital . . ." She covered her mouth with her hand. Her shoulders shook.

Baby watched.

"Come on," Lulu said. "Help me out, Princess! I'm fuckin' dying down here . . ."

Just then Mrs. Wong peered over the back gate, brandishing a large pair of pruning shears. *"You! You!"* she yelled at the girl.

Lulu spat again and stared at the old lady. Baby held her breath. Mrs. Wong had a small brown paper bag, and now she waved it at the girl like she was signaling to her with a flag. She reached over the gate and thrust the bag into the girl's hands. Lulu opened it and pulled out a round white bun. She turned it over and took a bite, and then another. Mrs. Wong gave a grunt and nodded, then she went back into her garden.

Baby let the curtain fall.

"Hey!" she heard Lulu call. "Thanks!" Then, like an afterthought, "Fuck you, Princess!"

"Hoi sam ma," Baby whispered to her sloping ceiling, in the dark.

■ ■ ■

"Bébé is in need of a name," Guy said.

"Baby will choose her own name when she's ready," Cayenne said. "That's the deal, right, Baby?"

"What's in a name?" asked Julien. He was Guy's customer, a poet from San Francisco who had come up to buy pot. "Would a rose by any other name smell as sweet?"

"Rose is pretty good," Baby said. "I like Rose."

Baby liked Julien. Cayenne did too. She thought he was TDH—tall, dark and handsome, plus he had brought lots of money. He was funny and imitated Guy's accent. "I wan' ze wheeeeelchair, man," he said, pointing at a plastic freezer bag on the kitchen table and counting out the bills.

"Rose is a terrible name," giggled Cayenne. She was in a mood to-night. There weren't enough chairs so Baby was sharing hers. Now Cayenne pulled Baby's head down into her lap and nuggied her scalp with a knuckle, acting playful. She did that sometimes when she wanted to impress a guy, to show she wasn't just somebody's mother.

"Cut it out," Baby said. She stood up and went to stand behind Julien. Her hair was tousled. "I like Rose. *Je m'appelle Rose.*"

Cayenne sniffed. "Flowers' names are so bourgeois."

Guy lit a joint and handed it to Julien, who took a long toke. "Oh, yeah, man," he said. "Iss ze fuckin' wheeeeeelchair!"

"How come you need a wheelchair?" Baby asked, bumping her hip into the back of Julien's chair. "Are you a cripple or something?"

Julien snorted, rocking forward as he exhaled. Cayenne laughed, too, high and tinkly.

"Oh, Baby, that's priceless," she said. "He's talking about the pot, silly. It messes you up so bad you need a wheelchair. That's all."

Baby continued bumping her hip against Julien's chair. "I know," she said. "I just think it's stupid."

Julien caught his breath and looked at her. Tears from the smoke and laughter sparkled in his dark eyes. "She's pouting," he said admiringly. "She's mad."

"I am not. I just think it's fucking dumb, is all."

"Oooh," Julien said. "Such language!"

"Yeah," Cayenne warned. "Watch it."

"Look at that lip," Julien said. He flicked a red curl from Baby's cheek and fingered her mouth. He pinched her bottom lip and tugged. His fingertips were hard and smelled like burnt tar.

"Cut it out, fuckface," Baby said. It hurt her to talk with him pinching her lip and her words came out funny. He held on.

"Hey, Mama," Julien said to Cayenne. "You got yourself one bitchy little baby . . ."

"Julien," Cayenne said. "Watch out for her, she—"

"Ow!" cried Julien, as Baby bit down on his finger. "Bloody hell!"

"—bites," Cayenne concluded, as Baby thundered up the stairs.

■ ■ ■

Baby lay on her bed, toes still scraping the ceiling. Guy hadn't gotten around to cutting off the legs. He'd meant to, but he kept forgetting. The sound of their voices from the kitchen dipped and swelled.

"I want more wine," Cayenne cried. "We have to celebrate. Look!"

The alley was empty, but the wind was up. The pylons were creaking, and a seagull cawed as it flew overhead.

"It's from that publishing place," Cayenne said. "The one I sent my chapter to? They liked it!" Her words were like bubbles, rising in the broth of her laughter.

Baby's heart started to pound.

"Listen." There was a pause, then Baby heard her mother reading. " 'Thank you for sending us your fascinating manuscript. *Ships in the Night* promises to be a real steamy bodice-ripper and we're thrilled to be in a position to help you launch this promising new romance . . . ' "

Her mother's breathless words bruised Baby's heart. *No*, she whispered into the dark. *Don't tell them. Tell me!*

Downstairs they were clinking their glasses. Guy wanted to see the letter. Cayenne was saying, "It must be all your positive energy, Julien." Baby rolled onto her stomach and buried her face in the pillow. After a while she took off her pants and crawled under the covers. She tried listening just to the wind, but still she could hear their voices.

"Where's the bathroom?" Julien asked.

"Come on, I'll show you," Cayenne said.

Baby heard their chair legs scrape. Guy said, "He don't need you to help him piss."

"Don't be silly," Cayenne said. "I have to check on Baby."

Baby listened to their feet, climbing the stairs. She shut her eyes and slowed her breathing. Outside her bedroom door, their voices changed, soft and slurred and secret.

"In here," Julien whispered.

"No! That's Baby's room . . ."

"Where, then?"

"Oh, Julien. Not now. I can't . . ."

"Come on. Ships in the night, right?"

The floorboards creaked under the shifting weight of their bodies. Baby barely breathed at all. She could hear pushing sounds against the wall, and other sounds, too—puffs of air, or like a low throat humming.

"We're writers," Julien was murmuring. "Kindred souls . . ."

"*Cayenne!*" Guy called, and after all the hushing it made Baby's heart leap.

"The bathroom's over there," Cayenne said loudly as she clattered down the stairs.

Baby breathed again and listened to the *shuush* of Julien peeing. In the kitchen, Guy and Cayenne were fighting. Baby got out of bed and crept toward the landing. She sat on the top step and hugged her bare knees.

"We were just talking," Cayenne was saying. She was leaning against the kitchen table, holding the side of her head. "He's a poet. We're kindred souls."

Guy was putting on his jacket. "*Bien,*" he said. He picked up a piece of paper from the table. It was Cayenne's letter. He waved it in front of her face. "So now you need money for your book, you can go and suck his kindred dick, eh?"

"Give me that," Cayenne said. She grabbed Guy's arm but he laughed and held the letter out of her reach. Her breasts were heaving. "Don't be so mean, *mon amour,*" she pleaded. "I'll pay you back. It's just until the novel starts to sell . . ."

Baby peered through the balustrades at her mother's teary upturned face. The tears were real. She must still care, Baby thought. Things must still be romantic. She heard a noise behind her and remembered Julien in the bathroom. She crept back to her bedroom. Downstairs, she heard the back door slam. She knelt by the window, drawing aside the faded cloth and pressing her hot forehead to the cool glass. She watched Guy descend the rickety steps and walk out into the alley. After a moment Cayenne ran after him, catching up with him at the Dumpster. Baby chewed her thumbnail as she watched them go.

The door to her bedroom opened, sucking the wind in from the alley through the crack, and the thin curtains billowed. The fabric caught the light from the streetlamp, so that what Julien saw, as he stood in the doorway, was a half-clothed Baby, enveloped in a lucent field of yellow and cornflowers. Her hair was tousled, and flaming tendrils blew across her forehead. She was kneeling on her little bed in her underpants as though in prayer. In a garret. She stared at him, then slowly she held out her hand. It was too much to ask, of a poet, to resist.

"Don't be scared," Julien said, approaching the bed.

"Do you have any money?" Baby demanded.

■ ■ ■

Cayenne lay on Baby's bed, staring up at the ceiling. "Canada is a backwater, Baby," she said. "We're getting stale here, don't you think? It's time we went back home. I was thinking maybe San Francisco. That's a *real* city. We can live in one of those cute Victorians and I can finish my novel. Julien said it's a fine community for writers. Wouldn't that be fun?"

Outside in the alley, the streetlamps had just come on. Baby pressed her lips to the cold glass. "I hate San Francisco," she said.

"How do you know?" Cayenne said. "You've never been there." She was wearing a peasant blouse with a lace-up front, wrapping the laces around her fingers so that the tips turned white. "Why are you doing this?" she said. Her voice tightened, rising into a whine. "Why are you ruining everything?"

Baby didn't answer. Down below, a chicken truck from Hung Lung Enterprises rattled through the alley past the streetlamp, sending a hooker stumbling into the spill of the light. Stacked high with empty chicken cages, the truck left a wake of feathers, floating in the air.

Cayenne sighed and sat up. She looked out the window. "That's the same girl," she said. "Isn't it?"

The hooker looked like Lulu, milky-eyed and confused. Glancing up toward the light, she caught sight of a wafting feather. Then another, falling, like snow. "Whooo whoooo," she laughed like a loon, then she doubled over and started to cough. Baby recognized the cough. She wanted to knock on the pane. Maybe they could have been friends, but now it was too late. Dazed, Lulu spun, a demented ballerina in a snow dome, reaching out to catch the feathers as they drifted down. Baby let the curtain drop.

"You just want Julien to fuck you."

Cayenne pinched her arm, hard. "Listen," she said. "It's not what you think. Julien and I have a special relationship. We're from the same tribe." Then she put her arms around Baby and gave her a big hug. "Trust me, hon. You'll change your mind when we get to San Francisco, I promise."

When we get to San Francisco, Baby thought, pulling away and rubbing her arm. The words stuck in her head. "When we get to San Francisco, I'm changing my name to Lulu."

"Lulu?" Cayenne said. "God, that's awful!"

"*L*'s are sensual. You said so."

"Whatever." Cayenne shrugged, then her eyes got dreamy. "Anyway, I'm thinking of changing the whole story. It's all going to take place in Canada, see? In the Pacific Northwest. The heroine's this poor Indian girl, and the villain's a French fur trapper, and maybe there's a Chinese drug dealer . . ."

Baby looked back out the window. Lulu was still there, spinning and coughing. Baby could hear Mrs. Wong next door, yelling something to the landlord in Cantonese. She glanced at Cayenne, then she tapped on the pane of glass. When Lulu looked up, she waved.

Cayenne didn't seem to notice. She was stretched out on the bed again, staring at the lowering ceiling. "I can still call it *Ships in the Night*," she was saying. She pulled out her letter, folded many times, from her bosom. She sighed. "Did I read you what they wrote? It's going to be a real steamy bodice-ripper, Baby . . ."

Baby climbed over her mother's legs. She took a thin wad of bills from her underwear drawer and stuffed it into her jeans pocket. She paused at the doorway.

"*Hoi sam ma?*" she asked, giving her mother another chance.

Cayenne still didn't get it.

"*Tao-che*," Baby said, and then she bolted.

SEPARATION ANXIETY

from **AMERICAN SON**

■ ■ ■

Brian Ascalon Roley

I

Today Tomas has to deliver a dog to a celebrity in Brentwood Park. I have not been to a celebrity's house before, and this morning I woke early and waited for him to get up so I could help. He walks into the kitchen and fixes a bowl of cereal without saying a word. Though yesterday he told me I could come, he does not normally take me on these trips, and I wonder if I should ask him again to make sure. But he looks too touchy to be bothered. Finally he finishes eating. There is still sleep in his face as we go out back and as he swings the wire door off the cage. I reach in and retrieve Johan, the best of the pups, who pants with an energy that comes from being young, though he is large already and fully trained. Tomas goes in and grabs Buster—Johan's mother—and drags her onto the grass. She stays close by him, making anxious circles.

Cut it out, Buster, he says, looking down on her. What you so worked up about?

She must sense we're gonna sell her son.

No shit.

BRIAN ASCALON ROLEY, born in 1966, is a biracial Filipino American who grew up in a household of Filipino immigrants to Los Angeles. His first novel, *American Son*, is the first part of a trilogy in progress. It was published to much acclaim and was considered by the *Los Angeles Times* to be one of the best books of 2001. He is currently at work on a new novel, as well as a nonfiction book on the relationship between ethnicity and religion.

No shit, I say. If it's so no shit then why'd you ask her why she's so excited.

I'm just making talk with her, Junior.

He turns away to rub her under her chin reassuringly, pressing his cheek down against the back of her neck. She whimpers and rubs her side against him like a cat, then sits down on her haunches again.

Are you gonna sell Buster, too? I say.

What do you think?

No.

Without a word for me, he rubs her fur to shake off bits of dirt and dried-up leaves. Then why'd you bring her out? I say.

He pats Buster's side seriously and lets his hand rest there. It's the last time she'll get to see her son. I want her to see him to the last.

We take the dogs through the house—Johan for the last time—and it seems to me a shame that our mother is not home to see him off. They seem to sense something is wrong, and they quicken their pant. Johan breaks free and scrapes across the kitchen linoleum towards the far end where, when he was a pup and allowed to live inside, we used to put out his dog dish. He sniffs in the corner, confused, and even shoves his nose up against the wall at the memory of where he used to push the dish against it.

Tomas hollers. Johan looks up, ears perked, and comes dutifully back.

In the meantime, Buster has wandered into and out of our mother's room, where she still sleeps, as if today might be the last time *she* would smell it.

Tomas lets the dogs into the car first, and they climb in back. Their fear—if they ever had any—has transformed into excitement, and as they peer out at me their breath fogs the windows. Their noses leave moist dots on the glass. Tomas gets inside. As I reach for my door he leans over and locks it.

The handle does not move. What you doing? Open the door.

You aren't coming.

Don't be stupid, I say. Let me in.

You deaf?

I try the handle harder again, though it will not budge. The dogs have their claws clambering against the glass, watching me. Tomas looks forward, inserting the key and revving the engine.

He pretends to be warming up the car, though he is waiting for me to plead.

Come on, Tomas, I finally say. Let me come with you.

He turns to me and rolls the window down a crack.

Why should I?

I want to see this celebrity's house.

He looks me up and down and shakes his head.

One look at you and they'll think these dogs were raised by a bunch of wimps.

I look aside and do not answer him, pretending to stare off at the neighbor's cactus plant. Nails scraping against the glass sound like keys clicking.

The door snaps open.

When I turn to him, he throws some of his clothes and junk off the seat onto the floor.

All right, you don't have to cry, he says. Come on in.

I do not move. I'm not crying, I say.

I'm not going to ask you again, he says. So you can come along and look at the house or stay behind.

Without a word I get in and we pull out and the car humps over the lump in the asphalt, a great warp above a tree root, and the dogs fall against my seat back and I can hear their eager panting.

■ ■ ■

We pass beneath the 405 overpass, entering its shadows, and above us I can see patches of sky between the bellies of the freeways that appear blindingly bright and blue, and the sun flickers over the dogs' faces until we come out into the daylight again. The dogs watch the sun, then the wetbacks who stand in golden shafts amid the shadows waiting to get picked up for work, short little men who smoke cigarettes and talk in groups.

Here the dogs peer at the buildings we pass: the mix of discount stores West LA people come down to shop in; taquería stands for the wetbacks who live three or four families to an apartment close by; a Starbucks on the way to the on-ramp that looks posh once you get beyond the iron railings that protect it.

I wonder if the dogs can see our reflections in the rapidly passing glass, in mirrored and tinted storefronts. In these reflections I can make out Tomas, me, and the dogs—just barely—and it looks as though they are looking at me, but I doubt they can see anything. They cannot even see the images on a television screen.

II

We stop at the Brentwood Country Mart and have the cheese pizzas we used to come for with our mother each time we visited our Tita Dina, who lives close by. It is strange how they have this covered courtyard with benches surrounding a tree; it feels somehow rustic, even though we are in the middle of a great urban city, and the people who frequent it are rich and mostly Jewish, from Brentwood Park. Daylight floods in pleasantly and we have always loved sitting here, but it seems sad without our mother this time. Tomas buys the pieces and folds mine over like a taco for me, the New York way our father showed us, then he gets some fries from the chicken stand and brings out the little cups of barbecue sauce they have that we always loved to dip them in, and he shakes the garlic salt seasoning on.

Dig in, he says, and folds his own piece over.

A few people watch us eat. Probably they are taking note of Tomas. A fortyish woman in slender black bicycle pants and a pink T-shirt. An older woman I recognize who works at the toy store. The wetback behind the pizza counter who spoke a few words of Spanish to my brother. Tomas did not understand the Spanish, though he nodded and tried to make it look as if he understood. I wonder if Tomas senses all this attention as he hunches over his piece. Probably he does, though he pretends not to, or at least not to care. In those days when we came with our mother or aunt nobody ever paid any attention to us, except at the toy store where they knew us, or the market where we bought chocolates, and the bookstore where Tomas used to read magazines and talk to the old skinny man who ran it and smelled like shoe polish and who would recommend to him all the Michener books my brother loved because they would take you to faraway places. Even after he stopped reading them, I would scour his old copies and buy the latest books. The same skinny old man still works there; he looks the same, but didn't recognize us walking in. He watched Tomas carefully as he paused to look over a few magazines and then told him not to look unless he was going to buy one. Tomas crumpled the one he was reading back into its slot and made his way to order our pizza.

Tomas buys a couple of drumsticks for the dogs and lets me feed them once we get into the car. As we roll up Twenty-sixth Street you can see the Santa Monica Mountains up ahead. Their sadly wrinkled sides face south, sunbathed in worn shades of purple and blue. My fingers are covered with slobber and sticky, plum-colored barbecue sauce that does not come fully off onto a napkin. We pull off San Vicente, and immediately it is as if we are in the countryside. There are mailboxes here, on the streets. There are no sidewalks. On some blocks you can see huge lawns leading to houses that look like they belong in the countryside or on some farm, but on other blocks the houses are barely visible, surrounded by fences and trees and gates with intercoms and video cameras.

This is a cool neighborhood, I say. It's just like being out in the countryside.

Tomas ignores me. He concentrates on the road. From the way his tendons rise on the back of his hand, gripping the wheel, I can see how tense he is, though he tries not to show it. Probably it is his car which makes him nervous, a white Oldsmobile, the type Mexican gangsters prefer because they can pile so many people into the backseat. He studies the houses and gates and fences and intercoms, the manicured lawns and cobblestone driveways. Strangely there are no cars parked on the curbs here; they are parked beyond the gates in the driveways, Mercedes, BMWs, and some utility vehicles too. The dogs circle about the backseat, worry in their eyes. It could be they have picked up my anxiety, or maybe they sense that something will soon happen to change their lives forever.

Look for the address, Tomas says.

I can't make them out, I say. None of them have numbers on the curbs and you can't see past the fences into the houses.

Sometimes we pass iron gates, and I get a glimpse of a house and then only trees and fences again.

I tell him to slow down.

He looks at me, the amused asshole grin of this morning on his face again. You nervous or something?

No. I just can't read the numbers.

You can't read numbers? A lot of good it does you to bury your face in those books you read.

I could read them if you'd slow down.

We round a corner and enter a canopy of tree branches that tunnel above us like interlaced fingers—between its knuckled branches, the sun is nervous and flickering. The lawns appear brighter from this shade.

Just cool down and relax, Junior. I cleaned out the car in case we get pulled over.

I told you, I say. I just can't read them.

Often in this car we get pulled over, and sometimes the cops make us get out and put our hands on the warm hood and they frisk us. They run their hands over our back and sides and along our inner thighs. Tomas complains about it at family dinners and says they are perverts and racists, but Tita Dina tells him he is getting what comes to him for dressing like a Mexican and driving a hoodlum car.

Finally we get to a white brick house that has narrow columns, fronted by a circular drive. I can see all this through the gate, which is wrought iron, unlike those of the neighbors' houses. Through a window above the front doors I make out that this house has a three-story entryway, and an enormous chandelier of dangling glass hangs from the ceiling.

This is it, I say after spotting the numbers above the country mailbox. As we pull up closer I can see it is aluminum, with a little red metal flag.

Dang, he says. That's some kind of a house.

I don't know. I think I'd like mine to be closed in like the neighbors'.

You mean you want it to be all fenced up and hidden?

Sure.

Why? he says. You afraid some photographers are gonna try and take your picture?

I do not answer him.

His eyes stay on me, then he looks forward and grins. I wouldn't count on it, Junior, he says. You'd have to be pretty famous for somebody to want to take a picture of a person with a face like yours.

Mom has said he should not tease me like this, but I do not remind him. I look out my window.

He continues observing me, carefully.

What you looking at so intently, Junior? he says. Haven't you ever seen a bush before?

There is a white rosebush before me which I have not noticed until now. But I do not look away from it.

I got news for you, Gabe. Celebrity bushes are the same as the ones owned by you and me.

You don't own anything, I tell him. Only Mom owns bushes. You have to have a job to afford a house.

I make plenty with the dogs and stolen stereos.

That's not a real job. It doesn't count.

Okay, Mr. Stockbroker, he says as we pull up to the gate. He stops and lowers his window before a white intercom perched on a metal stand. Tomas pushes a red button. We wait. He tries again and after a minute a lady's voice that sounds Mexican—probably the maid—asks what we want.

We've come to sell some dogs, he says into the box.

Again, the sound of static. Then the crackled voice comes on and says they don't take solicitors.

No, listen, Tomas says. We have the dogs with us now.

We no take solicitations, it says.

Then the static clicks off.

Tomas frowns and hits the side of the intercom and presses the button. I already talked to the señor of the casa, he says to the voice when it comes on again.

You speak to him already?

Sí.

There is a pause, and then the voice says *okay* and the gate slowly swings open. Its iron bottom scrapes along the driveway. You'd think they'd get a faster motor if they can afford a house like this, he says.

That was really great Spanish, Tomas, I say.

Fuck you, he says.

III

We pull up behind a black Land Cruiser that sits high on extra-tread snow tires, and in the polished paint a sunny, ghostlike reflection of our white car warps and twists as it nears. The dogs are nervous, thumping against my seat back.

Tomas pops open his door and gets out, pulling Johan after him.

Should I bring Buster out too? I say. She looks at me, then at Tomas—confused—and then to Johan, before laying the side of her head against my bare forearm.

No.

But don't you want her to see Johan off? I thought that was the whole point.

It is, he says.

I pause.

So?

So Buster *is* coming to see us off, but I didn't say anything about you coming inside, he says.

I am silent.

I don't want you coming in and fucking it up, he says.

He tells Johan to sit and the dog does, then my brother pulls the seat up again and Buster scrambles out. By now Johan has gotten excited again, and I hear his panting all the way from the passenger seat. His head turns back and forth as he looks rapidly around, making half circles like a cat. Buster comes up beside him, and he looks at her quickly, almost nudging her, but moves away again, distractedly, as he takes in his new surroundings.

I'm not gonna fuck it up, I say.

You'd fuck it up just looking the way you do.

What does that mean?

I mean take a good look at those clothes you're wearing. One look at that and they'll take the offer back for sure.

I don't think they'd care what I wear, I say, and come out of the car and force myself to hold my words. I want to ask him why he is being such an asshole, and when will he get over it, but I am beginning to wonder if he has actually become one. My eyes tear and the sun blinds me. If I cried maybe he would stop, but to prevent this from happening I stare hard at the house, studying it. Through the glass in the front double doors a brown-skinned woman approaches. She wears cheap jeans and a faded red T-shirt, probably a maid. She opens the door and steps outside.

She stands on the brick porch, a hand on her hip, regarding us suspiciously. No doubt she has heard some of our arguing. Tomas composes his face into his hardened unreadable expression.

He leans over and whispers to me, not turning or looking me in the eye. Calm down. And behave yourself if you think you can.

I *am* calm.

You can come in if you want, but don't say a word, he says. And don't stand too close to me or the client.

He mumbles something to himself about it not being hard for me to not say a word and then turns his back to me and climbs halfway up the porch towards the maid. She studies him—probably wondering if he is a real Mexican, or what other hot country he might have come from— glancing once towards me, then back to Tomas again. He has worn his thin T-shirt again so the white client can see the Virgin of Guadalupe through it. In front of her he seems embarrassed, though, and he keeps it turned away.

I grab Buster's collar and whisper for her to be quiet. She stops whimpering.

The lady sets her hands on her hips and regards her. She makes a lot of noise, the woman says.

It's not the one you're going to get.

She looks at Tomas as if surprised to hear his voice. This noise, it sounds like this one is not very happy.

Tomas nods seriously. She's the mother.

It takes a moment for the gears in the woman's mind to put it together and then I see the understanding pass behind her eyes.

Oh, she says, and nods her head. This one is the mother. I see.

We wanted her to say goodbye, he explains.

She nods and comes up to me—no longer suspicious—and reaches down and clenches the fur at the back of Buster's neck, then starts squeezing in a way meant to be rubbing. The woman is so close to my face now I can smell her hair spray.

Yes, she says. It is hard for a mother to see her child go.

She regards me as if for the first time.

Hello.

I mumble a greeting after I lower my eyes. Still, I can feel her smiling as she studies me. My face turns red.

She turns over her shoulder to Tomas, not letting go of Buster's neck. Ustedes son hermanos?

He looks like he doesn't understand but doesn't want her to know this.

She wants to know if we're brothers, I tell him.

I know that.

He glares at me and I shut up, but she faces me now and expects an answer.

Sí.

Yo creo que no.

I nod. Mi madre tampoco lo cree.

She bites her lip and thinks a moment.

Se parecen por la forma de sus ojos, she says, and then turns to Tomas: You do not seem so. But I can tell it in the shape of your eyes.

When he catches me looking at him he glares at me, and I look down. Even with the woman still rubbing her neck, Buster manages to rub her side against my jeans, and keeps pressed there, whimpering. The woman notices this.

This is your dog? she says to me.

I shake my head. No. It's my brother's. And my mom's.

She smiles. But she goes to you when she knows her son will be leaving.

She's only a dog, I say, then look down again. She can't know he's going.

The woman smiles. A mother knows.

She lets go of Buster's neck, then reaches over again to scratch behind her ear—a last time—then starts up the stairs, leading us inside. Tomas goes first and I hesitate in the doorway, not knowing if he wants me to go in, but the maid turns to me and makes several rapid friendly waves for me to enter—as if I were silly for thinking otherwise.

I duck my head and follow.

IV

Most people wonder what sorts of homes celebrities live in, probably picturing something modern: white carpets and trendy furniture, marble gourmet kitchens, a view onto an exercise room with chrome equipment. But we find our celebrity in a dark room with wood-paneled walls and an old pool table with lions carved on its legs. Tomas runs a finger over the green cloth, and I do too. It is feltless and bare as silk. The table has no pockets. The man comes up to us, pulling his robe string tighter, and looks out the French doors at the canyon view. At its bottom rests a golf course covered with brilliant sand traps shaped like oval moons. There are hills and valleys of sunny grass surrounded by mansions. I knew none of this was here. The drapes are held back by gold ropes, their braidlike tassels dangling.

He turns back to us and I see that he does not have the mustache he has on the TV show. His hair is thinner—the shiny scalp shows through the blown-dry strands—and his skin is far tanner, almost leathery beneath his eyes. But his eyes are as alive and young as the cop character he plays. He studies us sharply.

So you've brought the dog, he says. He has some sort of a southern or western accent, which surprises me since in the movies he always talks like a blue-collar cop from New York City.

Yeah, Tomas says.

The man shakes his head. But there's two. I don't remember asking for two.

This one's the mother, Tomas says. It's her pup you're going to get.

The man studies the dogs. He scratches their heads with his thick fingers, like a man who has been around animals, not like the urban detective he normally plays. He does not seem a bit afraid of them. He returns to Buster and sets his cheek against her ear and scratches firmly under her neck.

This is a nice one.

Tomas nods.

A lovely animal, the man says.

She's got good genes. Johan has them too.

The man purses his lips and nods to himself thoughtfully. He's a good dog, he agrees. He returns to Buster and she comes up and sets her side against him. But this one's better.

Tomas leans a hip against the pool table.

Johan is younger.

The mother's friendly.

Johan is too, my brother adds. He's just nervous now.

The man sets his cue stick on the carpet, gripping it upright like a staff, and his thumb rubs the tip. His thumb comes off, covered by green chalk. He looks firmly at my brother. Look. I grew up on a farm in Georgia. We had dogs like this one—American bulldogs. They're great guard dogs, but they aren't German. So don't try conning me about animals.

The man's thumb stops moving, very still on the tip, and his face is pushed close to my brother's, and though I can tell this bothers Tomas, he tries not to show it, and he does not lean back.

I'm not trying to con you, mister.

Just because I live in Brentwood doesn't mean I haven't been around the block. We used to hunt with hounds. Big yellow-eyed beasts. They could chew up a bear, clobber it down with a jaw. But I know these American bulldogs well, and they're good dogs. Once upon a time they used to kill bulls for British audiences until the nineteenth century when the government there got soft and made it illegal. He shakes his head, the pool cue in his hand now like a rifle. Then they got to figure out what to do with the dogs. They bred some of them into what's now your cute little condo brat English bulldog, and others they shipped over to the Unites States south where some rednecks taught them a few tricks. Did a pretty good job, I'd say. But they haven't been to Germany as far as I know.

I never told you they came from Germany, Tomas lies. I didn't mean to give you that impression. I only meant that I train them with German techniques.

Oh yeah, I know.

The man uprights his cue stick and chalks it and walks up and leans over the table, aiming, and slams the cue ball into another. They fly about the table. Then he returns and stares at Tomas again.

Tomas runs a nervous finger across his sweaty forehead, beneath his bandanna. Probably he is annoyed with this man for disbelieving him, even though he lied. He wants to do something—hit or yell at him or take the dog off and forget it, but the man had agreed to a price far too high—eight thousand dollars—and Tomas does not want to lose it.

They're techniques I got from the LAPD, Tomas says, trying to hold his stare. You can call my friend on the force right now if you want to. He'd be happy to talk.

The man shakes his head dismissively. There's no need for that. He studies Johan. No. What bothers me is this one's got a small skull. And his cranium above his eyes is too shallow, shows he isn't as smart as his mother.

Tomas starts to speak but the man turns away from him, towards the Mexican lady. What do you think, Lucinda?

She puckers her lips distastefully. I do not care about the size of the skull.

I know you don't.

She comes over and rubs Buster. I like this one.

I could tell you did. Why?

This one, she has a bigger heart than the boy. He is too young and restless. The woman shakes her head as she studies Johan. You will never know how such a young one will turn out.

Tomas looks angry that the maid would interfere with the sale. Actually, he's the quietest one in the litter, he says. Sleeps all night.

She crosses her arms. I don't think so.

My brother must be standing ten feet away from her. He stares at her meanly, keeping his face turned from the man. Hey, do you think you could get us a glass of water or something? he says. It's getting hot in here.

I stiffen.

She does not look pleased. She turns to me. What would you like, little one?

I shrug. A Pepsi?

She nods and does not ask Tomas what he wants and starts towards the kitchen, but the man comes over and touches her shoulder. I'll get it, honey, he says, then looks hard at Tomas. My wife's been busy all morning, he says. I'll get you your water if you're so thirsty.

Tomas's face goes red. His arms hang loosely at his sides.

She's not my maid, you know, the man says.

Tomas attempts not to hesitate. I didn't think she was your maid, mister. I was only thirsty.

The man does not answer my brother but looks towards the window, at the sunbathed mountains and the shadow of a cloud that drifts over its curves and ridges. Sunlight catches a pool table corner.

We just didn't want to get the wrong glasses or anything. Gabe will get us the water.

Hearing my name, I come to attention. All their eyes fall on me.

Sure, I tell them.

No, the man says. I'll get it.

He stops me with a heavy hand and leaves the room. We stand awkwardly with the lady. Tomas occupies himself by rubbing Johan, not looking up. I try to catch his eye but he hides his face from me.

When the man returns he sets the glasses on the bar counter so I have to get them and give one to Tomas. The way the lady watches me I get the feeling she does not think I should have to do this.

The man's arms are crossed, and he stares at Tomas.

Look. I'm paying you eight thousand dollars. I'm overpaying you as it is. Even the mother can't be worth that much.

My brother tries not to look away. Well, she ain't for sale.

Then you'd better leave.

Tomas shifts his weight from one foot to another and his hands are in his pockets. The lady glances at me, then touches the celebrity's arm and says: Wait. I like this dog. The mother.

He looks at her wearily. You really do, honey?

Really.

He scratches the stubble on his chin in a grave and thoughtful manner. You love it?

She nods, turning briefly to me and winking.

He sighs. He turns to Tomas. Okay, son. You heard the woman. She wants this dog. How about I buy both of them from you for the inflated sum of nine thousand dollars each.

Tomas looks like he wants that money real bad. I can't, he finally says, his voice threatening to break.

That's eighteen thousand dollars.

I know it.

You are turning down a lot of money for two dogs.

Tomas looks at his feet, then back up again. I can't.

Well then. How about I pay you eight thousand for the boy dog and twelve thousand for the mother. That's twenty thousand.

Tomas presses his finger into the railing and he watches as his thumb knuckle goes white.

Please, mister. She's a pet. Can't you just buy the boy dog?

My brother has not pleaded with anybody like this in years. Probably not since our father left us, and he had to do a lot of pleading back then. There is almost hurt in his voice and he looks down at Johan. Listen. I promise you I'm not conning you. This one boy dog's my favorite dog next to Buster. His head's small, that's true, but his ears are shaped so you know he's physically balanced and his temples are placed right up to it, not too high or low, which shows he's got a good temperament.

He looks aside and shudders a deep breath. His shirt grows at his chest and his biceps expand outward, to make room, then fall alongside his ribs again. The man studies him for a long time. He finds a checkbook and writes Tomas a check and takes Johan's leash. After rubbing him, he looks at Buster and shakes his head. He dwells on her for a very long time.

I'm sorry. I can understand she's your pet. But if you ever change your mind about this dog, we can deal. I assure you she'd have a good home with her son. You call us. You call *me*.

Sure, Tomas says, pocketing the check.

On our way down the steps he wipes a shoulder against his eyes. It could be the wind—I am not sure—but I am so surprised that without thinking I blurt out, Are you *crying*?

His knuckles hit me hard, so fast I didn't see it coming. My tongue prods at the shreds of my inner cheek, and salty blood floods my mouth.

Jesus, I say, why'd you do that?

Then his fist comes into my gut, sending me forward at the waist, then his elbow comes around the sharp bone of it, sending me sideways onto the driveway, the concrete meeting my temple. The surface feels grainy against my cheek and the torn pieces inside stick to my molars.

Don't you fucking talk disrespect to me.

I wasn't disrespecting you.

Don't you overstand me with your Flip, peasant Spanish.

I was only answering the lady's questions, I start to say, but am interrupted by the bottom of his shoe, the gum and sole and dirt pressing into that part of my face where I feel things the most.

IMMIGRATION BLUES

from THE MAN WHO (THOUGHT HE) LOOKED LIKE ROBERT TAYLOR

■ ■ ■

Bienvenido Santos

—*I'm only trying to help you. We should help each other in this country.*

—*Look who's talking. You the guy who run away when you see an old Pinoy approach you. You tell me that yourself. You can't deny.*

—*That's different. Most of these o.t.'s are bums.*

—*Ina couple more years, you'd be one of 'em.*

—*Not me. I save. I make no monkey business. When I retire I'll have everything I need.*

—*Except friends.*

—*Who need friends. Besides, I got friends.*

—*That's what you think. You're gonna lose one now. These guys you're scare are our countrymen.*

—*Who told you I'm scare? I just avoid 'em, that's all. Some of 'em give me bad time, like I'm a sucker.*

—*You look like one, that's why. But don't you see, these old guys are lonely.*

Born in Tondo Manila, in 1911, BIENVENIDO SANTOS was one of the most important, beloved, and widely read writers from the Philippines. His books include the short story collections *You Lovely People* and *Scent of Apples*; two books of poetry; and five novels, including *The Praying Man, The Man Who (Thought He) Looked Like Robert Taylor*, and *What the Hell for You Left Your Heart in San Francisco*. During his lifetime, he taught at Ohio State University and Wichita State University. In 1980, he was awarded an American Book Award for *The Scent of Apples*, his only book to be published in the United States. Santos died in 1996.

—Lonely, my balls! After the soft talk come the soft touch, the cry story.

—How I pity you. . . . Because you should've experience the other vice versa. Like I have. They take you to their homes, feed you till you burp. Especially those Pinoys who don't have no contact with other Pinoys. They show you off to their American wife like lost brother. Like they never get a chance to speak the dialect for years and they just keep talking, never mind the wife who don't understand. And when it's time for you to leave, you know you aren't going to see each other no more. Their eyes shine like they're crying. . . .

—I seen tearful fellow myself, but I think he got sore eyes. He should've been ina hospital.

—Have you been to their homes? The walls, they're cover with Philippine things. They're always shoving albums to you. Some of 'em even got the map of Philippines embroidered somewheres. But what's the use, my smart aleck paisano, you won't recognize loneliness even it's serve to you on a bamboo tray. . . .

■ ■ ■

Through the window curtain, Alipio saw two women, one seemed twice as large as the other. In their summer dresses, they looked like the country girls he knew back home in the Ilocos, who went around peddling rice cakes. The slim one could have passed for Seniang's sister as he remembered her in the pictures his wife kept. Before Seniang's death, they had arranged for her coming to San Francisco, filing all the required petition papers to facilitate the approval of her visa. She was always "almost ready, all the papers have been signed," but she never showed up. His wife had been ailing and when she died, he thought that, at least, it would hasten her sister's coming. The wire he had sent informing her of Seniang's death was not returned nor acknowledged.

The knocking on the door was gentle. A little hard of hearing, Alipio was not sure it was distinctly a knocking on wood that sounded different from the little noises that sometimes hummed in his ears in the daytime. It was not yet noon, but it must be warm outside in all that sunshine otherwise those two women would be wearing warm clothes. There were summer days in San Francisco that were cold like winter in the mid-West.

He limped painfully towards the door. Until last month, he wore crutches. The entire year before that, he was bed-ridden, but he had to force himself to walk about in the house after coming from the hospital. After Seniang's death, everything had gone to pieces. It was one bust after another, he complained to the few friends who came to visit him.

"Seniang was my good luck. When God decided to take her, I had nothing but bad luck," he said.

Not long after Seniang's death, he was in a car accident. For about a year, he was in the hospital. The doctors were not sure he was going to walk again. He told them it was God's wish. As it was he was thankful he was still alive. It was a horrible accident.

The case dragged on in court. His lawyer didn't seem too good about accidents like his. He was an expert immigration lawyer, but he was a friend. As it turned out, Alipio lost the full privileges coming to him in another two years if he had not been hospitalized and had continued working until his retirement.

However, he was well provided. He didn't spend a cent of his own money for doctor and medicine and hospitalization bills. Now there was the prospect of a few thousand dollars coming as compensation. After deducting his lawyer's fees it would still be something to live on. There was social security, partial retirement pension. It was not bad. He could walk a little now although he still limped and had to move about with care.

When he opened the door, the fat woman said, "Mr. Palma? Alipio Palma?"

"Yes," he said. "Come in, come on in." He had not talked to anyone the entire week. His telephone had not rung all that time. The little noises in his ears had somehow kept him company. Radio and television sounds lulled him to sleep.

The thin one was completely out of sight as she stood behind the big one who was doing the talking. "I'm sorry, I should have phoned you first, but we were in a hurry."

"The house a mess," Alipio said truthfully. He remembered seeing two women on the porch. There was another one, who looked like Seniang's sister. Had he been imagining things? Then the thin one materialized, close behind the other, who walked in with the assurance of a social worker, about to do him a favor.

"Sit down," Alipio said, passing his hand over his face, a mannerism which Seniang hated. Like you have a hangover, she chided him, and you can't see straight.

There was a TV set in the small living room crowded with an assortment of chairs and tables. There was an aquarium on the mantel piece of a fake fireplace. A lighted bulb inside the tank showed many colored fish swimming about in a haze of fish food. Some of it lay scattered on the edge of the mantelpiece. The carpet beneath it was sodden and dirty. The little fish swimming about in the lighted water seemed to be the only sign of life in the room where everything was old, including, no doubt, the magazines and tabloids scattered just about everywhere.

Alipio led the two women through the dining room, past a huge rectangular table in the center. It was bare except for a vase of plastic flowers as centerpiece.

"Sorry to bother you like this," the fat one said as she plunked herself down on the nearest chair, which sagged to the floor under her weight. The thin one chose the near end of the sofa that faced the TV set.

"I was just preparing my lunch. I know it's quite early, but I had nothing else to do," Alipio said, pushing down with both hands the seat of the cushioned chair near a movable partition, which separated the living room from the dining room. "I'm not too well yet," he added as he finally made it.

"I hope we're not really bothering you," the fat one said. The other had not said a word. She looked pale and sick. Maybe she was hungry or cold.

"How is it outside?" Alipio asked. "I have not been out all day." Whenever he felt like it, he dragged a chair to the porch and sat there, watching the construction going on across the street and smiling at the people passing by. He stayed on until it felt chilly.

"It's fine. It's fine outside. Just like Baguio."

"You know Baguio? I was born near there."

"We're sisters," the fat one said.

Alipio was thinking, won't the other one speak at all?

"I'm Mrs. Antonieta Zafra, the wife of Carlito. I believe you know him. He says you're friends. In Salinas back in the thirties. He used to be a cook at the Marina."

"Carlito, yes, yes, Carlito Zafra. We bummed together. We come from Ilocos. Where you from?"

"Aklan. My sister and I speak Cebuano."

"She speak? You don't speak Iloco."

"Not much. Carlito and I talk in English. Except when he's real mad, like when his cock don't fight or when he lose, then he speaks Iloco. Cuss words. I've learned them. Some."

"Yes. Carlito. He love cockfighting. How's he?"

"Retired like you. We're now in Fresno. On a farm. He raises chickens and hogs. I do some sewing in town whenever I can. My sister here is Monica. She's older than me. Never been married."

Monica smiled at the old man, her face in anguish, as if near to tears.

"Carlito. He got some fighting cocks, I bet."

"Not any more. But he talks a lot about cockfighting. But nobody, not even the Pinoys and the Latin Americanos around are interested in it." Mrs. Zafra appeared pleased at the state of things on the home front.

"I remember. He once promoted a cockfight. Everything was ready, but the roosters wouldn't fight. Poor Carlito, he did everything to make 'em fight like having them peck at each other's necks, and so forth. They were so tame. Only thing they didn't do was embrace." Alipio laughed, showing a set of perfectly white and even teeth, obviously dentures.

"He hasn't told me about that; I'll remind him."

"Do that. Where's he? Why isn't he with you?"

"We didn't know we'd find you here. While visiting some friends this morning, we learned you live here." Mrs. Zafra was beaming at him.

"I've always lived here, but I got few friends now. So you're Mrs. Carlito. I thought he's dead already. I never hear from him. We're old now. We're old already when we got our citizenship papers right after Japanese surrender. So you and him. Good for Carlito."

"I heard about your accident."

"After Seniang died. She was not yet sixty, but she had this heart trouble. I took care of her." Alipio seemed to have forgotten his visitors. He sat there staring at the fish in the aquarium, his ears perked as though waiting for some sound, like the breaking of the surf not far away, or the TV set suddenly turned on.

The sisters looked at each other. Monica was fidgeting, her eyes seemed to say, let's go, let's get out of here.

"Did you hear that?" the old man said.

Monica turned to her sister, her eyes wild with fright. Mrs. Zafra leaned forward, leaning with one hand on the sofa where Alipio sat, and asked gently, "Hear what?"

"The waves. They're just outside, you know. The breakers have a nice sound like at home in the Philippines. We lived near the sea. Across that water is the Philippines, I always tell Seniang, we're not far from home."

"But you're alone. It's not good to be alone," Mrs. Zafra said.

"At night I hear better. I can see the Pacific Ocean from my bedroom. It sends me to sleep. I sleep soundly like I got no debts, I can sleep all day, too, but that's bad. So I walk. I walk much before. I go out there. I let the breakers touch me. It's nice the touch. Seniang always scold me, she says I'll be catching cold, but I don't catch cold, she catch the cold all the time."

"You must miss her," Mrs. Zafra said. Monica was staring at the hands on her lap while her sister talked. Her skin was transparent and the veins showed on the back of her hands like trapped eels.

"I take care of Seniang. I work all day and leave her here alone. When I come, she's smiling. She's wearing my jacket and my slippers. Like an Igorot. You look funny, I says, why do you wear my things? She chuckles, you keep me warm all day, she says. We have no baby. If we have a baby . . ."

"I think you and Carlito have the same fate. We have no baby also."

"God dictates," Alipio said, making an effort to stand. Monica, in a miraculous surge of power, rushed to him and helped him up. She seemed astonished and embarrassed at what she had done.

"Thank you," said Alipio. "I have crutches, but I don't want no crutches. They tickle me." He watched Monica go back to her seat.

"It must be pretty hard alone," Mrs. Zafra said.

"God helps," Alipio said, walking towards the kitchen as if expecting to find the Almighty there.

Mrs. Zafra followed him. "What are you preparing?" she asked.

"Let's have lunch," he said. "I'm hungry. Aren't you?"

"We'll help you," Mrs. Zafra said, turning back to where Monica sat staring at her hands again and listening perhaps for the sound of the sea. She did not notice nor hear her sister when she called, "Monica!"

The second time, she heard her. Monica stood up and went to the kitchen.

"There's nothing to prepare," Alipio was saying, as he opened the refrigerator. "What you want to eat? Me. I don't eat bread, so I got no bread. I eat rice. I was just opening a can of sardines when you come. I like sardines with lots of tomato sauce and hot rice."

"Don't you cook the sardines?" Mrs. Zafra asked. "Monica will cook it for you if you want."

"No! If you cook sardines, it taste bad. Better uncooked. Besides, on top of the hot rice, it gets cooked. You chop onions. Raw not cooked. You like it?"

"Monica loves raw onions, don't you, Sis?"

"Yes," Monica said in a voice so low Alipio couldn't have heard her.

"Your sister, is she well?" Alipio asked, glancing towards Monica.

Mrs. Zafra gave her sister an angry look.

"I'm okay," Monica said, a bit louder this time.

"She's not sick," Mrs. Zafra said, "but she's shy. Her own shadow frightens her. I tell you, this sister of mine, she got problems."

"Oh?" Alipio exclaimed. He had been listening quite attentively.

"I eat onions," Monica said. "Sardines, too, I like."

Her sister smiled. "What do you say, I run out for some groceries," she said, going back to the living room to get her bag.

"Thanks. But no need for you to do that. I got lots of food, canned food. Only thing I haven't got is bread," Alipio said.

"I eat rice, too," Monica said.

Alipio had reached up to open the cabinet. It was stacked full of canned food: corned beef, pork and beans, vienna sausage, tuna, crab meat, shrimp, chow mein, imitation noodles, and, of course, sardines, in green and yellow labels.

"The yellow ones with mustard sauce, not tomato," he explained.

"All I need is a cup of coffee," Mrs. Zafra said, throwing her handbag back on the chair in the living room.

Alipio opened two drawers near the refrigerator. "Look," he said as Mrs. Zafra came running back to the kitchen. "I got more food to last me . . . a long time."

The sisters gaped at the bags of rice, macaroni, spaghetti sticks, sugar, dried shrimps wrapped in cellophane, bottles of soy sauce and fish sauce, vinegar, ketchup, instant coffee, and more cans of sardines.

The sight of all that foodstuff seemed to have enlivened the old man. After all, it was his main sustenance, source of energy and health.

"Now look here," he said, turning briskly now to the refrigerator, which he opened. With a jerk he pulled open a large freezer, crammed full of meats. "Mostly lamb chops," he said, adding, "I like lamb chops."

"Carlito, he hates lamb chops," Mrs. Zafra said.

"I like lamb chops," Monica said, still wild-eyed, but now with a bit of color tinting her cheeks. "Why do you have so much?" she asked.

Alipio looked at her before answering. He thought she looked younger than her married sister. "You see," he said, "I read the papers for bargain sales. I can still drive the car when I feel all right. It's only now my leg's bothering me. So. I buy all I can. Save me many trips."

Later they sat around the enormous table in the dining room. Monica shared half a plate of the boiled rice topped with a sardine with Alipio. He showed her how to place the sardine on top, pressing it a little and pouring spoonfuls of the tomato sauce over it.

Mrs. Zafra had coffee and settled for a small can of vienna sausage and a little rice. She sipped her coffee meditatively.

"This is good coffee," she said. "I remember how we used to hoard Hills Bros. coffee at . . . at the college. The sisters were quite selfish about it."

"Antonieta was a nun, a sister of mercy," Monica said.

"What?" Alipio exclaimed, pointing a finger at her for no apparent reason, an involuntary gesture of surprise.

"Yes, I was," Mrs. Zafra admitted. "When I married, I had been out of the order for more than a year, yes, in California, at St. Mary's."

"You didn't . . ." Alipio began.

"Of course not," she interrupted him. "If you mean did I leave the order to marry Carlito. Oh, no. He was already an old man."

"I see. We used to joke him because he didn't like the girls too much. He prefer the cocks." The memory delighted him so much, he reared his head up as he laughed, covering his mouth hastily, but too late. Some of the tomato-soaked grains of rice had already spilled out on his plate and the table in front of him.

Monica looked pleased as she gathered carefully some of the grains on the table.

"He hasn't changed," Mrs. Zafra said vaguely. "It was me who wanted to marry him."

"You? After being a nun, you wanted to marry . . . Carlito? But why Carlito?" Alipio seemed to have forgotten for the moment that he was

CHARLIE CHAN IS DEAD 2

still eating. The steam from the rice passed across his face, touching it. He was staring at Mrs. Zafra as he breathed in the aroma without savoring it.

"It's a long story," Mrs. Zafra said. She stabbed a chunky sausage and brought it to her mouth. She looked pensive as she chewed on it.

"When did this happen?"

"Five, six years ago. Six years ago, almost."

"That long?"

"She had to marry him," Monica said blandly.

"What?" Alipio said, visibly disturbed. There was the sound of dentures grating in his mouth. He passed a hand over his face. "Carlito done that to you?"

The coffee spilled a little as Mrs. Zafra put the cup down. "Why, no," she said. "What are you thinking of?"

Before he could answer, Monica spoke in the same tone of voice, low, unexcited, saying, "He thinks Carlito got you pregnant, that's what."

"Carlito?" She turned to Monica in disbelief. "Why, Alipio knows Carlito," she said.

Monica shrugged her shoulders. "Why don't you tell him why," she said.

"It's a long story, but I'll make it short," she began. She took a sip from her cup and continued, "After leaving the order, I couldn't find a job. I was interested in social work, but I didn't know anybody who could help me."

As she paused, Alipio said, "What the heck does Carlito know about social work?"

"Let me continue," Mrs. Zafra said.

She still had a little money, from home, and she was not too worried about being jobless. But there was the question of her status as an alien. Once out of the order, she was no longer entitled to stay in the country, let alone get employment. The immigration office began to hound her, as it did other Filipinos in the same predicament. They were a pitiful lot. Some hid in the apartments of friends like criminals running away from the law. Of course, they were law breakers. Those who had transportation money returned home, which they hated to do. At home they would be forced to invent lies as to why they had come back so soon. They were defeated souls, insecure, and no longer fit for anything.

They had to learn how to live with the stigma of failure in a foreign land all their lives. Some lost their minds and had to be committed to insane asylums. Others became neurotic, antisocial, depressed in mind and spirit. Or parasites. Some must have turned to crime. Or just folded up, in a manner of speaking. It was a nightmare. She didn't want to go back to the Philippines. Just when she seemed to have reached the breaking point, she recalled incidents in which women in her situation married American citizens and, automatically, became entitled to permanent residency with an option to become U.S. citizens after five years. At first, she thought the idea was hideous, unspeakable. Other foreign women in a similar situation could do it perhaps, but not Philippine girls. But what was so special about Philippine girls? Nothing really, but their upbringing was such that to place themselves in a situation where they had to tell a man that they wanted to marry him for convenience was degrading, an unbearable shame. A form of self-destruction. Mortal sin! Better repatriation. A thousand times.

When an immigration officer finally caught up with her, he proved to be very understanding and quite a gentleman. He was young, maybe of Italian descent, and looked like a star salesman for a well-known company in the islands that dealt in farm equipment. Yet he was firm.

"I'm giving you one week," he said. "You have already overstayed by several months. If, in one week's time, you haven't yet left, I shall have to send you to jail, prior to deportation proceedings."

She cried, oh, how she cried. She wished she had not left the order, no, not really. She had no regrets about leaving up to this point. Life in the convent had turned sour on her. She despised the sisters and the system, which she found tyrannical, inhuman. In her own way, she had a long series of talks with God and God had approved of the step she had taken. She was not going back to the order. Even if she did, she would not be taken back. To jail then?

But why not marry an American citizen? In one week's time? How? Accost the first likely man and say, "You look like an American citizen. If you are, will you marry me? I want to remain in this country."

All week she talked to God. It was the same God she had worshipped and feared all her life. Now they were palsy walsy, on the best of terms. As she brooded over her misfortune, He brooded with her, sympathized with her, and finally advised her to go look for an elderly Filipino, who was an American citizen, and tell him the truth of the matter. Tell him that if he wished, it could be a marriage in name only. If he wished . . . Otherwise . . . Meanwhile He would look the other way.

How she found Carlito Zafra was another story, a much longer story, more confused. It was like a miracle. Her friend God could not have sent her to a better instrument to satisfy her need. That was not expressed well, but amounted to that, a need. Carlito was an instrument necessary for her good. And, as it turned out, a not too unwilling instrument.

"We were married the day before the week was over," Mrs. Zafra said. "And I've been in this country ever since. And no regrets."

They lived well and simply, a country life. True, they were childless, but both of them were helping relatives in the Philippines, sending them money, goods.

"Lately, however, some of the goods we've been sending do not arrive intact. Do you know, some of the good quality material we send never reach my relatives. It's frustrating."

"We got lots of thieves between here and there," Alipio said, but his mind seemed to be on something else.

"And I was able to send for Monica. From the snapshots she sent us, she seemed to be getting thinner and thinner, teaching in the barrio, and she wanted so much to come here."

"Seniang was like you also. I thank God for her," Alipio told Mrs. Zafra in such a low voice he could hardly be heard.

The sisters pretended they didn't know, but they knew. They knew practically everything about him. Alipio seemed pensive and eager to talk so they listened attentively.

"She went to where I was staying and said, without any hesitation, marry me and I'll take care of you. She was thin then and I thought what she said was funny, the others had been matching us, you know, but I was not really interested. I believe marriage means children. And if you cannot produce children, why get married? Besides, I had ugly experiences, bad moments. When I first arrived in the States, here in Frisco, I was young and there were lots of blondies hanging around on Kearny Street. It was easy. But I wanted a family and they didn't. None of 'em. So what the heck, I said."

Alipio realized that Seniang was not joking. She had to get married to an American citizen otherwise she would be deported. At that time,

Alipio was beginning to feel the disadvantages of living alone. There was too much time on his hands. How he hated himself for some of the things he did. He believed that if he were married, he would be more sensible with his time and his money. He would be happier and live longer. So when Seniang showed that she was serious, he agreed to marry her. But it was not to be in name only. He wanted a woman. He liked her so much he would have proposed himself had he suspected he had a chance. She was hard working, decent, and, in those days, rather slim.

"Like Monica," he said.

"Oh, I'm thin," Monica protested, blushing deeply. "I'm all bones."

"Monica is my only sister. We have no brother," Mrs. Zafra said, adding more items in her sister's vita.

"Look!" Monica said, "I finished everything on my plate. I haven't tasted sardines for a long time now. They taste so good, the way you eat them. I'm afraid I've eaten up your lunch. This is my first full meal. And I thought I've lost my appetite already."

Her words came out in a rush. It seemed she didn't want to stop and paused only because she didn't know what else to say. But she moved about, gaily and at ease, perfectly at home. Alipio watched her with a bemused look in his face as she gathered the dishes and brought them to the kitchen sink. When Alipio heard the water running, he stood up, without much effort this time, and walked to her, saying, "Don't bother. I got all the time to do that. You got to leave me something to do. Come, perhaps your sister wants another cup of coffee."

Mrs. Zafra had not moved from her seat. She was watching the two argue about the dishes. When she heard Alipio mention coffee, she said, "No, no more, thanks. I've drunk enough to keep me awake all week."

The two returned to the table after a while.

"Well, I'm going to wash them myself, later," Monica said as she took her seat.

"You're an excellent host, Alipio," Mrs. Zafra commended him, her tone sounding like a reading from a citation on a certificate of merit or something. "And to two complete strangers at that. You're a good man," she continued, the citation-sounding tone still in her voice.

"But you're not strangers. Carlito is my friend. We were young together in the States. And that's something, you know. There are lots like us here. Old timers, o.t.'s, they call us. Permanent residents. U.S. citizens. We all gonna be buried here." He appeared to be thinking deeply as he added, "But what's wrong about that?"

The sisters ignored the question. The old man was talking to himself.

"What is wrong is to be dishonest. Earn a living with both hands, not afraid any kind of work. No other way. Everything for convenience, why not? That's frankly honest. No pretend. Love comes in the afterwards. When it comes. If it comes."

Mrs. Zafra chuckled, saying, "Ah, you're a romantic, Alipio. I must ask Carlito about you. You seem to know so much about him. I bet you were quite a . . ." she paused because what she wanted to say was "rooster," but she did not want to give the impression of overfamiliarity.

But Alipio interrupted her, saying, "Ask him, he will say, yes, I'm a romantic." His voice had a vibrance that was a surprise and a revelation to the visitors. He gestured as he talked, puckering his mouth every now and then, obviously to keep his dentures from slipping out. "What do you think? We were young, why not? We wowed 'em with our gallantry, with our cooking. Boy, those dames never seen anything like us. Also, we were fools, most of us, anyway. Fools on fire!"

Mrs. Zafra clapped her hands. Monica was smiling.

"Ah, but that fire is gone. Only the fool's left now," Alipio said, weakly. His voice was low and he looked tired as he passed both hands across his face. Then he lifted his head. The listening look came back to his face. Now his voice shook as he spoke again.

"Many times I wonder where are the others. Where are you? Speak to me. And I think they're wondering the same, asking the same, so I say, I'm here, your friend Alipio Palma, my leg is broken, the wife she's dead, but I'm okay. Are you okay also? The dead they can hear even they don't answer. The alive don't answer. But I know. I feel. Some okay, some not. They old now, all of us, who were very young. All over the United States. All over the world . . ."

Abruptly, he turned to Mrs. Zafra, saying, "So. You and Carlito. But Carlito he never had fire."

"You can say that again," Mrs. Zafra laughed. "It would have burned him. Can't stand it. Not Carlito. But he's a good man, I can tell you that."

"No question. Da best," Alipio conceded.

Monica had been silent, but her eyes followed every move Alipio made, straying no farther than the reach of his arms as he gestured to help make clear the intensity of his feeling.

"I'm sure you still got some of that fire," Mrs. Zafra said.

Monica gasped, but recovered quickly. Again a rush of words came from her lips as if they had been there all the time and now her sister had said something that touched off the torrent of words. Her eyes shone as in a fever as she talked.

"I don't know Carlito very well. I've not been with them long, but from what you say, from the way you talk, from what I see, the two of you are different . . ."

"Oh, maybe not," Alipio said, trying to protest, but Monica went on.

"You have strength, Mr. Palma. Strength of character. Strength in your belief in God. I admire that in a man, in a human being. Look at you. Alone. This huge table. Don't you find it too big sometimes?" Monica paused, her eyes fixed on Alipio.

"I don't eat here. I eat in the kitchen," Alipio said.

Mrs. Zafra was going to say something, but she held back. Monica was talking again.

"But it must be hard, that you cannot deny. Living from day to day. Alone. On what? Memories? Cabinets and a refrigerator full of food? I repeat, I admire you, sir. You've found your place. You're home safe. And at peace." She paused again, this time to sweep back the strand of hair that had fallen on her brow.

Alipio had a drugged look. He seemed to have lost the drift of her speech. What was she talking about? Groceries? Baseball? He was going to say, you like baseball also? You like tuna? I have all kinds of fish. Get them at bargain price from Safeway. But, obviously, it was not the proper thing to say.

"Well, I guess, one gets used to anything. Even loneliness," Monica said in a listless, dispirited tone, all the fever in her voice suddenly gone.

"God dictates," Alipio said, feeling he had found his way again and he was now on the right track. What a girl. If she had only a little more flesh. And color.

Monica leaned back on her chair, exhausted. Mrs. Zafra was staring at her in disbelief, in grievous disappointment. What happened, you were going great, what suddenly hit you that you had to stop, give up, defeated, her eyes were asking and Monica shook her head in a gesture that quite clearly said, no, I can't do it, I can't anymore, I give up.

Their eyes kept on talking a deaf-mute dialogue. Mrs. Zafra: Just when everything was going fine, you quit. We've reached this far and you quit. I could have done it my way, directly, honestly. Not that what you were doing was dishonest, you were great, and now look at that dumb expression in your eyes. Monica: I can't. I can't anymore. It's too much.

"How long have you been in the States?" Alipio asked Monica.

"For almost a year now!" Mrs. Zafra screamed and Alipio was visibly shaken, but she didn't care. This was the right moment. She would take it from here whether Monica liked it or not. She was going to do it her way. "How long exactly, let's see Moni, when did you get your last extension?"

"Extension?" Alipio repeated the word. It had such a familiar ring like "visa" or "social security," it broke into his consciousness like a touch from Seniang's fingers. It was almost intimate. "You mean . . ."

"That's right. She's here as a temporary visitor. As a matter of fact, she came on a tourist visa. Carlito and I sponsored her coming, filed all the papers, and all she had to do was wait another year in the Philippines, but she couldn't wait. She came here as a tourist. Now she's in trouble."

"What trouble?" Alipio asked.

"She has to go back. To the Philippines. She can't stay here any longer."

"I have only two days left," Monica said, her head in her hands. "And I don't want to go back."

Alipio glanced at the wall clock. It was past three. They had been talking for hours. It was visas right from the start. Marriages. The long years and the o.t.'s. Now it was visas again. Were his ears playing a game? They might well, as they sometimes did, but his eyes surely were not. He could see this woman very plainly, sobbing on the table. She was in great trouble. Visas. Oh, oh! Now he knew what it was all about. His gleaming dentures showed a half smile. He turned to Mrs. Zafra.

"Did you come here . . ." he began, but Mrs. Zafra quickly interrupted him.

"Yes, Alipio. Forgive us. As soon as we arrived, I wanted to tell you without much talk, 'I'll tell you why we're here. I have heard about you.

IMMIGRATION BLUES

Not only from Carlito, but from other Filipinos who know you, how you're living here in San Francisco alone, a widower, and we heard of the accident, your stay in the hospital, when you came back, everything. Here's my sister, a teacher in the Philippines, never married, worried to death because she's being deported unless something turned up like she could marry a U.S. citizen, like I did, like your first wife Seniang, like many others have done, are doing in this exact moment, who knows? Now look at her, she's good, religious, any arrangement you wish, she'd accept it. But I didn't have a chance. You welcomed us just like old friends, relatives. Later, every time I began to say something, she interrupted me. I was afraid she had changed her mind and then she began to talk, then stopped without finishing what she really wanted to say, why we came to see you, and so forth."

"No, no!" Monica cried, raising her head, her eyes red from weeping, her face wet with tears. "You're such a good man. We couldn't do this to you. We're wrong. We started wrong. We should've been more honest, but I was ashamed, I was afraid! Let's go! Let's go!"

"Where you going?" Alipio asked.

"Anywhere," Monica answered. "Forgive us. Forgive me, Mister Alipio."

"What's to forgive? Don't go. We have dinner. But first, *merienda*. I take *merienda*. You do also, don't you?"

The sisters exchanged glances, their eyes chattering away.

Alipio was chuckling. He wanted to say, talk of lightning striking same fellow twice, but thought better of it. A bad thing to say. Seniang was not lightning. At times only. Mostly his fault. And this girl Moni? Nice name also. How can she be lightning?

Mrs. Zafra picked up her purse and before anyone could stop her, she was opening the door. "Where's the nearest grocery store around here?" she asked, but like Pilate, she didn't wait for an answer.

"Come back, come here back, we got lotsa food," Alipio called after her, but he might just as well have been calling to the Pacific Ocean. Mrs. Zafra took her time although the grocery store was only a few blocks away. When she returned, her arms were full of groceries in paper bags. The two met her on the porch.

"*Kumusta*," she asked, speaking for the first time in the dialect as Monica relieved her of her load. The one word question meant much more than "how are you" or "how has it been?"

Alipio replied, as always, in English. "God dictates," he said, his dentures sounding faintly as he smacked his lips, but he was not looking at the foodstuff in the paper bags Monica was carrying. His eyes were on her legs, in the direction she was taking. She knew where the kitchen was, of course. He just wanted to be sure she wouldn't lose her way. Sometimes he went to the bedroom by mistake. Lotsa things happen to men of his age.

SURROUNDED BY SLEEP

■ ■ ■

Akhil Sharma

One August afternoon, when Ajay was ten years old, his elder brother, Aman, dove into a pool and struck his head on the cement bottom. For three minutes, he lay there unconscious. Two boys continued to swim, kicking and splashing, until finally Aman was spotted below them. Water had entered through his nose and mouth. It had filled his stomach. His lungs collapsed. By the time he was pulled out, he could no longer think, talk, chew, or roll over in his sleep.

Ajay's family had moved from India to Queens, New York, two years earlier. The accident occurred during the boys' summer vacation, on a visit with their aunt and uncle in Arlington, Virginia. After the accident, Ajay's mother came to Arlington, where she waited to see if Aman would recover. At the hospital, she told the doctors and nurses that her son had been accepted into the Bronx High School of Science, in the hope that by highlighting his intelligence she would move them to make a greater effort on his behalf. Within a few weeks of the accident, the insurance company said that Aman should be transferred to a less expensive care facility, a long-term one. But only a few of these were

AKHIL SHARMA was born in Delhi, India, in 1971. He immigrated to the United States with his family when he was eight. His novel, *An Obedient Father*, was published in the United States in June of 2000. One of the most acclaimed debuts of 2000, it won the prestigious PEN Hemingway Award and the Susan Kaufman PEN Prize from the American Academy of Arts and Letters. His short stories have appeared in *The New Yorker* and the *Atlantic Monthly*, and have been anthologized in *The Best American Short Stories, The O. Henry Award Winners*, and textbooks on creative writing.

any good, and those were full, and Ajay's mother refused to move Aman until a space opened in one of them. So she remained in Arlington, and Ajay stayed, too, and his father visited from Queens on the weekends when he wasn't working. Ajay was enrolled at the local public school and in September he started fifth grade.

Before the accident, Ajay had never prayed much. In India, he and his brother used to go with their mother to the temple every Tuesday night, but that was mostly because there was a good *dosa* restaurant nearby. In America, his family went to a temple only on important holy days and birthdays. But shortly after Ajay's mother came to Arlington, she moved into the room that he and his brother had shared during the summer and made an altar in a corner. She threw an old flowered sheet over a cardboard box that had once held a television. On top, she put a clay lamp, an incense-stick holder, and postcards depicting various gods. There was also a postcard of Mahatma Gandhi. She explained to Ajay that God could take any form; the picture of Mahatma Gandhi was there because he had appeared to her in a dream after the accident and told her that Aman would recover and become a surgeon. Now she and Ajay prayed for at least half an hour before the altar every morning and night.

At first, she prayed with absolute humility. "Whatever you do will be good because you are doing it," she murmured to the postcards of Ram and Shivaji, daubing their lips with water and rice. Mahatma Gandhi got only water, because he did not like to eat. As weeks passed and Aman did not recover in time to return to the Bronx High School of Science for the first day of classes, his mother began doing things that called attention to her piety. She sometimes held the prayer lamp until it blistered her palms. Instead of kneeling before the altar, she lay face down. She fasted twice a week. Her attempts to sway God were not so different from Ajay's performing somersaults to amuse his aunt, and they made God seem human to Ajay.

One morning, as Ajay knelt before the altar, he traced an Om, a crucifix, and a Star of David into the pile of the carpet. Beneath these, he traced an "S," for Superman, inside an upside-down triangle. His mother came up beside him.

"What are you praying for?" she asked. She had her hat on, a thick gray knitted one that a man might wear. The tracings went against the weave of the carpet and were darker than the surrounding nap. Pretending to examine them, Ajay leaned forward and put his hand over the "S." His mother did not mind the Christian and Jewish symbols—they were for commonly recognized gods, after all—but she could not tolerate his praying to Superman. She'd caught him doing so once, several weeks earlier, and had become very angry, as if Ajay's faith in Superman made her faith in Ram ridiculous. "Right in front of God," she had said several times.

Ajay, in his nervousness, spoke the truth. "I'm asking God to give me a hundred per cent on the math test."

His mother was silent for a moment. "What if God says you can have the math grade but then Aman will have to be sick a little while longer?" she asked.

Ajay kept quiet. He could hear cars on the road outside. He knew that his mother wanted to bewail her misfortune before God so that God would feel guilty. He looked at the postcard of Mahatma Gandhi. It was a black-and-white photo of him walking down a city street with an enormous crowd trailing behind him. Ajay thought of how, before the accident, Aman had been so modest that he would not leave the bathroom until he was fully dressed. Now he had rashes on his penis from the catheter that drew his urine into a translucent bag hanging from the guardrail of his bed.

His mother asked again, "Would you say, 'Let him be sick a little while longer'?"

"Are you going to tell me the story about Uncle Naveen again?" he asked.

"Why shouldn't I? When I was sick, as a girl, your uncle walked seven times around the temple and asked God to let him fail his exams just as long as I got better."

"If I failed the math test and told you that story, you'd slap me and ask what one has to do with the other."

His mother turned to the altar. "What sort of sons did you give me, God?" she asked. "One you drown, the other is this selfish fool."

"I will fast today so that God puts some sense in me," Ajay said, glancing away from the altar and up at his mother. He liked the drama of fasting.

"No, you are a growing boy." His mother knelt down beside him and said to the altar, "He is stupid, but he has a good heart."

■ ■ ■

Prayer, Ajay thought, should appeal with humility and an open heart to some greater force. But the praying that he and his mother did felt sly and confused. By treating God as someone to bargain with, it seemed to him, they prayed as if they were casting a spell.

This meant that it was possible to do away with the presence of God entirely. For example, Ajay's mother had recently asked a relative in India to drive a nail into a holy tree and tie a saffron thread to the nail on Aman's behalf. Ajay invented his own ritual. On his way to school each morning, he passed a thick tree rooted half on the sidewalk and half on the road. One day, Ajay got the idea that if he circled the tree seven times, touching the north side every other time, he would have a lucky day. From then on, he did it every morning, although he felt embarrassed and always looked around beforehand to make sure no one was watching.

One night, Ajay asked God whether he minded being prayed to only in need.

"You think of your toe only when you stub it," God replied. God looked like Clark Kent. He wore a gray cardigan, slacks, and thick glasses, and had a forelock that curled just as Ajay's did.

God and Ajay had begun talking occasionally after Aman drowned. Now they talked most nights while Ajay lay in bed and waited for sleep. God sat at the foot of Ajay's mattress. His mother's mattress lay parallel to his, a few feet away. Originally, God had appeared to Ajay as Krishna, but Ajay had felt foolish discussing brain damage with a blue God who held a flute and wore a dhoti.

"You're not angry with me for touching the tree and all that?"

"No. I'm flexible."

"I respect you. The tree is just a way of praying to you," Ajay assured God.

God laughed. "I am not too caught up in formalities."

Ajay was quiet. He was convinced that he had been marked as special by Aman's accident. The beginnings of all heroes are distinguished by misfortune. Superman and Batman were both orphans. Krishna was separated from his parents at birth. The god Ram had to spend fourteen years in a forest. Ajay waited to speak until it would not appear improper to begin talking about himself.

"How famous will I be?" he asked, finally.

"I can't tell you the future," God answered.

Ajay asked, "Why not?"

"Even if I told you something, later I might change my mind."

"But it might be harder to change your mind after you have said something will happen."

God laughed again. "You'll be so famous that fame will be a problem."

Ajay sighed. His mother snorted and rolled over.

"I want Aman's drowning to lead to something," he said to God.

"He won't be forgotten."

"I can't just be famous, though. I need to be rich, too, to take care of Mummy and Daddy and pay Aman's hospital bills."

"You are always practical." God had a soulful and pitying voice and God's sympathy made Ajay imagine himself as a truly tragic figure, like Amitabh Bachchan in the movie "Trishul."

"I have responsibilities," Ajay said. He was so excited at the thought of his possible greatness that he knew he would have difficulty sleeping. Perhaps he would have to go read in the bathroom.

"You can hardly imagine the life ahead," God said.

Even though God's tone promised greatness, the idea of the future frightened Ajay. He opened his eyes. There was light coming from the street. The room was cold and had a smell of must and incense. His aunt and uncle's house was a narrow two-story home next to a four-lane road. The apartment building with the pool where Aman had drowned was a few blocks up the road, one in a cluster of tall brick buildings with stucco fronts. Ajay pulled the blanket tighter around him. In India, he could not have imagined the reality of his life in America: the thick smell of meat in the school cafeteria, the many television channels. And, of course, he could not have imagined Aman's accident, or the hospital where he spent so much time.

■ ■ ■

The hospital was boring. Vinod, Ajay's cousin, picked him up after school and dropped him off there almost every day. Vinod was twenty-two. In addition to attending county college and studying computer programming, he worked at a 7-Eleven near Ajay's school. He often brought Ajay hot chocolate and a comic from the store, which had to be returned, so Ajay was not allowed to open it until he had wiped his hands.

Vinod usually asked him a riddle on the way to the hospital. "Why are manhole covers round?" It took Ajay half the ride to admit that he did not know. He was having difficulty talking. He didn't know why. The only time he could talk easily was when he was with God. The explanation he gave himself for this was that, just as he couldn't chew when there was too much in his mouth, he couldn't talk when there were too many thoughts in his head.

When Ajay got to Aman's room, he greeted him as if he were all right. "Hello, lazy. How much longer are you going to sleep?" His mother was always there. She got up and hugged Ajay. She asked how school had been, and he didn't know what to say. In music class, the teacher sang a song about a sailor who had bared his breast before jumping into the sea. This had caused the other students to giggle. But Ajay could not say the word "breast" to his mother without blushing. He had also cried. He'd been thinking of how Aman's accident had made his own life mysterious and confused. What would happen next? Would Aman die or would he go on as he was? Where would they live? Usually when Ajay cried in school, he was told to go outside. But it had been raining, and the teacher had sent him into the hallway. He sat on the floor and wept. Any mention of this would upset his mother. And so he said nothing had happened that day.

Sometimes when Ajay arrived his mother was on the phone, telling his father that she missed him and was expecting to see him on Friday. His father took a Greyhound bus most Fridays from Queens to Arlington, returning on Sunday night in time to work the next day. He was a bookkeeper for a department store. Before the accident, Ajay had thought of his parents as the same person: Mummy-Daddy. Now, when he saw his father praying stiffly or when his father failed to say hello to Aman in his hospital bed, Ajay sensed that his mother and father were quite different people. After his mother got off the phone, she always went to the cafeteria to get coffee for herself and jello or cookies for him. He knew that if she took her coat with her it meant that she was especially sad. Instead of going directly to the cafeteria, she was going to go outside and walk around the hospital parking lot.

That day, while she was gone, Ajay stood beside the hospital bed and balanced a comic book on Aman's chest. He read to him very slowly. Before turning each page, he said, "O.K., Aman?"

Aman was fourteen. He was thin and had curly hair. Immediately after the accident, there had been so many machines around his bed that only one person could stand beside him at a time. Now there was just a single waxy yellow tube. One end of this went into his abdomen; the other, blocked by a green bullet-shaped plug, was what his Isocal milk was poured through. When not being used, the tube was rolled up and bound by a rubber band and tucked beneath Aman's hospital gown. But even with the tube hidden it was obvious that there was something wrong with Aman. It was in his stillness and his open eyes. Once, in their house in Queens, Ajay had left a plastic bowl on a radiator overnight and the sides had drooped and sagged so that the bowl looked a little like an eye. Aman reminded Ajay of that bowl.

Ajay had not gone with his brother to the swimming pool on the day of the accident, because he had been reading a book and wanted to finish it. But he heard the ambulance siren from his aunt and uncle's house. The pool was only a few minutes away, and when he got there a crowd had gathered around the ambulance. Ajay saw his uncle first, in shorts and an undershirt, talking to a man inside the ambulance. His aunt was standing beside him. Then Ajay saw Aman on a stretcher, in blue shorts with a plastic mask over his nose and mouth. His aunt hurried over to take Ajay home. He cried as they walked, although he had been certain that Aman would be fine in a few days: in a Spider-Man comic he had just read, Aunt May had fallen into a coma and she had woken up perfectly fine. Ajay had cried simply because he felt crying was called for by the seriousness of the occasion. Perhaps this moment would mark the beginning of his future greatness. From that day on, Ajay found it hard to cry in front of his family. Whenever tears started coming, he felt like a liar. If he loved his brother, he knew, he would not have thought about himself as the ambulance had pulled away, nor would he talk with God at night about becoming famous.

When Ajay's mother returned to Aman's room with coffee and cookies, she sometimes talked to Ajay about Aman. She told him that when Aman was six he had seen a children's television show that had a character named Chunu, which was Aman's nickname, and he had thought the show was based on his own life. But most days Ajay went into the lounge to read. There was a TV in the corner and a lamp near a window that looked out over a parking lot. It was the perfect place to read. Ajay liked fantasy novels where the hero, who was preferably under the age of twenty-five, had an undiscovered talent that made him famous when it was revealed. He could read for hours without interruption, and sometimes when Vinod came to drive Ajay and his mother home from the hospital it was hard for him to remember the details of the real day that had passed.

One evening, when he was in the lounge, he saw a rock star being interviewed on "Entertainment Tonight." The musician, dressed in a sleeveless undershirt that revealed a swarm of tattoos on his arms and shoulders, had begun to shout at the audience, over his interviewer, "Don't watch me! Live your life! I'm not you!" Filled with a sudden desire to do something, Ajay hurried out of the television lounge and stood on the sidewalk in front of the hospital entrance. But he did not know what to do. It was cold and dark and there was an enormous moon. Cars leaving the parking lot stopped one by one at the edge of the road. Ajay watched as they waited for an opening in the traffic, their brake lights glowing.

■ ■ ■

"Are things getting worse?" Ajay asked God. The weekend before had been Thanksgiving. Christmas soon would come, and a new year would start, a year during which Aman would not have talked or walked. Suddenly, Ajay understood hopelessness. Hopelessness felt very much like fear. It involved a clutching in the stomach and a numbness in the arms and legs.

"What do you think?" God answered.

"They seem to be."

"At least Aman's hospital hasn't forced him out."

"At least Aman isn't dead. At least Daddy's Greyhound bus has never skidded off a bridge." Lately, Ajay had begun talking much more quickly to God than he used to. Before, when he had talked to God, Ajay would think of what God would say in response before he said anything. Now, Ajay spoke without knowing how God might respond.

"You shouldn't be angry at me." God sighed. God was wearing his usual cardigan. "You can't understand why I do what I do."

"You should explain better, then."

"Christ was my son. I loved Job. How long did Ram have to live in a forest?"

"What does that have to do with me?" This was usually the cue for discussing Ajay's prospects. But hopelessness made the future feel even more frightening than the present.

"I can't tell you what the connection is, but you'll be proud of yourself."

They were silent for a while.

"Do you love me truly?" Ajay asked.

"Yes."

"Will you make Aman normal?" As soon as Ajay asked the question, God ceased to be real. Ajay knew then that he was alone, lying under his blankets, his face exposed to the cold dark.

"I can't tell you the future," God said, softly. These were words that Ajay already knew.

"Just get rid of the minutes when Aman lay on the bottom of the pool. What are three minutes to you?"

"Presidents die in less time than that. Planes crash in less time than that."

Ajay opened his eyes. His mother was on her side and she had a blanket pulled up to her neck. She looked like an ordinary woman. It surprised him that you couldn't tell, looking at her, that she had a son who was brain-dead.

■ ■ ■

In fact, things were getting worse. Putting away his mother's mattress and his own in a closet in the morning, getting up very early so he could use the bathroom before his aunt or uncle did, spending so many hours in the hospital—all this had given Ajay the reassuring sense that real life was in abeyance, and that what was happening was unreal. He and his mother and brother were just waiting to make a long-delayed bus trip. The bus would come eventually to carry them to Queens, where he would return to school at P.S. 20 and to Sunday afternoons spent at the Hindi movie theatre under the trestle for the 7 train. But now Ajay was starting to understand that the world was always real, whether you were reading a book or sleeping, and that it eroded you every day.

He saw the evidence of this erosion in his mother, who had grown severe and unforgiving. Usually when Vinod brought her and Ajay home from the hospital, she had dinner with the rest of the family. After his mother helped his aunt wash the dishes, the two women watched theological action movies. One night, in spite of a headache that had made her sit with her eyes closed all afternoon, she ate dinner, washed dishes, sat down in front of the TV. As soon as the movie was over, she went upstairs, vomited, and lay on her mattress with a wet towel over her forehead. She asked Ajay to massage her neck and shoulders. As he did so, Ajay noticed that she was crying. The tears frightened Ajay and made him angry. "You shouldn't have watched TV," he said accusingly.

"I have to," she said. "People will cry with you once, and they will cry with you a second time. But if you cry a third time, people will say you are boring and always crying."

Ajay did not want to believe what she had said, but her cynicism made him think that she must have had conversations with his aunt and uncle that he did not know about. "That's not true," he told her, massaging her scalp. "Uncle is kind. Auntie Aruna is always kind."

"What do you know?" She shook her head, freeing herself from Ajay's fingers. She stared at him. Upside down, her face looked unfamiliar and terrifying. "If God lets Aman live long enough, you will become a stranger, too. You will say, 'I have been unhappy for so long because of Aman, now I don't want to talk about him or look at him.' Don't think I don't know you," she said.

Suddenly, Ajay hated himself. To hate himself was to see himself as the opposite of everything he wanted to be: short instead of tall, fat instead of thin. When he brushed his teeth that night, he looked at his face: his chin was round and fat as a heel. His nose was so broad that he had once been able to fit a small rock in one nostril.

His father was also being eroded. Before the accident, Ajay's father loved jokes—he could do perfect imitations—and Ajay had felt lucky to have him as a father. (Once, Ajay's father had convinced his own mother that he was possessed by the ghost of a British man.) And, even after the accident, his father had impressed Ajay with the patient loyalty of his weekly bus journeys. But now his father was different.

One Saturday afternoon, as Ajay and his father were returning from the hospital, his father slowed the car without warning and turned into the dirt parking lot of a bar that looked as though it had originally been a small house. It had a pitched roof with a black tarp. At the edge of the lot stood a tall neon sign of an orange hand lifting a mug of sudsy golden beer. Ajay had never seen anybody drink except in the movies. He wondered whether his father was going to ask for directions to somewhere, and, if so, to where.

His father said, "One minute," and they climbed out of the car.

They went up wooden steps into the bar. Inside, it was dark and smelled of cigarette smoke and something stale and sweet. The floor was linoleum like the kitchen at his aunt and uncle's. There was a bar with stools around it, and a basketball game played on a television bolted against the ceiling, like the one in Aman's hospital room.

His father stood by the bar waiting for the bartender to notice him. His father had a round face and was wearing a white shirt and dark dress pants, as he often did on the weekend, since it was more economical to have the same clothes for the office and home.

The bartender came over. "How much for a Budweiser?" his father asked.

It was a dollar fifty. "Can I buy a single cigarette?" He did not have to buy; the bartender would just give him one. His father helped Ajay up onto a stool and sat down himself. Ajay looked around and wondered what would happen if somebody started a knife fight. When his father had drunk half his beer he carefully lit the cigarette. The bartender was standing at the end of the bar. There were only two other men in the place. Ajay was disappointed that there were no women wearing dresses slit all the way up their thighs. Perhaps they came in the evenings.

His father asked him if he had ever watched a basketball game all the way through.

"I've seen the Harlem Globetrotters."

His father smiled and took a sip. "I've heard they don't play other teams, because they can defeat everyone else so easily."

"They only play against each other, unless there is an emergency— like in the cartoon, when they play against the aliens to save the Earth," Ajay said.

"Aliens?"

Ajay blushed as he realized his father was teasing him.

When they left, the light outside felt too bright. As his father opened the car door for Ajay, he said, "I'm sorry." That's when Ajay first felt that his father might have done something wrong. The thought made him worry. Once they were on the road, his father said gently, "Don't tell your mother."

Fear made Ajay feel cruel. He asked his father, "What do you think about when you think of Aman?"

Instead of becoming sad, Ajay's father smiled. "I am surprised by how strong he is. It's not easy for him to keep living. But, even before, he was strong. When he was interviewing for high-school scholarships, one interviewer asked him, 'Are you a thinker or a doer?' He laughed and said, 'That's like asking, "Are you an idiot or a moron?" ' "

From then on, they often stopped at the bar on the way back from the hospital. Ajay's father always asked the bartender for a cigarette before he sat down, and during the ride home he always reminded Ajay not to tell his mother.

Ajay found that he himself was changing. His superstitions were becoming extreme. Now when he walked around the good-luck tree he punched it, every other time, hard, so that his knuckles hurt. Afterward, he would hold his breath for a moment longer than he thought he could bear, and ask God to give the unused breaths to Aman.

■ ■ ■

In December, a place opened in one of the good long-term care facilities. It was in New Jersey. This meant that Ajay and his mother could move back to New York and live with his father again. This was the news Ajay's father brought when he arrived for a two-week holiday at Christmas.

Ajay felt the clarity of panic. Life would be the same as before the accident but also unimaginably different. He would return to P.S. 20, while Aman continued to be fed through a tube in his abdomen. Life would be Aman's getting older and growing taller than their parents but having less consciousness than even a dog, which can become excited or afraid.

Ajay decided to use his devotion to shame God into fixing Aman. The fact that two religions regarded the coming December days as holy ones suggested to Ajay that prayers during this time would be especially potent. So he prayed whenever he thought of it—at his locker, even in the middle of a quiz. His mother wouldn't let him fast, but he started throwing away the lunch he took to school. And when his mother prayed in the morning Ajay watched to make sure that she bowed at least once toward each of the postcards of deities. If she did not, he bowed three times to the possibly offended god on the postcard. He had noticed that his father finished his prayers in less time than it took to brush his teeth. And so now, when his father began praying in the morning, Ajay immediately crouched down beside him, because he knew his father would be embarrassed to get up first. But Ajay found it harder and harder to drift into the rhythm of sung prayers or into his nightly conversations with God. How could chanting and burning incense undo three minutes of a sunny August afternoon? It was like trying to move a sheet of blank paper from one end of a table to the other by blinking so fast that you started a breeze.

■ ■ ■

On Christmas Eve, his mother asked the hospital chaplain to come to Aman's room and pray with them. The family knelt together beside Aman's bed. Afterward, the chaplain asked her whether she would be attending Christmas services. "Of course, Father," she said.

"I'm also coming," Ajay said.

The chaplain turned toward Ajay's father, who was sitting in a wheelchair because there was nowhere else to sit.

"I'll wait for God at home," he said.

That night, Ajay watched "It's a Wonderful Life" on television. To him, the movie meant that happiness arrived late, if ever. Later, when he got in bed and closed his eyes, God appeared. There was little to say.

"Will Aman be better in the morning?"

"No."

"Why not?"

"When you prayed for the math exam, you could have asked for Aman to get better and, instead of your getting an A, Aman would have woken."

This was so ridiculous that Ajay opened his eyes. His father was sleeping nearby on folded-up blankets. Ajay felt disappointed at not feeling guilt. Guilt might have contained some hope that God existed.

When Ajay arrived at the hospital with his father and mother the next morning, Aman was asleep, breathing through his mouth while a nurse poured a can of Isocal into his stomach through the yellow tube. Ajay had not expected that Aman would have recovered; nevertheless, seeing him that way put a weight in Ajay's chest.

The Christmas prayers were held in a large, mostly empty room: people in chairs sat next to people in wheelchairs. His father walked out in the middle of the service.

Later, Ajay sat in a corner of Aman's room and watched his parents. His mother was reading a Hindi women's magazine to Aman while she shelled peanuts into her lap. His father was reading a thick red book in preparation for a civil-service exam. The day wore on. The sky outside grew dark. At some point, Ajay began to cry. He tried to be quiet. He did not want his parents to notice his tears and think that he was crying for Aman, because in reality he was crying for how difficult his own life was.

His father noticed first. "What's the matter, hero?"

His mother shouted, "What happened?" and she sounded so alarmed it was as if Ajay were bleeding.

"I didn't get any Christmas presents. I need a Christmas present," Ajay shouted. "You didn't buy me a Christmas present." And then, because he had revealed his own selfishness, Ajay let himself sob. "You have to give me something. I should get something for all this." Ajay clenched his hands and wiped his face with his fists. "Each time I come here I should get something."

His mother pulled him up and pressed him into her stomach. His father came and stood beside them. "What do you want?" his father asked.

Ajay had no prepared answer for this.

"What do you want?" his mother repeated.

The only thing he could think was "I want to eat pizza and I want candy."

His mother stroked his hair and called him her little baby. She kept wiping his face with a fold of her sari. When at last he stopped crying, they decided that Ajay's father should take him back to his aunt and uncle's. On the way, they stopped at a mini-mall. It was a little after five, and the streetlights were on. Ajay and his father did not take off their winter coats as they ate, in a pizzeria staffed by Chinese people. While he chewed, Ajay closed his eyes and tried to imagine God looking like Clark Kent, wearing a cardigan and eyeglasses, but he could not. Afterward, Ajay and his father went next door to a magazine shop and Ajay got a bag of Three Musketeers bars and a bag of Reese's peanut butter cups, and then he was tired and ready for home.

He held the candy in his lap while his father drove in silence. Even through the plastic, he could smell the sugar and chocolate. Some of the houses outside were dark, and others were outlined in Christmas lights.

After a while, Ajay rolled down the window slightly. The car filled with wind. They passed the building where Aman's accident had occurred. Ajay had not walked past it since the accident. When they drove by, he usually looked away. Now he tried to spot the fenced swimming pool at the building's side. He wondered whether the pool that had pressed itself into Aman's mouth and lungs and stomach had been drained, so that nobody would be touched by its unlucky waters. Probably it had not been emptied until fall. All summer long, people must have swum in the pool and sat on its sides, splashing their feet in the water, and not known that his brother had lain for three minutes on its concrete bottom one August afternoon.

PAPIER

from *GRASS ROOF, TIN ROOF*

■ ■ ■

Dao Strom

I.

It was a grand story with many events and an inconclusive ending, and it left her with an ache in her brain and heart, a feeling akin to wanting. Wanting tinged with amazement and understanding—the ending would always be inconclusive—and this was why the story worked as well as it did; this was why it was so affecting and rending and lingering. For many nights afterwards, she went to sleep wishing she could live this story and picturing herself after the experience a wiser, sadder, nobler person. Or she liked to imagine meeting a man who had lived through such an experience, a humble, beaten man whose integrity only she would recognize, and she would be his friend. She wouldn't ask for more than that.

She had been introduced to the story by a man whom she knew only by his first name, Gabriel. He was a French war correspondent living intermittently in her country and his own. When she met him in 1969, she was twenty-four years old, unwed with one son, then a toddler, from a previous relationship, and she was taking French and English literature and language classes at the Saigon University where Gabriel often came to visit the teachers, many of whom worked on the side as interpreters. She had aspirations of being a writer or artist; she

---

DAO STROM was born in 1973 in Saigon, Vietnam. She emigrated to the United States in 1975 and grew up in northern California. Her first novel, *Grass Roof, Tin Roof*, was published in 2003. She is currently at work on a second novel.

hadn't decided yet which kind. On her first date with Gabriel they saw an American movie about the life of Vincent Van Gogh, starring Kirk Douglas. The theater was mostly full of American GIs and foreign news correspondents and their Vietnamese dates or associates—other English-speaking, local advocates of Democracy—writers, teachers, print and broadcast news reporters and employees, students, businessmen, travel guides and ambitious prostitutes. Tran did not align herself with this latter group, and trusted Gabriel did not either, though she knew it would look suspect, a local woman on the arm of a foreign man. Her foreign man, the Frenchman, however, was obviously not a soldier; for her sake, he wore his press jacket (she had insisted on this, wanting the distinction to be clear, but had told him it was because she liked him better in the jacket). His build was also too slight and reserved for a soldier, and he was older, with a long face and faintly smiling, thin lips. Tran thought Gabriel's deep-set eyes—with their yellowish-hazel color, behind wire-framed glasses—held an intellectual, disenchanted cast.

The movie was maudlin and heroic, this in a time when such sentiment in the movies was still cathartic—though it is likely any movie featuring the likes of Kirk Douglas would've been cathartic at that time, at that outpost. Already a sense of hopelessness and consternation pervaded the streets, though people seemed to be laughing, selling, buying, venting opinions and eating and drinking with all the usual fervor; it was this fervor, in fact, that seemed now volatile and dangerously indifferent. Tran felt watchful in public places. And though she would in all sensible mind claim not to admire any military, she looked with a naïve respect, even a deferent longing, toward the American military men, for the very details of their dress and physicality (the size and stoutness of their bodies, the muted colors and fitted cut of their clothes, their sweat rings that seemed evidence to her of their formidability rather than—as it seemed with the local militia men, whose uniforms always sagged—their inability to cope) had in her mind aligned itself with a concept of order.

Tran was wiping her eyes when the lights came up at the end of the film, and when Gabriel asked why, she replied in her cautious French, "I understand very well the melancholy of the life of an artist." She had actually meant to use the word *l'angoisse*, but when *la mélancolie* slipped out of her lips she realized this was more right: a more subdued, less violent—more poetic, even—portrayal of the pain she had meant.

Suddenly the small theater trembled in a great ground shudder and there was a muffled boom and the noise of commotion outside. Inside, people began to panic and run for the exits. Gabriel took hold of Tran by both shoulders, pushed her into a corner against the stage. She felt the rough efficiency of his body pressed suddenly, unsexually, against hers—she felt more conscious of this than of the rumbling walls, which she had already surrendered her fate to in the first instant. With intensity Gabriel was watching the crowd, craning his neck. His body blocked Tran's view and she found herself staring at the fine brown hairs of his chest visible through the folds of fabric between his shirt buttons. She closed her eyes. Then the shaking stopped. They made their way toward an exit, and when they came out onto the street they saw the throng of people gathered in front of the bookstore and mail depot, its front now blown open and billowing black smoke. Three Vietnamese civilians writhed on the sidewalk in front of the mess, crying in pain; a few local policemen and Americans were running toward them. Gabriel directed Tran to wait at the back of the crowd. "I have to work," he said. Then he took his camera out of the small canvas satchel he wore slung over his shoulder. Tran watched his back (his shirt half-untucked, the seat of his pants rumpled) pushing through the crowd.

Later, much later, they would define the bombing as fate—not necessarily to say their relationship was doomed, but that this omen was representative of what was to come, or the nature of how things were to open between them.

■ ■ ■

The novel he had recommended to her was an American classic, *Gone With the Wind*. They read passages together ("If you want to learn English you must read this story," he'd said, "there is not much good about the English language except this story"). It was Gabriel's favorite American novel for a couple of reasons: one, he saw it as a great depiction of "the American insistence upon naïveté"; and, two, he liked those literary classics by authors who had never intended to be authors, who said all they needed to in one book alone. There was something more honest, more respectable, this way, he theorized, as if the book, the story itself, had forced its way out of the reluctant author, rather than the other method, where the story became tangled up in an author's ego. This author was a woman (which appealed to Tran) in the 1930s, and the novel had a good dose of everything: the rise and fall of vanities and so-cieties, births and deaths, unrequited loves, illegitimate children, an ir-repressible heroine, a scandalous hero. And at the center of it, a civil war between North and South, something relevant. Occasionally Tran and Gabriel would discuss the parallels between life and literature and politics and cultures, which spanned years and seas.

Tran did not always understand Gabriel's theories but was drawn in by his wry spirit, the nonchalance with which he delivered his well-informed and devastating perceptions about current politics, the same politics that only distressed Tran's Vietnamese colleagues and some-times confused Tran; she could easily find merit in every point of view. In fact she somewhat admired Gabriel, his aloofness, his sense of com-edy, which was almost cruel and thus took on another quality—acer-bic, tragic, self-denying. How did one become like this, she wondered, so intellectual and so resigned yet *not* resigned, by sheer virtue of his commitment to that very attitude? The more time she spent with him, though, the more she began to see cracks in his mask. When they prac-ticed reading in her language, his accent was slow and clumsy and al-most embarrassingly earnest. The way he would point to objects on the street (phone booth, gutter pipe, spokes of a bicycle wheel) or a part of her body, and ask her the words that named these places, these ap-pendages. His candor and his deep, eager, fumbling voice repeating after her at first surprised her; she saw a man who desired to be some-one other than he was, whose knowledge and wit encumbered rather than enlightened him. She understood then the grace, the simplicity, he saw in her—and the lack of which he despised in himself. Thus did clumsiness and a hidden vulnerability become the characteristics she associated with *white*. His white body, covered in dark curling patches of hair, was long and awkward and remorseful when they made love. His white linen shirts, wrinkled and sweat-stained. His white skin that seemed so thin and unsuitable a cover, especially under the tropical sun, and made nudity look unnatural (she soon developed the impres-sion that white people were meant always to be clothed, that it was their more natural state). Yet he was her vessel and gateway both, to a strange vision of power and regret, to so much of the outside world she didn't know how else she would ever reach. Though she did not think she loved him, at times she felt sympathy for him.

When Gabriel's assignment in Saigon ended in 1971, he returned to

France; someone else had always been there waiting for him. Tran was not mournful and told him confidently that she wished him well and would not miss him, that theirs had been what it was for the time it was—an intimacy enabled yet limited by the temporal circumstances of war, a situation wherein people like him (more than her) could for a period disinhabit the more regulated life to which they must eventually return. Tran was not an impractical woman; back in 1966, when the man who was her son's father had denied any involvement with her, she had learned her first lesson about the potential disappointments of love. In short, she had learned not to count on reciprocation. He had been a slightly older man, an established schoolteacher in their community, and he had introduced her to much about philosophy and the creative life. For the first few months after discovering she was pregnant with his child she had pursued him, demanding either money or that he marry her, and he had laughed her off, claiming that her relationship with him was merely a schoolgirl fantasy. Where the live proof came from, he had said, he would leave to speculation. Tran had felt crushed, indignant, humiliated. She went to a fortune-teller who informed her she should not try to marry before the age of thirty, as all her lovers would either die or leave her. And a man from far off would come for her one day. "I tell this to many women, it is true, to keep their hearts awake, their hopes up, but to you I mean it," the fortune-teller had said. And for the first time in her life Tran had experienced the resolve of *knowing*. Yes, she would have the child, but she did not want or need the father. Her own father was shamed and her mother heartbroken when Tran announced her decision. But they could hardly deny the presence of new life when actually it did arrive.

■ ■ ■

It is said love can move any mountain is how she began her version of the story, *and love comes to us when we are not looking, when we have turned our backs on its very possibility, have resigned ourselves to the longing. Yet when it comes, we know it from the first moment the would-be object of our affection appears. We know love by both the dread and excitement in our hearts, by the resistance our minds raise against what our hearts are straining toward; we know it by the fact that we cannot stop it once it starts to happen and suddenly the world is full of a sense of great and imminent change just ahead: the most minute detail overflows our senses now with the indescribable pleasures of hope.*

It was heavy-handed and sentimental and she recognized this, but it was the best she could do on a first try. She also believed that what came out first was rawest and truest, and should not be revised, to uphold its integrity. She had no diligence for backtracking. She was a young writer. Eager to expel her words.

■ ■ ■

Her story was commissioned to appear as a daily serial novel in one of the city's independent newspapers. A writer friend had secured the assignment for Tran, and it was to be her first citywide publication. A big step, for she had previously published only a few articles and short stories in reviews and smaller papers. "This editor, you have heard of him, he can help you," her writer friend assured her, "as he has helped many like us."

The man her friend spoke of was the paper's chief founder and editor, but because of his notoriety in politics, he and others had decided his affiliation would be best maintained as an unofficial relationship. Only his close colleagues knew his role. He filtered decisions through a young, posing editor in chief, and any actual writing he did he credited to other writers (some of whom existed, some of whom did not). His physical presence in the office was explained as visits to friends or consultations as a technical adviser. He shared a semiprivate office with the senior reporters, and entered and exited the same way most of the staff did, through a back-alley entrance. For the most part, he was not recognized and went about inconspicuously under his assumed name. He had assumed names at least five other times in the past fifteen years, and had still been jailed four times for what the ever-shifting government had labeled "the creation and advocation of slander and/or immorality." He had been dubbed a "gadfly." But he took no side wholeheartedly when it came to the subject of the war—not the Communist, not the American, not the South Vietnamese—for he believed them each to be a flawed system. Rather, he believed the true source of all troubles between humans ran someplace far deeper than politics.

It was under his latest name, Le Hoang Giang—a nom de plume alluding to the evanescent quality of autumn, translated literally from the Chinese as "yellow river"—that Tran met him.

He was thirty-four years old, an unassuming presence, slender, with kind eyes, a long, gentle face, and a warm smile. His hair was black, his skin very brown. A hint of knowing and humor lingered about the edges of all his expressions, as if he were continually assessing but withholding judgment. In a crowd, he was likely to retreat, to stand against a wall or leave without warning or good-bye.

"Tell me your idea," he said brusquely the first time she sat down before him. As she began to speak, he rested one hand on the side of his face and fixed his lucid gaze upon her.

"I want to write a love story based on the American novel *Gone With the Wind*—you have probably heard of it," she told him. "I want to set it in our country, but follow the same story line as the original. At least in essence I want to follow it."

He smiled as he leaned back in his chair and looked out the window. On the opposite side of the street below was a sidewalk café that was a popular hangout for the paper's writers and supporters; it occurred to Tran he could have been staring out the window minutes ago and seen her seated at a table down there, awaiting her appointment with him. It was raining, and the sound of water beating on the tin roofs was like nails in a metal can. Rain dripped in heavy streams from the eaves outside the open window.

"I read that book a long time ago," said Giang. "I found it moving. And so thorough. You must've been just as moved by it as I was."

It didn't seem necessary to respond, but out of respect Tran said, "Yes, Uncle." She felt she must address him formally, as her elder.

He looked at her again. "What will happen in your version of the story?"

She told him: instead of Atlanta at the crumbling of the United States Confederacy, it would be the northern port town of Haiphong at the climax of French rule. The heroine would be from a rice farm in a small northern village, and her family devout French-influenced Catholics. The family would be forced to flee south at the advance of the Viet Minh, and the story would follow that passage, which would bring the heroine to Haiphong.

"But mostly I want it to be a love story," explained Tran. "The heroine is torn, you see, because she is in love with a childhood friend who has gone off to fight for the Viet Minh. Then there will be a second man, who is committed to neither the French nor the Viet Minh—he just wants his own personal freedom—and he falls in love with the heroine and pursues her though she tries to deny him. She herself is apolitical. She doesn't want to go any further south simply because she is waiting for her childhood love to find her again. Maybe my story will reflect some contemporary issues. The heroine might find herself suddenly on opposing sides from the man she loves and once could trust, but mostly, to be honest, I'd like for my story to focus on the personal, emotional lives of its characters. When it comes to literature, that's what I'm truly interested in, you see."

"Yes," said Giang, seeming bemused, "life is never interesting unless one is in love with another who is in love with something or somebody else." He was looking at her now, but Tran felt as if he were speaking more to the space behind her than to her directly. "It is no new thing, you know," he said, "this story of men going off to war and women waiting in anguish for them to return. Every continent in the world knows this story."

Tran didn't speak, unsure if he meant to belittle her ideas.

He sat forward, laying his forearms on the desktop, his back slightly bowed as if he were about to stand. He turned his face toward the window for a moment. She could hear the hum of activity on the floor below, voices and typewriters and drawers slamming and laughter and footsteps. Finally Giang spoke: "I want you to write whatever you wish, and I will see that it gets published. Do you know, little sister, that is all I want to do myself? I am starting to think the only reprieve we will ever get from this war is when we are able to create—and it won't lie in our hands, but in our minds alone." He smiled sadly. "Every day I am more tired. Last night we were up very late, working. As usual." He laid his hands flat upon the desk. She noticed they were large, his fingers long and tapered.

"Thank you, Uncle," she said finally, understanding it was time for her to go.

■ ■ ■

Phuong-Li did not care for politics. To her it was a futile way to expend one's energies, and she did not understand the tension it stirred between people, the long heavy silences and sharp looks and charged nonchalance that passed now between her peers who held varying views. Phuong-Li merely wanted to play with old friends as they had when they were children, chasing each other about in the rice fields or laughing at something simple like the nickname Snake she had given one boy be-

cause he could not pronounce his words correctly and he spit when he talked fast.

"Why do you call me that?" the boy asked her once.

"That is my secret," Phuong-Li teased him, and her other friends giggled.

The boy, because he was fond of her, was flattered by her attention, no matter what the reason, so he answered to the name Snake.

Phuong-Li liked to recall these small, clever childhood games; they gave her a sense of importance, of secret control. Years later she saw the boy she had called Snake. He was now nineteen years old and had been away at school. What kind of school she did not know exactly, for she'd never asked. School was school, that vague process a few children, usually boys, went through. And when they returned, people bowed with deeper respect to these sons, and mothers blushed with adulation if it was their own sons returning in such style, for to parents schooling meant potential wealth. To Phuong-Li, it meant very little.

He came to her family's house with another neighborhood friend, and when Phuong-Li's little brothers opened the door, the friend asked for her. Snake hung back, his hands in his pockets, and he looked at his feet. When Phuong-Li came to the door, he waited to see if she would recognize him before he spoke. She did, and jumped forward to embrace him. Time and what she considered to be maturity had made her magnanimous toward all past acquaintances, close or not. He raised his face and smiled, showing warmth and something else, a certain light at seeing her again. It was in her eyes as well, though she did not realize it.

"You've grown up to be so pretty," he exclaimed.

"And you've learned how to speak properly!" she teased him.

Later, he smoked cigarettes with her older brothers while discussing politics and life in the city. She did not listen to their words, did not recognize that they were secretly probing one another with statements meant to provoke responses that would reveal their true allegiances. She did notice a tension in the air, although it only made her lament to herself: Why could they not all get along like old friends, like they used to, instead of indulging in all this tiresome talk? She admired the way Snake spoke, though, his easy mannerisms, the fierceness that lay beneath his composed veneer, showing itself only in small movements—the quick, forceful lift of his chin at a sound in the kitchen, the brusqueness

with which he struck his matches. She thought he must be saying impor-
tant, intelligent things, even if she did not understand them.

No, she cared nothing for politics. After that day, all she cared about
was love.

■ ■ ■

In the spring of 1972, Tran was in her seventh week of writing daily installments. She woke early in the morning and brewed herself a cup of
coffee in the apartment where she now lived with her six-year-old son.
They lived alone, the two of them, because Tran had felt her sisters and
religious mother could not understand the life of a writer, especially
when it was a woman who sought such a life.

Tran stood over the small stove in the far corner of the first-floor room,
gazing each morning at the wall as she fried an egg for her son, her
thoughts drifting to another world, of horses and hoop dresses and colored silks, of idle, well-educated, well-mannered women, servants announcing visitors in doorways of parlors. Tall, handsome, white-skinned
men in waistcoats. They bowed and kissed the ladies' hands. And from
this place her thoughts would then drift into the world of Vietnam. But
she was unable to conjure any images of a parallel world here, only a
vague sense of longing. The world of Vietnam was too visceral and in-
congruent next to the polished drama of the America in her mind. Even
her imagined version of Vietnam—the bustling port town of Haiphong in
1954, the setting of her story—was humid and overcrowded and raw. (It
resembled present-day Saigon, the only experience of a city from which
she had to draw.) There were no equivalents here to the panoramic views
of rolling green hills outside windows of estate houses, as existed in that
other land. Even the war here was not so noble and deeply felt a calamity
as it seemed to be there. Here the war was bogged down by the clearly un-
romantic facts of industry and contradicting chains of command, and it
often stretched on for months without incident. And when an incident did
occur it was always outside the city limits, far enough away to seem almost—though not entirely—irrelevant. As for the views outside Tran's
windows, they were of the stucco walls of neighboring buildings. The
inner walls of her own apartment (which she would stare at for hours each
morning as she typed) were pale blue and cracked. The only decorative
architectural elements were the concrete blocks with rough-edged patterns of ellipses and curved diamonds cut into them, which fitted into the

windows as screens. When the sunlight came through, it cast these patterns in shadow on the concrete floor.

Tran slid the egg she had cooked into a bowl and set it before her son, Thien. While Thien ate, she combed his hair. Sometimes she would tell him a tidbit of what she was working on in her head. "Maybe today is the day Phuong-Li will encounter her old Uncle Minh in the market," she would say. (Writing a serial novel was as much an adventure as reading one, she had found. She turned in her installments daily or weekly without much revision or forethought, and the pieces were published immediately, taken out of her hands, cemented in ink that quickly. It made plot seem to her a live, unpredictable factor she was stumbling blindly after, trying to keep up with it.)

Thien would respond appropriately, because he had been following along; all the names of persons his mother spoke of he accepted in the same way, whether they were fictional or real. "Will Uncle Minh punish her for how she ran away last week?"

"But she knows Uncle Minh's secret, that he married his wife for her money, because she has met her Uncle Minh's other daughter, remember? The one no one is supposed to know about."

"Uncle Minh is a bad man," Thien might say, and often Tran was proud of his astute judgments.

After breakfast each morning she walked her son to the end of the alley where it met an avenue. There he joined several other boys, and Tran watched as they raced across the avenue and through the gates to their school. Then she walked—smiling but not speaking to anyone she passed—back to the apartment. And once inside, she would sit down to write.

II.

They came to her apartment in the middle of the night and woke her. With Giang were two men, young reporters she had seen around the newspaper office. One waited, smoking, behind the wheel of Giang's car while the other stood outside her door. Giang waited, halfway down the alley, pacing in the predawn light.

"He says you must come with us. He's heard a rumor. It's important we investigate this," said the man at her door.

Tran did not hesitate to wake her son and take him over to the woman next door. Tran had been asked before to accompany reporters on their outings—they knew she would be interested in the outings as research, or sometimes they just wanted an extra eye along—but this was the first time Giang (whom she knew by reputation to be one of the more esteemed senior reporters) had singled her out. The woman next door, herself a mother of five and familiar with Tran's erratic schedule, welcomed Thien.

Tran fumbled for her camera and notebooks and left with the men.

The road out of the city was narrow and bumpy. As it was still the dry season, dust rose in their wake. Once, they stopped and the two younger men got out of the car to urinate by the side of the road, their cigarettes still poking from their lips, while Giang and Tran waited. The unwoken world outside the car's dirty windows was cool and blue and silent, and this made Tran aware of the silence between her and Giang. But she did not think much of it. She told herself he was just treating her as one of the men and there was no need between men to fill silences. Secretly she felt flattered; she felt her inclusion in this excursion to be significant. Proof that her insights or opinions had been heard by him and others, and noted. Especially in this time when men disregarded women's minds. She had done all she could not to appear a typical woman: she wore her hair short and spoke casually about sex, passionately about existentialism. She wanted to show them her mind was sharp. She could handle as much as they could.

The men got back in the car and they resumed driving. The city disappeared behind them into a crooked, cramped, hazy line on the horizon. Clumps of listing, bamboo-roofed shacks appeared at intervals alongside the road. They drove past swamps and groves of tall, reedy trees and a few early travelers on the road toting straw baskets of rice or produce or prodding along their pigs and cows. The reporters arrived near the village of Ha-Kan just after dawn, where they stopped at the edge of a rice field. Giang cut the car's engine and they listened to the rustling of the rice stalks, the twittering of birds, the whirring of crickets.

"This hamlet was raided early this morning by the VC. Some of the village children fled to the jungle. They were then chased back out of the jungle by certain members of the South Vietnamese army and shot while trying to hide in a herd of water buffalo. These children will probably end up tallied among the VC dead, my source tells me. But I want to record some evidence of the truth before then. Do you have your cameras ready?" Giang turned to the young reporters.

They went on foot by a small path through the trees, across a narrow arm of the river. The sky's faint colors changed and deepened above them like the images in a photograph developing, slowly. The fog uncurled from where it lay, low, around their knees; it seemed sentient, damaged, angry even, as if it did not want them to walk through. Then something solid came into the morning. They began to see purple water buffalo carcasses on the road, matching the pale purple swath of sky still lingering above the wet fields like a bruise.

Once there, the four walked among the bloated purple-black bellies that were like mounds of dark earth, Tran and the two reporters wondering why they had been brought to look at dead animals and daring not to express disappointment for fear of appearing callous to the cause. Brown-black blood ran out of each wide nostril. The animals' coats were mangy and smelled faintly like iron. Tran knelt to look more closely at a hoof. The last time she had stood this close to a water buffalo was as a child—when her family still lived in the far northern countryside where the air was so crisp it woke your skin in the morning. Tran found herself looking at the buffalo now with affection. Yet she knew it was not the death of animals they were here to mourn.

When she glanced up, Giang was watching her (his mouth slightly open, he seemed to be searching for something), and in that fleeting look she recognized something, if for only a flash. The depth with which he was watching her watch the dead buffalo—it was as if their faint understanding of whatever this incident might mean was profoundly the same. She saw it surprised him, but it did not surprise her. She knew then that some form of a romance would occur between them.

However: Love was not roses or white towers or any such nonsense. Rather, it was a call from some darker well of the heart possessing no regard for the rules of life, for the ideals of human sacraments, even. What love required of its participants would occur heedless of violence and happiness alike (she would write this into her story somehow later).

Breaking the spell, Giang said, with what seemed like a levity both concentrated and painful, "It must be the season for children to turn into buffalo."

■ ■ ■

That evening, she followed him at a distance as he walked into the city's quarter of poorhouses, a place she had never been before and knew no virtuous woman should go, and soon her curiosity turned to ire. "What kind of man is he? For what unspeakable intention can he be skulking about among such dwellings?" Her thoughts churned viciously. "Who is she? What does she have that I don't have?" He was leading her down an alley with foul-smelling gutters. She lifted her skirts, remembering herself in front of the mirror that very morning, turning this way and that, trying on dress after dress in anticipation of seeing him and thinking desperately, "It will not do, it will not do."

Now she thought, "This is what I have dressed for."

She followed him into a narrow alley behind a row of houses, and when he stopped at a door, she hid, flattening herself against the cool stone wall. He rapped three times on the door, paused, then rapped three more times in a deliberate rhythm.

The door opened, a shaft of yellow light fell upon his face—he was so handsome still!—and he stepped inside, and the door closed. She did not see the face of the person who had admitted him.

How long would she wait? And for what, should she find out? Would the truth about him only disgust and force her to see plainly that he inhabited worlds in which she had no place? She wished that she were older, her life less sheltered—she wished she'd known more hardship. Maybe then she would have acquired some of that roughness, that bitterness, that would have made her a woman for whom he would risk shame. Anything, she thought, anything but to be the one spying and desperate and lonely—oh so!—in the shadows of "real" life.

■ ■ ■

They drove back to the city with their notes and film, and once home set about writing what they believed to be the truth about the alleged massacre that had occurred in Ha-Kan. During a discussion in Giang's office, Tran tried to interject some of her own ideas, but in their eagerness the reporters talked over her. After making a few attempts she retreated, consoling herself in her head: You don't even care about politics. You're a fiction writer. You're writing a love story, more valuable in its own way.

Once, Giang gave her a small, patient smile; he had caught her eyes wandering. She was no longer confident about why she'd been invited to come along on the investigation in the first place.

The next day the story ran. When Tran arrived at the newspaper office in the afternoon as usual to turn in her daily installment, which she had spent the morning writing, she was surprised at being greeted with nods and cheers from other staff members. She—it appeared—had written the story, with the field help of the two young reporters; there was no mention of Giang. Photographs of the raided, burning hamlet ran next to an exposé on an allegedly corrupt general's career and crimes. Beneath his photograph ran a long list of names—other government and military officials and their illegal activities. Bewildered, Tran read the story and stared at her name in print above it. When she asked, no one knew where the two young reporters were.

"In and out as usual, those boys," said one clerk.

"I underestimated you," said another, coming forward to shake her hand.

■ ■ ■

This was how it began. In the following months Tran's popularity grew—her notoriety, in fact—as more articles were printed under her name. Articles of a slyly observant, condemnatory, apolitical bent—never siding with any of the official parties, only pointing out their contradictions. Colleagues said about Tran's pen name (which she had chosen rather naïvely at the beginning of her work for the paper, as she'd noticed most writers used pen names) that now it made sense. "Trung Trinh, master of the woman's style of attack," they said, joking that they'd previously not understood why a romance fiction writer would choose a pen name that made reference to the Trung sisters—Vietnam's legendary women warriors who had risen up in rebellion against their Chinese overlords in the first century A.D.

Tran was surprised to find that even when she said little or nothing, her character was meritoriously assessed: people took her silence as knowing. They deferred to her in discussion, even when she made only vague comments. Giang had explained she need only nod and say she was "still thinking about it" if anyone asked a question she couldn't answer; in private, he briefed her on the subjects of the articles. Gradually, she felt her confidence grow, her own writing develop irony. She learned how to absorb necessary information quickly; she appropriated gumption. Though she saw herself becoming somewhat a pawn in this game of his, she also couldn't deny her new freedom. Her wit was sharper, as she now knew the inner workings of the paper. Sentiments, false hopes, the old *yens* of her former romanticism, could no longer sway her. And though she knew her new skepticism threatened to desensitize her to the actual issues about which they were writing, she could not fathom going back. Her previous position seemed now unconnected and vulnerable and embarrassingly innocent.

They worked late many nights. They worked with their heads bent over documents or photographs, and Tran slowly became more knowledgeable—and even on occasion contributed to—these stories attributed to her. Giang made it clear she was doing him a favor—he was grateful, solicitous, charismatic. They were great friends, he would say, each helping the other by doing the very thing each wished to do most, and was this not the philosophy of self-fulfillment unfolding as ideally as it should? Was this not Equality, that beautiful, modern, Western thought? He wrote his stories, she wrote hers. The romantic nature of her fiction protected him—the censors were slow to examine political articles written by a woman romance writer. And yet the people knew.

(The reason he had chosen her was simple: he had to choose someone he wouldn't mind divulging his secrets to, and it was always, he said later, better to choose a person he thought might be a potential lover.)

It began in the midst of those late nights, the pressure, the exhilaration of secrecy shared, emotions fueled not only by personal but also worldly concerns. She knew he already had a wife and children, but she didn't worry about this or feel guilty. She didn't hope he would leave his family, either. According to Tran's own Buddhist-Existentialist-derived concept of Truthful Living it was the circumstances in which one lost all sense of time and consequence and reason that revealed when one was living one's true destiny. And so she reveled in the immediacy of their suspended moments, in which she thought neither of futures or pasts, nor of fantasies or realities. She became *shell, cavern, empty well:* she became replete. A sensation of sheer life, of Meaningful Living (how else could she put it?) loomed over her like a great umbrella. As a lover he was gentle, compassionate and warm, appropriately woeful at the could-have-beens of their situation.

She liked the way men looked at her during this time: with energy, with challenges, with a curiosity that was intellectual and spirited—and liked how they would joke with her and tell her frank things about other women she knew they'd never shared with a woman. They trusted, even feared, her; for here was one woman who couldn't be and didn't need to be fooled or wooed. Concerning love, she told herself she was practicing the Buddhist paradox of "living simultaneously": immersion and nonattachment together.

She kept busy. She was tenacious and vigilant at her work. During this period her writing sprang from her without her prescience: her fiction became more violent—sometimes this surprised her—as the calamities of war caused her characters to act out undue passions.

■ ■ ■

"School is more important than God." One morning Tran found herself saying this to her son.

Thien had been contesting her and asking questions she couldn't answer with tact. Questions concerning the rituals they did or did not perform, as Catholics, that might put them out of favor with God. It was his grandmother's—Tran's mother's—influence; Thien had been spending his afternoons at his grandmother's house while Tran was at the newspaper office. That morning, Thien wanted to practice his penmanship by copying out prayers, instead of doing his French vocabulary homework. Tran was at the stove fixing his breakfast.

"You won't do well in school just because you believe in God, God is not your teacher." This was the best way Tran could think of to emphasize the importance of keeping education and religion separate—in her mind, the former was crucial while the latter was optional. "You need to do well in school if you don't want to end up like the kids on the street or in the countryside who can't even spell their own names!" Thien bowed his head, and Tran asked him a question in French: "*Où est le gâteau?*" She meant "cake," but he heard "boat."

"*Le bateau est à l'océan*" replied Thien, glumly.

She tried to smile, teasing. "*Et est-ce que tu aimes manger le bateau?*"

He looked at her and frowned. Then he walked to the corner of the kitchen and sat on the floor, pulling his knees into his chest and burying his face in his arms. He yelled, *"J'ai pas faim!"*

She set his breakfast on the floor before him. "Let it get cold then," she snapped in Vietnamese.

Tran had scheduled her son's days to be full; she wanted him to become cultured. This meant art lessons, music, English, French, literature, drama—even soccer (it was the European sport of choice, as Tran understood). How could she explain to Thien that it was in *these* activities that he would find salvation, not in his grandmother's sad, persistent prayers? She saw her mother as a victim of submission; her husband, Tran's father, was a philanderer (as so many Vietnamese men were), while God constantly required her to be on her knees. She had spoiled her sons, too, and two were now dead from drink and war; the richest one was a gambler and ruthlessly selfish; and the other two were lost to her, having "died" into lives of vice. *Saigon has become like Babylon*, she lamented. Now the old woman lived an ascetic existence of cooking, cleaning and performing other duties with her unmarried daughters and their illegitimate children (Tran was the only one who'd acquired the means or drive to move out on her own). A houseful of unweddable women and a wayward husband. Neighbors looked on them with pity. Tran had grown up terrified of becoming like her mother or older sisters. She saved her allowances for months just to buy a book; she lied about running errands in the marketplace in order to attend forums on French literature.

"You're only a half-woman, that's what I hear people say," said her son, after he had begrudgingly begun to eat the food on his plate.

Tran was at her desk, sipping her coffee. "Who says this?"

"The other ladies, when they come to Grandma's house. Because you're never with me, and you don't know how to cook or clean properly. They say you walk like a rooster and smoke cigarettes and drink beer like the men, and that's why no man wants to marry you. What man wants to marry a woman who's like a man?"

"I walk like a rooster?" Tran was appalled and amused by this, thinking Thien must be misrepeating what he had heard.

"Yes, a rooster," said Thien emphatically. Then he stood and demonstrated, with his hands on his hips and his elbows sticking out.

From what Tran could gather, it had to do with her chest—the women were claiming she pushed it forward when she walked—and the bold uncouthness of her high-heeled boots that made her gait stiff and unfeminine and her footsteps loud, as if she meant to always announce her presence well ahead of her arrival.

"They are just jealous," said Tran. She felt miffed but slightly triumphant, too.

That afternoon she took Thien to his grandmother's house. She was thinking she would hire a maid soon, to lessen his visits to his grandmother. Tran and her mother did not converse in either a friendly or a strained manner; they nodded and gave each other perfunctory information. Tran's mother brought a plastic bag out of the bedroom and immediately set items on the floor around Thien. Wooden cars, a toy helicopter, green plastic soldiers, some items that were not toys but appeared still to hold interest for him—an empty tin can with a colorful label, an assortment of mismatched chopsticks. As she was leaving, Tran saw her mother moving toward Thien with a plate of rice cakes.

Her colleagues greeted her jovially as she entered the office. Shaking that morning's issue, one reporter (whom Tran sensed fancied her) exclaimed, "And how does the beautiful, mysterious Trung Trinh find time to be both subversive and romantic? What a remarkable woman!"

"Ah, but does it not take one to have the other? Does each simply not lead to the other?" teased another colleague. He was the same age as Tran, a photojournalist who kept mostly to himself and exhibited a carefree nature no matter the severity of his subject matter.

"Quan the philosopher," said the first reporter, not without admiration.

"Quan the skeptic," said Tran coyly; then reticently, coolly, removed her jacket and seated herself at her typewriter. She had her own desk now and composed her daily installments in the office, often finishing minutes before the deadline.

Quan nodded and smiled. He shouldered his camera bag and walked away.

"So," shouted a woman from a desk nearby. "What are the lovers up to today, Miss Tran?"

Tran glanced across the large room toward the stairs leading to the upstairs office where Giang worked. "Today I think I will put them on a boat," she said grimly, "with a cake."

■ ■ ■

The boy was four now, and sometimes she saw too much of his father in him. She had only married the man because it had been expected of her as it had been expected of her true beloved to marry his arranged bride. The general's daughter. Now they worked side by side, caring equally for each other's sons. All the men were gone. What did it matter anymore, the old rivalries among women? They all had love at stake now. Talk of fleeing was circulating in whispers in wash circles. The general's daughter was secretly packing, weeping as she sorted memorabilia and made wrenching, frivolous decisions over items of sentimental value. Passions passed, Phuong-Li had learned, but true love was lasting. It did not need reciprocation, it did not require consummation, it knew nothing of time. It knew nothing of safety.

Today was the boy's birthday, and she would take him down to the water to watch the fishing boats. The boy loved boats. He was always asking her to "watch, watch" as he did one trick or another. Phuong-Li was not particularly patient with children and tired quickly of his enthusiasm. She sat in the sand and touched her ribs. It had been four years ago—oh, how she had hated being pregnant! She remembered. Too well. She drew circles in the sand. No, it could not be happening again, not so soon, could it? Out on the water fishermen's nets arched through the air and landed, imprinting their grids on the shifting surfaces of the waves and catching sunlight in tiny squares of silver— fleeting seconds at a time—before sinking down into the warm darkness below.

■ ■ ■

A team of government police barraged the office the following morning. Rumors had been circulating of such police action against other newspapers. Semantics of certain ordinances were being interpreted now in stricter fashion and enforced, in order to tighten censorship rules. The police stopped at Tran's desk and ordered her to come with them. She protested, demanding to know why, and the men stood in indignation around her—the reporter who fancied her tried to lie that he was in fact Trung Trinh, a man writing under a female alias; Quan the photojournalist yelled uncharacteristic (for him) curses; other reporters said, "Take us instead. Are you so cowardly you must pick on our women staff members alone?" Only Giang kept his face down, melted into the background, left by the back door.

The police held her for interrogation. As they laid before her all the pages of the past episodes of her serial novel, they asked her to explain details of fashion and etiquette and dialogue between characters; they demanded to know what subversive messages each of these items encoded. She denied having encoded anything, but they insisted again that she "explain the codes." In the end, they pushed her to her knees and lashed her hands with a bamboo cane, a symbolic gesture, they assured her, not meant to cripple literally (they knew it was more important to break spirit than body). Maybe next time she lifted her pen she would hesitate.

Tran sobbed into her welted hands. The baby inside her kicked.

Later that night, she did not consider where the smoke would go, or that it would have to rise. Her son was coughing when he crawled down the ladder of their sleeping loft and peeked in at her on her knees before the small metal pail in the middle of her papers on the floor. She had been burning the original manuscript pages of all her serial episodes, although she knew this, in fact, erased nothing.

"Mama? What are you doing?"

"It is only me," said Tran, glancing up at the blur of her son through her heat-fogged eyeglasses.

III.

In the eighth month of her second pregnancy, Tran was facing a trial, the newspaper was facing shutdown, and neighbors and many other people she encountered daily were either denying or praying in the face of coming changes in the political climate. In the countryside, entire families were lynched, their heads strung from tree limbs, mouths agape. This, among a long list of horrors the approaching Communist takeover was likely to bring. At the National Cemetery, mass graves had been dug and filled as bodies were shipped in by the truckload, with no time or means for proper identification. Reporters took gruesome snapshots of bloodied bodies and bulging eyes—the dead looked stunned. Suicide in the cities increased.

Tran moved cumbersomely through these months, continuing to believe only in the newspaper's single-minded rebellion, the artists' cause of freedom of speech, which aligned itself with neither the approaching forces nor the failing and corrupt current government. She had spoken to no one of her pregnancy until it had made itself plainly visible and other women had begun—without acknowledging the pregnancy directly—to bring her extra food and pull out chairs for her to sit during meetings. Giang was the only person she had told before this point, and he had shaken his head. As if it were the bearing of his *own* feelings about the situation—and not the bearing of the child, exactly—that would be most taxing. This had been enough to tell Tran he had no intention of supporting her. But Tran had been through this once before, and this time she figured it was best not to raise a fight or ask for compensation or even acknowledgment. She knew Giang's reputation was more important to him than anything else. Nothing was personal that was not political here. They passed each other in the halls now with lowered eyes. Hers was not the only alias he used anymore; he had begun using it less ever since the first few visits from the police. And no one was interested in or entertained by her serial lately, either. For some reason it was not the same—with the writer so regrettably, unmentionably pregnant. Everyone, it seemed, shared a sense of chagrin and karma.

Giang's wife began to visit the newspaper offices regularly to bring him meals. She dressed tastefully, her hair done up immaculately. (Tran would not look up from her desk or would look up only briefly as the other women called out greetings to Giang's wife.) She was an attractive but vain woman who Tran knew from hearsay fancied herself a poet, but her poems had been published only because of her husband's influence, and she had never shed her true desire for wealth despite her husband's unflagging idealism. Tran also knew from hearsay that though the wife was aware of her, they did not speak of the other woman. At least he has granted us this much, Tran thought. But she wasn't sure whom he was really protecting.

In the end she went to the courtroom alone.

■ ■ ■

What have we done wrong? I would ask God, if I believed in Him. Oh these sad, sad days. You want to understand that the world works justly, and that war with all its atrocity and catastrophe is simply part of the greater Order, the yin to the yang of prosperity and peace we had for x number of years, et cetera. You want to believe in the story of the man who lost his donkey but won a horse. You want to believe in Philosophy. But my children, my unborn and my son, there is much that is unfair and I cannot explain why to you, though I bring you into this world to face it. I feel it crucial to tell you (should I not return or be able for whatever reasons to say it to you in person): I am sorry.

■ ■ ■

"This is it?" said the managing editor. "This is your installment?" The page he held in his hand was more than half blank, more than half white.

Tran nodded.

LIVE-IN COOK

from *THE BOOK OF SALT*

■ ■ ■

Monique Truong

When I applied for the position as live-in cook, I did not know about the house in Bilignin. I assumed that the lives of the two American ladies and therefore mine would be centered in Paris on the rue de Fleurus. They did not inform me during the interview about their seasonal migration. Not that it would have made a difference to me then. I had been in Paris for over three years. I had interviewed with and even worked for an embarrassing number of households. In my experience, they fell into two categories. No, in fact, there were three.

The first were those who, after a catlike glimpse at my face, would issue an immediate rejection, usually nonverbal. A door slam was an uncommonly effective form of communication. No discussion, no references required, no "Will you want Sundays off?" Those, while immediately unpleasant, I preferred. Type twos were those who might or might not end up hiring me but who would, nonetheless, insist on stripping me with questions, as if performing an indelicate physical examination. Type twos behaved as if they had been authorized by the French government to ferret out and to document exactly how it was that I had come to inhabit their hallowed shores.

"In Paris, three years," I told them.

MONIQUE TRUONG was born in Saigon in 1968 and moved to the United States at age six. She graduated from Yale University and the Columbia University School of Law, going on to specialize in intellectual property. She coedited, along with Barbara Tran and Luu Truong Khoi, the anthology *Watermark: Vietnamese American Poetry & Prose. The Book of Salt* is her first novel. She lives in Brooklyn, New York

"Where were you before?"

"Marseilles."

"Where were you before that?"

"Boat to Marseilles."

"Boat? Well, obviously. Where did that boat sail from?"

And so, like a courtesan, forced to perform the dance of the seven veils, I grudgingly revealed the names, one by one, of the cities that had carved their names into me, leaving behind the scar tissue that formed the bulk of who I am.

"Hmmm . . . you say you've been in Paris for three years? Now, let's see, if you left Indochina when you were twenty, that would make you . . ."

"Twenty-six, Madame."

Three years unaccounted for! you could almost hear them thinking. Most Parisians could ignore and even forgive me for not having the refinement to be born amidst the ringing bells of their cathedrals, especially since I was born instead amidst the ringing bells of the replicas of their cathedrals, erected in a far-off colony to remind them of the majesty, the piety, of home. As long as Monsieur and Madame could account for my whereabouts in their city or in one of their colonies, then they could trust that the *République* and the Catholic Church had had their watchful eyes on me. But when I exposed myself as a subject who might have strayed, who might have lived a life unchecked, ungoverned, undocumented, and unrepentant, I became, for them, suspect. Before, I was no more of a threat than a cloistered nun. Now Madame glared at me to see if she could detect the deviant sexual practices that I had surely picked up and was now, without a doubt, proliferating under the very noses of the city's Notre-Dames. Madame now worried whether she could trust me with her little girls.

Madame, you have nothing to worry about. I have no interest in your little girls. Your boys . . . well, that is their choice, she should have heard me thinking.

The odds were stacked against me with this second type, I knew. But I found myself again and again shamefully submitting. All those questions, I deceived myself each time, all those questions must mean that I had a chance. And so I stayed on, eventually serving myself forth like a scrawny roast pig, only to be told, "Thank you but no thank you."

Thank you? Thank you? Madame, you should applaud! A standing ovation would not be inappropriate, I thought each time I have just given you a story filled with exotic locales, travel on the open seas, family secrets, un-Christian vices. *Thank you* will not suffice.

My self-righteous rage burned until I was forced to concede that I, in fact, had told them nothing. This language that I dipped into like a dry inkwell had failed me. It had made me take flight with weak wings and watched me plummet into silence. I was unable to tell them anything but a list of cities, some they had been to and others a mere dot on a globe, places they would only touch with the tips of their fingers and never the soles of their feet. I was forced to admit that I was, to them, nothing but a series of destinations with no meaningful expanses in between.

Thank you but no thank you.

The third type, I called the collectors. They were always good for several weeks' and sometimes even several months' worth of work. The interviews they conducted were professional, even mechanical. Before I could offer the usual inarticulate boast about my "good omelets," I was hired. Breakfast, lunch, and dinner to be prepared six days a week. Sundays off. Some immediately delegated the marketing to me. Others insisted on accompanying me for the first few days to make sure that I knew the difference between a *poularde* and a *poulette*. I rarely failed them. Of course, I had never been able to memorize nor keep an accurate tally of the obsessive assortment of words that the French had devised for this animal that was the center, the stewed, fricasseed, sautéed, stuffed heart, of every Frenchman's home. Fat chickens, young chickens, newly hatched chickens, old wiry chickens, all were awarded their very own name, a noble title of sorts in this language that could afford to be so drunk and extravagant toward what lay on the dinner table. "A chicken" and "not this chicken," these were the only words I needed to navigate the poultry markets of this city. Communicating in the negative was not the quickest and certainly not the most esteemed form of expression, but for those of us with few words to spare it was the magic spell, the incantation that opened up an otherwise inaccessible treasure trove. Wielding my words like a rusty kitchen knife, I could ask for, reject, and ultimately locate that precise specimen that would grace tonight's pot.

And, yes, for every coarse misshapen phrase, for every blundered, dislocated word, I paid a fee. A man with a borrowed, ill-fitting tongue,

I could not compete for this city's attention. I could not participate in the lively lovers' quarrel between it and its inhabitants. I was a man whose voice was a harsh whisper in a city that favored a song. No longer able to trust the sound of my own voice, I carried a small speckled mirror that showed me my face, my hands, and assured me that I was still here. Becoming more like an animal with each displaced day, I scrambled to seek shelter in the kitchens of those who would take me. Every kitchen was a homecoming, a respite, where I was the village elder, sage and revered. Every kitchen was a familiar story that I could embellish with saffron, cardamom, bay laurel, and lavender. In their heat and in their steam, I allowed myself to believe that it was the sheer speed of my hands, the flawless measurement of my eyes, the science of my tongue that was rewarded. During these restorative intervals, I was no longer the mute who begged at this city's steps. Three times a day, I orchestrated and they sat with slackened jaws, silenced. Mouths preoccupied with the taste of foods so familiar and yet with every bite even the most parochial of palates detected redolent notes of something that they had no words to describe. They were, by the end, overwhelmed by an emotion that they had never felt, a nostalgia for places they had never been.

I did not willingly depart these havens. I was content to grow old in them, calling the stove my lover, calling the copper pans my children. But collectors were never satiated by my cooking. They were ravenous. The honey that they coveted lay inside my scars. They were subtle, though, in their tactics: a question slipped in with the money for the weekly food budget, a follow-up twisted inside a compliment for last night's dessert, three others disguised as curiosity about the recipe for yesterday's soup. In the end, they were indistinguishable from the type twos except for the defining core of their obsession. They had no true interest in where I had been or what I had seen. They craved the fruits of exile, the bitter juices, and the heavy hearts. They yearned for a taste of the pure, sea-salt sadness of the outcast whom they had brought into their homes. I was but one within a long line of others. The Algerian orphaned by a famine, the Moroccan violated by his uncle, the Madagascan driven out of his village because his shriveled left hand was a sign of his mother's misdeeds, these were the wounded trophies who had preceded me.

It was not that I am unwilling. I had sold myself in exchange for less. Under their gentle guidance, their velvet questions, even I could disgorge enough pathos and cheap souvenir tragedies to sustain them. They were never gluttonous in their desires, rather the opposite. They were methodical. A measured, controlled dosage was part of the thrill. No, I was driven out by my own willful hands. It was only a matter of time. After so many weeks of having that soft, steady light shined at me, I began to forget the barbed-wire rules of such engagements. I forgot that there would be days when it was I who would have the craving, the red, raw need to expose all my neglected, unkempt days. And I forgot that I would wait, like a supplicant at the temple's gate, because all the rooms of the house were somber and silent. When I was abandoned by their sweet-voiced catechism, I forgot how long to braise the ribs of beef, whether chicken was best steamed over wine or broth, where to buy the sweetest trout. I neglected the pinch of cumin, the sprinkling of lovage, the scent of lime. And in these ways, I compulsively wrote, page by page, the letters of my resignation.

Before joining my Mesdames' household, I thought that a home was a home, a Madame was a Madame, a city was . . . well, even then I knew that Paris was a city and that many other places were not. So I suppose it might have made a difference if I had known. I might have asked for more money, hazard pay, months-in-the-middle-of-nowhere pay, you-cannot-pay-me-enough-to-live-here pay.

Of course, my Mesdames are going to Bilignin again this year. My Mesdames are very regular. They like routines and schedules. They do not like to deviate from the chosen paths of their lives. GertrudeStein, after all, burned sixty candles on her birthday cake this month, and Miss Toklas will burn fifty-seven in April. She has a French document, though, that lists her as being born on a day in June. There have been years when my Madame waits until then to grow older. I do not know what she has planned for 1934. I suppose it depends on how she is feeling about her age, advancing. I would wager, though, that Miss Toklas will celebrate in June again this year because June means that my Mesdames will be in Bilignin. When I began working for them back in the autumn of 1929, they had just finished their first summer in their country house. My Mesdames' routine there was just beginning.

When summer comes to Paris, my Madame and Madame pack their clothes and their dogs into their automobile, and they drive themselves and their cargo down to the Rhône Valley to the tiny farming village. I am left behind to lock up the apartment and to hand the keys over to the concierge, whom I have always suspected of being overly glad to see these two American ladies go. I have seen him in his first-floor window watching the young men who come to court Gertrude-Stein, and I have seen him shaking his head unable to comprehend the source of the attraction. With my Mesdames already on the road for over a day, I pack up whatever warm-weather garments I have that year, and I go and splurge on a hat for the hot summer sun. If I find a bargain, then I also treat myself to lunch at an establishment with cloth on the table and an attentive waiter who is obliged to call me "Monsieur." I then take what is left of the money that my Mesdames gave me for a second-class train ticket, and I buy a third-class one instead. I sleep all the way down to Bilignin, where I open up the house and wait several more days—as my Mesdames drive at a speed that varies somewhere between leisurely and meandering—before I hear the honking of their automobile and the barking of two weary dogs. I wait for them on the terrace. I have plates of sautéed livers for Basket and Pépé and for their Mesdames bowls of thick cream, dolloped with last summer's strawberry preserves. There are smiles all around, except for Basket and Pépé, who greet me with the usual disdain. My Mesdames admire my new hat, which signals that the summer in Bilignin has officially commenced.

I have the hat because the house there, while spacious enough to be called a *petit château,* has no running water, and I am often outside in the gardens, where there is a pump. I also have the hat because in Bilignin as in Paris I have Sundays off. The farmers in the village are gracious enough and at first simply curious enough to invite me, the first *asiatique* they have ever seen, into their homes. And their sons, I have to admit, are handsome enough to make me accept each and every time. All the families in this area make their own wine, so drinking is never a problem, and generosity fills my glass till I thirst for just a bit of water. I have found that water at the end of these nights eases my entry back into Monday. Though sometimes there is not enough water in the sea for me. I awake the next morning to the sound of Miss Toklas slamming pots and pans in the kitchen. These are pots and pans that she and no one else would need for the preparation of the simple breakfast of fruit and fresh sheep's milk cheese that she and GertrudeStein prefer when they are in Bilignin. I climb down the narrow staircase that leads from my room to the kitchen, and I do the only thing that I know how when I am faced with an angry Madame.

"It is my health — " I lie.

"But I am improving as we speak," Miss Toklas finishes my usual speech for me.

I had overheard a *femme de ménage* from Brittany use those exact words in the home of a previous Monsieur and Madame, and I had her teach them to me. They are vague enough to cover most household mishaps and oversights and also have the assurance of in-progress improvement tacked on at the end. When she asked me why I wanted her to repeat it, I told her I thought the sentence clever and useful. The *femme de ménage* agreed, but she said that she could not take credit for it, as she herself had overheard an Italian nanny employ the same words in another household some years back. We servants, in this way, speak the same language learned in the back rooms of houses and spoken in the front rooms on occasions such as these. Miss Toklas and GertrudeStein have also developed an apparent appreciation for this sentence. On subsequent Mondays when my head is again too heavy with wine, my Mesdames' breakfast conversation floats up to my bedroom window, like pieces of burnt paper, from the terrace down below. Amongst their otherwise incomprehensible English words, I recognize the phrase "It is my health" said in a fair approximation of a laborer's heavily accented French. Laughter usually ensues. No matter, I think, as I turn over on my side. Laughter in this case is a good or, at least, a nonthreatening sign. Of course, I try not to indulge in this sort of behavior very often, not more than two or three times during the season. It is just that drink is cheaper in Bilignin. In fact, it is free. The farmers there ask very little of me, and when they do they seem to enjoy, unlike their Parisian cousins, the sounds of the French language faltering on my tongue. Sometimes they even ask to hear a bit of Vietnamese. They close their eyes, trusting and sincere, and they imagine the birds of the tropics singing.

In the summer my Mesdames kindly overlook my Monday-morning absences. Halfway through the season, Miss Toklas even suggests that I take Mondays off for "my health." Of course, she also reduces my pay by one day. But life in Bilignin does not require a full wallet, so I gladly accept the change in the terms of my employment. I also gladly accept the additional glasses of wine and whatever else comes my way every Sunday and Monday night. The farmers in Bilignin work and drink like horses. The two activities do not seem to affect each other in any significant way. I, however, begin losing my appetite and my body weight right along with it. By the end of the summer, GertrudeStein, when greeting me, finds it necessary to repeat herself: "Well, hello, Thin Thin Bin." Binh is my given name, but my Madame merrily mispronounces it, rhyming it instead with an English word that she claims describes my most distinctive feature.

A cook who has no desire to eat is a lost soul. Worse, he is a questionable cook. Even when I can no longer take a sip, a bite, a morsel of any of the dishes that I am preparing for my Mesdames, I never forget that tasting is an indispensable part of cooking. The candlelight flicker of flavors, the marriage of bright acidity with profound savoriness, aromatics sparked with the suggestion of spice, all these things can change within seconds, and only a vigilant tongue can find that precise moment when there is nothing left to do but eat. For a less experienced cook, such a turn of events, the sudden absence of appetite, would be disastrous. Imagine a portrait painter who attempts to practice his art with his eyes sealed shut. I, thankfully, am able to maintain the quality of my cooking with the help of my keen memory. My hands are able to re-create their movements from earlier times. My loss in body weight, however, I cannot hide and shows itself as a forlorn expression on my face, one that both my Madame and Madame have yet to notice.

When we are in Bilignin, Miss Toklas loses all interest in matters of the kitchen. She leaves that all to me. From May through September, Miss Toklas's heart lies in the gardens, where she too may be found from the early morning till the hour just before the setting sun. I have heard her cooing from the vegetable plots. She does not know that she emits the sounds of lovemaking when she is among the tomatoes. I have heard her weep with the juices of the first strawberry full in her mouth. And I have seen her pray. GertrudeStein has seen her too, but she thinks that my Madame is on her knees pulling out weeds. The god that Miss Toklas prays to is the Catholic one. I have seen the rosary wrapped around her wrist, the beads trickling one by one through her fingertips. From the second-story windows of the house, GertrudeStein sees her lover toiling in a garden, vines twisted around her hands, seeds falling in a steady rhythm from her palms.

Miss Toklas is in a garden, GertrudeStein, but it is divine. The Holy Spirit is in her when she pulls the tiny beets, radishes, and turnips from the ground. When she places their limp bodies in her basket, she believes that she knows the joys and anguishes of the Virgin Mother. And along with her raptures, she is ashamed, GertrudeStein. Because, my Madame has begun to think of life without you, to plan for it in incriminating ways. Miss Toklas knows that *she* would never be the first to go. She could never leave her Lovey so alone in this world. A genius, she believes, needs constant care. She is resolved to the fact that you, GertrudeStein, will be the first to go, and then what will she do, so alone in this world without you? And, that, GertrudeStein, are the words that end all of her prayers.

This past summer was my Mesdames' fifth and my fourth in Bilignin. About a week before we were scheduled to close up the house for the season, Miss Toklas came into the kitchen loaded down with baskets of squash, new potatoes, and the last of the summer tomatoes. As she sorted through the bounty, making it ready to be packed for the journey home, she looked over at me plucking a chicken for that night's supper. Even from behind an updraft of flying feathers, I could see that she was studying my face. Madame, do not worry, a few weeks back in Paris and I will be my old self again, I thought. After a short while, Miss Toklas cleared her throat and suggested that this year, maybe, I should ride back to Paris with GertrudeStein, herself, and the dogs. She could just as easily send the crates of vegetables back to the city by rail, she told me. I accepted the offer without hesitation. I have often watched with envy as Basket and Pépé ride away, Basket's ears flapping or in the case of Pépé's twitching in the wind, to take, as my mother would say, The-Long-Way-Home. Along with their Mesdames, these two dogs take in the sights and stop, I imagined, for impromptu meals whenever GertrudeStein's stomach begins to flutter with the moths of hunger.

For the farmers of Bilignin, the end of the summer season is marked by two events, the departure of the two Americans and their *asiatique* cook and the gathering of the grapes. The gathering is a festival where the younger farmers of Bilignin meet their future wives or lovers, but then again they do not do that sort of thing there. The wine casks and jugs from the past vintage have to be emptied to make way for the new. That requires almost as much work as the actual removal of the fruits from the vine. But that is why the farmers of Bilignin work *and* drink like horses. I am fine after the first bottle, but then I turn red. As these farmers and others have pointed out, I look as if I have been burnt by the sun. My cheeks, I am embarrassed to admit, are crimson. I cannot pass it off as a blush because the color is too intense. But beyond this red cast, I remain remarkably unaffected. Well, that is until I pass out. The line between being awake and not is easy for me to overstep, as I never see it coming. One moment I am sitting at one of the long tables set outside under the harvest moon for the occasion, and the next I am being slapped and doused with water. I take *that* as my signal to begin my walk back to my Mesdames' house. There, I am greeted by Basket and Pépé, who delight in the task. They begin to bark as soon as I open the iron gate to the gardens. They continue to bark as I unlock the door to the kitchen, where they are sitting in wait. These two act very undog-like at moments like these. They never jump on me, sniffing and nip-ping. They are obviously not happy to see me. His Highness and the Pretender to the throne do not have a drop of fear or protective instinct directed toward me either. These two sit by the stove and bark, bored by the whole affair but apparently obligated by a pact with each other to call attention to the time and the state of my arrival. When they are in Bilignin, Miss Toklas and GertrudeStein must sleep like dogs—well-mannered ones, that is. I never see their bedroom light turn on when I enter the gate, and I never hear them rustling about upstairs when I am in the dark kitchen below. Basket and Pépé, despite their mean-spirited efforts, always fail to rouse my Mesdames from their bed to come and see their cook, red, wet, and bleary-eyed.

Well, except for last summer when His Highness and the Pretender scored a great victory. Granted I did help their cause by throwing up and then passing out before I could reach the stairway to my room. Their noses must have been offended by the strong smell of alcohol that my vomit released into the room. I can imagine that their barking then reached a particularly persuasive pitch. Pépé does have a ten-dency to emit a eunuch-worthy howl when he is in pain or when there have been too many days of rain. I remember groping for the stairs one moment, and then the next I am being doused with water for the sec-ond time that night or, maybe, it was already morning. I looked over at the pool of vomit on the floor and nearby pair of sandals standing slightly apart. "Bin, you will take the train tomorrow. GertrudeStein and I will take the vegetables with us in the automobile," said a voice that, I am afraid, like the sandals, belonged to Miss Toklas. The sandals then padded away, gently slapping the tile floors of the dark house.

The next day, I walked around the house, somber and silent, closing the shutters and putting cloth over the furniture. The last of the summer vegetables caught a ride back to Paris with my Mesdames. Basket's ears were flapping. Pépé's were twitching. The usual traveling circus took off in puffs of dust as GertrudeStein waved, "Good-bye, Thin Thin Bin." Miss Toklas was in no mood for pleasantries and kept her hands on her lap.

Good-bye, GertrudeStein.

Really, Madame, what was I supposed to do in Bilignin? It was never part of our original bargain. I spend my months there and never, never see a face that looks like mine, except for the one that grows gaunt in the mirror. In Paris, GertrudeStein, the constant traffic of people at least includes my fellow *asiatiques*. And while we may never nod at one another, tip our hats in polite fashion, or even exchange empathy in quick glances, we breathe a little easier with each face that we see. It is the recognition that in the darkest streets of the city there is another body like mine, and that it means me no harm. If we do not acknowledge each other, it is not out of a lack of kindness. The opposite, GertrudeStein. To walk by without blinking an eye is to say to each other that we are human, whole, a man or a woman like any other, two lungfuls of air, a heart pumping blood, a stomach hungry for home-cooked food, a body in the constant search for the warmth of the sun.

GertrudeStein, in Bilignin you and Miss Toklas are the only circus act in town. And me, I am the *asiatique*, the sideshow freak. The farmers there are childlike in their fascination and in their unadorned cruelty. Because of your short-cropped hair and your, well, masculine demeanor, they call you "Caesar." Miss Toklas, they dub "Cleopatra" in an ironic tribute to her looks and her companionship role in your life. As for your guests who motor into Bilignin all summer long, they are an added attraction. Last summer, the farmers especially enjoyed the painter who hiked through their fields with clumps of blue paint stuck in his uncombed hair. There was also a bit of commotion over the young writer who wore a pair of lederhosen to walk Basket up and down the one street of that village. As for me, the farmers there are used to me by now. Only when they are very drunk do they forget themselves. At the grape gathering this year, one of them asked, "Did you know how to use a fork and a knife before coming to France?" That was followed by "Will you marry three or four *asiatique* wives?" Then a usually quiet farmer, a widower who lives alone with his dog, which he claims is more sweet-tempered than his now departed wife, asked, "Are you circumcised?" I looked around at my hosts and then up at the harvest moon. Why do they always ask *this* question? I wondered. I could only assume that their curiosity about my male member is a by-product of their close association with animal husbandry. Castrating too many sheep could make a man clinical and somewhat abrupt about such things, I thought. The morning after, they never recall asking me this question. In a matter of a few short hours, everyone in that village loses their memory. Everyone except me. Believe me, I have tried. But no matter how much I drink, I am still left with their voices, thick with alcohol, and their faces burnt raw by the sun.

MS. PAC-MAN RUINED MY GANG LIFE

■ ■ ■

Ka Vang

Mandy stole my boyfriend, Tiny. The RCB, or the Red Cambodian Bloods, called him Tiny because he stood at six feet with iron arms. He was big for a Khmer. Everyone respected him because of his size, except me. I didn't like Tiny because, well, he was tiny, about the length of a fortune cookie and as thick as a Bic pen.

A Puerto Rican mama, Mandy had yellow fever. Every three months, an Asian brother passed her to another like a coat that had been worn, but lost its appeal. She met up with Tiny at a party that I didn't attend because I was working. Within minutes, Mandy was wrapped around Tiny tighter than a bun around a hot dog.

Being dumped didn't bother me at all. Well, maybe just a bit. But Tiny was no trophy to be fought over. He didn't care that his father was killed in a Khmer Rouge labor camp because he wore glasses, or that his mother was raped by boys his age when Pol Pot's people came to his village. The killing fields were the streets of south Minneapolis for him.

KA VANG is an award-winning Hmong writer born in 1975 on a CIA military base in Laos just days before the country fell to Communism. She came with her family to the United States in 1980, and was formerly the first Hmong reporter for the *Saint Paul Pioneer Press* and the *Chicago Tribune*. She studied political science at the University of Minnesota, as well as literature and theater at the Imperial College in London, England, and African American history at Xavier University in New Orleans. Her writing addresses many aspects of historical and contemporary life in the Hmong community, drawing upon both traditional folklore and modern imagery to create a vivid record of her people's experiences.

Tiny was only interested in getting high and getting laid, and it didn't have to be in that order.

But, when you live the life of a gangsta girl, a woman stealing your man, particularly if she was from a rival gang, was a major sign of DIS-RESPECT, and therefore a serious justification for war.

"What about your rep?" my home girls implored, trying to convince me to jump Mandy. "Gurl, if I waz you, I'd cap her ass."

"It ain't like that," I replied, pushing down a hand made up into a sign of a gun.

It had been a while since our last gang fight and now my girls were itching to do damage. Mandy suddenly emerged as a convenient target. Last night, we jumped two black bitches for cutting us off on University Avenue. Like a scene out of a bad seventies car flick, we chased them down, trying to run them off the road until they pulled over somewhere between Snelling and Vandalia. Getting out of their beat-up Oldsmobile, they look like typical ghetto holes with cheap gold shimmering on their ears, fingers and necks. The first girl reminded me of Lil' Kim, short and flamboyant and the second, well, she was just plain ugly. But there were five of us and only two of them.

Nikki, my best friend, did a pretend karate kick she saw in a movie just to scare them as we approached cursing and threatening. She loved to perpetuate the myth that all Asians knew kung fu. We jumped on them with our brass knuckles and razor blades, and left them bleeding by the side of the road.

"I don't want to throw down, at least not for him," I told Nikki as we sat on my bedroom floor. "His father was killed by Pol Pot's regime and he thinks that stands for a specialized Khmer joint!"

"Cindy, you are the only one who cares about this shit," said Nikki, twisting her head in a circle. "Besides, you're Hmong, not Khmer, so why the fuck do you care? This is Saint Paul, not Southeast Asia. Think about the now, the hea! You can't let any ol' hole steal your MAN!"

Her fingers were in my face, accusing me of not protecting my property, our property. She made it clear that we would go to war. In a way, being in a gang is a lot like being in a democracy, the majority is right even when it becomes tyrannical.

"All right! Tonight at Louis's Billiard, her ass is grass!" I screamed, surprised by the hardness in my voice. Already my heart was hardening and my emotions evaporating so I could bring myself to hurt someone, even take a life.

We called our homeboys and told them we needed backup. About five of us gathered at my house in the late afternoon, and started to plan our war strategy. We brought every scissors, hammer, screwdriver, nail and tool we found in our fathers' toolboxes and wrapped them in duct tape so our fingerprints wouldn't be on the weapons if the cops ever got a hold of them.

Next we put tape on the gun. The one gun we all shared, which I was still holding from the last time we shot a Laotian girl for looking at Nikki the wrong way.

Sam, our backer who had a beef with Tiny's gang, picked us up at seven and took us to a gas station where we changed ten dollars into quarters and divided them among the five of us. The change came in handy if the cops came and we had to flee the scene on foot. That way, we could call home base, Sam's celli, from a gas station to be picked up. We had partners to run with just in case someone was shot or needed help. It wasn't the invasion of Normandy, but it was a scheme that worked. My only concern was that Louis's was located on a hill and it was January in Minnesota. The snow and ice were the unseen enemy.

We got to Louis's before Mandy and Tiny. I didn't see fear in my girls, and they didn't see fear in me. But my right toe covered beneath the thick sock twitched from anxiety at the thought of breaking open a head like a coconut with my bare hands. Only one part, an unseen part, feared. My mouth was foul and my soul had enough hate to turn a man into stone like Medusa, but this was reality and not a myth.

I played my favorite old-school video game, Ms. Pac-Man, to shake off any doubts. I pretended the ghosts were Mandy and Tiny, and I was chomping them up to be stronger. Chomping away, first the cherries, strawberry, and then the banana, which meant I reached the highest level of the game.

"Damn!"

"Whussup, second thoughts?"

"No. This is my highest score and I'm dead. Hey, can you spare me a quarter?"

"But the quarters are for—"

"Now, three-two-one! Nikki, please! I need that quarter. I've got to beat this game."

She hesitantly handed me a quarter. Thirty seconds later she handed me another quarter, and another.

"That's enuff, gurl! You should be keeping an eye on the door unless you want Mandy to come up in hea and blow your brains into the machine. Your back is towards the door!"

"Thought you got my back?"

The clicking sounds of billiard balls hitting each other and rolling to the pockets faded into the darkness when Mandy and Tiny arrived with some of Tiny's gang members.

He took one look at me and motioned his crew to exit. They were gone and there would be no fight. I turned back to the machine, back to defeating Ms. Pac-Man, a truly worthy opponent.

But it wasn't over for my friends. They crowded around me with their smeared lipstick mouths yapping and gawking at me to pursue Mandy and Tiny. Like a mindless zombie, I headed towards the door. My hands slipped into my jean pocket for the scissors. Walking into the cold Saint Paul night from the musky billiard hall, my excited breath formed a line of smoke from my mouth to the dry sky. Mandy and Tiny were about to get into their car when I screamed their names.

"Come over here!"

Tiny walked towards me like John Travolta from *Saturday Night Fever*. Mandy followed closely behind.

"Is Mandy your new girl?"

"Yeah," he said in his typical slow drawl.

"Why'd you dump me?"

"'Cos."

"'Cause what?"

"'Cos you're a crazy hole. Woman, I don't want no girl who's gonna be in my face, riding my ass about getting a job, fighting for my rights as a color man. I just don't care 'cos I just wanna have fun. And lately, you haven't been fun. You changed . . ."

It was about the sex. For men, it's about the G-thang. I knew I should have placed more of a priority on that, but I really didn't care for it.

My home girls urged me in Hmong to hit Mandy and they would follow. One of Tiny's hangers-on, Joe, got all tough and stepped up.

"Why yo bitches in my boy's face?"

"This is between the girls," said Sam, who cocked the gun in his pocket loudly.

"Yo, like you said, um, it's between the girls," replied a frightened Joe.

Nikki got tired of the rhetoric and took out a screwdriver from her pocket. She stabbed Mandy in the chest with it. Mandy let out a howl as Nikki drilled it into her coat and deeper. The next moments happened so fast that it is hard to explain all the details. I followed Nikki's lead and thrust the scissor into Mandy's stomach. The other girls hammered Mandy with their fists and weapons. But she was tough. Her hard fist slammed into my face and back. We were like bees attacking her and she was swatting us off.

I stopped and saw Tiny's worried face. He was too selfish to truly care for Mandy, but he didn't like an unfair fight. Tiny couldn't lift a finger to help Mandy for fear of Sam shooting him and his homies. But I still don't think he would have interfered even if he had a gun. He couldn't risk going to war with Sam, at least, not over a woman.

I tried yanking the scissor out of Mandy, but it was caught in something, maybe her coat, or skin? After three or four tries, I managed to pull it out and slashed her across the face.

Mandy laid in the ground moaning in agony. A circle of blood formed on the snow underneath her. We took turns kicking Mandy until we heard police sirens in the distance.

"Let's go!" Nikki said.

We dropped our weapons and scattered. Nikki and I, who were partners, started running down the hill into an unlit alley along University Avenue. I slipped and rolled, and twisted my ankle. Pain shot through my leg as I tried to stand up. Limping down through the alley, I couldn't keep up with Nikki.

"Whassup with your foot?"

"Sprained ankle," I huffed.

The sirens got closer. The Five-O must have seen us run into the alley.

"Into the garbage bin before it's too late," she said.

Nikki, who was more athletic, pushed me into a Dumpster behind a Vietnamese restaurant on University Avenue. My face landed on a pile of old pho noodles. It took me three years to eat noodles again. The Dumpster reeked with the rudest, most obnoxious odor, which penetrated my clothes, hair and skin. Nikki jumped in and crawled to the other side.

The siren came closer, but as the squad car approached it was turned off. We heard the wheels of the car on the snow. Silently and slowly it stalked us. I expected the lips of the bin to open and blinding lights from a flashlight to shine on my face. My parents would be disappointed with me again when they came to pick me up from juvenile hall. My mother would cry and my father would threaten to kill me. Then it dawned on me that I had just turned eighteen, so I wouldn't get off as easy. I had forgotten about my birthday, which raised the stakes.

We waited in the bin for hours, not saying a word. Not even when I felt a million small and slimy creatures crawling up my arms. After a while I could make out Nikki's large watery eyes in the dark. Then I saw her doing the same thing I was, slowly picking off the maggots from her body. My right ankle throbbed with pain, but I couldn't move to rub it, worried that I would give away our hiding place.

Were the police waiting for us to emerge like filthy pigs from the pen? Maybe they wanted to play a joke on us and the entire gang strike force was waiting for us to appear.

But there were no lights, no handcuffs, and no police dogs, only our shadows as we climbed out of the garbage bin.

I vomited all the way to the nearest gas station. We found a pay phone, but it was broken, so we walked to another station about a half a mile away. Afraid that the cops were still looking for us, we hid in doorways as cars drove by. The ice and cold made it difficult for the both of us to move faster.

"I think gangs have it easier in Cali," I said trying to make light of our situation. Nikki was not amused. I wondered if Mandy was dead. Would Tiny still find her pretty with that scar I made on her left cheek?

Nikki was becoming increasingly frustrated and took out a pack of smokes. I knew she thought I had let my home girls down by my unwillingness to jump Mandy. I had become useless.

She took out a cig and placed it in her mouth without lighting it up. She was trying to quit.

When we got to the second pay phone, we realized we were out of quarters.

"Where are they?" she screamed.

"In the Ms. Pac-Man game."

"Cindy? Why did you do that? How will we reach Sam now!"

"I forgot. I had a good game," I said defensively. "Look, I never told you to give me all of your quarters!"

Reeking like a bad Vietnamese restaurant with my ankle sprained, I knew it was the last gang fight for me. I had turned eighteen, and would no longer get a slap on the hand if I were caught. Tiny was right, my interests changed. But more importantly, I had changed. The role of being a gangsta girl was becoming too narrow for all that I wanted to do with my life. Even if Tiny didn't care about his future, I did about mine.

"I think this is it for me," I turned to Nikki and said.

Somehow she wasn't surprised.

"It's about time. I always knew you didn't have it in you. I wondered how long you'd last. I've got a bad habit that I am also trying to quit so I understand, but the others won't."

"I can take care of myself."

"I've got your back."

She pulled out a paper clip from her pocket and I started to laugh. The paper clip method was an old-school way to trigger the phone into thinking a quarter was put in. Of course, it no longer works on these new pay phones with the calling card feature. We called Sam to come and pick us up.

A week later, my girls and I met in a school parking lot, where they beat me to a pulp. It was a small price to pay for getting out of a gang.

UNTITLED STORY

■ ■ ■

José Garcia Villa

1

Father did not understand my love for Vi, so Father sent me to America to study away from her. I could not do anything and I left.

2

I was afraid of my father.

3

On the boat I was seasick and I could not eat. I thought of home and my girl and I had troubled dreams.

4

The blue waves in the young sunlight were like azure dancing flowers but they danced ceaselessly to the tune of the sun, to look at them

Born in Manila in 1908, JOSÉ GARCIA VILLA emigrated to the United States in 1930. He published four books of poetry and one short story collection in the United States, and a number of books in the Philippines. The recipient of numerous awards, prizes, and honors in his lifetime, the reclusive Villa died on February 8, 1997, in New York City. *The Anchored Angel: Selected Writings by José Garcia Villa* was published by Kaya Press in 1999.

made me dizzy. Then I would go to my cabin and lie down and sometimes I cried.

5

We were one month at sea. When I arrived in America I was lonely.

6

I window-shopped at Market Street in San Francisco and later when I was in Los Angeles I went to Hollywood but I remained lonely.

7

I saw President Hoover's home in Palo Alto but I did not care for President Hoover.

8

In California too I saw a crippled woman selling pencils on a sidewalk. It was night and she sat on the cold concrete like an old hen but she had no brood. She looked at me with dumb faithful eyes.

9

The Negro in the Pullman hummed to himself. At night he prepared our berths and he was automatic like a machine. As I looked at him I knew I did not want to be a machine.

10

In the university where I went there were no boys yet. It was only August and school would not begin until September. The university was on a hill and there the winds blew strong. In my room at night I could hear the winds howling like helpless young puppies. The winds were little blind dogs crying for their mother.

11

Where was the mother of the winds? I lay in bed listening to the wind-children crying for their mother but I would fall asleep before their mother had returned to them.

12

During the day the little blind puppies did not whimper much. It was only at night they grew afraid of the dark and then they cried for their mother. Did their mother ever come to them? Maybe their mother had a lover and she loved this lover more than the little blind puppies.

13

I had nothing to do and I wrote home to my friends but my friends did not write to me.

14

One day a boy knocked at my room. He was young and he said he was alone and wanted to befriend me. He became dear to me.

15

The boy's name was David. He was poor and he wore slovenly clothes but his eyes were soft. He was like a young flower.

16

When David was sick I watched over him.

17

Afterwards David would not go anywhere without me.

18

Of nights David and I would walk through the streets and he would recite poetry to me.

"Sunset and evening star
And one clear call for me . . ."

This was the slowness of David, the slowness of the sunset, of the evening star.

19

One night David came to me and said he was returning home the next morning. He could not earn enough money on which to go to school.

20

I died in myself.

21

After David had gone I walked the streets feeling I had lost a great, great something. When I thought of him it hurt very much.

22

School opened in September. At my table in the dining hall we were eight. I liked Georgia, Aurora, Louise and Greg. There was another girl and her name was Reynalda but she was a little haughty.

23

The boys were Joe and Wiley. Joe came from David's town and when I asked him about David he said they had been like Jonathan and David in high school. Joe loved David and David, who was far away now, became a bond between Joe and me.

24

Sometimes Joe and I got sore at each other but when we thought of David we became friends again.

25

Joe wanted to become a preacher and Wiley would be a sports editor. I did not know what I wanted to be. First when I was a boy I wanted to be a movie actor but later I did not want to be a movie actor. I wanted to paint but Father objected to it because he said painters did not make much money.

26

Father was a moneymaker. When he had made it he did not want to spend it. When I needed money I went to my mother and she gave it to me because she was not a moneymaker.

27

Then I fell in love with Georgia. Georgia had golden hair and I became enamored of it. In my country all the girls were blackhaired. I asked Georgia to let me feel her hair and when I ran my fingers through it I became crazy about her.

28

Georgia and I went running around. Afterwards she wrote me love letters.

29

In one letter she called me My Lord, in another Beloved. But I called her just Georgia although sometimes I called her Georgie. When I called her Georgie I smiled because it was like a boy's name.

30

One day Georgia and I quarrelled and many nights thereafter I walked the streets muttering to myself. I did not know what I was saying. I called myself, "You . . ." but the sentence did not get finished. I would look at the sky and behold the stars and talk to myself.

31

One night I stopped talking to myself. I was no longer incoherent and the sentence on my lips that began with "You . . ." got finished.

32

The finished sentence was beauteous as a dancer in the dawn. The sentence was finished at night but it was not like the night but like the dawn.

33

Later Georgia and I made up but everything was not as it used to be. The finished sentence was beauteous like a dancer in the dawn. After a time I did not care for Georgia nor she for me.

34

I went to school but I did not like going to school.

35

I said to myself I would be through with girls and love only the girl back home. I wondered if what had happened to me had happened too or was happening to Vi. As I thought it I got angry not at myself but with Vi.

36

A girl should be constant.

37

I was angry with Vi and in my fancy I saw many pictures of her with other boys. She was dancing and smiling and she had no thoughts of me.

38

Finally I dreamt Vi had got married and I woke up crying. Then I was no longer angry with Vi but with my father who had separated us. I wrote Father an angry letter blaming him. I said I would quit studying and did not care if he cut me off.

39

I was very angry I became a poet. In fancy my anger became a gorgeous purple flower. I made love to it with my long fingers. Then when I had won it and it shone like a resplendent gem in my hands I offered it to my father.

40

My father could not understand the meaning of the gorgeous purple flower. When I gave it to him he threw it on the floor. Then I said, "My father is not a lover."

41

I picked the flower and it lived because my father refused it.

42

One morning at breakfast I told Wiley and Joe and the girls that I was quitting school and leaving for New York that afternoon. At first they would not believe me but I was quiet and pensive throughout the meal and finally they believed me. They wanted to know why I was leaving but I told them I did not know it myself.

43

At lunch they looked at me wistfully and I said, "This is our last meal together." I became very sad.

44

I shook their hands and Louise and Aurora asked me if I would write to them. When I left the table they followed me softly with their eyes until I turned at the door.

45

Joe and Wiley walked with me to my room at the dorm. They did not want to leave me and in my room I said they must go for I must pack my things. They wanted to help me but I said I was not packing many things. I made them go after we had shaken hands and promised to write each other. Joe and Wiley wanted to go to the station to see me off but I begged them not to. It would make me feel bad, I said.

46

And so I made Joe and Wiley go but when they had left my room I went to the window and looked at them long and I cried. I liked Joe and Wiley and Aurora and Louise—why was I leaving them?

47

Then I lay on the bed without moving. All the time I knew I was not truly leaving for New York yet I felt greatly hurt. In myself I was leaving and behind me I would leave Joe and Wiley and the girls. I would be lonely again as when I had first come to America.

48

I had said I was leaving for New York but it was not true. I was a liar because I had felt like telling a lie and I was angry with my father and in my mind I wanted to do something rash like leaving college and going about starving in a big city like New York.

49

In the big city of New York, where I had never been, I was hungry and without money. I lived in a little dark room and it was dark and ugly for the rent was cheap. There was only one little window in the room and it was tight to open.

50

One night I opened the little window and a piece of paper blew in. It settled on the floor and then my mind began to work about it.—I am not alone. A lover is waiting for me outside. She has written me a letter calling me to her side. . . . "I will go to you, sweetheart," I whispered tenderly.

51

Then a strong wind blew in and the paper moved.—It is a white flower trembling with love. It is God's white flower.—It made me think of my gorgeous purple flower which my father had refused and I wanted it to become God's white flower. Make my purple flower white, God, I prayed.

52

In New Mexico I had prayed before about my father, mother and sisters but in New York I prayed about a flower.

53

In New York it was colder than in New Mexico.

54

I wanted to buy a new suit and go to see a new UFA film but I had no money.

55

Because I wanted to have a new suit and to see a new German film and I had no money I walked around in the streets. I looked at the haberdashery windows and gazed at the new styles. There was a wine-colored suit with padded shoulders and if I only had money I could have it. It cost sixty-five dollars.

56

In front of the big cinema it was very bright. In San Francisco I saw the Fox Theatre and I thought it was very big but this was much bigger. It was very lavish. Rich young ladies and thin gay gentlemen poured in. They laughed goldenly.

57

Then I got tired walking and I returned to my little dark room and the dark made me want a woman.

58

It was cold in the room and I thought if I had a woman I would not feel so cold. We would share each other's warmth.

59

"Warming woman, warming woman," I sang. How beautiful the words. How beautiful the thought.

60

Then I turned on the light and in the lighted room I took a book and read. The story was about a liar. I thought of myself. I had lied to Joe and Wiley and to Aurora and Louise and to every one at the table. It had occurred to me to lie and I did and now I was living up to my lie.

61

All these adventures in New York I have been telling you about happened in my room as I lay on the bed crying because I was a liar. But I was not afraid to cry.

62

Later I dressed and pretended I was going to the station where I was leaving. After a time when I got dressed I did not want to merely pretend and I left my room to go to the station.

63

On the way I met Aurora. She walked with me to the street corner to bid me good-bye. She held my hands long and her hold was tight. Her hands were soft like flowers and thin like roots but they were strong lovers. Her hands made cruel love to my hands.

64

"Write to me," her mouth said—but her hands, "Have we not touched the touch to last us forever? the touch of music that knows no forgetting?"

65

When I had already gotten into the bus and the bus started Aurora did not move. She stood at the corner, her eyes following me. She stood there long, immobile, and I waved my hand at her but only her eyes moved. Her hands that had been lovers were quiet now. Her whole body has become a quiet lover. As the bus moved away, in the far corner she was no longer a quiet lover but a song of serenity.

66

In the bus strange thoughts came to me: I have touched her hands. Why do I not love her the way I loved Georgia? Why have I not asked to touch her hair? Maybe if I touched her hair I would love her like I was maddened by Georgia. . . . I should have touched her hair. She would have liked it. We would have become lovers.

67

As to Georgia I did not bid her good-bye and I did not care. —I touched her hair. I ran my fingers through her hair. After I finished the sentence that was beauteous as a dancer in the dawn I did not care to touch her hair. —In the bus I could not understand why and it made feel sad.

68

I got off at the station and waited for the 5:30 train. It came and then it left. I watched it till I could not see it. I wondered if I was in it.

69

Had I bidden myself good-bye?

70

Afterwards I walked through the town as if I had gone out of myself. I looked for myself vainly. I was nowhere. I was now only a shell, a house. The house of myself was empty.

71

My god had flown away and carried with him my gorgeous purple flower. Will Father laugh now?

72

Where had my god fled? Where was he taking my purple flower which my father had refused?

73

In the morning, on the campus, I met Aurora and she said I fooled her. Later everybody said I fooled them. But to Aurora, as I thought of her as she stood at the street corner, her hands making love to my hands, and of her when she was a song of serenity, I said: "Your hands have told me an unforgettable story. Your song of serenity has awakened me. Now let me feel your hair . . ."

74

My god was in her hair. My god was there with my purple flower pressed gently to his breast. I opened his hands and he yielded to me my flower. I pinned it to Aurora's hair. And as the purple petals kissed the soft dark of her hair, my flower turned silver, then white—became God's white flower. Then I was no longer angry with my father.

EYE CONTACT

an outtake from **AMERICAN KNEES**

■ ■ ■

Shawn Wong

Being the only two Asians at a party, they tried to avoid each other, but failed. They touched accidentally several times. They watched each other furtively from across the room.

Aurora Crane had arrived first. They were her friends, her office mates, and it was their party. Raymond Ding was only a guest of her boss, who was the host of the office party. A visitor from out of town invited at the last minute. A friend of a friend in the city for only three days to do some business. When he arrived at the front door, she knew before he did that they were the only two Asians at a party. With dread she knew her boss would make a special point of introducing him to her and that one by one her friends, the loyal, would betray her and pair her with him. They would probably be introduced several times during the evening. It made sense to them. There was no real covert activity, no setup, no surprise blind date, no surprise dinner companion seated not so coincidentally next to her. She was not at home with mother meeting not so coincidentally her mother's idea of a "nice Japanese boy." She had a boyfriend (unfortunately in another city and

---

In addition to the publication of his two novels, *Homebase* and *American Knees* (which is being adapted into a film), SHAWN WONG has edited or coedited six anthologies, including the landmark *Aiiieeeee! An Anthology of Asian American Writers*. He has been a writer and a teacher for over thirty years and has known the editor of this anthology, Jessica Hagedorn, during that same period, which means Wong has shared many of his significant writerly and nonwriterly coming-of-age experiences in her company or under her influence. He was born in Oakland, California, in 1949.

not Asian and a lover none of the loyal had met and to add to the further misfortune, some knew she had moved away from him to define a future without him making it very complex in her mind, but simple in the minds of the now distrustfully loyal).

Prior to the impending introductions, she wondered when they would make eye contact, when he would realize they were the only two Asians at the party. She hoped to God he wasn't an insecure Asian male who would only talk to her. She hoped to God he wouldn't see her as every Asian boy's answer to the perfect woman—half white, half Asian, just enough to bring home to Mother while maintaining the white girl fantasy. This gets somewhat complex, certainly more complex than *Love Is a Many-Splendored Thing*. Aurora Crane is Eurasian Jennifer Jones. Is the Asian boy William Holden? He'd like to think so.

When he eventually gets around to asking, "What are you?" will it be any different than any other obnoxious bore? Or would he simply be overly curious, but too polite to ask? It would be that slow realization creeping over his face, the ponderings and machinations that nestle in the eyes, the slight squint as if squinting can detect racial ancestry and blood lines. He would ask finally when she noticed he was no longer listening to her and merely watching her talk, all the while trying to decipher and calibrate the skin tone, the shape of her eyes, the color of her hair. In the past, the truly devious and ignorant would ask where she was from. A city in California was not the answer. Where are your parents from? Also from California was not the answer. Sometimes she would return the favor and ask where the interrogator's parents were from because, ha ha, nearly everyone in Washington, D.C., was from somewhere else, a standard cliche. The truly inept (which were sometimes failed devotees of the truly devious and ignorant) would blurt out the question, "What nationality are you?" American and my parents. "What are you, you know, what race?" Was ethnicity so hard a word to use? "Oh, how wonderful to be Japanese and Irish! You're so pretty." At which point some D.C. matron and patron of the arts would exclaim to her friend, "Miriam, don't you think she's pretty? That skin coloring!" Sometimes they reach out and touch her skin without asking.

"Don't you think he's pretty?" Annie, the betrayer from work, nudged Aurora. She was, of course, referring to the visitor from the Orient. "Maybe he's a Japanese businessman in town to argue against import duty and the trade deficits, but then he's kind of tall."

Aurora, without looking at him, replied, "His suit is the wrong color. Euro-trash natural shoulders olive brown, not Brooks Brothers American cut charcoal grey. Handpainted tie. West Hollywood is about as far east as this guy goes."

Asian people could tell she was part Asian, perhaps not part Japanese, but something. They would know at first eye contact. This eye contact thing between Asian men and Asian women was where the war began.

This is how it happens.

An Asian woman and an Asian man are the only two people on opposite sides of an intersection waiting to cross the street. First there's usually one momentary point of eye contact to register race. He looks to see if he knows you or your relatives. If he doesn't, the competition begins. The men always weaken first. They look at the traffic, check the lights, check the wristwatch, then walk, never making eye contact again. At the critical point when eye contact should occur between the only two people on the street caught between the boundaries of a crosswalk, the men chicken out and check the time again or run as if they were late. Just once she'd like to shock one of these boys and say, "Hey, home. What it is?" Whenever she was with her black friend Steve Dupree on the street and heard him say that to another black man, she would ask if he knew that man. The fact that he never did made her wonder why it wasn't ever possible between two Asians. Was it distrust and suspicion? Was it historical animosity? Was it because Japan invaded China and Korea? Mao versus Chiang Kai-shek? Chinatown versus Japantown? Fourth generation Chinese American versus fresh off the boat?

Since the "mysterious and exotic visitor from the east" didn't have any Polo trademarks on his clothes, Aurora ruled out Korean and decided he was Chinese. She set out to find the most typically Chinese feature about him, but couldn't find the usual landmarks: cheap haircut with greasy bangs falling down across the eyebrows, squarish gold rimmed glasses askew because there's no bridge to hold them up, polyester balls on his pants with a baggy butt, a shirt tucked in way too tight, and perhaps a slab of jade on a thick 24 kt gold chain around his neck. He had none of the above except for a gift for the host and hostess in a plastic shopping bag. *Please, please*, Aurora thought, *let it be oranges!* Oh, it would be so Chinese to bring oranges. And, of course, the plastic shopping bag—Chinese Samsonite. He was made.

She knew she was being cruel. She had to be cruel in order to steel herself for the impending introductions. Why she needed to be cruel, she wasn't sure, but she found herself now looking for and analyzing the most un-Asian features about him. Okay, the clothes were certainly Melrose Avenue, West Hollywood, all natural fiber, beautiful colors. No man dressed like that in D.C., which was a lawyer's dark grey or navy blue and red tie town. No exceptions. Maybe on Saturdays they would walk on the wild side and wear a yellow tie. She doubted if Asian American men in West Hollywood dressed like him. That gave Aurora a clue. Okay, he was tall, nearly six feet, which gave Asian men that attitude that they're tall enough to qualify to flirt with white women eye to eye and not have to resort to either dominance or the cleverness of their shorter counterparts with the Napoleon complex.

"Isn't he pretty, Ro?" Annie repeated.

"He's obviously got some Wonder Bread squeeze at home who dresses him."

"Well there's one you don't have to make over," Annie said. "We deserve once in a while to find one that's already been made over with the cute clothes, contact lenses, cute haircut, nice shoes by some other woman. Jeez, the work we put into some of these guys, then they leave us because they're so presentable and de-polyesterized."

Aurora was reloading another salvo about a Chinaman shopping on Melrose Avenue in a four wheel drive Jeep Cherokee with a golden retriever, when Annie said what she always said about Aurora's analysis of men, "Yeah, yeah, I know, we weren't born cynical."

Aurora looked away when she saw her boss leading the Chinaman by the arm to the front room where she was sitting. Instead of the impending introduction she feared, she heard her boss announce, "Everybody, this is Raymond Ding from San Francisco. This is everybody." Turning to Ding, her boss continued, "I'll let everybody introduce themselves, and the food's coming soon." That was it.

When Ding surveyed the room and nodded hello, he didn't do a double-take on Aurora, instead said hello to the group, nodded his head. Those of the loyal closest to him began a discussion of San Francisco out of which Aurora heard snatches of conversation about fog and Italian food. Maybe he thought he was too good for her.

Aurora didn't know if she was relieved or disappointed. She was willing to give him a chance. Later, through some miscalculation on both their parts they had ended up at the food table together, each entering the dining room from different doors. She handed him a plate by the buffet. They spoke briefly about the food and exited the same separate doors. Upon re-entering the living room again by separate entrances they noticed that their seats had been taken by others. A piano bench large enough for two remained. From across the room, he made eye contact, didn't look away, and motioned for her to share the chair.

Brave Chinese boy, she thought.

"Do you play?" he asked pointing with his dinner plate to the piano. He wished those weren't his first words to her. Prop dependent, boring, and unoriginal introductory comment. Raymond suddenly felt like an interloper who sidles up to an attractive woman at a piano bar only to realize the vacant seat beside her belongs to her boyfriend only temporarily absent. Of course, he'd never do that anyway, unless the woman spoke to him first.

Her answer was a simple truth, "No." The intonation in her "no" closed doors, broke hearts, melted romantic inscriptions on sterling silver keepsake lockets with acid.

He said, "Food looks good." Prop dependent, boring, unoriginal again. Should he say something funny now like, "My how your eyes slant in this rich light. Hey, it's tough to get that *yin/yang* thing just right. How about that war bride thing?"

Aurora snaps a carrot stick in her mouth. Perhaps, Aurora thought, she should speak a little to the "Oriental" at hand just in case people were watching. "Was it Ray or Raymond?"

"Either way is fine, but go easy on the Ding jokes."

"Aurora Crane."

Raymond smiled. He was being witty and clever in his mind. He knew without asking that her parents had named her Aurora because of the aurora borealis, a child of many colors. Perhaps her girlhood friends teased her and called her "AB" for short. She was looking away from him after her introduction as if she were bracing herself for questions about her name, but Raymond posed the questions only in his mind and smiled to himself at the answers.

Back to back they entered conversations on opposing sides of the room. At first they spoke at the same time, each conversation drowning out the conversations on the opposite side of the room. The piano bench had a sensory induced demilitarized zone in which all touch and invasion should be avoided. But each time she laughed she leaned back touching, no, grazing him slightly. Each time after the first touch, the feeling lingered as if they were holding a flower petal between them without bruising it, or a potato chip, depending on how sentimental the touch. The touching worked its way into their conversations as each one of them paused in their own talk to eavesdrop on the other while feigning to pay attention to their own. Their touching became a way of flirting with each other. A simple touch from one would cause the other to stop their conversation, stutter over a word, be distracted. They would need this information later in order to gauge and measure the ground on which they would talk when the time came.

The Chinese "six breaths of nature" moved between them: wind, rain, darkness, light, *yin*, and *yang*. The perfect blend of each breath of nature settles the heart, mind, and body. Indeed, if something were to begin between Raymond and Aurora, neither one of them paid much attention to the fact that it had been raining for days, it was dark, a bright piano lamp was glaring in their eyes as they spoke and each of them now were situated antagonistically back to back rather than allowing the complementary *yin* which is dark and feminine and the *yang* which is light and masculine to find a sense of place between them. But then, that was just so much Orientalism under the rug.

He wanted to begin again. He prepared for a new beginning knowing that the conversation would eventually turn and it would include the two of them together. The piano bench's north and south would be joined together. The longer the delay, the later the party went, the more impossible to get over this Asian thing between them. Solve the dilemma, get the facts about each other's preference for lovers not of their own race. Nothing personal, you know. It's an individual thing, that love thing. We can get on with it, maybe even be friends, double date to prove how comfortable we are with voicing our racial preference to each other honestly and forthrightly. How adult of us; how politically correct.

Was she part Korean or Japanese? he wondered. Or maybe he was altogether wrong and she was native Alaskan or Indian or Latino? What a relief that would be.

He tells her in his mind, with his back turned to her, "Let's say we've just arrived here in America from a foreign country; you from

Korea, Ceylon, or Mongolia, me from the Forbidden City. I say to you at the supermarket checkout line where we meet, 'Hi, how are you?' in broken English. You, having just learned about standing in the express lines, look down and say, in Korean, 'You have two too many items.' I give you my salami and oatmeal cookies because you only have four items. You buy them and leave.

"The next time I see you, you're taking English and Pre-Nursing classes at Seattle Central Community College. In the school cafeteria, I say, 'Hey, how *are* you? What's your major?' You buy green Jell-O and leave.

"The next time I see you, you're getting an MBA degree from Kansas and dating a Jayhawk, 6910" power forward, full scholarship. He's no walk-on. You're his tutor. I see you in the library. I ask, 'Would you like to read my *Wall Street Journal?*' You put down your copy of *Die Zeit* and glare at me. I say, 'I'm majoring in social work.'

"The next time I see you, you're at a dude ranch in Arizona wearing cowboy boots with your jade. I resist calling you 'slim.'

"The next time I see you, you're buying leopard print black tights at Bloomingdale's. You're wearing a black suede dress with fringe. You've changed your name from something with too many syllables to Connie. 'How about some espresso, Connie?' I ask. You look down at the women's socks in my hands and I explain, 'I buy women's socks because I have small feet.'

"The next time I see you, you're trading in your Toyota and buying a Ford Bronco 4WD equipped with monster mudder tires and a chrome brush guard. Safest car in America. *You'll never get in it with that skirt*, I think. 'What's she got under the hood?' I ask. You peel out in reverse.

"The next time I see you, you're anchoring the news on television. 'How's the weather and what's the score?' I ask."

He feels Aurora rise from the piano bench, glances up at her as she gathers some empty plates to take to the kitchen. When she returns someone else has taken her place on the piano bench. Raymond and Aurora's eyes meet. He wants her to come and sit on his lap, sit on the floor beside him with the arm casually draped across his leg, share a glass of wine. Eye contact, then it's gone.

He rises from the bench because there isn't a place for her to sit, makes the same motion he made when they first shared the bench. She shakes her head and points at him, then at the kitchen. *Follow me.*

In the kitchen they talk for nearly an hour. No one interrupts them because they're the only two Asians at the party. Private and natural. There's an occasional "oh, I'm glad you two have met." Guarding against any further cleverness, he withholds anymore prop dependent glib comments and she finds out he's actually a little shy. He doesn't squint to determine her ethnicity. She doesn't leave him guessing. Their conversation is complementary. She offers information and he fills in the blanks without asking embarrassing questions. "I'd like to study Japanese at a language school in Kyoto," she tells him. He responds by asking if her mother is *Issei* or *Nisei*. She says she's *Nisei* and that her Irish American father met her while buying strawberries from the family farm.

She finds herself not needing to explain herself or her identity. Twice she reaches out and pulls him toward her to keep him from backing into someone carrying a tray of food. When the danger passes each time, he retreats a step. Perhaps he should have read Sun Tzu's *The Art of War*.

In just this hour of talk, Raymond sees that Aurora is not the kind of woman who places stuffed animals in her car or would wear a dress with a zipper from the neckline to the hemline. She doesn't buy Tupperware.

Two days later, this is how she made him kiss her. He was leaning against a column at the top of the stairs on the portico of the Lincoln Memorial. She walked toward him saying something he couldn't hear and leaned next to him, covering his arm with her back. She nestled. He put his arm around her waist. She denies this to this day claiming her eyesight isn't that good and she simply misjudged how close she was to him, yet at the time she didn't move away. They kissed at the top of the stairs of the Lincoln Memorial, at lunch time, in full view of school children on a field trip from North Carolina. He suddenly felt too conspicuously Chinese. She held him close and he kissed her on her neck just under her left ear which was exactly the right thing to do. She didn't breathe until she whispered in his ear, "Public and demonstrative Asian love. A rare sight."

One of the little southern white children asked their teacher, "Are they making a movie?"

Three years later, in San Francisco, they were packing their separate things and parting.

■ ■ ■

Raymond watches Aurora walk across the room and sit on the floor in front of the dresser. She pulls open a drawer and begins to sort through it, placing her things in a box. Raymond remembers their first kiss at the Lincoln Memorial was followed by several weeks of absence as Raymond returned to San Francisco. In the space between them they flirted, she scolded, he reminisced about their delicate kiss, she changed the subject, he probed politely the boundaries of their intimate talk, and she questioned his motives. With each answer, Raymond discovered the power of his voice in her ear. And with each answer he moved the boundaries closer to her heart.

He tells her a week after kissing her, "I miss you."

"Because of one kiss, Ray?"

"Another kiss under the ear."

Raymond doesn't know Aurora at all, except for their talk at the party, except for a kiss that grew out of an abrupt infatuation stalled by distance. If he were there he would know what to do.

"What would you do if you were here?" Aurora offers her own answer, "Would you take me on a *date*, Ding?"

"Maybe we're past the formal date period."

"We never had a date."

"The Lincoln Memorial."

"That wasn't a date. I met you there after work and you go and kiss me."

"You wanted me to kiss you."

"*I wanted it.* Listen to you! That'll stand up in court, bud."

"You know it's true."

"Cliche number two."

"What did you do today?" Raymond wonders if she would let him wimp out and change the subject.

"I got my first photo in the newspaper."

Raymond is relieved and pushes congratulations to her much too loudly.

"Yes, Ray," Aurora sighs, "years of training, months of hauling camera equipment around and setting up lights for other photographers and just when the newspaper is short staffed I get my chance and the editor sends me out on my own to do what? Take a photo of the President? Perhaps some visiting King? Stalk a bad boy Congressman? No, none of the above, I, Aurora Crane, hit the big time, hit the pages of print with a photo of a pothole in front of the White House."

"Is your name on it? Send me one. Signed 'Love and kisses.' "

"When are you coming back?"

"Do you want me to?"

Raymond finds out later that Aurora doesn't say the word "yes" much, one simply knows when she agrees. "I wish I were there now," Raymond says while searching for some way to find some detail, some familiarity in imagining her at home, but he's never been to her apartment and has seen her in only two different dresses. He resists asking, "What are you wearing?"

"I'm in bed," Aurora says. "Say it again."

"I wish I were there." There is a silence on the line then he hears her breathing change.

"What does your room look like?" Raymond retreats.

"It's a mess."

"Let me guess. The shoes are thrown in a jumbled mess on the closet floor, there are old magazines and newspapers on the floor, an old coffee cup from this morning sits on the bed stand with a little cold coffee in the bottom, the bookshelf is too small for all your books, there are photographs unframed and thumb-tacked to the wall, none of the photographs are your own, there are sweat pants, jogging shoes, and a bra lying on the floor. You're wearing an extra large Columbia University T-shirt in bed."

Aurora is silent.

"Aurora?"

"Where are you calling from?"

"Home."

"Did you talk to my roommate? You have a sister you're not telling me about? You left out the color of my panties."

"No. And, no to the second question. I was being polite on the third. The panties on the floor have purple dots and the ones you're wearing have Mickey Mouse on them."

"You're wrong, they're both on the floor."

"I guess this means we're past the formal date period." Raymond's breathing has changed.

"I'm wet."

Without hesitation Raymond proposes a scene in a lower voice, raising the humidity over the phone. "You are seated on top of your desk when I come into the room. Your legs are crossed. I walk up to you and put my hand under your knees and uncross your legs."

"What are you doing?"

"I'm doing the same thing you're doing."

"I didn't know forty year old Asian men masturbate."

She knows he's thirty-nine, but he lets it go. "We can even use the other hand to calculate logarithms on our Hewlett-Packard calculators." Aurora doesn't laugh. Her breathing sounds muffled as if she's talking from underneath the covers of her bed. "The backs of your knees are moist as I hold them down on the desk. I slide my hands up the sides of your thighs, feeling the muscles of your thighs tighten. I'm moving so slowly that you relax. Your legs part slightly. I can feel your breathing on my neck. I reach around your hips, up the fabric of your panties to the waistband."

"I have tights on."

"I reach for the waistband of your tights."

"You can't get to them from where you are."

"My fingers are feathers. You can barely feel them, but they can lift you, they can warm you, they have a tropical humidity of their own. Your tights melt away. Your panties are a warm breeze that comes up suddenly then vanishes, exposing a humid scented moss. My feathers flutter and nestle on the mound. My tongue is an orchid petal."

"That's too pastoral, but I like the fluttering."

"I'm trying to be polite on our first seduction. More graphic, dear?"

"No."

"How about mythic and heroic?"

"Yes, try mythic."

Like the voice that narrates NFL Films, Raymond is mythic and heroic. "The pulsating and golden aura of my manhood rises majestically in the east and blocks the sun. It presses, advances, draws you quivering toward me. It beckons you to embark on a voyage on the surging waves of a melting earth, a field of erupting, heaving mountains pouring white hot magma down down down to the crashing waves

of the ocean pounding the burning sand of your desire. We are reborn.
We are immortal. Come with me. Come."

"Your manhood blocks the sun?"

"Yes, child."

"How big is this golden aura of manhood?"

"How big do you want it to be?"

"Big as a cucumber."

"How about a pickle?"

"I'm hanging up."

Long distance phone sex and making love with Aurora in person are
the same seduction to her. A good lover must be articulate first and
skillful and attentive second. Aurora's bedtime stories. Raymond has to
flirt, and be romantic, and be seductive, and undress her, and make
love to her in complete sentences and full paragraphs. She wants to be
the center of his fantasy while they're making love. Each time the details must be different; different clothing, different order in which the
clothing comes off, different circumstances, different places. They are
characters in a story that has a beginning and a middle.

She pins Raymond to the wall and pulls his shirt out of his pants,
presses her face to his chest and tries to smell him through the fabric of
his shirt. She unbuckles his pants, lets them slide to the floor around
his ankles, and blocks his attempts to kick his shoes off and free his
pants by placing her knee between his legs. She wants him to be
slightly hobbled and awkward.

She whispers in his ear and pressures him, "What do you want to
do to me?" She wants him to think and be coordinated and be skillful
at the same time. She turns her back to him and leans against Raymond, pinning him between her and the wall. She reaches behind her
and tucks her fingers in the waistband of his underwear and pushes
them down. He lifts her skirt. She stands on his shoes so that she's
taller and accepts the way he nestles his erection between her legs.
She likes the feeling of him being hard against the crotch of her panties. He presses his penis against the fabric pretending to be frustrated
by his inability to enter her. He covers her right hand with his own
hand and places it on the buttons of her blouse. He kisses her neck
and watches her unbutton her blouse. He kisses her under her ear and
whispers his story. The story is told slowly so that Raymond never has
to change his mind, or revise, or edit. The sex stories he tells Aurora

are plotted to indulge Aurora's point of view and descriptively polite in his choice of words. It is Aurora who interrupts and poses questions. Her questions are partly her own voice and partly Raymond's. She says the words "suck" and "cunt" and "fuck" deliberately as if she were quoting Raymond, as if Raymond had said them, as if one could hear the quotes surrounding each word. Each question pursues Raymond's motives and each question can only be answered with "yes." She likes to hear him say "yes." Sometimes he stops in mid-sentence as he searches for ways of speaking with his hands. Aurora unbuttons, unhooks, unsnaps, unzips.

■ ■ ■

It's very hot. Very humid. We couldn't sleep the night before. In our exhaustion the following afternoon we've fallen asleep fully clothed on our bed in a hotel room with enormous windows and billowing white curtains.

We're bathed by the filtered sunlight of the opaque curtains. We're only one floor above a noisy street. Each time the breeze separates the curtains, there's a view across the street of other buildings, of windows mirroring the reflection of our hotel.

Are we in a foreign country? I'm not sure. The noise from the street stirs you from your deep sleep.

My hand rests inside your loose blouse cupping your breast. Before opening your eyes you can feel my thumb brush lightly against your nipple each time your breathing rises and falls. You push my hand away and the sweat pooled there is cooled by the breeze pushing through the curtains.

Was it a tire screech or a bottle shattering against the pavement that woke you? You unbutton your blouse, but you're too tired to sit up and shed it from your damp back. Your skirt is twisted and gathered and folded in the sheets. Some of the fabric of the skirt is matted against your thighs where you've been sweating. It irritates your skin. You push your skirt off. You're not wearing underwear and worry about the curtains parting.

You're beginning to remember your dream. You're angry with me. Something you dreamt made you angry. I was with two women and we were laughing at you and how you discovered my infidelity. You're angry now for being naked and vulnerable while I'm fully clothed and disloyal. Your heartbeat is pushed by your anger. Another bottle shatters on the street. You weren't dreaming, you say.

Your fear wakes me. You turn on your side and look into my brown eyes before I'm fully awake to see where I've been, to confirm my infidelity. Instead of seeing guilt and fear, you see a sleepy insouciance. Your anger changes to irritation at having been woken by your rapid heartbeat. By the time your hand reaches across and feels my slow heartbeat, you are convinced of my innocence.

"A little boy, a woman's fear," you whisper. I can't hear you over the noise from the street. Other people are talking. We are in a foreign country.

I lift your hand from my chest and place your palm against my forehead. "It's hot." You feel my cheeks with the cool backside of your hand. When I lick my dry lips you rest a fingertip on the tip of my tongue. I expect to taste the salt of my own sweat, instead I taste you. You push your finger down against my tongue. I take your hand from my mouth and place it back down there, our fingers intertwine, you push my finger inside you, pull my hand from you, brush the wetness against your clit. My finger is cradled by yours. You teach me each delicate stroke. "The curtains," you say, "people can see us." My tongue circles your nipple. "We are in a foreign country," I whisper.

■ ■ ■

After Raymond and Aurora make love, she lays her head against his chest, listens to his rapid heartbeat, his deep breathing, and she feels his body heat. Aurora is always amused by his exhaustion which she once thought was an exaggerated performance as if he were trying to please her. Aurora thought that men could not be so consumed by their orgasm, that in reality they are only consumed by the satisfaction of having completed a task that required coordination, timing, and unselfishness. *How was I?*

■ ■ ■

Aurora accepts and shoulders the guilt for why she and Raymond are separating. He's hurt but rarely shows it. He tries to be strong and tries to say things that are meant to be ironic and wry as if they had just met, as if she had no knowledge of how much he loved her. He can do this because he knows she still loves him. He thinks if he can keep Aurora talking and if he pretends he's strong, she'll be able to find her belief again. He tries not to give in to everything Aurora wants. Raymond picks an argument, but he's not very good at it.

"It's the age thing."

"It's not the age thing."

"It's the voice of experience thing."

"It's not the experience thing."

"I give too much advice."

"I ask you for advice."

"I'm Chinese and you're not."

"It's not racial."

"I'm a bad lover."

"You know the answer to that."

"I think your friends are young and silly."

"Some of them are."

"I patronize."

"You never patronize."

"I'm perfect."

"It's my fault, not yours."

"It's not your fault."

"I think I'm frightened by something."

"What is it Aurora?"

They both know, but can't say. It's hard for Aurora to believe in her own safety, that she can feel protected, that she believes she wants Raymond to protect her. Protect her from what? From what happens, from what ifs? No. It's identity. A sense of self. She wants to be as strong by herself as she is with Raymond. She wants to have a "son's" sense of the world. She wants an inheritance from her father. She wants her father to pass his power and authority to her as if she were a son. Perhaps he has already, she thinks. She wants people to witness and acknowledge King Lear handing the kingdom over to the loyal daughter. *Give me the pocket watch from Grandpa, turn over the business, pat me on the back when I follow you into the Navy, live your life through me, your son, and grab me another beer, will ya?* The witnesses Aurora sees only hear her saying, "Hey, sailor." She can't be part of the same inheritance. She's not white. She's part white, but it still makes her not white. Was Raymond the father that makes sense and joins two mutually agreeable identities together? He's more than just my lover, Aurora admits. It upsets her that Raymond knows he's not as strong without her. Has she had enough chances to prove herself, like Raymond has? "I'm older," Raymond has said more than once, "maybe I know there are things I simply can't do anymore, I can't prove anymore, or there are things I don't want anymore, or things I accept as is." Aurora remembers how Raymond talks about himself like a car, "As is, no warranty."

Raymond wonders if it is racial. Raymond argues with himself about race and gender, about race and identity being a flimsy excuse, a coverup, a scapegoat. He's interrogating himself and his answers sound defensive. "What is it you don't know? What is it you can't find out with me?" he wants to ask her.

Aurora wonders if it is racial. Perhaps Raymond makes too much of the race issue. Their union was never always just love and desire and friendship. Race was always present in public and in private. Sometimes she felt that he treated his ancestry as a gift to her that would make sense of who she was. She knew she didn't have to be with Raymond to simply say to herself that she was Japanese American and that she felt Japanese American even though some people found it difficult to see it in her face. Being with Raymond people assumed she was Asian and didn't have to guess. She found herself explaining less, but at the same time wanting to harbor the definition of herself that she had to defend against while growing up. Sometimes it was "the age thing" between them. Raymond knew himself better because he was older. Aurora sometimes wanted to be more adrift, more unsure, make more decisions. Raymond and Aurora fit together. There's a common bond. People can see it when they're together. She likes being in a city with a huge Asian population. She can identify with the city in the same way she can be identified with Raymond.

The first few months with Raymond was like being in a college ethnic studies class as they compared notes about being Asian in America and being biracial. Raymond spoke of the sixties and self-determination, then the seventies and used terms like "multicultural" that she had only heard in school and never between two lovers. Perhaps Raymond and Aurora were no different, neither one really knew they were Asian when they were young and each had to prove it in their own way. For Raymond the opportunity to find his identity came in the sixties. Negroes became Blacks and Raymond became "Asian American" without a hyphen. She knew all this information in a general way, yet Aurora would listen and be kind, but in reality only wanted to know how long Raymond's hair was and what he wore. Sometimes he lectured in bed about Berkeley in the sixties.

Aurora is afraid that she'll never forget the way she and Raymond make love.

"How can you be afraid of that?" Raymond asks. "Is that something you want to forget?"

Weeks later, after their separation, Aurora is sitting on the edge of the bed, her bathrobe is untied and hangs open, she is naked underneath. The phone rings. She doesn't move to answer it, instead her phone machine answers. When she hears Raymond's voice, she pulls her bathrobe close around herself. He sounds distracted, admits there is no reason he called, then says there was a reason, but he's forgotten. Then he remembers that he called to tell her his new phone number, but he doesn't tell her. He'll call again.

THE BROWN HOUSE

■ ■ ■

Hisaye Yamamoto

In California that year the strawberries were marvelous. As large as teacups, they were so juicy and sweet that Mrs. Hattori, making her annual batch of jam, found she could cut down on the sugar considerably. "I suppose this is supposed to be the compensation," she said to her husband, whom she always politely called Mr. Hattori.

"Some compensation!" Mr. Hattori answered.

At that time they were still on the best of terms. It was only later, when the season ended as it had begun, with the market price for strawberries so low nobody bothered to pick number twos, that they began quarreling for the first time in their life together. What provoked the first quarrel and all the rest was that Mr. Hattori, seeing no future in strawberries, began casting around for a way to make some quick cash. Word somehow came to him that there was in a neighboring town a certain house where fortunes were made overnight, and he hurried there at the first opportunity.

It happened that Mrs. Hattori and all the little Hattoris, five of them, all boys and born about a year apart, were with him when he paid his first visit to the house. When he told them to wait in the car,

---

HISAYE YAMAMOTO was born in 1921 in Redondo Beach, California. In 1986, she received the American Book Award for Lifetime Achievement from the Before Columbus Foundation. Her work has been published and anthologized widely. *Seventeen Syllables and Other Stories* received the 1988 Award for Literature from the Association of Asian American Studies. Two of the stories in that renowned collection were the basis for a 1991 American Playhouse / PBS film, *Hot Summer Winds*.

saying he had a little business to transact inside and would return in a trice, he truly meant what he said. He intended only to give the place a brief inspection in order to familiarize himself with it. This was at two o'clock in the afternoon, however, and when he finally made his way back to the car, the day was already so dim that he had to grope around a bit for the door handle.

The house was a large but simple clapboard, recently painted brown and relieved with white window frames. It sat under several enormous eucalyptus trees in the foreground of a few acres of asparagus. To the rear of the house was a ramshackle barn whose spacious blue roof advertised in great yellow letters a ubiquitous brand of physic. Mrs. Hattori, peering toward the house with growing impatience, could not understand what was keeping her husband. She watched other cars either drive into the yard or park along the highway and she saw all sorts of people—white, yellow, brown, and black—enter the house. Seeing very few people leave, she got the idea that her husband was attending a meeting or a party.

So she was more curious than furious that first time when Mr. Hattori got around to returning to her and the children. To her rapid questions Mr. Hattori replied slowly, pensively: it was a gambling den run by a Chinese family under cover of asparagus, he said, and he had been winning at first, but his luck had suddenly turned, and that was why he had taken so long—he had been trying to win back his original stake at least.

"How much did you lose?" Mrs. Hattori asked dully.

"Twenty-five dollars," Mr. Hattori said.

"Twenty-five dollars!" exclaimed Mrs. Hattori. "Oh, Mr. Hattori, what have you done?"

At this, as though at a prearranged signal, the baby in her arms began wailing, and the four boys in the back seat began complaining of hunger. Mr. Hattori gritted his teeth and drove on. He told himself that this being assailed on all sides by bawling, whimpering, and murderous glances was no less than he deserved. Never again, he said to himself; he had learned his lesson.

Nevertheless, his car, with his wife and children in it, was parked near the brown house again the following week. This was because he had dreamed a repulsive dream in which a fat white snake had uncoiled and slithered about and everyone knows that a white-snake dream is a sure omen of good luck in games of chance. Even Mrs. Hattori knew this. Besides, she felt a little guilty about having nagged him so bitterly about the twenty-five dollars. So Mr. Hattori entered the brown house again on condition that he would return in a half hour, surely enough time to test the white snake. When he failed to return after an hour, Mrs. Hattori sent Joe, the oldest boy, to the front door to inquire after his father. A Chinese man came to open the door of the grille, looked at Joe, said, "Sorry, no kids in here," and clacked it to.

When Joe reported back to his mother, she sent him back again and this time a Chinese woman looked out and said, "What you want, boy?" When he asked for his father, she asked him to wait, then returned with him to the car, carrying a plate of Chinese cookies. Joe, munching one thick biscuit as he led her to the car, found its flavor and texture very strange; it was unlike either its American or Japanese counterpart so that he could not decide whether he liked it or not.

Although the woman was about Mrs. Hattori's age, she immediately called the latter "mama," assuring her that Mr. Hattori would be coming soon, very soon. Mrs. Hattori, mortified, gave excessive thanks for the cookies which she would just as soon have thrown in the woman's face. Mrs. Wu, for so she introduced herself, left them after wagging her head in amazement that Mrs. Hattori, so young, should have so many children and telling her frankly, "No wonder you so skinny, mama."

"Skinny, ha!" Mrs. Hattori said to the boys. "Well, perhaps. But I'd rather be skinny than fat."

Joe, looking at the comfortable figure of Mrs. Wu going up the steps of the brown house, agreed.

Again it was dark when Mr. Hattori came back to the car, but Mrs. Hattori did not say a word. Mr. Hattori made a feeble joke about the unreliability of snakes, but his wife made no attempt to smile. About halfway home she said abruptly, "Please stop the machine, Mr. Hattori. I don't want to ride another inch with you."

"Now, mother . . ." Mr. Hattori said. "I've learned my lesson. I swear this is the last time."

"Please stop the machine, Mr. Hattori," his wife repeated.

Of course the car kept going, so Mrs. Hattori, hugging the baby to herself with one arm, opened the door with her free hand and made as if to hop out of the moving car.

THE BROWN HOUSE

The car stopped with a lurch and Mr. Hattori, aghast, said, "Do you want to kill yourself?"

"That's a very good idea," Mrs. Hattori answered, one leg out of the door.

"Now, mother . . ." Mr. Hattori said. "I'm sorry; I was wrong to stay so long. I promise on my word of honor never to go near that house again. Come, let's go home now and get some supper."

"Supper!" said Mrs. Hattori. "Do you have any money for groceries?"

"I have enough for groceries," Mr. Hattori confessed.

Mrs. Hattori pulled her leg back in and pulled the door shut. "You see!" she cried triumphantly. "You see!"

■ ■ ■

The next time, Mrs. Wu brought out besides the cookies a paper sackful of Chinese firecrackers for the boys. "This is America," Mrs. Wu said to Mrs. Hattori. "China and Japan have war, all right, but (she shrugged) it's not our fault. You understand?"

Mrs. Hattori nodded, but she did not say anything because she did not feel her English up to the occasion.

"Never mind about the firecrackers or the war," she wanted to say. "Just inform Mr. Hattori that his family awaits without."

Suddenly Mrs. Wu, who out of the corner of her eye had been examining another car parked up the street, whispered, "Cops!" and ran back into the house as fast as she could carry her amplitude. Then the windows and doors of the brown house began to spew out all kinds of people—white, yellow, brown, and black—who either got into cars and drove frantically away or ran across the street to dive into the field of tall dry weeds. Before Mrs. Hattori and the boys knew what was happening, a Negro man opened the back door of their car and jumped in to crouch at the boys' feet.

The boys, who had never seen such a dark person at close range before, burst into terrified screams, and Mrs. Hattori began yelling too, telling the man to get out, get out. The panting man clasped his hands together and beseeched Mrs. Hattori, "Just let me hide in here until the police go away! I'm asking you to save me from jail!"

Mrs. Hattori made a quick decision. "All right," she said in her tortured English. "Go down, hide!" Then, in Japanese, she assured her sons that this man meant them no harm and ordered them to cease crying, to sit down, to behave, lest she be tempted to give them something to cry about. The policemen had been inside the house about fifteen minutes when Mr. Hattori came out. He had been thoroughly frightened, but now he managed to appear jaunty as he told his wife how he had cleverly thrust all incriminating evidence into a nearby vase of flowers and thus escaped arrest. "They searched me and told me I could go," he said. "A lot of others weren't so lucky. One lady fainted."

They were almost a mile from the brown house before the man in back said, "Thanks a million. You can let me off here."

Mr. Hattori was so surprised that the car screeched when it stopped. Mrs. Hattori hastily explained, and the man, pausing on his way out, searched for words to emphasize his gratitude. He had always been, he said, a friend of the Japanese people; he knew no race so cleanly, so well-mannered, so downright nice. As he slammed the door shut, he put his hand on the arm of Mr. Hattori, who was still dumfounded, and promised never to forget this act of kindness.

"What we got to remember," the man said, "is that we all got to die sometime. You might be a king in silk shirts or riding a white horse, but we all got to die sometime."

Mr. Hattori, starting up the car again, looked at his wife in reproach. "A *kurombo!*" he said. And again, "A *kurombo!*" He pretended to be victim to a shudder.

"You had no compunctions about that, Mr. Hattori," she reminded him, "when you were inside that house."

"That's different," Mr. Hattori said.

"How so?" Mrs. Hattori inquired.

The quarrel continued through supper at home, touching on a large variety of subjects. It ended in the presence of the children with Mr. Hattori beating his wife so severely that he had to take her to the doctor to have a few ribs taped. Both in their depths were dazed and shaken that things should have come to such a pass.

■ ■ ■

A few weeks after the raid the brown house opened for business as usual, and Mr. Hattori took to going there alone. He no longer waited for weekends but found all sorts of errands to go on during the week which took him in the direction of the asparagus farm. There were nights when he did not bother to come home at all.

On one such night Mrs. Hattori confided to Joe, because he was the eldest, "Sometimes I lie awake at night and wish for death to overtake me in my sleep. That would be the easiest way." In response Joe wept, principally because he felt tears were expected of him. Mrs. Hattori, deeply moved by his evident commiseration, begged his pardon for burdening his childhood with adult sorrows. Joe was in the first grade that year, and in his sleep he dreamed mostly about school. In one dream that recurred he found himself walking in nakedness and in terrible shame among his closest schoolmates.

At last Mrs. Hattori could bear it no longer and went away. She took the baby, Sam, and the boy born before him, Ed (for the record, the other two were named Bill and Ogden), to one of her sisters living in a town about thirty miles distant. Mr. Hattori was shocked and immediately went after her, but her sister refused to let him in the house. "Monster!" this sister said to him from the other side of the door.

Defeated, Mr. Hattori returned home to reform. He worked passionately out in the fields from morning to night, he kept the house spick-and-span, he fed the remaining boys the best food he could buy, and he went out of his way to keep several miles clear of the brown house. This went on for five days, and on the sixth day, one of the Hattoris' nephews, the son of the vindictive lady with whom Mrs. Hattori was taking refuge, came to bring Mr. Hattori a message. The nephew, who was about seventeen at the time, had started smoking cigarettes when he was thirteen. He liked to wear his amorphous hat on the back of his head, exposing a coiffure neatly parted in the middle which looked less like hair than like a painted wig, so unstintingly applied was the pomade which held it together. He kept his hands in his pockets, straddled the ground, and let his cigarette dangle to one side of his mouth as he said to Mr. Hattori, "Your wife's taken a powder."

The world actually turned black for an instant for Mr. Hattori as he searched giddily in his mind for another possible interpretation of this ghastly announcement. "Poison?" he queried, a tremor in his knees.

The nephew cackled with restraint. "Nope, you dope," he said. "That means she's leaving your bed and board."

"Talk in Japanese," Mr. Hattori ordered, "and quit trying to be so smart."

Abashed, the nephew took his hands out of his pockets and assisted his meager Japanese with nervous gestures. Mrs. Hattori, he managed to convey, had decided to leave Mr. Hattori permanently and had sent him to get Joe and Bill and Ogden.

"Tell her to go jump in the lake," Mr. Hattori said in English, and in Japanese, "Tell her if she wants the boys, to come back and make a home for them. That's the only way she can ever have them."

Mrs. Hattori came back with Sam and Ed that same night, not only because she had found she was unable to exist without her other sons but because the nephew had glimpsed certain things which indicated that her husband had seen the light. Life for the family became very sweet then because it had lately been so very bitter, and Mr. Hattori went nowhere near the brown house for almost a whole month. When he did resume his visits there, he spaced them frugally and remembered (although this cost him cruel effort) to stay no longer than an hour each time.

One evening Mr. Hattori came home like a madman. He sprinted up the front porch, broke into the house with a bang, and began whirling around the parlor like a human top. Mrs. Hattori dropped her mending and the boys their toys to stare at this phenomenon.

"Yippee," said Mr. Hattori, "banzai, yippee, banzai." Thereupon, he fell dizzily to the floor.

"What is it, Mr. Hattori; are you drunk?" Mrs. Hattori asked, coming to help him up.

"Better than that, mother," Mr. Hattori said, pushing her back to her chair. It was then they noticed that he was holding a brown paper bag in one hand. And from this bag, with the exaggerated ceremony of a magician pulling rabbits from a hat, he began to draw out stack after stack of green bills. These he deposited deliberately, one by one, on Mrs. Hattori's tense lap until the sack was empty and she was buried under a pile of money.

"Explain . . ." Mrs. Hattori gasped.

"I won it! In the lottery! Two thousand dollars! We're rich!" Mr. Hattori explained.

There was a hard silence in the room as everyone looked at the treasure on Mrs. Hattori's lap. Mr. Hattori gazed raptly, the boys blinked in bewilderment, and Mrs. Hattori's eyes bulged a little. Suddenly, without warning, Mrs. Hattori leaped up and vigorously brushed off the front of her clothing, letting the stacks fall where they might. For a moment she clamped her lips together fiercely and glared at her husband.

But there was no wisp of steam that curled out from her nostrils and disappeared toward the ceiling; this was just a fleeting illusion that Mr. Hattori had. Then, "You have no conception, Mr. Hattori!" she hissed. "You have absolutely no conception!"

■ ■ ■

Mr. Hattori was resolute in refusing to burn the money, and Mrs. Hattori eventually adjusted herself to his keeping it. Thus, they increased their property by a new car, a new rug, and their first washing machine. Since these purchases were all made on the convenient installment plan and the two thousand dollars somehow melted away before they were aware of it, the car and the washing machine were claimed by a collection agency after a few months. The rug remained, however, as it was a fairly cheap one and had already eroded away in spots to show the bare weave beneath. By that time it had become an old habit for Mrs. Hattori and the boys to wait outside the brown house in their original car and for Joe to be commissioned periodically to go to the front door to ask for his father. Joe and his brothers did not mind the long experience too much because they had acquired a taste for Chinese cookies. Nor, really, did Mrs. Hattori, who was pregnant again. After a fashion, she became quite attached to Mrs. Wu who, on her part, decided she had never before encountered a woman with such bleak eyes.

THE KEEPER

from *FATHER OF THE FOUR PASSAGES*

■ ■ ■

Lois-Ann Yamanaka

Sonny Boy, son of Sonia, the only one I did not kill. Three, I killed. Number One in cartilaged pieces on a surgical tray. #2, like a dead feeder fish, flushed out and down. A third, buried in a jar behind my mother's house, fetal marsupial, naked pink.

Sonny Boy, son of Sonia, stop your crying on this bed, your purple wail without breath. Feel the squinting of my eyes, the gritting of my teeth, the closing of my fists. Here is my hand to cover your mouth. Here are my fists to crush your skull. Do you want to die?

They're smoking and drinking to your birth downstairs. And I'm the single artist mother, breast-feeding lounge singer mother, earth righteous minority mother. But I can't make you stop. Shh, they can hear you, godfuckingdammit.

LOIS-ANN YAMANAKA is the author of a book of poetry, *Saturday Night at the Pahala Theatre*; the novels *Wild Meat and the Bully Burgers*, *Blu's Hanging*, *Heads by Harry*, and *Father of the Four Passages*; as well as a young adult novel, *Name Me Nobody*, and an illustrated children's book, *Snow Angel, Sand Angel*. She is at work on a novel, *Behold the Many*. She is the recipient of the Pushcart Prize XVIII and XIX, the Asian American Studies National Book Award, the Elliot Cades Award for Literature, the Asian American Literary Award, and a Lannan Literary Award, among others. Born in Hololehua, Molokai, in 1961 and raised in Hilo, Pahala, and Keauhou-Kona on the Big Island of Hawaii, she lives in Honolulu, Hawaii, with her son.

Your body stiffens. Fists clench. You cry without sound. A blue boy. Let me bounce you, let me slap you, let me sing to you, let me choke you, let me throw you out the window.

I blow on your face. And in one long draw, you breathe me in.

I am the keeper of words. This is your word to keep: *God/the/son*.

Dear Number One,

You are my first dead baby, a baby boy.

I am on the green bed in Granny Alma's Kalihi house. Alone, so Alone. My face is puffy and flushed. Scared, I'm scared. My belly is a round ellipsis. I don't know who to tell. About you.

Your aunt Celeste comes into the room and stares at me. My mouth opens, but no words come out. And then she knows.

You are in me.

And you need to come out.

She turns without a word from the doorway of the green room. You are four months old, she tells Granny Alma. Call Dr. Wee, who sits two pews in front of Granny at church every Sunday.

He will suck you out of me.

But you want to stay.

Salamander fingers, you cling to my wet walls until your body rips apart. You are the color of tendon in my sweet stew, little pod, with eyes, black beads, like a rat's. Your aunt Celeste's lovely eyes.

Love,

Your mother, Sonia Kurisu, age 17

I hate my sister Celeste. Celeste who always reminds me that she raised me the best she could. Poor thing. Poor her. The kind of girl who's forced into substitute mommydom too early. Lots of sad stories about girls like her.

She found our mother wedged between her bed and the wall, an empty vial of Seconal, bent spoon, lighter, and small syringe on the floor. Celeste was ten. I was nine.

Grace was fading out, eyes rolling slowly, a groan, a mutter. We walked her dragging feet to the living room couch. Celeste put herself between Grace's legs and held her body up against the picture window. Head floating on a neck made of rubber. "Call 911, you moron. Don't just stand there."

Grace took several short gasps for air.

Purple mommy.

So I blew in her face. A long breath that she held, her head falling.

"She's leaving," Celeste screamed. I dropped the phone, the cord spinning the receiver. And she was still.

I saw the couch indent beside Grace. I smelled the rotting carcass of goat, a maggot-filled belly, the explosion of flies wet with intestinal fluid and excrement. Her head slid in the direction of the Specter. Celeste covered her nose and mouth.

"Get up, Mommy, the Devil's come to get you. Stand up, Mommy. Grace!" I screamed at her.

I witnessed the summoning of the Seraphim as my mother willed her body to rise. She stumbled to the front door and leaned her body over the porch railing, her arms and head hanging. Breathing, breathing, until the ambulance rushed up our driveway and drove us all away.

Who the fuck knows why the police called our Aunty Effie, who wasn't even a real aunt, to take us to her house. Our stay would be indefinite. I heard her calling the church's prayer tree late into the night.

"Grace. That's what I said. Grace Kurisu. The waitress at the 19th Hole. Painkillers and alcohol. She has that good-for-nothing husband. Oh, the big girl, Celeste's, all right. She's a strong Christian. Sonia, the little one, keeps talking about the Devil. The poor thing's screwed up, I tell you. I'll call Frannie and all the deacons."

She told the story of my mother over and over again to anyone and everyone who wanted to know every goddamn detail of our lives and the Appearance of the Angel of Death, in Hilo of all places.

At eleven o'clock, the phone went still. I heard Aunty Effie brushing her dentures and a short time later, a muffled snore from behind her bedroom door. Celeste nudged me, motioning me to follow her. We left through the front door into the cool Hilo night and walked home.

It was Celeste who walked me to school every day, fed me canned goods and rice for breakfast, and told me what to say when the CPS social worker came looking for us. She got me on the sampan bus after school, down the icy corridors of the hospital, and into the room where Grace spent the next six nights. Every night, we were deposited at Aunty Effie's. And every night by twelve, Celeste made sure we slept in our own beds.

Sister/Mother, it all sounds so loving.

But she of the iron-fisted mommydom became the Sadist.

And I of the get-the-shit/mind/soul-beaten-out-of-me-or-else became the Masochist.

So your word, Celeste Kurisu-Infantino, twenty years later, I still fucking hate you, wife of Sicilian not Portagee, Michael Infantino; mother of Tiffany, fat and full of acne, and Heather who draws cat's claws in God's eyes, keep it for me, my: *Sister/sadist.*

Dear Number One,

So who am I to blame a substitute mother for your death by suction? She raised me the best she could, right?

Love,

Your Mom, Sonia, age now

Now:

I am on a black futon in a wet, warm room, red scarves over dusty lamps. Windows closed, curtains drawn, no sound but heartbeat and breath. Sonny Boy is asleep beside me.

When will I stop fucking up?

The pregnancy attention was what I wanted. I loved it. All of them giving me the best chair in the house. All of them putting pillows under my feet. All of them rubbing my belly for good luck. Feeding me, indulging me, venerating the earth mother. O, the possibility of bringing forth life from your body! they marveled.

When will I wash my hair?

Mark promised to buy a bottle of Prell, the fucking flake. My best, childhood forever friend, my little Markie, digging out on me every time I fuck somebody not to his liking. I miss him, I need him, I call him. But he's gone.

When will I stop fucking up?

I'm too selfish to do this mommy shit. Mark could do it. Mark who mothered me over the years. Mark who fathered me over the years. Mark who brothered me over the years. Come back and take care of this fucking screaming baby. Come back and take care of me.

When will the bleeding stop?

This afterbirth blood smells rancid and old.

When will I stop fucking up?

This isn't a dog I can tie up in the rain. Watch it shiver on a blanket soaked with urine and shit. Starve it, no money for dog food. Give it one kind pat a day. Beat the howling out of him. Watch him die. Bury him in the backyard. No more dog. Was tired of him anyway.

When will I rest?

My body aches from rocking, carrying, strolling, bouncing this boy who cries in steady, staccato bursts until he's blue:

Four to six in the evening, nonstop, he's fucking shrieking.

Ten to twelve, shut the fuck up, I put my hand over his mouth, dig my nails into his cheeks.

Four to six in the morning, nauseated, I weave my fingers into his hair and squeeze.

Ten to twelve, crying, I fall to the floor, watch him drop off the bed headfirst.

And in between, he sleeps. Maybe.

Overstim, they tell me. Darken the room. Talk in hushed tones.

Colic, they tell me. Turn him on his belly. Turn him on his back. Don't eat cabbage or refried beans.

These days and nights that blur in a myopic haze. And no one to talk to but this horrible pod my body made.

I hear somebody leaving next door. Lucky you.

They're all leaving Las Vegas. They write songs and movies about this phenomenon. Leaving Las Vegas with empty pockets, and the eternal struggle:

Should I use my last dollar to eat a hot dog or put it in this slot machine? Dumb fuck, you should've eaten.

I hear somebody moving in next door.

And the mailman's shoving envelopes under my door.

A letter from my father, a man who knows about leaving. Lucky him. Never looked back. Never wanted to look back.

Sweet Sonia,

A man stands in front of an old Chinese hotel in Kuala Lumpur, Malaysia. A concessionaire sells him watermelon juice. The man takes in the smell of peanut pancakes, coconut rice, and goat curries.

He's looking for a place to spend the night in the midst of all the clatter and clang of the streets. The man wanders into a China-town. There's a Chinatown in every city of this world.

He finds a small Chinese hotel. Rooms, 25 ringgits, which is about four dollars. He sleeps early and long, full of rolls filled with chicken curry and cheeses. He drinks a delicious Chinese tea and falls into a steady slumber.

The next morning, he wakes full of huge red welts and an incredible pain that pulses through his muscles and into his bones. Are these mosquitoes? He searches the space of the room.

In the late afternoon, he passes a little mom-and-pop store full of cluttered shelves of strange bottles, dusty cans, and the odor of fermenting fish and mint leaves. The old woman sells him a can of insect repellent.

He returns to his tiny room overlooking a night market full of foreign sounds. The languages, sweet Sonia, the languages that he wishes to inhabit his body on lonely nights so he could speak to someone, these languages sound like music, like Italian opera or Hawaiian slack key. He knows the meaning of the melody from some place summoned inside his memory, and that he cannot understand the lyric does not matter.

This night, the man sprays his room before retiring to the voices outside of his terrace window over the streets that skein into alleys and crossings. But as he dozes, bedbugs begin to drag themselves from the crammed space of the bed.

These Malaysian bedbugs full of blood, his blood, are not lice with white, translucent bodies. These look like dog ticks, huge and gray, with two red lines on their backs that look like eyes. He presses into one of the dazed bugs and leaves the mark of his fingernail in its body. Hundreds of bedbugs pour out of the tears in the mattress.

The man sleeps well this night.

And the two red lines that look like eyes on the backs of the bedbugs? These are the marks on his body left by the bites—two tiny red lines etched all over him, front and back like shingles, the day he leaves Kuala Lumpur, languid and feverish.

May this letter find you in good health.

Your father,
Joseph Kurisu

I keep all of your letters, Father.

You who I search for. You whose words find me. The beauty therein. The emptiness without.

Now you keep this word: *Seek/and/you/shall/find.*

■ ■ ■

Joseph left us for good in the time of blood. We all bled, Mama, Celeste, and I, the three house dogs, females in heat—stained panties, dog diapers, and sanitary napkin belts on the clothesline, bloody pads wrapped in newspaper in the trash. He had been planning to flee this all along, the bloodletting.

Grace could've slit her veins and he'd have run.

She came home from a long waitressing shift at the 19th Hole to find Joseph packing his duffel bag again. Hadn't he told her he would be leaving?

She said nothing to him. "Did you eat dinner?" she asked me.

I shook my head.

"Dammit, Celeste, why didn't you cook for your sister?"

"Where's Joseph going?" I whispered to my mother.

"Did Jack's call him today? Did he drive the Japan tour to the volcano?" she asked Celeste.

"No, Mama," she replied.

I was eleven and bleeding for the first time. I hit myself over and over until my vagina bruised and swelled. I stayed home from school for days.

Grace tore open a can of Spam and dropped the slabs of pink meat in sizzling oil. "Goddamn you, Celeste, can't you even cook some rice?" she said, slamming dishes into the sink.

■ ■ ■

"I'm out of here," he'd said to me earlier that day.

"Take me with you," I begged. I'd skipped school. Joseph didn't mind when he was the good father of some of my memory. Then, he loved the company. "Please, Daddy, don't leave me."

"No room in my duffel," he replied flatly.

"Then put me in a box," I told him. "I'll be a good girl. I promise."

"You are a good girl," he said, placing his warm hand on my face. "But Daddy's traveling light. No room for you. Sorry, pal."

I grasped on to his hand. "You love me, Daddy?" I asked.

"True love is freedom, kiddo," he answered after a long silence. "Freedom with a capital F."

■ ■ ■

"Joseph!" my mother yelled. And when he didn't answer, she picked up the empty Spam can and walked down the hallway. "Where the fuck are you going? How the hell am I going to pay the bills? Who's going to take care of me?"

"Get out of my face," he said to her in his fierce monotone.

I listened to the thud of her body against the wall. She slashed his face that night. He let her cut him open. Then he slung his duffel over his shoulder and turned once to look at me with vulnerable, fiery eyes, his hand stopping the bleeding. "See you, kiddo," he said with a mock two-finger salute.

Celeste clambered over the couch to stop Grace from hurting him more. I helped her pry the can from my mother's fingers.

"Run, Joseph, run!" I screamed. "Daddy!" I held out my arms to him. He paused for a moment, then turned toward the door.

"Run, Joseph!" my mother cried. "Wake up, Sonia, you stupid little girl." And then my mother turned her hatred on me. It would be days before I returned to school with black eyes and a bruised face. Celeste and I took the can from her fingers and laid her body down.

"I'm sorry, Sonia," she said. "Oh, look at your face. Celeste, baby, look at what I've done."

He was there, outside the picture window, looking back at the house he would not see for the next few years. I want to believe he placed it inside his memory for summoning on a lonely night. But he gave me that mock salute with a cocky smirk and a jerk of his eyebrows. I pulled the curtains shut.

Dear #2,

You are my second dead baby, another boy. Here is a picture of me the day before you died.

I am in the small bedroom I grew up in at Granny Alma's house. I'm in my embroidered jeans and hippie gauze blouse. I'm wearing a crocheted bikini top, rose-colored, black-rimmed shades perched on my head.

There's a green bamboo bead curtain hanging from the doorway, hanging ferns in macramé plant baskets.

A long string of blinking Christmas lights encircling the windows. Fake snow sprayed on the jalousies.

I'm burning coconut incense in a small brass urn. Sitting cross-
legged, leaning against my bed covered with a paisley gauze bedspread.

I'm reaching out one hand to you, see me, you must, and making a peace sign with the other.

One day, #2, the word will parallel the image.

Merry Christmas,

Your mother, Sonia Kurisu, age 18

I never celebrate Christmas. Never.

I was twelve, Celeste thirteen. Joseph was gone.

Sweet Sonia, the name I had given to the girl who received his letters, knew he was in Thailand. This was the year Grace brought home
a five-foot Christmas tree, a small but beautiful tree, which cost us all
possibility of our own presents wrapped in red and green ribbons.

This was the tree she wanted to put in a rusty coffee can filled with
rocks on the black lacquer table that Joseph had shipped back piece by
piece from Chiang Mai. She wanted to give the illusion that it stood
from floor to ceiling when we took the Christmas Eve photo, Celeste
and I in red dresses, hiding the table with our bodies so he could see
that fine tree, a Noble Fir.

That fuck you, Joseph, tree. We're doing just fine, you fucking selfish asshole.

When Grace placed the tree on the table, the tip bent on the ceiling, sending asbestos snow into its branches. And Bing crooning I'm
dreaming of a white Christmas on the Muntz stereo.

"You don't need the table, Mama," Celeste suggested. "Why don't
you just put the tree on the floor. Never mind if it's short."

She got her face slapped twice. I kept my mouth shut.

"Go get me the hacksaw from outside, Sonia," my mother said. "Get
me a ruler from your schoolbag too."

My mother measured and marked. Her hair, flecked with rosewood,
head down, wild hair jerking with the frantic tug of the hacksaw
through wood. My mother cut off the legs of the lacquer table, one by

one, wonderful smell of the fine rosewood and the snow of sawdust in our hair. In Celeste's wet eyelashes, on her sweaty nose, dust in my cough, I tasted roses in my astonished mouth.

We had no money whenever Joseph left us. He'd just leave.

Celeste wore a velvet yoked muumuu with butterfly sleeves. Me, a red pinafore with a lacy white blouse, both charged at the National Dollar Store. Where would she send the pictures?

"Stop, Mama. Please," I whispered. "We don't even know if Daddy—"

"Shut your mouth, you hear me, Sonia? Smile, dammit. C'mon, Celeste, big smile. Look at the camera. Sonia, you knock off that crying."

Later that Christmas morning, with the money Granny Alma sent for Grace to buy presents for us from her, she bought two airline tickets. Two one-way tickets to Honolulu.

At the airport, Grace was monotone. "Say goodbye to me," she said. I stared at Celeste, my mouth agape.

"Mama?" Celeste gasped.

"I'll send your things later," she said, turning.

"No, Mama. What's going on?" I asked. "Why are you sending us away?"

She refused to answer me.

"You take care of Sonia, Celeste. Tell Granny Alma she's allergic to shrimp." She gave her a push. "Go, there's your flight." Celeste took my hand in hers.

"I hate you," I said to my mother, who never turned back to look at me.

So I say it every day. Every day until the day she turns to look at me and hear me. Listen, Mama, keep this word:

Burn/in/Hell.

WHAT IF MISS NIKKEI WERE GOD(DESS)?

∎ ∎ ∎

Karen Tei Yamashita

March again already. Imagine. Another March, another year. Dekasegi are always counting the years like birthdays. For Miss Hamamatsu, this was year 3. She arrived in March on her fifteenth birthday, by most standards a fully formed woman. Blame it—womanhood, her full hips and breasts—on her Italian blood. Okay, blame her large dark eyes and her elegant nose on the Italians too. But the long silky black hair, the high cheekbones, the Shiseido perfect skin—blame that on the Japanese. She was that stunning mixture of Euro and Asian that feeds the filmic imagination. Her features represented the full measure of occidental beauty, all gracefully accented in the exotic. To top it off, she carried these Venus-like qualities with an easy Brazilian charm, as if the sun anointed her naked body, the sands and spume kissed her heels, her smile sparkled for everyone, and all of this in the middle of the industrial city, Hamamatsu, known as the home of Yamaha and Suzuki. Pianos and motorcycles. It all made perfect sense, for in Hamamatsu, among Brazilians who labored to produce those keyboards and racing monsters, and who likewise judged this contest of

Born in 1951 in Oakland, California, raised in Los Angeles, educated in Minnesota, KAREN TEI YAMASHITA lived for nine years in Brazil, the setting for her novels *Through the Arc of the Rain Forest* and *Brazil-Maru*. A third novel, *Tropic of Orange*, is set in L.A. "What if Miss Nikkei Were God(dess)?" is excerpted from *Circle K Cycles*, a book of mixed genres reflecting the lives of Brazilians in Japan. Currently, Yamashita lives between the San Francisco Bay Area and L.A. and teaches at U.C. Santa Cruz.

representative beauty at the local disco, she was known as Miss Hamamatsu '96. High priestess of music and speed.

But that was last year, and here she was, still at the same job, making
multiple copies of Brazilian television shows for video rental distribution. The room where she worked was tucked away behind two storage
rooms, warehouses for boxes of imported Brazilian products. To get to
this back room, you had to negotiate a constantly changing maze
around walled cartons of Cica tomato paste, hearts of palm, Knorr
chicken soup cubes, Nestlé's sweetened condensed milk, Kimura
polvilho, and Sadia gelatin. The video thing was a somewhat clandes-
tine operation, but no one seemed to be too concerned about it. The
police probably knew about it, but they would only investigate if a formal complaint were made, and who was going to complain about
copyright violations of television shows half the globe away? The Japanese police wouldn't even know where to start. Who was Jô Soares to
them? Or the Corinthians? *Fantástico?*

Still, Miss Hamamatsu '96, staring at walls stacked to the ceiling
with JVC video recorders, dreamed of working somewhere else, in the
open, in an office that had a window at least and young men passing to
and fro who would of course turn their heads to appreciate her beauty.
Such a waste, but then again, it was better than working in a factory,
having to wear those ugly blue uniforms, subjecting her hands and
nails to dirt and grease from machinery, bending over inspection lines
of aluminum parts, minute after minute, hour after hour, day after day.
This was work her poor mother had to do. She had been spared such a
fate, but she would make it up to her family one day.

She was literally walled in by JVC recorders, 150 of them stacked in
precarious towers of 10, side by side, a spaghetti of cables and electric
cords snaking along the floor. In addition, scattered TV monitors of different shapes and sizes were lodged in between and on top of the
VCRs, all flashing several different or identical shows. After two years of
this, except for having to read the show titles on the tapes, she could
probably perform her task in the dark, plopping fifty tapes into fifty
VCRs at a time and hitting all the record buttons. Between recording
functions, she was busy rewinding tapes, packing them for shipment, or
slapping new labels over the old ones from a ticker tape of show titles
run off a word processor / inkjet printer system. Used video cassettes got
recycled over and over, and boxes of them were stacked everywhere. By

the end of the week, last week's shows had to be reproduced from masters, categorized, and separated for distribution. She had no idea how many stores rented these videos, but she assumed they must take these copies and make more of their own. Some dekasegi in Kyushu was probably watching a fuzzy version of his team's winning penalty kick. Was it a goal or wasn't it? Home was a copy of a copy of a copy of a copy, further away than she could imagine.

At the moment, the blonde spectacle of Xuxa, a live Brazilian Barbie doll in a silver miniskirt and matching boots, bounced around a dozen of her prepubescent mini-replica Xuxettes. Like other girls her age, Miss Hamamatsu had grown up with the Xuxa Show, dreamed of being a Xuxette. She mimed the Xuxette routine on the small square of available floor space. One, two and kick and, three, four and turn, and . . . Miss Hamamatsu, like Xuxa, was a natural, and of course she loved little children. The Japanese had nothing like Xuxa. Miss Hamamatsu imagined she could bring this phenomenon to Japan as a measure of friendship. She would have Japanese and Brazilian children on her show, her little princes and princesses, talk to all the children out there, make heartfelt speeches about being kind to foreigners, bring those poor little kids who suffered from ijime* onto her program and make everyone feel sorry for them. If things were going to change in the world, they would change because of children. That was going to be her message. The show was over. Stop. Eject.

Stop. Eject. Stop. Eject. Stop. Eject. Stop. Eject. Stop. Eject. Stop. Eject. Stop. Eject . . .

Jorginho popped his head in the door. "Oba!"

"Oi," she answered, grateful that he hadn't caught her dancing this time. Sometimes he would stand in the doorway watching her until she noticed. It was really irritating, but she had to appreciate his appreciation. He was just about the only one around who noticed her in this dungeon, slaving among the tapes.

"Anything good?" he asked, rummaging through the week's titles. "How about saving me a copy of this?" He held up a tape.

She glanced at the title. *Chitãozinho e Xororó.* They were a popular country music pair everyone was listening to in Brazil.

---

*ridicule

"Leandro and Leonardo are coming to Japan," he nodded with inside knowledge about another musical pair. "I know the producers for the event. They're planning a tour in seven cities. They've got big backers, and they're going to rake it in."

"Are they coming to Hamamatsu?"

"If they don't, it'll be a big mistake. We're one of the biggest Brazilian communities. They'll probably get a sold-out event here. The fans will·be clamoring."

"It won't matter if you're a fan or not. It'll be something to look forward to for a change," Miss Hamamatsu sighed.

Jorginho pointed to the tape of Chitãozinho and Xororó. "Don't worry, there'll be more. I'm going to see about bringing these guys to Japan too. Just let me make my contacts."

She smiled encouragingly. Jorginho had big plans. Well, they all had big plans. If you didn't have some kind of plan, you weren't a proper dekasegi. Then she pouted. "What about the Miss Nikkei Contest? Have you already abandoned that idea?"

"Worried?" he taunted her.

Ignoring him, she examined a master copy, copying down its title for duplication. It was Monday's episode of the current prime-time Globo novela: *O Rei do Gado*. It had arrived on a Varig flight that morning in a suitcase with other copies. She was possibly the first person living in Japan to see that episode. She had work to do. "It's time to watch my novela," she announced. "Don't you have work to do?"

"Oh my dear," he spoke affectionately to her. "If there's a Miss Nikkei in this world, it's you. There's not a day that passes that I don't think of you." He smacked her a kiss. "We're going to get you out of this video hell and make a lot of money with that pretty face of yours. Speaking of pretty faces—" He presented her with a large envelope.

"The photos!" she exclaimed.

"Proofs," he corrected. "Look them over, and we'll decide which ones to reproduce."

She scanned the tiny representations of her face and body. There were luscious exposures of her full lips and eyes filled with desire. There were nude poses, poses in string bikinis, poses in miniskirts, jeans, fitted jersey dresses. It was enough to drive any man crazy.

"And I've got some good news," he started in with a bit of suspense. "I met this guy whose sister used to be a model. Well, she's not a model any longer. Had kids. Put on weight. She's maybe in her thirties now. She just got a divorce, and she's thinking of joining this brother in Japan, see? So I got him thinking that he could invest some of that money he's been saving in his sister and open up a modeling school."

"Is this for real?"

"He showed me her old photos. She was a real stunner. Worked all over. New York. Paris." He waved his hands toward those distant locations. "It would take someone like her who knows the ropes to make this happen. I went out with him this weekend to look for places to open shop. All she's got to do is put up a sign. All the girls from the Miss Hamamatsu contest will come running."

"Including Miss Hamamatsu herself." She did a mock model walk up to the VCRs and back.

"Girl." He shook his head. "All that Brazilian beauty. There's got to be a way. Japan has this tropical gold mine and doesn't even know it."

She looked at her watch. "Jorginho, really, I've got to do the Monday novelas, or I'm in trouble."

"How about it? Karaoke tonight?"

"Maybe. I'll let you know." She brushed him off while shoving in the tapes for *O Rei do Gado*. It was the story of two Italian immigrant families coming to Brazil at the turn of the century. The Mezengas and the Berdinazzis. Antônio Fagundes plays the father Mezenga. Tarcísio Meira plays the father Berdinazzi. In the beginning they are friends with neighboring coffee farms. Then they get in a fight over the boundaries and become enemies. The son (played by Leonardo Bricio) and the daughter (played by Letícia Spiller) of the respective families fall in love, but of course it's a forbidden love, a Romeo and Juliet story.

The theme song was beautiful. She could sing the entire song. There were scenes filmed in Italy. And scenes of coffee plantations and farm life in Paraná in the early part of the century. It was all so romantic. She felt it was her story too, the story of her Italian side. Imagine. Her grandmother could have been Letícia Spiller. Miss Hamamatsu sank into the full sensation of the novela moment; it was one of the perks of her job.

■ ■ ■

The second week in March, she was making copies of director Tizuka Yamazaki's film, *Gaijin*. "Tizuka will be in Japan next month,"

Jorginho said, always in the know. "She's going to travel around to decide on a site for the sequel, *Gaijin 2*. In the meantime, she'll drum up interest for the old movie and try to get some sponsors for the new project."

Miss Hamamatsu had never even seen the first *Gaijin*. The heroine played by Kyoko Tsukamoto can't marry the man she loves, so she gets on a ship headed for Brazil with another man she doesn't love and leaves Japan forever. Like *O Rei do Gado*, this story is set in about the same time period. Kyoko has a hard life in Brazil working in the fields of a coffee plantation where Antônio Fagundes, this time, plays an Italian overseer who feels compassion for Kyoko's difficulties. The husband she comes to Brazil with dies of typhoid fever. By now she has a kid, and she can't pay off her debts to get out of her contract, so she decides to flee the plantation in the middle of the night. Antônio Fagundes follows her on horseback, but in the end helps her to escape. At the end of the movie, they meet years later in São Paulo. He's a labor organizer, and she's raising her child. Miss Hamamatsu wept at the end. It was her story too. Her mother was Japanese; her father was Italian. Her mother could have been Kyoko Tsukamoto; her father Antônio Fagundes.

Jorginho continued, "I know the people involved in producing *Gaijin 2*. I'm going to talk to them and get them involved in the Miss Nikkei Contest. There's a way this can work for everyone. We'll attract every gorgeous Brazilian woman in Japan. Who knows who might turn up? The future face or faces of actresses for this new movie, of course." He paused to reassure her. "I'm thinking of you, my dear, of course, but they don't need to know that."

It all made curious sense. In the novela, *O Rei do Gado*, Leonardo Bricio and Letícia Spiller, despite their feuding families, marry and have a son. Then the novela jumps ahead several years, and Antônio Fagundes, who played old man Mezenga in the first episodes, loses 20 pounds in 2 weeks and returns to play the grandson, Bruno Mezenga, the man who becomes the King of Cattle. She imagined further episodes: the King of Cattle becomes involved in an even more impossible and forbidden love affair with a beautiful Japanese woman. She, Miss Hamamatsu, would be the love child of this forbidden love.

Jorginho was ebullient with his ideas that day. "This is going to be a high-class event with high-class sponsors. Guaranteed. I've been talking to the KDD telephone people, to Varig, JAL, the Banco do Brasil. Everyone's enthusiastic. This is exactly the kind of event they're interested in promoting."

"Have you set a date and a place?" she asked.

"I'm looking into the Act City Plaza concert hall. Leandro and Leonardo are going to be booked there, too." Jorginho made a motion in the direction of the city's center, a large phallic tower planted in a music complex built to celebrate Yamaha and its theme for Hamamatsu: The City of Music. The Japanese called it Akuto Shiti. While Yamaha probably had international pretensions for its music center, it probably hadn't thought about a country music group from Brazil, not to mention a Miss Nikkei Contest. There in full regalia and pomp and circumstance, Miss Nikkei would proclaim her reign.

Thus Miss Hamamatsu imagined herself crowned in a diamond tiara, gliding down the walkway in that grand auditorium, her jeweled gown and velvet cape trailing behind her. Everything would be golden and glittering, lights flashing, stereophonic music swelling.

Meanwhile, she plastered labels onto video copies of *Gaijin*. The copies were probably illegal, but shouldn't every dekasegi see this film? A romantic story based on our history.

"I just thought of something," Jorginho congratulated himself. "How about this? We get Antônio Fagundes and Kyoko Tsukamoto, the original actors in *Gaijin*, to be the judges in the Miss Nikkei contest. Can you believe it? Now all we need is the participation of a former Miss Brazil."

Miss Hamamatsu smiled. Imagine.

■ ■ ■

The third week in March, Miss Hamamatsu was looking over the large head shots of herself in black and white.

"My God, you're photogenic," exclaimed Jorginho. "There's not a bad take in the entire batch."

"Except when I was making faces." She made a face.

"Even those are wonderful. Shows you have personality. There's an actress behind that gorgeous face." He patted her cheek affectionately.

"Now what?"

"Now we make up a portfolio. I'm going to print up a résumé for you."

She looked at him quizzically.

"I know. I know." He waved away her concerns. "I'll have to make some of it up, but who's going to check up on all the marvelous work you've done in Brazil?" He winked. "You'll see how we impress them. Put it on letterhead. All very professional with a slick folder. We put together a bunch of small folders to give away, to send out into the marketplace, test the waters, you know, send to magazines and newspapers. Then we have a large portfolio to take to meetings."

"Jorginho, you know I give most of the money I make to my mother, poor thing, for expenses. She sends all her money to Brazil to take care of her mother and my little brother there. Sure, I'm saving something for myself, and every once in a while I really splurge, but what I'm trying to say is that I can't go to meetings without dressing up a little."

"That's why these photos are important. Maybe we can interest a clothing company to have you wear their line of clothing and of course get free clothing in exchange. I'm in touch with the exclusive importer of a Brazilian brand of lingerie. When they see these photos, you're going to be their bra and panty pinup girl."

"It's going to take more than lingerie to dress this girl."

"So, we start with the basics."

"And don't forget makeup and hair."

"No problem." Like a magician, he pulled out a magazine. "Here's the latest copy of *Nova*, just in."

She flipped through this Brazilian version of *Cosmopolitan*. There was an article on skin care and nutrition, on shaping the face with cosmetics and matching makeup to skin tone, on pedicures, on hair color, on the latest in Fall fashions (it would be autumn in Brazil), and on orgasms. She sighed. Being beautiful was a full-time job. How she would like to check into a bona fide beauty salon once in a blue moon. Brazilian women went to each other's houses. Her mother's friend Arlete did hair and nails. Her girlfriend Flávia did depilation and face masks. They shared cosmetics and exchanged clothing. If she stepped into one of those fancy Japanese places, there was no telling how she would come out. There were Nikkei girls who you could swear were Japanese. They spent their money on the Japanese styles, and their bodies fit into those hipless pants and dresses. She was longer in the torso and legs and wider in the hips and bust. Imported Brazilian clothing for an imported Brazilian body; it took some finances to keep up her looks.

Jorginho looked over her shoulder at the magazine's advertisements. "I had an inspiration this morning. All we need is a video camera."

"You want to tape me?" she asked in mock surprise.

"Better than that. For example, this lingerie importer. We could do an ad for their lingerie. A commercial. I know a guy who used to work for Globo TV in Rio. I could get him to do the camera work."

"But where are you going to place this commercial? On Japanese TV?"

"It's amazing I never thought of it." He put his arms up and looked around the room. "This is our mother lode. This is where it can all start!"

Miss Hamamatsu gave him her full smile but looked confused.

Jorginho pointed at the video tapes. "Like a trailer or intros, understand? Or we could slip our commercials in at the regular breaks. Can you imagine the kind of money we could make, not to mention the exposure? These videos go out to dekasegi all over Japan."

"Do dekasegi buy a lot of lingerie?"

"Okay, not just lingerie. How about jeans? You look sensational in jeans."

"Can you believe it?" She patted the Brazilian tag on the pocket. "This imported pair cost me ichi man yen."

Jorginho calculated 10,000 yen—about 80 dollars. His eyes wandered lovingly over her bottom as she bent over to retrieve used tapes. "No wait! How about meat? We're importing hundreds of tons of Australian beef into Japan every month. You could do a meat commercial. Wear a cowboy hat. Sing a country music tune with a barbecue going on behind you. I'm not kidding. I know the owner of a meat distribution company. Leave it to me."

With the mention of beef, her mind wandered back into the continuing saga of O Rei do Gado. The first generation of Mezengas and Berdinazzis gradually die off. The second generation sells the coffee farms, exchanging their inheritances for even bigger ventures. Mezenga becomes the King of Cattle and Berdinazzi becomes the Dairy King, and they still hate each other. Raul Cortês plays Berdinazzi, the Dairy King. Miss Hamamatsu thought he was perfect in his role, gradually growing old over the course of the novela. She thought about this incredible opportunity to pretend to be someone else for months and in full public TV view until practically everyone in Brazil knew even the most intimate things about this other you. Maybe being in a commercial wasn't the same thing, but imagine: she could become the Queen of Beef.

■ ■ ■

The fourth week in March, Jorginho said, "I think we've got a bite. I sent your photos to this magazine operation." He waved a shiny copy in the air.

She could see the pose of a woman in a string bikini, down on all fours, the most prominent part of her—her buttocks—pressed against the glossy surface of the magazine's cover.

Jorginho reassured her. "This is a high-class operation. Look at the quality of these photos, the quality of the paper. It's sophisticated stuff. And prominent exposure. They are doing big business not only with the dekasegi crowd here in Japan but in Brazil as well. After all, beautiful women are beautiful anywhere. I told them they should put some Japanese translations in the margins. Japanese men are crazy for Brazilian women. They could get this market as well. How about it? You could be the foldout in the next issue." He unzipped the crisp protective cellophane of the magazine and dropped the foldout from the slick pages. A woman, naked except for a cowboy hat and boots, hung there, a limp tribute to Brazilian country music no doubt, and yet, the Queen of Beef. The dekasegi girlfriend of the month.

Bruno Mezenga is unhappily married to the bitchy Sílvia Pfeiffer, who is having an affair with a gigolo. In the meantime, Mezenga meets Luana played by Patrícia Pillar who is involved in the Movimento dos Sem Terra. She comes with a group of landless peasants and squats on Mezenga's land. Bruno Mezenga proves that his land is in use and that he's a good man, so Luana falls in love with him. It's true love. And besides, Patrícia Pillar is so rapturously beautiful even in jeans, without makeup, and playing an idealistic activist, he'd be stupid not to fall in love with her. The secret is that Luana is really a Berdinazzi and doesn't know it. Fate is at the crossroads.

As a dekasegi, Miss Hamamatsu appreciated the message of the downtrodden, those without land. They had every right to take over land held by absentee landlords and make it productive. Was there no justice in this world? She would be the Japanese mestiça Patrícia Pillar, the righteous and beautiful Luana. She with other dekasegi would take over Japanese contract companies and production lines. One day she would meet a powerful and princely Japanese executive who would sympathize with her plight and fall madly in love with her. It would be a true but forbidden love and eventually, after many episodes, their love would bring two feuding families—Japanese and dekasegi Nikkei—together and change the world.

The naked Queen of Beef still flapped between the porn pages, and Jorginho continued. "Listen, it's a beginning. Everyone has to start somewhere. It's understandable why this magazine has really taken off. All these single dekasegi men are living in dorms with other men. All they see is other men, work double shifts and overtime round the clock. Girl, have you no pity? A life of drudgery. What have they got to look forward to? They miss their girlfriends. They don't get any action. If they go to discos, it's one woman to ten men. You women can pick and choose. When a beauty like you comes along, it's natural that we should want to spread the bounty around. It's just a photo. What's the harm of a little imagination?"

Miss Hamamatsu looked around at her video recorder world. All at the same time, 150 VCRs were making 150 copies. *O Rei do Gado* was on all the monitors, but at slightly different moments in the same episode. It was disconcerting to watch. Bruno Mezenga embraces Luana; they kiss passionately. Their theme music surrounds them as the romantic moment is caught from several angles. All the monitors stuttered this image in various stages like a singing round. Since this current novela was picking up popularity, it was necessary to make more and more copies. It was a big seller in all the stores. Next week, maybe all the dekasegi women would be watching this scene, and all the dekasegi men would be staring at the naked Queen of Beef. Imagine.

Jorginho replaced the centerfold. "Actually, the guys at this magazine are looking to expand their horizons. They're interested in exploring the video end of the business. This is in the future of course, but it's a marketing opportunity they'd be foolish not to take advantage of. I'm working on them to sell my idea about commercial inserts in video rentals. I think they're interested in investing in it, you know, as a start. You have to start somewhere."

Miss Hamamatsu followed the kisses around the room, copied from one VCR to the next, 150 times. The scene closed. *To be continued.* Then the credits came up. She ejected the master copy and inserted another with the next episode. "I guess you're right," she agreed. "I imagine you have to start somewhere."

"Of course they're going to invest in the Miss Nikkei Contest. Their investment will bring us over the top. Hey." He pulled her away from her work and caught her in an embrace. "I'm also planning a ballroom dance with Miss Nikkei and her entire court. It's going to be the event of the year!" he exclaimed. He took his queen in a precarious waltz around her electronic prison. "By the end of the year, my dear, we'll be dancing our first dance." He ended with an exaggerated bow and she with a grand flourish.

Then she hurried to push all the play/record buttons.

Jorginho paused to worship her. A moment of reverence and then the theme song. Miss Nikkei. She was the best of both worlds.

THAT WAS ALL

■ ■ ■

Wakako Yamauchi

Last night I dreamed about a man I hadn't thought about in many years. He was my father's friend, a hold-over from his bachelor days. As far back as I can remember, starting somewhere in the late twenties, Suzuki-san visited us—though not frequently—and my earliest memory of him begins with these visits when at four or five, I used to run from him. I hated the feel of his hands; they were tough and calloused from farm work. My father's bachelor friends were constantly reaching for me—perhaps they were amazed that he, bachelor of bachelors, had settled down to domesticity with this beautiful woman, himself not so handsome, not so cunning (still not losing his bachelor ways—the drinking, the gambling), and had this scrawny kid, or perhaps they were recalling other children spawned in other wombs and brought to life only by seeing and feeling me and remembering. At that early age I suspected something sinister about their caresses, because I did not find this touch-touch attitude in men with families. Japanese people rarely touch, and my father . . . I cannot recall the warmth of my father's hand, except the sharp snap of it against my thigh when I misbehaved.

Born in 1924 in Westmoreland, California, the playwright and author WAKAKO YAMAUCHI has this to say about her work: "It took forty years, Garrett Hongo, and the Feminist Press to get *Songs My Mother Taught Me* published. I'm proud to say that the *Hungry Mind Review* (now called *The Ruminator*) has included it in the *100 Best American Books of the 20th Century*. Over these past decades I have continued writing, covering some of what I learned along the way, some mysteries that still elude me, joys that persist, and many of the bad habits that cling like burrs on an old dog's shanks."

My father acted as though I should accept these attentions from his friends as accommodations to him. I thought they were more for my mother's sake.

Raised on that desert farm under the patronage of two adults wrapped in their own set of problems and isolated from peer values, my imagination was left to run rampant. Although I cannot now believe it was entirely a misconception, I had the suspicion that all men were secretly and madly in love with my mother, who was the most beautiful and charming of all women. Magically emerging from that desert floor, she endured the harsh daylight realities and blossomed in the cool of the evening. After the bath. And I was sure no man in his proper mind could resist her. My father, I thought, was not in his proper mind.

My mother was a perfect Japanese wife except with my father in the bright light of day when she did the bulk of her nagging. My father's strength was his silence which he applied in varying pressures from Arctic chill to rock mountain imperturbability to wide open, no horizon, uninhabitable desert silence. My mother's emotional variances were my barometer: today she sings—fair and mild; today she remembers Japan—scattered showers; today he has made her unhappy again.

Suzuki-san lived in Niland 30 or 40 miles from us in a treeless landscape of sand and tumbleweed. I don't know why this area, not so distant, seemed more desolate than where we lived, maybe because where we lived there was a mother and father and a child, and where Suzuki-san lived, there was only him and two bleak structures, a kitchen and a bedroom, and the land beyond this complex and ranch was untouched from year to year, century to century—only the desert animals pocking its surface and the rain streaking the sand in a flash flood now and then. That seemed awesome to me.

I remember a visit to his homestead. I was six or seven. It was winter and my mother bundled me in a heavy coat and packed the car with pillows and blankets and we drove for what seemed hours. I was disappointed when we got there because there was no one and nothing to play with and in this incredibly boring place, the sun was blinding, the wind biting, and my mother was again in the kitchen cooking and mending Suzuki-san's clothes, and my father was walking up and down the furrows with Suzuki-san. I tried staying with my mother but the kitchen depressed me; without a woman's touch, it looked like the inside of a garage—no embroidered dish towels, crocheted potholders, nor a window with a swatch of dotted swiss fluttering.

I walked along with my father and Suzuki-san but their frequent stopping to examine plants, scratch the earth, turn over equipment, bored me and I wandered off to the desert. My father was not alarmed; on that windswept land a few loud bellows carried for miles and would quickly draw me back to him. Besides, there was no shrub taller than myself I could hide behind, no ditch I could drown in, and snakes and vipers were not considered a threat.

I wandered around looking for—I don't know what—maybe some indication that someone had been here before me and left something for me, and finding nothing, I stood by the fine pure sand the winds had pushed against a shrub and mused that it was possible I was the first person who had ever been on this particular mound of sand and put my shoe to that dust that began with creation and then my hand and then my cheek and then my hair and finally rolled myself on it and fell asleep.

My mother said later, brushing the sand from my coat with hard quick hands, "I think she rolled in the dirt," and my father said contemptuously, "Like a dog," and Suzuki-san looked at my mother with those bemused eyes that pretended to know something he didn't and I grew very angry and denied it all.

It was his mocking eyes that I disliked.

Intuitively I knew that my father, close to 40, and my mother, perhaps not yet 30, had abiding ties with Suzuki-san that started earlier than my arrival, perhaps somewhere back in Japan in Shizuoka, and perhaps on something less mysterious than appeared on the surface. I thought later maybe Suzuki-san had loaned my father a vast sum of money.

Suzuki-san was unlike my father's other bachelor friends, who still followed the crops along the length of California, cutting lettuce in Dinuba, harvesting grapes in Fresno, plums, peaches, and finally strawberries in Oceanside and those little known places—Vista, Escondido, Encinitas. They spent their money as soon as they got it—drinking, gambling, carousing—until at the southernmost end of the state, they looked for us and stayed two or three months eating my mother's cooking, and drinking my father's wine, oblivious to my mother's sighs which grew deeper as the visits wore on. Although Suzuki-san drank with my father too, he never permitted himself the coarse laughing and out-of-control drunkenness characteristic of the other roustabouts. Also Suzuki-san leased a parcel of land and farmed it like a family man—although he had no family that anyone spoke of either here in America or in Japan—nor did he show any apparent need for family, nor did my father or mother show interest in seeing him married. The need only surfaced now and then when he would catch me unaware and hold me squirming in his sandpaper grasp. Or sometimes it showed in the way he looked at my mother with his amused eyes. Perhaps when these needs were strongest, Suzuki-san came to us and ate with us, often bringing something special for my mother to cook, examining each morsel on his *hashi* before bringing it to his lips and chewing slowly—movements as sensual and private as making love. Once when he caught me watching him, he laughed and slipped some food into my mouth in a gesture so intimate I flushed warm and my father coughed suddenly. Those days he would stay overnight, sleeping on a cot in the kitchen and leaving in the morning after my mother's good breakfast.

Then about the time I turned fifteen, something very strange happened to me.

Suzuki-san was visiting us on this summer evening. We had finished supper; the day's warmth was still with us as we sat on the porch fanning away gnats and insects that flew past us toward the light of the small kerosene lantern. The air was still and the cicadas hummed without beginning or end. Suzuki-san returned from his bath stripped to his waist and sat next to me.

In the half dark I saw his brown body and smelled his warm scent and in the summer night with the cicadas' pervasive drone in my ear and the scent and sight of Suzuki-san's body assailing my better judgment, I fell in love.

I sat in the protective shadows of the night and watched the face I'd never before regarded as handsome and scrutinized the eyes that always seemed to mock me. I wondered about the wasted years this man had kept his perfect body to himself, never giving or receiving the love that was most certainly available to him. I wondered why he continued to work in his self-imposed exile and what future he hoped for himself . . . and whom he would share it with. An indescribable loneliness and sorrow came over me. I wished he would touch me again. He'd long ago stopped that.

Then he looked at me. My stomach turned and roiled with things terrible and sublime and sensual and sexual and rotten that I was unable to contain. They passed through me and fouled the still night. My father grunted and walked away. My mother glared at me and fanned the air away from herself and Suzuki-san.

I was mortified. I was betrayed by my mother, who should have found a way out for me. Instead she separated herself, denied me, and remained aloof, the lady of evening dew, and I . . . I was humiliated. Suzuki-san's eyes did not change. I went into the house.

That was all, that was all.

A few years later my father, unable to stave off the economic disaster that was our inexorable fate, moved us on to Oceanside. And a few years after that, war with Japan broke out and changed the course of our lives and we along with thousands of Japanese and Japanese Americans, were incarcerated in Arizona. Maybe Suzuki-san was also in the same camp. I don't remember seeing him.

And I fell in love at least three times thereafter—each time with the same brown body, the same mocking eyes—and the last time, I was drawn into a tumultuous love affair that spanned twenty-five years and ended on a rainy January morning. And perhaps I should add, I have not loved since.

And last night I had this dream:

I was living in a lean-to which I instinctively knew was part of Suzuki-san's house. The house itself was in terrible disrepair. It looked like a wrecking ball had been put to it. The floors buckled and the walls caved inward.

I felt I should offer to do something for the man who kindly shared his house with me, battered though it was. I was thinking of my mother who had so long ago done his cooking and mending. I went about gathering clothes I might wash for him. While going from room to room I passed a cracked and dusty mirror and in the fragmented reflection, I saw myself—older than my mother had ever been, older than I remembered myself to be.

I found two items to wash: an ancient pair of twills, moldy and stiff but unworn, and a sock, which I recognized as my own, half filled with sand.

Then I saw him in one of the rooms.

As it is with dreams, I was not surprised when I saw he was the same man I remember on the summer night when I so suddenly fell in love. He was naked to the waist, his body was tight and brown, he wore the same pants. In my head I thought, "He hasn't changed at all—still 35 . . . what would he want with this fifty-year-old woman I've grown to be?" But my mouth said, "I hope you're not paying a lot of rent for this place."

He said, "The rent is cheap."

It was my fault. I should not have started a conversation sounding so shrewish. I looked in his face to see if I could find some recognition of me . . . the me that he once wanted to hold . . . the me that was part of my mother's evening dew . . . the me that was gone forever.

I watched him until he could avoid me no longer and in my dream his eyes mocked me again . . . as they have always done.

A PERSONAL BIBLIOGRAPHY

First, a warning: This is definitely not a complete listing of works of fiction by Asian and Asian American authors who write in English. I am happy to report that since the publication of the original *Charlie Chan Is Dead* in 1993, there are many, many more writers around than I had included in that first edition's "Selected Readings" list. Obviously, some of the writers on this revised list have written many more books of fiction than I am able to note here. And because of space constraints, I have regretfully had to omit books of poetry and nonfiction by Asian and Asian American authors that have had an enormous influence on me. I have included books by several Philippine, British, Canadian, Caribbean, and Pacific Islander authors. Nowadays, with a little effort and computer know-how, one can actually order these once hard-to-find books through the Internet. It was a delightful challenge to put together this personal bibliography of novels and short-story collections. Here then, alphabetized by author:

Alexander, Meena. *Manhattan Music*. San Francisco: Mercury House, 1997.

———. *Nampally Road*. San Francisco: Mercury House, 1991.

Ali, Monica. *Brick Lane*. New York: Scribner, 2003.

Alumit, Noel. *Letters to Montgomery Clift*. San Francisco: MacAdam/Cage Publishing, 2002.

Apostol, Gina. *Bibliolepsy*. Manila: University of the Philippines Press, 1996.

Bacho, Peter. *Nelson's Run*. Holliston, Mass.: Willowgate Press, 2002.

——. *Dark Blue Suit and Other Stories*. Seattle: University of Washington Press, 1997.

——. *Cebu*. Seattle: University of Washington Press, 1991.

Brainard, Cecilia Manguerra. *When the Rainbow Goddess Wept*. Ann Arbor: University of Michigan Press, 1999.

Bulosan, Carlos. *America Is in the Heart*. Seattle: University of Washington Press, 2000.

——. *The Cry and the Dedication*. Philadelphia: Temple University Press, 1995.

——. *The Laughter of My Father*. New York: Harcourt, Brace & Co., 1944.

Cao, Lan. *Monkey Bridge*. New York: Viking, 1997.

Cha, Theresa. *Dictee*. Berkeley: Third Woman Press, 1995.

Chai, Arlene J. *The Last Time I Saw Mother*. New York: Fawcett Columbine, 1996.

Chan, David Marshall. *Goblin Fruit: Stories*. New York: Context Books, 2003.

Chang, Diana. *The Frontiers of Love*. Seattle: University of Washington Press, 1994.

Chang, Lan Samantha. *Hunger*. New York: W. W. Norton, 1998.

Chang, Leonard. *Over the Shoulder: A Novel of Intrigue*. Hopewell, N.J.: Ecco Press, 2001.

——. *Dispatches from the Cold*. Seattle: Black Heron Press, 1998.

——. *The Fruit 'n Food*. Seattle: Black Heron Press, 1996.

Chao, Patricia. *Monkey King*. New York: HarperCollins, 1997.

Chaudhuri, Amit. *Real Time: Stories and a Reminiscence*. New York: Farrar, Straus & Giroux, 2002.

——. *A New World*. New York: Knopf, 2000.

——. *Freedom Song*. New York: Knopf, 1999.

Chee, Alexander. *Edinburgh*. New York: Welcome Rain Publishers, 2001.

Cheng, Terrence. *Sons of Heaven*. New York: William Morrow, 2002.

Cheong, Fiona. *Shadow Theatre*. New York: Soho, 2002.

———. *The Scent of the Gods*. New York: W. W. Norton, 1991.

Chin, Frank. *Gunga Din Highway*. Minneapolis: Coffee House Press, 1994.

———. *Donald Duk*. Minneapolis: Coffee House Press, 1991.

———. *The Chinaman Pacific and Frisco R. R. Co.: Stories*. Minneapolis: Coffee House Press, 1988.

Chin, Sara. *Below the Line*. San Francisco: City Lights Books, 1997.

Chiu, Christina. *Troublemaker and Other Saints*. New York: Putnam, 2001.

Choi, Susan. *American Woman*. New York: HarperCollins, 2003.

———. *The Foreign Student*. New York: HarperFlamingo, 1998.

Chong, Kevin. *Baroque-a-Nova*. New York: Putnam, 2002.

Choy, Wayson. *The Jade Peony*. New York: Picador, 1997.

———. *Paper Shadows*. New York: Picador, 2000.

Chu, Louis. *Eat a Bowl of Tea*. Seattle: University of Washington Press, 1961.

Chua, Lawrence. *Gold by the Inch*. New York: Grove Press, 1998.

Chuang, Hua. *Crossings*. New York: Dial Press, 1968.

Davenport, Kiana. *Song of the Exile*. New York: Ballantine, 1999.

———. *Shark Dialogues*. New York: Maxwell Macmillan, 1994.

Davies, Peter Ho. *Equal Love: Stories*. New York: Houghton Mifflin, 2000.

———. *The Ugliest House in the World*. New York: Houghton Mifflin, 1997.

Desai, Anita. *Diamond Dust: Stories*. New York: Houghton Mifflin, 2000.

———. *Journey to Ithaca*. New York: Knopf, 1995.

———. *Baumgartner's Bombay*. New York: Knopf, 1989.

Desai, Kiran. *Hullabaloo in the Guava Orchard*. New York: Atlantic Monthly Press, 1998.

Dinh, Linh. *Fake House*. New York: Seven Stories Press, 2000.

Divakaruni, Chitra Banerjee. *The Vine of Desire*. New York: Doubleday, 2002.

———. *The Unknown Errors of Our Lives: Stories*. New York: Doubleday, 2001.

———. *Sister My Heart*. New York: Doubleday, 1999.

———. *The Mistress of Spices*. New York: Anchor Books, 1997.

———. *Arranged Marriage: Stories*. New York: Anchor Books, 1995.

Far, Sui Sin. *Mrs. Spring Fragrance & Other Writings*. Champaign: University of Illinois Press, 1995.

Fenkl, Heinz Insu. *Memories of My Ghost Brother*. New York: Dutton, 1996.

Figiel, Sia. *They Who Do Not Grieve*. New York: Vintage, 2000.

———. *Where We Once Belonged*. New York: Kaya Press, 1996.

Galang, M. Evelina. *Her Wild American Self: Short Stories*. Minneapolis: Coffee House Press, 1996.

Ganesan, Indira. *The Journey*. New York: Beacon Press, 2001.

———. *Inheritance*. New York: Knopf, 1998.

Grace, Patricia. *Dogside Story*. Honolulu: University of Hawai'i Press, 2001.

———. *Baby No-Eyes*. Honolulu: University of Hawai'i Press, 1998.

———. *Potiki*. New York: Penguin Books, 1986.

Gunesekera, Romesh. *Heaven's Edge*. New York: Grove Press, 2002.

———. *The Sandglass*. New York: New Press, 1998.

———. *Reef*. New York: New Press, 1995.

———. *Monkfish Moon*. New York: New Press, 1992.

Gupta, Sunetra. *The Glassblower's Breath*. New York: Grove Press, 1993.

———. *Memories of Rain*. New York: Weidenfeld, 1992.

Hagedorn, Jessica. *Dream Jungle*. New York: Viking, 2003.

———. *Danger and Beauty*. San Francisco: City Lights Books, 2002.

———. *The Gangster of Love*. Boston: Houghton Mifflin, 1996.

———. *Dogeaters*. New York: Penguin Books, 1991 (New York: Pantheon, 1990, in hardcover).

Hamid, Mohsin. *Moth Smoke*. New York: Farrar, Straus & Giroux, 2000.

Hara, Marie. *Bananaheart and Other Stories*. Honolulu: Bamboo Ridge Press, 1994.

Holthe, Tess Uriza. *When the Elephants Dance*. New York: Crown, 2002.

Ishiguro, Kazuo. *When We Were Orphans*. New York: Knopf, 2000.

———. *The Remains of the Day*. New York: Knopf, 1989.

———. *An Artist of the Floating World*. New York: Putnam, 1986.

———. *A Pale View of Hills*. New York: Putnam, 1982.

Iyer, Pico. *Abandon*. New York: Knopf, 2003.

———. *Cuba and the Night*. New York: Knopf, 1995.

Jen, Gish. *Who's Irish?: Stories*. New York: Knopf, 1999.

———. *Mona in the Promised Land*. New York: Knopf, 1996.

———. *Typical American*. New York: Houghton Mifflin, 1991.

Jin, Ha. *The Crazed*. New York: Pantheon, 2002.

———. *Bridegroom: Stories*. New York: Pantheon, 2000.

———. *Waiting*. New York: Pantheon, 1999.

———. *Ocean of Words: Army Stories*. Cambridge Mass.: Zoland Books, 1996.

Kadohata, Cynthia. *In the Heart of the Valley of Love*. New York: Viking, 1992.

———. *Floating World*. New York: Viking, 1989.

Kamani, Ginu. *Junglee Girl*. San Francisco: Aunt Lute Press, 1995.

Kang, Younghill. *The Grass Roof*. New York: Follett, 1959.

———. *East Goes West*. New York: Follett, 1937.

Keller, Nora Okja. *Fox Girl*. New York: Viking, 2002.

———. *Comfort Woman*. New York: Viking, 1997.

Kim, Suki. *The Interpreter*. New York: Farrar, Straus & Giroux, 2003.

Kingston, Maxine Hong. *Tripmaster Monkey: His Fake Book*. New York: Knopf, 1989.

———. *China Men*. New York: Knopf, 1980.

———. *The Woman Warrior: Memoirs of a Girlhood Among Ghosts*. New York: Knopf, 1976.

Kogawa, Joy. *Obasan*. New York: Anchor, 1994.

———. *Jericho Road*. Toronto: McClelland and Stewart, 1977.

Kuo, Alexander. *Lipstick and Other Stories*. Hong Kong: Asia 2000, 2001.

———. *Chinese Opera*. Hong Kong: Asia 2000, 1998.

———. *Changing the River*. Berkeley, Calif.: I. Reed Books, 1986.

Kureishi, Hanif. *Intimacy*. New York: Faber, 1998.

———. *Love in a Blue Time*. New York: Scribner, 1997.

———. *The Black Album*. New York: Scribner, 1995.

———. *Buddha of Suburbia*. New York: Viking, 1990.

Lahiri, Jhumpa. *The Namesake*. New York: Houghton Mifflin, 2003.

———. *Interpreter of Maladies*. New York: Houghton Mifflin, 1999.

Lai, Larissa. *When Fox Is a Thousand*. Vancouver, B. C., Press Gang, 1995.

Lau, Evelyn. *Other Women*. New York: Simon & Schuster, 1996.

Law-Yone, Wendy. *Irrawaddy Tango*. New York: Knopf, 1993.

———. *The Coffin Tree*. New York: Knopf, 1983.

Lê, Thi Diem Thúy. *The Gangster We Are All Looking For*. New York: Knopf, 2003.

Lee, Chang-rae. *A Gesture Life*. New York: Riverhead Books, 1999.

———. *Native Speaker*. New York: Riverhead Books, 1995.

Lee, C. Y. *Flower Drum Song*. New York: Penguin Books, 2001.

Lee, Don. *Yellow*. New York: W. W. Norton, 2001.

Leong, Russell Charles. *Phoenix Eyes and Other Stories*. Seattle: University of Washington Press, 2000.

Lieu, Jocelyn. *Potential Weapons: A Novella and Short Stories*. Saint Paul: Graywolf Press, 2004.

Lim, Shirley Geok-Lin. *Joss and Gold*. New York: Feminist Press, 2001.

———. *Two Dreams: New and Selected Stories*. New York: Feminist Press, 1997.

Lin, Ed. *Waylaid*. New York: Kaya Press, 2001.

Linmark, R. Zamora. *Rolling the R's*. New York: Kaya Press, 1995.

Liu, Aimee. *Cloud Mountain*. New York: Warner Books, 1997.

Loh, Sandra Tsing. *If You Lived Here, You'd Be Home by Now*. New York: Riverhead Books, 1997.

Louie, David Wong. *The Barbarians Are Coming*. New York: Putnam, 2000.

——. *Pangs of Love*. New York: Knopf, 1991.

Lum, Darrell. *Pass On, No Pass Back*. Honolulu: Bamboo Ridge Press, 1990.

Meer, Ameena. *Bombay Talkie*. New York: High Risk Books/Serpent's Tail, 1994.

Mo, Timothy. *Sour Sweet*. New York: Random House, 1985.

——. *Monkey King*. New York: Doubleday, 1980.

Mootoo, Shani. *Cereus Blooms at Night*. Vancouver, B. C.: Press Gang, 1996.

——. *Out on Main Street and Other Stories*. Vancouver, B. C.: Press Gang, 1993.

Morales, Rodney. *When the Shark Bites*. Honolulu: University of Hawai'i Press, 2002.

——. *Speed of Darkness*. Honolulu: Bamboo Ridge Press, 1988.

Mori, Kyoko. *Stone Field, True Arrow*. New York: Picador, 2001.

Mori, Toshio. *Unfinished Message: Selected Works of Toshio Mori*. Salinas: Heyday Books, 2002.

——. *Yokohama, California*. Seattle: University of Washington Press, 1985.

——. *The Chauvinist and Other Stories*. Los Angeles: Asian American Studies Center (UCLA), 1979.

Mukherjee, Bharati. *Desirable Daughters*. New York: Theia, 2002.

——. *Leave It to Me*. New York: Knopf, 1997.

——. *Holder of the World*. New York: Knopf, 1993.

——. *Jasmine*. New York: Grove Weidenfeld, 1989.

——. *The Middleman and Other Stories*. New York: Grove Press, 1988.

——. *Wife*. New York: Penguin Books, 1987.

——. *Tiger's Daughter.* New York: Houghton Mifflin, 1971.

Murayama, Milton. *Plantation Boy.* Honolulu: University of Hawai'i Press, 1998.

——. *Five Years on a Rock.* Honolulu: University of Hawai'i Press, 1994.

——. *All I Am Asking for Is My Body.* Honolulu: University of Hawai'i Press, 1988.

Murray, Sabina. *The Caprices.* New York: Houghton Mifflin, 2002.

Naipaul, V.S. *Bend in the River.* New York: Knopf, 2001 (reissue).

——. *Guerrillas.* New York: Vintage International, 1975.

Nair, Meera. *Video: Stories.* New York: Pantheon, 2002.

Ng, Faye Myenne. *Bone.* New York: Hyperion, 1993.

Ng, Mei. *Eating Chinese Food Naked.* New York: Scribner, 1998.

Nguyen, Kien. *The Tapestries.* Boston: Little, Brown, 2002.

Nuñez, Sigrid. *For Rouenna.* New York: Farrar, Straus & Giroux, 2001.

——. *Naked Sleeper.* New York: HarperCollins, 1996.

——. *A Feather from the Breath of God.* New York: HarperCollins, 1995.

Okada, John. *No-No Boy.* Seattle: University of Washington Press, 1979.

Ondaatje, Michael. *Anil's Ghost.* New York: Vintage, 2001.

——. *The English Patient.* New York: Vintage, 1996.

——. *Coming Through Slaughter.* New York: Vintage, 1993.

Ong, Han. *Beneficiary.* New York: Farrar, Straus & Giroux, 2004.

——. *Fixer Chao.* New York: Farrar, Straus & Giroux, 2001.

Ozeki, Ruth. *All Over Creation.* New York: Viking, 2003.

——. *My Year of Meats.* New York: Penguin Books, 1998.

Pak, Gary. *Ricepaper Airplane.* Honolulu: University of Hawai'i Press, 1998.

——. *The Watcher of Waipuna and Other Stories.* Honolulu: Bamboo Ridge Press, 1992.

Pak, Ty. *Moonbay: Short Stories.* New York: The Woodhouse Inc., 1999.

Realuyo, Bino. *Umbrella Country.* New York: Ballantine Books, 1999.

Rizzuto, Rahna Reiko. *Why She Left Us.* New York: HarperCollins, 1999.

Roley, Brian Ascalon. *American Son*. New York: W. W. Norton, 2001.

Romero, Sophia G. *Always Hiding*. New York: William Morrow, 1998.

Rosca, Ninotchka. *Twice Blessed*. New York: W. W. Norton, 1992.

——. *State of War*. New York: W. W. Norton, 1988.

Rushdie, Salman. *The Satanic Verses*. New York: Picador, 2000.

——. *Shame: A Novel*. New York: Picador, 2000.

——. *East, West*. Toronto: Vintage Books Canada, 1996.

——. *The Moor's Last Sigh*. Toronto: Vintage Books Canada, 1996.

——. *Midnight's Children*. New York: Penguin Books, 1995.

Ruthkowski, Thaddeus. *Roughhouse: A Novel in Snapshots*. New York: Kaya Press, 1999.

Sakamoto, Kerri. *Electrical Field*. New York: W. W. Norton, 1999.

Santos, Bienvenido. *What the Hell for You Left Your Heart in San Francisco*. Manila: New Day, 1987.

——. *The Man Who (Thought He) Looked Like Robert Taylor*. Manila: New Day, 1983.

——. *The Praying Man*. Manila: New Day, 1982.

——. *Scent of Apples: A Collection of Stories*. Seattle: University of Washington Press, 1979.

Seth, Vikram. *An Equal Music*. New York: Broadway Books, 1999.

——. *Suitable Boy*. New York: HarperCollins, 1993.

——. *The Golden Gate: A Novel in Verse*. New York: Random House, 1986.

Shankar, S. *A Map of Where I Live*. Portsmouth, N.H.: Heinemann, 1997.

Sharma, Akhil. *An Obedient Father*. New York: Farrar, Straus & Giroux, 2000.

Shigekuni, Julie. *A Bridge Between Us*. New York: Anchor Books/Doubleday, 1995.

Sone, Monica. *Nisei Daughter*. Boston: Little, Brown, 1953.

Stapleton, Lara. *The Lowest Blue Flame Before Nothing*. San Francisco: Aunt Lute Books, 1998.

Strom, Dao. *Grass Roof, Tin Roof*. New York: Houghton Mifflin, 2003.

Tan, Amy. *The Joy Luck Club*. New York: Putnam, 1989.

Tharoor, Shashi. *Riot*. New York: Arcade, 2001.

——. *The Five Dollar Smile and Other Stories*. New York: Arcade, 1993.

——. *Show Business*. New York: Arcade, 1992.

Truong, Monique. *The Book of Salt*. New York: Houghton Mifflin, 2003.

Tyau, Kathleen. *Makai*. New York: Farrar, Straus & Giroux, 1999.

——. *A Little Too Much Is Enough*. New York: Farrar, Straus & Giroux, 1995.

Ty-Casper, Linda. *Wings of Stone*. New York: Readers International, 1986.

——. *Awaiting Trespass* (*A Pasión*). New York: Readers International, 1985.

Umrigar, Thrity. *Bombay Time*. New York: Picador, 2001.

Uyemoto, Holly. *Go*. New York: Dutton, 1995.

——. *Rebel Without a Clue*. New York: Crown, 1989.

Villa, José Garcia. *The Anchored Angel*. New York: Kaya Press, 1999.

Villanueva, Chea. *Jessie's Song and Other Stories*. New York: Masquerade Books, 1995.

Wang, Ping. *Foreign Devil*. Minneapolis: Coffee House Press, 1996.

——. *American Visa: Short Stories*. Minneapolis: Coffee House Press, 1994.

Watanabe, Sylvia. *Talking to the Dead and Other Stories*. New York: Doubleday, 1992.

Wong, Norman. *Cultural Revolution*. New York: Persea Books, 1994.

Wong, Shawn. *American Knees*. New York: Simon & Schuster, 1995.

——. *Homebase*. New York: Plume, 1991.

Yamada, Mitsuye. *Desert Run: Poems and Stories*. New York: Kitchen Table Press, 1988.

Yamamoto, Hisaye. *Seventeen Syllables and Other Stories*. New York: Kitchen Table Press, 1988.

Yamanaka, Lois-Ann. *Father of the Four Passages*. New York: Farrar, Straus & Giroux, 2001.

——. *Saturday Night at the Pahala Theatre*. Honolulu: Bamboo Ridge Press, 1999.

——. *Blu's Hanging*. New York: Farrar, Straus & Giroux, 1997.

——. *Wild Meat and Bully Burgers*. New York: Farrar, Straus & Giroux, 1996.

——. *Heads by Harry*. New York: Farrar, Straus & Giroux, 1993.

Yamashita, Karen Tei. *Circle K Cycles*. Minneapolis: Coffee House Press, 2001.

——. *Tropic of Orange*. Minneapolis: Coffee House Press, 1997.

——. *Brazil-Maru*. Minneapolis: Coffee House Press, 1992.

——. *Through the Arc of the Rainforest*. Minneapolis: Coffee House Press, 1990.

Yamauchi, Wakako. *Songs My Mother Taught Me*. New York: Feminist Press, 1994.

ANTHOLOGIES

Asian Women United of California. *Making Waves: An Anthology of Writings by and About Asian American Women*. Boston: Beacon Press, 1989.

Bao, Quang, and Hanya Yanagihara, eds. *Take Out: Queer Writing from Asian Pacific America*. New York: Asian American Writers' Workshop, 2000.

Brainard, Cecilia Manguerra, ed. *Fiction by Filipinos in America*. Manila: New Day, 1993.

Carbo, Nick, and Eileen Tabios, eds. *Babaylan: An Anthology of Filipina and Filipina American Writers*. San Francisco: Aunt Lute Books, 2000.

Cerenio, Virginia, and Marianne Villanueva, eds. *Going Home to a Landscape: Writings by Filipinas*. Corvallis, Ore.: Calyx Books, 2003.

Chan, Jeff, Frank Chin, Lawson Fusao Inada, and Shawn Wong, eds. *Aiiieeeee!: An Anthology of Asian American Writers*. Washington, D.C.: Howard University Press, 1974.

Chan, Jeffery Paul, Frank Chin, Lawson Fusao Inada, and Shawn Wong, eds. *The Big Aiiieeeee!: An Anthology of Chinese American and Japanese American Literature*. Salinas: Meridian Press, 1991.

Chin, Marilyn, and David Wong Louie, eds. *Dissident Song: A Contemporary Asian American Anthology*. Santa Cruz: Quarry West, 1991.

Chock, Eric, and Darrell Lum, eds. *The Best of Honolulu Fiction: Stories from the Honolulu Magazine Fiction Writing Contest*. Honolulu: Bamboo Ridge Press, 1999.

——. *Best of Bamboo Ridge: The Hawaii Writers' Quarterly*. Honolulu: Bamboo Ridge Press, 1986.

Fenkl, Heinz Insu, and Walter Lew, eds. *Kori: The Beacon Anthology of Korean American Fiction*. Boston: Beacon Press, 2001.

Francia, Luis, and Eric Gamalinda, eds. *Flippin': Filipinos on America*. New York: Asian American Writers' Workshop, 1996.

Gamalinda, Eric, Frank Stewart, and Alfred Yuson, eds. *Century of Dreams: New Writing from America, the Pacific, and Asia*. Honolulu: University of Hawai'i Press, 1997.

Hagedorn, Jessica, ed. *Charlie Chan Is Dead: An Anthology of Contemporary Asian American Fiction*. New York: Penguin Books, 1993.

Hara, Marie, and Nora Okja Keller, eds. *Intersecting Circles: The Voices of Hapa Women in Poetry and Prose*. Honolulu: Bamboo Ridge Press, 1999.

Hong, Maria, ed. *Growing Up Asian American: An Anthology*. New York: William Morrow, 1993.

Kim, Elaine, Lilia Villanueva, and Asian Women United of California, eds. *Making More Waves: New Writing by Asian American Women*. Boston: Beacon Press, 1997.

Kono, Juliet, and Cathy Song, eds. *Sister Stew: Fiction and Poetry by Women*. Honolulu: Bamboo Ridge Press, 1991.

Kudaka, Geraldine, ed. *On a Bed of Rice: An Asian American Erotic Feast*. New York: Anchor Books/Doubleday, 1995.

Lim, Shirley Geok-lin, and Cheng Lok Chua, eds. *Tilting the Continent: Southeast Asian American Writing*. Moorhead, Minn.: New Rivers Press, 2000.

Lim, Shirley Geok-lin, Mayumi Tsutakawa, and Margarita Donnelly, eds. *The Forbidden Stitch: An Asian American Women's Anthology*. Corvallis, Ore.: Calyx Books, 1989.

Lim-Hing, Sharon, ed. *The Very Inside: An Anthology of Writing by Asian and Pacific Islander Lesbian and Bisexual Women*. Ottawa, Ont.: Sister Vision, 1994.

Maira, Sunaina, and Rajini Srikanth, eds. *Contours of the Heart: South Asians Map North America*. New York: Asian American Writers' Workshop, 1998.

Mendoza, Louis, and S. Shankar, eds. *Crossing into America: The New Literature of Immigration*. New York: New Press, 2003.

Moua, Mai Neng, ed. *Bamboo Among the Oaks*. Minneapolis: Minnesota Historical Society Press, 2002.

Nam, Victoria, ed. *Yell-oh Girls: Emerging Voices Explore Culture, Identity, and Growing Up Asian American*. New York: Quill, 2001.

Shah, Sonia, ed. *Dragon Ladies: Asian American Feminists Breathe Fire*. Cambridge, Mass.: South End Press, 1997.

Srikanth, Rajini, and Esther Iwanaga, eds. *Bold Words: A Century of Asian American Writing*. Rutgers, N.J.: Rutgers University Press, 2001.

Tan, Joel, ed. *Queer PAPI Porn: Gay Asian Erotica*. San Francisco: Cleis Press, 1998.

Tran, Barbara, Monique Truong, and Luu Truong Khoi, eds. *Watermark: Vietnamese American Poetry & Prose*. New York: Asian American Writers' Workshop, 1998.

Watanabe, Sylvia, and Carol Bruchac, eds. *Into the Fire: Asian American Prose*. New York: Greenfield Review Press, 1996.

———. *Home to Stay: Asian American Women's Fiction*. New York: Greenfield Review Press, 1990.

Women of South Asian Descent Collective, ed. *Our Feet Walk the Sky: Women of the South Asian Diaspora*. San Francisco: Aunt Lute Books, 1993.

Wong, Shawn, ed. *Asian American Literature: A Brief Introduction and Anthology*. New York: HarperCollins College Publishers, 1996.

*Grateful acknowledgment is made for permission to reprint the following copy-
righted works:*

   "Rico" from *Dark Blue Suit and Other Stories* by Peter Bacho. Copyright
© 1997 by University of Washington Press. Used by permission of the University of Washington Press.

   "Homecoming" by Carlos Bulosan. Used by permission of Aurea Bulosan
Gentile.

   "Melpomene Tragedy" from *Dictee* by Theresa Hak Kyung Cha (Tanam
Press). Copyright © 1982 by Theresa Hak Kyung Cha. Used by the permission
of the Estate of Theresa Hak Kyung Cha.

   "Moon" by Marilyn Chin. Copyright © Marilyn Chin, 1993. First appeared in *Charlie Chan Is Dead*, edited by Jessica Hagedorn (Penguin Books,
1993). By permission of the author.